HAWAIIAN
MYTHOLOGY

HAWAIIAN MYTHOLOGY

Martha Beckwith

with a new introduction by
Katharine Luomala

UNIVERSITY OF HAWAII PRESS
HONOLULU

*Originally published in 1940 by Yale University Press for the
Folklore Foundation of Vassar College*

First printing by University of Hawaii Press 1970
Second printing 1971

Paperback printing 1976, 1979, 1982

Library of Congress Catalog Card Number 70-97998

ISBN 0-8248-0514-3

Manufactured in the United States of America

CONTENTS

PART THREE: THE CHIEFS

HAWAIIAN MYTHOLOGY

PART FOUR: HEROES AND LOVERS
IN FICTION

INTRODUCTION

WHY, after thirty years, should Beckwith's *Hawaiian Mythology* be reprinted? Why, for the last twenty-five years, have scholars and amateurs alike sought for either new or used copies of this book which has become a rarity?

To begin with, it was the first, and is still the only, scholarly work which charts a pathway through the hundreds of books and articles, many of them obscure and scarce, and through the little-known manuscripts that record the orally transmitted myths, legends, traditions, folktales, and romances of the Hawaiian people. Beckwith herself saw it as a "guide to the native mythology of Hawaii" (p. xxxi), and by mythology she meant "the whole range of story-telling" (p. 2).

Secondly, from the vantage point of Hawaiian oral narrative the book directs the reader into similar material from peoples elsewhere in Polynesia who are closely related to the Hawaiians, reminding him of relevant narratives from areas west of Polynesia and occasionally even east of Hawaii. The southern Pacific comparison Beckwith offers as "an important link in tracing routes of intercourse during the period of migration of related Polynesian groups" (p. 5). However, except to summarize immediately the hypothesis current in 1940 and to make her detailed comparisons throughout the book, she is unconcerned with migration theory as such. Consequently, under the silent weight of testimony, the reader envisages for himself the Pacific being criss-crossed every which way by sailing families who passed on their lore wherever they found listeners.

Beckwith, it is soon evident, in naming the book *Hawaiian Mythology* gave it an overly limited and modest title. The title does not reflect her comprehensive consideration of the oral art of the Hawaiians and other Polynesians in relation to their total culture. It thoroughly infuses every chapter, but it is up to the reader to extract references to economic life and oral art concerning it and put together a topical chapter on economics for himself. Writing to me in May 1955, four years before her death, of her wish to have me revise her book and bring out a second edition, Miss Beckwith said, "My special interest in writing the mythology was to produce a book which covered what I conceive to be the province of a true mythology—not merely a series of tales, but, with the tales as major illustration or formal expression, to point out the ideas of the relation of man to the world he lives in, geographic, historic, social and political, which result in such expression, and to connect the particular forms of expression developed in Hawaii to those common with his throughout the known Polynesian area. This last has been done pretty sketchily as was perhaps necessary to preserve unity and be manageable in a single volume. . . ."

Four is the Polynesian ritual number, so I shall cite but one more of several additional values that might be named. What a wealth of ideas and problems she discovered in preparing her guide! Again writing to me in May, she said, "I do like to see things as wholes as far as possible. Then one gets to know where the unexplored problems come in. There are still several in Hawaiian mythology that ought to be looked into. We must talk about them when I see you. . . ." The problems she discovered, but left only partially explored, are a heritage for this generation of scholars who will appreciate the enriched implications that time and new data have given to her ideas.

A new edition, Miss Beckwith wrote me, would, she hoped, bring the work up to date "with bibliography and checked for misprints or what I fear most, notes misplaced, since the original idea was to insert the note directly in the text in parentheses and in printing the present form said references might easily have got misplaced." She was more anxious about these errors than about the incorporation of new data. In answer to my suggestion that, even with her failing strength, she might still bring out articles that would put the new research into perspective, she wrote, "I am not so keen about the new material because that can always be put into another article, as you say, although I do love a single thorough text on a subject to save the scholar's search over out-of-the-way references. For example, I don't suppose anybody ever uses my maiden article on 'Dance Forms of Moki and Kwakiutl Indians' which Dr. Boas kindly had printed in the Americanist Journal, out of whose same theme as suggested by Dr. Boas, Ruth Benedict wrote her real masterpiece."

Her weakening eyesight and the aftereffects of a stroke prevented her at eighty-four years of age from undertaking alone a revision of her book, although she had begun a piece here and there. For myself, I could not then imagine when I would find the time. Moreover, the book as she had first written it, misprints and misplaced references notwithstanding, was uniquely hers—a monument of permanent and irreplaceable value just as she had created it. Perhaps she did come to realize that for me to make revisions in her book, even with her permission, was in my mind equivalent to tampering. Now, although the petty errors remain and the various updated additions and revisions have not been made, at least her major wish is being granted, for she said, "But I do want the book to continue in use and how can it when the new people in the field who have come along must depend on a library copy or possibly have no such copy at hand?"

For those who did not have the good fortune to know this scholarly gentlewoman I shall quote, with permission of the American Folklore Society, most of the commemorative essay I wrote about her for the *Journal of American Folklore* (volume 75, 1962, pages 341–353).

Martha Warren Beckwith, president of the American Folklore Society in 1932–1933, was a major contributor to ethnography and folklore, most notably of two regions separated by a continent, the Pacific and the Caribbean.

Miss Beckwith's formal career in ethnography and folklore did not begin until her mid-thirties. She had already spent more than ten years, after graduating from Mt. Holyoke College, as a teacher of English at Elmira, Mt. Holyoke, Vassar, and Smith Colleges when in 1906, after studying anthropology under Franz Boas at Columbia University, she received her M.A. degree. In 1918, when she was forty-seven years old, she received her Ph.D. In 1920 she returned to Vassar, which she had left in 1913 after four years in the English

Department, but now her position was that of research professor on the Folklore Foundation and associate professor of comparative literature. The latter title was dropped in 1929, but
the research professorship continued until Miss Beckwith's
retirement in 1938. The Vassar Memorial to her in 1959 says
of the research professorship that it "was probably unique in
the history of American college education—and perhaps is
even to this day. It was made possible by the generosity of a
Mr. and Mrs. Alexander of Hawaii, was arranged by them
anonymously through a lawyer so that even President Mac-
Cracken did not know the identity of the donors until after
Miss Beckwith's retirement, and was given solely for Miss
Beckwith. Even in this day of giving to colleges and univer-
sities by foundations we might remark this practice for
serious consideration."[1]

The Folklore Foundation developed from the close ties
between the Alexander and Beckwith families on the island
of Maui in the Hawaiian Islands. Miss Beckwith, born in
Wellesley Heights, Massachusetts, on January 19, 1871, went
as a young girl to the Hawaiian Islands with her parents,
George Ely and Harriet Winslowe (Goodale) Beckwith, both
schoolteachers. There were kinfolk in the islands; "cousins"
is the general term used to describe those who are interrelated
by many and intricate lines of descent from early missionaries. Miss Beckwith was the grandniece of Mrs. Lucy
Goodale Thurston, who with her husband had been among
the pioneer missionaries; and Miss Beckwith, though not
born in the islands, became an adopted "cousin."[2]

Her father, who taught at Royal School and Punahou College, also developed a plantation at Haiku, Maui, that was
later taken over by Alexander and Baldwin. It was on Maui
that Miss Beckwith became a friend of Miss Annie M.
Alexander, who was to become well known, particularly at
the University of California at Berkeley, for her sponsorship
and support of research in zoology, paleontology, botany, and
other fields. Miss Alexander's interest in scholarship and her
devotion to her friends is reflected also in the Vassar Folklore
Foundation. In 1951 Miss Beckwith dedicated the climax of
her research, her study of the Kumulipo, a Hawaiian creation
chant, "To the memory of Annie M. Alexander, Lifelong

Friend and Comrade from early days in Hawaii, Whose generous sponsorship has made the author's research possible."[3]

To Miss Alexander, whom I met when I was a freshman at Berkeley and already set to become an ethnographer and folklorist, I owe my meeting with Miss Beckwith and much encouragement and assistance in my own study. After I had written my master's thesis on American Indian folklore at Berkeley, the two deflected me into Polynesian study with the suggestion, already well plotted by them secretly without my knowledge, that I immediately join Miss Beckwith, who was then at Bishop Museum, to help her with her manuscript on *Hawaiian Mythology*. I left four days later on the *Malolo*.

Although best known for her work on the Hawaiian Islands, Miss Beckwith had also done fieldwork, or had made short visits productive of studies, in other parts of the world. She wrote from firsthand acquaintance about the folklore and ethnography not only of the Hawaiians but of the Jamaicans (both Negroes and East Indians), the American Indians (among others the Mandan, Hidatsa, and Oglala), the Portuguese residents of Goa, and present-day Americans (folk festivals, college superstitions, and Dutchess County folklore).

She made four trips to Jamaica, usually of five or six weeks at a time during her vacations in the summer of 1919, the winters of 1921 and 1922, and the spring of 1924. She also made four trips to the Dakotas. In the summer of 1926 she worked principally at Pine Ridge Reservation in South Dakota, mainly with the Oglala, and in the summers of 1929, 1931, and 1932 at Fort Berthold Reservation in North Dakota, principally with the Mandan and Hidatsa. This American Indian fieldwork was done, she noted, at the suggestion of Franz Boas. She spent the spring of 1927, while on a trip around the world, in Portuguese India, which is singled out for mention because she inspired the collecting of lore there which was later published.

But always there were the return trips to the Hawaiian Islands, and they became increasingly frequent in later years. Her first year after retirement in 1938 from Vassar College, with the title of professor emeritus of folklore, was spent in the islands. Her headquarters as usual was at Bishop Museum where she was honorary research associate in Hawaiian folklore during the years when she was most actively and continuously engaged in translating the Hawaiian manuscripts stored there. She translated, edited, and wrote explanatory notes and prefaces to the manuscripts of Kepelino, Kamakau, and other Hawaiian writers of the period of the Hawaiian monarchy. She prepared for her later work on creation chants and mythology, and continued with her large work *Hawaiian Mythology*. "Not before 1914 did the actual shaping of the work begin," she wrote in the preface to this book which was published in 1940, a year short of her seventieth birthday, and dedicated to celebrate the seventy-fifth anniversary of Vassar College and the twenty-fifth year of Henry Noble MacCracken's presidency.

As soon as World War II had ended and she was able to obtain transportation, she left Berkeley, her new home since retirement, to visit the islands again. Now the translation and study of the Kumulipo was her main interest. It was published in 1951 when she was eighty years old. She made only one more visit to the islands after that, and her manuscript notes on the Hawaiian medicinal herbs that she collected then are now at Bishop Museum. Although a small part of the massive Kamakau translation with which she had been more closely associated than published acknowledgments hint was printed in Honolulu in 1961, she wanted no part in it, even if she had been asked, because she did not want her name connected with it unless she could do the total revision which she felt necessary to meet her standard of quality for publication.

The deep springs of the tremendous energy on which she drew all through her life are illustrated by her last visit to the Hawaiian Islands in 1951. She had only recently suffered from what had been feared would be either a fatal or a severely disabling stroke. Proving the doctors wrong on both scores, she recovered so well that she soon set out for the islands. She tramped around Maui with her remaining childhood friends and informants as she enthusiastically collected herbs regarded by Hawaiians as of medicinal value. She participated in a busy round of social activities on Maui and Oahu, and went swimming whenever she was near the ocean.

Late one overcast wintry afternoon she pointed out to her
shivering companion, half her age, the distant reef to which
she had thought nothing of swimming in her youth even after
a long day of picnicking and riding horseback around the
island. Then she plunged into the rolling breakers and started
swimming as vigorously as if she intended not only to reach
the reef but break her youthful record in doing it. Ocean
"bathing," as she called this activity, she heartily recom-
mended for improving her companion's lesser energy.

In the eight years remaining to her after that, only her
failing eyesight seemed to handicap her continuing to write
for publication, but she was able to read what was being published in the many fields of her interest and to comment on
her reading in letters to her friends, and to plan for the dis-
posal of her remaining research papers and exceptionally
fine library.

Miss Beckwith was a dedicated scholar with great powers
of concentration. If she were working alone, she was quite
likely to forget appointments and the passage of time. If she
were working with informants, translators, or other associates, her absorption sometimes disconcerted and wearied
them, for she could sit for hours almost motionless except for
moving pencil or tapping finger, focusing upon the manifold
possibilities of the translation of a native phrase or the rich
symbolism of a character. I recall a distinguished professor of
anthropology, her contemporary, telling me, still with emo-
tion decades after the occurrence, how he had enjoyed her
rapt attention to his explanation of his subject until he had
suddenly felt exploited (and probably as if he were one of his
own Indian informants). That more than one ethnographer
has forgotten that informants want to be assured from time
to time of their value as human beings and not merely as
information-relaying machines was vividly dramatized a few
years ago for the Anthropological Society of Hawaii by some
Micronesian guest speakers who burlesqued in pantomime
the dedicated ethnographer-fidgeting informant situation
which they had experienced when, after World War II, the
Coordinated Investigation of Micronesian Anthropology
blitzed their islands.

However, the association with Miss Beckwith provided a

rigorous training and discipline in the standards of sound
scholarship which successfully drew from some of her informants not only their information for the immediate project
at hand, but enabled them to continue independently later
with confidence and respect for themselves as original con-
tributors to scholarship. She generously noted with apprecia-
tion the names of the numerous people who had assisted her
in any way, but her point of view seems to have been predominantly that she was merely the intermediary who had
helped them preserve for their people and science what might
otherwise have been lost forever in the face of rapid cultural
change. She expected as much of them, therefore, as of herself.

Her dedication to her work accompanied an absentmind-
edness with regard to many events in the outside world or a
strong perturbation when she was aware of them and they
violated her standards. Many a story about Miss Beckwith
begins, "Do you remember the time she . . . ," and has the
polished smoothness and kindly humor of affectionately retold family folklore. (See footnote 11.) Miss Beckwith herself,
because of her semidetachment, often described most enter-
tainingly bits and pieces of modern American culture that
had captured her amused attention. For all her love of her
research she liked to entertain her friends, and despite her
reserve she expressed in time of her friends' elation or heart-
break a penetrating intuition and sympathetic under-
standing. How aptly the Vassar Memorial describes her:
"She was an inspiring teacher of the comparatively few students she recognized as promising, but she was no more interested in the average student than she was interested in the
political and social problems of modern life. She had many
warm friends, however, who appreciated her single-minded
devotion to scholarship and her courage in the many difficulties of research in her chosen field. She was a charming
and beautiful woman, the best type of Victorian lady and
scholar."

E. S. Craighill Handy, who is himself a lifelong specialist
in Polynesian culture and who knew Miss Beckwith and her
work well, wrote more than twenty years ago that she "has
been equally a pioneer in unearthing literary materials and
discovering living sources of authentic knowledge."[4] This

was true not only in the Pacific but in the Caribbean, and, in
fact, wherever she happened to be.

Her interest in Hawaiian literary materials is worth em-
phasizing because she showed it from the beginning of her
career when she selected the romance of Laieikawai to translate and study for her doctoral dissertation. The romance was
a nineteenth-century newspaper serial based upon an oral
narrative which Haleole, a creative writer, reinterpreted in
the hope of founding a Hawaiian literature. At the beginning
of this century, when Miss Beckwith was starting out in anthropology, the emphasis was more on recovering or recon-
structing the pre-European culture of natives than on what
the natives had done with European culture. Alien European
influences were weeded out of source materials to reveal the
old. Miss Beckwith, it appears, early realized the significance
of studying the post-European period in itself, of describing
it as it existed, and of valuing it, first and foremost, regardless
of what alien influences blended with the old, as still the culture of the natives. That she did not always fully enough sort
out native from European traits and track down all the foreign strands led to some criticism of both her Caribbean and
Pacific research. E. G. Burrows, for example, differed with
her on how to evaluate the Christian influences on Hawaiian
mythology and on the descriptions of Hawaiian culture by
Kepelino, Kamakau, and other compatriots of Haleole.[5]

Miss Beckwith, it seems, read the accounts written by
native Hawaiians of the nineteenth and twentieth centuries
as if she were Hawaiian. She saturated herself in the materials
and was carried along by the continuity that she recognized
as present in Hawaiian tradition despite the dynamic pro-
cesses of change in pre-European or post-European times.
However the tradition might change, it was ever-Hawaiian,
for the Hawaiian had selected, consciously or unconsciously,
in terms of his own system of values from a vast arc of cultural possibilities, to use Benedict's phrase. Introduced traits,
whether Tahitian or European, in Hawaiian tradition must
somehow harmonize or reflect an earlier, existing matrix or
they would not have been accepted.

This point of view can be discovered, I think, not only in
Hawaiian Mythology and in the preface to the translation of

Kepelino but in the study of the Kumulipo. In the latter work, Miss Beckwith writes of trying to see the creation chant "in the light of Polynesian thought" with the aid of her Hawaiian associates.[6] She recognized that the prayer chant was "ancient and pre-Christian" but that it may have undergone rearrangements. It was still to her the Kumulipo of the Hawaiians.

How do the Hawaiians accept her intensive scholarship? I do not attempt to say but cite what struck me as poignantly indicative. Idly looking through a manuscript deposited in Bishop Museum and written by a Hawaiian who took a compatriot to task about his translation and interpretation of a certain legend, I came to a line in which the critic informed his compatriot that as for the word Ka-aloha-lani it should be Ka-alohi-lani, and as a clincher of the truth of his assertion he added "(see Beckwith Haw. Mythology)."

Despite the training the students of Boas got in folklore and the work many of them have done in it, Martha Beckwith was one of the few to become better known as folklorist than anthropologist although she also contributed to the ethnography of Hawaii, Jamaica, and Dakota Indians. Ethnography and oral narrative art are united in her work; one illuminates the other. That this is not more widely realized stems perhaps from her unwillingness or inability to emphasize the interpretations that flash up from her assemblage of empirical data. Often they are hidden among the data where those who consult her writings only for reference material too easily overlook them or maybe discover them only after the insights have been more dramatically presented in the work of others. Her basic procedure, exemplified in the Polynesian research, was, I think, to bring to light source data that might otherwise be overlooked and lost, to draw from them their inherent organization, and to sketch the outlines of their structure. She did not seek as a rule to solve a specific problem or to test a particular hypothesis, but to make a clearer overall map of the field than existed so that later more problem-oriented followers might benefit. In a way this applies to her monograph *Folklore in America* of less than a hundred pages which are devoted mainly to "Definition of the Field" of folklore in general and to "Method of Folklore" rather than to the title of the monograph. The work has had less notice than it deserves. Of one of its contributions, Daniel G. Hoffman wrote, on page 226, of the *Journal of American Folklore* in 1959, twenty-nine years after its publication:

I have found no theoretical discussion which supersedes Martha Beckwith's suggestions, made almost thirty years ago, about the nature of those groups in America among whom folklore is found. She proposed that isolation through time of a group with its own distinctive culture, and the resultant stability of that culture, were the prerequisites for folklore. She found the isolation to be either spatial, occupational, linguistic, religious, or racial, or any combination of two or more of these factors. We can verify these criteria by mentioning the findings of some of our principal collectors and folk historians. . . .

In presenting the Hawaiian text of the romance of Laieikawai and her literal translation, Miss Beckwith prefaces them with a fine analysis of Hawaiian narrative art as revealed through this romance and other Hawaiian narratives, discusses Hawaiian narration in relation to that of the rest of Polynesia, and dwells extensively on the interaction of narrative with the rest of the aristocratic culture, and calls attention to the sociological importance of the customs mentioned in the narratives. Similar analyses appear in her later studies. Dorothy D. Lee, in a discerning review of that important work *Hawaiian Mythology*, writes:

For me, the value of this work lies in the fact that it is the only study of mythology I know in which the writer has not intentionally or unconsciously, interfered with the ideas which are presented. . . . She draws no distinctions where the Hawaiian does not draw them. She has steeped herself so thoroughly in her material, that she accepts what most of us would have tried, at best, to justify. In this way, she can transfer directly to the reader, Hawaiian concepts unacceptable to the reasoning of the Euro-American mind. . . . Out of Miss Beckwith's presentation emerges a world of thought in which identity is not delimited and not exclusive, where identities merge and overlap and divide without confusion. Here the concept is active and real. It is treated with respect; it is not explained away either rationally or on historical grounds; neither is it squeezed into an acceptable shape through the mold of scientific thought. . . .[7]

Beckwith's pioneering in research was as varied as her regions for doing fieldwork. The importance of her work in translating Hawaiian source material, garnering information on the culture, and creating paths for later students to follow in the chaotic and complex jungle of Hawaiian mythology are familiar to all. Little known, however, is her first paper, published in 1907, which probably summarizes part of her M.A. thesis in anthropology at Columbia University under Franz Boas. In the tribes studied and the point of view expressed, it recalls the work of Ruth Benedict, a later student of Boas. Beckwith once mentioned in passing to me that Boas had indeed called Mrs. Benedict's attention to her study and suggested developing certain lines of it. In this study on Hopi and Kwakiutl dance forms Beckwith sought to show "how two groups, sufficiently isolated to exhibit distinct cultural types, have developed distinct dramatic forms along the lines of their social and economic interests." Besides singling out their distinct forms she also pointed out how differently each culture, following its own peculiar and dominant bent, had interpreted even the traits which they shared, as, for example, that of having certain dancers play the part of fools.

Climaxing Beckwith's series of papers and monographs on her Jamaica fieldwork was her book published in 1929, *Black Roadways: A Study of Jamaican Folk Life*, of which many, predominantly favorable, reviews appeared in scientific journals and literary supplements of newspapers. The long, detailed, and generally complimentary review by Melville J. Herskovits is of particular interest because of his specialization as an Africanist.[8] The book, he wrote, is "the first ethnographic study of the life of any New World Negro which, to my knowledge, has been attempted. She tries to see the culture of the Jamaicans as a whole, and she describes it as a unit as she would describe the culture of any distinct people." Her descriptions of customs were so detailed that he felt able to identify some as not merely African in origin but specifically, say, as Yoruba or Ashanti. Whatever defects the book had in treatment, he said, were those of a first study. It did not pay enough attention to examples of individual behavior or to variations from accepted patterns. Herskovits differed with some of the interpretations which he regarded as not taking into consideration the information from other New World Negro groups or from African tribes. Miss Beckwith's published rejoinder pointed out that she was not here attempting a comparative study as she had attempted in some of her earlier Jamaican reports; and she defended her interpretations with which Herskovits had differed.

Herskovits' review further states that *Black Roadways* "stimulates questions that, in the search for their answers, force one to a consideration of the neighboring Negro people of the New World, and thus lead the way toward the examination of yet another major problem, the question of unity of New World Negro culture." He concluded that "the book is a pioneer ethnological account of a New World Negro group" and he "hoped that later students will build on its facts, and be stimulated by its interpretations to further study."

His hope was to be realized, for during the last decade some Yale graduate students in anthropology have done fieldwork in Jamaica. Two or three whom I talked to at some anthropological meetings in Philadelphia in the summer of 1956 asked me to tell Miss Beckwith if I should see her in Berkeley on my way back to Honolulu how much they admired the accuracy and range of her Jamaica research. They had apparently found it a solid foundation on which to build.

Beckwith's *Jamaican Folklore* is listed by J. Mason Brewer in his survey of Afro-American folklore as one of the collections "exemplifying the techniques of sound research in their respective ways."[9]

Although Herskovits felt that Beckwith did not tell enough about individual behavior in *Black Roadways*, American anthropologists in the late 1920s were only gradually shifting from generalized descriptions of culture to more consideration of individual personality in culture. As a matter of fact, in going over Beckwith's Jamaican publications on folklore, I had been impressed at how much data she gave about informants, her field situation, quotations of informants' personal views, and the like. I contrasted this amount with the page of information I had scraped together about narrators from published records of other American anthropologists relative to a widely diffused American Indian tale which I had once studied intensively. In the *Kumulipo*, published at the end of Miss Beckwith's career, one of the outstanding features is her presentation of individual Hawaiian interpretations of the symbolism of the chant.

Probably the freshness and relative fullness with which Beckwith sometimes describes a Jamaican, Indian, or Hawaiian cultural situation in which she was a participant-observer reflects her combined training in English literature and anthropology. One even catches some of the flavor of the larger social circle in which she moved on her field trips. Certainly one wishes for far more than she gives of the living quality of a culture but much comes through. Martha Beckwith undoubtedly enjoyed her study of folklife, for she called such study her hobby in one of her official biographies, but those who knew her would probably agree with me that she never pretended or tried to be "just one of the folks." Her results are never those of a dilettante, but of a scholar.

The only direct evaluation of Beckwith's Siouan work, however, which anthropological studies on the Dakota cite and quote, appears in William N. Fenton's article which surveys far more than the Iroquois folklore referred to in his title.[10] In considering the adequacy of collections from various American Indian areas, Fenton remarks, "The Plains, particularly to the north, seem well covered." And among the northern Plains tribes "represented by substantial collections" he lists the Teton Dakota, Mandan, and Hidatsa studied by Miss Beckwith. He also lists her among the collectors who "have sometimes analyzed their own materials," and among the few "notable exceptions" who have applied a rigorous method of analysis and followed it through. The Dakota examples he mentions in his discussion of native classification of narrative forms appear derived from Beckwith's Dakota studies. In discussing the problem of collecting narratives, he points out that Boas' ideal of getting all the folklore in the native language sometimes resulted in a collector's never getting around either to translating the stories or to getting them printed if he did translate them. He continues, "Yet there is a middle ground between scientific accuracy and mere story collecting. Beckwith makes a pretty good case of taking materials in Indian English, allowing for lapses of Indian memory and not retouching the material to enhance its attractiveness. Unless we listen to reason the folk materials and the story tellers will vanish before students are trained" (to know the Indian language in which to collect and translate the narratives). To amplify Fenton's statement, it may be noted that Beckwith's method, as described in her prefaces to the Dakota collections, was to get most of the stories narrated in the native dialect and translated directly into English by an interpreter. That she apparently recorded a few stories in the native language is suggested by her statement that a month passed before her interpreter could dictate the English translation of a certain narrative to her.

Another area of Beckwith's pioneering was in American regional folklore. With her fellow anthropologists she worked on New World Negro and American Indian folklore and culture, but she also ranged into the folklore and customs of historical America. Her too-brief chapter titled "Folklore in America" in her monograph of that name shows her varied interests. She wrote several reviews of books on American regional culture by Constance Rourke and other writers. As a member of the National Committee in 1934 of the National Folk Festival she wrote descriptions of the folk festivals she attended. The Vassar Memorial to her refers to President Henry Noble MacCracken's raising money for her students to collect folklore in Dutchess County. His book on the history of the county refers to the "rich harvest" of this work and cites examples of county popular beliefs.[11] While the Vassar students collected and published Dutchess County superstitions, Beckwith collected and published the superstitions of Vassar students.

As a trained anthropologist teaching comparative literature and folklore at Vassar, Beckwith seems to have served as a liaison between anthropology and the humanities. Her statement[12] that "American scholars . . . are looking with more sympathy upon the part folklore has played in the cultural background of the past out of which literary narrative has taken shape" is perhaps an indicator of the interest she aroused among her colleagues in comparative literature by her articles on "The English Ballad in Jamaica," "Polynesian Analogues to the Celtic Otherworld and Fairy Mistress Themes," and "Punjab Legend in Relation to Arthurian Romance." She was studying ballad, myth, folktale, and cult "alive" in Jamaica and Hawaii, and through her abundant cross-cultural references she was revealing to her colleagues in the humanities what could be learned in their fields through the study of living cultures. What her anthropological colleagues learned from the Celtic, Scandinavian, and other literary references is hard to say. Her detailed footnotes with their references ranging far in space, time, and cultural level are to me, at least, twinkling, if sometimes puzzling, beacons to mark the common humanity of storytellers and chanters, whether ancient or modern Greek and Hindu, medieval Celt and Scandinavian, or modern Hawaiian and Jamaican. Though hints of possible common origin of parallels in far-separated cultures appear in one of the early papers on the Otherworld and Fairy Mistress themes, one of the last papers, "Polynesian Story Composition," which deals with the same themes, perhaps reflects her final views. There she seems to eschew a common origin for similarities in world-wide stories with these themes and to describe the Polynesian variants as perhaps taking shape in Samoa and spreading eastward into other archipelagoes which reinterpreted them and used them as symbols, couched in terms of personalized nature philosophy and romantic fiction, to describe particular historical events.

Beckwith's interest in Celtic folklore and Gaelic literature appears as one of the numerous strong and luminous threads woven throughout her work. The interest shown in her work by Gaelic scholars and poets, some who had taken refuge in the United States during the first quarter of this century after Irish political difficulties, is marked. Ella Young, poet and folklorist, who lectured in the United States in the 1930s and made this country her home, writes of lecturing at Vassar and of getting Martha to go to New York for a few days: "I want her to meet some of my Irish friends who, on their part, are eager to acquaint themselves with the author of those books on Hawaiian folklore, the holder of the Vassar Chair in Mythology. . . . Boris Artzybasheff is showing us New York. . . ." (He was also illustrating Young's latest book on Irish folklore.) Young continues, "Ireland and the Irish make a stir in New York. Joseph McGarrity is giving a party; a poet himself, a magic-master of words, he is eager to show Martha Beckwith some Irish poets and let her hear songs in Gaelic that she may compare them with songs she has listened to in her native Hawaii. . . ."[13] Earlier, during four months from January through April 1923, Ireland had come to the Hawaiian Islands, when Padraic Colum, sponsored by the Hawaiian Legend and Folklore Commission and Yale University, retold Hawaiian tales for children in four books, two of which include Beckwith among those to whom Colum dedicated the retellings.[14]

The world range of her interests made clear to her the common humanity of mankind expressed through his oral narrative art. In whatever group she found herself, she was at ease, and through her dignity and graciousness made the gathering that of "cousins." Her wish to have her ashes returned to Maui was expectable. She wrote on the first page of her preface to *Hawaiian Mythology* "of a childhood and youth spent within sound of the native hula drum at the foot of the domelike House of the Sun on the windy island of Maui. There, wandering along its rocky coast and sandy beaches, exploring its windward gorges, riding horseback above the cliffs by moonlight, when the surf was high or into the deep forests at midday, we were aware always of a life just out of reach of us latecomers but lived intensely by the kind, generous race who chanced so many centuries ago upon its shores." She was buried on February 24, 1959, in the old cemetery at Makawao, Maui, where her parents, brother, and sister also lie, as well as her friend Annie Alexander. High on the quiet bluff, visited by shifting sun, wind, and rain, "some friends who had been her playmates at Haiku and cousins assembled . . . just as the sun was setting behind the West Maui Mountains. And then a tropical rain came over us and we were shrouded in a lovely mist as we placed a fragrant flower lei for Martha. Three Hawaiian women came and sang her favorite hymn. The sky was then aglow with colors as a beautiful rainbow appeared at the close of this fitting and simple memorial. . . ."[15]

Not *Vale*, but *Aloha*, Martha Warren Beckwith.

KATHARINE LUOMALA
Professor of Anthropology

HONOLULU, HAWAII
JUNE 1969

NOTES

1. (Vassar Memorial), a manuscript loaned to me by Mrs. Dorothy (Beckwith) H. Thomas, headed "At a Meeting of the Faculty of Vassar College held March ninth, nineteen hundred and fifty-nine, the following Memorial was unanimously adopted: . . . ."
2. Biographical details relating to Miss Beckwith come from a variety of sources. Among them are *American Women*, vol. 3 (1939–1940): 66; *Directory of American Scholars*, 3rd ed., p. 49. New York, 1957; "In Memoriam," *One Hundred and Seventh Annual Report*, pp. 37–38. Honolulu: Hawaiian Mission Children's Society, 1959; *Honolulu Star-Bulletin*, Feb. 4, 1959; *Honolulu Advertiser*, Feb. 5, 1959; prefaces to Beckwith's publications.
3. See the appended bibliography of Beckwith's publications.
4. Review of *Hawaiian Mythology*. *American Sociological Review* 6 (1940): 984.
5. Review of *Hawaiian Mythology*. *Journal of American Folklore* 54 (1941): 213–214, 230–232. Beckwith's reply is in *JAF* 55 (1942): 254–256.
6. *The Kumulipo*, p. 184.
7. Review of *Hawaiian Mythology*. *American Anthropologist* 43 (1941): 293–295.
8. Review of *Black Roadways*. *JAF* 43 (1930): 332–338. For Beckwith's reply, see "A Rejoinder." *JAF* 44 (1931):222–223.
9. "Afro-American Folklore." *JAF* 60 (1947): 381.
10. "Iroquois Indian Folklore." *JAF* 60 (1947): 383–397. See particularly pp. 388, 389, 392, 394.
11. Henry Noble MacCracken, *Blithe Dutchess. The Flowering of an American County from 1812*. New York: Hastings House, Inc., 1958, p. 218.
    While the girls collected Dutchess lore and Beckwith collected Vassar lore, President MacCracken recorded Beckwithiana. The following story I had heard told orally from time to time from Miss Beckwith's friends and was once informed that Dr. MacCracken had written it down for publication, but I never had located his account. An appeal to one of Miss Beckwith's cousins brought an immediate reply on January 25, 1962, with a typed copy of "When Poughkeepsie Saw the Hula," as reprinted in the *Christian Science Monitor*, April 2, 1951, from *The Hickory Limb* by Dr. MacCracken. The letter of inquiry to the cousin had raised the question of the authenticity of this legendary experience, and the cousin wrote, "And I can assure [you] that it is true, because Martha thought the world of him, and I am cer-

tain that he would not tell a lie. Moreover, the whole episode is so characteristic of Martha, that I have no doubt that it is true." Neither do I. This is Dr. MacCracken's story:

Sometimes the unexpected self-assertion of women professors came from the same dynamic that makes professors absent-minded—devotion to truth in one's special field. Among my best friends on the faculty was Miss Martha Beckwith, who held at Vassar the chair of Folklore, a rare if not unique position. In her researches she had lived with the Hawaiians of the older stock, Negroes in Jamaica highlands and reservation Indians.

"Come, Miss Monnier," she said one day; "the paper advertises a genuine Hawaiian hula at the theatre. I want you to see it. A car just went by with a big poster, too. Genuine hula, think of it!"

Miss Monnier's protests were of no avail. Off they went to the theatre on Main Street. At the door the usher asked for tickets. "Nonsense," said Miss Beckwith, "I am an authority." Awed and puzzled, the doorman let them through. They marched down to a central seat. The vaudeville was on, and the "hula" girls, from West Forty-Second Street, of course, capered on.

"This is unscholarly," said Miss Beckwith. "I must protest."

"Please, Martha, don't make a scene. What is the use?"

Martha arose and addressed the audience. "In the interest of truth," she said, "I must denounce this performance. It has nothing about it that in any way represents the true hula, except the skirt, and even that is artificial. You are being taken in."

The theatre was in an uproar. "Go ahead, old lady. Speak your mind. Tell us about the hula!" "Sit down!" Miss Martha did not sit down. She told them what the true hula was, until the petrified manager came to life and started off the hula once more.

"Come, Mathilde," said the scholar; "we will not stay for such an unscholarly performance." Miss Monnier followed Miss Beckwith's stately withdrawal while the customers cheered.

12. *Folklore in America*, pp. 62–63.

13. Ella Young, *Flowering Dusk: Things Remembered Accurately and Inaccurately*. Toronto: Longmans, Green & Co., 1945, pp. 215, 216.

14. *The Bright Islands* was dedicated to Martha Beckwith and Herbert Gregory; *Legends of Hawaii* was dedicated to them and to a number of other people.

15. Mrs. Thomas in a letter to me December 12, 1961.

BIBLIOGRAPHY OF MARTHA WARREN BECKWITH

Abbreviations

AA   *American Anthropologist*
JAF   *Journal of American Folklore*
JPS   *Journal of the Polynesian Society*
MAFS   *Memoirs of The American Folklore Society*
PFFVC   *Publications of the Folk-Lore Foundation of Vassar College*

"From Prattville to Fall River." *Sierra Club Bulletin* 3 (1901): 288.

"Dance Forms of the Moqui and Kwakiutl Indians." In *Proceedings of the International Congress of Americanists, Fifteenth Session, Quebec, 1906*, vol. 2, pp. 79–114. Quebec, 1907.

"The Hawaiian Hula Dance." *JAF* 29 (1916): 409–412.

"Hawaiian Shark Aumakua." *AA* 19 (1917): 503–517.

"The Hawaiian Romance of Laieikawai." In *U.S. Bureau of American Ethnology, Thirty-third Annual Report, 1911–1912*, pp. 285–666. Washington, D.C., 1919.

"Hawaiian Riddling." *AA* 24 (1922): 311–331.

Review of *The Fornander Collection of Hawaiian Antiquities and Folk-lore*, T. G. Thrum, ed. *AA* 24 (1922): 376–380.

Folk-Games of Jamaica, with music recorded in the field by Helen H. Roberts. *PFFVC*, no. 1. Poughkeepsie, 1922.

"Some Religious Cults in Jamaica." *The American Journal of Psychology* 34 (1923): 32–45.

"Signs and Superstitions Collected from American College Girls." *JAF* 36 (1923): 1–15.

"Polynesian Analogues to the Celtic Otherworld and Fairy Mistress Themes." In *Vassar Mediæval Studies*, edited by Christabel Forsyth Fiske, pp. 29–55. New Haven: Yale University Press, 1923.

Christmas Mummings in Jamaica, with music recorded in the field or from phonograph records by Helen H. Roberts. *PFFVC*, no. 2. Poughkeepsie, 1923.

Preface (signed) and footnotes (some of which are signed "Ed.") to *Hawaiian Stories and Wise Sayings*, by Laura C. S. Green. *PFFVC*, no. 3. Poughkeepsie, 1923.

The Hussay Festival in Jamaica, with music recorded by E. Harold Geer. *PFFVC*, no. 4. Poughkeepsie, 1924.

Introduction (signed) to *Hawaiian String Games*, by Joseph E. Emerson. *PFFVC*, no. 5. Poughkeepsie, 1924.

Jamaica Anansi Stories, with music recorded by Helen H. Roberts. *MAFS*, vol. 17. New York, 1924.

With Laura C. Green, "Hawaiian Customs and Beliefs Relating to Birth and Infancy." *AA* 26 (1924): 230–246.

"The English Ballad in Jamaica: A Note Upon the Origins of the Ballad Forms." *Publications of the Modern Language Association* 34 (1924): 455–483.

Jamaica Proverbs. PFFVC, no. 6. Poughkeepsie, 1925.

Review of *Norwegian Fairy Tales*, by H. Gade and J. Gade. *JAF* 38 (1925): 139–141.

Review of *At the Gateways of the Day* by P. Colum, *Hawaiian Legends* by W. R. Rice, *More Hawaiian Folk Tales* by T. G. Thrum, *Hawaiian Historical Legends* by W. D. Westervelt. *JAF* 38 (1925): 325–327.

With Laura C. Green, "Hawaiian Customs and Beliefs Relating to Sickness and Death." *AA* 28 (1926): 176–208.

Untitled preface (unsigned) and footnotes (signed "Ed.") to *Folk-tales from Hawaii*. Second Series, by Laura S. Green. *PFFVC*, no. 7. Poughkeepsie, 1926.

Notes on Jamaican Ethnobotany. PFFVC, no. 8. Poughkeepsie, 1927.

"A Note on Punjab Legend in Relation to Arthurian Romance." In *Medieval Studies in Memory of Gertrude Schoepperle Loomis*, pp. 49–74. New York: Columbia University Press, 1927.

With Laura S. Green, "Hawaiian Household Customs." *AA* 30 (1928): 1–17.

Review of *Santal Folk Tales*, by P. O. Bodding. *JAF* 41 (1928): 174–177.

Jamaica Folk-Lore, with music recorded in the field by Helen H. Roberts. *MAFS*, vol. 21. New York, 1928. This is a republication of *PFFVC*, no. 1, *Folk-Games of Jamaica; PFFVC*, no. 2, *Christmas Mummings in Jamaica; PFFVC*, no. 6, *Jamaica Proverbs;* and *PFFVC*, no. 8, *Notes on Jamaican Ethnobotany*. The pagination is not continuous. An "Addenda," pp. 47–67, has been added to *Christmas Mummings*. An "Index," pp. 80–82, and an "Addenda," pp. 84–95, have been added to *Jamaica Proverbs*.

Foreword (signed) and footnotes (signed "Ed.") to *Folk-Tales from Hawaii*, by Laura S. Green. This is another edition of *PFFVC*, no. 3, *Hawaiian Stories and Wise Sayings;* and *PFFVC*, no. 7, *Folk-tales from Hawaii*. Honolulu: Hawaiian Board Book Rooms, 1928.

Introduction (signed) and footnotes (signed "Ed.") to *The Legend of Kawelo*, by Laura C. Green. *PFFVC*, no. 9. Poughkeepsie, 1929.

Black Roadways: A Study of Jamaican Folk Life. Chapel Hill: University of North Carolina Press, 1929.

Myths and Hunting Stories of the Mandan and Hidatsa Indians. PFFVC, no. 10. Poughkeepsie, 1930.

"Mythology of the Oglala Dakota." *JAF* 43 (1930): 339–442.

Folklore in America, Its Scope and Method. PFFVC, no. 11. Poughkeepsie, 1931.

"Black Roadways: A Rejoinder." *JAF* 44 (1931): 222–223.

Review of *California Indian Nights Entertainments*, by E. W. Gifford and G. H. Block. *JAF* 44 (1931): 310–311.

Review of *American Humor*, by Constance Rourke. *JAF* 44 (1931): 311–313.

Kepelino's Traditions of Hawaii. Bernice Pauahi Bishop Museum Bulletin 95. Honolulu, 1932.

Myths and Ceremonies of the Mandan and Hidatsa. PFFVC, no. 12. Poughkeepsie, 1932.

"Hawaiian Riddles and Proverbs." *The Friend* 102 (1932): 332–333.

"The White Top Festival." *JAF* 46 (1933): 416.

Note (signed) and footnotes (unsigned) to *Hawaiian Folk Tales.* Third Series, by Mary Wiggin Pukui. *PFFVC*, no. 13. Poughkeepsie, 1933.

Review of *Die geheime Gesellschaft der Arioi*, by W. E. Mühlmann. *AA* 35 (1933): 378–380.

Mandan and Hidatsa Tales. Third Series. *PFFVC*, no. 14. Poughkeepsie, 1934.

Review of *Signs, Omens, and Portents in Nebraska Folklore*, by M. Cannell and *Proverbial Lore in Nebraska*, by E. L. Snapp. *JAF* 47 (1934): 266–267.

Review of *Three Lectures on Chinese Folklore*, by R. D. Jameson. *JAF* 47 (1934): 396–398.

Review of *Dakota Texts*, by E. Deloria. *AA* 37 (1935): 342–343.

Foreword (signed) and footnotes to *The Legend of Kawelo and Other Hawaiian Folk Tales*, by Laura C. S. Green and Mary K. Pukui. Reprint of *PFFVC*, no. 9, *The Legend of Kawelo*, and *PFFVC*, no. 13, *Hawaiian Folk Tales*. New material added. Honolulu, 1936.

Introduction (signed) to "Folk Tales from New Goa, India," edited by Sarah Davidson and Eleanor Phelps. *JAF* 50 (1937): 1–51. (The numerous comparative footnotes throughout the article and the outlines of the first nine stories together with their classification by the Aarne-Thompson scheme are probably also by Beckwith although unsigned.)

Review of *Suriname Folk-Lore*, by M. J. Herskovits and F. S. Herskovits. *JAF* 50 (1937): 412–415.

Mandan-Hidatsa Myths and Ceremonies. MAFS, vol. 32. New York, 1938.

Review of *The Book of Folk Festivals*, by D. G. Spicer and *British Calendar Customs. Scotland*, vol. 1, by M. M. Banks. *JAF* 51 (1938): 357–358.

"National Folk Festival, Washington. Mountain Folk Festival, Berea College." *JAF* 51 (1938): 442–444.

Hawaiian Mythology. New Haven:Yale University Press, 1940. Reprint. Honolulu: University of Hawaii Press, 1970.

"Polynesian Mythology." *JPS* 49 (1940):19–35.

Review of *English Folklore* and *Haunted England*, by C. Hole. *JAF* 55 (1942): 180–181.

"A Reply to the Review of *Hawaiian Mythology.*" *JAF* 55 (1942): 254–256.

Footnotes (signed) to "Games of My Hawaiian Childhood," by Kawena Pukui. *California Folklore Quarterly* 2 (1943): 205–220.

Review of *The Roots of American Culture*, by C. Rourke. *JAF* 56 (1943): 222–223.

"Polynesian Story Composition." *JPS* 53 (1944): 177–203.

Review of *Primitive Education in North America*, by G. A. Pettitt. *JAF* 60 (1947): 312–314.

Review of *Sumerian Mythology*, by S. N. Kramer. *JAF* 60 (1947): 446–448.

"Function and Meaning of the Kumulipo Birth Chant in Ancient Hawaii." *JAF* 62 (1949): 290–293.

Review of *Hawaiian Legends in English and Annotated Bibliography*, by A. Leib. *JAF* 62 (1949): 330–331.

The Kumulipo, A Hawaiian Creation Chant. Translated and edited with commentary. Chicago:University of Chicago Press, 1951.

"The Jew's Garden, Etc." *JAF* 64 (1951): 224–225.

Original Introduction (signed) to "Mid-Hudson Song and Verse," edited by Constance Varney Ring, Samuel P. Bayard, and Tristram P. Coffin. *JAF* 66 (1953): 43–68.

The remainder of Martha Warren Beckwith's papers are in the library at the University of California at Berkeley and in the Bernice P. Bishop Museum, Honolulu.

PREFACE

THIS guide to the native mythology of Hawaii has grown out of a childhood and youth spent within sound of the hula drum at the foot of the domelike House of the Sun on the windy island of Maui. There, wandering along its rocky coast and sandy beaches, exploring its windward gorges, riding above the cliffs by moonlight when the surf was high or into the deep forests at midday, we were aware always of a life just out of reach of us latecomers but lived intensely by the kindly, generous race who had chanced so many centuries ago upon its shores.

Not before 1914 did the actual shaping of the work begin. The study covers, as any old Hawaiian will discover, less than half the story, but it may serve to start specific answers to the problems here raised and to distinguish the molding forces which have entered into the recasting of such traditional story-telling as has survived the first hundred years of foreign contact.

To the general student of mythology the number and length of proper names in an unfamiliar tongue may seem confusing. Hawaiian proper names are rarely made up of a single word but rather form a series of words recalling some incident or referring to some characteristic significant of the person or place designated. To a personal name an epithet may be affixed, such as "o ka lani" which means literally "of the heavens" but is translated by Hawaiians by the term "heavenly" as a title of endearment or adoration. The name of the parent is often added with the causal possessive "a" meaning "child of," as in Umi-a-Liloa, which may be read "Umi, child of Liloa." In many cases the definite article "ka" becomes a part of the name and hence the preponderance in Hawaiian of names beginning with this syllable. Since recognition of its composition is essential to its proper accent, in cases where this is known with a good degree of probability through native informants, the name has been hyphenated upon its first appearance and occasionally throughout.

With the analysis of the name in mind, the pronunciation offers little difficulty. There are no silent letters. Theoretically at least, each vowel represents a distinct sound; each consonant is voiced as a distinct syllable ending in a vowel sound. Words written alike but different in meaning are to be distinguished, however, only by their spoken accent, as Ka-u', The-breast, which names a district on Hawaii, and ka'u for the summer season. A third form, ka'u, for the possessive pronoun of the first person singular, pronounced with a glottal stop, is written with the inverted apostrophe called a hamzah, indicative of a lost consonant sound in the *k* range. Besides the five vowel sounds, pronounced as in Italian, only seven consonants were recognized in the reduction of the language to writing by the early American missionaries and these do not differ from the same signs in English; the shifting of *l* to *r*, *k* to *t*, *p* to *f*, and *w* to *v* characteristic of various Polynesian dialects and recognized in the oral speech of old Hawaiians is hence ignored in the written form.

The effect upon Hawaiian speech of this melodious heaping up of sound without articulation is altogether pleasing and lends itself easily to the chanting of long poetical recitations such as Hawaiians of the old days delighted in, as in the shorter and more varied poetry of dance and celebration.

My thanks are here rendered to the trustees, director, and staff of the Bishop Museum in Honolulu for their aid and cooperation; to the president, trustees, and faculty of Vassar College for their interest in and recognition of the work of the Folklore Foundation under which, since 1920, this work has been carried on; and to Professors Franz Boas and William Witherle Lawrence of Columbia University, whose encouragement and advice have been so often and so generously given.

There are also many names to be recalled with grateful remembrance of those who have contributed directly toward the making of this book: Joseph Emerson, Stephen Desha, Mary Pukui and her mother Mrs. Wiggin, Emma Olmsted, Laura Green, Pokini Robinson, Ernest and Pearl Beaglehole, Kenneth Emory, Katharine Luomala, Frank Stimson, David

Malo Kupihea, Peter Buck, Edward Handy, Margaret Tit-
comb, Thomas Wahiako, Daniel Hoʻolapa, Hattie Saffrey
Rhinehardt, Emma Taylor, Rachel Kekela Kaiwiaia, Jonah
Kaiwiaia, Kilinahi Kaleo, William Pogue, Hezekiah Ikoa,
Lyle Dickey, Ethel Damon, Marie Neal, Lahilahi Webb.

Finally, thanks are especially due for the unstinting care
of the publishers under whose expert hands the laborious task
of setting up so composite a mass of material in convenient
form for reference has been successfully achieved.

HAWAIIAN
MYTHOLOGY

COMING OF THE GODS

HOW traditional narrative art develops orally among a nature-worshiping people like the Polynesians can be best illustrated by surveying the whole body of such art among a single isolated group like the Hawaiian with reference to the historical background reflected in the stories and to similar traditions among allied groups in the South Seas. Something of the slant of thought upon which society is regulated must be realized as it is brought out in particular instances. For this purpose a division of the subject into stories of gods and ghosts, of ancestors as they appear in the genealogies of chiefs, and of fiction in the form of legend and romance has been here adopted, although one form often overlaps another.

Hawaiians use the term kaao for a fictional story or one in which fancy plays an important part, that of moolelo for a narrative about a historical figure, one which is supposed to follow historical events. Stories of the gods are moolelo. They are distinguished from secular narrative not by name, but by the manner of telling. Sacred stories are told only by day and the listeners must not move in front of the speaker; to do so would be highly disrespectful to the gods. Folktale in the form of anecdote, local legend, or family story is also classed under moolelo. It is by far the most popular form of story-telling surviving today and offers a rich field for further investigation, but since no systematic collecting has been done in this most difficult of forms for the foreign transcriber, it is represented here only incidentally when a type tale has become standardized in folklore. Nor can the distinction between kaao as fiction and moolelo as fact be pressed too closely. It is rather in the intention than in the fact. Many a so-called moolelo which a foreigner would reject as fantastic nevertheless corresponds with the Hawaiian view of the relation between nature and man. A kaao, although often making adroit use of traditional and amusing episodes, may also proceed quite naturally, the distinction being that it is consciously composed to tickle the fancy rather than to inform the mind as to supposed events.

The Hawaiians worshiped nature gods and these gods entered to a greater or less extent into all the affairs of daily life, played a dominant part in legendary history, and furnished a rich imaginative background for the development of fictional narrative. Hence the whole range of story-telling is included in the term mythology. Among Hawaiians the word for god (akua) is of indeterminate usage. Thus any object of nature may be a god; so may a dead body or a living person or a made image, if worshiped as a god. Every form of nature has its class god, who may become aumakua or guardian god of a family into which an offspring of the god is born, provided the family worship such an offspring with prayer and offerings. The name kupua is given to such a child of a god when it is born into the family as a human being. The power of a kupua is limited to the district to which he belongs. In story he may be recognized by a transformation body in the form of animal or plant or other natural object belonging to him through his divine origin, and by more than natural powers through control over forms of nature which serve him because of family descent. As a human being he is preternaturally strong and beautiful or ugly and terrible. The name comes from the word kupu as applied to a plant that sprouts from a parent stock, as in the word kupuna for an ancestor. So the word ohana, used to designate a family group, refers to the shoots (oha) which grow up about a rootstock. The terms akua, aumakua, and kupua are as a matter of fact interchangeable, their use depending upon the attitude of the worshiper. An akua may become an aumakua of a particular family. A person may be represented in story as a kupua during his life and an aumakua if worshiped after death. A ghost (lapu) is called an akua lapu to designate those tricky spirits who frighten persons at night. Nonhuman spirits who dwell in the myriad forms of nature are the little gods (akua li'i) regularly invoked in prayers for protection. "Little gods who made not heaven and earth" they were called in contempt, after the introduction of Christianity had brought the scientific viewpoint to the contemplation of the forms and forces of nature.

An animistic philosophy thus conditions the Hawaiian's whole conception of nature and of life. Much that seems to us wildest fancy in Hawaiian story is to him a sober statement of fact as he interprets it through the interrelations of gods with nature and with man. Another philosophic concept comes out in his way of accommodating himself as an individual to the physical universe in which he finds himself placed. He arrives at an organized conception of form through the pairing of opposites, one depending upon the other to complete the whole. So ideas of night and day, light and darkness, male and female, land and water, rising and setting (of the sun), small and large, little and big, hard and light (of force), upright and prostrate (of position), upward and downward, toward and away from (the speaker) appear paired in repeated reiteration as a stylistic element in composition of chants, and function also in everyday language, where one of a pair lies implicit whenever its opposite is used in reference to the speaker. It determines the order of emergence in the so-called chant of creation, where from lower forms of life emerge offspring on a higher scale and water forms of life are paired with land forms until the period of the gods (po) is passed and the birth of the great gods and of mankind ushers in the era of light (ao). It appears in the recitation by rote of genealogies in which husbands and wives are paired through literally hundreds of generations. It is notable that in similar genealogies such as the Hebrew, in which, as introduced by the missionaries, Hawaiians showed extraordinary interest, males alone are recorded.

Gods are represented in Hawaiian story as chiefs dwelling in far lands or in the heavens and coming as visitors or immigrants to some special locality in the group sacred to their worship. Of the great gods worshiped throughout Polynesia, Ku, Kane, Lono, and Kanaloa were named to the early missionaries. They are invoked together in chant, as in the lines:

> A distant place lying in quietness
> For Ku, for Lono, for Kane and Kanaloa.

They are recognized by the appearance of whatever natural phenomena have been associated with their worship by tradition or ritual custom, as color, scent, cloud or rainbow forms, storm signs, and the notes of birds. Each had a place in family worship. The first three, at all events, had, by the time of Captain Cook's landing, been drawn into the national temple worship. Subordinate gods attached to the families of the great gods were invoked by those who hoped to gain through them special skills or success in some particular form of activity. Even thieves had their patron god. Some of the names of these departmental gods as recorded in Hawaii are to be found attached to South Sea deities; others are of native origin. The elaborate cycle of story centering about the family of the fire goddess Pele of the volcano bears every mark of such local development.

The original character of these great gods is hard to determine. Buck thinks they were of human origin, chiefs whose superior ability in life or the mystery which surrounded them on earth led to their deification after their death or disappearance. I believe that they were at first conceived as nature deities of universal significance, like Pele, and their identification with a particular human being, perhaps as an incarnation of the god, came later. So Captain Cook was worshiped as Lono because the people thought the god, or possibly the chief who impersonated the god, had returned to them in the form of this impressive stranger. Worshipers of a god were sometimes identified with the god after their death. It also happened that a man acquired the name of an ancestor during life as a sobriquet. A certain Hawaiian chief was called Wakea because he had a child by his own daughter, a departure from custom like that narrated in the myth of the first parent. An episode told in the life of Lono the god seems to have become mixed up with the quarrel of the chief Lono-i-ka-makahiki with his wife Kaikilani. Thus confusion arises through the habit of doubling names and we are unable to say in particular instances whether the god or his namesake, or which namesake in the historical sequence, is alluded to. But divinity is thought of in Polynesia as lying dormant in the idea and manifesting itself in form only when it becomes active—an activity represented among a people obsessed by the social importance of genealogical descent as a succession of births. It seems to me therefore probable that different immigrant families brought with them the gods and ritual familiar to them in the south, and developed local or personal gods in competition with a rival's claim to sources of aid from the spirit world. The particular form such a god took depended upon some dream or incident which suggested that a god had thus manifested himself to them.

Hawaiian mythology recognizes a prehuman period before mankind was born when spirits alone peopled first the sea and then the land, which was born of the gods and thrust up out of the sea. In Hawaii, myths about this prehuman period are rare. No story is told of the long incubation of thought which finally becomes active and generates the material universe and mankind; the creation story in Hawaii begins at the active stage and conforms as closely as possible to the biblical account. No story is told of the rending apart of earth and heaven, after the birth of the gods. No family of gods is represented, no struggle of the son against the primeval father, no story of the ascent to the heaven of the gods after esoteric wisdom, no myth of Tiki and the first woman, or one so obscured as to remain doubtful. Even Wakea and Papa, whose figures play a dominating part in Hawaiian myth and story, are represented as parents upon the genealogical line, not as the Sky and Earth deities their names imply. Thus the imagination, which in Polynesian groups in the South Seas plays with cosmic forces, in Hawaii is limited to human action on earth, magnified by incarnations out of a divine ancestry. Cosmic myths are either absent or told in terms of human society.

The comparison of Hawaiian stories with versions from the southern Pacific offers an important link in tracing routes of intercourse during the period of migration of related Polynesian groups. When the peopling of Hawaii took place cannot be clearly demonstrated. It was probably some centuries after the Christian era and perhaps first by way of Micronesia, from whence the earliest Polynesian voyagers may have spread out fanwise over the eastern Pacific. The firstcomers

to the Hawaiian group may have chanced upon these uninhabited islands. They may have followed flights of migrating
birds or observed currents which brought strange pieces of
wreckage to their shores. There is no archaeological evidence
to show that any people of a different culture had lived here
before them. Later migrations certainly took off from Tahiti,
as is distinctly recorded in old chants and legends and further proved by linguistic identities and corresponding forms
of culture between the two areas. Thus Hawaii, although for
many centuries finally cut off from contact with the parent
group, retained a considerable body of common tradition and
still kept the memory of the ancestral bonds with "Kahiki" as
the rootstock (kumu) of the family line. All were branches
(lala) from the parent stock. The plot of many Hawaiian
romances and hero tales turns upon such a claim to relationship with a chief in Tahiti through whom the child of the
humbler parent lays claim to divine lineage.

Hawaii was a large and fertile land. After the hardships
and struggles of early colonization the social order became
stabilized, long voyages ceased, chiefs settled down to a life
of leisure, and aristocratic arts and amusements flourished.
Even in the humblest family, story-telling furnished entertainment for long evenings. In the courts of chiefs it was a
popular amusement on the occasion of a journey or a visit.
Genealogies and local legends were carefully preserved. Traditional hero tales and romances were spun out long into the
night by means of song and dialogue, one detail following another according to a fixed pattern, or an episode being introduced from another legend to prolong the tale. A contemporary incident might be adroitly narrated in terms of some
legendary episode; an old tale localized or moved forward
into the cycle told of a contemporary chief; a story of gods
made over into one of human exploit.

But a tale once composed retained its general form, even
much of its detail. Since the habit of memorizing does not
easily die out, a comparatively large body of such traditional
story has been preserved, for the most part from oral recitation. Hawaiians today readily distinguish stories invented on
a foreign pattern, of which, after the coming of the whites,

they were prolific composers. It was through the introduction
of the new art of letters that the missionaries won their most
spectacular success over the minds of the leaders of the nation. Very soon after their arrival, the reduction of the language to writing was followed by the setting up of the first
printing press west of the Rockies. The missionaries specialized in biblical knowledge, but free versions of foreign tales
from Persian epic, *The Arabian Nights,* Shakespeare, Wal-
ter Scott, and lesser romancers of the day fill the pages of
Hawaiian newspapers after the sixties. Wild romances were
composed upon the foreign model with a setting of passion
and mystery borrowed from other than native sources. The
popular romance of Leinaala is said to have been inspired by
the love passages in the Song of Solomon, and the magic employed is distinctly other than Hawaiian or even Polynesian.

Happily, however, some Hawaiian editors believed that the
old stories handed down from their forefathers through oral
recitation had equal claim to the interest of their readers. A
call was sent out for such transcriptions and, from the period
of the sixties, many such legends were committed to writing
and printed as continued stories in the weekly journals. A
single tale might run on for years, as happened in the case of
one whose translation I had attempted, only to find that the
transcriber had died without bringing the story to a conclusion. Luckily the mother of my interpreter was able to furnish the gist of the ending from her familiarity with the legend as told in the section of the country from which she came.

Through the picture given in these recitals the background
of old Hawaiian culture may be actually realized. It is that
of a people divided into strict classes as chiefs, priests, commoners, and slaves, holding prerogatives according to inherited rank down to their minutest subdivisions, and of land
similarly subdivided, parceled out by each district chief to
his followers during his own lifetime and returned to his successor for redistribution after his death. Each such ruling
chief represented a family group (ohana) claiming a divine
ancestor of whom he was the oldest male of pure blood in direct descent, or lacking such, the female of highest rank, and
through whom he inherited the land rights for his district,

commanded the services of his relatives and hangers-on, and appointed his heir at death. From time to time this orderly system of inherited descent was broken by the usurpation of a popular leader, inferior in blood but ambitious for land and power and encouraged by a discontented faction within the following or by a powerful relative from a neighboring district. Many of the legends turn upon such a conflict with the old order, in which an adventurer of a younger branch leads a popular revolt.

It was under such an astute and powerful leader that the Kamehameha line was rising to power at the time of Cook's discovery of the islands in 1778. The complete success of the first Kamehameha and his final domination over the group was due not only to unusual strength of character but also to his readiness in adopting foreign ways of warfare and in following the advice of white men salvaged from the crews of looted foreign vessels, by which qualities he proved himself a capable dictator. The express commands of the dying chief, loyal to the old gods under whom he had won victory, were nevertheless powerless to prevent the final overthrow of the old religious system upon which had depended the stability of the social order. General demoralization had followed the economic changes which took place as a result of the conquest. Land was redistributed to the victors, old families were dispossessed and their holdings given to warring adventurers. Moreover, for forty years the presence of white strangers and contact with other countries had weakened respect for the old system by which law had been regulated upon religious tapus. Young Hawaiians visiting America on whaling ships around the Horn asked for teachers for their people. Almost immediately upon the death of the old chief in 1819 the rejection of the eating tapus between men and women took place. In 1820 the first missionaries sent out from Boston by the American Board of Missions were allowed to land and to take up their mission of teaching a new faith and imposing the standards of a foreign civilization. Within a few years after this event the whole nation followed their chiefs in repudiating the national worship and adopting the Christian religion. Social and political changes took western patterns. The uniting of the nation under a single ruler (moi) as in European countries was followed by the setting up of a constitutional form of government after the American model, the dividing up of lands for individual ownership, and the abolition of the class system. Chiefs and slaves were alike under the new law of Christian democracy. Destructive war ceased, however political intrigue might continue.

Foreign contacts of this period must certainly have influenced story-telling, especially those traditional narratives which are comparable with Bible incidents like the creation, flood, and fall of man, or episodes also which would have seemed indecent to the foreign listener. Borrowings from southern groups must have occurred, too, after interrelations were again established with neighbors of their own blood. Hawaiians joined whaling expeditions in very early days, and had intercourse with China and the Northwest Coast. Mexican cowboys were introduced into Hawaii to help in the development of cattle ranches and may have contributed some episodes from their own stock of racy story-telling. Modern interpolations certainly occurred and are to be recognized in tales collected direct from more than one native narrator and recorded in Hawaiian text. It is likely too that the long novelistic passages which occur in romances published for Hawaiian readers, as well as the handling of dialogue and incident to create a picture of life, are imitated from English models. It is highly probable that the almost complete absence of cosmic imagination already noticed is due to suppression under the influence of the hard-headed incredulity of the literal-minded English and Americans who became their mentors. But those tales which Hawaiians themselves accept as genuine are easily to be distinguished from the spurious. The strangeness of the concepts to our own culture and their consistency with Polynesian thought prove a minimum of foreign influence. Many episodes or whole histories correspond with southern types. Only in certain cases is this correspondence so close as to prove a late borrowing. In every case, however recently remodeled, the story is firmly based on native tradition and remains true in detail to native Hawaiian culture.

Despite the breakdown of classes, Hawaiians of chief stock take pride today in preserving family genealogies, possibly at times distorted by a desire to aggrandize their claim to rank. Blue blood is still to be recognized in some fine old Hawaiians who do honor, in the dignity of their lives, to their inherited tradition. Many old Hawaiian chiefs during the first hundred years of foreign contact remained on their holdings in the back country conducting their lives much according to the old pattern, retelling their family tales or those belonging to their own locality, repeating their family chants and genealogies, treasuring their family gods or setting up new gods for immediate protection against want or sorcery. In everything relating to the past the family bond remained sacred. The old pride of rank did not easily lose its hold upon the imagination. About the places where the old gods walked, where the forefathers dwelt, lingered still their active influence for good or evil; wahi pana (storied places) they are called. Even today a mere child of the district will point them out. Local entertainers may always be found ready to tell the legend, embellished by a chant at emotional moments to break the monotony of recital.

On the edge of the royal fishponds below Kalihi, in a house built for King Kalakaua, lives David Malo Kupihea, holding among his kindred, who have settled close about him, a position corresponding in humble fashion to the old patriarchal dignity of the past. Beyond the soft fringe of overhanging cassias shimmer the surfaces of the ponds outlined in enduring stone, and there are dusty exhalations from neighboring dump-heaps to which the once royal area has been consigned as the creeping population of the city seeks to build up firm land upon the bordering marshes. There Kupihea rules alike over fishponds and dump-heaps. As tradesmen come and go it is to "papa" that they appeal for adjudication. Descended from a long line of sorcery priests of Molokai in the high-chief class, educated in the best English-speaking schools of Honolulu side by side with the children of the newcomers, inheriting from his fathers the office of guardian of the royal fishponds, he keeps his love for the old learning taught by the elders of his own blood, and takes an even emotional interest in discussion with those who show a willingness to learn.

According to Kupihea the great gods came at different times to Hawaii. Ku and Hina, male and female, were the earliest gods of his people. Kane and Kanaloa came to Hawaii about the time of Maui. Lono seems to have come last and his role to have been principally confined to the celebration of games. At one time he was driven out, according to Kupihea, but he returned later. Kane, although still thought of as the great god of the Hawaiian people, is no longer worshiped, but Ku and Hina are still prayed to by fishermen, and perhaps Kanaloa—Kupihea repeating to me softly the prayer with which he himself invoked the god of fishes.

Of the coming of the gods he had explicit evidence to offer: "Ku and Hina were the first gods of our people. They were the gods who ruled the ancient people before Kane. On [the island of] Lanai was the gods' landing, at the place called Ku-moku. That is the tradition of our people. Kane and Kanaloa [arrived there], but not Lono. Some claim that Lono came to Maui. It is said that at the time Kamehameha quartered his men at Kaunakakai on Molokai before the invasion of Oahu, he went to Lanai to celebrate the Makahiki [New Year] festival and on that occasion he said, 'We come to commemorate the spot where our ancestors first set foot on Hawaiian soil.' So it seems as if it must be true that the first gods who ruled our people came to Lanai."

II

KU GODS

KU and Hina, male or husband (kane) and female or wife (wahine), are invoked as great ancestral gods of heaven and earth who have general control over the fruitfulness of earth and the generations of mankind. Ku means "rising upright," Hina means "leaning down." The sun at its rising is referred to Ku, at its setting to Hina; hence the morning belongs to Ku, the afternoon to Hina. Prayer is addressed to Ku toward the east, to Hina toward the west. Together the two include the whole earth and the heavens from east to west; in a symbol also they include the generations of mankind, both those who are to come and those already born. Some kahunas teach a prayer for sickness addressing Ku and Hina, others address Kahikina-o-ka-la (The rising of the sun) and Komohana-o-ka-la (Entering in of the sun). Still others call upon the spirits of descendants and ancestors, praying toward the east to Hina-kua (-back) as mother of those who are to come, and toward the west to Hina-alo (-front) for those already born. The prayer to Ku and Hina of those who pluck herbs for medicine emphasizes family relationship as the claim to protection. All are children from a single stock, which is Ku.

Ku [or Hina], listen! I have come to gather for [naming the sick person] this [naming the plant] which was rooted in Kahiki, spread its rootlets in Kahiki, produced stalk in Kahiki, branched in Kahiki, leafed in Kahiki, budded in Kahiki, blossomed in Kahiki, bore fruit in Kahiki. Life is from you, O God, until he [or she] crawls feebly and totters in extreme old age, until the blossoming time at the end. Amama, it is freed.[1]

Ku is therefore the expression of the male generating power of the first parent by means of which the race is made fertile and reproduces from a single stock. Hina is the expression of

1. *AA* 28: 201–202.

female fecundity and the power of growth and production. Through the woman must all pass into life in this world. The two, Ku and Hina, are hence invoked as inclusive of the whole ancestral line, past and to come. Ku is said to preside over all male spirits (gods), Hina over the female. They are national gods, for the whole people lay claim to their protection as children descended from a single stock in the ancient homeland of Kahiki.

The idea of Ku and Hina as an expression of common parentage has had an influence upon fiction, where hero or heroine is likely to be represented as child of Ku and Hina, implying a claim to high birth much like that of the prince and princess of our own fairy tales. It enters into folk conceptions. A slab-shaped or pointed stone (pohaku) which stands upright is called male, pohaku-o-Kane; a flat (papa) or rounded stone is called female, papa-o-Hina or pohaku-o-Hina, and the two are believed to produce stone children. So the upright breadfruit (ulu) tree is male and is called ulu-ku; the low, spreading tree whose branches lean over is ulu-hapapa and is regarded as female. These distinctions arise from analogy, in the shape of the breadfruit blossom and of the rock forms, with the sexual organs, an analogy from which Hawaiian symbolism largely derives and the male expression of which is doubtless to be recognized in the conception of the creator god, Kane.

The universal character of Ku as a god worshiped to produce good crops, good fishing, long life, and family and national prosperity for a whole people is illustrated in a prayer quoted by J. S. Emerson as one commonly used to secure a prosperous year:

O Ku, O Li! (?) Soften your land that it may bring forth. Bring forth where? Bring forth in the sea [naming the fishing ground], squid, ulua fish. . . .

Encourage your land to bring forth. Bring forth where? Bring forth, on land, potatoes, taro, gourds, coconuts, bananas, calabashes.

Encourage your land to bring forth. Bring forth what? Bring forth men, women, children, pigs, fowl, food, land.

Encourage your land to bring forth. Bring forth what?
Bring forth chiefs, commoners, pleasant living; bring about
good will, ward off ill will.[2]

Here again, in the antithesis between sea and land, is another illustration like that between male and female of the
practical nature of prayer, which sought to omit no fraction
of the field covered lest some virtue be lost. The habit of antithesis thus became a stylistic element in all Hawaiian poetic
thought. Imagination played with such mythical conceptions
of earth and heaven as Papa and Wakea (Awakea, literally
midday). Night (po) was the period of the gods, day (ao)
was that of mankind. Direction was indicated as toward the
mountain or the sea, movement as away from or toward the
speaker, upward or downward in relation to him; and an innumerable set of trivial pairings like large and small, heavy
and soft, gave to the characteristically balanced structure of
chant an antithetical turn. The contrast between upland and
lowland, products of the forest and products of the sea, and
the economic needs dependent upon each, shows itself as a
strong emotional factor in all Hawaiian composition. It was
recognized economically in the distribution of land, each
family receiving a strip at the shore and a patch in the uplands. It was recognized in the division of the calendar into
days, months, and seasons, when those at the shore watched
for indications of the ripening season in the uplands and those
living inland marked the time for fishing and surfing at the
shore. It modified the habits of whole families of colonizers,
some of whom made their settled homes in the uplands and
in the forested mountain gorges. It determined the worship
of functional gods of forest or sea, upon whom depended success in some special craft.

A great number of these early gods of the sea and the forest are given Ku names and are hence to be regarded as subordinate gods under whose name special families worshiped
the god Ku, who is to be thought of as presiding over them
all. As god of the forest and of rain Ku may be invoked as:

2. *HHS Papers* 2: 17–20.

Ku-moku-hali'i (Ku spreading over the land)
Ku-pulupulu (Ku of the undergrowth)
Ku-olono-wao (Ku of the deep forest)
Ku-holoholo-pali (Ku sliding down steeps)
Ku-pepeiao-loa and -poko (Big- and small-eared Ku)
Kupa-ai-ke'e (Adzing out the canoe)
Ku-mauna (Ku of the mountain)
Ku-ka-ohia-laka (Ku of the ohia-lehua tree)
Ku-ka-ieie (Ku of the wild pandanus vine)

As god of husbandry he is prayed to as:

Ku-ka-o-o (Ku of the digging stick)
Ku-kulia (Ku of dry farming)
Ku-keolowalu (Ku of wet farming)

As god of fishing he may be worshiped as:

Ku-ula or Ku-ula-kai (Ku of the abundance of the sea)

As god of war as:

Ku-nui-akea (Ku the supreme one)
Ku-kaili-moku (Ku snatcher of land)
Ku-keoloewa (Ku the supporter)
Ku-ho'one'enu'u (Ku pulling together the earth)

As god of sorcery as:

Ku-waha-ilo (Ku of the maggot-dropping mouth)

These are only a few of the Ku gods who play a part in Hawaiian mythology.

The Ku gods of the forest were worshiped not by the chiefs but by those whose professions took them into the forest or who went there to gather wild food in time of scarcity. Ku-mauna and Ku-ka-ohia-laka were locally worshiped as rain gods. Canoe builders prayed to the canoe-building gods for aid in their special capacities: Ku-moku-hali'i their chief; Kupa-ai-ke'e (Kaikupakee, Kupaikee), explained as adz (kupa) which eats (ai) the superfluous parts (ke'e), and worshiped as inventor of the bevel adz for hollowing out the canoe; Ku-pulupulu (Ku-pulupulu-i-ka-nahele) called "the chipmaker"; Ku-holoholo-pali (-ho'oholo-pali) who steadies the canoe when it is carried down steep places; Ku-pepeiao-loa and -poko, the "long-" and "short-eared" gods of the seat braces by which the canoe is carried. They prayed also to the female deities: Lea (La'e, Laea) who appeared in the body of a flycatcher (elepaio) and tapped the trunk to show if it was hollow, and Ka-pu-o-alakai (Ka-pua-) who presided over the knot (pu or pua) by which the guiding ropes (ala-kai) were held to the canoe; goddesses identified in some legends with Hina-ulu-ohia (Woman of the ohia growth) and Hina-pukuia (Woman from whom fishes are born), wives respectively of the gods of fishing and of upland cultivation, Ku-ula-kai and Ku-ula-uka, and sisters of the first three canoe builders' gods named above. Some equate Ku-pulupulu with the male Laka, called ancestor of the Menehune people, and hence with Ku-ka-ohia-laka, god of the hula dance. When the people of Ka-u district hear for the first time the sound of the kaeke drum and flute, as La'a-mai-kahiki passes their coast on one of his visits from the south, they say, "It is the canoe of the god Ku-pulupulu," and they offer sacrifices.[3]

Ku-ka-ohia-laka is worshiped by canoe builders in the body of the ohia lehua, the principal hardwood tree of the upland forest. His image in the form of a feather god is also worshiped in the heiau with Ku-nui-akea, Lono, Kane, and Kanaloa.[4] He is the male Laka worshiped in the hula dance. That is why the altar in the dance hall is not complete without a branch of red lehua blossoms.[5] In Tahiti, Rarotonga, and New Zealand, Rata is the name of the ohia tree.[6] In the cave of this god in Ola'a on Hawaii grows an ohia lehua which is looked upon in that district as the body of the forefather,

3. Malo, 113, 168–179; Kamakau, *Ke Au Okoa,* December 9, 1869; J. Emerson, *HHS Papers* 2: 17; N. Emerson, *Pele,* 201–202; Westervelt, *Honolulu,* 97–104; For. Col. 4: 154–155; Rice, 97; Thrum, *Tales,* 113, 215–216.

4. For. Col. 6: 14.   5. *Ibid.* 5: 364 note 1.

6. Malo, 115–116 note 5.

Laka. It bears only two blossoms at a time. If a branch is broken blood will flow. The story of its origin is as follows:

Ku-ka-ohia-a-ka-laka and his sister Ka-ua-kuahiwa (The rain on the ridges) come from Kahiki to Hawaii and live, Ku with his wife at Keaau and Kaua with her husband in the uplands of Ola'a. When the sister brings vegetable food from her garden to her brother at the sea, her stingy sister-in-law pretends that they have no fish and gives her nothing but seaweed to take home as a relish. In despair at this treatment, Kaua transforms her husband and children into rats and herself into a spring of water. Her spirit comes to her brother and tells him of her fate. He visits the uplands, recognizes the spot as she has directed in the dream, and, plunging into the spring, is himself transformed into the lehua tree which we see today.[7]

Hina-ulu-ohia (Hina the growing ohia tree) is the female goddess of the ohia-lehua forest. In the genealogies, legends, and romances she appears as mother of Ka-ulu, the voyager, and wife of Ku-ka-ohia-laka; Kailua on the northern side of Oahu is their home. As wife of Kaha'i she is mother of Wahieloa and grandmother of Laka at Kauiki in Hana district of Maui. In the shape of an ohia tree she protects Hi'i-lawe, child of Kakea and Kaholo, and Lau-ka-ieie the daughter of Po-kahi. To both god and goddess the flowering ohia is sacred and no one on a visit to the volcano will venture to break the red flowers for a wreath or pluck leaves or branches on the way thither. Only on the return, with proper invocations, may the flowers be gathered. A rainstorm is the least of the unpleasant results that may follow tampering with the sacred lehua blossoms.

Ku-mauna (Ku of the mountain) is one of the forest gods banished by Pele for refusing to destroy Lohiau at her bidding.[8] He is said to have lived as a banana planter in the valley above Hi'ilea in Ka-u district on Hawaii which bears his name. There he incurred the wrath of Pele and was overwhelmed in her fire. Today the huge boulder of lava which re-

7. Green and Pukui, 146–149.
8. N. Emerson, *Pele*, 201–202.

tains his shape in the bed of the valley is worshiped as a rain
god. As late as 1914 a keeper escorted visitors to the sacred
valley to see that the god was properly respected and his influence upon the weather restrained within bounds for the
benefit of the district. The legend runs as follows:

A tall foreigner comes from Kahiki and cultivates bananas of
the iholena variety in a marshy spot of the valley. Pele comes
to him in the shape of an old woman and he refuses to share his
bananas with her. She first sends cold, then, as he sits doubled
up with his hands pressed against his face trying to keep warm,
she overwhelms him with a stream of molten lava. In this shape
he is to be seen today encrusted in lava.

Sick people are sometimes brought to a cave near the place
where stands Kumauna and left there overnight for healing.
In case of drought an opelu fish is brought from the sea and
struck against the rock in order to call the rain god's attention to the needs of his worshipers. In case a fish of the proper
variety is lacking, a rare plant growing in the vicinity, which
has leaves mottled like the sides of the opelu, may be used as
a substitute. But all this must be done with the greatest reverence. Visitors to the valley are warned to be quiet and re-
spectful lest a violent rainstorm mar their trip to the mountains. The story told of Johnny Searle has become a legend
of the valley and a warning to irreverent foreigners. About
the year 1896, while Johnny Searle was manager of Hiʻilea
sugar plantation, there occurred a prolonged drought and
one evening as he was riding home down the valley with a
party of Hawaiian goat hunters he raised his gun and shot at
the Kumauna boulder, exclaiming, "There, Kumauna! Show
your power!" The shot broke off a piece from a projecting
elbow, which some say he took home and threw into the fire.
His companions fled. That night (as the story runs) a cloud-
burst rushed down the valley and flung great stones all over
the back yard of the plantation house, where they may be
seen today as proof of the truth of Kumauna's power.[9]

9. N. Emerson, *Pele*, 201–202; J. Emerson, *HHS Reports* 27:
33–35; local informants.

Rain heiau were still to be found in early days on Hawaii.
A famous healing kahuna of Ka-u nicknamed Ka-la-kalohe,
who worshiped his god the sun in Honokane gulch, is said to
have been constantly appealed to by the white planter to invoke rain or sunshine.[10] In the Chatham islands an old Moriori could raise a favorable wind for fishing by tapping on
the trunk of a special kopi tree. Other trees or rocks sent "a
deluge of rain" in response to tapping.[11] In Samoa two spirits, Foge and Toafa, have charge of the rain. When a company go out after doves, offerings are made to them of taro
and fish in order to insure fair weather. But if someone follows and strikes the stone which is dedicated to the two spirits, a thunderstorm will fall.[12] In Nanduayalo in the Lau
islands a small rock below high-water mark brings a tidal
wave if anyone strikes it or breaks off a piece.[13]

A fisherman might choose any one of various fishing gods
to worship, and the tapus which he kept depended upon the
fish god worshiped.[14] Ku-ula-kai (Ku of abundance in the sea)
was one of these gods, some say the one who had control over
all the gods of the sea. Reddish things were sacred to him.
The fisherman's heiau set up at a fishing beach is called after
him a kuula. The god lived as a man on earth on East Maui
in the land called Alea-mai at a place called Leho-ula (Red-
cowry) on the side of the hill Ka-iwi-o-Pele (The bones of
Pele). There he built the first fishpond; and when he died he
gave to his son Aiai the four magic objects with which he controlled the fish and taught him how to address the gods in
prayer and how to set up fish altars. The objects were a decoy stick called Pahiaku-kahuoi (kahuai), a cowry called
Leho-ula, a hook called Manai-a-ka-lani, and a stone called
Kuula which, if dropped into a pool, had the power to draw
the fish thither. His son Aiai, following his instructions, traveled about the islands establishing fishing stations (ko'a) at
fishing grounds (ko'a aina) where fish were accustomed to
feed and setting up altars (kuula) upon which to lay, as
offerings to the fishing gods, two fish from the first catch:

10. Green and Pukui, 137–139.

11. Skinner, *Mem.* 9: 62, 63.   12. Stuebel, 149.

13. Hocart, 214, cf. 217, 218.   14. Malo, 274.

one for the male, the other for the female aumakua. Some accounts give Aiai a son named Punia-iki who is a fish kupua and trickster and helps his father set up fishing stations.

In this story the god Ku-ula-kai who supplies reproductive energy to all things of the sea is represented by his human worshiper. The man Kuula who served the ruling chief of East Maui as head fisherman has a place on the genealogical line stemming from Wakea. The fishpond over which he presided, the place where his house stood, the bones of the great eel he slew, the stone of victory (Pohaku o lanakila) set up by his son at the famous surfing beach of Maka-ai-kuloa to commemorate his triumph—all are pointed out today by natives of the locality in verification of the story. At the stone Maka-kilo-ia (Eyes of the fish watchman) placed by Aiai on the summit of Kauiki, fishermen still keep a lookout to watch for akule fish entering the bay. A haul of 28,000 were drawn up there only a few years ago. It is the old fishing technique still practised, both in its practical and its religious aspect, which is referred to Kuula's teaching. All the places named in the legend of Aiai remain as authentic fishing grounds and stations for fishermen in island waters. Nor is the old practice of offering fish from the first catch to the god upon the fish altar entirely forgotten.

STORY OF KUULA

Wahiako version. While Ka-moho-ali'i (The shark chief) is ruling chief over Hana, the god Kuula is living in human form at Leho-ula by the sea with his wife Hina-puku-ia (Hina-pupu-kae) while his brother Ku-ula-uka (Sacred one of the uplands), god of cultivators, is living in the hills with Hina's sister Hina-ulu-ohia (Laea) as his wife. The chief finds the food supply diminishing and his people in want. He appoints Kuula-kai head fisherman and Kuula-uka head cultivator for the whole island. Kuula-kai builds a fishpond with walls twenty feet thick and ten feet high and an inlet for the fish to go in and out at. The pond is always full of fish because of Kuula's power, and men crowd to see the wonder he has made. Finally appears an enemy who breaks down the walls of the fishpond. At Wailau on Molokai lives a handsome chief named Kekoona who has kupua power and can turn himself into an eel three hundred feet long. He sees the fishpond swarming with fish and slips in through the inlet, but when he has fed well he cannot get out without breaking down the wall. He goes away and hides in a deep hole about seven hundred feet beyond Alau island called "Hole of the ulua" because it is a feeding place for ulua fish. The chief's kahuna points out the enemy and his hiding place. Kuula fishes for the eel with the famous hook Manaiakalani baited with roasted coconut meat and attached to two stout ropes held by men standing on opposite sides of the bay. These draw the hooked eel to shore, Kuula kills him with a stone, and there his body lies turned to stone with one jaw smashed and the other gaping. The dog Poki is set to watch him and may be seen also turned to stone looking off to Molokai where the friends of the chief are bewailing him. Often one hears a shrill sound like mourning and the bubbles that push up into the rock pools are the tears of those who mourn.

The dead chief's favorite determines to revenge himself upon Kuula. He gets himself appointed Ka-moho-ali'i's messenger to the fishpond and one day when the chief has sent him for a fish and Kuula has given him instructions how to prepare it by cutting off its head, baking it in the oven, slicing, and salting it, he throws away the fish and pretends that Kuula's words were directed toward the chief's own body. The chief orders Kuula to be burned in his house with all his family. Because he is a god, Kuula knows of the order and prepares to save himself, his wife, and son. He bequeaths to his son Aiai his magic objects and his power of drawing the fish, instructs him about setting up fishing stations, and bids him escape with the smoke when it turns to the west; then he and his wife escape into the sea "carrying with them all the things for the people's good." Aiai escapes with his calabash from the house when the smoke turns to the west, and hides in a hole in the cliff. Three gourds pop in the fire and all believe that the three inmates of the house are consumed. A storm arises and all those who have taken part in the burning are killed.

Meanwhile the fish have followed Kuula and Hina and the pond is empty. The chief threatens the people with death if no fish is brought him. Aiai is befriended by a little boy named

Pili-hawawa and to save the family of his friend he drops the kuula stone into a pool and the fish swarm into the pool. The first fish that the chief eats slips down his throat whole and chokes him to death.

LEGEND OF AIAI

The first fishing ground marked out by Aiai is that of the Hole-of-the-ulua where the great eel hid. A second lies between Hamoa and Hanaoo in Hana, where fish are caught by letting down baskets into the sea. A third is Koa-uli in the deep sea. A fourth is the famous akule fishing ground at Wana-ula mentioned above. At Honomaele he places three pebbles and they form a ridge where aweoweo fish gather. At Waiohue he sets up on a rocky islet the stone Paka to attract fish. From the cliff of Puhi-ai he directs the luring of the great octopus from its hole off Wailua-nui by means of the magic cowry shell and the monster is still to be seen turned to stone with one arm missing, broken off in the struggle. Leaving Hana, he establishes fishing stations and altars along the coast all around the island as far as Kipahulu. At the famous fishing ground (Ko'a-nui) in the sea of Maulili he meets the fisherman Kane-makua and presents him with the fish he has just caught and gives him charge of the grounds, bidding him establish the custom of giving the first fish caught to any stranger passing by canoe. Another famous station and altar is at Kahiki-ula.

At Hakioawa on Kahoolawe he establishes a square-walled kuula like a heiau, set on a bluff looking off to sea. On Lanai he fishes for aku at cape Kaunolu and there (some say) finds Kane-apua fishing. At cape Kaena a stone which he has marked turns into a turtle and this is how turtles came to Hawaiian waters and why they come to the beach to lay their eggs, and this is the reason for the name Polihua for the beach near Paomai. On Molokai he lands at Punakou, kicks mullet spawn ashore with his foot at Kaunakakai, and at Wailau where Koona lived and where he finds the people neglecting to preserve the young fish, he causes all the shrimps to disappear and then reveals their retreat to a lad to whom he takes a fancy. This is a rocky ledge called Koki and hence the saying "Koki of Wailau is the ladder to the shrimps." Kalaupapa is still a famous fishing ground because of the stone Aiai left there. A good place for fishing with hook and line on Molokai is between Cape-of-the-dog and Cape-of-the-tree.

On Oahu, Aiai lands at Makapu'u and makes the stone Malei the fish stone for the uhu fish of that place. Other stones are set up at grounds for different kinds of fish. The uhu is the common fish as far as Hanauma. At Ka-lua-hole the ahole fish run. The fish still spawn about a round sandstone (called Ponahakeone) which Aiai placed outside Kahuahui. It is Aiai's son Punia who, instructed by Aiai, sets up the Kou stone for Honolulu and Kaumakapili; the kuula at Kapuhu; a stone at Hanapouli in Ewa; and the kuula Ahuena at Waipio. The fishing ground outside Kalaeloa is named Hani-o; grounds for Waianae are Kua and Maunalahilahi; for Waimea, Kamalino; for Laiemaloo, Kaihukuuna. The two, father and son, visit Kauai and Niihau and finally Hawaii, where the most noted fishing grounds are Poo-a, Kahaka, and Olelomoana in Kona; Kalae in Kau; Kupakea in Puna; I in Hilo.[15]

STORY OF PUNIA-IKI

(a) *Thrum version.* At Kakaako, Aiai lives with a friendly man named Apua. The chief Kou is a skilful aku fisher at his grounds from Mamala to Moanalua. At Hanakaialama lives Puiwa and she seeks Aiai for a husband and they have a son Puniaiki. One day while she is busy gathering oopu and opae the child cries and when he asks his wife to attend to it she answers him saucily. Aiai prays and a storm raises a freshet which carries away fish and child downstream. He sees Kikihale, daughter of Kou, pick up a large oopu from the stream and recognizes his child transformed into a fish. The chiefess makes a pet of it and feeds it on seamoss. One day she is amazed to find a man child in its place. She determines to have the child reared to become her husband, and this comes to pass. When she reproaches him for doing nothing but sleep, he sends her to ask for fishhooks from her father, but burns as useless the innumerable

15. Thrum, *Tales,* 215–249 (from the Hawaiian of Moku Manu); Thomas Wahiako, sheriff for Hana district, Maui, June 10, 1930 (and other local informants); For. Col. 6: 172–175; J. Emerson, *HHS Papers* 2: 17–20; Ellis, *Tour,* 88.

hooks which Kou sends him. In a vision Aiai appears to him at
Kaumakapili where is the famous lure Kahuai which he had
from his father Kuula. With this in hand, Punia fills the canoe
with aku, which fairly leap into the canoe after the lure.[16]

(b) *Fornander version.* Kuula and Hina live at Niolopa,
Nu'uanu, and are famous for their luck in fishing. This comes
from a pearl fishhook named Kahuoi, which is guarded by the
bird Ka-manu-wai at Kau-maka-pili. When it is let down into
the water the fish jump after it into the canoe. Kipapalaulu, ruling chief of Honolulu, steals the hook. Hina bears the child Aiai
and throws him into the Nu'uanu stream. He is borne downstream to the bathing place of Kipapalaulu's daughter Kaua-
elemimo near the rock Nahakaipuami [pointed out today in the
Nu'uanu stream]. The chiefess brings up the beautiful child and
takes him for her husband. When about to bear a child she
craves aku fish and Aiai bids her ask her father for his pearl
fishhook and a big canoe for fishing. He makes a great haul of
fish, which he brings to his wife, but the hook he returns to the
care of the bird, which has been ailing since the loss but which
now recovers strength.[17]

STORY OF PUNIAKAIA

Puni-a-ka-ia (Hankering after fish), the handsome son of
high chiefs of the northern districts of Oahu named Nu'upia
and Hale-kou, who live at Kaneohe, nurses the fish Uhu-makaikai, parent of all the fishes, and his pet drives fish into his nets.
He marries a pretty, well-behaved woman named Kaalaea, to
whom he and his father and mother bring gifts according to
custom. She gives herself alone by coming to him and placing
herself in his lap. He goes to live with her family but they insult
him for doing nothing but sleep and he goes away to Kauai,
takes a high chiefess to wife, and lays a wager to bring in a
great catch of fish. His pet fish in the pool at Nu'upia, apprised
by his mother of the wager, sends him fish enough to win the
whole island of Kauai. He gives these away to the men who have
taken him across to Kauai and returns to Oahu with his new
wife.[18]

16. *Tales,* 242–249.   17. For. Col. 4: 554–559.
18. *Ibid.* 5: 154–162; Dickey, *HHS Reports* 25: 19.

The theme of the stolen luck-bringing fishhook is common
in the South Seas. It occurs again in Hawaii in the story of
Iwa the master thief, which appears in a later chapter.

New Zealand. Tau-tini, son of Tari's sister Hine-i-taitai, recovers the fishhook which Ra-kuru, brother-in-law of Tari, stole
from Rari.[19]

Tokelau. Kalokalo-o-ka-la, child of the Sun in Fakaofa,
starts up a tree to visit his father in order to get a lucky fishhook as a bridal present for his wife. Directed by an old blind
woman whose eight taro sprouts he has broken off and whose
sight he has restored, he passes stinging insects, then crabs,
goes through a spinning door, and finds his father. He is given
a bundle and told not to open it, but does so and is swallowed by
a shark because the Sun is angry. The hook falls into the sea
and is taken by the Fiji chief and shaped into a lucky spoon
bait. Hina's husband tries it and is so pleased with it that he
carries it away with him. The whole wedding party except Hina
are in consequence drowned. Hina returns to her father and her
child Tautini gets possession of the shell and is successful in
bonito fishing until he loses the hook.[20]

Samoa. 'Alo'alo is sent to heaven after the lucky fishhook in
order to satisfy his wife's pregnancy craving for fish. He disobeys the tapu and falls into the sea near Fiji and the hook he
has obtained is lost.[21]

Tonga. (*a*) An old man's daughter is taken to the sky. A man
crawls up the fishline leading to the sky and she bears twins.
The twins are sent to their grandfather for "the hook for pulling up land." The old man tells them to select a bright hook, but
they take the dull one and it turns out to be the lucky hook.[22]

(*b*) Maui-kisikisi comes to Manu'a after a lucky fishhook,
meets the fisherman's wife Tavatava-i-Manuka, and wins from
her the secret that the dull-looking hook is the one he must take.

19. White 1: 170–172.   20. *JPS* 32: 168–170.
21. Krämer 1: 412–416.   22. Gifford, *Bul.* 8: 20.

"Tavatava-i-manuka" has become the saying for one who has betrayed a secret.[23]

At the time of Cook's discovery of the Hawaiian group, priests of the strictest religious order followed the Ku ritual. According to the Ku worship any public calamity which threatened the whole people, like prolonged drought, was to be averted by the erection of a special form of heiau (luakini) in which was observed a prolonged ritual involving the whole people as participants and demanding exorbitant offerings to the gods in the shape of pigs, coconuts, redfish, white cloth, and human victims. This was especially the practice in time of war. The ruling chief alone could erect such a heiau, but subject to the advice of the priests, who picked out a favorable site and decided whether an old heiau was to be repaired or a new one set up. Tradition was consulted to determine the plans of heiau whose erection had been followed by success in battle. Variations in plan might occur, but all must include the essential parts laid down at the time of the building of the first heiau by the gods at Waolani on Oahu, and it was to the national god Ku-nui-akea that such a heiau was erected.

Ku-nui-akea was represented in the heiau by a block of ohia wood freshly cut under strict ritual ceremonies. A human sacrifice was offered as payment for the tree both at the spot where it was cut down and at the posthole where the image was set up. In the forest the gods of the growing tree were invoked in a prayer which seems, with its reiterative phrasing, a very old one:[24]

> Ku of the forest, Ku-lono, strike gently,
> Ku-pulupulu, Ku-mokuhali'i, strike gently,
> Cut a pathway, strike gently,
> Cut a pathway above, strike gently,
> Cut a pathway below, strike gently,
> Hew down the ohia Ku-makua, strike gently,
> Hew down the ohia of the forest, strike gently,
> Hew down the ohia of the moist forest, strike gently,
> Hew down the ohia of the koa forest, strike gently. . . .

23. Reiter, *Anthropos* 2: 446; *JPS* 20: 166.
24. Kamakau, *Ke Au Okoa*, February 24, 1870.

The public ceremonies at the heiau covered ten days, or might be extended if the auspices were unfavorable. They have not been studied in detail, but the accounts include a circuit run about the images in the heiau carrying the portable gods and led by a naked man impersonating Ka-hoali'i; recitation of sacred "binding prayers" during a period of complete silence, called an aha (assembly); dedication of the mana (sacred) sanctuary where the priests assembled for two days to chant prayers; another aha ceremony followed by a symbolic "binding of the heavenly to the earthly realm" by means of a rope of sennit run around the inside of the sacred house; the offering to Ku of a human victim or of an ulua fish whose eye was plucked out for Ka-hoali'i; the cutting of the god's navel string, represented by a girdle of coconut leaves, in a ceremony corresponding to that for a chief's son, and the girding of the god and of each of the other images with a loincloth; the dressing with white tapa of the three-tiered prayer tower, into which the priest then entered; a visit to the mountains by priests and people carrying the portable war gods of the chiefs and returning with shouts and singing, bearing branches of koa trees to make a temporary booth; the sacrifice of a pig and its entire consumption, each man in the group sharing the feast; a ceremonial bath in the sea from which each returned with a piece of coral in his hand and piled it upon a heap outside the temple; and finally the presentation by the female chiefs of the ruling family of a great loincloth for Ku.

The occasion of the offering of human sacrifices brought together only those of rank and those who had prepared themselves under careful discipline. It followed, according to Kamakau, a strict period of prayer during which the audience all "sat firmly on their buttocks, the left leg crossed over the right leg in the position called ne'epu and the left hand crossed over the right." At the command of the priest everyone held up the right hand pointing toward heaven, kept this position while the group prayed in unison, and then went back to the first position, all exactly at the same time and without moving the body. A mistake meant death to the awkward or careless. If the body to be offered was that of a chief

slain in battle the ruling chief took hold of the hook Manai-
kalani (the famous hook that drew up land), which hung
from a cord, and hooked it into the mouth of the victim, at
the same time reciting the prayer which condemned the traitor, and the body was laid on the altar with each arm embrac-
ing the body of a hog laid on either side of the dead man.
After a war there might be many such victims.[25]

Four feather war gods were worshiped in the heiau in the
time of Kamehameha as visible forms of the god Ku-nui-akea
under the Paao priesthood. These gods are described by Kamakau as "sticks of wood below, draped in folds of tapa . . .
and at the head a very fine feather hung dangling so as to
cover the head. When the god was consulted to know the
truth, the feather stood straight up, whirling about like a
waterspout as if full of electricity, and flew from its place
and rested on the head of a person and trembled on his head,
his arm, or shoulder. This was a sign that the god would help
and bless him in war and give him prosperity."[26] Impotent
gods who remained obstinately passive were rejected by war
leaders or the battle was called off. Kawelo, the story says,
smashed the god Ku-lani-hehu with a club and called it a
coward because it showed not even a flutter of feathers when
consulted about the success of his expedition to Kauai.[27]

Kukailimoku is the most famous of the Ku gods of battle
owned by Kamehameha. Kalakaua describes the image as "a
small wooden figure, roughly carved, with a headdress of yellow feathers." This god was said to utter cries during a battle which could be heard above the sounds of the fight. It was
supposed to represent the god Kaili of Liloa, which was given
to Umi at the time when the rule over the land was given to
Hakau, to have been carefully preserved and worshiped by
Umi, and to have descended to Keawe-nui-a-Umi and from
him to his son Lono-i-ka-makahiki. Ka-lani-opu'u gave it to
Kamehameha.[28] This was not, however, the original Kaili

25. Malo, 210–248; Pogue, 21–22; Kamakau, Ke Au Okoa, February 17 to March 3, 1870; Handy, Bul. 34: 278–282.

26. Ke Au Okoa, March 17, 1870; Kuokoa, July 6, 1867.

27. For. Col. 5: 28–31.

28. Ibid. 4: 188, 190; 5: 464; Kalakaua, 44.

god, according to some old Hawaiians. The original god (akua) was a stone (or gourd) about the size of two fists, bound about with sennit, and having at the top two feathers from the mythical bird called Hiva-oa, which were secured by prayer. When Kamehameha conquered all the islands, the saying was "E ku kaili moku," that is, "Kaili has risen over the islands." This expression became attached to the image. After the abolition of the tapu by the chiefs after Kamehameha's death, the keeper of Kaili in Kohala made a canoe and placed the god in it, together with food, awa, and tapa cloth. He wept over the god, saying, "O Kaili, here is your canoe, here is food, here is awa, here is tapa; go back to Kahiki." Then he set the god adrift on the ocean and by the mana of the god the canoe sailed onward to Kahiki and was never seen again.[29]

All of these war gods were ultimately regarded as gods of sorcery. It was for this reason that Kamehameha was careful to secure the gods of the islands over which he had gained rule. Ku-ho'o-ne'e-nu'u was the god of the Pakaka temple at Kou (Honolulu) and the principal god of Oahu ruling chiefs. Ku-ke-olo-ewa was worshiped on Maui and became a god of Kamehameha when he gained possession of that island. Ku-kaili-moku was the most powerful sorcery god of Hawaii until the rise of the famous sorcery god of Molokai, Ka-leipahoa, whose story will be told later.

Ku-waha-ilo (Ku maggot-mouth) was by tradition a man-eater and the god responsible for the introduction of human sacrifice. Ellis's story is that, after Umi's victory over his elder half-brother Hakau, the voice of "Kuahiro his god" was heard demanding more men for the sacrifice, until eighty of the enemy had been offered. The legend runs that when the body of Hakau himself was laid on the altar the god came down from heaven in a pillar of floating clouds with thunder and lightning and dark clouds, and "the tongue of the god wagged above the altar."[30]

In fiction the place of this god is in the heavens. He pours

29. Given, July, 1935, by Mrs. Lahilahi Webb.
30. Ellis, *Tour*, 272; Kamakau, *Ke Au Okoa*, March 17, 1870.

"death-dealing bolts" in the Aukele legend.[31] In the Ana-elike romance his coming is preceded by earthquake and heavy winds, then by a tongue carrying victims in its hollow, followed by the body.[32] In the Hainakolo romance he is a man-eater with terrible bodies such as a whirlwind, an earthquake, caterpillars, a stream of blood, a mo‘o body with flashing eyes and thrusting tongue.[33] All these manifestations are among the bodies of the Pele family of gods, and Ku-waha-ilo's name is one of those given for the husband of Haumea and father of Pele. Male chiefs worshiped him as a god of sorcery under the name of Ku-waha-ilo-o-ka-puni.[34] In the legend of Hawaii-loa he is the god worshiped by the man-eaters of the South Seas, because of whom Hawaii-loa forbids further intercourse with southern groups.[35] In a Hawaiian newspaper he is invoked as:

> Ku with the maggot-dropping mouth,
> Ku big-eyes,
> Ku little-eyes,
> Ku long-eyes,
> Ku short-eyes,
> Ku rolling-eyes,
> Ku strolling about in the rain,
> Ku like a seabird,
> Ku the parent,
> Ku of the uplands,
> Ku of the ohia tree,
> Ku of the low-lying islands,
> Ku mountainward,
> Ku seaward,
> Ku with a mouthful of maggots,
> 　　Return! Return!

31. For. Col. 4: 76–85.　　　　32. Rice, 20, 22–24.
33. Westervelt, *Gods and Ghosts,* 165–170.
34. Malo, 114.　　　　35. For. Col. 6: 279–280.

III

THE GOD LONO

HENRY thinks that the Hawaiian Lono as "Great Lono dwelling in the waters" (Lono-nui-noho-i-ka-wai) is the Tahitian god Ro'o, messenger of the gods and especially of Tane, who "sets himself in the cloud" and feeds upon it, is born and matured there, and travels on with it.[1] Lono in Hawaii is associated with cloud signs and the phenomena of storms. According to some old Hawaiians, the god "with head hidden in the dark clouds above" (po'o huna i ke ao lewa) is primarily Lono. In the address of the priest to the returning Lono at the Makahiki he is associated with the clouds:

> Your bodies, O Lono, are in the heavens,
> A long cloud, a short cloud,
> A watchful cloud,
> An overlooking cloud; in the heavens (it is),
> From Uliuli, from Melemele,
> From Polapola, from Ha'eha'e,
> From Omao-ke-ulu-lu,
> From the land that gave birth to Lono.
> Behold Lono places the stars
> That sail resplendent through the heavens.
> High resplendent is the great image of Lono;
> The stem of Lono links our dynasties with Kahiki,
> Has lifted them up,
> Purified them in the ether of Lono. . . .[2]

In prayers to Lono the signs of the god are named as thunder, lightning, earthquake, the dark cloud, the rainbow, rain and wind, whirlwinds that sweep the earth, rocks washed down ravines by "the red mountain streams [stained with red earth]

1. 369–371.
2. Malo, 191–192, translation by N. B. Emerson.

rushing to the sea," waterspouts, the clustering clouds of heaven, gushing springs on the mountains.

> Lono the rolling thunder,
> The heaven that rumbles,
> The disturbed sea,

says the chant.

The Lono order of priests in the days of Kamehameha set up heiaus to pray for rain, abundant crops, or escape from sickness and trouble. A prayer to Lono, recorded in the Fornander collection under Thrum, shows how, after the coming of Kane and Kanaloa and the establishment of the ancestral line through Kumuhonua and Lalohonua and its spread over the island through Wakea and Papa, from whom were born the chiefs, there came Lono also from the ancestral birthplace, to whom were offered the redfish, the black coconut, the whitefish, and the growing awa; to Kane and Kanaloa were made sacred the red fowl, the pig, and awa: "Ku, Kane, and Kanaloa are supreme in Kahiki." The coming of Lono is heralded by cloud signs in the heavens and finally:

> Lono and Keakea-lani,
> Living together, fructifying the earth,
> Observing the tapu of women,
> Clouds bow down over the sea,
> The earthquake sounds
> Within the earth,
> Tumbling down there
> Below Malama.[3]

Kea in the chant is the goddess Nuakea. Nuakea, descended from Maweke of Oahu, lived on earth as a prophetess and became the wife of Keolo-ewa, ruling chief of Molokai and son of Kamauaua.[4] Her name is coupled with Lono's in the ceremony for weaning a boy child, in which the symbolic gourd of Lono plays an important part. The common people remembered the fructifying powers of Lono in the shape of a symbolic food gourd, which, like the stone of Kane, was used for

3. For. Col. 6: 505–506.   4. For. Pol. Race 2: 31–32.

family prayers only. Each householder kept in his house of worship, called the mua, a food gourd (hulilau) called kuaahu (altar) or ipu (gourd) of Lono, covered with wickerwork and hung by strings to a notched stick. Inside the gourd were kept food, fish, and awa, and a little piece of awa was tied to the handle outside. Morning and evening the pious man took down the gourd, laid it at the door of the house, and, facing outward, prayed for the chiefs, commoners, and for the good of his own family, then ate the food from the gourd and sucked the awa.[5] The gourd prayer quoted by Malo for the ceremony at the weaning of a male child invokes both Lono and (Nua)kea, the goddess who provides milk for the nursing mother and is now petitioned to stop the supply. Both god and goddess are called upon to eat the food provided, Kea to see to the child's prosperity, Lono to send propitious cloud omens, and both to guard against the malice of sorcery. After this ceremony the child is transferred to the men's house and eats no more with the women.[6] The chant runs:

My vine branch this; and this the fruit on my vine branch. Thick set with fruit are the shooting branches, a plantation of gourds. . . .

How many seeds from this gourd, pray, have been planted in this land cleared-by-fire? have been planted and flowered out in Hawaii?

Planted is this seed. It grows; it leafs; it flowers; lo! it fruits —this gourd-vine.

The gourd is placed in position; a shapely gourd it is.

Plucked is the gourd; it is cut open.

The core within is cut up and emptied out.

The gourd is this great world; its cover the heavens of Kua-kini.

Thrust it into the netting! Attach to it the rainbow for a handle! . . .

Lono as god of fertility was celebrated in the Makahiki festival held during the rainy season of the year, covering a

5. Kamakau, *Kuokoa*, August 24, 1867; *HAA* 1910, 56–57; 1911, 156.

6. Malo, 120–127.

period of four months from about October to February. During this time the regular tapu days were suspended; the people left off their ordinary occupations and practised athletic games. Meanwhile ritual ceremonies took place and a procession moved through each district collecting offerings out of the abundance provided by the god in response to the prayers and offerings of the preceding year.

Lono-makua (Father Lono) was the name given to the material form which represented the god at this time. It was a straight wooden post or mast about ten inches in circumference and ten to fifteen feet long "with joints carved at intervals," says Malo, and a figure at the upper end which Alexander identifies as a bird. Near the top was tied a cross-piece about sixteen feet long to which were hung feather wreaths, imitations of the skeleton of the kaupu bird, and at each end long streamers of white tapa cloth which hung down longer than the pole. This was the so-called "Long-god" of the Makahiki.

Before the Long-god was brought out, fires were lighted on the beach and the people bathed ceremonially in the sea and put on fresh garments. This bathing festival was called hiʻu-wai (water-splashing).[7] For five days thereafter the high priest was kept blindfolded and "merry-making, boastful demonstrations of prowess, and boxing were the occupations of the day." Offerings to the god were collected from each district. The Long-god was borne along the seacoast, the procession moving clockwise, with the land side to the right. A Little-god was in the meantime borne along through the uplands in the opposite direction, followed by the people, who gathered huge packs of edible fern as they went, and returned that same evening to the point of departure. It might take twenty days for the Long-god to make the circuit. At each chief's place the carriers were fed, the chief's wife hung a fresh tapa-cloth girdle about the god, and the chief clasped an ivory tooth ornament upon it. "Hail to Lono!" cried the people while the priest prayed to the god and pointed out the clouds from Tahiti which were the signs of his coming. Mean-

7. Malo, 190, 202; Kepelino, 96, 193; Pogue, 19.

while the keepers of each god hung bundles of roasted taro tops on the sides of their houses to break the tapu on labor. Fires were lighted on the night of Kane, and if they burned brightly and there was no rain the bandage was removed from the eyes of the high priest and the next day all could go fishing and eat the fish caught. When the Long-god returned, the ruling chief sailed out in a boat to meet the god and on his return he was met by a company of spearmen; one of these threw a spear which he or his attendant parried, and another touched him with a spear. A mock battle followed and that night the ruling chief offered a pig in sacrifice at the heiau. A naked impersonator of Ka-hoali'i spent the following night in a temporary booth and the next day all the people feasted on roast pig. A large-meshed net, the net of Maoloha (Maoleha), filled with vegetable food was shaken out and if none clung to the net it was a sign of a prosperous year. A structure of wickerwork was sent out to sea "to take Lono back to Kahiki" and an unpainted canoe "coursed back and forth in the sea." Finally, to free the pork tapu it was necessary for the ruling chief to spend a night in each of four booths in succession; and to free the fishing tapu on the aku fish, which alternated for six months with that for the opelu, the Kahoali'i impersonator ate an eye of an aku fish and one of a man killed in sacrifice. "Now began the new year," concludes Malo.[8]

During the passage of the Long-god from district to district, offerings for the god were collected in the form of vegetable food, live animals, dried fish, bark-cloth garments, ornaments, and other valuable property. If the offering was considered too small, the god remained overnight until more could be gathered, and the land overseer was likely to be dispossessed. In Kamehameha's day a kind of game was made of such an event; the pole was let down, and the whole following were at liberty to raid the district and take what property they pleased, but if anyone took anything after the pole was set straight again, he was subject to the owner's retaliation.[9]

8. Malo, 186–210; Pogue, 18–19; Kamakau, *Ke Au Okoa*, February 17, 1870; For. Col. 6: 34–44.

9. Kamakau, *Kuokoa*, July 6, 1867.

A comparison of harvest festivals reported from other South Sea groups shows that the idea is common, but the form each takes and the god to whom the occasion is dedicated must be regarded as dependent upon the special social system and special religious setup locally developed within the group. In Tahiti, a first-fruit festival is celebrated called the parara'a matahiti, beginning in December or early January and invoking Roma-tane (Ro'o-ma-tane), god of Paradise.[10] In the Marquesas, harvest festivals are celebrated in the autumn at the seasons of ehua and mataiki.[11] In Fiji, the Lord from Hades comes to the Tailevu coast in December and pushes the young yam shoots through the soil. Silence is imposed during this moon; at the end a great shout is raised and the news is carried from village to village that pleasure and labor are again free for all.[12] In Tonga, at the time of presentation of the first fruits, the sports of wrestling, club-fighting, and boxing are indulged in.[13] In San Cristoval, at the time of first fruits, the priest offers sacrifice as the news is sent forward from village to village and the people go forth, the men bearing weapons and sham-fighting as they go, the women carrying a fire stick for the sacrifice. They chant a song and set up symbols at a sacred tree in order that the creepers may be strong for climbing, the cooking successful, the adzes sharp, the craftsmen skilful at house building, the mat making prosperous. They burn sacrifices of puddings made from the first crops. Then they send on word to the next village, where a similar ceremony is performed.[14]

The legend given by Henry Lyman of the way in which Lono came to institute the Makahiki games is as follows:

LEGEND OF THE MAKAHIKI

Lono sends out two of his brothers as messengers to find him a wife on earth. They travel from island to island and finally in the Waipio valley on Hawaii beside the falls of Hi'ilawe they find the beautiful Ka-iki-lani dwelling in a breadfruit grove

10. Henry, 177.   11. Handy, *Bul.* 9: 218.
12. Thomson, 114.   13. Collocott, *Bul.* 46: 53.
14. Fox, 80–81.

companioned by birds. Lono descends on a rainbow and makes her his wife and she becomes a goddess under the name of Ka-iki-lani-aliʻi-o-Puna. They live at Ke-ala-ke-akua and delight in the sport of surfing. A chief of earth makes love to her and Lono hears him singing a wooing song. He is angry and beats her to death, but not before she has assured him of her innocence and her love for him. Lono then institutes the Makahiki games in her honor and travels about the island like a madman challenging every man he meets to a wrestling match. He builds a canoe such as mortal eyes have never seen since, with a mast of ohia wood and a sail woven of Niʻihau matting and cordage twisted from the coconuts of Keauhou. The people bring heaps of provisions and pile them up before him. Forty men bear the canoe to the launching place, but Lono sails forth alone. His words of promise to the people are that he will return to them, not by canoe but on an island shaded by trees, covered over by coconuts, swarming with fowl and swine.[15]

The story opens much like the version given by Ellis of the institution of the Arioi society by the god Oro, in the person of Oro-tetefa as Mühlmann thinks, whom he takes to be the earthly Oro and perhaps a historical person.[16]

LEGEND OF ORO

(a) *Ellis and Mühlmann versions.* Oro desires a wife of the daughters of Ta-ata, the first man. He sends his two brothers, Tu-fara-pai-nuʻu and Tu-fara-pai-raʻi, to seek for such a wife. They visit island after island and finally at Moua-tahataha-rua (Red-ridged mountain) on Borabora they find the beautiful Vai-raumati. Oro makes of the rainbow a pathway to earth. He finds the girl bathing at Ovaiaia at Vai-tape on Borabora and makes her his wife. Hoa-tabu-i-te-rai is the child born to him. His younger brothers come in search of him, Oro-tetefa and Uru-tetefa. Finding the wife and having no suitable gift to present to her, one turns himself into a pig and a bunch of red feathers and the other makes the offering. To reward his broth-

15. Thrum, *Tales,* 108–116; see Handy, *Bul.* 34: 112.
16. *Tour,* 75.

ers, Oro deifies them and makes them leaders of the Arioi society.[17]

(b) *Moerenhout version.* Oro himself descends to earth on
the island of Borabora and with his two sisters, the goddesses
Teouri and Oaaoa, attends all the festivals where women are
gathered. At Vaitapé he finds a girl of rare beauty bathing in
the pool Ovaiaia, Vairaumati by name. The sisters approach
her on his behalf and she consents to have an affair with him
provided he is young, handsome, and a chief. Each night he descends on a rainbow to his bride. His brothers come to seek him
and, finding him with the girl and having with them no presents
to offer, one takes the body of a pig, the other of a bunch of red
feathers and, retaining also their human bodies, they present
their gifts. That night the pig bears seven little ones which are
dedicated to the Arioi, which a man named Mahi now initiates
at Oro's request. Oro quits Vairaumati in a column of flame after
bidding her name the child Oa-tabou-te-ra'i (Sacred friend of
the gods). This child becomes a great chief and rules well. At his
death he ascends to the heavens where his father and mother
dwell.[18]

The likeness between this late Hawaiian Lono story and
that collected early in Tahiti as the origin of the Arioi society under the patronage of Oro does not argue for an original identity of Lono with the Tahitian god Oro, whose worship at the great temple at Raiatea probably arose later than
the migration period to Hawaii. The theme of the descent of
a god from heaven to a beautiful woman of earth is a stock
theme in Polynesian mythology and recurs repeatedly in Hawaiian chant and story. Further investigation is needed to
prove that it originally belonged to the Lono myth, tempting
as is the hypothesis. Its application to the figure of this new
god—who is said to have been introduced late from Maui
into the orders of priesthood and who was worshiped without human sacrifice as a god of peace and of fructification of
the earth, in contrast to the severe Ku ritual directed toward

17. Ellis, *Researches* 1: 231–234; Mühlmann, 37–40.
18. Moerenhout 1: 484–489.

the preservation of the ruling chief in time of war or danger
from sorcery and the enforcement of the tapu system upon
which a chief's rank and power depended—would explain
some mythical allusions which are now obscure. But the
theme uniformly connected with the Lono myth and his institution of the Makahiki games is the jealousy motive and
this does not appear in the Tahitian Oro myth, although it
bears some resemblance to an episode in the life of the navigator Hiro. It gets mixed up in Hawaii with the late history
of a grandson of Umi named Lono-i-ka-makahiki, to which
it does not belong. A song of the god Lono in an epic form unusual in Hawaiian poetry is quoted in translation in the notes
taken on the visit to Honolulu of H.M.S. *Blonde* in 1825.
The allusion in the fourth couplet is to the play of pieces in
the game of checkers (konane) in which Lono and his wife
are engaged, but its secret meaning, divined by the chief,
suggests getting rid of the lady's present lover in favor of
the one who sends the message.[19]

SONG OF LONO

Rono [Lono], Etooah [akua or god] of Hawaii, in ancient
times, resided with his wife at Karakakooa [Kealakekua or
Path of the gods].

The name of the goddess, his love, was Kaikirani-Aree-Opuna
[Kaikilani-ali'i-o-Puna]. They dwelt beneath the steep rock.

A man ascended to the summit, and from the height thus addressed the spouse of Rono:

"O Kaikiranee-Aree-Opuna, your lover salutes you: keep this,
remove that: one will still remain."

Rono, overhearing this artful speech, killed his wife with a
hasty stroke.

Sorry for this rash deed, he carried to a morai the lifeless
body of his wife, and made great wail over it.

He traveled through Hawaii in a state of frenzy, boxing with
every man he met.

The people astonished said, "Is Rono entirely mad?" He re-
plied, "I am frantic on her account, I am frantic with my great
love."

19. Byron, 20–21.

Having instituted games to commemorate her death, he embarked in a triangular boat (piama lau), and sailed to a foreign land.

Ere he departed he prophesied, "I will return in after times, on an island bearing coconut trees, and swine, and dogs."

A second question of relation with the Oro figure in Tahiti arises in connection with the Arioi society, of which Oro was the patron god.[20] The dramatic dances whose performance was an important part of the program of this society correspond to the schools of dancing in Hawaii organized under expert leaders and dedicated to gods of the hula, whose elaborate performances on the island of Hawaii were witnessed by Vancouver in the latter part of the eighteenth century. That these were connected with the Makahiki festival and hence must have been on this island under the patronage of the god Lono is proved by the fact that Kamehameha and his queen were obliged at this time to withdraw before the dance "as they are prohibited by law from attending such amusements, except on the festival of the new year [that is, the Makahiki festival]" and that the performance itself on that day "was contrary to the established rules of the island" and only permitted out of compliment to the foreign visitors.[21]

The hula dance in Hawaii is developed in connection with the Pele deities, and these deities are invoked together with Lono in the prayers offered to Kane in the heiau. Laka is the male god named as patron of the hula dance. He is represented in the ohia lehua tree, whose red blossoms were used for decoration of the altar in the religious ceremonies of the dance. Emerson identifies Lono with Laka, and there is some ground for the association in the fact that in the Ku ritual Lono is invoked with Ku in prayers connected with the setting up of the Ku image cut from an ohia lehua tree of the forest. Lono-makua, the name given to the Long-god of the Makahiki festival, is also the name of Pele's fire keeper as

20. Mühlmann; Ellis, *Researches* 1: 229–247; Henry, 230–246; Moerenhout 1: 484–489; Handy, *Bul.* 79: 61–65; 9: 39–42; N. Emerson, *Songs of the Hula.*

21. Vancouver, 5: 63–75.

represented in the fire sticks, symbol of fertilization. Laka as a form of Lono, god of fertility, would give a further objective idealization, in the fiery red flowers of the lehua which grows native on the mountainside about the volcano, to the symbolic association between fire and fertilization. Lightning is also an attribute of storm clouds as well as the rolling thunder. The word Lono belongs not only to the idea of sound but also to that of hurling, as a spear. On the Kumuhonua genealogy Laka is named as the son of Kumu-honua (Earth foundation) and Lalo-honua (Earth below), thirty-six generations earlier than Wakea and Papa, the first parents of the Kane people. It is tempting to think that this Laka, god of the wildwood, son of Ku (Kumuhonua), the ancestral god of the first Hawaiian immigrants through union with a woman from below, came to be replaced after the rise of the Kane gods by the great god Lono dwelling in the heavens.

The relation of the god Lono to the Kamau-nui family of Maui, from whom Kamapua'a the hog man is descended and with whom the Kamauaua family of Molokai seem by their name to be connected, will be discussed in connection with the legend of the hog kupua. It would seem likely that Lono was the god worshiped by this family. Lono names are common in the Kamapua'a story and appear on the genealogical line of ruling chiefs of the island of Maui. The close relation felt between a god and his offspring or his worshiper on earth makes it increasingly difficult to disentangle the threads of myth from those of accumulated legend and to identify figures in story or in ritual worship which have branched off from the main source through the storyteller's instinct for fresh combinations out of an old stock of tradition, or the worshiper's for dreaming such a recombination.

IV

THE KANE WORSHIP

KANE was the leading god among the great gods named by the Hawaiians at the time of the arrival of the missionaries in the islands. He represented the god of procreation and was worshiped as ancestor of chiefs and commoners. According to the possibly late edition of the Kumuhonua legend, he formed the three worlds: the upper heaven of the gods, the lower heaven above the earth, and the earth itself as a garden for mankind; the latter he furnished with sea creatures, plants, and animals, and fashioned man and woman to inhabit it.

An account of the creation of the world which appears in the genealogical legend of Kumuhonua, the first man fashioned by the gods, represents Kane as playing a dominant role as creator, but assisted by Ku and Lono, a trilogy called lahui akua (union of gods) or he papa Kane (Kane class) said to be worshiped under the name of Ku-kauakahi.[1] The worship of Tane (Kane), Ro'o (Lono), and Tu (Ku) by the manahune in Tahiti, to whose mythology belong the Polynesian figures also of Atea (Wakea), Ti'i (Ki'i or Tiki), and Maui, is closely comparable with the Hawaiian Kane worship.[2]

LEGEND OF CREATION

(*a*) *Fornander version* (1). In the first era Kane dwells alone in continual darkness (i ka po loa); there is neither heaven nor earth. In the second era light is created and the gods Ku and Lono, with Kane, fashion the earth and the things on the earth. In the third era they create man and woman, Kumu-honua (Earth beginning) and Lalo-honua (Earth below). In the fourth era Kane, who has lived on earth with man, goes up to

1. For. Col. 6: 271.   2. Henry, 398–399.

heaven to live and the man, having broken Kane's law, is made subject to death.[3]

(b) *Fornander version* (2). The three gods Kane, Ku, Lono come out of the night (po) and create three heavens to dwell in, the uppermost for Kane, the next below for Ku, and the lowest for Lono, "a heaven for the parent (makua), a heaven for Ku, a heaven for Lono." Next they make the earth to rest their feet upon and call it "The great earth of Kane" (Ka-honua-nui-a-Kane). Kane then makes sun, moon, and stars, and places them in the empty space between heaven and earth. He makes the ocean salt, in imitation of which the priests purify with salt water. Next an image of man is formed out of earth, the head out of white clay brought from the seas of the north, south, east, and west, the body out of red earth (apo ula) mixed with spittle (wai nao). The right side of the head is made of clay brought from the north and east, the left side is made of clay from the south and west. Man is formed after the image of Kane with Ku as the workman, Lono as general assistant. Kane and Ku spit (or breathe) into the nostrils, Lono into the mouth, and the image becomes a living being. "I have shaped this dirt (lepo) ; I am going to make it live," says Kane. "Live! live!" respond Ku and Lono. The man rises and kneels. They name him Ke-li'i-ku-honua (The chief Ku(mu)-honua) or Honua-ula because made out of "red earth." They give him a delightful garden to live in called Kalana-i-hauola, but later Paliuli, situated in the land of Kahiki-honua-kele (The land that moved off), and fashion a wife for him out of his right side and call her Ke-ola-Ku-honua (or Lalo-hana). "Great Hawaii of the green back and mottled seas" this land is called. A law is given him but he breaks the law and is then known as Kane-la'a-(kah)uli, "a god who fell because of the law."[4]

In the original garden of Kumuhonua and Lalo-hana his wife, are to be found the pig, dogs of various varieties, mo'o of many sorts. A tapu tree, sacred apples which cause death if eaten by strangers, and tapu bark cloth forbidden to all but the

3. For. Col. 6: 335.   4. Col. 6: 267, 268, 273–276.

high chiefs are spoken of. Some think that the laau (law or tree) which caused the expulsion of the pair from the garden refers to these things. The garden, which is very sacred, goes by a multiplicity of names. It is the great white albatross of Kane that drove them out of the garden (Ka Aaia-nukea-nui-a-Kane). Kumuhonua-mokupuni is the land to the eastward to which Kumuhonua retreats after he has broken the law, and he returns to Kapakapa-ua-a-Kane and is buried in a place called Kumu-honua-puʻu, which was afterwards called Ka-puʻu-poʻokanaka (The hill of human heads).[5]

(c) *Kepelino version.* Kane as a triad, Kane, Kana (Ku), Lono, exists alone in the deep intense night which he has created, and brings about, first light, then the heavens, then the earth and the ocean, then sun, moon, and stars.[6] Kane existing alone chants,

> "Here am I on the peak of day, on the peak of night.
> The spaces of air,
> The blue sky I will make, a heaven,
> A heaven for Ku, for Lono,
> A heaven for me, for Kane,
> Three heavens, a heaven.
> Behold the heavens!
> There is the heaven,
> The great heaven,
> Here am I in heaven, the heaven is mine."

During the first five periods the heavens and earth are created and the sun, moon, and stars, and plants to clothe the earth. In the sixth period man is formed.

Kane, Ku, Lono, conceived as a single godhead, mold Kumuhonua, the first man, out of wet soil and he becomes living soil. They make him a chief to rule over the whole world and place him with his wife Lalo-honua in Ka-aina-nui-o-Kane (The great land of Kane), where they live happily until Lalo-honua meets the "Great seabird with white beak that stands fishing" (Aaia-nui-nukea-a-ku-lawaia) and is seduced to eat the sacred apples

5. For. Col. 6: 273–276.   6. 14–17.

of Kane. She goes mad and becomes a seabird. The seabird carries them both away into the jungle, the trees part and make a path for them, but the trees return to their places and the path is lost, hence the name "Hidden land of Kane" for this first garden home. . . . Death is the penalty for Kumuhonua because he did not keep the command of the god. He gains the name Kane-la'a-uli and is jeered at by the people as he goes weeping and lamenting along the highway. For countless years he dwells as a refugee on the hill called Pu'u-o-honua, then he returns to Kahiki-honua-kele and is buried on a mountain called Wai-hon(u)a-o-Kumuhonua. There his descendants also are buried and the place is called "The heaping place of bones" (O-ke-ahuna-iwi).[7]

(d) *Kamakau version.* Kane, assisted by Ku and Lono and opposed by Kanaloa, makes the heaven and the earth. All is chaotic. Nothing exists but the upper regions and the spirit gods. Kane excels among the gods in wisdom and power. The triad of gods unite in forming the world. They begin on the twenty-sixth day of the month, the day dedicated to Kane, and in six days, including the days of Kane, Lono, Mauli, Moku, Hilo, Hoaka, form the heavens and the earth. The sabbath or holy day of Ku is established on the seventh day.[8]

On Oahu between Kualoa and Kaneohe lies the first land planned by the gods. On the eastern flank of Mololani (a crater hill on Mokapu), at a place where fine red earth is mixed with bluish and blackish soil, the first man is formed by the three gods Kane, Ku, Lono. Kane draws a likeness of the gods with head, body, hands, and legs like themselves. Then he makes the image live and it becomes the first man. The gods place him in a house of kou wood and name him Huli-honua because he is "made out of earth." The first man notices that his shadow always clings to him. While he sleeps the god makes a good-looking woman and when he awakes she lies by his side. He calls her Ke-aka-huli-lani (The shadow from the heavens).[9]

7. 24–35, 42–47.
8. *Ke Au Okoa,* October 14, 1869.
9. *Ibid.* October 21, 1869.

(*e*) *Westervelt version*. On the island-like peninsula of Mokapu on Oahu is the crater hill Mololani. On the east side near
the sea red earth lies beside black soil. Kane makes an image of
a man out of earth. . . . Ku and Lono catch a spirit of the air
and give Kane's figure life. They name him Wela-ahi-lani-nui.
The man notices his shadow (aka) and wonders what it is. The
woman is torn out of the man's body by the god Kane; Ku and
Lono heal the body. When the man sees her he names her Ke-
aka-huli-lani after his own shadow.[10]

The similarities here to biblical stories have made readers
suspicious of the stories of the forming of man out of earth
and of the fall of man and his being driven out of a sacred
garden. It is, however, much more likely that familiarity with
the biblical stories has lent a coloring and an emphasis to traditions which were genuinely native than that the Hawaiians
have invented these stories in direct imitation of Bible accounts. In the southern groups, Tane (Kane) makes a woman
out of sand. In Tahiti, although Ta'aroa (Kanaloa) is the
great first mover, Tane is the god of beauty who adorns the
earth and Tu(Ku) is the "builder."

The worship paid to Kane was of a simple character, without human sacrifice or laborious ritual. "Life is sacred to
Kane" (ua kapu ke ola na Kane), was the saying. Kane worshipers were called he papa la'a (a consecrated class) as distinguished from image worshipers.[11] The heiau to Kane at first
contained no images until image worship became popular,
when they were introduced into all heiau. Ellis found the
name Kane-nui-akea attached to a stone image from Kauai
brought to the heiau of Kauai-kahaloa at Puapua'a in Kona,
Hawaii, and with it two wooden gods called Kane-ruru-honua
(Kane shaking the earth) and Rora-maka-ehe (probably
Lono with flashing eyes) and a feather god called Ke-kua-ai-
manu (The bird-eating god).[12]

A family altar called Pohaku-o-Kane (Stone of Kane)
was set up to Kane in the shape of a single conical stone from

10. *Honolulu*, 70–74.
11. For. Col. 6: 266; Kepelino, 58.
12. *Tour*, 88; *HAA* 1908, 70.

a foot to eight feet in height, plain or with slight carving, and planted about with ti plant, where members of a family went to pray to their aumakua and ask forgiveness for the broken tapu to which they ascribed any trouble that had come upon them. Here they sought protection from their family god with offerings and prayer. They came early in the morning, chewed awa while a pig was baking, and, when all was ready, ate under tapu, leaving no remnants and clearing away all rubbish. The place for setting up the stone and the offering to be made were revealed in a dream to the kahuna they consulted. The stone itself was sprinkled with water or with coconut oil and covered with a piece of bark cloth during the ceremony. It is possible, since the Kane stone is generally regarded as an emblem of the male organ of generation, that this covering is similar to the reported practice, before worshiping an image in which sex organs were displayed, of covering those parts with tapa cloth.[13]

Each family worshiped Kane under the name of its own family Kane god, or aumakua, but invoked also all other Kane gods whose aid it desired. Kamakau lists thirty such aumakua and adds, with his customary love for exaggeration, "There were thousands and thousands of names to fit the work done, but all referring to one god. There was one altar and only one place to offer food, the stone of Kane, and among all inspired by a Kane god, one keeper should not despise another. They should all eat the sacrifices and offerings together; the difference lay in the law of each god and the things dedicated to each." The prayer to the aumakua must hence be inclusive. It enumerates first the male aumakua, then the female, and begins, "Stoop down, heaven! listen, earth! hearken, pillars of earth, aumakua at the rising and the setting of the sun, from that tapu point to this tapu point! Here is the offering and the sacrifice, a sacrifice to the god because we are in trouble," and concludes, after enumerating the gods of the heavens, "To all male aumakua and to all the chiefly ancestral aumakua, to you I appeal. Brush aside the dark-

13. Kamakau, *Ke Au Okoa*, March 3, 1870; Thrum, *More Tales*, 267–270.

ness, brush aside death, brush aside trouble. It is I [name of suppliant], chief one of your children in this life. Return, that we may have mana (sacred power)." The same invocation is repeated to the female aumakua and their names are listed.[14]

An example of Kane worship in the name of one of these lesser deities is illustrated in the description given by Kamakau of the place held by Kane-hekili (Kane in the thunder) as an aumakua on the island of Maui. Kane-hekili as god of thunder is associated with Kane-wawahi-lani (Kane breaking through heaven), Ka-uila-nui-maka-keha'i-i-ka-lani (Lightning flashing in the heavens), Ka-hoali'i, and other gods whose names suggest the lively phenomena of a thunderstorm. Humpbacked forms may be seen driving through the air at such times, led by Na-kolo-i-lani, or by the humpbacked brothers of Pele. During such a storm all containers should be turned bottom side up; all persons should lie face downward and make no outcry. Silence is the law (tapu) of Kane-hekili. Two stones in the cave of Ke-ana at Kahuku on Oahu are said to be the bodies of two boys who disobeyed their mother's injunction to keep silence during a thunderstorm.

Kane-hekili is the god worshiped by those who claim an aumakua in the thunder. Thunder is the divine form of the god. When he comes to his worshipers in a dream, he is seen in his human form with his feet standing on earth and his head touching the clouds, one side of his body black and the other side white. Such a mark on the body is hence the sign of one given to Kane-hekili. Anyone born with a birthmark on the right side is said to be so given. Ulumeheihei, the friend of Kamehameha and governor of Maui after the setting up of the kingdom, was one who had this sign. Kahekili, the last ruling chief of Maui, was tattooed on one side of his body to show that he belonged to the family of the thunder god. A kahuna named Kahekili who at one time kept the heiau of Pakana-loa, erected back of Keanae on Maui at a place where violent thunderstorms occur, came to be regarded as possessed by the spirit of Kane-hekili. He was feared as a sor-

14. *Ke Au Okoa,* October 27, 1870.

cerer, but any plot against his life seemed invariably to be checked by a violent thunderstorm. When he died, his brother-in-law sought his body inside the heiau and carried away the head to Lanai and worshiped it as a god. Parts of the body were distributed, and men became known as worshipers of "eyes of Kahekili" or "mouth of Kahekili."[15]

Chiefs who count their genealogy direct from Kane, whether on the Ulu or Nanaulu line, rank among the hoaliʻi or high tapu chiefs as distinguished from the lower grades of chiefs with a less distinguished family genealogy. Descent is therefore of vital importance and the privileges enjoyed by Kane worshipers are on the basis of such rank, which gives them command of tapus comparable to those of the gods. They are in fact gods (akua) in name as in effect, with power over life and death because of the awful sacredness with which their presence is regarded. They are "chiefs with the tapus of gods" (na liʻi kapu akua) as compared with the tapus enjoyed by the lesser chiefs (na liʻi noa). They are "chiefs of the ikupau" as compared with "chiefs of the ikunuʻu" who share the right to temporal power alone and the ordinary tapus of chiefs.

The name of Ka-hoaliʻi is given to "a mythical ancestor worshiped as a god," deity of the walled heiau at Kawaipapa, Papaʻa, Kauai, and said to be the possessor of the two famous axes of old times from the gods Haumapu and Olopu with which he "cut asunder the government [aupuni] so that it fell." It was with these axes that the kahuna must touch the ohia tree selected for the building of a luakini heiau before the tree was felled and brought down from the forest.[16] On various ceremonial occasions the god was impersonated as a dark man, completely naked, with stripes or patches of white on the inner sides of his thighs. At the Makahiki festival he occupied a booth of lama wood during the period of the freeing of the various food tapus, and at the close of the period, when the aku fish were freed, the eyeball of a fish and that of a human victim were given him to swallow. At the building of

15. *Ke Au Okoa,* March 31, 1870; Westervelt, *Gods and Ghosts,* 124–125; J. Emerson, *HHS Papers* 2: 15.

16. Malo, 206 note 33; Kepelino, 12; *HAA* 1907, 42; 1910, 59–60.

a luakini heiau he was again impersonated by a naked man who led the running. At the dedication ceremony of a heiau for the circumcision of a young chief, a night was given up to this god during which none dared come outside lest he die. The priests passed about praying the people to come out and the official who sought human sacrifices, called the Mu, tried to entice out the unwary in order to secure a victim.[17]

The law (tapu) of this god was called Puʻu-koa-maka-ia (Hard eyeball of a fish) with reference to the human eyeball which was the offering he demanded. Kamakau asserts that a chief possessed by the spirit of Ka-hoaliʻi might invoke this law at any time when the followers of the chief were assembled. All must then look steadfastly at the chief thus possessed and anyone might be selected as victim and his eyes gouged out and swallowed in a cup of awa.[18] Maui, when he recovers his wife from Bat, has to be appeased with the eyes of the abductor offered to him in a cup of awa before his injured feelings are pacified.[19] Kuʻi-a-lua, god of the art of bone breaking (lua), demands of his pupils that they eat an eyeball of a victim after finishing their course of training.

The drinking of a victim's eye with the kava as an offering to deity is reported from other groups. In Tahiti, when human victims were sacrificed, says Ellis, the eye was given to the king.[20] In the Marquesas, the spirit of the brother-in-law of Tiki is caught up to the sky and sacrificed and the eyes are consumed with the kava.[21] In New Zealand eyes are scooped out and swallowed in order to obtain the spirit of the owner, says Taylor.[22]

In myth Ka-hoa-liʻi or an equivalent is represented as a god of the underworld, who occupied "the subterranean region through which the sun passes each night from west to east." In the legend of Kana, Ka-hoa-lei (or liʻi), vexed by Niheu, withholds the sun and leaves the people in darkness until Kana visits the land to the far east, blackens his hands to resemble those of the god, and gets handed up to him the

17. Malo, 197–199 note 25, 220–221; For. Col. 6: 10, 24–26.
18. Kamakau, *Ke Au Okoa*, March 17, 1870.
19. Thrum, *More Tales*, 259.   20. *Researches* 1: 342–352.
21. Handy, *Bul.* 69: 133–134.   22. 147.

sun, the stars, and the cock that signals the dawn.[23] So in the legend of Aukele, that hero secures the water of life in the same manner from the servants of the underworld deity Kamoho-ali'i at the pit of the far eastern edge of the world where the sun comes up.[24] Kane himself is said to have come to Hawaii from the east, and old Hawaiians make the front door face the east as a sign of Kane worship and turn toward the sun when they offer their morning prayer.[25]

Chanted prayers to the gods were an important part, perhaps the important part, of temple worship. The most sacred of these were uttered by the high priest and for this ritual a scaffolding was erected within the temple area called the Lananu'umamao because built in three stages, called nu'u (earth), lani (heavens), and mamao (far off but not beyond hearing). This last and most sacred stage was entered by the high priest and ruling chief alone. The whole structure was covered with white bark cloth (oloa). On the floor of the temple platform surrounding the structure stood the images, the chief image directly in front of the staging. On each side of the tower were sometimes placed arches of bent saplings, three on a side, and these were supposed to bend if the offering (or prayer) was acceptable. This oracular response of the gods may be compared with the drum placed over a high chief's threshold, whose sounding or silence indicated the rank of the one entering, or the cord similarly hung across the entrance which fell to the ground of itself before a high chief, but under which one of lower rank must stoop.

Prayers were offered at each step of the scaffolding. Some were offered at the altar before ascending the tower. A series of prayers used in the Kane worship and recited by an old Hawaiian from Kauai named Robert Luahiwa to Mr. Theodore Kelsey are here given as translated by Miss Laura Green in order to show the highly exalted religious feeling with which the high gods were approached by the priest who ut-

23. Rice, 102–105.

24. *Ibid.*, 102–105; Ellis, *Tour*, 296; Dibble, 17; For. Col. 4: 86–96.

25. For. Col. 6: 275.

tered the prayer, the audience meanwhile sitting motionless in perfect stillness until, at the word noa, the tapu was "freed" and they might resume their customary liberty of movement. The word amama with which the prayer concludes is pre-Christian and not connected with the Christian amen.

The first prayer is little more than an enumeration of the names of Kane as the subordinate forms by which the one god who embraces them all is worshiped. It is the prayer "given by Kane when he began to offer prayer in the heiau of Kuikahi, at Hanapepe, Kauai, near the stream of Manawai-o-puna" and "is calling on the lesser Kanes to do their duty and aid him."

The second prayer is one offered by Kane to the assembly (papa) of gods from the steps of the oracle. It is significant that the female gods of growth, Laka and Hiʻiaka, are invoked with Kane, and that the plants used for temple decoration are included among the names of Kane: the fragrant myrtle (maile), the ieie vine or climbing pandanus, the sacred lehua and dracaena trees out of which images were carved. Pele, Kapo, and the male and female Ku gods are also invoked. The enchanted stone Kapolei, formerly belonging to Kauai, is mentioned.

The third prayer is offered at the altar. Lono of the heavens, Hiʻiaka, and Laka are invoked with "red Kane." At the fourth prayer the priest is within the "six" arches and upon the steps of the scaffold. Here the reciter breaks off. The most sacred prayers, those uttered from the prayer tower, are not reported.

The same reciter gives a fifth prayer offered when gathering plants in the mountains for temple decoration. The guardian spirits are invoked to return and possess the plants. "Produce sacredness, produce freedom, freedom for me, a man," prays the gatherer, and then begins to pluck the leaves with prayer. The address to Kane-i-ka-pahuʻa (Kane the thruster) is said to be to Kane in the guise of an owl, who thrusts with wings and talons at the enemies of his worshipers in time of battle and turns aside their weapons. The word may also mean "dancer." Kane-i-ka-pahu-wai is "Kane with a calabash of water" which he pours out upon the earth below.

1. THE PRAYER OF KANE	1. KA PULE A KANE
O Kane-Kanaloa!	E Kane Kanaloa!
O Kane-of-the-great-light-ning-flashes-in-the-heavens,	E Kane-kauila-nui-makeha-i-ka-lani,
O Kane-the-render-of-heaven,	E Kane-i-ka-wawahi-lani,
O Kane-the-rolling-stone,	E Kane-i-ke-poha(ku)-ka‘a,
O Kane-of-the-whirlwind,	E Kane-i-ka-puahiohio,
O Kane-of-the-rainbow,	E Kane-i-ke-anuenue,
O Kane-of-the-atmosphere,	E Kane-i-ke-pili,
O Kane-of-the-rain,	E Kane-i-ka-ua,
O Kane-of-the-heavenly-cloud,	E Kane-i-ke-ao-lani,
O Kane-standing-before-the-pointed-clouds,	E Kane-i-ka-maka-o-ka-opua,
O Kane-standing-before-the-heavenly-clouds,	E Kane-i-ka-maka-o-ka-ao-lani,
O Kane-in-the-cloud-above,	E Kane-i-ke-ao-luna,
O Kane-in-the-cloud-floating-low,	E Kane-i-ke-ao-lewa-lalo,
O Kane-in-the-cloud-resting-on-the-summit,	E Kane-i-ke-ao-pali-luna,
O Kane-in-the-cloud-over-the-low-hills,	E Kane-i-ke-ao-pali-lalo,
O Kane-of-the-heavenly-star,	E Kane-i-ka-hoku-lani,
O Kane-of-the-dawn,	E Kane-i-ke-ao,
O Kane-of-the-clouds-on-the-horizon,	E Kane-i-ka-opua,
O Kane-of-the-red-rainbow,	E Kane-i-ka-punohu-ula,
O Kane-of-the-great-wind,	E Kane-i-ka-makani-nui,
O Kane-of-the-little-wind,	E Kane-i-ka-makani-iki,
O Kane-of-the-zephyrs,	E Kane-i-ke-aheahe-malie,
O Kane-of-the-peaceful-breeze,	E Kane-i-ka-pa-kolonahe,
O Kane-of-the-strong-thrust,	E Kane-i-ka-pahu‘a-nui,
O Kane-of-the-great-water-source,	E Kane-i-ka-pahu-wai-nui,
O Kane-of-the-little-water-source,	E Kane-i-ka-pahu-wai-iki,
O Kane-traveling-mountain-ward,	E Kane-i-ka-holoholo-uka,
O Kane-traveling-seaward,	E Kane-i-ka-holoholo-kai,

O Kane-dwelling-in-the-mountain,	E Kane-noho-uka,
O Kane-dwelling-by-the-sea,	E Kane-noho-kai,
O Kane-dwelling-by-the-upper-precipice,	E Kane-noho-pali-luna,
O Kane-dwelling-by-the-lower-precipice,	E Kane-noho-pali-lalo,
O Kane-gazing-upward,	E Kane-ha-lo'-luna,
O Kane-gazing-downward,	E Kane-ha-lo'-lalo,
O Kane-glancing-at-the-upper-spaces,	E Kane-ha-lo'-lewa-luna,
O Kane-glancing-at-the-lower-spaces,	E Kane-ha-lo'-lewa-lalo,
Sleeping-Kane,	Kane-moe,
Kane-sleeping-in-the-great-light,	Kane-moe-awakea,
Kane-of-the-coral,	Kane-kokala,
Kane-of-the-long-coral,	Kane-kokala-loa,
Kane-of-the-quaking-coral,	Kane-kokala-lu-honua,
Kane-of-the-steadfast-coral,	Kane-kokala-ku-honua,
Kane-of-the-sharp-pointed-coral,	Kane-kokala-i-ke-kiu,
Kane-of-wafted-coral,	Kane-kokala-i-ke-ahe,
Kane-the-swift-runner,	Kane-i-ka-holo-nui,
Kane-the-slow-runner,	Kane-i-ka-holo-iki,
Kane!	O Kane!
Kane! Lono!	O Kane! O Lono!
I will live through all of you, my gods.	E ola no au ia' oukou a pau e o'u mau akua.

2. THE PRAYER OF KANE TO THE ASSEMBLY OF GODS	2. KA PULE A KANE I KA PAPA PULE HAHAU ILOKO O KA PAPA O KE KUAHU
O Kane-of-the-great-lightning,	E Kane-ka-uila-nui,
O Kane-of-the-great-proclaiming-voice,	E Kane-leo-lono-nui,
O Kane-of-the-small-proclaiming-voice,	E Kane-leo-lono-iki,

Silently listening in the mountains—

E hoolono ana oe i ke kuahiwi—

In the great mountains,

I ke kuahiwi nui,

In the low mountains,

I ke kuahiwi iki,

O Kane-of-the-thunder,

E Kane-hekili,

O Kane-of-pale-flowers (or guardian of innocent children),

E Kane-hoopuakea,

O Kane-of-the-maile,

E Kane-i-ka-maile,

O Kane-of-the-fern,

E Kane-i-ka-palai,

O Kane-of-the-ginger,

E Kane-i-ka-awa-puhi,

O Kane-of-the-ieie,

E Kane-i-ka-ieie,

O Kane-of-the-lehua-blossom,

E Kane-i-ka-pua-lehua,

O Kane-of-the-yellow-blossom,

E Kane-i-ka-pua-lena,

O Kane-of-the-scattering-seed,

E Kane-i-ka-pua-lalahua,

O Kane-in-the-flash (of lightning),

E Kane-i-ka-olapa,

O Kane-of-the-intense-heat,

E Kane-i-ka-haoa,

O Kane-of-the-hala-pepe,

E Kane-i-ka-hala-pepe,

O Kane-of-the-big-fern,

E Kane-i-ka-palai-nui,

O Kane-of-the-small-fern,

E Kane-i-ka-palai-iki,

O Kane-of-the-sharp-point,

E Kane-i-ke-kiu,

O Kane-of-the-fire,

E Kane-i-ke-ahi,

O Kane-of-the-mist,

E Kane-i-ka-ohu,

O Kane-of-the-fog,

E Kane-i-ka-noe,

O Kane-of-the-big-smoke,

E Kane-i-ka-uahi-nui,

O Kane-of-the-little-smoke,

E Kane-i-ka-uahi-iki,

O Kane-in-the-shadow,

E Kane-i-ke-aka,

O Kane-in-the-shadow-of-Kapolei,

E Kane-i-ke-aka-o-Kapo-lei,

O turning-Kane,

E Kane-huli,

O Kane-turning-completely,

E Kane-hulihia,

O Kane-turning-completely-to-Kahiki,

E Kane-hulihia-i-Kahiki,

To Kahiki east, to Kahiki west.

I Kahiki-ku, I kahiki-moe.

Arise, O Pele!

E ala oe e Pele!

Arise, O Hiiaka-in-the-bosom-of-Pele,

E ala oe e Hiiaka-i-ka-poli-o-Pele,

Arise, O Woman-in-green,
Arise, O red Kapo,
O Kapo, return-n-n!
A petitioning voice to you all,
  my guardians,
The male aumakua,
The female aumakua,
Turn all of you.
Guardians of the night and of
  the day,
I am your offspring,

To me, the man, grant life!

E ala oe e Wahine-oma'o,
E ala oe e Kapo-ula,
E Kapo -ho' —i a-a—!
He leo lono no ia' oukou a pau,
  e o'u mau kiai,
Na ku kane,
Na ku wahine,
E huli mai oukou a pau.
E na aumakua o ka po a ma
  ka ao,
Owau nei la ka oukou pulapula
  nei,
Ia'u, i ke kanaka, e ola no a-
  a—!

3. THE PRAYER AT THE ALTAR

Spread out the showers that
  all may be cleared,
That the heavens may be
  cleared of the lightning;
Great are the crashing peals!
On the highest pinnacle great
  Lono-of-Kane will hear.
O Hiiaka, O Hiiaka, hear me!
I only am swaying a prayer,
Help me to sway my petition,
  O Kane!
In the great assembly he is—
  understands
And gives freedom to me, O
  Kane-of-Lono!
O Kane of the great red voice,
O Kane of the blazing voice,
O Kane of the smoking voice,
O red-voiced Kane in the mist,
O Laka, O Laka, hear me!
O Laka of the beautiful forest!

3. KA PULE ANA I KE KUAHU

Pahala ka ua kala i mahiki,

Mahiki ka lani a ka uila nui;

Nui na kalo kani uina!
Lohe o Lono-nui-a-Kane i ka
  poha kau.
E Hii e, e Hii ho'i e!
Owau wale no ke hina nei,
E hina pu a'e no kaua, e
  Kane e!
I ka aha nui o ia, ua ike no a

Ua noa no ia'u, e Kane-o-
  Lono, e!
E Kane-leo-ula-nui,
E Kane-leo-ula-i-ke-ahi,
E Kane-leo-ula-i-ka-uahi,
E Kane-leo-ula-i-ka-noe, e,
E Laka e, e Laka ho'i,
E Laka i ka ulu wehiwehi!

O Kane, inspire me with hope,

Granting me knowledge,
Granting me power,
Granting me skill,
Granting me great wisdom—
That I may receive knowledge, skill,
Power from you all,
Ye guardians of the night and of the day!
The prayer is ended, it is free.

E hooulu mai ana oe ia'u nei, e Kane,
Ho mai he ike,
Ho mai he mana,
Ho mai he akamai,
Ho mai he ike nui—
I loaa ia'u ka ike, ke akamai,

Ka mana, mai ia' oukou,
I na aumakua o ka po, a me ke ao!
Amama, ua noa.

4. THE PRAYER ON THE STEPS NEAR THE ALTAR

O Kane of the proclaiming voice,
O Kane of the great proclaiming voice,
O Kane of the small proclaiming voice,
You are listening on the pinnacle,
You are listening to the ocean,
You are listening to the rain,
You are listening to the great wind,
You are listening to the rumbling,
You are listening to the murmuring sound,
O Kane, give heed (to *me*)!
O Kane, behold!
Turn and look at me,
Thy offspring, Ku.
I am Ku above,
I am Ku below,
I am Ku of Kahiki,

4. HE PULE IA I KA PAPA KUAHU

E Kane-leo-lono e,

E Kane-leo-lono-nui e,

E Kane-leo-lono-iki e,

E hoolono ana oe i ka wekiu,

E hoolono ana oe i ke kai,
E hoolono ana oe i ka ua,
E hoolono ana oe i ka makani nui,
E hoolono ana oe i ka halulu,

E hoolono ana oe i ka oe' iki,

E Kane ho'i e!
E Kane ho'i a!
E huli mai oe a nana ia'u nei
I kau pulapula nei, o Ku.
Owau nei la o Ku-iluna,
Owau nei la o Ku-ilalo,
Owau nei la o Ku-i-Kahiki,

I am Ku of great Kahiki,
I am Ku of sleeping Kahiki,

Recumbent and listening
Unto the copious rain that
cleanses all—
Cleansing the heavens of Kane.
The eyes of Kane flashing
upward,
The eyes of Kane flashing
downward,
Descending, standing and
stepping on the foundation
below.
This is wholly I, from head to
foot,
And do not fail to recognize
me
As a man, a descendant from
a mother of many,
A mother of few,
Give me life!
Produce sacredness, produce
freedom, freedom for me.
The prayer is finished, it is
free.

Owau nei la o Ku-i-Kahiki-nui,
Owau nei la o Ku-i-Kahiki-
Moe,
E moe ana a hoolono ana
A pala ka ua kala i mahiki—

Mahiki ka lani a Kane.
Owa ka maka o Kane-iluna,

Owa ka maka o Kane-ilalo e,

Ilalo noa a ku a hehi i ka
papa o lalo.

Owau okoa no keia, mai luna
a lalo,
A mai hoohewahewa mai oe
ia‘u
I ku kanaka, i ke kumulau loa,

I ke kumulau iki,
E ola no e!
Elieli kapu, elieli noa. Noa no
ia‘u nei!
Amama, ua noa.

5. A CHANTED PRAYER FOR THE PLANTS

Kane, Kanaloa!
Kane-of-the-flashing-light-
ning-of-the-heavens,
Kane-render-of-heaven,
Kane-of-the-rolling-stone,
Kane-of-the-surface-stone,
Kane-of-the-whirlwind,
Kane-of-the-rainbow,
Kane-of-the-atmosphere,
Kane-of-the-rain,

5. PULE OLI I KA NAHELE

Kane, Kanaloa!
Kane-ka-uila-nui makeha i ka
lani,
Kane-ka-wawahi-lani,
Kane-i-ka-pohakaa,
Kane-i-ka-pohakau,
Kane-i-ka-puahiohio,
Kane-i-ka-anuenue,
Kane-i-ke-pili,
Kane-i-ka-ua,

Kane-of-the-cloud-of-heaven,
Kane-of-the-horizon-cloud,
Kane-of-the-heavenly-star,
Kane-of-the-horizon-cloud,
Kane-of-the-floating cloud,
Kane-of-the-wind,
Kane-of-the-sun,
Kane-of-the-star,
Kane-of-the-owl,
Kane-of-the-drum,
Kane-of-the-water-source,
Kane-traveling-mountainward,
Kane-traveling-seaward,
Kane-traveling-the-upper-
 precipice,
Kane-traveling-the-lower-
 precipice,
Kane-sleeping-at-midday,
Kane-of-the-coral,
Kane-of-the-long-coral,
Kane-of-the-short-coral,
Kane-of-the-upper-coral,
Kane-of-the-lower-coral,
Kane-of-the-northwest-wind,
Kane-of-the-zephyr,
Kane-running,
Kane-the-swift-runner,
Kane-the-slow-runner,
Kane-of-long-Lono,
Kane-of-short-Lono,
Kane of Lono, oh!
You are listening to the mur-
 muring waters!
Produce sacredness, produce
 freedom!

Kane-i-ke-ao-lani,
Kane-i-ka-maka-o-ka-opua,
Kane-i-ka-hoku-lani,
Kane-i-ka-opua,
Kane-i-ke-ao,
Kane-i-ka-makani,
Kane-i-ka-la,
Kane-i-ka-hoku,
Kane-i-ka-pahua,
Kane-i-ka-pahu,
Kane-i-ka-pahuwai,
Kane-i-ka-holoholo-uka,
Kane-i-ka-holoholo-kai,
Kane-i-ka-holoholo-pali-luna,

Kane-i-ka-holoholo-pali-lalo,

Kane-i-ka-moe-awakea,
Kane-i-ke-kokala,
Kane-i-ke-kokala-loa,
Kane-i-ke-kokala-iki,
Kane-i-ke-kikala-iuka,
Kane-i-ke-kokala-ikai,
Kane-i-ke-kiu (makani),
Kane-i-ke-ahe,
Kane-i-ka-holo,
Kane-i-ka-holo-nui,
Kane-i-ka-holo-iki,
Kane-o-Lono-nui,
Kane-o-Lono-iki,
Kane-o-Lo-o-no e!
Hoolono ana oe e Kane i ka
 wai e!
Elieli kapu, elieli noa!

V

KANE AND KANALOA

IN his character as a culture god the name of Kane is generally coupled with that of Kanaloa. About Kanaloa as a god apart from Kane there is very little information. He is god of the squid, called in the Kumulipo Ka-heʻe-hauna-wela (The evil-smelling squid). A prayer quoted by Emerson invokes Kanaloa in this character to heal one under the influence of sorcery:

> Kanaloa, god of the squid,
> Here is your sick man,

and ends with an excellent objective description of squid catching.[1] In the Kumulipo genealogical chant there appear, during the eighth era which ushers in the period of human life (ao) as distinguished from the period of the gods (po), the woman Laʻilaʻi and the three males, Kane, a god, Kiʻi, a man, and Kanaloa, the great octopus. Fishermen still solicit his protection, but on the whole the squid is today looked upon with distrust as an aumakua.

This attitude is reflected in a tendency by Hawaiian antiquarians to equate Kanaloa with the Christian devil. His name is associated with various legends of strife against Kane in which Kanaloa and his spirits rebel and are sent down to the underworld. In the legend of Hawaii-loa belonging to the Kumu-honua epic account of the Kane tradition, Kanaloa is the leader of the first company of spirits placed on earth after earth was separated from heaven. These spirits are "spit out by the gods." They rebel, led by Kanaloa, because they are not allowed to drink awa, but are defeated and cast down to the underworld, where Kanaloa, otherwise known as Milu, becomes ruler of the dead.

The legend places Kane and Kanaloa in opposition as the

1. Malo, 149–150 note.

good and evil wishers of mankind. When Kane draws the figure of a man in the earth, Kanaloa makes one also; Kane's lives but Kanaloa's remains stone. Kanaloa is angry and curses man to die. He makes all kinds of poisonous things. It is he who seduces the wife of the first man in this version. Kanaloa of the great white albatross of Kane is the name given to him as responsible for driving the first man and the first woman out of the garden spot the gods have provided for them.[2]

In similar stories of opposing creators reported by Codrington from New Hebrides, Tagaro is the good, Suqe the evil wisher of mankind. In Aurora, Tagaro makes things and tosses them in the air; what he catches is good for mankind, what Suqe catches is evil.[3] On Whitsuntide island, whatever Tagaro did or made was right; Suqe was always wrong.[4] On Lepers' island Suqe shares the creation with Tagaro, but makes things wrong.[5] In the Banks islands the same stories are told of Qat and Marawa the spider:

Qat and Marawa (Spider) each makes a man. Qat makes his live after six days, but Marawa, after bringing his to life, buries him again and he rots, and this is the origin of death.[6]

Kanaloa, like Kahoali'i, is also associated with the underworld, as in the chant in which Hawaii is spoken of as "fished up from the very depths of Kanaloa."[7] Tangaroa is god of the ocean in the South Seas, Tane of land and of plant and animal life. The use of salt water for purification is, however, ascribed to Kane in Hawaii and such water is called "tapu water of Kane" (wai tapu a Kane), the particle a instead of o denoting direct handiwork rather than simple possession.[8] To Kane is ascribed the bringing of food plants to Hawaii. The heiau of Ka-mau-ai (The heap of vegetable food) at Keauhou, Kona, dedicated to Kane, is said to be the site of the

2. For. Col. 6: 267–268; Kamakau, *Ke Au Okoa,* October 21, 1869; Westervelt, *Honolulu,* 70–74.
3. Codrington, 168.   4. 169.
5. 171.   6. 157–158.
7. For. Pol. Race 2: 18.
8. For. Col. 6: 273; *AA* 28: 176, 180.

introduction of cultivated food plants.[9] Pigs, coconuts, breadfruit, awa, and the wauke plant from which bark cloth is made are sacred to Kane.

In these culture activities, however, Kane is generally coupled with Kanaloa, and there exists a vast amount of popular and mythical lore in which the two gods are named together. Both are invoked by canoe men, Kane for the canoe building, Kanaloa for its sailing.[10] In a chant consecrating a new canoe in which "Kanaloa the awa-drinker" is specified, both gods are invoked as "active" (he miki oe).[11] Both are deities of the heiau of the po'okanaka class called Hauola at Hoea, Waiawa, on Kauai.[12] They are worshiped as gods at Kohala and a temple is built for them.[13] The east is spoken of as the "high road traveled by Kane" or the "red road of Kane," the west as the "resting-place of Kane," or the "much-traveled road of Kanaloa." The northern limit of the sun in the celestial ecliptic is called the "black shining road of Kane" and the southern limit on the celestial ecliptic that of Kanaloa. The celestial equator is the "road to the navel of Wakea" (ala i ka piko o Wakea) and "red road of the spider" (alaula a ke ku'uku'u).[14]

Prayers accompanying the bringing of offerings couple the names of the gods: "O Kane, O Kanaloa, here is the taro, the bananas, here is the sugar-cane, the awa. See, we are eating it now."[15] Or: "Here is food, O Gods, Kane and Kanaloa! here is food for us. Give life to us and our family. Life for the parents feeble with age. Life for all in the household. When digging and planting our land, life for us."[16]

Kane and Kanaloa are described in legend as cultivators, awa drinkers, and water finders, who migrated from Kahiki and traveled about the islands. One account says that they lived at Alakahi in Waipio valley on Hawaii with some of

9. *HAA* 1908, 72–75.
10. Bastian, *Heilige Sage,* 131.
11. Malo, 173. 12. *HAA* 1907, 39.
13. Westervelt, *Honolulu,* 37.
14. For. Pol. Race 1: 42–43, 127.
15. Rice, 117. 16. Westervelt, *Honolulu,* 33.

the lesser gods, Maliu, Kaekae, Ouli (Uli), where they cultivated bananas and led a simple life. Kanaloa was tall and
fair, Kane was dark, with curly hair and thick lips.[17] According to Lyons,[18] "Kane and Kanaloa were from Kahiki (foreign gods). They came traveling on the surface of the sea
and first caused plants for the food of man to grow." Kamakau says that they "came from Kahiki in the shape of human
beings," were sighted off Keei, landed on Maui. The time was
that of "Wakalana, father of the Maui brothers." Their
coming was coincident with that of Haumea, and she "gave
birth to strange noisy creatures," perhaps with reference to
the introduction of pigs to Hawaii, an animal sacred to the
Kane worship.[19]

The two are also connected with fishponds. Ke-awa-nui and
Ke-awa-iki who live at Mokapu point are visited by Kane
and Kanaloa, and they build the Paohua fishpond.[20] There is
a famine on Lanai. A fisher boy comes daily to a little hut he
has erected for his god and lays a bit of fish there, saying, "O
god, here is a bit of fish for you." Kane and Kanaloa are so
pleased with his piety that they bring the famine to an end.[21]
They are said to have been followed from Kahiki by the ama-
ama fish (mullet), and when an old Hawaiian visited the
mainland a few years ago and found mullet there, she was
convinced that Kane and Kanaloa must have traveled in that
country. Fish altars are set up to Kane-ko'a along streams to
increase the catch of oopu fish. Kane and Kanaloa are said
to have been worshiped with awa and whitefish (aholehole)
on their arrival from Kahiki.

It is as awa drinkers that the water-finding activities of
these gods are employed in some stories, because awa is their
principal food and they must have water with which to mix
it. "Awa-iku" are said to be beneficent spirits that act as
messengers for Kane to ward off the evil influences of the

17. Thrum, *More Tales,* 259–260.
18. *JPS* 2: 174.
19. *Ke Au Okoa,* March 31, 1870.
20. McAllister, *Bul.* 104: 185.
21. Bastian, *Heilige Sage,* 131–133.

"mu" spirits and manage the winds, rains, and other things useful to man.[22] An old hula song danced today alludes to this awa-drinking propensity of the god:

> Ua maona a Kane i ka awa,
> Ua kau ke kaha i ka uluna,
> Ke hiolani a la i ka moena,
> Kipu i ke kapa a ka noe.

> "Kane has drunk awa,
> He has placed his head on a pillow
> And fallen asleep on a mat,
> Wrapped in a blanket of mist."[23]

Fragmentary legends point to a struggle among the gods for the privileges of awa drinking. Both Maui and Kaulu rob the garden patch of the gods.

Local legends abound in which the gods Kane and Kanaloa are represented as traveling about the country establishing springs of water and seeing that they are kept clear for drinking purposes or for uses of the chiefs. Here "Kanaloa acts as the urge, Kane as the executor."

LEGENDS OF KANE AND KANALOA AS WATER FINDERS

Kane and Kanaloa go into the precipitous mountains back of Keanae on Maui and lack water. They discuss whether it can be obtained at this height. "Oi-ana (Let it be seen)!" says Kanaloa; so Kane thrusts in his staff made of heavy, close-grained kauila wood (*Alphitonia excelsa*) and water gushes forth. They open the fishpond of Kanaloa at Luala'ilua and possess the water of Kou at Kaupo. They kill the kahuna Koino at Kiko'o in Kipahulu because he is guilty of defilement at mealtime. They cause sweet waters to flow at Waihee, Kahakuloa, and at Waikane on Lanai, Punakou on Molokai, Kawaihoa on Oahu.[24] On Kauai they leave few springs because they are not recognized as gods. The impress of their forms as they slept is left on the rock

22. Malo, 140–141 note 10.
23. N. B. Emerson, "Hula," 130.
24. Kamakau, *Kuokoa*, January 12, 1867.

above the pool of Mauhili in the Waikomo stream in Koloa district where, on the cliff below, are two pointed rocks named Waihanau and Ka-elelo-o-kahawau.[25] Two holes are pointed out just below the road across Ohia gulch beyond Keanae on Maui where Kane dug his spear first into one hole and then into the other with the words, "This is for you, that for me." The water gushing from these apertures is called "the water of Kane and Kanaloa."[26] The gods land at Hanauma on Oahu and springs flow at various places where the two mix awa on their way to Waolani in Nu'uanu valley. In Manoa valley they see a pretty girl and both gods try to seize her. The attendant changes into a great rock in their path, a spring of water trickles where the girl stood, and over it lean two ohia trees, symbols of the gods. This is the spring called "Water of the gods," which was sacred to Kamehameha.[27]

It was at the time of the migration of Kane and Kanaloa from Kahiki that the "stones of Kane" were set up and the "waters of Kane" were "brought forth from hills, cliffs, and rocks." Emerson quotes from Kauai a hula song composed in the popular question-and-answer repetitive form, beginning,

> "A query, a question
> I put to you,
> Where is the water of Kane?"
> "At the Eastern Gate
> Where the sun comes in at Ha'eha'e
>   (easternmost point of Hawaii),
> There is the water of Kane."

The stories of the spring-finding activities of the gods are not to be interpreted as alluding to the skill with which irrigation was applied to taro plantings in upland or in wet taro cultivation. The legends make no mention of such uses for the water springs which the gods caused to gush out of rocks. They simply express the mystery which even to an old Hawaiian today belongs to such a phenomenon. The native who

25. *HAA* 1907, 92.   26. Local information.
27. Green and Pukui, 112–115; Westervelt, *Honolulu*, 32–37; Bastian, *Heilige Sage*, 132–133; McAllister, *Bul.* 104: 152.

accompanied us to the outlet of a tunnel just put through in
the back country of Ka-u district on Hawaii to bring water
from the upper valleys showed an excitement which scarcely
a Niagara or a Boulder Dam could arouse in our own country. Such places are celebrated as sacred spots (wahi pana).
It is said that the heiau of Kau-maka-ula (Thy red eyes)
built by the chief Kamehaikaua after the flood of Ka-hina-
li'i was repaired by the kahuna Kahonu for the young chief
Kekua-o-ka-lani and a house erected for him at Maliko where
he was reared at the "waters of Kane and of Kanaloa" in the
Puna-lu'u division of the Koolauloa district on Oahu. The
strange thing about the heiau was that the eyes of all the pigs
in the district turned red as the tapu nights approached, and
during the tapu nights of Kane and of Kanaloa the sound of
piping and whistling and drumming could be heard at the
heiau.

> The man-fishing net of Lono,
> The braided net of Kamehaikaua,

runs the chant, with reference, Thrum says, to the "fish"
sacrificed at the Makahiki, and the division of the heiau area
called the "net" (upena) where the victim was snared.[28] Kane
as the spear thruster and god of gushing waters has phallic
symbolism. The thruster is the male, the spring of water,
which Hawaiians think of as the source of life, is the female
in the generative process. Hence Kane's aspect as "Kane of
the water of life."

28. Thrum, *More Tales,* 117–120.

VI

MYTHICAL LANDS OF THE GODS

IN myth Kane and Kanaloa are represented as gods living in the bodies of men in an earthly paradise situated
in a floating cloudland or other sacred and remote spot
where they drink awa and are fed from a garden patch of
never-failing growth. Often this land is located upon one of
the twelve sacred islands under the control of Kane believed
to lie off the Hawaiian group "within easy reach of and having frequent intercourse with it." These islands are frequently mentioned in ancient chants and stories before the
last Paao migration from Tahiti. Today they are called the
"lost islands" or "islands hidden by the gods." At sunrise or
sunset they may still be seen on the distant horizon, sometimes touched with a reddish light. They may lie under the
sea or upon its surface, approach close to land or be raised
and float in the air according to the will of the gods. They
are sacred and must not be pointed at.[1]

The land of Kane-huna-moku (Hidden land of Kane) is one
of these islands. Here live Kane and Kanaloa with other spirits who are Kane's direct descendants; such as, "Kane of the
thunder," "Kane of the water of life," "Kane who shakes the
earth," twenty of whom are listed by Rice. It is a middle
land between heaven and earth where spirits enjoy all the delights of earth without labor and without death, and "in extreme old age return to earth, either in the bodies of men or
as spirits," or "become gods and live in the clouds."[2] Kepelino calls it the land where the first man was made. Here he
lived until Kumuhonua transgressed the law of Kane and was
driven from this good land. "There is no land to be compared
to it in excellence."[3] Hawaiians today say that this land had
its birth from Niu-roa-hiki, a land belonging to Hawaii but

1. Rice, 31.   2. *Ibid.*, 116, 125–128.
3. 46.

which does not approach these islands, and that those who have kept the tapus may go there after death.

Kane-huna-moku is still worshiped as an aumakua or guardian spirit, who will bear away his worshiper in the body at death. Some thirty years ago a family who worshiped Kane-huna-moku, living at Hana on the island of Maui, fixed upon a certain day when the island would pass by and take them away in the flesh. When the day came there were strange shapes in the clouds and excitement ran high. There are also stories of those who have caught sight of the hidden island. Mrs. Pukui relates, from the account given her by her grandmother when she was a child in Ka-u on Hawaii, that when Kane-huna-moku passes by one can hear cocks crowing, pigs grunting, see flickering of lights and waving of sugar cane and persons moving about the island. An old woman is its guardian. She holds an implement of destruction for anyone who lands without invitation. On the island is a pool of water called Ka-wai-ola-a-Kane which keeps people young and heals all manner of diseases.[4]

In myth Kane-huna-moku appears off Wailua on Kauai and carries off Kauakahi-ali'i, who thus disappears forever.[5] Waha-nui and his voyagers pass it on their way to "tread on the breasts of Kane and Kanaloa" and see men on the island "gathering coral for food."[6] Two fishermen from Pu'uloa were blown off to this island and brought back breadfruit to Hawaii.[7] The old Hawaiian saying is, "Here the breadfruit grew and was eaten (Ulu no ka ulu, a ai no)." In the chant of Kumulipo, when birds are born "they cover the land of Kanehunamoku."[8]

Of two important Hawaiian myths of the hidden island of Kane and Kanaloa, one is a secular story which tells of a pious worshiper who is allowed to visit the land and taste its delights before returning to his ordinary life on earth, the other an esoteric myth purporting to relate the establishment of the land and the life of its ruler. Of the first, Rice's version is

4. Kepelino, 189; Kamakau, *Ke Au Okoa,* October 13, 1870.
5. Dickey, *HHS Reports* 25: 28.
6. For. Col. 5: 518.   7. *Ibid.* 678.
8. Liliuokalani, 19.

by far the fullest, but concludes with an *Arabian Nights'* touch which can hardly belong to a native original.

LEGEND OF MAKUAKAUMANA

(a) *Rice version.* Makua-kau-mana is a pious worshiper of Kane and Kanaloa who lives in north Oahu at Kaulua-nui with his only son, whose mother died at his birth, and cultivates daily his garden patch, being careful always to call upon his gods in so doing. The two gods visit him in the disguise of strangers, note his piety and his hospitality to strangers, and give him a digging stick and a carrying pole to relieve his labor. They come again disguised as old men and teach him how to pray, offer sacrifices, and keep the tapus for Kane-huli-honua, giver of land, and Kane-pua'a, god of rich crops; for Hina-puku-ai, goddess of vegetable food, and Hina-puku-i'a, who gives abundance of fish. A third time they come dressed like chiefs and bring a red loincloth (malo pukuai) and a colored bedspread (kuina-kapa-papa'u). To test Makua's steadfastness they complain that his son has broken the eating tapu of the gods. Makua would have slain his son, but the gods stay his hand. They send a great fish and when Makua goes to dive from its back, they cause the fish to swallow him and bear him away to the hidden land of Kane-huna-moku where he may live with Kane and Kanaloa in the "deathless land of beautiful people." It is, however, forbidden to weep in this land and the gods prepare an illusion in which he sees his son forced into the sea by his wife and a shark devouring him. Makua cannot restrain his tears. He is accordingly borne back to his old home and cast upon the beach, where his son rejoices over him but his friends reproach him for losing the joys of that good land. He lives to a good old age and is buried on Oahu.[9]

(b) *Green version.* A certain pious man calls so constantly upon his gods that they weary of attending to him upon so trivial occasions. They carry him to their paradise underseas, where they appear to him in human bodies and chide him gently for his simplicity before returning him to his mourning friends.[10]

9. 116–132.   10. 61–63.

(c) *Westervelt version.* At Kaipapau near Hauula, north Oahu, lives an old kahuna who has Kane and Kanaloa as his gods. They come to visit him, rest and drink awa with him, and for his piety give him ulua fish, never known before in those waters. They forbid him to go down to the beach, whatever noise of shouting he may hear. A great fish comes inshore near a place called Cape-of-the-whale and the people use its back to leap from. The kahuna cannot resist joining the sport. The fish swallows him and carries him away to Tahiti.[11]

(d) *Kohala version.* A whale gets stranded on the coast of Kohala and men begin cutting it up. Hamumu comes along with taro, gets on the head of the whale, begins to cut, and is carried away to Kahiki. There he learns temple building and other arts. He returns inside a coconut shell whose contents have been cleaned out through the eye and the shell sealed up with gum. This is the origin of the building of the Mo'okini temple of Kohala to which belongs the Hulahula ritual.[12]

(e) *Lanai version.* In time of famine a fisherman builds a hut by the sea and comes daily with the fish he has caught to lay a morsel before the god, although this god he does not know by name. One day two men appear, to whom he gives what he has. The next morning they inform him that they are Kane and Kanaloa who have heard his prayers. A time of plenty follows, and a terraced heiau is built on the spot.[13]

The story probably belongs to the popular South Sea myth of Longa-poa and the tree of plenty discussed under Haumea. Closely corresponding concepts are contained in the myth of the hidden island, Kane-huna-moku, the conclusion of which is discussed under that of the Mu and Menehune people. Thrum does not say where he obtained the story.

MYTH OF KANEHUNAMOKU

Kane and Kanaloa are lords over the children of the gods who peopled the earth in early days. Kane-huna-moku (Kane's

11. *Honolulu,* 145–147.   12. *HAA* 1925, 77–78.
13. Bastian, *Heilige Sage,* 132.

hidden island) is their son. When he is born, thunder crashes and lightning flashes. From the union of Mano-i-ku(kiu)-lani (Male head of the clouds in the blue sky) and of Hihikalani (Female head of the rolling clouds) arose a mist out of which blood-tinted pyramidal clouds separated. Kane-huna-moku is therefore descended from these two.

When he becomes a man he desecrates the flower garden of Kaonohi, whose pool is called Mano-wai, and is banished with Kaonohi to a floating land where their people are to be dwarfs who build upon rocky soil. He comes to himself in this land and questions where he is. He sees an abundant growth of trees and fruits, drinks of a spring, but cries, "Where am I, living in the shadow of night, below, below?" A mysterious voice bids him to continue "over the blue ocean, the deep sea, the red sea" because of his pride, and upon its asking him what he desires, he asks for a wife who shall be Kaonohiula. The voice answers from the budding ti plant. Thunder and lightning play. Many white chicks come running toward him. The voice tells him that his land is sacred and shall not be seen in the light of day. It shall be seen only at certain tapu periods in July and August. When it hovers near Haena, Kauai, then he shall be near "on the floating land of Kaonohiula."

This land is a beautiful floating cloud of Kane and Kanaloa. Ka-onohi-ula is his companion there. Bowling is to be their favorite sport. The children of Kane-huna-moku and Ka-onohi-ula in this land are a mo'o (Mo'o-nanea), a dog (Pili-a-mo'o), a caterpillar (Halulukoa), a beautiful girl with supernatural powers (Halalamanu), a girl of fire (Kuilioloa), Ioio-moa "endowed with sacredness, upholding family purity," and an ordinary child (Kaonui).

The land of Kane-huna-moku is composed of three strata, the outer called Kane-huna-moku after himself, the second called Kueihelani where live his wife and children and the dwarf people, the inner called Ulu-hai-malama where fragrant flowers grow. Uhawao and Uhalaoa are overseers of this garden and they lead the migration of the people of Kane-huna-moku toward vegetable growth. Kauhai is the one who sets in motion the island, which is driven through space by the wind, but only at night is it in motion. Kui-o-Hina is the one "who makes possible the equilibrium of Kane-huna-moku in the night of Mohalu (twelfth night of the moon as it begins to round and first of the Kane nights) as it revolves in space," as also during the periodical visits of Kane and Kanaloa on the night of Akua (full moon).[14]

Rice gives Ulu-koa (Barren breadfruit) as an alternative name for Kane-huna-moku. Ulu-koa is named by Kamakau as one of the unknown aumakua worlds of the dead by the "upright walls of Kane" to which the dead are conducted by Kane-huna-moku. Some say it belongs to Samoa. In the story of Anelike it is called Ulu-ka'a (Uala-ka'a). It is an island of women reached by a young swimmer who teaches the use of cooked food and weds its chiefess, as in the South Sea story of Kai, and which rolls (ka'a) up to the shore to bring wife or son to the husband and father.

The most famous of these floating islands is Paliuli, as it has come to be called regularly, although Pa-liula with reference to the twilight or mirage (liula), as in Westervelt's story of Ke-ao-melemele, would seem to be a more natural original. Fale-ula is the "bright house" in the ninth heaven in the Samoan creation story.[15] Paliuli is pictured as an earthly paradise of the gods "supposed to float above the clouds or to rest upon the earth at the will of its keeper" and also identified, like Kane-huna-moku and Ulu-koa, with the original paradise where the first two human beings were made and where they first dwelt, as in the chant,[16]

> O Paliuli, hidden land of Kane,
> Land in Kalanai Hauola
> In Kahiki-ku, in Kapakapaua of Kane,
> Land with springs of water, fat and moist,
> Land greatly enjoyed by the god.

In ancient story it is to be reached deep under the seas. In the Aukele legend the seeker after the water of life wings his way "straight toward the rising sun" and then descends a pit

14. *HAA* 1916, 140–147.   15. *JPS* 1: 186, 187.
16. For. Pol. Race 1: 77–78.

to reach the place where it is guarded. In the Kumulipo the lines run,

> Surely it must be dismal, that unknown deep,
> 'Tis a sea of coral from the depth of Paliuli.

Today the fertile land of Paliuli is definitely localized in the uplands of Ola'a in the forest between Hilo and Puna districts on Hawaii "west of Pana-ewa and a little east of the house of the Rev. Desha" at a place known as Thirteen Miles. Nauahi of Hilo is said once to have chanced upon this enchanted spot, but in an attempt to prove his boast and guide a friend to the spot he looked for the path again in vain; "The gods had hidden it." It is here that romance places the ever-fruitful garden of the gods, described as a land "flat, fertile, and well-filled with many things desired by man" where "the sugar cane grew until it fell over and rose again, the bananas fell scattering, the hog grew until the tusks were long, the chickens until the spurs were long and sharp, and the dogs until their backs were broadened out."

The three mythical lands already named are to be found, in the myth of Kalana-i-hauola, as appellations for the earthly paradise situated in the first land made by the gods, and as the place where the gods placed the first man and the first woman they had made. Kalana-i-hauola is in Kahiki-honua-kele (Kahiki the land that moved off), or in Mole-o-lani (Root of heaven), or in Hawaii-nui-kua-uli-kai-o'o (Greenbacked Hawaii of spotted seas) in Kahiki-ku. It has a multitude of names all belonging to Kane and referring to the nature of the land; as, Spirit land, Sacred land, Dark land, Tapu land, Hidden land, or to the traditional bark cloth, mountain apple, breadfruit, which the god has placed in that land; and it contains also the "water of the gods of Kane" (wai-akua-a-Kane) and the "water of life" (wai-ola) of Kane.[17] Kane as preserver is invoked as "Kane of the water of life."[18]

17. For. Col. 6: 266–268, 273–275.
18. Malo, 208.

This "water of life" is described as a spring "beautifully transparent and clear. Its banks are splendid. It had three outlets: one for Ku, one for Kane, and one for Lono; and through these outlets the fish entered the pond. If the fish of this pond were thrown on the ground or on the fire, they did not die; and if a man had been killed and was afterwards sprinkled over with this water, he did soon come to life again."[19]

In Maori tradition Taranga-i-hau-ola (Kalana-i-hau-ola) is the place "where the first members of mankind were created." Tiki, the creative being, comes from Taranga, the place of creation.[20] Hau (or Wai)-ora is the name of the third heaven, the place where the spirit of man comes to him at birth. To Hauora or Te-wai-ora-a-Tane comes the spirit of the child about to be born and from this heaven the soul is sent to the newborn child. When the body of the dead is burned, when all is consumed but the buttocks, the person conducting the operation pokes them up with a stick, causing sparks to fly upward, and this is said to take the spirit to the Wai-ora-nui-a-Tane.[21] Some Maori say that the moon is concerned with the giving of life to the child. "The moon is the real husband of all women. According to the knowledge of our ancestors and elders, the marriage of man and woman is of no moment; the moon is the true husband."[22] The moon, when it is wasted away, bathes in the lake of Aiwa (Aewa) in the living water (wai ora) of Tane and renews its life.[23] In Tahiti, Vai-ora-a-Tane, the Milky Way, is above in the highest heaven. It is called "the water for the gods to lap up into their mouths."[24] At a royal child's first bath he is said to be bathed in the Vai-ora-a-Tane.[25] In Tonga, in Bulotu where the gods live is the spring Vai-ola near the talking tree "under whose shadow the gods sit down to drink kava, the tree acting as master of ceremonies and calling out the name of

19. For. Pol. Race 1: 77–78.
20. Tregear, *TNZI* 20: 389–390.
21. *JPS* 6: 162.
22. *Ibid.* 8: 101; Izett, 12, 19, 20.
23. White 1: 141–142.   24. Henry, 356.
25. *Ibid.,* 184.

him to whom the bowl shall be carried." It is when the gods sail away from Water-of-life, people the earth, and lose the way back to Bulotu that they become mortal.[26] In San Cristoval life-giving power is attributed to water, which even causes conception.[27] In the rite of the child's first bath the water is "charmed" to take away sickness and give life.[28]

Similar stories of wandering islands are told in the Tuamotus. Uporu and Havaiki are two ancestral lands said to be visible to those on a ship halfway between. An ancient homeland called Hoahoamaitu is described as sinking beneath the waves. In a romance from Ana'a, Vaireia goes to meet Hinauru in the wondrously beautiful land of Hekeua which rises from the sea and to which no man has ever come before.[29] In the legend of Tane and Kiho-tumu, when Tane visits the older god, Kihotumu tests him by sending him to pursue the swiftly flying island Nuku-tere, where he has deposited his sacred diadem. If Tane succeeds in this quest his power will equal that of Kihotumu. The chant runs:

Here is the Sailing Island, the swiftly fleeing land,
Poised to depart on the long voyage to the far shore of Hivanui,
Great land of darkness,
Flocking birds, wheeling above the clouds, trail their fleeting shadows on the land,
The Vanishing-Isle is as a migratory bird flashing in undeviating flight, now launched upon the wind.[30]

The legend played a real part in South Sea island life. Marquesans know the hidden islands of the gods where the priests say food abounds and which may be seen on the horizon at sunset. They frequently leave home to go in search of them; more than eight hundred are known to have set out for these lands and only one canoe was ever heard from.[31] Fison describes Tongan efforts to reach the lands hidden by the gods.

26. Fison, 16–17.
28. *Ibid.*, 181.
30. Stimson, *Bul.* 111: 39–41.
27. Fox, 253.
29. Stimson MS.
31. Handy, *Bul.* 9: 19–20.

South Sea descriptions of an earthly paradise where the spirits of the dead are sent to enjoy the delights of earth without the fear of death differ only in detail from the Hawaiian myth. Rohutu noanoa (fragrant Rohutu) is the earthly paradise of the Arioi society in Tahiti, situated in the air above the mountain of Tamehani-unauna in the northwest of Raiatea, and invisible to human eyes. It is ruled by Romatane. Souls are directed thither by the god Tu-ta-horoa. There they enjoy all the delights of life without labor and are immune from death.[32] In Samoa, Bulotu is the paradise dominion of Save-a-siuleo, human above and fish below, with a house whose pillars are made of the bones of dead chiefs. Here the spirit bathes in the water of life and becomes strong again.[33] In Aitutaki, to avoid baking in Miru's oven, a piece of coconut and one of sugar cane are placed over the stomach of the dead. The soul will then go to Iva, where souls feast at ease under the guardianship of Tukaitaua.[34] In Rarotonga warriors may go to a paradise called "Tiki's reed house."[35] In Niue there is a "bright land of Siva" in the sky to which some dead go.[36] Among the d'Entrecastreux a few warriors go to the sky, where life is one great feast.[37] Some Andaman islanders say that souls go to live in the sky with a mythical being named Tomo, the first ancestor, where they have plenty of pork and dancing.[38] On San Cristoval souls, after living in Rodomana where they join their friends, swim on to the island of Maraba where is "a paradise of souls, feasting and dancing" and a "river of living water" called Totomanu where the soul bathes and, if it is that of a devout man, is absorbed into A'unua and becomes immortal without losing personality.[39] The Fiji elysium is an island to the northwest of Vitilevu called Burotu or Morotu. Here lives Hikuleo, the tailed god, beside the water of life and the speaking tree that calls out the order of precedence at the feast.[40] About 1885 a new

32. Ellis, *Researches* 1: 245–246, 397–398; Henry, 201; Moerenhout 2: 434.

33. Turner, 257–260.

34. Gill, 175.

35. *Ibid.*, 170.

36. *JPS* 2: 15.

37. Jenness, 146.

38. Brown, 169.

39. Fox, 235.

40. Thomson, 117.

religion spread in Fiji called the Tuka religion. Life immortal in Mburotu kula (red paradise) was the teaching of this religion. It told of a fountain of life, a house of sleep and pleasant dreams, "interwoven with poetry and romance." It was said to be allied to a religion invented in New Zealand by a "mad prophet" called Kooti, and it centered in the region of the mountain Kauvandra, on Viti-levu, shrine of the snake god Ndengei.[41]

Such hopes of an earthly paradise where the religious may enjoy the delights which are the perquisite of the gods whom they worship are common to many if not all priest-guided religions. In ancient Japan, Toko-yo-no-kuni is the "eternal land," the retreat of gods and spirits not to be reached by common man.[42] The Indian poet Somadeva tells of the heavenly abode of Siva, "untouched by the calamities of old age, death and sickness, . . . home of unalloyed happiness. . . . Wonderful are the magic splendours of the Vidyadharas, since they possess such a garden in which enjoyments present themselves unlooked for, in which the servants are birds, and the nymphs of heaven keep up a perpetual concert."[43]

The Kane-huna-moku aumakua worship in Hawaii is today plainly concerned with the fate of the spirit after death. The symbolism of the hidden islands in the original Kane worship seems rather to center in the birth of the child descended from high chiefs and his care before reaching maturity. The term Ulu-pa'a to designate "a girl before her first period of menstruation and a boy before hair develops on his body" would perhaps explain the persistence of the breadfruit (ulu) in the symbolism. The picture of the earthly paradise corresponds with the care taken of such a young chief who is brought up under tapu. It is significant that in the romances, as soon as a marriage is arranged for the young person so cared for, the place is shut up and activities are carried on elsewhere. The connection between this land and that in which the first man and the first woman are made argues

41. Brewster, 236–260; Thomson, 140–145.
42. Chamberlain, 87.
43. Penzer edition 8: 152, 162, 170.

still further that the underlying idea is of the period of maturing of the reproductive energy, both in man and in nature,
during which the god Kane repeats the process by which he
first produced man. The esoteric symbolism involving the
sexual life, the period of chastity to which high-born children
were subjected under tapu, the selected marriage, are very
well illustrated in the romances as they will appear later. It
looks as if an ancient teaching connected with Kane worship,
its phallic symbolism, and its interest in reproduction, had
been adapted to the biblical account of Adam and Eve in
Eden in a kind of harmonizing between the old teaching and
the new Christian mythology.

Other mythical lands mentioned in the Kane-huna-moku
myth and occurring constantly in chant, legend, and romance seem to be without the particular machinery of the
hidden land, although pictured as lands inhabited by the ancestral gods and closed after the migration of their descendants. Kuai-he-lani (Supporting heaven) is the name of the
cloudland adjoining earth and is the land most commonly
named in visits to the heavens or to lands distant from Hawaii. In the legend of Ka-ulu it is the place where Kane and
Kanaloa drink awa with the spirits (called also Lewa-nu'u
and Lewa-lani).[44] It is the chant name for the land from
which Olopana came[45] and which Kila visits;[46] the land in
which Pele was born,[47] or to which she goes after leaving Polapola;[48] the land from which came the grandparents of Kamapua'a;[49] the "legendary land" in which Mo'o-inanea cares
for the gods and where the children of Ku and Hina are born
and the parents live until all migrate to join Kane and Kanaloa on Oahu, when it is "shut up" by the mo'o guardians
and indeed called "the hidden land of Kane";[50] the land in
which Keanini is born and where he lives and from which he
departs for the underworld,[51] and that from which Ku-waha-

44. For. Col. 5: 364.   45. For. Col. 6: 321.
46. *Ibid.* 320.
47. N. Emerson, *Pele,* ix; Westervelt, *Volcanoes,* 5.
48. Rice, 7.   49. For. Col. 6: 251.
50. Westervelt, *Gods and Ghosts,* 148.
51. For. Col. 6: 345; Westervelt, *Gods and Ghosts,* 170, 182, 214.

ilo comes to woo the grandmother of Keanini in the Pukui version; the land in Kahiki to which Ka-pua-o-ka-ohelo-ai is banished by her parents and which is her mother's ancestral home;[52] the home of Laukia-manu's father in Kahiki, to which she travels on a banana shoot;[53] home of the Iku family to which Aukele belongs;[54] the land visited by Ku-a-lana-kila, keeper of Moku-lehua.[55] In the myth of Kane-huna-moku it is described as constituting the second stratum of the "floating land" created by Kane and Kanaloa for their son, and the home of his wife and children, inhabited by the Menehune and the Mu-ai-maia or banana eaters.[56] In the dirge to Kahahana[57] it is the land of the deified dead:

> Aia i Kuaihelani ka hele-ana-e
> O ka onohi ula o ka lani ko inoa.

> "There in Kuaihelani you have gone
> The rainbow of the heaven is your name."

It lies to the west, for two chiefesses who travel thence voyage eastward to Hawaii; after a voyage of forty days the sweet smell of kiele flowers hails their approach to its shores.[58] It is called in chant,

> The divine home land
> The wonderful land of the setting sun
> Going down into the deep blue sea,[59]

and a migration from Kuaihelani is described as

> The ali'i (chiefs) thronging in crowds from Kuaihelani
> On the shoulders of Moanaliha (Ocean).[60]

Above Kuaihelani lies Nu'u-mea(meha)-lani (Sacred raised place of the heavenly one), the land in the clouds to

52. For. Col. 4: 540–542.
53. *Ibid.* 596.
54. *Ibid.* 32, 108.
55. *Ibid.* 6: 320.
56. *HAA* 1916, 140–141.
57. For. Col. 6: 296.
58. *Ibid.* 4: 540, 546.
59. Westervelt, *Gods and Ghosts,* 146.
60. *Ibid.,* 208.

which Haumea retires in anger with all her retainers when the bird-man carries off her favorite grandchild, and whence she releases the hot season to parch the land;[61] the place to which she returns to dwell with the gods after the tree blossoms which she has received from Olopana in payment for his daughter's painless delivery;[62] the land above, to which Na-maka-o-kaha'i pursues the Pele sisters to spy out their movements;[63] the land to which Papa retires after her quarrel with Wakea;[64] the land above Ke-alohi-lani to which the guardian of that land "flies up" when he discovers the arrival of Ka-hala-o-mapuana and her carrier, in order to bring back with him his magician brother;[65] the land in "the highest place in the heavens" in which the mo'o guardian builds "out of clouds" in Ke-alohi-lani a house "turning like the ever-moving clouds" for Ke-ao-melemele, the child of Ku and Hina;[66] the inner third stratum of the floating land created as a home for Kane-huna-moku and his family and surrounded by a garden of fragrant flowers.[67] In all these cases it is thought of as a land in the heavens situated above Kuaihelani or its equivalent. Fragrance, brightness, elevation, and a special sacredness are the attributes of this mythical land. According to Emerson, Nu'umealani is the aumakua of clouds.[68]

Accustomed as they are to dividing up the universe according to rank, Hawaiians easily think in terms of above and below, drawing an invisible line in space between Kuaihelani and Nu'umealani, between Lewa-lani, that region of air which lies next to the heavens of the gods, and Lewa-nu'u which lies below, next to the treetops. Here spirits may live in the bodies of human beings and enjoy the delights of earth. We say of men who live on a scale beyond that enjoyed by most that they "live like gods"; the Polynesians say of their gods that they live like men in the enjoyment of earthly abundance.

61. *HAA* 1926, 12.   62. Westervelt, *Honolulu,* 49.
63. For. Col. 4: 106.   64. Malo, 24.
65. *RBAE* 33: 554.
66. Westervelt, *Gods and Ghosts,* 127–129.
67. *HAA* 1916, 143.   68. *HHS Papers* 2: 15.

VII

LESSER GODS

T HE great gods each had his own form of worship, his priests and heiaus, his own special symbols of ritual distinction. "Ku by fives" is the old saying. Conquering chiefs took pains to recognize in their worship the gods of the lands they took over. Nothing is more characteristic of Hawaiian religion than the constantly increasing multiplicity of gods and the diversity of forms which their worship took.[1] Even of the heiau Thrum says there was "no one alike."[2] Besides the great gods there were an infinite number of subordinate gods descended upon the family line of one or another of the major deities and worshiped by particular families or those who pursued special occupations. Says Malo, "Each man worshiped the akua that presided over the occupation or profession he followed, because it was generally believed that the akua could prosper any man in his calling."[3] Says another: "Below the four great gods were fifty lesser gods [some say forty, others an indeterminate number], each named after some attribute of the god appropriate to the special department over which he presided; fifty Kane gods, fifty Lono gods, and also subordinate gods. Over these the great gods presided. These in turn ruled fifty lesser Kane, Ku, Lono [and Kanaloa] deities, and so on, the whole system comparable to a tree with trunks, branches, twigs."[4] Some worshiped their gods in the form of images. "There were many of them, about forty or twice forty of feather idols," says one describing the ceremonial of a royal sacrifice.[5] Others worshiped without any concrete form. Kepelino distinguishes between the way in which were regarded the gods who were worshiped by the forefathers, "the gods who made heaven and earth," and the spirits (uhane), a numberless body, "millions upon

1. Malo, 112. 2. *HAA* 1907, 50.
3. 112–115; For. Pol. Race 2: 60.
4. Given by Miss Laura Green. 5. For. Col. 6: 10.

millions," whom he divides into the bodiless spirits of the air (uhane lewa) created by Kane to serve the gods, and the bodiless spirits of the dead who have become guardian spirits (aumakua) for their descendants on earth.[6] In order not to omit any one of the host of lesser deities formed out of the spittle of the god when he was shaping the earth, it was customary to add to or open an invocation with the formula, "Invoke we now the 40,000 gods, the 400,000 gods, the 4,000 gods" (E ho'oulu ana i kini o ke akua, Ka lehu o ke akua, Ka mano o ke akua), and to add to these ritual numbers expressive of an innumerable multitude such identifications as, "the ranging of the gods by rank, the circle of the gods, the coming together by twos, the coming together by threes, the murmur of the gods," with reference to "that countless rout of little gods . . . whose shouts (ikuwa) were at times distinctly to be heard."[7]

All forms of nature were thus thought of as bodily manifestations of spirit forces. The hierarchies of the gods corresponded to the social system, which recognized a minute classification of society into ranks according to blood inheritance. National worship of the great gods, conducted by ruling chiefs, was an expression of descent from a common stock. The slave class who bore no such relationship were hence outcasts; they lived apart and were forbidden intermarriage or even association, except of a limited sort, with the freeborn. Worship of a god as special guardian or aumakua of a particular family was also an expression of kinship and commanded the service of whatever nature spirits belonged, either by descent or by adoption, to the family of the god. Even the great gods Ku, Kane, Lono, Kanaloa might be addressed in prayer as "aumakua." Romances and hero tales are rich with implications of this relationship in which nature shares in the signs and acclamations which attend the footsteps of a divine offspring. Says a Fornander story:

At sight of Kila the crowd began to shout, admiring his beauty. Even the ants were heard to sing in his praise; the birds

6. 10–19.
7. N. Emerson, "Hula," 21–24; Malo, 114.

sang, the pebbles rumbled, the shells cried, the grass withered, the smoke hung low, the rainbow appeared, the thunder was heard, the dead came to life, the hairless dogs were seen and countless spirits of all kinds. . . . All these things mentioned were the people of Moikeha, who, upon the arrival of Kila his son, caused themselves to be seen in testimony of Kila's high rank.[8]

And again, at the appearance of another divine chief:

The woods rejoiced, the winds, the earth, the rocks; rainbows appeared, colored rain-clouds moved, dry thunder pealed, lightnings flashed.

Ka-onohi-o-ka-la (Eyeball of the sun), who lives in the sun, when he puts off his divine nature and comes to earth in a human body thus announces his approach:

When the rain falls and floods the land, I am still here. When the ocean billows swell and the surf throws white sand on the shore, I am still here; when the wind whips the air and for ten days lies calm, when thunder peals without rain, then I am at [the border of the heavens]. When the thunder peals again, then ceases, I have left the taboo house at the borders of Kahiki . . . my divine body is laid aside, only the nature of a taboo chief remains and I am become a human being like you.[9]

Compare the ascent to heaven of Tawhaki in Maori legend, who divests himself on the top of a mountain of his earthly garment and clothes himself with lightning,[10] and the journey of Paliula's brother to Hawaii in his divine form of lightning in the romance of Ke-ao-melemele; or the account from Tahiti of Tafa'i's apotheosis.[11] In Mangaia:

"Birds, fish, reptiles, insects, and *specially inspired priests*, were reverenced as incarnations, mouth-pieces, or messengers of the gods. . . . The earth is not made, but is a thing dragged up from the shades; and is but the gross outward form of an invisible essence still in the underworld. . . . Many of their gods were originally men whose spirits were supposed to enter into

8. For. Col. 4: 168.
10. White 1: 55.
9. *RBAE* 33: 554.
11. Henry, 558–559.

various birds, fish, reptiles, and insects; and into inanimate objects, such as the triton shell, particular trees, cinet, sandstone, bits of basalt."[12]

American Indian peoples far removed from the South Seas cherish a similar attitude toward animate nature. When a warrior of the Omaha takes a new name it is necessary to announce it to the thunder, rocks, hills, trees, worms, animals, and birds. Riggs is quoted as saying of the Dakota Sioux, "They pray to the sun, earth, moon . . . to any object, artificial as well as natural, for they suppose that every object, artificial as well as natural, has a spirit which may hurt or help, and so is a proper object of worship."[13] Of Siwash, god of earth of a California tribe, the story says:

So he took some of the people and of them he made high mountains, and of some smaller mountains. Of some he made rivers and creeks and lakes and waterfalls, and of others, coyotes, foxes, deer, antelopes, bears, squirrels, porcupine, and all other animals. Then he made out of the other people all the different kinds of snakes and reptiles and insects and birds and fishes. Then he wanted trees and plants and flowers and he turned some of the people into these things. Of every man or woman that he seized he made something according to its value.[14]

Specifically comparable with the Hawaiian concept is the American Indian assertion that "each class of animals or objects of a like kind possesses a peculiar guardian divinity which is the mother archetype."[15] It is this class god who is worshiped as an aumakua through the particular member of the species recognized as a child of the god. Nor are natural objects alone thus regarded. A sledge introduced early from the Northwest Coast was worshiped, says Ellis, under the name of Opae-kau-ari'i (Crab for a chief to rest on).[16] Worshipers of Nu'u, guardian of excrement, were forbidden to allow fire to touch their excrement.[17] Some saw their old gods

12. Gill, 20, 21, 32; cf. 16.   13. *RBAE* 3: 324–325; 11: 434.
14. *JAFL* 15: 38.   15. *RBAE* 11: 434.
16. *Tour,* 99.
17. Emerson, *HHS Papers* 2: 15.

in printed words (palapala). They say that "in ancient times
the gods came to Hawaii from overseas with their families
and followers and peopled the group. Up to that time only
spirits dwelt here. For a long time they lived with their people
as visible, personal gods, but when they became disgusted
with their evil ways they left them and went elsewhere. But
they left a promise that some day they would return in di-
minutive size and speaking strange tongues so that the people would not recognize them. When the white men came with
their strange language and their art of printing, the tradition was recalled to the minds of some: 'E ho'i mai ana makou mai ka aina e mai, e olelo ana i na olelo malihini, a iloko o
na hua makali'i, a e ho'ohewahewa no kekahi o oukou i ko
oukou akua' (We shall return from a foreign country speaking a strange language and in little forms, and some of you
will not recognize your gods). The Hawaiians hence felt that
their gods had returned in the Bible. The size of the type
used in its printing caused them to think that their gods had
come in that shape."[18]

Star lore has yet to be recorded from Hawaii. Stars were
named and were associated with gods and chiefs, but no star
incarnations or apotheoses are related in Hawaiian story.
Sun and moon are represented in myth, either as habitations
of gods who descend and live on earth in human form, or as
divine bodies of gods who are worshiped as aumakua by their
descendants. At noon when the body casts no shadow the full
strength of the sun passes into its worshiper. Ka la i ka lolo
(the hour of triumph, or, literally, the sun on the brain) it
is called. The very small part played even in ritual story by
so striking a natural object as the sun, which we know had
its worshipers, leads one to suspect a suppression of myth
which was phallic in nature or else was so tied up in sorcery
as to invite secrecy. First perhaps Ku and then Kane were
looked upon as the male procreative gods into whose family
on earth the whole Wakea genealogy is drawn. Maui with,
in some groups, his dazzling phallus may be regarded in the
same light.

18. From Mrs. Pukui to Miss Green.

The wind god (or goddess) La'ama'oma'o causes the wind and storm to arise, but in story the action is altogether concerned with the human means of attaining control over these powers. La'ama'oma'o himself is worked into the migration legend of Moikeha as a helpful companion who stops off at Hale-o-Lono in Kaluakoi on Molokai (a cave on the north coast near Kalaupapa) or at Waipio, as the party coasts along the islands.[19] Maui is said to have obtained the "Gourd of constant winds" (Ipu-makani-a-ka-maumau) from the kahuna Kaleiiolu in Waipio valley to fly his kite by.[20] The famous tale of Paka'a, which belongs to a period rather late in the history of the ruling chiefs of Hawaii but is probably put together out of much older material, also shows the wind god well under the influence of his human worshipers through their knowledge of the chants which enumerate his attributive names, and their possession of the bones of his keeper (kahu).

LEGEND OF PAKA'A

Rice version. Paka'a is the son of the head steward of Keawe-nui-a-Umi and of La'a-ma'oma'o, daughter of a chief at Kapa'a on Kauai [note the play on the name], whom the steward marries incognito and leaves with child upon return to his master, without revealing to the family his high rank but bestowing upon the mother the customary tokens of his paternity. The fatherless boy is despised by the mother's family. He invents the use of a sail and wins a racing contest. The mother gives him a finely polished calabash containing the bones of his grandmother Loa, who in her life had controlled the winds of every district from Hawaii on the east to Kaula on the west of the group, and teaches him how to open the calabash and call the name of whatever wind he desires, and she then sends him to seek his father.

The boy is recognized by the tokens and at his father's death succeeds to his father's offices of chief councilor, diviner, treasurer, and navigator for the chief. Jealous enemies conspire against him and the office of navigator is taken from him. He

19. Kamakau, *Kuokoa*, January 5, 1867; Malo, 114; Kalakaua, 255–256; For. Pol. Race 2: 53.

20. Westervelt, *Maui*, 114–118; *Gods and Ghosts*, 59–60.

leaves the ruler in anger and hides himself on a remote coast of Molokai [at a spot where the foundation of his house is pointed out today] and there takes a wife and engages in agriculture against the coming of his chief. To his son Kuapaka'a he teaches all his own lore of the winds and rains [some hundreds of which are quoted in the Fornander version]. When Keawe comes seeking his favorite, he conceals himself, but the boy calls up a storm and brings the party ashore, where the chief is entertained in the old style and becomes even more wistful over the loss of his old friend and servant, until finally the navigators who have usurped his place are drowned in a storm and the chief himself is constrained to put to death the others who have plotted against him.[21]

The account makes no claim for Paka'a as a personified wind god and it is only through material possession of the ancestral bones and the no less important oral recitation of the sacred names that godlike power becomes his. All this is in line with definite priestly training and has nothing to do with allegory.

Wind imprisonment by noted magicians occurs in other South Sea areas.[22] Cloud shapes, rainbows, and other such appearances are, like the stars, definitely connected with chief families and their comings and goings. There is no attempt to dramatize the phenomena themselves save in relation to the human action in which they play a part in the service of the family to which they belong. Stories in which nature spirits are the actors represent them as marrying, fighting, giving birth, exactly like human beings, but colored with the attributes of the forms they represent. Poliahu, goddess of the snow-covered mountain, who vamps the lovers of the lady of Paliuli, wears a white mantle and cold is her attribute. It is often to secure the powers obviously belonging to the object, or to some other object, generally analogous in name or attribute, whose nature it is believed to share, that natural objects are worshiped as gods.

21. Rice, 69–89; Kamakau, *Ke Au Okoa,* December 15, 1869—January 5, 1870; For. Col. 5: 72–135; Thrum, *More Tales,* 53–67.
22. Dixon, 55, and notes 63–65.

For this reason stones in general have a potential power. Kane-poha(ku)-ka'a (Rolling stone Kane) is the subordinate Kane god who presides over stones. He was never represented by an image but came to his worshipers in dreams in human form with a head of stone. He was invoked by warriors to bless their weapons and make them "strong as rocks," and by farmers to bless their fields. The saying is, "He ola ka pohaku a he make ka pohaku," that is, "There is life in the stone and death in the stone," because stones are used as missiles to kill and as ovens in cooking. Stone working was a chiefly art, and an elaborate differentiation of stones suitable for working was known to the adept. Malo lists fifty-eight varieties and believes "there are many other stones that have failed of mention."

To secure a god to preside over games, large stones were selected and wrapped in tapa, and ceremonies were performed over such a stone in the heiau. If the owner of the god was unsuccessful more than once or twice, the stone god was thrown away. Rocks have sex: the solid rock, columnar in shape, is male; the porous rock, loaf-shaped or split by a hollow, is female. Chiefs and priests worshiped these rocks and poured awa over them as representatives of the god. If a stone of each sex was selected, a small pebble would be found beside them which increased in size and was finally taken to the heiau to be made a god. Iliili-hanau-o-Koloa (Birth pebble of Koloa) is the mother of rocks for Kau district, referring to the porous pebbles found especially at the beach of Koloa, Kau district, on Hawaii. Such stones were supposed to grow from a tiny pebble to a good-sized rock and to reproduce themselves if watered once a week. Care had to be taken lest they be stepped upon or otherwise treated with disrespect. Hence they were carefully wrapped in tapa and laid away on a high rafter of the house. At a child's naming day or on other special occasions such as marriages, wars, and fishing expeditions they were taken down and arranged on ti leaves, together with awa root, upon a mat or table and their wisdom and blessing invoked. Afterwards some member of the family would have a dream favorable or un-

favorable to the project in hand and this was regarded as
sent from the god. A similar idea is found in Tonga, where
black volcanic pebbles and white pebbles of coral, buried together, are believed to increase.[23]

According to Fornander, a priest consulted by a person
who wished to steal the property of another would divine the
result of the undertaking by a process of "odd or even" with
a pile of some fifty pebbles. If the would-be thief chose a pile
containing an odd number of stones and the pile left over for
the owner was even, the expedition would be lucky; if the re-
verse, unlucky. An odd number or an even number for both
sides was "bad." Pebbles used in the game of kimo (jackstones) and in the game of konane (a kind of checkers) are
regarded with that sanctity which surrounds the objects sacred to the use of chiefs.[24]

Special stones are regarded as sacred because of a traditional connection with old ancestors. They are gods (akua)
and it is bad luck to disturb them. According to Mrs. Pukui,
near the old Hawaiian hotel at Waikiki is a row of rocks called
Pae-ki'i to which it was the custom in old days to take strangers caught along the coast and suspected of a war trip or a
search for a human victim for their gods, and hold their
heads under water until they were drowned. This method of
putting to death was called kai he'e kai. An old Hawaiian
who was asked to point them out refused lest "our lives should
pay the forfeit."

Petroglyphs abound about the islands, some as picto-
graphs, a good many representing crude outlines of the human figure. The most interesting are in the form of cup-
markings surrounded by one or two rings. Those which
occur on the boundaries of Apuki land division in Puna are
used by the old Puna people as depositories for the child's

23. *Bul.* 61: 301; *JPS* 30: 230.
24. Malo, 40; Brigham, *Mem.* 1, No. 4; Ellis, *Tour,* 158; Kalakaua, 40; *HHS Reports* 25: 30; For. Col. 6: 72; Green, 123; *AA* 26:
243–244; Westervelt, *Gods and Ghosts,* 197; and local information
collected by Miss Green.

navel cord. The subject has been studied by Baker,[25] Stokes,[26] Ellis,[27] and mentioned by Dibble.[28]

Stones, as shown in the story of Kuula, are often worshiped as fish gods. Stories of fish gods and fish transformations are common, since, as a Fornander informant somewhat enigmatically remarks, "some of the beings who inhabited this world were gods and some were fishes, and this fact remains to this day."[29] Fish altars were built to a number of fishing gods besides Ku-ula, the great god of the fishing stations; to Kane-makua, Kini-lau (Multitude), Ka-moho-ali'i (Shark god of the Pele family), Kane-koa, Kane-kokala, and others.[30]

Birds are notably potential gods or spirit beings. In the machinery of romance migratory birds or those which nest in high cliffs are messengers for the high chiefs in the story. Thus plover (kolea), wandering tattler (ulili), tropic bird (koae), turnstone (akekeke, akikeehiale) are sent by the divine chiefs of the story, generally in pairs, to act as scouts or to carry messages from island to island. The plover, accompanied by the tattler, remains in Hawaii or flies on south from August until the following May or June, when it migrates to Alaska for nesting, leaving behind immature birds and cripples. Cartwright reports watching flights of these birds for two or three days at a time from the deck of an ocean steamer going south to Samoa.[31]

According to a Tongan story, Hama followed the tropic bird to sea to find out where it got its food and discovered the island of Ata.[32] In New Zealand thousands of birds assemble on Spirits Bay, where the spirits of the dead take their departure for the reinga (heavens), and leave New Zealand for northern Siberia. A Maori song runs,

> Whilst the fleet of canoes o'er the ocean are paddled
> The flocks of gods are above in the heavens flying.

25. See *HAA,* index.   26. BPBM Oc. Papers 4, No. 4.
27. *Tour,* appendix.   28. 88.
29. Col. 5: 266–272, 510–514; Emerson, *HHS Papers* 2: 12–13; Thrum, *Tales,* 270–274.
30. *HAA* 1910, 56.   31. *JPS* 38: 110–111.
32. Collocott, *Bul.* 46: 52–53.

The godwit (kuaka) arrives in October and leaves in March by way of Norfolk, New Hebrides, Solomon Islands, New Guinea, Timor, Celebes, Japan, China, to Siberia. "Who can tell of the nests of the kuaka?" is a Maori proverb.[33] On Ellis Island frigate birds are used by native pastors to send messages. Formerly natives sent pearl fishhooks in this way from island to island. The birds are kept on perches and fed fish. When they see another similar perch they alight upon it.[34] In Samoa the plover (Tuli) is the messenger of Tangaloa-a-lagi.[35] In a Marquesan legend the tropic bird (Kotae) and the swallow (Kopea) are sent to secure songs.[36]

In Hawaiian story subordinate deities and even the great gods appear in bird bodies. The spirits of relatives serve their descendants in this form. In Haleole's romance the chiefess of Paliuli is served by birds and rests upon their wings. Her house is thatched with royal yellow feathers. The notes of birds mark her progress. The story reads: "When rings the note of the oo bird I am not in that sound, or the alala, I am not in that sound; when rings the note of the elepaio then am I making ready to descend; when the note of the apapane sounds, then I am without the door of my house; if you hear the note of the iiwipolena, then I am without your ward's house; seek me, you two, and find me without."

The elepaio bird (*Chasiempis sandwichensis*) or flycatcher is a goddess worshiped by canoe makers. When a canoe was to be built, a priest would go to the forest, select a tree, and pray to the gods of the woods to bless it, then wait for an elepaio bird to alight on the trunk. If it merely ran up and down, the trunk was sound; but where it stopped to pick at the bark, that spot was sure to be found rotten and the builder would run a risk in making use of the trunk.[37]

Mythical birds called Halulu, Kiwaʻa, Iwa appear in the stories as bearers overseas or to the heavens.[38] The kiwaʻa is

33. *JPS* 16: 172–173; 21: 118–119.

34. Turner, 282.   35. Krämer 1: 392.

36. Handy, *Bul.* 67: 54.

37. Westervelt, *Honolulu,* 100; For. Col. 4: 458, 462.

38. Emory, *Bul.* 12: 12–13; Westervelt, *Gods and Ghosts,* 66–73; For. Col. 4: 42, 64–67; *RBAE* 33: 472.

said to be the pilot bird which conducts the navigator in to
the canoe shed at the landing place. Halulu in the Aukelenui
legend is the man-eating bird from Kahiki who can also take
human form. The heiau of Halulu at Kaunolu on Lanai was
the most important on that island. Of the reference in the
Kumulipo, "This is the landing-place of the bird Halulu,"
Hawaiians say that the name was given to a chief, also called
Hoolulu, brought here from foreign lands, who landed at
Kona on Hawaii and from whose line Beckley's grandmother
stems. The feathers that rise and fall on the heads of images
in answer to a kahuna's petition are said to come from the
mythical birds Halulu and Kiwaʻa—"Wonderful feathers,"
says Kamakau, "made out of particles of water from the
dazzling orb of the sun."[39] By Malo they are said, more pro-
saically, to come from the iwa or man-of-war bird (*Fregata
aquila*) found on the small islands off Kauai, Kaula, and
Nihoa.[40] Individuals of this species are worshiped under particular names. The bird Ka-iwa-kalameha is a great bird ancestress with dwelling places in all the islands and in Kahiki.[41]
Kiha-haka-iwa-i-na-pali is a great bird sent by Lonopele to
vomit over the canoe of Paao and sink it in the waves.[42]

A fourth seabird known in myth as the Aaia-nukea-nui-a-
Kane (Great white albatross of Kane), also written with the
termination a-ku-lawaia (standing fishing), is the white albatross (*Diomedea immutabilis*) which used to be seen commonly along the island coasts and was called "Kane's bird."[43]
So in Tahiti the common albatross is spoken of as the
"shadow" of Taʻaroa.[44]

Species of birds which are habitants of the islands hence
appear in myth as kindred and servants of gods who are
worshiped as family guardians, or the god himself may manifest himself on earth in bird form and be worshiped under the
name of his particular manifestation.

Vegetable growth is regarded by Hawaiians with more re-

39. *Ke Au Okoa*, February 24, 1870.
40. Malo, 65; For. Col. 6: 451 note 1.
41. Westervelt, *Honolulu*, 224.　　42. Kalakaua, 48.
43. Kepelino, 32; *Moolelo Hawaii*, 41; Thrum, *More Tales*, 71.
44. Henry, 386.

ligious awe than animal life because it is not so intimately associated with man. All life other than human springs from the gods since it is out of control of man. It is therefore alive with spirit force. Plants are thought of as transformation bodies of gods and as such take their place in myth.

In folk belief the wind god Makani-keoe (Makani-kau), one of the many gods of love named in Hawaiian lore, has control over plants and can himself take the form of a tree or cause plants to grow. A branch from his transformation form will serve as a love charm, but only a brave person can secure such an amulet because of the voices and visions which will pursue him. The sisters of Makani-keoe are Lau-ka-ieie, who owns the cowry shell Leho-ula, and Lau-kiele-ula, who becomes wife of Moanaliha-i-ka-waokele, one of the remote ancestors of the Kane line and father of the Maile sisters in the romance of Laieikawai. One turns into the sacred pandanus vine called ieie, the other into the sacred sweet-scented kiele blossom of the uplands. A folktale from Kau district on Hawaii tells how Makani-kau takes pity on a young husband turned out of the house by his wife's family because of his indolence, and reconciles the couple by conjuring up food for his protégé when all the land suffers from famine. Today in Kau when there is a family quarrel folk say, "Makani-keoe is gone from home," or "has come back" when the quarrel is patched up.[45]

Hawaiians are extravagantly fond of perfume, and fragrant plants are invariably associated with deity. Color is also indicative of divine rank, yellow and red being the colors sacred to chiefs. Yellow seems to be primarily the Kane color. The use of flower wreaths and decorations of woodland plants for a dance hall carries with it a sense of divinity which strengthens the emotional satisfaction with which such things are regarded. Certain red flowers are sacred to the gods and those whom they love. Like the red iiwi bird, so is the red iiwi blossom of the vine sacred. No one not beloved of the gods will dare to pick and wear it lest he be haunted by a headless woman carrying her head under one arm.

45. Green, 34–42.

Awa drink from the shrub of the pepper family (*Piper methysticum*) is invariably used in sacrifice to Kane gods. Different varieties are distinguished by their color and markings and by the size of the root sections. Babies were given the juice of the nene variety as a soothing syrup. "This is a fretful (onene) child and must be given the awa nene," is the saying. Only the most common variety could be used by the commoner; the rarer kinds were reserved for the chiefs. For the gods and on ceremonial occasions the moi (royal), hiwa (black), and papa (recumbent) were used, the papa, from which the moi was often an offshoot, being specially offered to female deities. The most highly prized was that which sprouted upon trees so that the roots to be gathered grew exposed on the tree. It was called awa "resting on trees" (kau laau) or "planted by the birds" (a ka manu).

Awa offered to a god was either poured or sprinkled over the image, or, if there was no image, the kahuna sprinkled it in the air and drank the remainder in the cup. The cups used were always made of polished coconut shells cut lengthwise in the shape called kanoa. The cups were never placed on the floor itself but on a piece of bark cloth spread before the priest or server, and never where they might be stepped over or otherwise desecrated. As soon as the ceremony was over, they were washed, placed in a net (koko), and hung from the rafters. The strainer was also carefully washed and hung in a tree to dry. The order of serving also was important. At the entertainment of a guest, it was considered an insult to the host if the guest refused the cup or passed the cup handed to him, as guest of honor, to an inferior chief. Before a war especially all chiefs drank together a cup of awa, which passed from hand to hand in order of rank. In passing the cup to a chief it was customary to utter some appropriate remark or sing a chant, but no particular form was fixed by tradition.

The preparation of the awa did not differ from the methods described for other groups. The young boys and girls who chewed the chiefs' awa were especially selected from the chief class for their perfect teeth. The peculiar sense of sacredness which associated the awa with the body of a god be-

cause of its narcotic effect was still further strengthened by
this ceremonial restraint and the exclusiveness put upon its
use.[46]

Coconut groves are among "those things on earth which
are worshiped." The grove at Kalapana was in old days tapu
to all but the descendants of a certain family of chiefs of
whom the following story is told:

LEGEND OF THE RECUMBENT COCONUTS OF KALAPANA

Long ago two young chiefs of Puna named Hinawale and
Owalauahi(-wahie) who were cousins and intimates stole away
incognito to tour the island. Returning after several months
they joined a group of men who were testing their strength by
attempting to bend to earth two full-grown coconut trees. Unrecognized they waited until all had failed, then they too made
the attempt. Hinawale grasped one tree, Owalauahi the other,
and with a strong downward pull laid them low. The people
shouted applause. Upon discovering that the men were their
own chiefs their joy knew no bounds.

The mother of Mrs. Pukui, who tells the tale, is descended
from one of these two chiefs. Visitors to the coconut grove today are shown Naniu-moe-o-Kalapana (The recumbent coconut trees of Kalapana) still flourishing as of old, although it
is said that the two original trees have been since replaced.
The story is told of Queen Emma that when she found the
trees dead and asked her men to bend two more to take their
place none could do so until the queen herself held a leaf of
each, when they were easily bent. A San Cristoval account of
the passage to the land of the dead tells how, at Hauihaiha,
the souls are supposed to bend down the fronds of a coconut
called Niu-tarau (Coconut of crossing).[47] Although not so
stated, the task is probably a test of chief rank. The play of
words in the Hawaiian is upon the word moe, which denotes
the rank of a high tapu chief and also refers to the position
of the growing trunks as they lie as if sleeping (moe) along
the ground.

46. Given by Mrs. Pukui.   47. Fox, 234.

A good deal of lore centers about the origin of food plants
or other plants useful in the economic life. Stories are told to
explain certain tapus upon them or customs connected with
them which are observed in particular families. A common
folktale is that of the relief of famine out of the body of a
god who is living on earth in human form and takes pity
upon his starving family. Sometimes he provides an oven of
food out of his own body, himself emerging unhurt. Sometimes a plant springs from his body at death, which is his
spirit body.

MYTH OF THE OVEN OF FOOD FROM THE BODY OF A GOD

(a) *Emerson version* (told to J. S. Emerson in 1883 at Kau-
pulehu, Kona, Hawaii). A stranger comes to the land and
takes a wife. The people have no food. He builds and heats an
imu (oven), lies down in it and is covered with earth. When it is
uncovered after a period suitable for cooking, the oven yields
all sorts of cooked food, while the man himself, perfectly untouched, is seen approaching from the sea. A stream of fresh
water called Wai-kawili (Mingling waters) is found welling up
at the sea where he has emerged after digging his way half a
mile from the oven into which he entered.[48]

(b) *Pukui version* (told to her when she was a child by an old
lady of Hilo named Kanui Kaikaina). Hina-i-ke-ahi (Hina in
the fire) is a kupua woman who lives at Hilo, Hawaii, with her
sister Hina-i-ka-wai (Hina in the water). During a famine
Hina-in-the-fire builds and heats an imu. After naming the various foods to be cooked therein and bidding the family uncover it
when they see a cloud shaped like a woman resting over it, she
lies down in it and is covered with earth. When they uncover the
oven, the food named is found within and Hina herself approaches from the sea wreathed with brown seaweed and goes
out swimming with Woman-of-the-coral, "one of the wives of
the god Ku." Her sister is jealous and attempts to duplicate the
feat, but nothing is found in the oven but her ashes because she
has not the same kupua gift as her sister.[49]

48. *HHS Reports* 27: 31–33.   49. Green, 57–59.

(c) *Westervelt version.* Hina, mother of Maui the demigod, has four kupua daughters, Hina-ke-ahi, Hina-ke-kai, Hina-ma-huia, Hina-kuluua (Kuliua). The first has power over fire, the second over the sea, the last over the rain (ua) ; Hina-mahuia is the fire goddess of southern Polynesia, Mafuie. After Hina has prepared the oven and is covered over, she journeys underground and emerges first at a still pool of fresh water called Moe-wa‘a, then from a great spring of water which bubbles up at the very shore [such as old Hawaiians used for a fresh-water bath after swimming (auau-wai)]. She commands them to open the oven and enough food is found within to last until the famine is ended. Her sister Kulu-ua repeats the experiment but lacks the power. Her body is burnt to ashes but her spirit escapes and appears as a cloud over the peaks in sign of rain. In some versions Maui is represented as seeking his sister's destruction.[50]

Stories of the introduction of the breadfruit tree take either a rational or a mythical turn. The rational legend is that Kaha‘i, son of Ho‘okamali‘i and grandson of Moikeha, brought the breadfruit from Upolo to Hawaii and planted it at Pu‘uloa, Kohala.[51] In the Fornander story of Namaka-o-ka-paoo, Hawaiian-born son of Ka-ulu-o-kaha‘i (Breadfruit of Kaha‘i), a great chief in Kahiki-papa-ia-lewa (Faraway land in space), a gourd containing the tokens his father has left for him the son deposits at the foot of the "breadfruit impersonation of his father" at Kualakai, which tree "is standing to this day."[52] An early schoolboy composition by W. S. Lokai says that two men who were out fishing were blown to the land of Kane-huna-moku, inhabited only by gods, and brought thence the breadfruit, which they planted at Pu‘uloa. Haumea came there to inspect it and spread it to other lands.[53]

The mythical tale is as follows:

50. *Maui,* 155–164.
51. Kamakau, *Kuokoa,* January 12, 1867; For. Pol. Race 2: 54; Col. 4: 392, 393.
52. *Ibid.* 5: 278.   53. *Ibid.* 678, 679.

ORIGIN MYTH OF THE BREADFRUIT

(a) *Lokai version.* The breadfruit tree grew up from the testes of a man who died for his family at Kaawaloa in Kona, Hawaii. The forty thousand and the four thousand gods first tried the fruit green, then cooked, and found it palatable, but when they heard where it came from they began to vomit and so spread the tree all the way between Kona and their home at Waipio.[54]

(b) *Pukui version.* The god Ku loves a woman of earth and the two live happily until there comes a famine. Bidding farewell to his wife, Ku stands on his head and disappears into the ground. None but his wife and child are able to pick the fruit.[55]

(c) *Lyman version.* A man named Ulu lives at Waiakea, Hawaii, and has a young son named Moku-ola, from whom the island of that name in Hilo bay is afterwards named. Ulu dies of famine, but, following the directions of the priests of the heiau at Puueo, the family bury his body near a spring of running water and remain all night within the house. During the night they hear the sounds of dropping leaves and flowers, then of heavy fruit, and in the morning find a breadfruit tree at their door, with the fruit of which the famine is relieved.[56]

In one story the coconut brought by Kane, "a man of very long bones," is said to have been formerly low, but when a servant was sent by his master to pick the coconuts, the tree lengthened as he climbed.[57] The idea is the same as that of the tapu upon picking breadfruit with which the Pukui version concludes.

Similar stories tell of the growth of a plant out of a human body after burial. The most famous of these is that told elsewhere of the lauloa taro that grew from the embryo child of Papa and Wakea. Others explain some family tapu upon a

---

54. For. Col. 5: 676–679.
56. Thrum, *More Tales,* 235–241.
57. For. Col. 5: 596–599.

55. Green and Pukui, 127.

particular plant. In Ka-u a legend is related to explain why
the family of a certain chiefess are careful to do no injury to
a gourd of a particular species used for household purposes
and to bury it carefully if broken. The story shows how a
natural happening may be interpreted as a myth.

LEGEND OF THE BITTER GOURD

A chiefess of a certain family dies and is buried in a cave.
From her navel grows a gourd vine. It finds its way to the garden of a chief of the seventh district, and there produces a fine
gourd. The chief thumps it to test its ripeness and the spirit of
the gourd complains to a kahuna in a dream. Kahuna and chief
trace the vine to its source and the gourd is thereafter treated
respectfully.[58]

Myths tell how a god who has lived on earth takes at death
the form of some plant. From the body of Kaohelo, sister of
Pele, grew the ohelo bushes so abundant on volcanic moun-
tainsides; "the flesh became the creeping vine and the bones
became the bush plant."[59] The ieie vine is said to be the form
in which the goddess Laukaieie was worshiped "when the time
came for her to lay aside her human body." Kamakau relates
of Hina-ai-ka-malama that "she found a sweet potato from
the moon of a kind called hua-lani (fruit-of-heaven)" and he
thinks it may be for this reason that she was said to be "nourished on the moon" (-ai-ka-malama). Her husband may thus
have had a legitimate reason for cutting off her foot when she
escaped to the moon, according to the popular story, in order
to preserve a planting of the precious new food which may
be conceived as the form her spirit took in its moment of deification.[60] Of Maikoha, banished son of Konikonia, the myth
says that he wandered away and died at Kaupo on Maui and
out of his body grew a wauke plant (*Broussonetia papyri-
fera*) of a hairy kind like the hairy Maikoha and useful for
beating out bark cloth.[61]

58. Green and Pukui, 140–143.   59. For. Col. 5: 576, 577.
60. *Ke Au Okoa,* October 21, 1869.
61. For. Col. 5: 270, 271.

MYTH OF MAIKOHA

(*a*) *Fornander version.* The youngest son of Konikonia and Hina-ai-ka-malama is a hairy man from whom sprang the wauke plant. The five girls in the family are Ka-ihu-koa, (Ka-) Ihu-anu, (Ka-) Ihu-koko, Ka-ihu-kuuna, Ka-ihu-o-palaai. The five boys are Kane-au-kai, Kane-huli-koa, Kane-milo-hai, Kane-apua, Maikoha. Maikoha breaks up the sacred things. The father tests the children by tying a beam to the back of the neck and to the chin to see which one is brave enough not to cry. Maikoha is judged guilty and banished. He travels to the place in Kaupo called Maikoha and becomes a wauke plant, which is hairy to this day. His sisters come to seek him and find his navel at the root of the plant. They journey on to Oahu where they marry chiefs and change into fishponds stocked with special kinds of fish. Ka-ihu-o-palaai becomes the wife of Ka-papa-o-puhi at Hono-uliuli in Ewa and stocks the fishponds of that region with fat mullet. The oldest, Ka-ihu-koa, becomes the wife of the handsome chief of Waianae and changes into the fishing ground just out from Kaena point where the ulua, amber fish, and dolphin abound. Ihu-koko becomes the wife of Ka-wai-loa at Waialua where the aholehole fish abound which followed her home. Ka-ihu-kuuna becomes the wife of Lani-loa at Laie and changes into a famous fishing ground for mullet. Kane-au-kai follows in search of his sisters in the form of a lump of pumice or a log of wood and is worshiped as a fish god by two old men at Kealia, Waialua.[62]

(*b*) *Westervelt version.* Maikoha's body is planted by his daughters at his own direction at Pu-iwa beside the Nuuanu stream. He is chief god of tapa makers; his daughter Lau-hu-iki taught the art of pounding the wauke bark, his daughter La'a-hana that of marking the pattern on the beater.[63]

Similar plant-origin stories occur in southern groups. In Tahiti, Rua-ta'ata in Raiatea, whose temple is Toa-puhi (Eel rock), and his wife Rumau-arii, whose temple is Ahu-noa, called also Ta-pari, have four children. In time of fam-

62. For. Col. 5: 270, and see Kane-au-kai.
63. Westervelt, *Honolulu,* 7, 65.

ine the people eat red clay for food. Rua-ta'ata pities his
hungry family and, taking leave of them, he goes outside the
cave where they live and becomes a breadfruit tree.[64] Three
children in the form of coconuts become trees which, in one
version, save the people from famine.[65] On Tonga the story is
told of Fevanga and his wife Fefafa on the island of Eneiki
who kill their leprous daughter to serve to the chief Laau
with his kava. Parts of her body are buried and from the
head grows a kava plant, from the intestines the sugar cane
which is the accompaniment of a kava-drinking ceremony.[66]
In Rarotonga, Tangaroa goes to Avaiki-te-varenga and
takes a wife. He does not like the rice food which his wife prepares. Her parent Vai-takere dies and sends them breadfruit,
which they prepare as tatapaka, mashed and mixed with coconut.[67] In another Rarotonga story a father dies for his starving son and from his body develops the first pig.[68] In a Maori
story Tu-taka-hinahina tells his son to watch his grave after
his death. It is a time of darkness. Two maggots develop
from his body. The son cooks them and the sun rises.[69]

Supernatural birth stories are not uncommon. In Samoa
the story is told of Sina who forgets to chew talo for the decoy pigeon. She flees and bears a child in the form of the pel-
let she forgot to chew. This, buried, produces the pula-au
taro.[70] In Tonga, Faimalie swallows the yam of Pulotu and
later gives birth to it on earth.[71] Among the Maori the story
goes that Rongo-Maui, younger brother of the star Whanui
(alpha Lyrae of Vega), introduced the kumara to this world.
His own body was the basket. He cohabited with Pani-Ti-
naku. She goes to the waters of Mona-riki to give birth and
learns a chant. Her offspring are the varieties of the sweet
potato.[72] Another story says that Pani gets kumara by stepping into the water and rubbing her stomach until her baskets are filled with sweet potatoes.[73] The Dusun of North

64. Henry, 423–426; Ellis, *Researches* 1: 68.

65. Henry, 421–423.

66. Gifford, *Bul.* 8: 71–75.

67. *JPS* 8: 65–66.

68. Gill, 135–138.

69. White 2: 48–51.

70. Buck, *Bul.* 75: 533.

71. Gifford, *Bul.* 8: 163.

72. *JPS* 28: 26.

73. White 3: 113–115.

Borneo say that the first man and the first woman were made out of earth. Their first child they cut up and out of its parts grew the different food plants.[74] In Tonga the Papaia is thought of as the excretion of a goddess on Eua.[75] See also the Hawaiian name for the coarse grass called "Excretion of (Kama) pua'a" (Kukaepua'a). The Japanese story is that the moon god Tsukuyomi is sent by his sister to earth and finds the goddess Ukemotshi. When he is hungry and asks for food, out of her mouth come all kinds of fish, animals, vegetables. He will not eat but cuts her in two in wrath and goes back to heaven. His sister laments this result and sends a messenger to see if the goddess is really dead. Out of her body come animals and food plants which the messenger takes back to heaven. These things become the food for the chiefs of the human race who until this time have eaten raw food. The sun goddess introduces agriculture into heaven as men on earth have practised it thereafter.[76] Somewhat similar is the Maori story of Rehua, who feeds his guests with birds that live upon the insects in his hair.[77] Among the Tami of New Guinea the wives of a fisherman who always has good luck in fishing are shocked to discover that he dips his own head into the water and fishes crowd about it. They cry him shame and he sits with his head on his knees and disappears into the earth and from the spot where he sat grows the coco palm.[78]

The myth of the coconut derived from an eel lover is found commonly throughout the South Seas but has not appeared in Hawaii.[79]

Tahiti. (*a*) Hina, whose gods are sun and moon, is espoused to a chief who has an eel body. She flees to the god Maui for help. He baits his fishhook, the eel swallows it, Maui cuts up the body and gives the head to Hina to take home and plant [in Gill's version the head is a gift from a god]. Hina forgets and puts the head down while she bathes at Pani and the head

74. Evans, 45–46.   75. Collocott, *FL* 46: 45–46.
76. Chamberlain, 59–60.
77. Grey, 50–53; White 1: 82–83; Taylor, 282–283.
78. Neuhauss, 546–547.   79. Dixon, 55, 56.

sprouts into a coconut. Her daughter carries the coconut to the Tuamotu group at Taka-horo in the atoll of Ana, whence the plant spreads.[80]

(b) Taitua bathes in the stream Teohu in the depths of Vaiari. She plays there with an eel. It pursues her and she flees. A trap is built for it and the eel caught. At night it tells her in a dream to bury the head and from this springs the coconut tree.[81]

Samoa. Sina has a pet eel for which, as it grows larger, she seeks a larger pool. She climbs a tree on the bank and shakes down the fruit into the water. As she gathers it, the eel strikes at and deflowers her. She flees and it follows. When it is killed, its buried head becomes a coco palm.[82]

Tonga. Hina weeps when her eel is taken from her bathing pool, cut in pieces and eaten. From its buried head grows the coconut.[83]

Mangaia. Ina-moe-aitu (-with a god lover) is wooed by the eel, Tuna. It sends a flood and floats to her home, bids her cut off its head and plant it, whence comes the coconut.[84]

Tuamotus. Tuna lives in the lake Vaihiria at Tahiti. Hina is his wife. Maui abducts her, Tuna follows, is destroyed by Maui, and from his head springs the coco palm.[85] The same story is told of Maui and Tekina from whose head grows the coco palm.[86]
[In Fakahina, on the other hand, Tehu, son of Tetahoa and Teahio, six generations ago brought the first coconut to that island from Tahiti or one of the western islands in the boat named Kayau.[87]]

80. Henry, 615–621; Gill, 80–81.
81. Baessler, *ZE* 37: 921–922.
82. Stuebel 4: 67–68; Turner, 243–245.
83. Gifford, *Bul.* 8: 181–183.   84. Gill, 77–79.
85. Seurat 20: 438–439; Caillot 1: 95–109.
86. Montiton, 343.   87. Audran 5: 126.

Pukapuka. The wife longs for a certain strange fish and the husband brings many kinds, none of which is the right one. Finally, by uttering a charm, he hooks Tuna the eel, who tells him to plant its head and give only the body to the wife. From the head grows the coconut tree, which bears two coconuts on the top branch, three on the next branch, four on the next, and so on. The husband tosses the nuts in the air to each of the islands in the eastern and western Pacific but forgets Pukapuka in the middle. So only a hard dry nut is left and it is hard to grow coconuts on Pukapuka.[88]

Kai of New Guinea. An eel husband seeks his wife. Her new husband cuts him in bits and out of his body spring yams. Before this, agriculture was unknown in the land.[89]

San Cristoval. A man marries a snake wife. Her son-in-law finds a snake coiled about his son and chops up her body. The coconut grows from her head.[90]

Extremely heterogeneous origin stories are told of other plants important in Hawaiian culture. Some of these center upon the discovery and naming of varieties. Some are fabulous, others rational. The fabulous either are connected with some mythical figure or are riddling tales whose significance is now lost.[91]

88. Beaglehole MS.   89. Neuhauss, 180–185.
90. Fox, 82–84, 93–98.
91. For. Col. 5: 656–659; 606–677.

VIII

SORCERY GODS

HAWAIIAN sorcery has never been studied in relation to its actual functioning in different localities or its influence upon mythology and the priesthood in particular aspects. A single center alone has been reported in any detail and this in too fragmentary a form to warrant a conclusive study. Besides this a few isolated examples are added and a few illustrative stories centering upon such practices, together with the somewhat extensive bibliography available upon the actual technique employed by such practisers of sorcery as the kahuna anaana (praying to death), the kahuna hoʻounauna (sending sickness or trouble), and the kahuna kuni (divination by burning). Enough has been reported to show that sorcery, although by no means universally practised, had become one of the strongest forces in shaping the life and character of the Hawaiian people and in determining the careers of their leaders. Kamehameha was extremely careful to secure for himself all the strong sorcery gods worshiped by the ruling chiefs of the islands over which he ruled and to set up god houses and keepers for their worship.

Sorcery was commonly practised through the use of fetchers made in the shape of an image (kiʻi), which was believed to be possessed by the spirit of a powerful ancestor, or perhaps by a nature spirit, who was worshiped for the purpose of bringing the mana of the god under control of its keeper. Or the bones of a dead member of the family might be preserved and worshiped in the same manner, called an unihipili. Or the body might be dedicated to some powerful god like that of the shark, ruled by Ka-moho-aliʻi; or of the moʻo ruled by the goddess Kalamainuʻu; or of thunder, ruled by Kane-hekili; or of the owl, ruled by Kukauakahi. The body of the dead would then be changed into that of a shark, moʻo, owl, or other form, recognizable to the family by some mark upon

its body, or to the kahuna who officiated at the dedication
ceremony by some sign of identification, and into this body
the spirit of the dead would enter. If it was then worshiped
by the family, it would take that family under its protection, punishing their enemies and providing them with good
things. Such protectors were called aumakua.

Valuable as such a god might be as a family protector, it
had its dangers as well. If its worship was neglected and its
tapus forgotten or disregarded, the aumakua visited vengeance with an incredible vindictiveness upon its own keeper and
his family. Moreover, because of the strong sense of family
descent, every such god became a link in the chain which
bound succeeding generations to the tapus imposed by their
ancestral guardians, the aumakua born into the family line.
On the other hand, the mana of the family aumakua from ancestral times became the right of every member of the family
as a kumu-pa'a should he at any time seek help from such a
guardian. If, however, a family god proved ineffective, it
might, it would seem, be disregarded for a stronger.

Spirits might also possess a living person, a keeper of the
god, or a member of his family, and convey messages in this
way. Such spirits were called akua noho (literally, sitting
gods) and a person into whom a god entered was regarded as
a god during the time of possession. Kamakau is careful to
show that although Kamehameha seemed to treat the keeper
of Kahoali'i himself as a god, it was because he really believed
that the god Kahoali'i entered into the body of its keeper
and it was this god, not the living man, whom he worshiped.
Hawaiian antiquarians insist that the image, animal, or object which the god entered had no power in itself but only the
spirit that possessed it. Sorcery began when these possessing
spirits were sent abroad to do injury to another.

As bits of a keeper's body were valued after the keeper's
death in securing the services of a spirit gifted with superior
mana, although not themselves gods, so chips, even scrapings
of an image, were charged with its mana, or objects associated with such an image could be also so charged and serve as
fetchers, under the same deity. Thus dealings in sorcery were
not confined to the chiefs and priests but spread among the

people. Not that everyone who kept an aumakua made use of the god for sorcery. In practice, however, such persons were feared by their neighbors. The chiefs tried to put down sorcery and made laws against it, but the secrecy with which it was thereafter practised only increased the terror. Counterpractitioners arose who fought sorcery with sorcery and the system thus increased in complexity.[1]

There is no reason for thinking that such sorcery practices originated in the Hawaiian group. Tahitian 'oromatua are described by Henry as "disembodied spirits of famous rulers and warriors of the nation, whose skulls were used as fetchers." Little images called ti'i are used by Tahitian sorcerers, carved out of stone, coral, or wood, especially pua wood from the marae, and dressed in white tapa bound with sacred sennit. These are possessed by demons (varua-ino) or "disembodied spirits of evil" ('oromatua-'ai-aru) or "long-toothed aumakua" ('oramatua-niho-roroa). They are kept in houses set up on stilts in a special marae under which sleep the "magicians" who are their adopted parents. Ti'i, the malicious first man, is connected with sorcery. He has a white heron as fetcher, which he sends out to destroy men. The god invoked to cure those afflicted by sorcery is Ro'o (Lono)-te-roro'o.[2]

History has concerned itself with political struggles in Hawaii which finally ended in the consolidation of the group under the rule of the Kamehameha line, and has neglected the obscure and deadly warfare carried on between rival orders of sorcery on the different islands or in neighboring villages on the same island.

The source of one of the oldest schools of sorcery in Hawaii is said to have come from the goddess Pahulu and was thus described by a Hawaiian informant descended from the Molokai Lo family of kahuna chiefs who claim Pahulu as their ancestress and Molokai as the center of the "strongest" sorcery in the whole group of islands.

1. Malo, 135–158; Kamakau, *Ke Au Okoa*, May 12—September 29, 1870; J. Emerson, *HHS Reports* 26: 17–39; Buck, *YUPA* No. 2: 1–19.

2. Henry, 203–209.

LEGEND OF PAHULU

About the time of Liloa and Umi, perhaps long before, chiefs flocked to Molokai. That island became a center for sorcery of all kinds. Molokai sorcery had more mana (power) than any other. Sorcery was taught in dreams. All these Molokai auma-kua were descendants of the goddess Pahulu.

Pahulu was a goddess who came in very old times to these islands and ruled Lanai, Molokai, and a part of Maui. That was before Pele, in the days when Kane and Kanaloa came to Hawaii. Through her that "old highway" (to Kahiki) starts from Lanai. As Ke-olo-ewa was the leading spirit on Maui who possessed people and talked through them, so Pahulu was the leading spirit on Lanai. Lani-kaula, a prophet (kaula) of Mo-lokai, went and killed off all the akua on Lanai. Those were the Pahulu family. Some say there were about forty left who came over to Molokai. The fishpond of Ka-awa-nui was the first pond they built on Molokai. Some came to Oahu and landed on the beach opposite Mokuli'i. The heiau of Pahulu is on the Kaneohe side of the Judd place about six hundred feet away from the old sugar mill at Hakipu'u and out in the water toward Mokuli'i. That is where they landed on Oahu. Near the old Judd place was a heiau for Kane-hoa-lani.

Three of the descendants of Pahulu entered trees on Molokai. These were Kane-i-kaulana-ula (Kane in the red sunset), Kane-i-ka-huila-o-ka-lani (Kane in the lightning), and Kapo. About four hundred trees sprang up in a place where no trees had been before, but only three of these trees were entered by the gods. The Lo family of Molokai, a family of chiefs and kahunas, are descended from Pahulu. Many of them are well-known persons today.

So far as can be discovered, with the exception of a few scattering references to Pahulu as the leading spirit (akua) of Lanai, nothing further is to be found in print about this goddess.[3] As for the Lo family, Andrews calls them "an or-der of priests who lived on the mountain Helemano [on Oahu?] and consecrated the bodies of the dead." The practice

3. For. Col. 5: 428.

of dedicating the dead to become guardian spirits of a family aumakua was not known in the earliest period of the settling of these islands and did not come in, Kamakau thinks, until after the time of Wakea and the establishing of the tapus of chiefs. But as precise references to gods worshiped by ruling chiefs in the heiau in the form of images are studied, it becomes certain that they were sought because of their power not only to care for the soul of their keeper but to discover and ensnare the souls of those who had prayed him to death.

The god of Maui called Lo-lupe (Olo-pue, Ololupe) is the god invoked in the rite of deification of the dead or restoration of the dead to life. He is represented in the form of a kite (lupe) shaped like a sting ray. Some say his is an errand of benevolence and not of crime, and that he is sent into the heavens to ensnare the souls of those alone who have done evil. Malo calls him "the deity who took charge of [the souls of] those who spoke ill of the king, consigning them to death, while the souls of those who were not guilty of such defamation he conducted to a place of safety." Warriors greatly feared this god. At the death of a ruling chief it was under the rule of Lo-lupe that the divining priesthood (kahuna kuni) worked to detect, by means of burning a part of the chief's body used as a "bait" (maunu), the secret enemy who had prayed him to death. Another branch of the priests' work was to dedicate the body and convert it into an aumakua. After Kamehameha's conquest of Maui he sent a messenger to Kahekili to ask for the image of Lo-lupe, but as it was in the care of the kahuna Ka-opu-huluhulu who would not give it up, Kahekili sent instead a chip of the poison god Kalai-pahoa and this became the Kane-mana-ia-Paiea (The mana power of Kane for Paiea, Paiea being a nickname for Kamehameha) which the chief kept to guard his life until the day of his death and for whom he built a god house and set up keepers.[4]

Other gods besides Lo-lupe who are named as conductors of the souls of dead chiefs are Ka-onohi or Ka-onohi-o-ka-la

4. For. Pol. Race 2: 239–240; Kalakaua, 49; Malo, 141, 143 note 3; Kamakau, *Kuokoa*, July 6, 1867.

(The eyeball of the sun) and Ku-waha-ilo (Ku of the mag-
got-dripping mouth). Kalakaua places the first in the skies
to receive the souls brought to him by Ku-waha-ilo, but some
say that Ka-onohi is the conductor and Ku-waha the receiver
and devourer of souls.[5] All the images of war gods named
under the Ku group are in fact sorcery gods. Kamakau
names Ku-keoloewa and Ku-ho'one'enu'u as forming with
Ka-onohi and Lo-lupe the Papa-kahui, an order (papa) of
gods kept by Kamehameha to act as guides for the souls of
the dead. It is, finally, at least significant that the god Ka-
hoali'i with his tapus of the white haupu bird and the eyeballs
of men, who was impersonated at religious ceremonies by a
naked man with a peculiar marking and was allowed free
eating with the chiefesses, and whose keeper had so powerful
an influence over Kamehameha, resembles so closely the description of the Tahitian Ti'i, god of sorcery, with his white
heron as a fetcher and his images of wood or stone or coral
which were sent out on errands of mischief.

One more reference in the story of Pahulu must be explained before taking up the central theme of the Pahulu legend, the entering of the gods into the trees on Molokai. The
story says that the Pahulu gods on Lanai were most of them
killed and the rest banished from Lanai by the prophet Lani-
kaula. Popular legend attributes to Kaululaau the mischievous son of Kakaalaneo of Maui, the clearing of that island of
the spirits who were its first inhabitants. Lanikaula's grove
of kukui trees and the place of his grave on the eastern point
of the island of Molokai facing Maui and Lanai are still
pointed out among the famous places on that island, and the
rock islet shown where he buried his excrement.

LEGEND OF LANIKAULA

Lani-kaula (Divine prophet), the famous prophet of Halawa
on Molokai, is said to have lived in the time of Kamalalawalu of
Maui. For fear of sorcery he used to carry his excrement out
secretly to a rock islet off the coast in order that no rival kahuna could get at it and put him to death by burning it (ka

5. Kalakaua, 49; Ellis, *Tour,* 107.

lawe maunu). His friend Kawelo came to visit him, spied upon him, and took some of the excrement to his own sacred fire of Ke-ahi-aloa and burned it there. Lanikaula knew that he must die. He called his sons to devise some means of burying his body so that none could find it. Finally it was decided to dig a pit and cover the body over with stones.

The fire of Kawelo, Ke-ahi-aloa, is said to have been kept constantly burning in order to fulfil a prophecy that as long as this fire on Lanai and the fire of Waha across the channel on Maui were kept up, dogs and hogs would not fail on those islands. Kawelo left his daughter, Waha his son in charge of the fire. One night the young people were busy with love making and the fires went out. Kawelo threw himself over the cliff of Maunalei and killed himself.[6]

LEGEND OF KALAIPAHOA

(a) *Kamakau version.* A man of Molokai named Kane-ia-kama (Kane-a-Kama) joins a gambling game at Hale-lono, the gambling place at Ka-lua-koi, and wins the stakes. On his way home he gambles again at the famous gambling place on Mau-naloa and loses everything he has except his bones, which he is afraid to stake. That night the god Kane-i-kaulana-ula (Kane in the red flush of victory) comes to him in dream and bids him stake his life the next day, promising him victory if he will take him as his god. In vision he sees this god lead a procession of gods, three of whom enter trees in a grove which springs up where no grove had been before. The next day he stakes and wins and gains back all that he has lost. From the nioi tree entered by the god he carves an image of his god. This is the Kalai-pahoa (Cut with a pahoa axe). Two other gods enter trees: Ka-huila-o-ka-lani (The lightning in the heavens) enters an ae tree, Kapo enters an ohe (bamboo). The wood of the Kalaipahoa tree is so poisonous that anyone upon whom a chip falls is killed by it. Every waste piece, after the image has been carved with proper prayers and offerings, is sunk in the sea.

The Kalaipahoa god belongs to the ruling chief of Molokai and Kane-ia-kama is its keeper. It is not used at this time for

6. Emory, *Bul.* 12: 18–19; For. Col. 5: 674.

sorcery. Later, in the time of Peleioholani (son of Kualiʻi) on
Oahu, Kamehamehanui on Maui, and Kalani-opuʻu on Hawaii,
an influential man of Kalae on Molokai named Kai-a-kea sets up
a god house to Pua and Kapo under the name of "The grove of
Maunaloa" (Ka-ulu-o-Maunaloa). He too has a vision and in
this waking vision there comes to him a procession of beautiful
women led by the god Pua and the goddess Kapo, who bid him
take them as his gods and tell him to go to a spring, where he
will find a flock of mud hens (alae) and a calabash containing
mana. He then begins to worship Kalaipahoa in the form of
these spirits. Not until these gods have passed to his daughter
are they used for sorcery. She prophesies that Oahu will pass
to Kahekili. When this happens her claim to be inspired by Pua
and Kapo is believed and she and her husband Puhene at Kapu-
lei are sought for purposes of protection and vengeance. Kamehameha has god houses built for both these gods when he becomes ruler over the islands.[7]

Such is Kamakau's account of the poison god called Kalaipahoa. Other versions say that the tree sprang up in a single
night during the time of the chief Kamauaua, father of
Kapeʻepeʻe and Keoloewa of Molokai. Three sisters came
from an unknown land and one of them entered into the tree
and poisoned it. Others say that Kane-kulana-ula entered the
tree in a flash of light just before it was felled and was unable
to escape. The grove is said to have been so poisonous that
birds fell dead as they flew over it.[8]

The flash of light which marks the entrance into the tree
of the god of lightning is a very old conception, preserved in
two South Sea areas in connection with gods of war and perpetuated in Hawaii in folk beliefs about Kalaipahoa sorcery.
The first Kalaipahoa image is said to have been cut into bits
and distributed among the chiefs after Kamehameha's death.
Bundles of blocks made out of nioi wood and graded in size,
if they had been brought into contact with the Kalaipahoa
were supposed to partake of its mana. They might be then

7. *Ke Au Okoa,* May 12, July 14, 1870.
8. Ellis, *Tour,* 68–69; For. Pol. Race 2: 239, 240 note 2; Malo,
113; Westervelt, *Gods and Ghosts,* 108–115.

used as fetchers and sent out at night in the form of a streak of light, large at the head and tapering into a tail. In Puna district twenty years ago obscure diseases like tuberculosis were invariably laid to sorcery and many reported seeing the Kalaipahoa poison fly from the house of the sorcerer to that of his victim. The fetcher as a streak of light may have a long history in Hawaii, since Ka-ili (The snatcher), described by Ellis in 1823 as a god seen at evening "flying about in the form of a comet,"[9] is the name of Liloa's war god bequeathed to his favorite son Umi, who eventually seized the rule from his less able and less devout brother. In New Zealand, the god Rongo-mai came to earth and led the attack of the Nga-ti-hau against the Nga-ti-awa in form "like a shooting star or comet, or flame of fire."[10] In Tahiti, Ave-aitu (Tailed god) is a god with a long tail who guides the hosts of Tane (Kane) in time of war.[11] Taylor says, probably in reference to the same figure, "The ancient image of Tane in Tahiti was represented as a meteor, cone-shaped with a large head, the body terminating in a point, with a long tail."

The idea of fetchers in the form of a streak of light may derive from a primitive idea like that reported from Dobu, where people believe that fire from the pubes of flying witches is seen at night.[12] This would explain such incidents in Hawaiian story as the display of her person by a supernatural woman to frighten off a malicious ghost, or the use of her skirt to raise a thunderstorm. Kapo with her flying vagina is worshiped as an akua noho. She is one of the daughters of the sorceress Haumea, who entered a growing tree to save her human husband, thereby so infecting it with deity as to be poisonous to all who cut it. From Haumea also came the mysterious tree out of which were cut the sorcery gods Kuho'one-'enu'u worshiped by Oahu chiefs as god of war, and Kukeo-loewa, god of war for Maui and Molokai. All the Pele family are linked with sorcery.

Another sorcery figure in the story is that of Pua, whom Malo names with Kapo as an akua noho feared, the one on Molokai, the other on Maui, because believed to take posses-

9. *Tour*, 90.   10. White 1: 109.
11. Henry, 379.   12. Fortune, 99, 152.

sion of people and cause swelling of the abdomen.[13] In Tahiti
pua wood is said to be a favorite for the carving of fetchers.
Puara'i names "a famous Tahitian warrior of old" worshiped
as one of three 'oromatua set up in the image house of the national marae of Tane at Maeva in Huahine.[14] The pua (bua)
tree is found in many South Sea stories at the entrance to the
land of the dead. Here then is another link with Tahitian
sorcery.

Some confusion in sex is perhaps to be explained by the
dual character of these sorcery gods. Male sorcerers seem to
work through a female companion as akua noho. A wooden
image of the Kalaipahoa poison god in the Bishop Museum
is realistically carved in the form of a female human figure
with knees slightly flexed, arms hanging away from the body,
fingers apart, and mouth open. A female figure of Keoloewa
in the same stylized position carries a small human figure on
its back. Keoloewa holds the same position in ancient tradition as the leading spirit of Maui that Pahulu is said to have
held on Molokai.[15] Ellis describes a Keoloewa image as of
wood dressed in native tapa with head and neck of wickerwork covered with red feathers to look like a birdskin, and
wearing a native helmet hung with human hair, the mouth
large and distended. It was placed in the inner room of the
temple at the left of the door, with an altar before it.[16] Keoloewa is said to have been worshiped as an akua noho up to
the time of Kamehameha.

Among other names connected with sorcery in Hawaii that
of Uli is the one most commonly invoked. Rice calls her the
sister of Manua, god of the underworld whose place Milu has
usurped in popular tradition, and of Wakea, god of the upper world[17] and an equivalent on the genealogical line to the
god Kane as spiritual procreator. The name Uli may hence
possibly be derived from that of Milu, goddess of the underworld in many South Sea mythologies. In Rice's account she
is to be found grouped with two brothers, like Kapo in the
Kalaipahoa story. On Molokai, Uli-la'a (laau?) is the god of

13. Malo, 155, 156, 158 notes 3, 4.
14. Henry, 203, 206.   15. For. Col. 4: 476.
16. Ellis, *Tour*, 66–67.   17. Rice, 93.

medicine, "a god of invincible laws."[18] Kamakau cites two
Uli goddesses, sisters to the chief Kuheilani son of Hua-
nui-ka-laʻilaʻi: Uli of the uplands, sorceress grandmother of
Kana and Niheu[19] and Uli of the seashore who marries a
fisherman at Kualakoi, teaches the art of praying to death,
and becomes the aumakua of the kahuna anaana who pray
people to death.[20]

Streaks of light, trees informed with deity—to these two
phenomena as part of the machinery of the poison-god legend
is joined a third element, that of the bird form as a transformation body of the flying god. A white hen and a flock of
white chickens Kamakau describes as part of the Kalaipahoa
keeper's outfit, reminiscent of the white haupu bird of Ka-
hoaliʻi, the white albatross of Kane, and in Tahiti the white
heron of Tiʻi. The feathered head of the image of Keoloewa
and the feathers from the mythical seabirds which wave from
the heads of sorcery gods of war may be emblems of the same
shape-shifting power. Uli is named with Maka-ku-koae and
Alae-a-Hina as gods invoked by sorcerers for the purpose of
bringing death to an enemy. Maka-ku-koae is the god who
brings madness (pupule) or raving insanity (hehena) or
imbecility (lolo).[21] Alae-a-Hina (Mud hen of Hina) is the
sorceress from whom Maui wrested the secret of fire. Mud
hen, tropic bird, plover are all birds implicated in the sorcery
pattern, perhaps because they are thought of as strangers,
birds from Kahiki, as also because of a certain eeriness in
their cry. Uli may be the Ulili, the wandering tattler which
migrates with the plover from Alaska for nesting.

A fourth element which these stories of the origin of orders
of sorcery have in common is the likeness to be observed in the
make-up of the group who initiate poison or healing. Uli is
associated with two brothers in one version of her story;
Haumea comes with Kane and Kanaloa "moving across the
sea"; two brothers accompany Pele, one of them called the
chief aumakua of those to whom bodies are dedicated to become sharks. The sorceress Kamaunu, grandmother of the
hog-man Kamapuaʻa, comes to Maui with two men both of

18. Malo, 145; Kalakaua, 50.　　19. For. Col. 4: 270.
20. Ke Au Okoa, July 21, 1870.　　21. Malo, 136, 140 note 3.

whom at different times claim her as wife. Stories of the introduction of medicine to cure disease caused by sorcery show a similar grouping. Two men and a woman are named among the "strangers" who scatter disease over the islands, and two brothers land with a sister on the eastern point of Hawaii and become aumakua respectively of plover and fowl. A formal element of this kind repeated in so many similar instances must derive from some common idea about which each school of sorcery practice has built up its legend. The two men perhaps represent the two keepers (kahu) whose business it is to care for the god and order its activities; the woman is the akua noho, the goddess who acts as their servant and goes forth on errands of sorcery; the bird body or the flash of light is the form she takes in her flight.

The object of Kamehameha in setting up god houses for the gods of the various island districts under his rule was to insure to his own service not only his own war god (and probably also god of sorcery) Kukailimoku, but also the gods of the chiefs subject to him. The Kalaipahoa sorcery on Molokai is only a single instance of the way in which rival schools of sorcery arose to terrorize the land, and their method was to draw into their own service such names as had already gained prestige as gods of possession (akua noho). One school borrowed its pattern from another.

Closely related to these schools of sorcery was the art of the healer. The herb doctor (kahuna-lapaau-laau) studied the properties of healing herbs to combat sickness. Tradition preserves the names of a number of these herb doctors who combined practical knowledge of the medicinal effect of herbs with the priestly office. Many of these doctors worked under the supposition that disease, especially when accompanied by swelling of the abdomen, was caused by the arts of sorcery. Lono-puha (Lono of the ulcer) is said to be the first to practise the art of healing through medicinal herbs in Hawaii, and to found a school upon this system. The Lono-puha order of kahunas diagnose by means of pebbles arranged to outline the body of a man and to show the parts of the body known to be attacked by a disease whose symptoms they understand. By feeling the body with the tips of the fingers and referring to the chart of pebbles to verify the part afflicted, they are able to name the disease and apply the proper remedies. Every step of the treatment must be accompanied by prayer to the aumakua of healing. The old order was revived in the time of Kamehameha under the famous kahuna Palaka, son of the herb doctor Puheke and direct descendant from Lonopuha. He is said to have cut open his father when he died to see the course the disease had taken and to have "thought out the enema to relieve pain," trying it first on a dog with the use of a polished bamboo as tube.[22]

LEGEND OF LONOPUHA

(a) *Emerson version.* Lono takes human form and becomes a farmer. One day he strikes his foot with his digging stick and a wound results which bleeds profusely. Kane comes to him and teaches him how to lay on a poultice of popolo leaves [still used effectively by Hawaiians for any open wound] and teaches him the properties of medicinal herbs. He is thus worshiped after his death as Lono-puha (Lono of the swelling), patron of the kahuna lapaau laau (herb doctor). At this same time too the stones of Kane were set up as altars for families to repair to for protection against trouble and sickness.[23]

(b) *Westervelt and Thrum version.* Lono is a handsome chief with red skin who lives on the western side of Hawaii and engages in farming. Ka-maka (-nui-ai-lono) passes by and predicts illness. Lono repudiates the idea, but at that moment strikes his foot with his digging stick and faints from loss of blood. A messenger follows the stranger with a pig and Kamaka returns and binds up the wound with a poultice of salt, leaves, and fruit. Lono, finding himself healed, follows the stranger and begs to become his disciple. Kamaka spits into his mouth, thus imparting his mana to Lono, then teaches him the use of healing herbs. He sends Lono to practise in Waimanu while he goes to live at Kukui-haele.[24]

22. Kamakau, *Ke Au Okoa,* August 25, September 15, 22, 1870.
23. Malo, 148–149 note 10.
24. Westervelt, *Gods and Ghosts,* 94–95; Thrum, *Tales,* 52–54.

MYTH OF LONOPUHA AND MILU

Thrum and Westervelt version. While Milu is chief in Wai-pio, some strangers arrive from Kahiki, landing first at Ni'ihau, then traveling through all the islands and settling at Kukui-haele above Waipio. Their names are Ke-alae-nui-a-Hina (a woman), Ka-huila-o-ka-lani, and Kane-i-kaulana-ula. Disease follows them wherever they go and many would have died had not Ka-maka-nui-a-hailono followed and healed those whom the strangers had made ill. This company seek the death of Milu, chief of Waipio. Milu appeals to Lono-puha and he assures him of immunity if he will remain within his house during a certain period, whatever the provocation. When a great bird flies over the village, Milu cannot resist coming out to see what the shouting is all about and the bird snatches away his liver, leaving him lying lifeless. Lono pursues the bird, sees where it disappears into a rock, and heals Milu by laying upon the wound a cloth soaked in the blood the bird has left scattered and by then applying healing medicines. A second tapu is laid not to go surfing. Milu one day disobeys and is swept under and his body never recovered.[25]

Lonopuha here seems to stand apart from the sorcery gods in the story as a practical practitioner. Other characters bear names directly connected with sorcery. Ka-huila-o-ka-lani and Kane-i-kaulana-ula are the gods who enter trees in the Kalaipahoa story. Here they are represented as strangers who settle in the upland above Waipio valley, accompanied, as in the Kalaipahoa story, by a woman sorceress of the Pele family, and seek the life of the chief Milu. Tradition gives the name of Milu to a chief of Waipio who is swept down into the underworld because of disobedience to Kane and becomes ruler of the land of the dead in place of the old god Manua. Sorcery practitioners who work by sending out "spirits of evil" to possess people are called priests of Milu (kahuna o Milu).[26] Obviously we have here to do with a contest of sorcerers.

25. Thrum, *Tales,* 50–57; Westervelt, *Gods and Ghosts,* 95–98.
26. For. Col. 6: 112.

Ka-maka-nui-a(ha)ilono (Kamaka) who imparts his healing knowledge to Lono is manifestly a sorcery kahuna who first possesses Lono and causes his foot to swell, then teaches him how to cure such wounds. He heals a number of persons who have fallen ill through the sorcery of the strangers from Kahiki, and would have cured Milu had he obeyed the imposed tapu. Kalakaua makes both these practitioners pupils of a third whom he calls Kolea-moku (Land plover?). He was a man of ancient days who was taught the medicinal arts by the gods and was himself deified after death and worshiped in the heiau at Kailua. His two disciples practised his arts after his death and were often able to drive away the evil spirits that caused sickness. They too were deified after death.[27] According to Malo, the heiau erected after recovery from illness was called either a Lono-puha or a Kolea-muku.[28]

Kolea-moku (muku) is probably another name for the aumakua of the kolea birds elsewhere called Kumukahi, who comes with Moikeha's company but stops off at the eastern end of the island of Hawaii and settles at the point of land that bears his name, where he is represented by a red stone at the extreme end of the point. Two of his wives, also in the form of stones, manipulate the seasons by pushing the sun back and forth between them at the two solstices. The place is called "Ladder of the sun" and "Source of the sun" and here at the extreme eastern point of land of the whole group, where the sun rises up out of the sea, sun worshipers bring their sick to be healed.[29] The legend says that Kumukahi can take the form of a plover, enter a medium, and cause him to do marvelous things.

LEGEND OF KUMUKAHI

Kumukahi came from Kahiki at the time of Pele, whose relative he was, together with a brother Pala-moa born in the shape of a cock (moa) and a sister named Sun-rise (Ka-hikina-a-ka-la). He was able to take the form of a man or of a kolea bird at will. Today his spirit is able to possess a medium (haka) so that the

27. Kalakaua, 50.   28. 147.
29. Local information given to Mrs. Pukui.

person can hold out his hand and an awa plant will grow right out of it, or, if a pig is brought in, the medium can speak and the pig will drop dead at his feet. A medium possessed by Pala-moa has similar powers but not so strong. Palamoa is god of fowls. His grandchild Lepe-a-moa (whose legend is told in detail on Oahu) was born in the shape of an egg.[30]

A native of North Kona relates how he witnessed with his own eyes similar powers exhibited by a kahuna who had the mana of a god.

One of the deputy sheriffs of North Kona named Joseph K. Nahale was being done to death by sorcery. An eel of the kauila (red) variety was caught, salted, and put in the sun to dry. The kahuna called the people to build up a fire and heat hard stones (ala). When the stones were heated he prayed and threw the eel into the fire. The eel "closed up and ran outside the fire." Had the eel died in the fire, Nahale would have died, but in this way the kahuna cured Nahale. At another time the same kahuna made a sign to cure a man who was ill. He sent the family to get a small banana plant. He prayed over the plant and it grew and a leaf appeared and a bunch of bananas. Everybody in the house ate from it. In half an hour it sprang up and ripened. This kahuna had power, but he never used it to kill people.

In all the stories here quoted sorcery is represented as brought in from abroad by parties of immigrants and as containing all the elements described in Tahiti in the Tane worship in connection with the figure of Ti'i, first man and magician, as practised in the heiaus to protect the lives of ruling chiefs and detect and punish their enemies. The connection of the name of Lono with this system will thus become clear if the Lono of the medical kahunas is thought of as the god Ro'o-te-roro'o who was worshiped in Tahiti by the prayer-healing kahunas in special marae (temples).[31]

In Hawaii the Ku ritual was practised in heiaus of a special class, belonged to the stricter order of priesthood, and could be employed by the ruling chief alone. It included hu-

30. *AA* 28 (1926): 187–190; Westervelt, *Honolulu*, 204.
31. Henry, 209–212.

man sacrifice and was set up by a war chief to protect him from enemy sorcery and insure his own success. The milder Lono ritual was practised in a heiau of an inferior class and without human sacrifice. It might be used, but not solely, by a ruling chief. Although no precise account has been given of the form which the worship took, it is likely that one of its objects was to invoke Lono as the god of healing to ward off evil influences.

Long journeys of Polynesian mythical heroes to the sun, to the underworld after fire, or to the upper heavens are, I venture to assert, more often than has been heretofore recognized built upon the idea of a sorcerer's quest after just such a system of control over the spirits who determine sickness and health, life and death. Folk versions have obscured this interpretation. The figure of Maui-tikitiki, son of Kalana and Hina, is generally conceded to represent the arch mischief maker of Polynesian mythology. Mischief making is sorcery, euphemistically phrased. In this art of sorcery all the Maui stories show him an adept. In Hawaii, where the kite-shaped god of the wind, Lo-lupe, is sent out to entangle the souls of enemies to the chief, we have a story of Maui as a kite flyer in control of the winds. The Polynesian story of Maui's visit to the underworld to obtain fire is a euphemistic folk version of the way in which he wrested from his sorceress grandmother her control of sorcery and threw it, as poison or healing, into the trees. The Hawaiian version in which he wins the secret from the little mud hen, the bird form taken by Pele sorceresses, is even more suggestive of a similar theme. When Kana goes to the underworld to restore the sun and moon to his people, when Aukele goes down into the pit of the sun in the east after the water of life, each of these heroes is defying the lord over death by sorcery. The water which restores to life is a literal rendering of the practice by which the healing kahuna brings back a patient to life at eastern points of the islands. Maui's journey through the body of his ancestress to secure everlasting life for man, an episode absent in Hawaii from the Maui cycle, is a story founded upon the common belief in a sorcerer's power to journey in the spirit to the land of the dead to pluck souls back into life.

IX

GUARDIAN GODS

THRUM shows Kane and Kanaloa dwelling at Ala-kahi in Waipio with "some of the lesser gods such as Maliu, Kaekae, Ouli [Uli], and a number of others," but, unfortunately, does not give his source for the tale. The mischief maker Maui meets his death while trying to steal bananas from the gods, an incident which suggests the story of the old woman roasting bananas on the road to the other world so common to quest stories not only of Hawaii but of the southern groups. Uli is the principal deity worshiped by sorcerers. She takes precedence of Haumea in this capacity. A sorcerer's prayer quoted by Emerson reads:

> E Uli e!
> E Uli nana pono,
> E Uli nana hewa,
> E Uli i uka,
> E Uli i kai,
> Eia mai la o (Puhi), he kanaka,
> He ia wawae loloa,
> Ke iho aku la,
> Ke kuukuu aku la,
> Nana ia (Puhi),
> He ia wawae loloa mai ka po'o a i ka hiu . . .
> O Uli!

> "O Uli, look upon the right,
> O Uli, look upon the wrong,
> O Uli, toward the mountains,
> O Uli, toward the sea, here is [the person cursed] a man,
> A fish with long legs,
> He is descending,
> He is being let down,
> Look upon the person cursed,
> He is a fish with long legs from head to tail. . . ."[1]

1. *HHS Papers* 2: 20–21.

Maliu (Accepted) is the name given to a deified deceased
chief, says Andrews. At the opening of the Kumu-uli genealogy recited by chiefs alone, Maliu is associated as a god
with Kane, Kanaloa, and Kauakahi (First war). Ku-kaua-
kahi is the owl god to whom bodies are offered to become owls.
It seems fairly evident that sorcery which depended upon the
practice of dedicating the dead to become family protectors,
and the preserving and setting them up for worship, was recognized if not inaugurated by the Kane worship.[2]

The legend of Pumaia tells how the spirit of a dead man
whose bones are worshiped may force the chief Kuali'i himself to respect a vow made to a god.

LEGEND OF PUMAIA

When Kuali'i builds the heiau of Kapua'a to his god Kane-
nui-(a)k(e)a, he demands the hogs of Pumaia, a hog raiser at
Puko-ula adjoining Waiahao in Kona district, Oahu, to use for
sacrifice. Pumaia keeps back one favorite pig which he has
vowed shall die a natural death. Kuali'i sends messengers to demand this last hog, but Pumaia kills each messenger until none
are left. Finally Kuali'i catches, binds, and kills Pumaia and
throws his bones into the pit with others. Pumaia's spirit advises
his wife where to find his bones. She and her daughter hide in a
cave at the top of the left-hand peak of the Nu'uanu pali and
worship his bones until Pumaia as a spirit is stronger than when
he was alive. Food and treasure are stolen from Kuali'i's men,
and the chief has no peace until he has built three houses, one
for the wife and daughter, one for their possessions, and a third
for the bones of Pumaia. The kahuna then prays over the bones
and restores them to life.[3]

The dedication of a corpse to become an owl, mo'o, shark,
or other animal form or a flame burning in the service of Pele,
may be an even older practice than that of using the dead as
fetchers to work for the prosperity of a family and carry
sickness or trouble to their enemies. A native pupil in the

2. Thrum, *More Tales,* 259–260; For. Pol. Race 1: 184; Kalakaua, 50.

3. For. Col. 4: 470–477.

schools of early days says rather dryly that the soul after death had three abiding places, "in the volcano, in the water, on dry plains."[4]

Owls (pueo) are among the oldest of these family protectors. In a legend from Maui, Pueo-nui-akea is an owl god who brings back to life souls who are wandering on the plains. The owl acts as a special protector in battle or danger. "The owl who sings of war" (Ka pueo kani kaua) says the chant.[5] The universal guardianship of the owl is expressed in the saying attached to it, "A no lani, a no honua" (Belonging to heaven and earth). The flight of an owl through the air was carefully watched by the leader of a defeated army and to the spot where it alighted he would lead his men, "protected by the wings of the owl." Many stories are told of escapes from imminent danger due to an owl. A warrior under Kamehameha in the thick of the battle was about to plunge over a precipice when an owl flew up in his face and he was able to thrust his spear into the earth and save himself from the leap. Napaepae of Lahaina, capsized in the Pailolo channel, swam all night and would have gone under had not an owl flapped its wings in his face and attracted his attention to land. A man escaping from the enemy in battle was saved from pursuit by an owl alighting at his hiding place. All these natural occurrences were interpreted as direct interventions of the owl as protector in danger.

Emerson thinks that owls were worshiped as a class and not as individual protectors. This may be generally true, but individual owl protectors are reported. Those who worshiped owls worshiped them under special names. At Pu'u-pueo lived the owl king of Manoa and drove the Menehune from the valley. A famous Oahu owl story is that of the owl war carried on in behalf of a man named Kapoi who, having robbed an owl's nest, took pity on the lamenting parent and returned the eggs. He then took the owl as his god and built a heiau for its worship. The ruling chief Kakuhihewa, considering this an act of rebellion, ordered his execution but at the moment of carrying out the order the air was darkened by flying owls

4. For. Col. 5: 572–577.   5. *Ibid.* 6: 300.

which had come to his protection. The places on Oahu where the owls made rendezvous for this battle are known today by the word pueo (owl) in their names, such as Kala-pueo east of Diamond Head, Kanoni-a-ka-pueo in Nuʻuanu valley, Pueo-hulu-nui near Moanalua. The scene of the battle at Waikiki is called Kukaeunahio-ka-pueo (Confused sound of owls rising in masses).[6]

Next in importance to the shark aumakua and possibly of older arrival in Hawaii are the moʻo, reptile forms of the lizard kind but of monstrous size, believed to inhabit inland fishponds. Says Kamakau:

> The moʻo that guarded these ponds were not the common gecko or skink; no, indeed! One can guess at their shape from these little creatures but this is not their real form. They had a terrifying body such as was often seen in old days; not commonly, but they were often visible when fires were lighted on altars close to their homes. Once seen, no one could preserve his skepticism. They lay in the water from two to five fathoms in length (twelve to thirty feet) and as black in color as the blackest negro. If given a drink of awa they would turn from side to side like the keel of a canoe in the water.

The goddess Kalamainuʻu (Ka-lani-mai-nuʻu, Kala-mai-mu) is the many-bodied moʻo aumakua to whom bodies were dedicated to become moʻo. Houses called puaniu were erected to her for deifying the dead.

Kiha-wahine is the most famous of these apotheosized human bodies. She was a chiefess on Maui and at death she was dedicated to become a moʻo and became herself a goddess and was worshiped in the heiaus on Maui and Hawaii. Her image there, dressed in deep saffron yellow or light yellow or a patterned tapa cloth, was but a symbol, Kamakau is careful to explain, of the spirit of the goddess herself, which was known through her entering into a living person or through visible revelation in "one of her terrible forms." Kamehameha set up her image in the heiau. In her name he carried his conquest

6. Kamakau, *Ke Au Okoa*, May 5, 1870; Westervelt, *Honolulu*, 131–137; Thrum, *Tales*, 200–201; *HAA* 1909, 45–46.

over the islands. He gave her the prostrating tapu; even those passing in canoes were obliged to observe this tapu. Uluma-heihei Hoapili of Maui, who later became an active friend of the missionaries and a leader in establishing the Christian church, was her keeper (kahu).

Appearances of Kiha-wahine are reported from various places on Maui. The old fishpond at Haneoo in Hana district is still thought of as her home. When there is foam on the pond she is at home and fish caught at this time will be bitter in taste. Modern ideas give her the form of a woman. A fin-like projection of rock near the center of the pond called Lauoho (combing) is where she sits to comb her hair. Kiha-wahine is also reported from the pool of Maulili in Waikomo stream in Koloa, Kauai. In the story of Puna-ai-koae she is the mo‘o woman who has a combat with Pele over the possession of the young chief as husband.[7]

Mokuhinia is another mo‘o aumakua belonging to Maui whose appearances at various places on West Maui are re-lated by Kamakau, one of these on the occasion of the death of a chief, and the most spectacular in 1838 when she showed herself to "hundreds of thousands" of people gathered at the pond of Mokuhinia. Lani-wahine is a mo‘o goddess of Ukoa pond, Waialua, on Oahu. She often appears in human form to foretell some terrible event. Kane-kuaana, once a living person whose body was worshiped to become a mo‘o, rules the land of Ewa between Halawa and Honouliuli and brings it prosperity. If fish were scarce her relatives would erect wai-hau altars and light fires and the waters would be filled with pearl oysters and fine fish. Hau-wahine is the mo‘o goddess of the ponds of Kawainui and Kaelepule in Koolau district on Oahu. She brings abundance of fish, punishes the owners of the pond if they oppress the poor, and wards off sickness. Walinu‘u and Wali-manoanoa are many-bodied ancestral mo‘o for whom pillars were set up in the heiau as memorials and who are worshiped as female deities upon whom depends

7. Kamakau, *Ke Au Okoa*, April 28, May 5, 1870; Malo, 114, 155; Kepelino, 18; *HAA* 1907, 92; Westervelt, *Gods and Ghosts*, 152–162; Thrum, *More Tales*, 185–196.

the prosperity of the government. Waka (Waha) is another mo'o goddess worshiped by female chiefs. She appears in romance as the guardian of Paliuli (Paliula) on Hawaii and of the young chief Kauakahiali'i on Kauai. Mo'o-inanea (Self-reliant mo'o) is also represented in romance as first-born child of Kane-huna-moku in Kuaihelani and head of the mo'o family in Kuaihelani before the emigration of the Ku and Hina family to Hawaii and the shutting up of the hidden island. She is the man-eating ancestress of Aukelenuiaiku in Kuaihelani.[8]

The mo'o deities thus far named are all female aumakua worshiped by chiefesses. Not all mo'o are female and not all are friendly. There are many legends of contests with unfriendly mo'o. Lani-loa is a mo'o who used to kill passers-by below Laie until cut up into the five little islands seen today off the coast as Malualai, Keauakaluapaaa, Pulemoku, Mokuaaniwa, and Kihewamoku.[9] The mo'o is one of the Pele family's terrible forms. Hi'iaka's journey to Kauai to fetch Pele's lover is delayed by many contests with evil mo'o gods. Pi'i-ka-lalau is a mo'o deity of Kauai who can take the form of a giant, a pigmy, or a mo'o and who fights a terrible battle against the chief Kauakahi on behalf of his friend Keli'ikoa.[10] The contest between Pele and the mo'o goddess for their human lover has already been mentioned. The mo'o, in fact, fights for the family of its keeper. A great mo'o is guardian of Paliuli and defends the place from intruders in the Laiei-kawai story. The head and tail of the mo'o guardian of Puna district on Hawaii are still shown, petrified into rock, one in the pool at Kalapana, the other in a clear pool called Puna-lua a half mile distant. Bathers must dive and touch the rock before attempting to swim there. Respect is felt for the little mo'o who sun themselves on dry banks and on the walls of houses. A person should never crush a lizard's egg lest he fall over a precipice.

8. Kamakau, *loc. cit.;* Malo, *loc. cit.;* Haleole; Westervelt, *Gods and Ghosts,* 116, 122; *HAA* 1916, 143; Dickey, *HHS Reports* 25: 26–28; For. Col. 4: 38–43.

9. Rice, 112.   10. *HHS Reports* 25: 27–28.

Mo'o worship has probably been brought to Hawaii. Mo'o are gods of the royal Oropa'a family of Tahiti.[11] A legend tells of a chief who is charmed by a mo'o who later bears him a son exactly resembling himself. He disowns the boy and has the mother killed. The boy's descendants are living to this day.[12] In Tonga gods are regarded as formless but might become incarnate in certain forms. For example, the god Toufa might appear as a particular man (his priest), as a shark, or as a gecko.[13] In New Zealand the lizard is connected with sorcery. It is placed under a boundary stone to cause sickness.[14] There are myths of the killing of monster lizards called ngarara or taniwha. Such monsters in Samoa are said to inhabit deep chasms or pools in the river.[15]

Most popular of all family guardians among a fishing people are shark aumakua. The manner of offering a corpse to become a shark is described in detail by Kamakau, together with the offerings required to pay the officiating kahuna and to feed the shark god; the ceremony at the offering; the appearance of the aumakua god or gods for its reception; and the gradual transformation of the body until the kahuna is able to point out to the awe-struck family the actual markings on the body of the shark singled out for worship, corresponding to the clothing in which the body of their beloved had been wrapped. Such a shark aumakua became the family pet. It was fed daily and was believed to drive food into the net, save the fisherman from death if his canoe capsized, and in other ways ward off danger. Like all these protecting guardians it had its evil uses as a fetcher to kill an enemy, but it must be remembered that this purpose was recognized as evil and that before Christianity came in and the skepticism of the whites refused to credit such superstition, the ruling chiefs came down with a heavy hand upon the practice of sorcery. On the whole the relation of a fisherman's family to its shark aumakua was a friendly and intimate one and the fact of the tangible presence of the pet robbed it of horror. There is scarcely a Hawaiian family of the old type

11. Henry, 383.   12. *Ibid.* 622–623.
13. Gifford, *Bul.* 61: 288.   14. Handy, *Bul.* 34: 180.
15. *JPS* 2: 211–215.

GUARDIAN GODS 129

who cannot claim today some such aumakua known by name
to the whole community.

The ancestral shark gods to whom the bodies of the dead are
dedicated are believed to have come from Kahiki and are worshiped as protectors of the whole district. They appear in
other than shark form, as owls, hilu fish, mo'o, or human beings, says Malo, and in such form associate with men or speak
to them in vision. The most important of these ancestral
sharks (mano kumupa'a) named by him are Ku-hai-moana,
Kane-huna-moku, Kau-huhu, Ka-moho-ali'i, and Kane-i-kokala. Ku-hai-moana (Ku-hei-moana) is called "the largest
and most celebrated of Hawaiian shark gods," thirty fathoms
long, with a mouth as big as a grass house. He is king shark
of the broad ocean, lives in deep water off Kaula islet, and is
said to be a man-eater and husband of Ka-ahu-pahau, but in
some tales the name is given to a female. Kane-huna-moku is
the fish form taken by the ruler of the hidden island. Kauhuhu is the fierce king shark of Maui who lives in a cave in
Kipahulu and also has a home guarded by mo'o deities at the
"Eel cave" (Ana-puhi) between Waikolo and Pelekunu on
the windward side of Molokai. Kane-i-kokala is a kindly
shark aumakua who saves people who are shipwrecked and
brings them safe to shore. The kokala fish are sacred to him,
and the folk of Kahiki-nui, which is peopled by his family,
says Kamakau, fear to eat these fish or to touch any food that
has come in contact with them or even to cross the smoke of
an oven where they are cooking.

Most celebrated of these ancestral shark gods is Ka-moho-
ali'i, Pele's many-bodied brother and the shark god to whom
all members of the Pele family offer corpses to become sharks.
His home upon a cliff on the northern edge overlooking the
crater is so sacred that even Pele dare not blow smoke across
it, and the mo'o goddess Kihawahine, when she had her celebrated tussle with Pele, feared to spew phlegm upon it.[16]
When Ka-moho-ali'i takes human form, he appears without
his loincloth, a privilege, says Emerson, which marks the
god![17] In the story of Laukaieie, he and his shark people are

16. Westervelt, *Gods and Ghosts,* 157.
17. *HHS Papers* 2: 10.

living at Kahoolawe.[18] Kauhi, the cruel husband of Ka-hala-o-Puna, who kills his wife in his shark form, is represented as a member of Kamohoali'i's family.[19] It seems fair to equate this shark deity with Ellis's Mo'oari'i to whom a heiau formerly stood on "almost every point of land projecting any distance into the sea" on the island of Molokai[20] and with Kalakaua's Moali'i, "a celebrated sea god of Molokai in shark form" and "principal shark god of Molokai and Oahu," who is worshiped by the Molokai chief Kaupe'epe'e, and fresh wreaths placed on his huge image on Haupu overlooking the ocean when an expedition comes or goes by sea.[21] He may be identical with Kahoali'i, the naked god of the Makahiki, to whom the eye of fish or man is dedicated in a cup of awa and whose possible relation with the Tahitian sorcery god Ti'i has already been pointed out. Mrs. Pukui recalls in corroboration of this identification the lines of a chant in which the cliff summit above the crater of Kilauea, so sacred to Kamohoali'i that smoke from the burning pit never touches it, is ascribed to Kahoali'i:

> Ka mahu a i luna o Wahinekapu,
> Ua kapu aku la ia Kahoali'i.

"The smoke rises above [the place called] Sacred-woman,
The place sacred to Kahoali'i."

It is on the whole as savior from sorcery that the shark aumakua is so universally worshiped in Hawaii.[22]

Similar shark worship of individual family guardians, sometimes those inspired by human spirits, is recorded from Tahiti[23] and illustrated in the story of Taruia.[24] In Tonga, Seketoa turns into a shark because his elder brother is jealous of him and tries to kill him. He is the guardian spirit of a special family. When the priest summons Seketoa with

18. Westervelt, *Gods and Ghosts,* 44–46.

19. *Ibid.,* 85.   20. *Tour,* 67.

21. 49, 77.

22. Kamakau, *Ke Au Okoa,* April 7–21, May 5, 1870; Thrum, *More Tales,* 288–292; J. Emerson, *HHS Papers* 2: 8–12.

23. Henry, 389–390.   24. *Ibid.,* 624, 630–631.

kava, first appear his attendants in the shape of two small fish, then appears Seketoa, first in the body of a dog fish, then as a small shark, and so on, increasing in size until he appears in his full length as Seketoa.[25] Tui-tofua, who goes away and turns into a man-eating shark because he is accused of annoying his father's concubines, finally appears in a company of six sharks who keep the reef clear for their own people.[26] In Mangaia a warlike chief is clubbed to death by the priest for wearing the sacred red flowers in the tapu region of the gods, and his spirit enters into an eel which has drunk his blood. Thence it passes into a huge white shark worshiped by a priestly tribe who make for it an image of rosewood.[27] In Fiji, a shark guardian carries a man ashore. A pet hawk, eel, lizard, or fresh water prawn may also become a guardian of the living.[28] In the Lau islands, the shark god Mami takes both human and shark form.[29] In Aurora, a man makes an image of a shark out of basketwork and when he wants to eat men he gets into the image; a bird thereupon flies upon the roof as a sign to an old woman and she breaks a stick; the image then goes into the water.[30]

The fullest reports come from San Cristoval. Here are reported the passing of the soul of the dead into the shark as its commonest incarnation; the transformation of a living person into a shark; and the "exchange of souls between man and shark," as Fox puts it, in which a shark becomes a man's familiar and acts for the man. A shark-man's power passes to his son, who is initiated at birth by the father crooking his arm like a shark's fin and putting the child under his arm. The child and his shark receive the same name. The two are so closely associated that if one dies the other dies. It is said that these are "sharks who have exchanged souls with living men." It is a process of adoption, and what injures one injures the other.[31]

25. Gifford, *Bul.* 8: 83–84; Collocott, *Bul.* 46: 56–58; *JPS* 24: 116–117.

26. Gifford, *Bul.* 8: 77–82.   27. Gill, 29–30, 288.

28. Thomson, 115–116.   29. Hocart, 211–212.

30. Codrington, 407–408.

31. Fox, 110–111, 115–116, 132–133; Codrington, 259.

Of traditional adventures with shark aumakua, Hawaiians tell many stories. Kamakau tells of a certain family descended from a shark, a member of which might be punished for breaking a tapu of the shark god by being "laid beside the shark in the sea for from two to four days close to the fin of the shark" and yet be brought up alive from this unpleasant experience. Unfortunately, the family of whom the story was told were all dead before Kamakau could secure corroboration of this remarkable event, but he saw the place where it happened and "my relatives of my parents' and grandparents' generation say that hundreds of people have seen them lying in the sea and returning to shore in a weakened condition after they had lain for as much as five days in the sea." It is further told (and the story compared with that of Jonah) that in the days of Kakaalaneo (or Eleio) of Maui, Kukuipahu of Hawaii was swallowed by a shark and lived inside its body many days and came ashore at Hana, Maui, with all his hair worn off, whereupon the daughter of the chief was bestowed upon him as a wife. He is said to have been saved because he was faithful in his offerings to the gods.[32]

The following stories are, with a few exceptions, stories recently collected, many of them never before recorded, and told as actual occurrences. They could be indefinitely extended from the lips of intelligent Hawaiians living today.

AUMAKUA LEGENDS

It is related that a girl of thirteen years of age, living at Waikapuna, a long sandy beach directly below Naalehu, Kau, dreamed that a lover appeared to her out of the ocean. Every morning when she told her parents this dream her father thought she had allowed some one liberties and wanted to conceal it, so he kept her carefully guarded. The dreams however continued. After a time the girl gave birth to a shark. Her parents recognized this as the offspring of an akua mano (shark god) called Ke-'lii-kaua-o-Kau, a cousin of Pele, and did not hold the girl responsible.

The young mother took the baby, wrapped it in green pa-

32. For. Col. 5: 660.

kaiea (a coarse seaweed) and cast it into the sea. The young shark was always recognizable by its green coat, and became the aumakua of that particular family. From that time they were careful not to partake of either shark flesh or pakaiea moss. Swelling of the abdomen would have followed the breaking of the shark tapu; incurable sores attacking the mouth, the breaking of the seamoss tapu.

As the shark never ate human flesh, it was a favorite in the neighborhood. One day a stranger, Kahikina by name, went out fishing and was attacked by two sharks. When he cried out for help he saw a small green shark coming toward him with great speed, which quickly attacked the man-eaters, slashing them with its tail until they fled. It then slipped under the canoe and carried it safely to the shore. So grateful was Kahikina that he returned next day with a huge awa root as offering and he also cleaned from the shark's back the barnacles and pebbles which had accumulated there. Ever after that the shark and the man became great friends. The shark would chase schools of fish toward the shore and all that the man caught he would divide between them.

Opuopele, brother of Kahikina, lived at Paula beach, Kau, and loved to go fishing. One day he had just thrown a stick of giant powder into Kawa-nui cove and dived off the cliff to gather the spoils when he found himself confronted by a shark on one side and a turtle on the other. Undismayed, he began to talk to the shark, saying, "There is your share, here is mine," at the same time offering the shark a fish and bagging one for himself. In this way the shark was pacified, and the old man returned to the shore with a gunny-sack half-filled with fish. When the wife was asked about this strange occurrence she answered that the shark always appeared when her husband went fishing and that he always shared the catch. She did not claim the shark as an aumakua but there was probably this deeper significance in the explanation.

A policeman in Lahaina was sent to Molokai to deliver some government money. He went in a whaleboat accompanied by his wife. In the middle of the channel between the islands of Molokai and Maui a storm came up which overturned the boat. They

tried to cling to its sides but the rough waves drove the boat
from them. The man prayed thus: "If I have any aumakua in
this ocean I pray you to carry me and my wife to the land."
The woman saw something red in the water and the next moment
saw that her husband was holding on to the tail of a shark
which had appeared to rescue them. The fish swam through the
rough waves and brought them safe to shore. [In one such
rescue the shark "fanned the waters" to keep the swimmer from
getting chilled, and gently pushed him along to safety. The idea
is that the shark belongs to the volcano deities and hence has
control over heat.][33]

A man and his wife live near the sea at Keanae; his sister and
her husband live in the woodland at Kau-palahalaha. Every day
the man goes out fishing, bidding his wife give fish to his sister
when she comes from her upland garden with vegetable food for
the family. The man's wife is stingy and gives her sister-in-law
only the tail end of a fish. This the woman in disgust drops into
a calabash. One night both husband and wife have a dream and,
rising, they find a live shark in the calabash. For many years
they keep it in a pool [which may be seen today at this place]
and make food offerings to it. Once, during high water, it is
washed down to the sea. It now lives in the hole called Lua-hi'u
(Hole of the tail) which may be seen near Mrs. Hardy's house
and which extends underground half a mile and comes out near
the Keanae wharf.[34]

At the bay of Pukoo on Molokai lived the kahuna Kamalo
who had the terrible Kauhuhu as his shark god. Kamalo's two
sons are killed by order of the chief Kupa for playing upon the
sacred temple drum (pahu kaeke) at the heiau of Iliili-o-pae.
Kamalo seeks revenge. With a black pig as a gift he seeks first
the famous seer Lanikaula, then Kaneakama, then Kahiwaka-
apu'u, and finally comes to the cave between Waikolu and Pelekunu where lives Kauhuhu guarded by Waka and Mo'o. Kauhuhu comes in on the eighth wave and listens to his petition.
Some months later the storm called Wai-o-koloa descends upon

33. Given to Miss Green by Mrs. Annie Aiona, 1923.
34. Given by Mrs. Hardy of Keanae, East Maui, 1930.

Mapulehu valley, its coming heralded by a rainbow spanning the valley, and all the inhabitants are swept into the sea and devoured by sharks. Kamalo's household alone escapes because of the sacred fence he has built and provisions stored at Kauhuhu's direction.[35]

Na-pua-o-Paula, a pretty girl on Hawaii, arouses the jealousy of a neighboring family. They give offerings to their shark aumakua to destroy her and she is carried away by a wave and devoured by a shark. Her mother goes to a sorcerer. A child is born who resembles the dead girl and is given her name. The other family are afflicted with swellings and die miserably.[36]

Women were supposed to be visited in dream by aumakua spirits who wished to have a child by them. The dreams would continue until the birth of the first child, and to this child the father would give a name (in dream). Such children were often born in the shape into which the father could change himself—shark, owl, caterpillar, stone—but they were more human than godlike in nature. Folktales tell how alliances with lovers of double nature were avoided. Some of these resemble the famous South Sea story of Hina and Tuna, the eel from whose head sprung the first coconut.

TALES OF ANIMAL LOVERS

Kumu-hea (or Mo'o), son of the god Ku, lives in the hill Pu'uenuhe at Hi'ilea in Kau district and is the god (aumakua) of the cutworm. He marries a girl, but comes to her only at night, for by day he is a worm (or mo'o). He does not support her. With the advice of her parents she ties a hemp string to his back and when he leaves her she follows him to the hill and discovers his true nature. He is angry. Cutworms attack the crop. The parents appeal to Kane, who cuts up the god; and hence the small peelua cutworms (or lizards) of today, which Hawaiians fear to injure.[37]

35. Thrum, *Tales*, 186–192; Westervelt, *Honolulu*, 193.
36. Green and Pukui, 154–157.
37. Green, 43; J. Emerson, *HHS Papers* 2: 12; Rice, 110.

Puhi-nalo is the eel lover of a girl of Waianae on Oahu. Her brothers discover that he is an eel-man, fight him, and hurl his body against the cliff, where it is to be seen today.[38]

Puhi and Loli (Eel and Sea-cucumber) turn into handsome men and court two girls. Their father watches the two men turn into fish again, catches them in a net, cooks them, and serves them up to the two girls. The girls vomit, one a tiny eel and the other a sea-cucumber, which the father burns to ashes. These are the children they would have had by the two lovers.[39]

Animal forms associated with the many-bodied Pele family are the mo'o, the brindled dog, the oopu fish. A brown-haired woman (ehu) belongs to the Pele family and may be Pele herself or one of her spirit followers in human form. Brindled dogs are called ilio mo'o to this day. The fresh-water oopu fish (*Eleotris fusca*) looks something like a mo'o and hence should not be eaten by any family who have a mo'o auma-kua. Molokai and West Maui people fear to eat it. The oku-hekuhe or owau variety of the goby fish (oopu) is one of the forms of the god Kane-lau-apua, according to Emerson. In Tahiti, goby fish are thought to be possessed by the spirits of premature births.[40] The following stories are told of the double nature of the goby fish. Many similar tales teach a wholesome respect for those potential favorites of deity whose gods resent cruelty or greed in their treatment.

STORIES OF OFFENDED AUMAKUA

A man of Molokai catches a dish of oopu of the o-kuhekuhe or o-wau variety. He bundles the fish up in ti leaves and lays them on the fire to broil. A voice speaks from the bundle and he flees in fright.[41]

Ka-hinano (Pandanus blossom) catches a dish of goby fish, cleans and salts them, then goes after material for mat weaving.

38. McAllister, *Bul.* 104: 117–119.
39. Green and Pukui, 170–173.   40. Henry, 390.
41. Green and Pukui, 176–177; N. Emerson, *Pele,* 194 note *c*.

A brown-haired woman comes to the house, calls to the fish, and replaces them alive in the creek.[42]

(a) Pae is the name of a brindled dog that used to come from the Koolau hills on Oahu to the villages at the sea. The chief's servants one day catch the dog and are carrying her away to bake for a feast when a brown-haired (ehu) woman appears and calls the dog to her. The tying strings drop off, and woman and dog disappear in a pool.[43]

(b) A spirit dog of kindly nature named Pae lives on Hawaii. She is once playing about in her dog body when an old couple catch and fatten her for a feast. A brindled dog comes to her aid at the last moment. They kill the old people and make their way to Oahu, where they live in the Nuuanu valley and Pae becomes "the dog of Koolau."[44]

A turtle kupua named Ka-wai-malino is picked up and brought home by an old couple. The children play with it and poke out an eye. The mother has a dream in which a beautiful woman with one eye inflamed begs her to take the turtle back to its home in the Wailuku river in Hilo, Hawaii.[45]

Manoanoa, a woman of Molokai, eats squid eagerly. Once when she has cut up a squid and placed the tentacles on a tree to dry she hears a voice say, "Eat the tentacles but spare the head!" and the squid jumps into the spring and disappears.[46]

Puni-he'e (Squid lover) has an inordinate fondness for squid. A neighbor warns him to beware lest the gods be angry. One day the squid comes to life in the pot and hangs itself over the door, and Puni-he'e flees in terror.[47]

Kumu-hana, a bird hunter, recklessly slaughters the plover (kolea) even when he does not need them to eat. His neighbor, who worships the plover god Kumu-kahi and has been made ill

42. Green, 111–112.   43. Ibid., 48–49.
44. Green and Pukui, 178.   45. Pukui MS.
46. Green and Pukui, 175.   47. Green, 46–47.

by contact with the smoke from Kumu-hana's oven, warns him against this sacrilege. Kumu-hana disregards the warning and is overwhelmed by a flock of plover, who enter his house and peck and scratch him to death. The place where he lived is called Ai-a-kolea to this day.[48]

Kilauname, a cultivator of Kau district, lives at a place called Waha-mo'o (Mo'o's mouth) between Naalehu and Waiohinu. Here he and his friend Mauna-kele-awa plant potatoes. When caterpillars attack the vines, instead of gathering them carefully into baskets and carrying them away as his friend does, he recklessly kills them. In revenge caterpillars overrun his vines and the man himself and eat him up alive.[49]

In Fiji a man named Kowika, a Soso of the fisher class from Mbau, ventures to the cave where Ratu-mai-Mbulu (Lord of Hades) is fed and shoots the god when he appears in snake form. As a result, until he does penance he is haunted by snakes. Snakes flow from the bamboo where he drinks and his sleeping mat is alive with them.[50]

Hawaiians delight to tell tales of the travels, wars, and adventures of famous shark gods, those friendly to man pitted against the man-eaters. Turner, hearing similar tales of shark wars in Samoa, was himself disposed to interpret them symbolically of human contests, but found that the natives took them literally, as they do, no doubt, in Hawaii.[51]

The famous shark goddess Kaahu-pahau and her brother (or son) Ka-hi'u-ka (The smiting tail), who lived in a cave at the entrance to Pearl Harbor and guarded Oahu waters against man-eating sharks, were reputed to have been born of human parentage, she as a girl with light hair, and to have changed into sharks. They were friendly to man and were fed as pets by the Ewa people whose district they guarded, and their backs scraped clean of barnacles by their keepers. When the new dry dock collapsed at Pearl Harbor about 1914 the supposition was that the shark guardians of the basin were

48. Green, 108–110. 49. *Ibid.*, 44–45.
50. Thomson, 114–115. 51. 214.

still active. Miss Green writes: "Today a floating dock is employed. Engineers say that there seem to be tremors of the earth at this point which prevent any structure from resting upon the bottom, but Hawaiians believe that 'The Smiting Tail' still guards the blue lagoon at Pearl harbor." Kaahu-pahau is called by Kamakau the sister of the sharks Kane-huna-moku and Ka-moho-ali'i and wife of Ku-hai-moana, father of Ku-pi'opi'o. The story that she is herself killed in the shark war against man-eaters is repudiated by Oahu Hawaiians, as also the accusation made by Kamakau that it was she herself who devoured the chiefess Papio because she was saucy to the keeper who reproached her for going swimming at the lagoon wearing the ilima wreaths which were sacred to the shark goddess. Kaahu-pahau was no man-eater.

STORY OF MIKOLOLOU'S ESCAPE

The shark Ke-ali'i-kaua-o-Kau (The war chief of Kau) is born at Ninole, Kau, where his last keeper died in 1878. With four companions he travels about the islands waging war against man-eaters. The man-eater Mikololou joins the party, is caught in the net of Kaahu-pahau at Pu'uloa and dragged up on the beach, and escapes death only by his tongue being swallowed by a dog, which then jumps into the sea and the tongue becomes Mikololou again. "Mikololou lived by his tongue" (I ola o Miko-lolou i ka alelo) is the saying, to imply that there is a way of escape out of every difficulty.

ROMANCE OF "THE LITTLE BROWN SHARK OF PU'ULOA"

Ka-ehu-iki-mano-o-Pu'uloa (The little brown shark of Pearl harbor) is born at Panau in Puna, Hawaii, and named after the red hair of the shark goddess Kaahu-pahau. For ten days his father Kapukapu feeds him on awa and his mother Holei on her milk. He is then put into the sea while his parents return to the uplands. He puts out to sea and pays a visit to each of the king sharks of Hawaii in turn, all of whom he wins by his deference. Ke-pani-la of Hilo, Kane-ilehia of Kau, Kua of Kona, Mano-kini of Kohala, Kupu-lena of Hamakua join him on his projected tour to Kaula and thence to Kahiki and return. The fierce king shark of Maui, who assumes a threatening attitude, is slain by the little shark entering his wide-opened mouth and devouring his inwards. Ka-moho-aliʻi, overgrown with sea moss, meets them kindly and consents to adopt the little red-haired shark. An elaborate ceremony takes place which gives Ka-ehu power to change into a hundred forms. The party visit Molokai and Oahu, where the adventure with Mikololou takes place and Kaahu-pahau gives them a token which will pass them safely by Ku-hai-moana, king shark of Kauai and Niʻihau. After a round of the South Sea islands, of which the Marquesas, Tahiti, and the Dutch Indies are mentioned, and a bath in the Yellow river of Kahiki [can this be an allusion to the Chinese river of death?] they return home and, as they arrive off Waikiki, encounter the man-eater Pehu on the watch for "crabs" and lure him inshore, where the natives put him to death. Arrived at Puna, the young hero is welcomed by his upland parents with appropriate feasting.[52]

Many local legends are told of shark-men, always to be known by the mark of a shark's mouth upon the back, who can change form from man to shark and who for a long time go undetected until it is noticed that an apparently disinterested warning to swimmers is always followed by a fatal attack by a man-eating shark. Thus Kawelo (Kawelo-maha-mahaia) of Kauai; Pau-walu of Wailua, Maui; Nenewe of Waipio on Hawaii; Kaai-poʻo of Kapaahu in Puna, Hawaii; another unnamed at Kawai-uhu in Kaalualu, Ka-u district, of Hawaii; Mano-niho-kahi at Laie, Oahu;[53] Kamaikaahui of Maui.

LEGENDS OF SHARK-MEN

Kamaikaahui lives at Muolea in Hana district of Maui. He was born in the form of a rat, then became a bunch of bananas, then a man with a shark's mouth at his back, over which he always wears a cloth to conceal the mark. He is a man on land and a shark in the sea. He farms by the highway and when

52. Thrum, *More Tales,* 293–308; Green, 102–107.
53. J. Emerson, *AA* 19: 508–510; Dickey, *HHS Reports* 25: 29.

people pass, going down to the sea, he warns them against sharks. Then he runs ahead of them by a back way and devours them. At last he is suspected. Seeing people on the shore ready to attack him, he leaves his clothes at a place called Kau-hala-hala and swims to Waipahu in Waikele on Oahu and becomes ruling chief of Ewa district, where he terrorizes the country until slain by Palila.[54]

Kawelo is a shark-man living on Kauai in the region of Mana. He has a shark mouth on his back, a tail and appendages on the lower part of his body. He can take the form, besides that of a shark, of a worm, a moth, a caterpillar, a butterfly, and thus escape an enemy. Two rocks shaped like grass houses, one under water in the Wailua river, the other a little below the cave of Mamaaku-a-Lono, represent his two houses as a shark and as a man. As a shark-man he lived between Kealia and Wailua and would eat up the children who ventured to swim out between those two places. Finally he was discovered and a long line of men formed who stoned him to death. He is identified with the famous chief Kawelomahamahaia (Kawelo with fins like a fish), grandfather of Kawelo and descended from Mano-ka-lani-po, who was believed to become a shark god (akua mano) at death.[55]

Pau-walu (Eight dead) lives at Wailua, Maui. He warns men as they go to the sea that eight will be dead before they return and a shark always kills eight of them as predicted. He is therefore suspected as a shark-man. Akeake the strong is born beside the stream Hau-ola and while yet a little boy starts about Maui fighting champions. After overcoming Lohelohe, he, with his companion Pakolea, spends the night at a friend's house named Ohia and learns about Pauwalu. The shark-man scoffs at so little an antagonist, but Akeake easily binds him, exposes the shark's mouth on his back, and casts him into the fire.[56]

54. For. Col. 5: 140–144, 372–374.
55. Dickey, *HHS Reports* 25: 33; N. Emerson, "Hula," 79 note *f;* Westervelt, *Honolulu,* 173.
56. Pukui MS.

Nenewe lives on Hawaii "beside the large basin at the bottom
of the waterfall on the west side of Waipio valley." As men go
to the sea to bathe at Muli-wai he warns them of the shark that
may eat them and, as one man is always lost at such times, the
people begin to suspect him. They catch him, pull off the cape
which he always wears, and expose the shark's mouth on his
back.[57]

Nanaue is the shark-man of Waipio in the time of Umi,
child of Ka-moho-aliʻi and Kalei. His maternal grandfather
feeds him meat, hoping to make a warrior of him, and he develops a taste for human flesh. When detected at Waipio he
turns into a shark and swims to Hana, where he marries the
sister of a petty chief. At Molokai he lives at Poniu-o-Hua.
When he is at last discovered the young demigod Unauna is employed to put him to death and the marks of the struggle are to
be seen on the Kainalu hillslope and on a grooved rock called
Puʻu-mano about which the ropes were wound which held the net
with which he was caught. The shark god punishes the desecra-
tion of a bamboo grove on this occasion by taking away the
cutting qualities of the bamboo from this particular grove of
bamboo unto this day.[58]

Mano-niho-kahi (Shark with one tooth) lives near the water
hole in Malae-kahana between Laie and Kahuku. When he sees a
woman going to the sea to gather fish or limu he warns her
against sharks, then comes himself and kills her. The chief lines
up all the men and detects the shark-man by the mark of the
shark's mouth on his back when the tapa garment which he
wears is dragged off.[59]

A similar story collected in Pukapuka runs as follows:

A man-eater, an atua-pule, lives in a hole. When two or more
go by to fish he stays inside; when only one, he comes outside
and kills him and drags him into his hole to eat. Two men steal

57. J. Emerson, *AA* 19 (1917): 509.
58. Thrum, *Tales,* 255–268; Westervelt, *Gods and Ghosts,* 59–65.
59. Rice, 111; J. Emerson, *AA* 19: 510.

upon him, entice him outside while they hide, and attack him together. He almost drags them in, but (in one version) a woman calls out to them to "brace the foot" or (in another version) to "lift it high" and they are able to save themselves. The atua slips away to the sea and goes to Samoa, leaving Pukapuka in peace.[60]

Among the Rarotongans a child whose father is Moe-tarauri, an ancestor of Iro, bears on his back a birthmark in the form of a centipede which is seen to writhe when the child is angry.[61]

60. Beaglehole MS.   61. *JPS* 25: 146.

X

THE SOUL AFTER DEATH

HAWAIIAN stories of going to the underworld after the soul of the dead and restoring it to the body are based on the Hawaiian philosophy of life, whose tendency is to dissociate the spirit or soul (uhane) from the body (kino) and to think of it with a quite independent life of its own apart from the body, which is dead or inert without it. The spirit may wander away from the living body, leaving it asleep or merely listless and drowsy, and visit another in dream or as an apparition (hihi'o) while the other is awake. Its exits from the living body are made through the inner angle of the eye, called lua-uhane. Since this habit of wandering is dangerous, lest the spirit be caught and prevented from returning to its body, the kahuna will perform a ceremony and place a special kind of wreath on the head of a person thus addicted.

Theoretically the kahuna alone can see the spirit (uhane) of the dead or dying, but practically everybody is afraid of the lapu or visible form of a dead person. It has human shape and speaks in the same voice as in life, but has the power of enlarging or contracting at will. It cannot change into another shape. The gods alone have this power, called "four-hundred-bodied" (kino-lau). But the dead may enter an object, especially a bone, and hence it is that Hawaiians fear to disturb human bones or to speak of sacred things lest they anger these spirits of the dead, who will then work them mischief. They fear to carry food, especially pork, at night lest they be followed. They will tie to the container a green ti leaf or bamboo or lele banana leaf as a command to the ghost to fly away (lele). This is called placing a law (kanawai) upon the food. But unless the leaves are fresh the law will not work.

To test whether a form is that of a spirit or of a living person, large leaves of the ape plant are laid down. A living person will tear the leaves in treading over them, a spirit will leave no trace. Or something is done to startle the supposed person, who will vanish instantly if a spirit. Another method is to look for the reflection of the person in a bowl of water. The reflection is the spirit of a living person; a mere spirit casts no reflection.[1] Fox enumerates a number of ways employed by natives of San Cristoval to test a stranger who looks like a human being but may be a spirit. Most of these tests are such as would betray ignorance of local ways or clumsiness in applying them.[2]

Restoration of the dead in Hawaiian story consists in bringing the body back to form if crushed, then in catching the released soul and restoring it to the body. Just as, in cases of fainting, manipulation begins at the feet and progresses upward, so in stories of bringing the dead to life the spirit is represented as pushed back into the body at the foot (instep or toe) and making its way upward with resistance, because fearful of the dark passages within the body, until a feeble crow announces the final resuscitation. Fragrant plants are wrapped about the body to tempt reëntrance by the reluctant spirit. Chants play a determining part in the process. A purifying bath is the final step, out of which the body emerges transfigured and full of renewed life. This process of resuscitation is called by Hawaiians kapuku or kupaku.[3]

The soul is often represented in such operations as fluttering about the body or over land or sea, visible to the eyes of the kahuna, who catches it in a gourd. Or it may already have joined the spirits in the underworld of the dead and must be brought or lured thence for return to the body. Thus we get a story of the Orpheus type of a visit by a mortal, aided by the gods, to the underworld. Three such legends are traditional in Hawaii: that of Maluae who brings his son back from the cleft of the underworld where he is being punished for eating a banana which is tapu to the gods Kane and Ka-

1. Westervelt, *Gods and Ghosts,* 89–92; For. Col. 5: 550–553; Rice, 13–14; and see Hiʻiaka.

2. 136–137.

3. Thrum, *Tales,* 150–152; J. Emerson, *HHS Reports* 9: 13–14; N. Emerson, *Pele,* 73–80, 131–152.

naloa; of Mokuleia whose god Kanikani-a-ula accompanies him to the realm of Manua after his wife Pueo who has hanged herself; and the famous legend of Hiku who goes on a similar errand to the realm of Milu after his wife Kawelu.[4] Only the first and last of these stories is told in detail. Besides these, the Westervelt Hainakolo version contains a long account of how the soul of Keanini is brought back from the realm of Milu by his grandson.[5] Hiʻiaka restores the soul of Lohiau in the Pele cycle. The folktale of Ka-ilio-hae (The wild dog) tells how the spirit of the young warrior at the doorway to the spirit world is met by his sister, who is an aumakua-hoʻ-oola (guardian spirit who brings back to life), and is taken first to the underworld and shown the spirits at play, but forbidden to join them lest he never be allowed to come back to life; then taught the passwords enabling him to enter the presence of the chief of the spirits; finally led home and forced back into his lifeless body through the foot.[6] The story resembles folk legends of a person who dies and comes back to life such as are common in every culture.[7]

LEGEND OF MALUAE

Maluae raises bananas for his gods in the uplands of Manoa at a place called Kanaloa-hoʻokau. For his family he raises other food. His son Kaaliʻi eats one of the tapu bananas and the gods cause the boy to choke to death over it. His spirit goes to the underworld while his body lies lifeless. The father thereupon ceases to feed the gods and refuses all food himself, wishing only to die with his son. The gods miss their daily offering and repent having punished the boy so severely. After forty days they promise to aid Maluae in bringing back his son's soul from Manua. They restore his strength and give him the canoe Makuʻ-ukoʻo which contains food, weapons, fire, and fresh water. He enters the roadway at Leilono in Moanalua and breaks through the cleft below the foundations of the earth where his son is

4. For. Col. 6: 337; Pol. Race 1: 83.
5. *Gods and Ghosts,* 203–219.
6. Westervelt, *Gods and Ghosts,* 100–107.
7. Green and Pukui, 120–121.

being punished for his sin, but not in the place set apart for the worst sinners, and he restores the spirit to its lifeless body.[8]

STORY OF HIKU AND KAWELU

(a) *Fornander version.* Hiku, or Hiku-i-ka-nahele (Hiku of the forest), son of Keaholu and Lanihau, lives at Kau-malumalu in Kona, Hawaii, on the slope of Hualalai. One day he goes out to amuse himself with his answering arrow Pua-ne, made from the stalk of a sugar-cane tassel. The arrow falls near the home of the beautiful Kawelu of the seashore and she picks it up and conceals it, in this manner luring Hiku into her house, where he remains six days "without being offered food" [that is, the favors of her body]. At the end of this time he leaves her angrily and when, too late, she follows and chants of her love and begs him to return, he conjures up vines and vegetation to block her way. The disconsolate chiefess strangles herself and her spirit goes down to Milu.

Hiku consults the kahunas as to her recovery. Following their directions, he is paddled out to the point where the sky meets the water, his body rubbed with rancid oil to simulate putrefaction, and a convolvulus vine let down into the sea on which he descends into Milu. There he invites the spirits to share in the new sport of swinging. When the spirit of Kawelu is thus tempted to grasp the vine, he gives the signal and the two are drawn back to the upper world. The spirit is borne to the house where her body is lying and crowded in from the feet up until she is completely resuscitated.

(b) *Emerson and Westervelt version.* Ku is the father of both Hiku and Kawelu (who are thus half-brother and sister and their marriage hence predestined); Hina is his mother, with whom he lives alone at her home on the mountainside. A place named Wai-o-Hiku marks the spot on the shore where his arrow fell. Ku accompanies his son on his journey to the underworld. The rope used is the ieie vine and it is let down at the traditional entrance to the spirit world in Waipio valley. In

8. Kamakau, *Ke Au Okoa,* October 13, 1870; Westervelt, *Gods and Ghosts,* 14–20.

Milu, Hiku takes part in a betting contest, with Kawelu as the stake, and completes her name chant. The soul of Kawelu is imprisoned in a coconut shell split lengthwise, such as sorcerers use for soul catching, when it tries to escape in the form of a butterfly.[9]

The theme of the unrecognized lover, which belongs to the Kahaʻi cycle and is evidently at the basis of the Hiku and Kawelu story, occurs in a tale from the Maori of the southern island which almost exactly parallels that of the Hawaiian Hiku and Kawelu.

Maori. (*a*) *Pare and Hutu.* Pare is a woman of high rank living with a single female attendant in a fine carved house, her food being passed in to her by three attendants. A stranger, Hutu, comes to the village and spins tops better and throws darts farther than any competitor. Pare comes out of her house to watch him. His arrow falls at her door and she takes it inside, thus forcing him to go in to recover it. She begs for his love and is refused because of his lower rank and the fact that he has a family at home. When persuaded that he has left her for good she hangs herself. Her retainers seize Hutu to kill him also. He offers to restore her to life. He chants to heal her injured body, then goes to fetch her spirit from the lower world. Hine-nui-te-po, to whom he has brought a token, directs him on his way and gives him a basket of food, because if he eats food in the lower world he will surely die. She shows him how to plunge head first so that as he meets the wind at the bottom he will land on his feet. When he reaches the lower world, Pare refuses to appear. He invents a new sport by bending down a tree and swinging out on its tip. Pare seats herself on his back and they are swung upward by the rebound until his hands grasp the roots of plants growing in the upper world. Creeping through the opening with his prize, he performs the ceremonies for bringing the soul back into the body and marries the revived woman.[10]

9. For. Col. 5: 182–189; Thrum (from Emerson), *Tales,* 43–50; Westervelt, *Gods and Ghosts,* 224–240; Malo, 143 note 3.

10. White 2: 163–167; discussed by Westervelt, *Gods and Ghosts,* 241–244.

(*b*) *Hikareia*. A lover, Hikareia, comes at night to make love
to his lady. She pushes him away, mistaking him for someone
else, but in the morning she discovers her mistake and, finding
him offended, drowns herself.[11]

(*c*) *Miru*. Kewa was a prince or ruler of the spirit world.
Miru had been educated in all the mysteries, a full knowledge of
which constitutes a perfect tohunga. By means of this knowledge, he, on the death of his sister, was enabled to follow her to
the spirit world, where he captured her spirit, and, bringing it
back, succeeded in making it enter her body, and thereby brought
her back to life. Meanwhile Kewa was completely foiled and deprived of his victim by this act of Miru.[12]

Marquesas. (*a*) Kena of Hiva-oa deserts his first wife. She
follows him in vain over mountain ridges and finally throws herself over a cliff and is killed. He takes a cousin for his second
wife. She is killed by a stratagem and her spirit goes down to
the fourth Havai'i. His mother aids him to descend into the lower
world to recover the spirit. Great difficulties attend the descent.
At the entrance to the fourth Havai'i are clashing rocks between
which his companion, who is holding on to the tailpiece of his
loincloth, is crushed to death. Kena escapes. The chiefess of the
land assists him to bathe and dress his wife and put her into a
basket, from which he is forbidden to release her on any pretext
whatever for ten days after their return. The first time he breaks
the tapu and has to repeat the journey, but the second time he
is more careful.[13]

(*b*) Tue-ato's wife has been strangled for infidelity but is
brought back by his sisters because of his grief. He must abstain
from her for thirteen days, but the first time he breaks the tapu
and the sisters are obliged to bring her back a second time.[14] In
a variant from Nukuhiva, Hahapoa goes to Havai'i to recover
his wife Hanau and breaks the tapu by letting her out of the
basket too soon.[15]

11. Beattie, *JPS* 29: 198.
12. Hare Hongi, *JPS* 5: 116–119.
13. Handy, *Bul.* 69: 117, 120.
14. *Ibid.* 113.   15. *Ibid.* 121–122.

(c) Te-noea-hei-o-Tona sends to Taaoa beach a coconut-sheath canoe which moves of itself and the beautiful Hina-tau-miha takes it into her cave. He follows and weds her. Two wild women beguile him away. She follows in pursuit and when he fails to return she hangs herself and her spirit goes to Havai'i.[16]

Similar stories of a journey to the other world to recover a soul that has left the body at death occur throughout the South Seas. In Tahiti, Tafa'i recovers his wife's spirit from the underworld and restores it to her body.[17] In Samoa the spirit of Sina, daughter of the king of Fiji, is recovered from the ninefold heaven and the girl comes back to life.[18] In another Samoan tale two lads see the gods handing about the soul of a dying chief and manage to snatch it away in the dark and restore it to the body.[19] In Tonga the handsome husband of the daughter of Hina and Sinilau is killed and his spirit goes down to Pulotu. Hina's brother brings it back to the body and restores him to life with the "life-affecting fan."[20] In Tokelau the wife's jealous sisters steal her husband's soul. The wife goes to seek it and restores her husband to life.[21] In Pukapuka:

Milimili dies and goes down to Po. His wife weeps. Tangata-no-te-Moana (Man of the ocean) is applied to by the woman's family gods and goes down to the house of Leva. The gods are unwilling to let the soul go but Tangata-no-te-Moana gets Tuli-kalo to beat the wooden gong so hard that it shakes the house, the gods rush out, and the rescuer throws the soul of Milimili to the family gods, who restore it to the body.[22]

In San Cristoval, to recover the live spirit of the dead it must be brought back from Rodomana (land of souls), from some sacred place, from the sea, or from the sky (Hatuibwaro's country). The "doctor" goes into a trance and his soul goes to Rodomana. A friend hides him. A dance is in progress. He goes in and seizes the unwilling soul or pushes it before him.

16. Handy, *Bul.* 69: 45–49.   17. Henry, 563–564.

18. Krämer 1: 121–124.   19. Turner, 142–143.

20. Collocott, *Bul.* 46: 17–20.

21. Burrows, *JPS* 32: 159–160.   22. Beaglehole MS.

The other souls try to stop him. He flies into the air with the soul.[23]

In the Hawaiian legends of Eleio, of Kahalaopuna, and of Pamano, restoration to life does not imply a visit to another world. The soul is caught fluttering apart from its dead body (kino wailua) and the body restored to life by crowding the soul back into it or by some other device. Eleio brings back to life a chiefess who becomes wife of Kakaalaneo of Maui and mother of the famous sorcerer Ka-ulu-laau, who drives the spirits out of the island of Lanai. Kahalaopuna is an innocent wife who dies at the hands of her jealous husband. The story is developed into a romance which provides a second husband for the loyal wife, from three to five restorations, and episodes of ghost testing and shark transformation. Pamano is a lover also killed out of jealousy, and his resuscitation is effected by two unihipili sisters. A school mistress in Kipahulu, to which district the story belongs, believes it must be true because of a rock resembling a human form and said to be that of Pamano, which used to lie face upward before someone pushed it over on its side.

STORY OF ELEIO

The Eleio family are independent chiefs living at Kauiki at the time when Kakaalaneo rules over the whole island of Maui. The "awa roots of Eleio" are among the famous things of Maui.[24] Eleio is a swift runner who can make the circuit of Maui three times in a day. It is his business to provide fish (or awa) from Hana at the east side of the island to the chief at Lahaina on the west side. He makes the run while the feast is preparing and by the time it is ready he is back with the fish (or with awa, prepared by chewing as he runs). Three times he is pursued on his way by a spirit named Ka-ahu-ula (The red cape) and once he is saved only by the prompt action of his sister Pohaku-loa, who lives at Kamaalea, in exposing herself and shaming the spirit away. He therefore changes his route from the north to the south side of the island. Here he encounters the spirit of the high chiefess Kanikaniaula who has come from Hawaii in dis-

23. Fox, 243–245.   24. For. Col. 5: 544, 610.

guise and married a low chief of Maui and her body now lies
lifeless. He pauses to perform the ceremony of restoration to
life, which involves building a bower of sweet-smelling plants,
offering the proper prayers and sacrifices, and when the spirit
approaches at the offering of awa, catching it and pushing it
into the body from the instep up. Kakaalaneo, impatient at his
messenger's delay, has an oven prepared to put him to death as
a punishment for his tardiness. Eleio appears with the rare
feather cape wrapped about his neck and leaps directly into
the oven, but is dragged from it to tell his story, and to offer the
restored chiefess as wife to Kakaalaneo.[25]

STORY OF KAHALAOPUNA

(a) The parents of Kahalaopuna are the twin brother and
sister Ka-au-kuahine (The rain of the mountain ridge) and Ka-
hau-kani (which names the Manoa wind), children of Akaaka
and Na-lehua-akaaka, names of a projecting spur of the ridge
back of Manoa and the red lehua bushes that grow upon it.
Rainbows still play about her former home and Manoa girls are
said to inherit her beauty. She lives under tapu in a house called
Kahaimano on the way to the spring of the Water-of-the-gods,
and is early affianced to Kauhi of a powerful family of Koolau
(or Waikiki), belonging some say to the Mohoali'i. Mischievous
persons pretend that they have enjoyed her favor. Kauhi believes them and determines that she must die. He leads her
through the wild forest to the uplands of Pohakea close to
Kaala mountain, where he beats her to death and buries her
body beneath a lehua tree under leaves. Her spirit flies to the
top of the tree and chants her story. Passers-by hear her and
tell her parents, who search out her body and, finding it still
warm, restore it to life.

(b) Nakuina version. The girl's family owl god follows and
she is restored to life only to return loyally to her husband, who
again beats her to death and finally buries her where the owl
cannot recover her. An elepaio bird (or her own spirit) bewails
her fate and a youth named Mahana finds and restores her by

25. For. Col. 4: 482–487; 5: 434.

the water cure called Kakelekele at the water cave of Mauoki in Kamoiliili, since called Wai-o-Kahalaopuna. Knowing that she will go back to her husband if he is allowed to live, Mahana learns the chants with which the girl pleads for life with her husband and renders them on a public occasion, declaring that he learned them from the girl herself, now living. Kauhi stakes his life that the girl's supposed form is that of a ghost. Tests are imposed. He loses and he and the two false accusers are put to death. His spirit, however, enters a man-eating shark, which lurks along the coast until it catches the girl out sea-bathing and finally consumes her body so that resuscitation is impossible.[26]

STORY OF PAMANO

Pamano is born in Kahiki-nui on the island of Maui in the days of Kai-uli the chief belonging to a famous Kaupo family. Pamano is son of Lono and Kanaio. He studies the art of the hula, becomes a proficient chanter, and is adopted by Kai-uli, at whose court his mother's brother Waipu is also residing. Kai-uli's pretty daughter Keaka is kept under strict tapu. Both Pamano and his intimate friend Koolau are in love with her, but they agree to have nothing to do with her without the other's consent. She, however, prefers Pamano and entices him into the house. When Koolau chants a song of reproach from without Pamano answers from within. The chief, seconded by Pamano's treacherous uncle and his jealous friend, decides that he must die by poison. Although warned by his unihipili sisters Na-kino-wailua and Hokiolele, he allows himself to be enticed in from surf riding, made drowsy with awa, poisoned, and chopped to pieces. The sisters find and restore him to life. A kaula (seer) tests him with ape leaves to see if he has a human or a ghost body. At a kilu dance given by Keaka and Koolau he reveals himself by chanting songs known only to himself and Keaka. He refuses to have anything to do with her while his enemies live, and Kaiuli, Waipu, and Koolau are ordered slain.[27]

26. For. Col. 5: 188–193; Nakuina, in Thrum, *Tales*, 118–132; Kalakaua, 509–522; Westervelt, *Gods and Ghosts*, 84–93.
27. For. Col. 5: 302–313; Kepelino, 12.

In Anaa of the Tuamotus:

Mehara, ruling chiefess of Ra'iatea, is courted by Pofatu of
Mo'orea. She gives a formal dance. Fago, a young chief of the
upper valley, dances so well that Mehara falls in love with him.
Pofatu is angry and has Fago cut into bits and sunk in the sea
in a basket. Fago's sister Pua recovers the body through her
guardian gods and by magic brings him to life. After avenging
himself on Pofatu he becomes Mehara's husband and rules her
people.[28]

The Hawaiian teaching illustrated in these stories is that
death to the body (kino) does not entail death to the spirit
(uhane) but follows separation between the two. The experiences of the soul after it leaves the body at death, according
to the teachings of the kahunas, follow a traditional pattern
based on very early traditional ideas but probably influenced
by later development of the aumakua belief. There is a place
of the dead, reached at some leaping place, with which is connected a branching tree as roadway of the soul. Elaborations
enter into these basic ideas as a result of the part conceived
to be played by the aumakua in protecting and sheltering the
soul and leading it to its aumakua world.

The worst fate that can befall a soul is to be abandoned by
its aumakua and left to stray, a wandering spirit (kuewa) in
some barren and desolate place, feeding upon spiders and
night moths. Such spirits are believed to be malicious and to
take delight in leading travelers astray; hence the wild places
which they haunt on each island are feared and avoided. Such
are the plains of Kama'oma'o on the island of Maui, the rough
country of Kaupea at Pu'uloa on Oahu, Uhana on Lanai,
Maohelaia on Molokai, Mana on Kauai, Halali'i on Ni'ihau.
In these desolate places lost spirits wander until some friendly
aumakua takes pity upon them.[29]

Gods like Ka-onohi-o-ka-la and Ku-waha-ilo bore to the
heavens the souls of chiefs "where it was supposed the spirits
of kings and chiefs sometimes dwelt, and afterwards returned

28. Stimson MS.
29. Pogue, 30–31; Kamakau, Ke Au Okoa, October 6, 1870.

them to earth, where they accompanied the movements and watched over the destinies of their survivors," writes Ellis.[30] In every case, the reception the soul met after separation from the body depended upon his relations with his aumakua. A person who has committed a sin against his aumakua, says Malo, is exhorted to obtain pardon while he still lingers at Pu'u-ku-akahi (First stopping place) before being conducted to Ku-akeahu (Heaping up place) where he must make the final leap into the underworld called Ka-pa'a-heo (The final parting).[31] At the first point his aumakua may succeed in bringing him back to life.

Milu is said to have been a chief on earth who, on account of disobedience to the gods, was swept down into the underworld at death and became its ruler. Both Kahakaloa on Maui and Waipio on Hawaii claim him as chief; Kupihea says that the Kahakaloa story is the older and the Waipio Milu story is patterned after it. According to the Waipio story, Wakea in his old age retired to Hawaii and lived at Waipio, and at his death he descended to the "Island-bearing land" (Papa-hanau-moku) beneath the earth and founded a kingdom there. Milu succeeded him as chief in Waipio and after Milu's death, due to disregard of the tapu set upon him by the god, Milu became associated with Wakea in the rule of the underworld. In the Kumu-honua legend Milu sets himself up against Kane and is thrust down with his followers "to the uttermost depths of night" (i lalo lilo loa i ka po). The name of Kanaloa is sometimes associated with this opposition to Kane and the quarrel said to be because awa was refused to Kanaloa and his followers.[32] Others call Manua the original lord of the underworld of the dead. Manua is said to be brother to Wakea and Uli and is spoken of in the chant of Nu'u as "the mischief maker."[33]

Entrance into the pit of Milu (Lua-o-Milu) is at a cleft on some high bluff overlooking the sea or in the edge of a valley wall, and a tree serves as the roadway by which the soul takes its departure. One such entrance is at Kahakaloa on the

30. *Tour,* 107.
32. For. Col. 6: 268.

31. Malo, 151 and note.
33. *Ibid.* 337; Kalakaua, 48.

island of Maui, another in Waipio valley on Hawaii, a third
in Moanalua on Oahu. Other leaping places of the soul (Leina-
ka-uhane) are named at different points about the island
coasts. Miss Green reports a leaping place for every district
of Hawaii.[34] Pogue and Fornander name leaping places for
each island.[35] Dibble speaks of "one at the northern extremity
of Hawaii, one at the western termination of Maui, and the
third at the northern point of Oahu."[36] Thus Ka-papa-ki'iki'i
is named on Ni'ihau; Mauloku on the islet of Lehua; Hanapepe on Kauai; Kaimalolo and Kaena on Oahu; in Wainene
between Koolau and Kona on Molokai; Hoku-nui on Lanai;
Keka'a and Kama'oma'o on Maui; and on Hawaii, at Maka-
hana-loa for Hilo district, Kukui-o-pae for Kohala, Kumukahi for Puna, Leina-akua (God-leap) for Kau.

The tree myth is given in considerable detail by both Kepelino and Kamakau. Malo makes no allusion to it.

(a) *Kepelino version.* The soul when it comes to the leaping
place encounters a tree called Ulu-la'i-o-walu which forms the
roadway into the other world. Little children are gathered about
it and direct the soul. One side of the tree looks green and fresh,
the other dry and brittle, but this is an illusion, for the dry
branch is the one which the soul should grasp to save itself from
being cast down into the world of the dead. It must climb on to
the top, being careful to lay hold of a dry twig which will grow
under its hand, and then descend the main trunk to the "third
level," where little children will again direct it how to escape
being cast down to Po.[37]

(b) *Kamakau version.* When the spirit comes to Leilono (perhaps Leina-o-Lono, "Leaping place of Lono") where grows the
tree Ulu-o-Leiwalo, if no aumakua is there to help it will catch
at a decayed branch and fall down to endless night, but if an
aumakua is at hand the soul may be brought back to revive the
body or it may be led into the aumakua world. At the leaping
place at Kaena point on Oahu is a circular clearing about two
feet in circumference which is the doorway to the aumakua

34. *AA* 28: 187.   35. Pogue, 30; For. Col. 5: 574.
36. 82.   37. 50–53.

world. Nearby is the tree with the "misleading" branches. A huge caterpillar guards the eastern boundary of this roadway, a mo'o the western, and if the soul is afraid of these guardians and strays away from the entrance, he will again need his au-makua to help him. The place is at the right side of the bluff toward Waialua and near the road to Keaoku'uku'u.[38]

(c) *Pukui version.* In Ka-u district on Hawaii the "casting-off" place of the soul is marked by an old kukui tree to which the soul must cling, laying hold of a green branch, which has the attributes of the dry, in order to be hurled more quickly with its companions into the "labyrinth that leads to the underworld" lest it lose its way and be left to wander as a stray soul over waste lands of earth.[39]

(d) *Emerson note.* Kane(lau)-apua in pursuit of Kane-lelei-aka (a spirit whose "real body" is in the heavens while its "shadow" flits upon the water) is advised to "start from the breadfruit tree of Leiwalo" and take a flying leap in order to reach his objective.[40]

Except for this myth of the leaping place with its arbo-real roadway, Hawaiian poets have not done much toward elaborating the story of the fate of the soul after its separa-tion from the body. There is no voyage of the soul overseas as in Mangaia; no drama of a pathway of the soul where it is tested and purged of earthly associations, as in Fiji; no vivid experience of adventures in the underworld, as in the South Sea stories, or of the literal "oven of Milu" into which the soul is cast for devouring by the goddess who presides over the dead. Open as the tree myth is to suspicion as influenced by our own myth of the "tree of life and death" which may have become known in early days through stories of the Alex-ander cycle or *The Arabian Nights* tales, Hawaiians claim it as a true native belief, and its wide distribution in the South Seas must argue for its genuine character in some form or other in Hawaii. Kepelino says: "This is not a variant of sa-

38. *Ke Au Okoa,* October 6, 1870.
39. *AA* 28: 187.   40. *Pele,* 194 note c.

cred story, this is a genuine Hawaiian legend. It is not a version taken from the stories of the Holy Bible. It is a strange
thing taught by the spirit. Perhaps the Hawaiians were mis-
taken. Perhaps a tree is not the roadway down to Po. Perhaps
these were words handed down from our first ancestors, but
(the meaning) lost because of the length of time gone by."

Kepelino's contention is sustained by comparison with
South Sea stories. In Rarotonga, Tiki climbs the "Pua tree
at the leaping place" (Pua-i-te-reinga), but, ignoring his
mother's warning to climb the green side, he is precipitated
for his folly into the underworld of Muru (Milu), and
hence men die.[41] In another story a girl is told to step on the
green branches as she climbs, as the dry will take her to spirit
land.[42] In Mangaia a great bua tree with fragrant blossoms
rises to conduct the soul to the underworld, the domain of
Miru, bearing a branch for each principal god. Each soul
climbs out on the branch of his own family god and either
falls thence into a great net from which he goes into the presence of Miru, or leaps into the expanse of the sky.[43] In Rarotonga the souls climb to an ancient bua tree and fall into the
net of Muru.[44] Gill describes Tane at Ukupolu climbing the
bua tree and arriving at Enuakura, spirit land of red feathers.[45] In Anaa of the Tuamotus, when Kihi-nui is stolen and
taken down to Po, the parents follow the taproot of a pua
tree down to the dark world of Ko-ruru-po where the dead
repair.[46] The Moriori dead travel to a point of land at Perau
westward, where they leap into the sea and cling to the root
of an ancient akeake tree (or vine), chiefs climbing over the
branches, commoners crawling under.[47] In the Fijian story of
the pathway of the soul across the island of Viti-levu, the way
leads past a tree where cling the souls of children, who ask
after their parents in the world of living men.[48] So far as I
know this is the only other association in this area of children
with the soul's pathway to the world of the dead.

41. *JPS* 29: 108–109.   42. Gill, 131–132.
43. *Ibid.*, 152–166.   44. *Ibid.*, 169.
45. 109.   46. Stimson MS.
47. Skinner, *Mem.* 9: 55–61; *JPS* 6: 167.
48. Thomson, 126–127.

The division of the world of the dead into compartments of greater or less desirability seems to have developed rather under the teaching of the priesthood as a means of political power than under that of the missionary doctrine. There is no evidence that American missionaries dwelt upon the horrors of hell to convert their hearers to seek after the joys of heaven. They were very young and very convinced and they preached to a people accustomed to tapus as the mark of acceptance by the gods. The sufferings therefore pictured in that part of the underworld ruled over by Milu, as in the chant,

> You die in the oven of Milu
> Established in the fire of Milu
> And unending death,

must be referred to threats of sorcery. We recall that sorcerers who kill by sending an evil spirit to entangle the soul (kahuna-ho'ounauna) are called priests of Milu. The spirits of Milu are called lapu (ghost) or hihi'o (apparition), those of Kane are the "spirits of the high places of the wind" who belong to the aumakua world. It is Milu who sends the soul that is unforgiven by its aumakua to "an unsubstantial land of twilight and shade, a barren and waterless waste, unblest by flower, or tree, or growing herb."[49] A sorcerer's prayer to destroy an enemy concludes,

> Bind, bind fast
> And cast down into the voiceless deep,
> Down, down, down to the bottom of the abyss.

It is possible that such imprecations have, as has been suggested by Gill for the South Seas, a literal implication. A distinction was made in burial customs between chiefs and commoners. The bones of the highest chiefs were carefully preserved and deposited in heiau or distributed among their families for veneration. The bodies of the lower chiefs were laid out straight and wrapped in many folds of tapa before depositing in caves for burial. Priests were disposed in the

49. Malo, 151 and note.

same fashion, but generally in the heiau where they had been keepers. The common people were bound into a sitting posture with their heads bent over their knees, and thrown down the mouths of inaccessible caves or pits. Kamakau describes two such pits on the island of Maui, one at Waiuli, "several miles" in depth and with a wide mouth so that it could be approached from various directions, the other at a cone in the crater of Haleakala called Ka-aawa, a name applied to an insect that destroys vegetation and also to an embryo hilu fish.[50]

Kamakau tells us Hawaiians were taught that there was a place of darkness called Milu and a place of light called Wakea. The aumakua were the intermediaries between the living and the dead.

Na aumakua mai ka po mai
Nana i na pua, hoʻokomo iloko o keia po o ka malamalama.

"Aumakua of the night,
Watch over your offspring, enfold them in the belt of light,"

pray the religious. Of the place of darkness he says, "The endless darkness is the darkness of Milu, the deep darkness, the strata with a deep cleft, the strata of bitterness. . . . Fire, darkness, and dreadful cruelty were in the keeping of the chief of that world."[51]

In Rice's legend of Makua-kau-mana, as in Kepelino, three worlds of the dead are taught. The "third world" is the world where Kane lives and where he takes people good enough to become gods. Bad people go first to a land "where men have done neither good nor evil and where they wait to be rescued," next to a world "where they see joy and sorrow," finally to the world "where they shall weep because of the heat which lasts day and night."[52] According to Kepelino, to the po of Kumuhonua go the spirits of those who have kept the law. To the "cold po" go those who descend by the tree of life and

50. *Ke Au Okoa*, October 6, 1870.
51. *Ibid.*, October 13, 1870.
52. Rice, 175.

death; it is a place without pain or happiness where the soul lives much as in this world. To the po of Milu go the law breakers, where there is "unending fire."[53] Dibble describes a "place of houses, comforts, and pleasures" enjoyed by the religious and a "place of misery below, called Milu" where the irreligious are thrust.[54]

The po of Kumuhonua, the world where the offspring of Kane live, is the aumakua world, the Papa-o-Laka, evidently taught by the kahunas as an urge to pious exertion, the imagery of which, as translated from Kamakau after Mrs. A. P. Taylor, is not without a ring of apocalyptic vision.

The aumakua world is a wide level world containing many dwelling places. . . . Many were the dwelling places but the world was one . . . many overseers ruled over by one great Lord. . . . In the aumakua world were a rolling heaven, a multiple heaven, a multitudinous heaven, a floating cloudland, a lower cloudland, the immovable standing walls of Kane, the horizon line enclosing the flat surface of the earth, the depths of ocean, the beauty of the sun, the brightness of the moon, the glories of the stars, and other places too numerous to mention which were called the aumakua world. . . . Many were the gates by which to enter the aumakua world. If a man or one of his descendants was related to the heavenly beings and was not a stranger to those who had rights in the heavens, then it was understood that he had a right to go to the heavens. If the aumakua of a man and his family belonged to the floating cloudland (just below the heavens), then he was prepared for the floating cloudland. If the aumakua of a man and his family belonged to the ocean depths then it was understood that there he had a right to go, and if the man and his family had an aumakua in the volcanic fire, there he had an irrevocable right to go, or if at Ulu-ka'a and the upright walls of Kane, then it was understood that he would be taken there. . . . And it was said that those who were taken to the floating cloudland and to the multiple heaven and to the other heavens had wings and had rainbows at their feet. These were not wandering spirits . . . these were the beloved of the heavens. . . . Those of heaven are

53. 48–55.   54. 82.

seen on the wings of the wind and their bounds are above the regions of earth and those of the ocean are gathered in the deep purplish blue sea of Kane, and so are all those of the whole earth belonging to the aumakua world; all are united in harmony. The world of endless darkness, the darkness of Milu, the deep darkness, the strata with a deep cleft, the strata of bitterness, the strata of misery, the strata of harshness, has many names given it in Hawaiian stories. That world was said to be an evil world, a friendless world, without family, a fearful world, a world of dread, a world of pain, a world to be patiently endured, a world of trouble, a cruel world. . . .[55]

Certainly this Papa-o-Laka, this aumakua world of Kane, must be considered a very considerable achievement by the priests of the Kane worship in thus spiritualizing the aumakua conception. It must never be forgotten that these aumakua changes of body had in them nothing symbolic. The transmutations were looked upon as absolutely literal. When Kamehameha went down to appease Pele and save his fishponds from an approaching lava flow, a certain chiefess accompanied the party whose child, lately dead, had been dedicated to the fire goddess, and the kahuna was able to point out to her the particular flame in the advancing flow which was her child's transformed body as a minister of Pele; whereupon the mother poured out a chant of love and greeting.

Descent to Milu is, on the other hand, merely a popular expression for death. A victor boasts,

> The youth kills with a single blow
> Lest he (the victim) go down to Milu
> And say he was struck twice.

It is not thought of as a place of torture. One informant thinks of the dead as dancing the hula olapa (drama dance), feasting on shadowy food, and leading a drowsy existence.[56] In the stories the spirits are found dancing with the eepa people and pleased with new sports, songs, and dances. There is competition. The gods may effect a way of escape, but there

55. Kamakau, Ke Au Okoa, October 13, 1870.
56. AA 28: 186.

is always reluctance on the part of the spirit, an idea easily derived from observation of the actual process of resuscitation. Ellis calls it "a land of darkness" where the dead lie beside streams under spreading kou trees surrounded by the emblems of chiefs.[57] The idea is of a shadowy world where people live much as in this world, but an unsubstantial world, a return to the Po, a spirit world.

One Hawaiian informant explains Po as a vast sea where forms live in the lower stages of life. It is out of this sea that land is born and the higher forms of life and man, who make up the world of light (Ao). "So each human being is formed in the spring of water within the uterus of the mother and emerges from it into human life. At death he returns to the Po again." Upon this general sense of the continuity of life is superimposed the idea of a kingdom of the dead where life appears much as in this world, an idea derived from experiences in trance or dream and found particularly useful in story-telling. The thought that man might have lived forever had not someone disobeyed the prohibition imposed is so widespread throughout the South Seas, and the stories told about this disobedience so various, as to preclude Christian teaching as its origin. The idea is of a cycle of life, the human rising out of the spirit world and at old age returning into the safe waters of that world again, to be guarded and reborn into the world of form, either as a human being or as some one of the many bodies which we see in nature, whose god has revealed itself as aumakua to the man during life and whose tapus he has punctually observed. The period of a man's life from birth to old age, "withered and dried like a mat of pandanus," may never be broken save by some sin against the aumakua which has aroused its anger. Even the dark arts of sorcery seem to depend upon an enemy's skill in catching the man at some point of vulnerability, some carelessness in observing the tapus of his god. Contests between aumakua are certainly pictured in story, one seeking the man's life, the other protecting it, but the broken law is the fundamental idea in all Hawaiian thought about accident or early death.

57. *Tour*, 275.

In the Maori account it is said that the offspring of Tane by Hine-te-tama would not obey Rangi and were swept down to Po; "by them mankind are drawn into a lower world."[58]

Family ties in the afterworld remain unbroken, and all Hawaiians believe in the power of spirits to return to the scenes they knew on earth in the form in which they appeared while they were alive. Especially is this true of the processions of gods and spirits who come on certain sacred nights to visit the sacred places, or to welcome a dying relative and conduct him to the aumakua world. "Marchers of the night" (Huaka'i-po) or "Spirit ranks" (Oi'o) they are called. Many Hawaiians and even some persons of foreign blood have seen this spirit march or heard the "chanting voices, the high notes of the flute, and drumming so loud as to seem beaten upon the side of the house." Always, if seen, the marchers are dressed according to ancient usage in the costume of chiefs or of gods. If the procession is one of gods, the marchers move five abreast with five torches burning red between the ranks, and without music save that of the voice raised in chant. Processions of chiefs are accompanied by aumakua and march in silence, or to the accompaniment of drum, nose-flute, and chanting. They are seen on the sacred nights of Ku, Lono, Kane, or Kanaloa, or they may be seen by day if it is a procession to welcome the soul of a dying relative. To meet such a procession is very dangerous. "O-ia" (Let him be pierced) is the cry of the leader and if no relative among the dead or none of his aumakua is present to protect him, a ghostly spearsman will strike him dead. The wise thing to do is to "remove all clothing and turn face up and feign sleep."[59]

58. White 1: 29.
59. Kepelino, 198–200; Westervelt, *Gods and Ghosts,* 251; Malo, 152, 154 note 4.

PART TWO

Children of the Gods

XI

THE PELE MYTH

HAWAIIANS believe that the volcano at Kilauea is inhabited by a family of fire gods presided over by the goddess Pele who governs the activities of lava flows. A kahuna brother Moho (Ka-moho-ali'i), two sisters, Pele and Hi'iaka (Hi'iaka-i-ka-poli-o-Pele), and a hump-backed brother named Kamakaua (Ke-o-ahi-kamakaua) are said to compose the original Pele family, all further additions being purely mythical. Traditional lists of volcano deities compiled by Ellis, Kalakaua, and Westervelt name at least five brothers and eight sisters, the brothers associated with the phenomena of thunderstorms and volcanic activities, the sisters with cloud forms, as translated by Ellis, who also uses the old *t* sound which later informants replace with a *k*.

ELLIS[1]	KALAKAUA[2]	WESTERVELT[3]
Ka-moho-arii	Kamohoalii (god of steam)	Kamohoali'i
Ta-poha-i-tahi-ora (Explosion in the place of life)	Kapohoikahiola (god of explosions)	Ka-poha-i-kahi-ola
Te-ua-a-te-po (The rain of night)	Keuakepo (Rain of fire)	Ke-ua-a-ke-po
Tane-hetiri (Kane of the thunder)	Kane-kahili	Kane-hekili
		Kane-pohaku-ka'a
		Kane-hoa-lani
		Kane-huli-honua
		Kane-kauwila-nui
		Kane-huli-koa
Te-o-ahi-tama-taua (Fire-thrusting child of war)	Keoahi-kamakaua	Ke-o-ahi-kama-kaua
		Lono-makua

1. *Tour*, 183–186. 2. 49. 3. *Volcanoes*, 69–71.

ELLIS	KALAKAUA	WESTERVELT
Pele	Pele	Pele
Makore-wawahi-waa (Fiery-eyed canoe breaker)	Makole-nawahi-waa	Hiiaka-makole-wawahi-waa
Hiata-wawahi-lani (Heaven-rending cloud holder)	Hiiaka-wawahi-lani	Hiiaka-wawahi-lani
Hiata-noho-lani (Heaven-dwelling cloud holder)	Hiiaka-noho-lani	Hiiaka-noho-lani
Hiata-taarava-mata (Quick-glancing-eyed cloud holder)	Hiiaka-kaalawa-maka	Hiiaka-kaalawa-maka
Hiata-hoi-te-pori-a-pele (Cloud holder embracing the bosom of Pele)	Hiiaka-hoi-ke-poli-a-pele	Hiiaka-i-ka-poli-o-Pele or Hiiaka-opio
Hiata-ta-bu-enaena (Red-hot mountain-holding cloud)	Hiiaka-kapuenaena	Hiiaka-kapu-enaena
Hiata-tareiia (Wreath-gar-landed cloud holder)	Hiiaka-kaleiia	Hiiaka-kaleiia
	Hiiaka-opio	

The Pele myth is believed to have developed in Hawaii, where it is closely associated with aumakua worship of the deities of the volcano, with the development of the hula dance, and with innumerable stories in which odd rock or cone formations are ascribed to contests between Pele and her rivals, human or divine. The myth narrates the migration or expulsion of Pele from her distant homeland and her effort to dig for herself a pit deep enough to house her whole family in cool comfort or to exhibit them in their spirit forms of flame and cloud and other volcanic phenomena. She approaches the

group from the northwest, tries island after island without
success, and finally settles on Hawaii at the crater Moku-a-
weoweo (Land of burning). Her brother Ka-moho-ali'i and
other male relatives assist in or accompany the journey. The
only female companion noted in the story is her pet little sister Hi'iaka. The myth continues at great length with an account of Pele's affair in spirit form with a handsome young
chief of Kauai of whom she is enamored and whom she determines to have for a husband; of sending her sister to fetch
him to share her home on Hawaii; of jealousy of her faithful
messenger; and of the sister's consequent defiance.

The Pele myth therefore falls into two parts: (1) the establishment of Pele's home at the volcano on Hawaii, (2) the
sending for her lover Lohiau to share this home. In the first
myth Pele is the dominant character, in the second her sister
Hi'iaka has assumed that position.

PELE LEGENDS

(a) *Migration legend.* Pele is one of a family of seven sons
and six daughters born to Haumea and her husband Moemoe
(Moemoe-a-aulii), all distinguished figures in old legend. Pele
is very beautiful with a back straight as a cliff and breasts
rounded like the moon. She longs to travel and, tucking her little
sister born in the shape of an egg under her armpit, hence
called Hi'iaka-i-ka-poli-o-Pele (-in the armpit of Pele), she
seeks her brother Ka-moho-ali'i. He gives her the canoe of their
brother Whirlwind (Pu-ahiuhiu) with Tide (Ke-au-lawe or Ke-
au-miki) and Current (Ke-au-ka) as paddlers, and promises to
follow with other members of the family. She goes by way of
Polapola, Kuaihelani "where Kane hides the islands," and other
islands inhabited by gods (Mokumanamana) to Ni'ihau, island
of the chiefess Fire-thrower (Ka-o-ahi), where she is hand-
somely entertained. Thence she visits Kauai and appears in the
midst of a hula festival in the form of a beautiful woman. Falling desperately in love with the young Kauai chief Lohiau, she
determines to take him for a husband. Passing southeast from
island to island, on each of which she attempts to dig a home in
which she can receive her lover, she comes finally to Hawaii and

there is successful in digging deep without striking water, an element inimical to her fiery nature.[4]

(b) *Expulsion version.* Pele is born to Kane-hoa-lani and Haumea in Kuaihelani. She sticks so close to Lono-makua, the fire god, as to cause a conflagration (or, as in the Aukelenuiaiku story, makes love to her sister's husband) and her older sister Na-maka-o-kaha'i, called "a sea goddess," drives her away. She takes passage in the canoe Honua-i-a-kea with her little sister carried in her armpit and accompanied by her brothers Kamoho-ali'i, Kane-milo-hai, Kane-apua, and others, and arrives at the Hawaiian group by way of the northwestern shoals. There Kane-milo-hai is left on one islet as an outguard and Kane-apua on another, but Pele pities this last younger brother and picks him up again. A group of songs relate the relentless pursuit of the party by the older sister until the two sisters encounter each other in Kahiki-nui on the island of Maui and Pele's body is torn apart and the fragments heaped up to form the hill called Ka-iwi-o-Pele (The bones of Pele) near Kauiki, while her spirit takes flight to the island of Hawaii and finds a permanent home on Hawaii.[5]

(c) *Flood version.* Pele is born in Kapakuela, a land to the southwest, "close to the clouds," and her parents are Kane-hoa-lani and Ka-hina-li'i, her brothers Ka-moho-ali'i and Kahuila-o-ka-lani. By her husband Wahieloa (Wahialoa) she has a daughter Laka and a son named Menehune. Pele-kumu-honua entices her husband from her and Pele travels in search of him. With her comes the sea, which pours from her head over the land of Kanaloa (Kahoolawe), never before so inundated, and her brothers chant,

> "A sea! a sea!
> Forth bursts the sea,
> Bursts forth over Kanaloa (Kahoolawe),
> The sea rises to the hills. . . ."

4. Rice, 7–10.
5. N. Emerson, *Pele,* xi–xvi; For. Col. 4: 102–107; Westervelt, *Volcanoes,* 8–12; cf. N. Emerson, "Hula," 187–189, where Pele is expelled on account of disrespect to her mother.

"Thrice" (according to the chant) the sea floods the land, then recedes. These floodings are called The-sea-of-Ka-hina-li'i.[6]

(d) *Unnatural birth version.* Pele's father is the man-eater Ku-waha-ilo who dwells in the far-off heavens. Haumea, her mother, belongs to the Pali (cliff) family. Two daughters are born, Na-maka-o-kaha'i from the breasts of Haumea, Pele from the thighs. Brothers are born; Ka-moho-ali'i from the top of the head of Haumea, Kane-hekili (Thunder) from the mouth, Kau-ila-nui (Lightning) from the eyes, and other children (from four to forty sisters) from various parts of Haumea. Hi'iaka is born in the shape of an egg and cherished as Pele's favorite.[7]

(d') Papa and Wakea are the parents of Pele, Ka-moho-ali'i, and Kapo. Kapo is born from Papa's eyes, Kamohoali'i from her head as a mist-crowned precipice.[8]

Local elaboration of the migration story describes in detail the localities on each island where Pele pursued her digging activities.[9] A famous dance song records the successive steps of Pele's advance from island to island, beginning:

> The blaze trembles,
> Bursts out above, below,
> The spade rattles in the cleft below.
> "What god is this digging?"
> "It is I, Pele,
> Digging a pit on Ni'ihau."[10]

As the oral recitation proceeds, recounting Pele's migration, old Hawaiian story tellers insert a song chanted in the oli (singing) style, such as the famous "Coming of Pele" describing the building of the canoe, the journey from the homeland, the family group who accompany Pele, their arrival on Hawaii, and their apotheosis at the volcano. "Kahiki" and "Polapola" as they occur in the song are today re-

6. Thrum, *Tales,* 36–38; Kepelino, *Bul.* 95: 187–188; Westervelt, *Volcanoes,* 7.

7. *Ibid.,* 64–71.
8. Westervelt, *Honolulu,* 30.
9. Green, 18–23.
10. N. Emerson, "Hula," 85–87.

ferred to the Society group, from which lands the party of
gods is represented as migrating.

> No Kahiki mai ka wahine o Pele
> Mai ka aina mai o Polapola
> Mai ka punohu a Kane mai ke ao lapa i ka lani
> Mai ka opua lapa i Kahiki
> Lapa ku i Hawaii ka wahine o Pele
> Kalai i ka wa'a o Honua-ia-kea
> Ko wa'a, e Kamohoali'i, hoa mai ka moku
> Ua pa'a, ua oki, ka wa'a o ke 'kua
> Ka wa'a o kalai Honua-mea o holo
> Mai ke au hele a'e, ue a'e ka lani
> A i puni mai ka moku, a e a'e kini o ke 'kua
> Iawai ka hope, ka uli o ka wa'a?
> I na hoali'i a Pele a e hue, e
> Me la hune ka la, kela ho'onoho kau hoe
> O luna o ka wa'a, o Ku ma laua o Lono
> Holo i honua aina, kau aku
> I ho'olewa ka moku, a'e a'e Hi'iaka na'i au ke 'kua
> Hele a'e a komo I ka hale o Pele
> Huahua'i Kahiki lapa uila
> Uila Pele e hua'i e
> Hua'ina hoi e.

"The woman Pele comes from Kahiki,
  From the land of Polapola,
  From the ascending mist of Kane, from the clouds that move
    in the sky,
  From the pointed clouds born at Kahiki.
  The woman Pele was restless for Hawaii.
  'Fashion the canoe Honua-ia-kea,
  As a canoe, O Kamohoali'i, for venturing to the island.'
  Completed, equipped, is the canoe of the gods,
  The canoe for (Pele)-of-the-sacred-earth to sail in.
  From the straight course the heavenly one turned
  And went around the island, and the multitude of the gods
    stepped ashore.
  'Who were behind at the stern of the canoe?'

'The household of Pele and her company,
Those who bail, those who work the paddles,
On the canoe were Ku and Lono.'
It came to land, rested there,
The island rose before them, Hi'iaka stepped ashore seeking
    for increase of divinity,
Went and came to the house of Pele.
The gods of Kahiki burst into lightning flame with roar and
    tumult,
Lightning flames gushed forth,
Burst forth with a roar."[11]

HI'IAKA MYTH

Emerson version. Pele has made her home with her brothers
and sisters at the crater of Mokuaweoweo. She falls into a
deep sleep during which her spirit leaves her body and, following the sound of the nose-flute (Kani-ka-wi) and the whistle
(Kani-ka-wa), arrives at the island of Kauai while a hula dance
is in progress. She takes the form of a beautiful woman and
wins the young chief Lohiau as her husband. Upon leaving him
on the third (or ninth) night, she bids him await her messenger
to bring him to the house she is making ready for him. [In Rice's
version this meeting precedes her digging experiments from
island to island.] In the meantime, her faithful sister has watched
over her inert body and is relieved to see it return to conscious-
ness. Pele calls for a messenger and Hi'iaka-i-ka-poli-o-Pele is
the only one of her household brave enough to face the dangers
of the way. The girl demands and is given the powers of a god
in order to pass through the ordeal in safety. Entrusting her
beloved lehua groves and her friend Hopoe to the care of her
sister and receiving her sister's last commands not to indulge in
embraces on the way and to return within forty days, she sets
forth on her perilous journey.

On the way she provides herself with women companions. Her
old nurse Pau-o-palai (Skirt of palai fern) accompanies her as
far as Kohala, where she remains with her husband Paki'i until
the girl's return. A half goddess named Wahine-omao (Thrush-

---

11. Roberts MS. collection, translation after Mrs. Pukui.

woman), daughter of Kai-palaoa and Puna-hoa, is the only one who makes the entire journey with her. Another girl, Papulehu, joins her on the way but has not the spiritual qualifications to survive even the first of the dangers encountered.

Choosing the upland path across Hawaii, the party must first exterminate the evil mo'o who make the way dangerous. With the help of the war gods Kuliliaukaua and Kekako'i and the shell-conch blowers Kamaiau, Kahinihini, and Mapu, Hi'iaka fights and overcomes a number of these monsters. The mo'o woman Panaewa, who impedes her way in the form first of fog (kino-ohu), then of sharp rain (kino-au-awa), then of a candle-nut (kukui) tree, she entangles the mo'o and her followers, the Na-mu and Na-wa in a growth of vine [or engulfs them in the sea]. Two mo'o, Kiha and Pua'a-loa (Long hog), are caught in a flood of lava, where their forms may be seen to this day. The shark at the mouth of Waipio valley who seizes swimmers cross-ing the bay is met and slain. Mo'olau, chief of the jumping mo'o (mahiki) in the land of Mahiki-waena, is defied, his followers put to rout, and the wounds bound up of two men the mo'o have mangled. Two mo'o, Pili and Noho, who make travelers pay toll at the bridge across the Wailuku river, are rent from jaw to jaw and the way opened for free traffic. The prudish ghost god Hinahina-ku-i-ka-pali, who objects to the girls swimming naked across the stream Honoli'i while holding their clothing above their heads, is reproved and put to silence.

Crossing to Maui, the girls avoid the attentions of the pad-dlers Pi'i-kea-nui and Pi'i-kea-iki and proceed along the coast. A maimed spirit named Manamana-i-aka-luea is seen dancing the hula mu'umu'u (maimed) and her spirit nature is tested by throwing a hala fruit and seeing her figure instantly vanish. Omao catches the spirit and the girls restore it to its lifeless body. Refused hospitality at the home of the chief Olepau [or Kaulahea] in Iao valley, Hi'iaka avenges the insult by catching his second soul, as it goes fluttering about while he lies sleeping, and dashing it against the rock Pahalele near Waihe'e. At the advice of the kahuna Kuakahi-mahiku, the chief's friends at-tempt to overtake and conciliate Hi'iaka but are tricked by con-cealing transformations. At the hill Pulehu the two take the shapes of an old woman and child with a dog; at Kalaula'ola'o, of girls stringing blossoms; at Kapua in Kaanapali they appear as women braiding mats for a new house. [In Rice's version other incidents occur and the chief is restored to life.]

Crossing next to Molokai, the girls choose the route along the dangerous windy side of the island and make the passage to Oahu from Kaunakakai. The single adventure described is the banishing of the lawless mo'o tribe who have robbed women of their husbands, and the slaying of the mo'o woman Kikipua who has stolen Oloku'i from his wife Papaua, deserted her own husband Hakaaano, and made a false bridge of her tongue to destroy travelers. Hi'iaka makes use of her skirt (pau) as a bridge, over which the girls pass safely. The mourning women whose husbands have been destroyed by the mo'o band she however reproves for indulging in useless hysteria.

Again choosing the rocky side of the island on Oahu, Hi'iaka addresses chants to the rocks Maka-pu'u and Malei, whom she recognizes as her own supernatural relatives; greets Pohaku-loa at Ka-ala-pueo (The owl road); and crushes the evil mo'o Mokoli'i at Kualoa. Kauhi, "with eye-sockets moist with the dripping dew from heaven," wishes to go with her and, when she refuses his company, struggles up to a crouching position. So his form may be seen today along the rock wall of Kahana. At Kahipa she reproves Puna-he'e-lapa and Pahipahi-alua for slipping away without a greeting. At Kehuahapu'u she listens to the sound of the sea, notices the uki plant, and admires the beauty of Waialua. At the plain near Lauhulu she chants the praises of the mountain Kaala. At Kaena point she apostrophizes its huge boulders and begs the Rock-of-Kauai, left at sea when Maui's fishline broke, to send her a canoe to cross to Kauai. It was from this point that her sister had listened to the music which lured her across the channel to Lohiau's feast.

The restoration of Lohiau takes place on Kauai. Arrived on that island, the girls are entertained at the house of the chief Malae-ha'a-koa, whose lameness they have cured, and learn of the death of Lohiau out of grief over the disappearance of the beautiful woman who came to him at the hula dance. Two women of Honopu, Kilioe-i-kapua and Kalana-mai-nu'u, relatives of Kilioe, have stolen his body from the place where his sister Kahua-nui had laid it, and hidden it in an inaccessible cave high up on the cliff Kalalau [but in some versions Kilioe is Lohiau's sister and the hider herself of the body]. Hi'iaka catches the fluttering spirit and destroys the two Honopu women by means of an incantation. She and Omao scale the cliff and for ten days, while the people below dance the hula, she recites the chants useful to restore a spirit to its body. At the end of this time Lohiau lives and all three descend on a rainbow and purify themselves in the ocean.

The return voyage is now to be undertaken. Meanwhile the forty days' limit set by Pele for the journey has been already covered and more delays are still before them. Between Kauai and Oahu the shark gods Kua and Kahole-a-Kane and the sea goddess Moana-nui-ka-lehua raise a storm to prevent the match between their divine relative Pele and a mere mortal like Lohiau. Hi'iaka chooses the overland route across the island of Oahu while the other two round the island by canoe. At Pohakea she climbs the ridge, looks across to her home on Hawaii, and voices a bitter lament when she sees her beloved forests in flames and her friend Hopoe wrapped in burning lava. Still true to her mission in spite of her sister's betrayal, she chants a warning to the two alone in the canoe to indulge in no love making. At Kou (Honolulu) the party is entertained by the famous prophetess Pele-ula, a former lady-love of Lohiau, and Hi'iaka contends with her hostess in a kilu game for his possession, but refuses to take advantage at that time of her success. [Some accounts state that at this point the three fashion visible bodies for themselves out of spittle and, leaving these behind, go in their spirit bodies to Hanauma bay, where they pass over to Maui.]

The death of Lohiau takes place as a climax to Pele's jealousy. Without waiting for an explanation from the two women who go ahead to acquaint Pele with the story of their adventures, the angry goddess, furious at the long delay, overwhelms them with fire. At this, Hi'iaka, for the first time and on the very edge of the crater in full view of her sister, accepts Lohiau's embraces. Pele calls upon her sisters to consume Lohiau, but they pity his beauty. She invokes her gods but they call her unjust and blow away the flame, for which disloyalty she banishes them to the barren lands of Huli-nu'u; and that is how Ku-pulupulu,

Ku-moku-hali'i, Ku-ala-nawao, Kupa-ai-ke'e, and Ku-mauna came to sail away and become canoe makers in other lands. Finally Pele herself encircles the lovers with flame. Hi'iaka has been given a divine body and cannot be hurt, but Lohiau's body is consumed.

The second restoration of Lohiau to life follows. Hi'iaka digs down after him through the earth, passing at the first stratum of earth the god of suicide, at the fourth the bodies of her two women friends, whom she restores to life. She is about to rend the tenth layer when Wahine-omao warns her against letting in the water upon her sister. Lohiau's spirit, fluttering overseas, first to Kauai, where he bids his friend Paoa seek Pele, then to La'a in Kahiki, is caught by Kane-milo-hai who has been left to guard the outposts of the group, and restored to life. At first he is listless, but La'a's bird messengers, Plover and Turnstone, rouse him to interest in human affairs. At Pele-ula's home he is reunited to Hi'iaka. [In Rice's version he is sent back to Kauai by canoe. In one legend Omao becomes the wife of Lono makua.][12]

The trance motive in the story of Pele's meeting with her lover depends upon the idea that a spirit can wander away from a living body (uhane-hele) and take the form of a second body (kinoho'opaha'oha'o), in which form it can carry on a life of its own apart from the body. The theme is rationalized in the Laieikawai romance where Aiwohikupua dreams of meetings with Laieikawai before he has ever seen her. In Tahiti it is recorded that the young chiefess of Huahine remained in such a condition for a month, during which time she met a lover who cherished and protected her.[13] In a Marquesan story two gods who desire the woman Teapo stop her breath and take her ghost to Havaii where she hears songs sung which she can repeat after she is restored to life.[14]

Few references to the Pele figure are to be found in other

12. N. Emerson, *Pele;* Westervelt, *Volcanoes,* 72–138; Rice, 10–17; Green, 22–27; For. Col. 6: 343–344; *HAA* 1929, 95–103; Kalakaua, 481–497.

13. Henry, 220–223; Ahnne 10: 43.

14. Handy, *Bul.* 69: 82–85.

groups. Gifford reports a Tongan female deity called Puako-
mopele with pig head and woman's body who rules all the
gods of Haapai and whose sacred animal is the gecko.[15] Allusions to Pele in Tahiti as deity of fire under the earth are said
to be due to late contact with the Hawaiian group:

The heat of the earth produced Pere (Conceiving heat), goddess of the fire in the earth (atua vahine no te vera o te fenua)
. . . a blond woman (vahine 'ahu) ; then came Tama-ehu (Blond
child) or Tama-tea. Fire was those gods' agent of power; it
obeyed them in the bowels of the earth and in the skies. They
were the chief fire gods.[16]

. . . The great goddess Pere (Consuming heat) must be goddess of spontaneous burning of the earth. Tama-'ehu (Blond
child), the brother of Pere, must be the god of heat in the nether
lands.[17]

. . . Pere has light down in the earth, without heat; above is
the fire ever burning. Awe-inspiring is the residence of Pere down
in the earth, great are her attendants that follow her below and
above the surface of the world.[18]

In Tahiti, the uninhabited islet of Tubai, most northern of
the group, is Pere's home during her visits to the south.[19] Ti-
'ara'a-o-Pere (Standing place of Pele) is the name of the assembly ground of the district of Tautira on Tai-a-rapu.[20]

Pele as goddess of volcanic fire is addressed in Hawaiian
chants by a number of names descriptive of volcanic activity.
Pele-ai-honua (eater of land) she is called because she destroys the land with her flames.[21] Ai-laau (Wood eater) in
the Pele myths is an old volcano god who retreats before Pele
or surrenders to her the pit he has dug.[22] According to Kamakau he is still an aumakua of volcanic fire to whom dead

15. *Bul.* 61: 294–295.   16. Henry, 359.
17. *Ibid.*, 417.   18. *Ibid.*, 144.
19. *Ibid.*, 104.   20. *Ibid.*, 86.
21. Green, 21.
22. Rice, 9; Westervelt, *Volcanoes*, 13.

bodies are offered to become flame.[23] Among the Maori, the descendant of Maui-mua who came to New Zealand in the Tearatawhao canoe is literally "Toi the wood eater" because he used raw fern-wood, the edible palm, and young fern sprouts for food and knew nothing of fire and of cultivated food.[24]

Pele's most common chant name is Pele-honua-mea (Pele of the sacred earth), reminiscent of the Maori Para-whenua-mea, a name which Percy Smith interprets as "effacement of nature due to the flood," Para-whenua-mea being, in Maori myth, the wife of Kiwa and mother of "the great ocean of Kiwa" or the Pacific Ocean.[25] Pele is the name by which the goddess is worshiped in her fire body. Ka-ula-o-ke-ahi (The redness of the fire) is her sacred name as a spirit. Kilinahi Kaleo, whom I here quote, gave a start when I pronounced the name, and lowered his voice in answering my question. Pele's name as a woman on earth, he told me, was Hina-ai-ka-malama. Clearly the Maui mythologists of Hana have taken this means to work into the Pele cycle their own famous Hina goddess of the moon, to whose connection with the flood story and with the Kaha'i-Laka cycle is now added a place in the pantheon of the hula dance and the romances woven about its festivals.

23. *Ke Au Okoa,* May 5, 1870.
24. *JPS* 2: 250; 3: 13; 22: 149.
25. *MPS* 3: 98 note 51, 159.

XII

THE PELE SISTERS

IN the Hiʻiaka myth Pele's messenger is represented as an expert in sorcery and the hula, arts of which the Pele family as gods of generation are special patrons. The whole Pele and Hiʻiaka cycle of stories is rehearsed episodically in the hula dance. Even the smallest incident may furnish a theme for the dance. The hula songs are not composed by mortals but taught by the Pele spirits to worshipers of Pele. Those who learn the dances are supposed to be possessed by the spirit of the Pele goddess of the dance. An error in the step shows that the patroness has rejected the dancer. Since Hiʻiaka is the supreme patroness of the hula, all prayer chants for the hula ceremonies are "named under" Hiʻiaka, even those dedicated to Ku and Hina. A chant that is "named" to a person becomes that person's property, no matter if it was composed in honor of another person, just as any other piece of property may be passed on to another. All prayer chants (mele pule) dedicated to Hiʻiaka are prayers of the ancients.

Training in the hula does not include the whole art of sorcery but every hula master must know the prayers to ward off sorcery (pule pale) and each pupil learns such a prayer for his protection. Even as late as Kalakaua's time kahunas were educated as priests of Pele. Some who wished to study sorcery would stay for a year or more at the volcano, make sacrifice, and dream a chant. This chant they would dedicate to Pele or Hiʻiaka. In offering sacrifice the kahuna must get all four gods to "work" with him by invoking each in prayer. He must include also the ancestral gods (kumu-akua), the guardian gods (aumakua), the deified gods (unihi). He would call upon "All the original ancestors of chiefs" (Na kumu-aliʻi a pau loa o ka po), "The descendants of chiefs" (Na-lala-aliʻi), "The chiefs who were last of their line" (Na-welau-aliʻi).[1]

1. N. Emerson, *Pele;* also, "Hula"; Helen Roberts, *Bul.* 29;

Dance motives are directly incorporated into the Pele and Hi'iaka story. One such is drawn about the figure of Hopoe, the beloved girl friend of Hi'iaka.

Hopoe is first seen by Hi'iaka dancing a hula beside the sea Nanahuki in Puna district. Hi'iaka takes her for a favorite. For her Hi'iaka plants the forests of red and white blossoming lehua to be found in that region. A flowering lehua tree is hence her emblem. When she is overwhelmed by Pele's impatient wrath she becomes changed into a rock, which used to stand balanced like a dancing figure just as the girl was caught by the lava, but is now fallen and lies near Keaau in Puna.[2]

Another dance incident is that of the maimed spirit who inspired the affection of Wahine-omao, a scene represented in the hula mu'umu'u (cut off).[3] A third is the reference to Kilinoe, the famous hula teacher of Kauai whose "unike, or sign of an expert," is essential to one who would dance the hula in public on Kauai.[4] Rice makes her the sister of Lohiau, Emerson connects her with the sirens who steal away Lohiau's body. A Malo note[5] gives the name to a (male) god of cliffs.

The most complete of these dance motives is to be found in the episode at Pele-ula's home in Nu'uanu valley where the two women compete in dance and chanted improvisation for the possession of a lover. The land of Pele-ula on Oahu has been placed by McAllister where Vineyard street crosses the Nu'uanu stream.[6] The soft rain that comes down the valley only as far as the present Judd street is still called "the rain of Wa'ahila of Nu'uanu" (ka ua Wa'ahila-o-Nu'uanu) after a chiefess whose name is commemorated in a hula in which she excelled and which was a favorite of Pele-ula.[7] The competition is represented as taking place during a kilu game, a

Green, 2–5; Malo, 155–157; For. Col. 6: 68–74; J. Emerson, *HHS Reports* 26: 17–39; Kamakau, *Ke Au Okoa*, July 21 to August 11, 1870.

2. Emerson, *Pele*, 11–14, 162–163, 227; For. Col. 6: 343–344; Rice, 10; Westervelt, *Volcanoes*, 87–95; local information.

3. N. Emerson, "Hula," 212–215.

4. Rice, 14.   5. 119.

6. *Bul.* 104: 83.   7. N. Emerson, *Pele*, 170 note.

popular pastime of chiefs comparable to our own kissing
games but a step more erotic, and including exhibitions of
dance and song which called for the highest development of
skill in these arts. The scene is placed on Oahu during Hiʻ-
iaka's return trip after the restoration of Lohiau in Kauai,
but there is reason to suppose that it belongs actually after
Pele's outburst of anger and the second restoration of Lohiau, and represents Pele's final effort to win back her lover
from her younger sister. This supposition is supported by
the fact that in Rice's version Hiʻiaka and Lohiau meet at
Pele-ula's home on Oahu after Lohiau's second restoration to
life. Originally perhaps the incident belonged to Kauai, where
Pele in her spirit body competes with his sister Kilinoe for
the embraces of her lover while her human body lies in trance.
It may be that a shift of interest in the characters of the story
has brought about the change of scene and actors.

As for the scene itself, there is no doubt that it was drawn
from life. Malo gives a detailed description of the games of
ume and kilu as practised in upper-class circles, ume a frankly
sexual game in which two lovers are sent out by the master of
ceremonies to satisfy their desire; kilu a sort of quoits in
which a gourd is spun to hit a stake in the form of a wooden
cone placed in front of the desired lover among the players
of the opposite sex, as they sit ranged, one on one side, the
other on the other side, of the space cleared for the game. A
score of ten hits entitles the player to the favors of the lover
for the night unless bought off with a gift of land or other
coveted commodity. This form of courting was, we are told,
a great favorite in the circles to which the chiefs belonged,
but from which all not members of the chief class were carefully excluded.[8]

The theme of the kilu game seems to have been a favorite
with composers of romance and is frankly realistic in treatment. The Pukui version of the Hainakolo romance represents the sister of the abandoned Hainakolo winning back
Keaunini to her sister in a kilu contest in which she competes
successfully in dance with the girl who has charmed him away

8. Malo, 281–287.

and in song recalls his mind to the scenes of natural beauty
which he has shared with his former wife, phrased no doubt
to include the erotic allusions so dear to Hawaiian ears but
which escape the foreign interpreter. It is at a kilu game at
the court of Kakuhihewa that Lono-i-ka-makahiki wins the
companionship of the visiting chiefess from Kauai and turns
the occasion to account by learning from her the chant called
Mirage of Mana which he later asserts was composed as
his name-song from childhood. Both Kawelo and Halemano,
after finding the arts of fishing and farming, which their elders prescribe, insufficient to win the love of ladies, become
experts in the hula and at a kilu game Halemano turns once
more the heart of the much wooed beauty of Puna to her
former husband. An episode in the romance of Laie-i-ka-wai
shows the beauty of Hana, Hina-i-ka-malama, competing
with a rival for her lover's favors.

A similar theme occurs in other groups. Stimson tells the
story from Anaa in the Tuamotus of Gana, Huri-te-papa,
and the princess Faumea, where Gana is the suitor of Faumea
in Tahiti-nui, but Huri-te-papa wins her by his dancing. So
in the story of Mehara the beauty is won by the best dancer.[9]
In Grey's story from the Maori, Kahureremoa comes as a
stranger to the dance hall and awakens love by her dancing.[10]
Te Ponga wins an ally whose heart he has stirred by his
graceful dancing.[11]

Such descriptions prove the popularity of the theme, in
which both individual dancing and organized games with
competitive dancing between experts are employed with the
romantic object of arousing the passion of love or of winning
back an estranged lover or one tempted to infidelity. The
scene is drawn from life and gives an excellent idea of social
life in upper-class circles in the old days. It must be observed
that in every instance decorum was strictly preserved and a
punctilious etiquette guarded the whole affair. No such scenes
of general license occurred as are described as taking place
at the mourning ceremonies of a chief.

9. Stimson MS. 10. 164–165.
11. 188–189.

The second element brought out in the episodes of the story, that of sorcery, is softened in the rationalized romance. Hi'iaka has obtained from her sister all her powers and is able to compete with her opponents in magic, prophetic vision, and healing power. Peleula is a famous makaula or seer, but Hi'iaka prevails over her. Waihinano, the pert sorceress who defies her on Maui, has been brought up by Kapo and Pua, but Hi'iaka catches and crushes to death the soul of the Maui chief for which they both contend. The kahuna who sends after her to conciliate her she deceives by transformations. She sees through the sorcery of her opponents, like that of the false bridge. She has, besides, power to heal and to restore the spirit to the body. She works through the application of fragrant herbs and through chanting. Here the theme of communal religious dancing is brought out in the nine days during which the whole community take part in a hula ceremonial while Hi'iaka is engaged in chanting prayers to restore the spirit to Lohiau's body.

A character whose part in the hula cycle is not very clear is that of Lohiau's friend Kaleiopaoa. Emerson makes him throughout a faithful friend and one to whom Lohiau's spirit flutters after death to acquaint him with the spot where his body lies and bid him go to Pele, presumably to induce her to restore his body to life. Paoa vows vengeance upon Pele and seeks her at Kilauea, where he finds an old woman surrounded by beautiful girls and pleases her by picking her out from among them by the heat of her hand. He avoids the poisoned food she offers. Pele becomes young and beautiful and the two become lovers. Rice's version, though briefer, tells a similar story but differs in conclusion. Pele gives Hi'iaka to Paoa as his wife and he returns with her to Kauai, but during the marriage feast Lohiau, restored to life, reveals himself at the kilu game and claims Hi'iaka, and Paoa casts himself into the sea for shame. The heiau with stepped platform whose ruins are to be seen at Kee, Haena, on Kauai, and which Emory calls "the famous court of Lohiau," is given by Thrum the name Kilioe and by Dickey that of Ka-ulu-o-Paoa.[12] Paoa is

12. *HAA* 1929, 84–94.

the name of Pele's digging stick with which she makes so
many fruitless (paoa) attempts to dig a pit for her island
home.[13] Emerson calls the paoa "Pele's divining rod."[14] The
name is singularly like that of the Kaleipahoa (Cut with
a stone axe), the famous poison god fashioned from the supernatural trees on Molokai which were entered by the three
Pele sorcerers Kane-i-kaulana-ula, Ka-huila-o-ka-lani, and
Kapo. It is probable that Paoa once occupied a more important place than he holds today in the Pele legend.

The prayers used in the hula dance are seldom addressed to
Pele, but to Laka as patron of the hula and to Kapo in her
character as "Red eel-woman" (Kapo-ula-kina'u) and "Red
Kapo of the myriad gods" (-kini-akua) and Hai(Hina-ai)-
ka-malama. Kapo is said to be the child of Haumea and the
god of the sorcery kahuna, Kua-ha-ilo (To breed maggots in
the back), equivalent to Ku-waha-ilo, and Laka is the child
of Kapo, "not in the ordinary sense but rather as a breath or
emanation." The two are "one in spirit though their names
are two."[15] Laka and Kapo therefore must be thought of as
different forms of the reproductive energy, possibly Kapo in
its passive, Laka in its active form, and their mother Haumea
as the great source of female fertility. In Laka all the goddesses of vegetation reappear. She is invoked at the altar in
the dance house as follows:

> Thou art Laka,
> God of the a'ali'i plant (deep-rooted),
> Laka from the uplands,
> Laka from the lowlands,
> Bring the i-e vine that grows in the wildwood,
> The maile that wreaths the forest,
> Red-beaked kiele flower of the god,
> The joyous rhythm of the dance,
> In honor of Hina-ai-ka-malama,
> The eel-woman,
> Red Kapo the eel-woman,

13. Westervelt, *Volcanoes,* 9–11.
14. *Pele,* xiv, xvi.   15. N. Emerson, "Hula," 47.

Laka art thou,
God of the altar here,
Come back, come back, dwell here at thine altar,
Bring it good luck.[16]

According to Daniel Ho'olapa, the prayer to the goddess Alalalahe is addressed to Laka, goddess of fruitfulness, represented (lines 12–19) as "the woman suspended in air, face upward, tossing this way and that, her limbs outspread, her voice choked. She is the fondled sacred one, the earth left over in the making. Her womb holds multitudes upon multitudes in the uplands and the sea. It is a single family that springs from her womb. She is the impregnated one, the fertilized, from whom descend generations of offspring, the family of Laka, fruitful as the stalk." In other words, Laka or Alalahe (Many-branching one) is the goddess of love, "the shining one" (alohi), the "beloved" (aloha).[17]

Kapo is said to have been born of Papa (or Haumea) while she was living up Kalihi valley on Oahu with Wakea her husband. Some say that she was born from the eyes of Papa. She is of high rank and able to assume many shapes at will.[18]

Poepoe version. Kapo-ula-kina'u, Ka-moho-ali'i, Pele-honua-mea are the three wonderful ones who came from Wakea and Papa. "A very sacred tapu of the gods rests upon her." Birds never sing about her tapu home up Kalihi valley. There at noon when the sun is shining brightly she may be seen on the hillside beyond the upland of Kilohana where stands her tapu stone into which she entered, shaped like a house in front, like a fish's tail behind.[19]

Kapo's power to separate her female sexual organ from her body gives her the name of Kapo-kohe-lele (Kapo with the traveling vagina) called also Kapo-mai-ele.[20]

16. Emerson, "Hula," 42.
17. Kepelino, 182–183; N. Emerson, "Hula," 23–48.
18. Westervelt, *Honolulu,* 29–30.
19. BPBM MS. col. quoted in McAllister, *Bul.* 104: 89.
20. For. Col. 6: 344.

When Kamapua'a attacked Pele near Kalapana, Kapo sent this kohe as a lure and he left Pele and followed the kohe lele as far as Koko Head on Oahu, where it rested upon the hill, leaving an impression to this day on the Makapu'u side. Then she withdrew it and hid it in Kalihi. When the Hawaiians dream of a woman without a vagina it is Kapo. Since Kapo does not like this part of the body, unless a medium possessed by Kapo wears a ti leaf protection she is in danger of having this part of her body torn at.[21]

As goddess of sorcery Kapo is worshiped principally on Maui where she acts as an akua noho or god who possesses the deified dead and gives commands or foretells events through their worshipers. Pua has a similar position on Molokai. These gods have power to bring diseases that can be cured only by placating the god or by appealing to a more powerful sorcery.[22] In the legend of the Kalaipahoa, Kapo is one of the three gods who enter the trees out of which the poison god is carved. In the Hi'iaka romance, she is living at Wailuku on Maui, and she is associated with Puanui in rearing Waihinano, the sorceress who is unable to defend her patron against Hi'iaka, whom she has flouted; possibly to be identified with Waialani, daughter of Kaohelo, whom Pele has offended by giving her berries to eat which are the body of her dead mother.

The myth of the deification of Pele's sister Ka-ohelo tells how the ohelo berries which grow in profusion about the volcano became sacred to Pele and why no one plucks and eats them without first making an offering to her. The story starts with a version of the migration legend.

LEGEND OF KAOHELO

The four sisters Pele, Hi'iaka, Malulani, and Kaohelo are born in Nu'umealani but migrate to Hawaii after the arrival of Aukelenuiaiku. Malulani settles on Lanai, the other three go on to Hawaii. Kaohelo instructs her son Kiha to bury her when she dies "on the navel of your grandmother at Kilauea" and out of her

21. From Mary Pukui.   22. Malo, 155–156.

flesh springs the creeping ohelo, out of her bones the ohelo bush; other parts of her body are thrown to Maui, Oahu, Kauai, and become ohelo bushes on those islands. The head Pele retains as the smoldering fire in the volcano and Kaohelo becomes one of Pele's gods.

Kaohelo's spirit forms a marriage with the spirit of the handsome Heeia on Oahu, who abandons her later for another woman. The little hills about the district of Heeia (the land division adjoining Kaneohe in Koolau) are formed by her from the body of Malulani, who has hanged herself out of grief for her sister. Kaohelo's spirit daughter Waialani comes to visit her relatives on Hawaii and is given some of the berries to eat which are the body of her mother. Blood flows from them as she eats and she vows never to see Pele again on earth.[23]

MYTH OF PU'U-HELE

(a) Pu'u-hele (Traveling hill) is a child born in the form of a bloody foetus to Ka-hina-li'i, mother of Pele and Hi'iaka. The sisters throw it away. The child crosses the channel of Alanui-haha between Hawaii and Maui and lands at Nu'u in Kaupo in the form of a beautiful woman. She passes on without speaking to Nu'u and makes friends with the beautiful Pu'u-o-maiai. Manawai-nui recognizes her and calls her by name. Kanahaha sees her and falls dead and a spring gushes to this day from the hill of that name. Leho-ula follows her as she continues her route along the coast. At Wanana-lua Pu'u-hele vows to remain. When Kai-hua-lele reproves her for trespass' she dies and through her power as a god her spirit body lives on in the form of the hill Kauiki at the seashore. The spirit body of her opposer lives in the form of the hill Kai-hua-kala in the uplands above Kauiki. From the fact that it is generally covered with clouds, this hill is used as a sign of fair weather in the often quoted lines of the chant,

> Fair weather on Maui
> when Kai-hua-kala is clear,
> Kai-hua-kala in the uplands,
> Kauiki beside the sea.

23. For. Col. 5: 576–580.

(*b*) The child Puʻu-hele is brought from Koloa, Kauai, by Lalawalu. She is peevish and bites at her nurse's breasts when a halt comes in the journey, until they reach Hana, where the child is satisfied to be left.[24]

Other stories occur which account for cone-shaped hills or rock islands of Maui as the bodies of members of the Pele family, often such as are transformed through the jealous wrath of the goddess.

MYTHS OF SACRED HILLS

The two hills beyond Maalaea bay on Maui are named Puʻu-hele and Puʻu-o-kali. They are moʻo beings and their first child is a daughter born of Puʻu-o-kali and named Puʻu-o-inaina. She is placed on the sacred island of Kahoolawe, called at that time Kohe-malamalama. She becomes the wife of the two sons of the kahuna of Hua, Kaakakai and Kaanahua, who take the form of birds and retreat to Hana-ula when the great drought comes and there alone rain falls. Puʻu-o-inaina takes Lohiau for her husband while he is living at Maalaea. Pele is angry and cuts her in two in the middle. The tail becomes the hill Puʻu-o-lai at Makena, the head becomes the rock islet of Molokini.[25]

Northwest of Lahainaluna is the hill Puʻu-laina, 647 feet in height. Puʻu-laina is the son of Eeke and Lihau (names of the summit crater of West Maui and the high peak back of Olowalu). These two are husband and wife. Eeke falls in love with Lihau's younger sister Puʻu-wai-o-hina from Kauaula and Lihau is about to kill Puʻu-laina but he is saved by the father. The god Hina-i-ka-uluau places a tapu on the two lovers but they break the tapu and are changed into two mountain ridges. Lihau gives Puʻulaina to Molokini for a husband. One of Pele's younger sisters desires him and when Molokini refuses to give him up she changes Molokini into an islet. Pele in anger transforms both mother and son into hills.[26]

24. For. Col. 5: 544–549; *Ke Alakai o Hawaii,* May 29, July 9, 1930.

25. For. Col. 5: 514–519.   26. *Ibid.* 532–535.

XIII

PELE LEGENDS

LOCAL legends abound of the swift retribution visited by Pele upon those who dare to offend her. Presumption and boasting bring immediate punishment. Rivals in love serve as explanatory theme for lava-rock formations. The popular chiefly sport of sled (holua) racing is worked into a number of legends in which a mere mortal dares competition with Pele. Kapapala, after competing successfully with Pele's pretty sisters, ventures to challenge Pele herself upon the waves of the volcano and is consumed.[1] Papa-lau-ahi is about to win a race to which Pele has challenged him when, looking back over his shoulder, he sees the goddess in her fire form at his back and is overwhelmed in a flood of lava.[2] The most famous of these competition legends is that of Kahawali, localized along a comparatively fresh lava stream running down to the sea from above Kapoho in the district of Puna. Lava rocks are said to mark the fate of members of Kahawali's family and of his favorite pig. The famous tree-molds (Papa-lau-ahi) above Kapoho are introduced as a group of hula pupils caught in the trail of Pele's wrath. For stories of destructive lava flows within historic times in which Pele is believed to have shown her wrath or her favor, see the historic account of the destruction of Keoua's army[3] and of Kamehameha's fishponds.[4]

LEGEND OF THE BOASTER

(a) A man with an eel body named Kani-lolou, who lived upon this group of islands before Pele's arrival, visits Kahiki-lani-nui-akea and boasts of the superior beauty of his own land. On his return he finds Kauai, Maui, and Hawaii overwhelmed with lava

1. Westervelt, *Volcanoes*, 33–34.   2. *Ibid.*, 29–30.
3. Ellis, *Tour*, 186–187; For. Pol. Race 2: 324–326; Kamakau, *Kuokoa*, April 27, 1867; Westervelt, *Volcanoes*, 146–151.
4. *Ibid.*, 146–151; Kamakau, *Kuokoa*, July 13, 20, 1867.

from mountain to sea. It is after this man that eels are called Puhi-kani-lolou.

(b) A man from Puna visits Kauai and boasts of the superior beauty of his own land. The prophet Kane-akalau foresees its ruin and upon the man's return to Puna he finds it overwhelmed with lava.[5]

LEGEND OF PAULA

Paula is a beautiful girl who lives in Ka-u district on Hawaii between Naalehu and Honoapu. Pele's lover once finds her with two companions engaged in her favorite sport of kimo (jackstones) and lingers to play with her. Pele came along looking for her lover, and there at the point called Ka-lae-o-kimo the two may be seen turned to stone just as Pele found them. The other two were also buried in lava, but only the pebbles they tossed are now visible.[6]

LEGEND OF KAHAWALI

The handsome young chief Kahawali lives near Kapoho in Puna district on Hawaii in the days of Kahoukapu the chief. He has a wife and two children named Paupoulu and Kaohe, a mother living at Kuki'i, and a sister Koae at Kula. His father and another sister named Kane-wahine-keaho live on Oahu. Kahawali is an expert in the hula dance and in riding the holua. At the time of the Lono festival, when the hula pupils have gathered for a public appearance, a sled race is arranged with his friend Ahua. Pele in the guise of an old woman offers to compete with him. Angry at the chief's rebuff, she pursues him down the hill in fire form. He flees first to the hill Pu'ukea, then hastens to bid goodby to his wife and children, pauses to say farewell to his favorite pig Aloi-pua'a, and has just time to greet his sister at Kula before escaping to the sea in a canoe which his brother has opportunely brought to land.[7]

5. Remy-Brigham, 36; Westervelt, *Volcanoes,* 31–32; For. Col. 5: 534.

6. Green, 55.

7. *Ibid.,* 3–9. See also Ellis, *Tour,* 219–223; Marcuse, 125–128; Thrum, *Tales* (from Ellis), 39–42; Kalakaua, 501–507; Westervelt, *Volcanoes,* 37–44.

STORY OF THE STINGY GIRL

Pele appears to two girls of Ka-u roasting breadfruit and asks for food and drink. One gives kindly, the other excuses herself on the ground that the food is dedicated to Laka. A flood of fire comes and destroys the home of the stingy girl, but the generous one has been warned and has set up the necessary protection.[8]

Many heiaus to the goddess Pele were erected in old days, especially beside lava streams and at the edge of the crater, and the bodies of the dead are still offered to the goddess in the belief that their spirits will live again with Pele in a beautiful home beneath the burning pit which is the goddess's material body, and go forth as her messengers in bodies of flame to avenge any infringement of her tapus and to work her will in the land. Only those connected with the Pele family by being born with a human body from one of the Pele spirits, or a direct descendant of one of these, or one outside the family who has been adopted and given a name (in dream) by Pele herself, have a right to such a burial. Ancestral gods of the Pele family, called kumu-paʻa (descended from the source), such as Haumea, Kane-hekili, Ka-hoaliʻi, Kane-wa-wahi-lani, Kauila-nui-makeha-i-ka-lani, No-kolo-i-lani, Ka-moho-alii, Polo, Hiʻiaka, Na-maka-o-kahaʻi, may bring their direct descendants into the Pele family. These are kumupaʻa who may be worshiped as aumakua. They do not belong among the supreme gods and their kahunas are not in the line of the old priesthood of Hikapoloa. The worship of Pele was not taught in the schools of the priesthood nor was her body deified. Pele's descendants alone worship her. Only actual relatives invoke her and become her keepers. Pele names are given to children born into her family, but such names belong to that individual alone and cannot be passed on to another, even to an own child. One such Pele name, given to an older sister of Mrs. Pukui, is Kukuena-i-ke-ahi-hoʻomau-honua (Kukuena in the fire which fertilizes the earth). Here "Kukuena" is the name of a sister of Pele who acts as guide

8. Green and Puki, 166–167; related also in North Kona.

to travelers[9] and the word "ho'omau" means literally to dampen or render moist, in allusion to the cool home beneath the volcano to which Pele admits those of her family on earth whose bodies are offered to her at death. An old Kona resident tells the following story:

In old days a man's mother said she was to go to Pele in the volcano. The son took her by the old road around through Kau called Ka-ala-Pele (The Pele road), not by the new road, and left her at a distance along the way and said, "If your god is a true god she will come and take you." As he left he looked back and the fire had flowed out and taken the body. He went back and there was no body to be seen. Napela was the son's name and he lived in Pahala, Kau, in 1881.[10]

The struggle between rival schools of sorcery set up by the Pele worshipers is perhaps worked into the legends which show Hi'iaka fighting the evil mo'o, who are primarily spirits of the damp woodlands and ponds of water; or the legend of Pele's sister Na-maka-o-kaha'i, who may have been originally a water spirit in spite of the fiery nature of her various transformation forms as the story is told today; or in the strife between Pele and the woman of the mountain top, Poliahu, for the fertile land of Hawaii; or in her fight with the amorous hog-man, Kamapua'a, whose gods are the storm signs inimical to fire. The legend of Puna-ai-koae and the demon wife carries the same implication. Of the three recorded versions, the Kamakau version is told to explain the origin of certain fishing customs and leaves the denouement incomplete. The Thrum and Westervelt versions, evidently from an identical source, stress the rivalry between the fire goddess and the water mo'o, whose images are set up in the heiau, one representing Haumea in her human form as Wali-nu'u, the other the goddess Kalamainu'u.

9. N. Emerson, *Pele,* 221 note *k.*

10. Given by Daniel Ho'olapa. See also Ellis, *Tour,* 183–187, 228–231, 262–263; Kamakau, *Ke Au Okoa,* March 31, 1870; Kalakaua, 139–140; Green and Beckwith, *AA* 28: 185–186; For. Col. 5: 572–575; Westervelt, *Volcanoes,* 63.

STORY OF PUNAAIKOAE

(a) *Kamakau version*. The mo'o woman Kalamainu'u lives in a cave at Makaleha in Laie, Waialua district, on Oahu. Going forth one day in search of a husband she finds the young Kauai chief Puna-ai-koae (Puna tropic-bird eater) surfing on the waves of Ka-lehua-weha, lures him to her own board and carries him away to Kaena point, where they land and, ascending the Waianae mountains to Pu'u-ka-pele, descend to the stream of Wailea on the west side of which her cave is still to be seen today. After several months of love making and feasting Puna longs again for surf riding and his wife fetches a board from the corner of the cave but warns him against speaking to anyone while he is away. On his way to the sea two relatives of the mo'o woman, Hinalea and Aikilolo, hail him and warn him of his wife's true nature. They tell him that the board he carries is in reality her mo'o tongue and that unless he can escape he must ultimately perish. He returns secretly to the cave and spies upon his wife in her mo'o form. Because of her nature as a spirit she knows what has happened and prepares to eat him, but since he shows no fear when she shows him her terrible forms, she forgives him and goes forth to slay his informants. They evade her for a time by creeping into a crack of the sea floor. Kuao and Ahilea tell her how to set a trap to catch them. Thus the basket trap for catching hinalea fish came to be invented, and Kalamainu'u is still an aumakua for catching hinalea fish in that vicinity.[11]

(b) *Emerson and Westervelt versions*. Puna is surfing at Waimanalo, Waikiki, when he encounters the mo'o-woman and is lured by her to Molokai and hidden away in her cave home. Her brother Hinale warns him as he is going to join the surfers, and he peeps in and sees his wife feeding on spiders and their webs. He pacifies her wrath and watches his chance to escape to the pit of Pele and put himself under the protection of his former wife's (Walinu'u's) family. He pretends to thirst after the ice-cold waters of Poliahu and gives his wife a gourd to fill which he has secretly punched with holes. During her absence he makes

11. *Ke Au Okoa,* January 6, 1870.

his escape. Kiha-wahine summons the moʻo gods and fills the pit of Pele with their phlegm, but the place sacred to Ka-moho-aliʻi is unharmed and the moʻo gods are many of them consumed with fire and Kiha-wahine is obliged to escape to the pond called Loko-aka (Shadow pond). Ounauna is the fellow who shows her how to make the fish basket to trap Hinale.[12]

The story of the escape from a cannibal wife is widespread throughout Polynesia, often connected with the trick of sending the monster on a fruitless errand (generally after water) in order to gain time for escape. The widespread motives of death by feeding with hot stones or by drawing up to a height on a rope and then cutting the rope, common in southern Polynesia (and throughout Africa), are not found in Hawaii, nor are the tricks, also well known, of substituting a dummy for the body or providing a speaking substitute. These are no doubt later embellishments. On the other hand, there is little doubt that the characteristically Polynesian motive of the woman who has a back which opens and devours all the fish while her family sleep was once a part of Hawaiian stories of a demon wife.[13]

Maori. (*a*) Ruru-teina is on his way home with his wife when he goes to fetch fire and is seized by a reptile-woman named Nga-rara-hu-ora. The rat people tell him that she is not a woman; then, to escape her revenge, they run, one into a stone, the other into the gable of the house. While the demon tries to get at them, Ruru runs away and with the help of his brother succeeds in burning the reptile-woman in a house prepared for the purpose and returns home to his wife.[14]

(*b*) Te-ruahine-mata-maori is a witch who recites incantations for the yam crop. Paowa goes to her house (presumably to learn the incantations). To escape her he sends her for water and by incantations dries up the streams. He burns her house and flees; she pursues swimming and he kills her by pretending

12. Thrum, *More Tales,* 185–196; Westervelt, *Gods and Ghosts,* 152–162.

13. Compare Dixon, 62, 69.   14. White 2: 26–30.

to feed her and pouring hot stones down her throat. From her armpits he recovers "sacred red garments."[15]

(c) Kurangai-tuku catches Hatupatu while he is out after birds. To escape her he sends her for food "at the sixth range" of hills and, when she pursues, takes refuge in a rock and she finally falls into a boiling hot spring and dies.[16]

(d) Houmea is the wife of Uta, whom she leaves to starve while she swallows his whole catch and pretends that fairies have taken it. She swallows her children, but they carry, one a carved staff, the other a barbed spear, and at their father's incantation come out alive. To escape her Uta sends her for water, dries up the springs by incantations so that she may have far to go, and escapes with the boys in the canoe, after directing the various parts of the establishment to answer for him when she calls. She pursues, is fed with fish, and finally with a hot stone which causes her death. The name Houmea is today applied to evil women, adulteresses, and thieves who dwell among men. Tu-ta-wake is her child, with whom come evil and daring.[17]

(e) Tu who dwells in Reiapanga is taken for a husband by a monster woman who comes swimming up to his canoe and is taken on board. He tries to escape but is brought back. Finally his sons come to find him and they succeed in burning her in the house.[18]

(f) Titipa by a trick makes off with Tautini's canoe. Tautini goes to Titipa's settlement and sends Titipa's wives after water, then dries up the springs and makes off with his canoe.[19]

(g) Rate sends Poua-haa-kai for water. By means of incantations he causes the water to recede, then kills Poua by feeding him red-hot stones.[20]

Tahiti. (a) Ro'o-nui, husband of Haumea, leaves her to return to the lower world (Po). Haumea is angry and turns cannibal. When their son Tuture-i-te-a'u-tama (Tuture the child

15. White 2: 55–59.

16. Taylor, 154–157; Grey, 116–118.

17. White 2: 167–172.

18. *JPS* 5: 195–200; 6: 97–106; 29: 136–138. The story is known also by the Moriori in the Chatham islands and in Manihiki.

19. White 2: 158–160.   20. *Ibid.* 3: 3–4.

swum for) eats cooked food, she eats her food raw. To escape her, Tuture sends her to fill water gourds in which he has bored holes, and himself sails away in the ship which he has built at the base of the mountain Viriviri-i-te-rai on the northeast coast of Tahiti. Haumea follows swimming. He kills her by pouring red-hot stones down her throat under pretence of food. Her body comes ashore at Haavai and she lives again as Nona-niho-niho-roa (Nona of the long teeth).[21]

(b) Hono-ura in jest sends his brother for a drink and pierces the water gourd. Three girls laugh at him and he is angry.[22]

Marquesas. (a) Huuti boasts that he will send his arrow into the ear of the mo'o woman at Otua named Te-mo'o-nieve. She conceals the arrow and when he comes to fell a tree for a canoe claims him for her husband. He objects to her food and, pretending to go away to prepare some for himself, returns to his companions and makes fun of her. She discovers his treachery and, throwing his companions into a sleep, brings him back to her cave. When he awakes he is terrified. As a beautiful woman she accompanies him home and bears him three boys and a girl before he dies.[23]

(b) Tuapuu is a demon wife who opens up her back and devours the whole catch of fish. The children discover this and give her eels to eat which kill her. . . . They flee but she comes to life and pursues. They climb a rock, the daughter lets down her hair for the mother to climb up, and when she is almost up they cut the girl's hair and the mother is killed.[24]

Rotuma. A man has a demon wife. He flees from her. She follows, overhears his talk with his first wife arranging a fishing expedition, and carries him away herself in place of the first wife, having roused him at midnight by crowing like a cock.[25]

Malay. A baboon carries a girl away to his home in the tree

21. Leverd, *JPS* 21: 1–3; cf. Henry, 554.
22. *Ibid.,* 526.   23. Handy, *Bul.* 69: 21–25.
24. *Ibid.* 37–45.
25. Romilly, *Letters,* 139–146.

and she has a child. She sends the baboon to fill a bamboo with water and pierces a hole in the bottom, then runs away.[26]

Three other folktales of demon wife or husband have been collected in Hawaii, most of them from the island of Maui, where an excellent story of a pursuing head was early set down by a student at the Lahainaluna school.

STORY OF THE DEMON HEAD

Mahikoa and his brother-in-law Pilikana go up to a place in the woods above Kaana-pali on Maui called Wahikuli to cut battens for a house. The wood catches from the fire they have kindled for warmth in the cave where they sleep. Pilikana awakes and tries to waken his brother-in-law, but Mahikoa is burned up to his head before he awakes. Pilikana flees, the head (po'o) pursues, calling out to him to wait and they will go home together. He runs toward the sea, where a prophet stands ready to help him, and as he falls exhausted the prophet spears the blazing head with splits of bamboo.

The spirit of the husband seeks his wife Keiki-wai-uli, but she, warned by the kahuna, refuses to go out to him or to send the children out. When the spirit enters the house, she slips out with the children and the house is burned to the ground with the demon spirit shut inside.[27]

STORY OF THE DEMON WIFE

(a) *Wahiako version.* Waiolola lives with his wife Kukui-ula at the place where the auto road to Kipahulu now ends. When his wife dies, he buries her by the front door and builds a small structure above her grave, where he goes to mourn for her. One night of the full moon a figure like his wife rises and asks that one of the children be sent to her. He sends the youngest and she devours the child and asks for another. He sends her the oldest and, taking the only remaining child in his arms, he flees, calling upon his sister Manini in chant as he goes. If he can reach the kahuna at the heiau called House-of-Lono (which stands today

26. *RASSB* 46: 65–71.
27. For. Col. 5: 528–533; Thrum, *More Tales,* 242–247.

a heap of ruins seaward of the road that turns down to Hamoa bay) he will be safe. His sister goes out and fights the spirit and he falls upon the threshold of the heiau with the child and is protected by the priest. The Kaupo end of Kipahulu is named Kukui-ula after this demon wife.[28]

(b) *Kekela version.* A man of Kipahulu loses his wife after she has born him five children. Instead of putting her body into a cave (lua-pao) he places her in front of the house. Some years later at night a voice calls to him from without to send out one of the children. He does so and she devours it. This happens each night until he has but one child left. A kahuna from Kauai gives him a couple of dogs to set upon the demon after persuading it into the house. The demon flees, he burns his wife's body, and the spirit never troubles him again.[29]

STORY OF FISHING WITH EYES

(a) *Maui version.* Kokole the husband and Kokole the wife live at the beach near Kipahulu, Maui. The wife sends her husband to the uplands after kukui nuts to string for torch fishing. Each time that she goes after fish she returns unsuccessful and complains that she is "robbed of her fish by the owner of the sea." A seer warns Kokole that his wife is not what she seems. He spies upon her and sees her throw out her eyes as bait. He catches the eyes and threatens to destroy them. She devours one of the children, he flees to the kahuna with the other, and the woman and her eyes are thrown into the fire.[30]

(b) *Oahu version.* At Na-maka-lele (Flying eyes) live Keawe and his wife Keana-haki. He plants in the hills and fishes at the sea. After the sixth child is born the woman's nature changes and she undertakes the business of fishing. Sending out her eyes as bait she makes a big catch, all of which she devours except a single fish with which she returns complaining of ill luck. Warned by a kahuna, Keawe follows and detects her. He catches her eyes and wraps them up in a small bundle and takes them

28. Told by Sheriff Wahiako, June 11, 1930.
29. MS. by Rachel Kekela.
30. MS. by Joseph Kaiwaaea of Kipahulu, 1930.

home with the load of fish. The sixth child sees where he puts the eyes, answers the mother's inquiries, and she can see again.[31]

Samoa. Lauti, jealous of Sina, steals her soul, places it in a basket, and gives it to her elders to keep for her. In the morning Sina is found dead. Her brother overhears Lauti's chant to her elders when she asks for the basket, imitates it and, having thus secured the basket, restores Sina to life. He finds Lauti fishing with her eyes, catches the eyes and puts to death the demon.[32]

Maori. Hatupatu finds an ogress using her lips as a spear to cast at birds. He throws his dart at the same bird she has thus speared, and when he goes to recover it, finds it stuck in her lips. He is handsome and she forgives him and takes him as her husband.[33]

The Hawaiian Kalamainu'u legend has a close variant in the Tahitian story of the cannibal woman Nona, grandmother by her daughter Hina of Hema, father of Kaha'i, and of Pu'a (Puna) who is the Maori Punga, ancestor of the eel family and their kin in the sea. As such it is associated with the Aikanaka-Hina cycle localized in the same district on the island of Maui from which most of the demon-wife folktale versions have been drawn. On the other hand it is connected with the Oahu story of how Haumea in the person of Wali-nu'u (Papa) lived with Makea (Wakea) up Kalihi valley on Oahu and saved him from death by entering into a tree. Puna is identified with Wali-nu'u's lover, and the two kupua women, Kalamainu'u and Haumea, are shown as rivals in love. They fight with their kupua bodies, fire and water, but their human bodies also enter into the scrap, as, according to Thrum, their images are represented in the heiau, Walinu'u with a broken nose and Kalamainu'u with blinded eyes. The wrappings of yellow tapa seem to indicate that they belong to the Kane worship.

31. McAllister, *Bul.* 104: 94–95.   32. Krämer 1: 136–139.
33. Grey, 116–118.

XIV

KAMAPUA'A

ONE of the most popular figures in Hawaiian mythical narrative is the being, half man and half hog, who goes by the name of Kama-pua'a (Hog-child). Tradition relates the immigration to the group of the Kamapua'a family during the colonizing period. An extended and racy account of his adventures as a kupua on these islands or in Kahiki appears in one of the fictitious narratives (kaao) collected from Fornander informants. Local legends and nursery tales further embellish his story. As wooer of Pele he is drawn into the Pele cycle and, according to Kamakau, the child of Pele by Kamapua'a becomes an "ancestor of chiefs and commoners" on these islands. In the genealogical chant of the Kumulipo there occurs, during the fifth period of the po, the birth of a being half hog, half god, of whom the chant says:

> His snout was of great size and with it (he) dug the earth,
> He dug until he raised a great mound,
> He raised a hill for his gods,
> A hill, a precipice in front,
> For the offspring of a pig that was born.[1]

The "mound" raised by the pig-god may perhaps be understood to refer to a powerful family of descendants.

The colonizing tradition represents Kamapua'a as the grandson of the sorceress Kamaunua-niho (Ka-mau-nui) and connects the family first with the island of Maui, then with Oahu and Kauai, and finally extends the adventures of the hog-man to Hawaii and Kahiki, from which land the family originally migrated.

1. Liliuokalani, 25.

LEGEND OF THE KAMAPUA'A FAMILY

The chiefess Ka-maunu-a-niho comes from Kahiki with her husband Humu (Aumu) and the chief Kalana-nu'u-nui-kua-mamao. They land at Kalahawai in Waihe'e on Maui and live in the uplands of Waihe'e, where Kamaunu takes Kalana for her husband and Humu retires to Kahiki. Her daughter Hina becomes the wife of Olopana, chief of the northern district of Oahu, and has a son who is named Kahiki-honua-kele (Kahiki the land that moved off) because of the family affiliation with Kahiki. Hina then takes Olopana's younger brother Kahiki-ula, chief of Kauai, as her husband and has two sons, named Kele-keleiaku(aiku?) and Kamapua'a.[2]

As a kupua, Kamapua'a is under the special protection of ancestral gods and himself godlike. As a man he is tall and handsome; "the big foreigner with sparkling eyes" (ka haole nui, maka olohilohi) he is called in chant.[3] Some say that he has bristles down his back which he conceals under a cape. He is able to change himself not only into a hog but also into fishes and plants of various kinds. He is said to have escaped Pele's fire by changing himself into the tough-skinned little fish known as the humuhumu-nukunuku-a-pua'a and when a pig is not available at a time of sacrifice this fish or some other of the hog-man's forms may be substituted, such as the coarse grass (panicum pruriens) called kukae-pua'a (pig excrement), patches of which mark his wanderings over the islands. His plant bodies are enumerated in one of his name chants, and the story is that he overcomes Lono-of-the-eight-fore-heads-of-stone by tangling each forehead (lae) in wild growth and the dog-man Ku-ilio-loa by stuffing himself in his weed bodies down the dog's throat and then cutting his way out. In these transformation fictions it is worth noting that the shape-shifting power to change into any given form also implies a duplication of such forms; he may himself take the form of a hog, but at his prayer the place is filled with hogs

2. Kamakau, *Ke Au Okoa*, March 31, 1870, quoted in For. Pol. Race 2: 43–44.

3. For. Col. 6: 335.

sent to his succor. He was occasionally worshiped as a god, if the report is correct that at Wainiha, Kauai, was a small paved heiau which had Kamapua'a for its deity.[4]

The fictitious narrative of Kamapua'a (Pua-pua'a) is said to have taken sixteen hours in the recital.[5] Most Hawaiians declare that he was born in Kahiki, but Westervelt tells of his birth on Oahu.

Kama-pua'a is born as a foetus at Kalua-nui on the northern coast of Oahu. His older brother Kahiki-honua-kele tries to throw him away, but when his mother comes out of her bath of purification she finds him lying on her skirt in the form of a baby pig. The brother therefore takes the pig to his grandmother and Kamaunu recognizes her kupua grandson and rears him until he is grown.[6]

The adventures of the hog-man thus born to Hina include, first, his strife with his stepfather Olopana on Oahu; second, strifes on Kauai, first with its chief Makali'i and his own father who is ruling under Makali'i, next with a rival chief in behalf of his father-in-law who has bestowed wives upon himself and his friend; third, strife in Kahiki with Lono-of-the-eight-foreheads-of-stone and his dog Ku-ilio-loa; fourth, strife as the wooer of Pele on Hawaii and Maui.

LEGEND OF KAMAPUA'A

Kamapua'a and Olopana. Kamapua'a grows up strong and rough and is unpopular with his stepfather Olopana, ruling chief of Koolau at Kailua. Kamapua'a lives in Kaliu-wa'a valley (Leaky canoe) and is led on by the supernatural fowl Kawauhele-moa to rob Olopana's hen roost and commit other depredations. Four times the guards, eight hundred strong and each time increasing in number, capture him in his hog shape and tie him to a pole; four times his grandmother releases him with a chant. Finally all his captors are slain except Makali'i, who escapes to bring the report. The whole district is aroused.

4. *HAA* 1907, 43.
5. J. Emerson, *HHS Papers* 2: 13–14.
6. *Honolulu,* 249–250.

Kamapuaʻa stretches his body as a bridge up which his household escape out of the valley and he retreats to Wahiawa and
engages in farming. Olopana consults a new prophet from Kauai
and learns how Kamapuaʻa may be rendered weak. Lonoaohi,
the old prophet whom Olopana has disgraced for failure to capture Kamapuaʻa, takes up the cause of the hog-man and when
he is brought bound to the heiau for sacrifice, instructs his sons
Black-hog and Spotted-hog to make a mere pretence of tying
him. In the morning when Olopana and his men come for the
sacrifice, Kamapuaʻa springs up and kills the chief and all the
men except Makaliʻi.[7]

Kamapuaʻa on Kauai. (*a*) Kamapuaʻa repairs to Kauai
where Makaliʻi the ruling chief over the greater part of the
island is fighting Kane-iki. With Lima-loa he courts Kane-iki's
pretty daughters and takes up his father-in-law's cause against
his uncle. With his war club Kahiki-kolo he kills the champions
and wards off the spears thrown against him. Makaliʻi hides between the knees of Kamaunuaniho and pacifies his nephew by
reciting all the land's name chants, which the love god Lono-iki-
aweawe-aloha teaches him out of compassion. Kamapuaʻa allows
him his choice of a place of banishment and he chooses to retreat to the mountains. Then come his father Kahiki-ula and his
brother Kahiki-honua-kele to do battle. Questioned by Kamapuaʻa, the father asserts that he has no other son, and the
brother replies that both his brothers are dead; "one Pele slew
and the other hung himself." At Hina's approach Kamapuaʻa
withdraws lest he slay his mother. Later he pays a visit to his
parents at Kalalau and is so angry when they do not recognize
him that only by chanting all his name songs and, as a last resort, by exposing herself naked can his mother pacify him. He
finally goes away to Kahiki with Kowea.

(*b*) Kamapuaʻa swims in fish form to Kipukai on the southeast coast of Kauai. Changing into a huge hog he roots up the
growing crops. The bristles down his back which reveal, when in
human form, his hog nature, he hides with a cape. While he is
sleeping in hog form in the spring called today Wai-a-ka-puaʻa,

7. For. Col. 5: 314–327; Westervelt, *Honolulu,* 250–257; Kalakaua, 142–147.

Lima-loa rolls a stone down to crush him, but he reaches out and throws a stone which wedges the rock on the hillside. He and Lima-loa become friends and he helps Lima-loa to court the two lovely sisters of the ruling chief of the Puna side of Kauai from Kipukai to Anahola, whom the friends find combing their hair at the two rock basins called Ka-wai-o-ka-pakilokilo (The water of the reflected image) which they are using as looking glasses. After taking the girls as his wives, he fights for their brother against the Kona side of the island from Koloa to Mana. In hog form, with the hands of a man to wield the club, he kills the Kona chiefs in battle and takes their feather capes and helmets, which he hides under his bed. Only through a spear wound which he has received in his hand is he discovered to the Puna chief as the one who has kept for himself the chief's own share of the booty. For this act Kamapua'a is banished.[8]

Kamapua'a and Lono-ka-eho. Kamapua'a flees from Kauai and goes away to Kahiki, where rival chiefs, Lonokaeho and Kowea, are at war. Kowea gives Kamapua'a his daughters as wives in order to win his championship. Kamapua'a calls upon his plant bodies to entangle the eight stone foreheads of Lono-kaeho as they strike down upon him, and when he has killed his foe he calls upon his hog bodies to "eat up" Lono and all his men. He then meets the dog-man Ku-ilio-loa and, stuffing his weed bodies into the warrior's open jaws, kills him from within.[9]

Kamapua'a and Pele. Kamapua'a comes to the crater of Halema'uma'u (Fern house) and, appearing upon the point sacred to Pele, woos the goddess in the form of a handsome man. Her sisters attract her attention to him. She refuses him with insult, calling him "a pig and the son of a pig." His love songs change to taunts and the two engage in a contest of insulting words. He attempts to approach her, but she sends her flames over him. Each summons his gods. Pele's brothers encompass him "above and below" and would have smothered him had not his love-making god lured them away at sight of a woman.

8. For. Col. 5: 342–363; Rice, 51–53; Westervelt, *Honolulu,* 261–267.

9. For. Col. 5: 326–333.

Kamapua'a threatens to put out the fires of the pit with del-
uges of water, but Pele's uncles, brothers, and the fire tender
Lono-makua keep them burning and again the hog-man's life is
in danger. His sister, chiefess of Makahanaloa, comes to his aid
with fog and rain. Hogs run all over the place. The pit fills with
water. The love-making god sees that if Pele is destroyed Kamapua'a will be the loser. The fires are all out, only the fire sticks
remain. These the god saves, Pele yields, and Kamapua'a has
his way with her. They divide the districts between them, Pele
taking Puna, Ka-u, and Kona (districts periodically overrun
with lava flows) and Kamapua'a ruling Kohala, Hamakua, Hilo
(the windward districts, always moist with rain).[10]

The two have a child named Opelu-nui-kauhaalilo who becomes ancestor of chiefs and commoners on Hawaii (Kamakau).

Kamapua'a leaves Hawaii and draws up a new home from the
ocean depths where he establishes a family. Pele, who now loves
him, tries in vain to draw him back with a love chant (Westervelt).

According to Kalakaua, the Pele myth is built up out of
an actual occurrence, in which a family of immigrants take
refuge in a mountain cavern from the unwelcome advances
of the hog-man and are overwhelmed by a stream of fiery lava
which pursues the attacking party down the mountain. The
supposition is that the flames from the burning lava are the
transformed bodies of the submerged family, who live today
in the volcano and manifest themselves in its activities. It is,
however, more than probable that the story is a rationalized
invention influenced by the popular aumakua conceptions of
Kalakaua's period.

Kalakaua version. About 1175, while the usurper Kam(a)iole
is ruling the island of Hawaii, a family of chiefs and priests
from a southern group, led by a kahuna named Moho, land at
Honoapu on the Ka-u coast and, proceeding along the coast to
Puna, settle in the foothills back of Keauhou. With Moho come

10. For. Col. 5: 332–343; Westervelt, *Honolulu,* 267–276; *Volcanoes,* 45–54; N. Emerson, "Hula," 228–232; Kalakaua, 147–154;
Kamakau, *Ke Au Okoa,* March 31, 1870; Ellis, *Tour,* 186.

his sisters Pele and Ulolu and his humpbacked brother Kamakaua. Kamapua'a has fled to Hawaii from Oahu and, hearing of
Pele's beauty, he comes to court her. She refuses him with insult, calling him "a pig and the son of a pig." He and his followers raid the settlement and kill all but the immediate family,
who take refuge in an underground cavern in a cleft of the
mountain. Kamapua'a's band push on, when there suddenly
bursts forth a stream of lava, submerging the cavern and driving the besieging party to take refuge in the sea.[11]

Other Pele connections occur in the Kamapua'a legend.
The same land from which Kamaunu and her brothers migrate is that which Aukele visits to seek Namakaokaha'i, older
sister of Pele, and it is at least plausible to conclude that Aukelenuiaiku is to be identified with the brother Kelekeleiaku
and possibly Kamapua'a with Namaka's brother Kane-apua
of that romance. The names of three sisters said to have been
born to Hina, the mother of Kamapua'a, are listed in chant
among the plant gods of the hog-man and two of them, Hau-
nu'u and Hau-lani, are names of wives of Haumea's grandsons for whom she made herself young again to take them as
husbands.[12] The Kamaunu and Pele families are represented
in myth as hostile, although in some way related. Malaehaa-
koa (or hoa), called the kahu of Hi'iaka, who recites to her
the hymn chanting the deeds and mysteries of Pele since the
beginning of her rule, a hymn which also names Niheu-the-
mischievous and Nuakea wife of Keoloewa of Molokai, is the
same who tells Olopana how to get control of Kamapua'a
by offering as a sacrifice objects in which the letters l-a-u occur. If Kamapua'a is equivalent to Kane-pua'a (Kane-
apua), who is worshiped as a god of agriculture to bring rain
and abundance to the crops, he would be, like her older sister
Namakaokaha'i, naturally pitted against Pele the fire-god-
dess and consumer of vegetation.[13]

The device of using springing plants to entangle a con-

11. 140–142, 148–154; For. Pol. Race 2: 44–45.
12. Kamakau, *Kuokoa,* January 12, 1867.
13. N. Emerson, *Pele,* 109–131; For. Col. 6: 492–499; 5: 322;
Pol. Race 1: 163.

testant or effect an escape is common in kupua stories. Hi'-
iaka uses it to overcome an evil mo'o; Kaulana-poki'i when
she avenges the murder of her brothers; Makani-keoe to protect his protégé; Kauakahi's sister to obstruct the path of
her brother's sweetheart or, as in the Green version, to hide
him away in a tree. Most famous of all such tree conceal-
ments is that of Haumea when she enters a tree with her husband in order to save him from his captors. In the Marquesas,
Ono-the-resurrected enters a temanu tree as a god and lives
on air.[14] In New Zealand, Tu-te-koro-pango conjures up
plants to obstruct the path to his home.[15]

The Olopana at Kailua on Oahu who is Kamapua'a's "uncle" is not to be confused with Moikeha's brother Olopana,
although it is impossible not to suspect a confusion between
Hina's desertion of her older husband for his younger brother
and Lu'ukia's of Olopana for Moikeha. Nor is the Lonokaeho
with the foreheads of stone generally identified with the chief
of the same name at Kahiki whom Paao calls upon to come
and rule Hawaii. The coupling with his name of the great
dog Ku-ilio-loa justifies a connection with the Lono-ka-ehu
(Lono the blond) who comes to the group from Kahiki with
his great dog of that name in search of his brother. Hawaiians called "ehu," with lighter skin, brown eyes, and curly
brown hair in contrast to the darker-skinned Hawaiians with
straight black hair, are associated in native belief with the
Pele family. Outlying villages show a number of such brown-
haired persons, said to be of pure native stock.

Fiction, however, plays with these names for its own purposes and it would be unsafe to draw any historical conclu-
sions from the use made by story tellers of such local associations. In Thrum's Kana legend Lonokaeho is the fourth man
of fame to whom Hakalanileo of Hawaii appeals in vain for
help to regain his wife.[16] He is represented as the wooer of
Maui's mother Hina in her cave on the Wailuku river in Hilo,
Hawaii, while Maui is away snaring the sun. The rock (eho)
into which he was changed still stands to attest the truth of
the story.

14. Handy, *Bul.* 69: 104–109.   15. White 1: 42.
16. *Tales,* 66.

The attack upon Lonokaeho in Kahiki is transferred in the Kaulu legend to Kailua, and that upon his companion to Kualoa on Oahu, the district from which comes Lonokaeho's daughter, who marries La'a-mai-kahiki in the Moikeha tradition and becomes mother of La'a's son Lauli-a-La'a. The "foreheads" of stone of Lonokaeho are alluded to in chant:

> He mau lani pohaku na Lonokaeho,
> No lani ka lae i ponia i ka wai niu,
> I haua i ka pua'a hiwa a Kane,
> I ka pua'a hiwa, puawa hiwa a Lono.

"Lono-ka-eho had foreheads of stone,
  Lono's was a forehead annointed with coconut milk
  [i.e., Lono belonged to the highest class of chiefs],
He was worshiped [?] with the black pig of Kane,
The black pig, the bundle of black awa of Lono."[17]

The "foreheads" perhaps refer to eight lines of chiefs from whom the heavenly one (lani) counts descent. Pio-ke-anuenue (Curve of the rainbow) he is elsewhere called in allusion to the pio rank to which he is born.

The "eight foreheads of stone" have interesting connections with the south. For central Polynesia and westward the number eight has special significance in sacred matters. In the Tahitian group, Ra'iatea has eight stones set up at the national marae to represent eight kings who have ruled in the past and the names of these kings are given to the eight sacred symbols of investiture of royal chiefs at Taputapuatea.[18] Borabora (called Vavau) and "first-born" after Ra'iatea is divided into eight districts.[19] Mo'orea (called Aimo'o) is so divided into eight arms by the natural ridges of the mountains as to carry the name of "the octopus" (fee).[20] The god Maui is called "Maui of the eight heads."[21] Eight directions of the cardinal points are known to mariners.[22] In the Tua-

17. For. Col. 6: 485.
18. Henry, 120, 193; *JPS* 21: 77.
19. Henry, 102.   20. *Ibid.*, 89.
21. *Ibid.*, 558.   22. *Ibid.*, 460.

motu group eight islands west of Fakarava (Havaiʻi) represent independent chieftainships.[23] In Samoa the heavens where the gods dwell are "eight-fold."[24] An eight-spiked club is described by Buck.[25] Moso-a-le-alofi slays the Tagaloa-of-the-eight-livers.[26] Eight is a sacred number in Fiji. A Fijian giant, Thanga-walu, came into the world two months after conception and rapidly grew to a height of sixty feet with a forehead "eight spans high." Another giant deity has eight eyes, another eight arms.[27] In Tonga, Alai-aloo (Eight foreheads) is a god frequently consulted for the cure of the sick;[28] the number eight is a favorite to associate with mounds;[29] Lolo-ma-tokelau's compound has a fence of eight cross-pieces.[30] On Easter island immigrants from Mangareva have made eight enclosures.[31]

On San Cristoval the number eight "seems to be connected with magical powers." In the story of the snake spirit named "Eight fathoms," when the snake is killed she comes to life again after "eight days" of rain. She makes her house of "eight leaves." She is cut into "eight pieces" and comes to life after "eight showers of rain." She submerges a village with "eight waves," a feat also performed by the hero Rapuanante.[32] To work magic a woman takes eight each of dracena leaves, coconuts, and dog's teeth.[33] There is a story of "eight dwarves." In Japan the princess bestows eight treasures, called "eight deities of Idzushi."[34] In Hawaii a sorcerer's prayer addressed to Kane and other gods begins, "To you who are the breath of the eighth night."[35] A famous Maui chief is named Child-of-eight-branches (Kama-lala-walu).

Some connect Kama-puaʻa with the god Lono, and Lono names certainly occur in his story. He wars with Kowea

23. Henry, 111–112. 24. Krämer 1: 22.
25. *Bul.* 75: 592–593.
26. Fraser, *RSNSW* 26: 279; Turner, 250.
27. Williams, 218. 28. Mariner 2: 107.
29. McKern, *Bul.* 60: 17. 30. Collocott, *FL* 46: 18.
31. Henry, 118. 32. Fox, 93.
33. *Ibid.,* 170. 34. Chamberlain, 261.
35. Rice, 23.

(Koea) against Lono-ka-eho in Kahiki. His foster father's priest Lono-aohi, whose sons are named Black-hog and Spotted-hog, becomes his ally. Lono-iki-aweawe-aloha is his love-making god. Signs and prophecies in the clouds are alluded to in his chants. A name chant runs:

> He miki he miki
> A i hanau mai oe, e Hina,
> Ka maka o ka pua'a,
> E lele ana i ke lani,
> E lele ana i ke kuahiwi,
> Ewalu maka o ke keiki pua'a a Hina,
> Na Hina oe,
> Na Kahikiula,
> Na Kahikilei,
> O Lonoiki oe,
> O Lononui oe,
> O kuu maka, o kuu aloha, e Lono e,
> Haina a moe i kuahu a Olopana;
> A ko kakou ali'i,
> Kou inoa, e o mai.

"Take care, take care,
  When you give birth, Hina,
  The eyes of the hog
  They glance to the heavens,
  And glance to the mountain,
  The son of Hina is a hog with eight eyes,
  By Hina art thou,
  By Kahikiula,
  By Kahikilei,
  Thou art little Lono,
  Thou art great Lono,
  My eye, my love, O Lono!
  Follow until thou liest on the altar of Olopana,
  The altar of our chief,
  This is your name, make answer."[36]

36. For. Col. 5: 314–317.

Although tradition sometimes lays the scene of Kama-pua‘a's birth in Kahiki, to which place his father's name Ka-hiki-ula is said to belong, and legends of his exploits in the Hawaiian group are told also of Kahiki, and he is said not to have died in Hawaii but to have retired to Kahiki and married a chiefess there, nevertheless local legends abound all over Hawaii which connect his name with various places now held sacred because of their connection with the hog-child. The valley of Kaliu-wa‘a (The leaky canoe) which cuts into the Koolau range of Oahu must be approached with reverence. Leaf offerings are made at the entrance to the valley; women at their monthly periods must wear a protection of ti leaves about their necks. Near the head of the valley a smooth furrow worn by water falling over the cliff is explained as the groove cut when he made a ladder of his virile member for his followers to escape their pursuers. A small hollow in a rock near the entrance to the valley is the place where he hid, and an upright slab on the cliff above is the transformed body of the man who pointed out his hiding place to his enemies.[37]

Most local stories, however, concern themselves with his amorous adventures. At Kamoiliili he sees two pretty women and pursues them. They are goddesses and disappear in the earth. When he digs for them, two springs of water burst forth known as the "springs of Kamapua‘a."[38]

Other women whom he pursues turn into springs, their male defenders into stone, and gashes in the earth are made by his snout. At a place near the coast in Puna called Lua-o-Pele, where the earth is torn up as if there had been a struggle, he is said to have overtaken the reluctant Pele and forced the fire goddess to submit to his embraces. They say that this is why today the sacred lehua trees "grow right down to the shore at this place alone." Pele's sister Kapo, aware of Pele's peril, sends her own wandering vagina (kohe-lele) to light upon a tree and attract Kamapua‘a from her sister. He follows it to Oahu, where its impression may be seen today on

37. Westervelt, *Honolulu*, 251–254; Thrum, *Tales*, 193–199.
38. Westervelt, *Honolulu*, 259–260.

the Makapu‘u side of Koko head where it rested before Kapo withdrew it and hid it in Kalihi valley. A Maui legend tells how, when Kapo is living at Wailua-iki with her husband Kuo‘u, Kamapua‘a comes to that island in his fish form and sees a rainbow resting over Kapo's house. Her husband is out fishing and she is beating tapa when the handsome stranger enters. Two men on the cliff signal to her husband and he comes running and gives Kamapua‘a a whack with his paddle. The kupua sends the husband flying over the cliff, called to-day Kuo‘u, and he falls in the shape of a huge stone pointed out today by the roadside. The gap between Wailua and Wailua-iki through which today runs a steep trail, still traveled by the mailman to the valley, was torn out at the time of this struggle. Kapo's house may also be seen and the mark of her vagina against the cliff. Similar stories of Kamapua‘a's attack upon Pele are among the popular stories told in this vicinity. In the pursuit Kamapua‘a loses his hair at a point called Huluhulu-nui (Many bristles), runs against the cliff at Pua‘a-ho‘oku‘i, and finally overcomes Pele at the hill called Ka-iwi-o-Pele (The bones of Pele). Such episodes are related with a keen relish for particular detail and rhythmical repetition, punning on place names and etiological references playing a determining part in the story.

XV

HINA MYTHS

HINA-HANAIA-I-KA-MALAMA (The woman who worked in the moon), said by Kilinahi Kaleo to be Pele's name as a woman on earth, identifies the Hawaiian goddess with the Tahitian who beats out tapa in the moon; Hina-papa'i-kua she is called in Hawaiian nomenclature. The home of Pele in this incarnation is at Kauiki on Maui where, as wife of Aikanaka on the Ulu line, she becomes weary of tapu restrictions and escapes to the moon. In a second even more mythical legend, she is lured up by a chief of Hawaii from a land underseas and from her calabash of food the moon and stars reach the skies.

MYTH OF HINAHANAIAIKAMALAMA

(a) *Fornander version.* Hina-ai-malama (Hina feeding on the moon) is the grandchild of Kai-uli and Kai-kea (Dark and Light sea) and child of Hina-luai-koa (-vomiting coral) and her younger brother Ku-kea-pua. The parents live under the sea in Kahiki-honua-kele and can take the form of pao'o fishes. They have ten children, Hina-a-ke-ahi, Hina-palehoana, Hina-luaimoa, Iheihe (in the form of a cock), Moahalehaku, Ki'ima-luhaku, Kanikawa (in the form of a hen), Lua-ehu, a boy in the form of an ulua fish, and two children who have human form, Hina-ai-malama and her younger brother Kipapa-lau-ulu. To Kipapa is entrusted the care of his beautiful sister. He neglects his charge and is banished, but his grandfather makes a crack in the ocean through which he crawls to the place above (Kawa-luna), leaving to his sister the calabash Kipapa-lau-ulu containing the moon and stars for her vegetable and fish food, and takes service with the chief Konikonia. So kindly is he treated that he returns after his sister and she becomes the chief's wife. The two have ten children, five girls and five boys, one of whom is banished for sacrilege and travels to Kaupo on Maui where he dies, and from his dead body springs the wauke plant for making bark cloth. His five sisters, coming in search of him, travel to Oahu where they wed chiefs and turn into the noted fishponds of that island stocked each with its special kind of fish. Kane-au-kai, another brother, comes floating after his sisters over the sea in the form of a rock (pumice?) and is taken for a god by two fishermen on the Waialua coast of Oahu.[1]

(b) *Malo and Fornander version.* The woman of Lalo-hana (or Wahine-i-mehani) is the daughter of Ka-hina-li'i and Hina-ka-alualu-moana (Hina who followed on the ocean). She lives in a country underseas outside of Waiakea, Hilo, Hawaii, where Konikonia is ruling chief (or outside Keauhou, Kona, where Lono is chief). The chief is bothered by always losing the bait and hook from his line when he goes fishing and Ku-ula, the brother of the underseas woman, who is in the service of the chief, tells him that it is his sister who has broken the chief's hooks. Konikonia orders him to fetch his sister to him. Ku-ula explains that he must set up images (ki'i) of her absent husband Ki'imaluahaku, tying them a fathom apart to a line beginning inside the chief's house and extending from boat to boat in the sea, and finally letting the end of the line drop down in front of the girl's house. She will believe that her husband has returned from Kahiki and will follow the images into the chief's house. The trick is successful; the girl lies down to sleep in the chief's house and is taken by the chief. After four days she sends for her food calabash (or coconut gourd) but its contents fly up to heaven in the form of the crescent moon, the bright part called kena, the dim part ana. Her brothers come in search of her, borne by their parents upon a wave of the sea, which mounts to the mountaintops and drowns all but the chief, his wife, and his family (ohana), who have escaped to the highest peak. This is the flood of Ka-hina-li'i. When the waters subside the chief returns to his own land.[2]

The two famous chants of the Kuali'i and the Kumulipo contain allusions to this fishing story. In the Kuali'i chant, Maui is represented as fishing with the hook Manai-ka-lani,

1. Col. 5: 266–273.
2. Malo, 307–310; For. Col. 6: 318.

baited with the red feathers of the mud hen (alae bird) to
draw together the "table of Laka," the "vast unbroken bottom of the sea." The scene is laid at Kauiki on East Maui,
home of the chiefs Kaiuli and Kaikea. The chief of the island
of Hawaii is supposed to be the fish for whom the hook is
baited.

(c) *Kuali'i version.*

> Kauiki bound to the mainland and towering high,
> Hina-ai-ka-malama (lived there),
> The alae (mud hen) of Hina was the bait
> (Of the fishhook) let down to Hawaii,
> Tangled with the bait into a bitter death,
> Lifting up the very base of the island,
> Drawing it up to the surface of the sea.
> Hidden by Hina were the wings of the alae,
> But broken was the table of Laka
> And the hook carried far down to Kea,
> The fish seized the bait—the fat large ulua,
> Luaehu, offspring of Pimoe. . . .

"Hina lived in the sea and spoilt the bait—the *alae*—so that
the islands were not drawn together as Maui wished," explains Lyons. The god of the land to be drawn up, called Kea
in the chant, is, Lyons thinks, Lono-nui-akea, and the "ulua
fish" is the chief Luaehu.[3]

A second reference to the same misadventure occurs in a
Kauai Maui story.

(d) If Maui can hook the fish Luehu on the night of Lono, he
can draw the islands together. The nine alae birds who have the
secret of fire warn the fish Luehu when the brothers are approaching. Hina teaches Maui how to trick the birds with an
image and himself hide and catch the youngest mud hen. The
place is shown near Holoholoku where the trick was carried out.
Maui now hooks the Luehu fish and the islands would have been
drawn together had he not, contrary to his mother's warning,
taken into his canoe a harmless-looking gourd bailer out of

3. *JPS* 2: 160.

which emerges a beautiful woman who seats herself behind the
paddlers. The crowd on shore shout their admiration of her
beauty, the brothers turn to look, and the islands drop away.[4]

The Kumulipo reference occurs in the latter part of the
fourteenth era, just before the enumeration of Maui's adventures and after the birth of Pau-pani-akea, "who is no other
than Wakea," and the hanging of the stars in the heavens.

(e) *Kumulipo version.*

Strewn are the seeds, the very small seeds in the heavens,
Strewn are the seeds of the gods, the sun is a god,
Strewn the seeds of Hina, who is the same as Lono-muku,
The food of Hina-hana-i-ka-malama, of Waka,
Found by Wakea in the deep ocean,
Among the sea coral, in the rough sea,
Hina-hana-i-ka-malama floated as a bailer,
Was taken into the canoe, hence called "Hina the bailer" (Hina-
    ke-ka),
Carried to the shore and put by the fire,
Coral insects were born, the eel was born,
The sea-urchin was born, the sea-egg was born,
The blackstone was born, the volcanic stone was born,
Hence she was called "Hina from whose womb came various
    forms" (Hina-opuhala-koa).[5]

The chant as it proceeds to the story of the "images" is variously rendered by Hawaiian translators.

(a) *Liliuokalani translation.*

Hina wanted food and Wakea provided,
Set his gods up and well bolstered,
Set them nicely in a row;
Then went after Hina-kaweoa to be his wife.
A fowl was born and clung to Wakea's back.
'Twas a stain, this fowl that grew on the back of Wakea,

4. Dickey, *HHS Reports* 25: 16–18.
5. Kalakaua, 61.

Wakea grew angry and tried to brush it off;
Wakea, provoked and annoyed,
Shook it off and it lit on the roof.
That fowl on the roof,
That fowl was a chief,
That came from the seed of Kaeoeo,
That climbs in space.
The heavens did swing,
The earth does swing
In the starry space.[6]

(*a'*) *Ho'olapa translation* (unpublished).

Hina wanted food. Wakea went to fetch it,
Set up images, propped them up,
Set them up proudly in a row,
Wakea in the form of Ki'i slept with "Hina the reddened one"
    (Hina-kaweoa),
A moa bird was born, perched on Wakea's back,
The moa scratched the back of Wakea,
Wakea was angry, tried to drive it away,
Wakea was angry, wrathful and troubled,
Tried to keep it off and it flew to the ridgepole,
The moa was a chief,
This was the seed of Kaeoeo (Kaweoa?)
Which spread over the sky,
All over the heavens,
All over the earth,
Yes, over the earth.

(*a''*) *Robinson translation* (unpublished).

Built up an image and set it on a foundation,
Built up images in a line,
Wakea seized and slept with Hinakaweoa,
The cock rested on the back of Wakea,
The cock scratched the back of Wakea,
Wakea was jealous, began to shrug his back,

6. 79.

Wakea was jealous, vexed and angry,
Banished the cock and it flew to the housetop,
The cock was on the housetop,
The cock was lord,
This was the seed of Kaeoeo
Begotten in the heavens,
The heavens shook,
The earth shook,
Even to the sacred places.

The various Hinas in this story are not very clearly differentiated. Thrum says that Hina-kawe(o)a is the mother of the Maui family and hence the same as Hina-nui-a-(ka)-lana (Hinanu), who is named as the mother of the priestly island Molokai, whom Wakea took to wife after Papa (Haumea) had left him in anger, and from whom the island is called Molokai-of-Hina.[7] Elsewhere she is called Hina-lau-ae,[8] whose sacred cave on Molokai dividing Mapulehu from Kaluaaha is called the root (kumu) of the island and is to be approached with reverence.

Hina-opuhala-koa is goddess of the corals and spiny creatures of the sea and appears sometimes as a woman, sometimes as a coral reef. According to Pukui, it is from a shell from her reef that Maui makes his famous fishhook to draw together the islands. In the Hilo folktale of Hina-i-ke-ahi she comes out of the sea with Hina after the purification by bathing of the goddess of fire.[9]

Hina-ke-ka (Hina the bailer), who floats up in the form of a gourd and is taken into Wakea's canoe, is here equated with Waka. In the Westervelt version of the Hainakolo romance, Waka is sent by the sorceress daughter of Pi'imoi, Hina-kekai, in the form of a great eel to prevent Lono-kai's approach to Kuaihelani. When the eel is drawn into the canoe and the head cut open there steps out a beautiful woman who attempts his seduction.[10] In the Kauai Maui legend the girl in the bailer is a sister of Maui's mother Hina.

As for the food calabash of Hina-i-ka-malama out of which

7. *More Tales*, 199.
8. *Ibid.*, 200–201.
9. Green, 59.
10. *Gods and Ghosts*, 211–214.

moon and stars escape to the heavens, although the myth may possibly refer to the determination of the planting calendar by the moon and the times of fishing by the rising and setting of the stars, it probably has reference to the spread of families of chiefs who sprung from the womb of the underseas woman taken to wife by the chief of Hawaii, or, more remotely, to the mythical relation believed to exist between the conception by the mother and the phases of the moon. On Oahu the name Kipapala(u)ulu is given to the ruling chief of Honolulu living at Kapu'ukolo by the sea, who steals the magic fishhook of Kuula, god of fishing. Kuula wins it again through the marriage to the chief's daughter of a child fished up out of the water, who turns out to be the child (or grandchild) of Kuula, and who sends his wife to ask the hook from his father-in-law for a fishing expedition and thus returns it to his own parent.[11]

The obscure symbolism of these undersea stories links Hina-hanai-a-ka-malama (Hina nourished on the moon) with the matings described in the story of Wakea and Papa, ancestors of the race, from which are descended the lines of chiefs on the various islands of the group. This undersea Hina further becomes the Hina-hanaia-i-ka-malama (Hina who worked in the moon) or Hina-i-ka-malama (Hina in the moon), stories about whom are localized about Kauiki at the eastern point of the district of Hana on the island of Maui and connect her with both the Aikanaka and the Maui legendary cycles. The work she does is tapa making, hence in Hawaii she takes the name of Hina-i-kapa'i-kua (Hina the tapa beater). As such she is often equated with Hina wife of Akalana and mother of the Maui brothers. As wife of Aikanaka and ancestress of the famous Polynesian heroes Kaha'i and Laka, she is represented as retreating to the moon out of weariness with her husband's tapus. "Above was Hana-ia-ka-malama" says the chant which tells how her grandson Kaha'i goes to seek his father by the path of the rainbow.[12] Westervelt has collected the following Kauiki story:

Hina lived on Kauiki and the board on which she beat out

11. For. Col. 4: 556.   12. For. Pol. Race 2: 17.

tapa cloth may still be seen in the shape of a long black rock
above the surf line below Kauiki. She tired of the labor and,
packing her calabash, started by the rainbow path to the sun
but, finding it too warm, she climbed instead to the moon, although her husband resisted her departure. There in the moon
she may be seen with her calabash by her side.[13]

The stories told of Hina in Hawaii point to an early connection with the Tahitian moon goddess Hina wife of Ru
(Lu), ancestor in Tahiti of the Maui brothers. Among the
many names given this goddess are those of "Hina who
stepped into the moon" and "Hina the tapa beater."[14]

As Hina-nui-ti-'a'ara (Great Hina of scented herbs) she is
invoked by fire walkers and in the ceremony of the ti (ki) oven,[15]
and is therefore always dressed in garments of scented ti leaves.[16]
As Hina-ta'ai-fenua and Hina-fa'auru-va'a she accompanies
Ru as canoe pilot in his voyagings to and from Tahiti. As
Hina-nui-te-araara (Great Hina the watcher) she watches in
the moon over travelers on earth at night and as Hina-tutu-ha'a
(Hina the cloth beater) over cloth beaters for the gods. On
earth her home is at the peninsula called Motu-tapu in Raiatea.
Not far inland she spreads out her tapa at a place called Tu-
tura'a-ha'a-a-Hina (Hina's place for beating cloth), where a
long stone represents the fallen breadfruit tree whose bark she
uses. One night she stepped into the moon and is hence called
Hina-i-a'a-i-te-marama (Hina who stepped into the moon).
From the banyan tree in the moon she stepped upon and broke
off a branch, which floated to Opoa and grew into a tree there
[a myth which strangely resembles the Hawaiian legend of
Haumea and the tree gods].[17]

Perhaps it is the popularity of this moon goddess in Hawaii which has brought her into the Pele cycle as one of the
forms taken by the fire goddess in her life on earth. In romance Hina-i-ka-malama is a beautiful chiefess of Hana district on Maui who contends with her rival, the snow goddess

13. *Maui*, 167–169.   14. Henry, 407–408.
15. *Ibid.*, 463.   16. *Ibid.*, 214.
17. *Ibid.*, 459–464.

Poliahu, for the embraces of their mutual lover. A Pele myth recounted by Westervelt from Hawaii represents Pele from the volcano on Maunaloa on the south side of the island as pouring fiery lava over the land while Poliahu from lofty Maunakea at the other end of the island spreads her cooling mantle of snow.[18]

Laie-i-ka-wai version. The young chief of Kauai when he goes to seek the beauty of Puna makes a vow to enjoy no other woman until he has won Laie. At Hana on Maui he is attracted by the lovely Hina-i-ka-malama as she rides the famous surf at Puhele, and he turns in at Haneoo. The chiefess falls in love with the handsome stranger and wins him at a game of konane (Hawaiian checkers). He excuses himself until his return and goes on to Hawaii, where he courts an even more beautiful chiefess in the person of Poliahu, who also promises him her hand. When he finally loses hope of winning Laie-i-ka-wai, he "claps his hands before his god" to free himself from his rash vow and proceeds to a marriage with Poliahu, whom he fetches home with a great cortege to Kauai. While the festivities are proceeding at Mana, the disappointed Hina, apprised of her lover's duplicity, appears and claims the forfeited stake. Aiwohikupua is obliged to relinquish himself to her embraces, but the angry Poliahu envelopes the lovers in alternate waves of unendurable heat and cold until they are obliged to separate, when the mountain goddess retires to her home attended by her three maidens, Lilinoe, Waiaie, and Kahoupokane, and Aiwohikupua finds himself bereft of both ladies.[19]

The episode gives opportunity for a realistic scene at a kilu game where the kaeke dance is being presented. Hauailike, a friend of Aiwohikupua, plays much the same secondary role as a lover of Hina-i-ka-malama as Paoa of Pele in the Hi'-iaka legend. Clearly the composer here has in mind Pele in her human form as Hina-i-ka-malama, and the whole episode must be regarded as inspired not only by the kilu contest between Pele-ula and Hi'iaka for Lohiau's affection, but by the traditional rivalry between the two mountain goddesses.

18. *Volcanoes*, 55–62.   19. Haleole, 378–383, 402–407, 474–491.

Among the ten children who are named as offspring of the sea goddess Hina-luai-koa through marriage with a brother of the same parents, as recounted in the myth of the undersea woman with which this chapter opens, the oldest-born is the daughter called Hina-a-ke-ahi (Hina of the fire), a name corresponding to Pele's in her character as a god. Hina-ai-malama (Hina who eats the moon), the youngest sister and the only one with a human body, has the name attributed to Pele as a woman on earth. In the Lalohana version the girl who feeds upon the moon is daughter of Ka-hina-li'i, parent in some versions of the migrating Pele family. The flood sent by her parents which sweeps over the island is called, as in the Pele migration version, the sea of Ka-hina-li'i. It must be clear by this time that "sisters" and "daughters" are often to be understood as manifestations of the same deity in several forms, each of which has its distinct place in myth and ceremonial. On the other hand deities drawn from different sources may become identified with a single dominating figure. Associated with the Tahitian Hina of the moon as the presiding genius of the ti oven is "a chieftainess of this world" called Vahine-nui-tahu-ra'i (Woman who set fire to the sky), who commands the lightning. The relation of this figure to the Kalaipahoa sorcery in the form of a streak of light and its close connection with the Pele family are doubly significant. Life through fertility of the female here on earth is the dominant conception of both fire and moon worship, and that of the unity of the race through descent from a divine ancestress is the social incentive for merging the two as different aspects of a single divinity, who is Haumea or Papa in Hawaii, Hotu (fruitfulness) in Tahiti.

The following abstracts from other Polynesian groups offer some interesting comparisons with the theme of the underseas (or underworld) woman drawn up to become a chief's wife and the mother of chiefs. The terms translated "upper" and "under" in some cases may mean "windward" (east) and "leeward" (west).

Samoa. (*a*) One of five "sons of ocean" named Papa-usu-i-au has for wife Gaogao-o-le-tai. Their children are Sina-lesae'e and

Pili. Sina goes above to Manu'a and becomes the wife of Tangaloa. Her brother follows and takes the chiefess of Manu'a for
his wife and their son becomes chief. There comes upward from
the land below a woman named Sau-mani-lalama to fish with
torches. She is snared and becomes wife to the chief (Tui) of
Manu'a and it is from Pili and his issue that divisions of labor
and island settlements are named.[20]

(b) To Light and Darkness is born Tagaloa-ui. He takes to
wife Sina-so'umani and Tae-o-Tagaloa is born and becomes the
first Tui-manu'a.[21]

Tahiti. (a) Ta'aroa has produced the "gods of the four
classes" and now wishes to produce mankind. He bids Hina go
to Ti'i-maaraatai, a man and her brother. He follows her and
himself taking the form of this Ti'i they become man and wife.
Their son is Ti'i. Hina's daughter Hina-ereere-monoi becomes
the wife of Ti'i and Taata (kanaka, man) is born. Transformed
into a beautiful young woman, Hina becomes his wife and Ouru
and Fana (Ulu and Nana) are born, from whom come the human race.[22]

(b) The oldest daughter of Ti'i and Hina, "she who ate
before and behind," is Hina-'ere'ere-manua. In order to lure
Hina from her tapu enclosure where she is kept by her parents,
Tu-ra'i-po or Ti'iti'i-po gets Matamata-arahu (Printer in charcoal) to display patterns of tattooing in charcoal. Thus the art
is taught in Tahiti.[23]

Mangaia. Wakea breaks out of the darkness of the underworld into the light of the upper world. He brings Papa upward, in one version luring her by sprinkling coconut meat in
the cave leading out from the underworld. From these two spring
the people of Mangaia.[24]

Marquesas. (a) After Hina and her brothers Fifa-the-greedy
and Paoe escape from their demon mother, Hina descends to
Havai'i and the brothers are taken into service by two chiefs,

20. *JPS* 4: 50–51.   21. Krämer 1: 419.
22. Ellis, *Researches* 1: 112–114.
23. Henry, 287.   24. Gill, 6–8.

Fifa by the greater chief of Hanaiapa and Paoe by his younger brother, the lesser chief. Hina has directed her brothers to keep her supplied with food and Paoe obeys her. The chief becomes curious and asks about his sister's beauty; Paoe looks up at the full moon and compares his sister to it in loveliness. The chief asks for her as his wife and she consents. The greater chief however desires Hina and she consents. He puts his brother to death, and she becomes the wife of the greater chief.[25]

(b) The woman living in Oʻo-vaʻu, a land "under" the sea, is drawn up in a net to become Pohu's wife.[26]

25. Handy, *Bul.* 69: 41–45. 26. *Ibid.* 115.

XVI

MAUI THE TRICKSTER

THE deeds of Maui, the well-known trickster hero of
Polynesia, are reported sporadically in Hawaii, always
minutely localized for each island, and centering especially about a point above Kahakuloa for West Maui,
Kauiki for East Maui, a cave on the Wailuku river above
Hilo for Hawaii, Waianae on Oahu, Wailua on Kauai. Most
of the principal episodes of the Maui cycle found in other
groups occur, but sometimes with considerable or complete
variation from forms familiar in the south. The search for
eternal life and the transformation of the sister-wife's lover
into a dog are absent and there is no report of culture traits
invented by Maui except perhaps that of the kite. Only in
the Kumulipo chant is there any indication of a complete
legendary cycle. That such a cycle existed in connection with
the Kane-Kanaloa legend is evident from such fragments as
we have. Maui is made a direct ancestor from Wakea on the
Ulu line; a list of his adventures or "strifes" (ka ua) occurs
in the fifteenth era of the Kumulipo. Except for a series of
encounters with Kane and Kanaloa for possession of the awa
drink, these correspond closely with the well-known series
from the south. It is unfortunate that early collectors neglected these stories, which today have probably been much
toned down from forms more nearly approaching the primitive versions obtained by Stimson from the Tuamotus, and
whose connection with the mythology has been lost.

That in spite of the fragmentary and modernized form in
which it survives the story is very old is evident from its wide
localization. Besides the Kauiki references, the particular
place is pointed out on East Maui near Kailua on the windward side of Kaumakanai above the beach of Pokihale where
the oven of the alae bird kupua was not long ago still visible. Not far off, the print of Maui's knee is still to be seen
where he stooped to drink at a stream. The reference to Hi-

na's cave home connects the story with an early period, as do the allusions to Kane and Kanaloa as banana eaters and kava drinkers. Maui's connection as a trickster and sorcerer with the Kane group is clearly demonstrated.

Setting aside for the moment the Kumulipo series, the following motives occur in Hawaiian versions:

(A) Mysterious birth (Poepoe MS. BPBM col.; For. Col. 5: 536–539; *HHS* 25: 16–17). In every case the supernatural father is a stranger, variously named as Hina-lau-ae, Makali'i from the heavens, "a man named Malo." The reputed father is Akalana.

(B) Pushing up the heavens (Westervelt, *Maui*, 31–32).

(C) Getting fire (Thrum, *Tales*, 33–35; Westervelt, *Maui*, 64–66; Kamakau, *Ke Au Okoa*, February 3, 1870; *Moolelo Hawaii* [1838], 41).

(D) Fishing up islands (Thrum, *More Tales*, 248–252; *HHS* 25: 17–18; *Moolelo Hawaii*, 41).

(E) Snaring the sun (Thrum [by Forbes], *Tales*, 31–33; For. Col. 5: 538–539; *Moolelo Hawaii*, 41).

(F) Rescue of (F1) mother from water monster (Westervelt, *Maui*, 7–8; local legends); (F2) wife from bat (Thrum, *More Tales*, 252–259); (F3) Maui's own rescue by an owl child (For. Col. 5: 538–541).

(G) Death (Thrum, *More Tales*, 259–260).

1. *Kumulipo version (after Ho'olapa)*.

Waolena was the husband, Mahuie was the wife,
Akalana was the husband, Hina-a-ke-ahi was the wife,
Maui-the-firstborn was born, Maui-the-middle-child was born,
Maui-the-littlest (ki'iki'i) was born, Maui-of-the-loincloth was born,
Girded with the loincloth of Akalana.
Hina-of-the-fire was pregnant and bore a cock,
Hina delivered her child in the form of an egg;
She had not lived with a cock
But a cock was born to her.
The cock crowed "alala!" Hina was puzzled,
She had not lived with a man but a child was born,

A mysterious child for Hina-of-the-fire.
Kia-loa and Kia-a-ka-poko were both angry,
The brothers of Hina,
Two of the four Kia.
Maui fought, those Kia fell,
Red blood flowed from the forehead of Maui,
That was Maui's first strife.
He fetched the bunch of black-stemmed awa from Kane and
    Kanaloa,
That was Maui's second strife.
The third strife was the quarrel over the strainer;
The fourth was that over the bamboo of Kane and Kanaloa;
The fifth strife was that at the gathering for the wrist-turning
    contest.
The sixth had to do with his descent;
Maui asked who was his father,
Hina denied that he had a father,
The loincloth (malo) of Kalana was his father.
Hina-of-the-fire wanted fish;
He learned fishing; Hina commanded,
"Go fetch your father,
There is the line, the hook,
Come-here-from-the-heavens (Manai-a-ka-lani), that is the hook
For grappling the islands together, out of the ocean."
He seized the great alae bird of Hina,
The bird sister of Pimoe;
This was the seventh strife of Maui.
The mischievous kupua it was whom he hooked,
The jaw, the mouth as it opened, of Pimoe,
The fish that was lord of the island that shakes the ocean.
Pimoe was pulled ashore dead by Maui.
He had pity for Mahanauluehu,
The child of Pimoe,
Maui brought him ashore and devoured all but the tail,
Pimoe lived through his tail,
Mahanauluehu was the tail he lived through.
Kane and Kanaloa were shaken from their foundation,
With the ninth strife of Maui.
Pe'ape'a carried away Hina-ke-ka,

The bat god was this Pe'ape'a,
This was the last strife of Maui,
He scratched out the eyes of the eight-eyed bat;
The strife ended with Moemoe.
Everyone knows of the strife of Maui with the Sun,
With the loop of the snaring cord of Maui;
Summer became the Sun's,
Winter became Maui's.
He drank the muddy waters of the plain
Of Kane and Kanaloa,
Strove by trickery,
Around Hawaii, around Maui,
Around Kauai, around Oahu;
At Kahalu'u is the afterbirth buried, at Waikane the navel
    string,
He died at Hakipu'u at Kualoa,
Maui-of-the-loincloth,
The famous kupua of the island,
A chief indeed.[1]

2. *East Maui versions:* (A) *Birth*, (C) *Finding fire*, (D) *Fishing up islands*, (E) *Snaring the sun*. Maui is not the child of Hina by Akalana in the natural way but is begotten one day when she has a longing for seaweed, goes out to the beach at Kaanomalo to gather some, and, finding a man's loincloth on the beach, puts it on and goes to sleep. The child born from this adventure is named Maui-a-Akalana and her husband says, "We have found our lord!"

Maui's first feat is getting fire from the mud hens while they are roasting bananas. Hina teaches him to catch the littlest one. He finds them at Waianae on Oahu. Each time he approaches they scratch out the fire. When he finally succeeds in seizing the littlest mud hen she tries to put him off by naming first the taro stalk, then the ti leaf as the secret of fire. That is why these leaves have hollows today, because Maui rubbed them to try to get fire. At last the mud hen tells him that fire is in the water (wai), meaning the tree called "sacred water" (wai-mea),

1. Kalakaua, 63–65; Liliuokalani, 81–82; translation after Hawaiian informants.

and shows him how to obtain it. So Maui gets fire, but he first rubs a red streak on the mud hen's head out of revenge for her trickery before letting the bird escape.

Maui's next feat is stopping the sun from moving so fast. Hina sends him to a big wiliwili tree where he finds his old blind grandmother cooking bananas and steals them one by one until she recognizes him and agrees to help him. He sits by the trunk of the tree and lassoes the sun's rays as the sun comes up. The sun pleads for life and agrees that the days shall be long in summer and short during the six winter months.

While Maui is still a child he goes fishing with his brothers and gets them to go far out to the fishing ground called Po'o directly seaward from Kipahulu and in a line with the hill called Ka-iwi-o-Pele. Here with his hook called Manai-a-ka-lani (Come from heaven) he catches the big ulua of Pimoe. For two days they pull at it before it comes to the surface and is drawn close to the canoe. The brothers are warned not to look back. They do so. The cord breaks, and the fish vanishes. That is why the islands are not united into one.[2]

(B) *Pushing up the heavens.* The sky presses down over the earth. A man "supposed to be Maui" says to a woman that if she will give him a "drink from her gourd" [a euphemistic expression] he will push up the sky for her. She complies and the man [standing on Kauiki] thrusts the sky upward. Today, although the clouds may hang low over the mountain of Haleakala, they refrain from touching Kauiki.[3]

3. *West Maui versions:* (A) *Birth.* Maui is the son of Hinalau-ae and Hina. The family lives at Makalia above Kahakuloa. While Maui is still unborn, some men out fishing see a handsome child diving from a high cliff into the sea, and they pursue. The child makes for home and returns to his mother's womb. Thus they know that a magician is to be born.[4]

Lanai variant. Pu'upehe is the supernatural son of Kapokoholua the father, Kapoiliili the mother, who live on the island of

2. BPBM Hawaiian MS. col. L9' (Poepoe col.); text from *Kuokoa,* June 27, July 4, 1863 (by Puaoaloa); translation from Mrs. Pukui.

3. Westervelt, *Maui,* 31–32.   4. For. Col. 5: 536–539.

Lanai, which goes at this time by the name of Ka-ulu-laau. For thirteen months Pu'upehe lives unborn and frightens his mother by speaking to her from her womb and playing the ghost as a spirit abroad, in which form he sends fish to his father's line through his god Pua-iki and learns the arts of warfare by over-hearing an expert teaching others how to kill Pu'upehe's father. He demands awa to chew and tobacco, both of which seem to be new customs to his parents. When he leaves his mother's body it becomes flat; when he returns it is again swollen.[5]

Maori variant. Whakatau, son of Apakura, is formed by the god Rongo out of Apakura's apron when she leaves it one day on the sand. Kites are seen flying in the air but no one is visible because Whakatau is under the sea. One day he comes out on shore and is pursued, but no one can catch him but his mother Apakura.[6]

(E) *Snaring the sun.* The sun goes so fast that Hina has trouble in drying her strips of bark cloth. Maui observes the sun from Wailohi and sees where it rises. He fashions strong cord of coconut fiber from Peeloko (Paeloko) at Waihee. The sun is rendered tractable and Maui then turns to punish Moe-moe, who has derided his effort. Moemoe flees until overtaken north of Lahaina, where he is transformed into the long rock beside the road today.[7]

(F3) *Maui's rescue.* While Maui is away snaring the sun, his mother bears an owl-child. Maui is kind to the owl. Once he is taken prisoner and is to be offered in sacrifice at Moali'i. Hina and the owl, hearing of his danger, follow him. The owl releases him and Hina sits down, covers him with her clothing and pretends to pick fleas. Thus he is saved.[8]

4. *Kauai versions:* (A) *Birth.* Hina, the mother of Maui, dreams in Kahiki of surf riding at Wailua on Kauai with a handsome man. Her brother Nu-lo-hiki turns himself into a canoe in which Hina sails to Wailua and takes for her husband the man of her dreams. This man is Makali'i who has come from

5. *Ibid.* 554–561.

6. Grey, 72–73; cf. Westervelt's story of Maui obtaining a wind gourd to fly his kite, *Maui,* 114–118.

7. Local informant.   8. For. Col. 5: 538–541.

the skies, to which he returns after the birth of Maui and his eight brothers. The canoe is left at Molokua and becomes the first coconut tree on the island. Up this tree Maui climbs to visit his father.

(D) *Fishing.* If Maui can hook the fish Luehu on the night of Lono, he can draw the islands together. The nine alae birds (mud hens) give warning to Luehu of his approach. His mother teaches him to make an image in his place and himself hide and seize the youngest alae. The place where he catches the bird is shown in a taro patch near the navel stone of Holoholoku. He now catches the big fish, and the islands would have drawn together had he not, contrary to his mother's warning, taken into his canoe a bailer that comes floating on the water and which turns into a beautiful woman. The crowds cheer the wonder, the brothers turn to look, and the big fish escapes the hook and the islands slide apart again.[9]

5. *Hilo (Hawaii) versions:* (F1) *Rescue of mother.* Hina, mother of Maui, lives in a cave by the Wailuku river in Hilo on Hawaii where she beats bark cloth. While Maui is away at Aleha-ka-la (now called Hale-a-ka-la) snaring the sun, Lono-kaeho (some say Kuna the eel) comes to woo her and when she refuses him he almost drowns her. She calls to Maui for help and he throws about Lono-kaeho the snares with which he has overcome the sun and turns him into a rock which stands there today. The stone image of Hina could in old days be seen with water dripping from its breasts, but a landslide has covered it.[10]

6. *Waianae (Oahu) versions:* (A) *Birth.* Akalana is the father, Hina-kawea the mother of Maui-a-ka-lana and his two brothers, Maui-mua, Maui-ikiiki. Maui and his mother live in a cave on the south side of Waianae on Oahu where Hina makes her tapa. The fishhook Manai-a-ka-lani, the snare with which Maui snared the sun, the places where he made his adzes, are to be seen there to this day. The father of Maui goes to Kahiki and his descendants people all the lands of the southern ocean as far as New Zealand.[11]

9. Dickey, *HHS Reports* 25: 16–18.
10. Given by Mary Pukui; cf. Westervelt, *Maui,* 7–8.
11. Kamakau, *Ke Au Okoa,* October 21, 1869.

(D) *Fishing*. Maui-kupua, his mother and brothers live at Ulehawa, Maui and his mother in a cave called Kane-ana, in Waianae district. Maui wishes to unite the islands. His mother sends him to Ka-alae-nui-a-hina, who tells him he must hook Uniho-kahi at the fishing station of Ponaha-ke-one off Ulehawa. Maui and his brothers paddle out to the fishing ground with the hook Manai-a-ka-lani. He tells his brothers to catch the bailer (kaliu) they will see floating by, and himself takes it into the canoe. When they reach the fishing station the bailer has become transformed into a beautiful woman. She accompanies Maui's hook into the sea and bids Uniho-kahi open his mouth, as she and Maui have been disputing about the number of his teeth. When he obeys she hooks him fast. The brothers paddle. Maui bids them not look back; but they disobey, the hook comes loose, and the islands separate again.

(F2) *Rescue of wife from bat*. On another occasion the brothers go fishing. All catch sharks except Maui, who hooks a moi fish and an ulua. He has taken these to the heiau Lua-eha and has swallowed half of a fish, beginning at the head, when he looks up and sees Pe'ape'a-maka-walu (Eight-eyed bat) making off with his wife Kumulama. He drops the fish but is unable to overtake the abductor. His mother Hina sends him to his grandfather Ku-olo-kele in the land of Ke-ahu-moa, where he sees a humpbacked man coming, hurls a stone at him, and straightens out his back. The stone may be seen today at Waipahu where Ku-olo-kele hurled it. The grateful grandfather shows Maui how to fashion a bird-shaped ship (a kite) out of feathers, ti leaves, and ieie vine, in which he flies through the air to Moana-liha and sees "the houses of Limaloa" and the people gathered on the shore. The chief Pe'ape'a orders the strange bird brought into the house. When the chief sleeps, Maui waits until all eight eyes are closed and then cuts off the chief's head and flies away with his wife to Oahu, where he drains all eight of the bat's eyes in a cup of awa.

(G) *Death*. Maui goes to live in Hilo on Hawaii and makes himself unpopular with his tricks. He one day visits the home of Kane and Kanaloa and their party at Alakahi in Waipio valley and attempts to spear with a sharp stick the bananas they are roasting by the fire. He is detected and his brains dashed out.

They color the side of Alakahi peak and tinge red the shrimps in the stream. A rainbow is formed of his blood.[12]

No comprehensive study of Maui variants can here be attempted. An interesting comparison with Stimson's findings from the Tuamotus will be useful as containing some fresh and striking similarities with Hawaiian myth, either in the Maui cycle itself or in other connections which link with it.

Tuamotus. (*a*) *Composite version.* Maui-tikitiki-a-Ataraga is the child of Ataraga by Huahega whom Ataraga seeks at her bathing place. He snares the sun; gains his real father's recognition; slays Mahuika; fishes up Tahiti and Little Tahiti; rescues Hina from Tuna the eel and, when Tuna follows with a flood, stays the water by exposing his phallus, then kills Tuna, from whose head springs the first coconut; when Peka steals Hina, he gets into the body of a golden pheasant and, flying to Peka's home, gets taken in as a pet in spite of the mother's warning, cuts off Peka's head, and flies away with Hina; transforms Hina's lover Ri, and his friend who comes to seek vengeance, into dogs; when he sees Huahega's hair turning gray, goes to exchange stomachs with Rori the sea slug in order that men may not die, but his brothers raise a shout and he vomits it up again and hence men die.[13]

(*b*) *Anaa version.* Maui-tikitiki (Wonder worker the vigorous) is fifth son of Ataraga and the chiefess Huahega, daughter of the magician Mahuike who controls fire, to whose home Huahega retires after the birth of her fifth son. He gains recognition by his father, seeks his mother and gains recognition by her family, but, refused by Mahuike a house like his older brothers, he kills Mahuike in a tossing contest. He snares the sun with a rope made from the hairs of his mother's head. With the help of his brothers he fishes up the land of Havaiki from the ocean bottom. He takes to wife the daughter of Tiki, who is Tuna's wife, and kills Tuna, from whose head springs the coconut tree named Niu-roa-i-Havaiki. Peka-nui (Great bat) carries off Hina and Maui changes into a snipe, follows "the road of the

12. Thrum, *More Tales,* 248–260.
13. *Bul.* 127: 5–52.

bird," slays Peka as in the other version, and recovers his wife.
He falls ill and is told to crawl into the shell of Tupa the crab
so that he may change his skin and go on living like the crab. In
order to do so he must swallow Rori-tau's entrails, but as he is
doing this his brothers come along and cause him to vomit them
up. He turns Hina's lover Ri and Ri's friend Togio into dogs.
Maui's brothers go to the sun; one is killed in the sun's heat, the
other returns and Maui goes to get his brother's body (or pretends to go) to bury it in the heavens. He makes his marae tapu
while pretending absence on an errand to the sun, so that he
may enjoy, without his mother's knowledge, the two girls (from
the heavens), the Dawn-maid and the Maid-of-the-Moon. He
sends home the Dawn-maid but keeps the Maid-of-the-Moon as
his wife.[14]

All the familiar incidents of the Polynesian Maui cycle except that of pushing up the sky are contained in these Tuamotu versions. The parallel to the Hawaiian story of Maui
and the eight-eyed bat is very close. The incident in the Tuamotu story of the religious tapu imposed in order to conceal
an amorous affair is to be compared with the Hawaiian Wakea and Papa infidelity episode in which Wakea imposes tapu
nights in order to embrace his daughter Hoʻohoku-ka-lani.
A close parallel also occurs at the conclusion of the Laieikawai romance, where the sun-god husband pretends an errand
to earth in order to gratify his passion for his wife's sister.
Hina-nui-a-(ka)lana is named in the chant of the birth of
islands as mother of the priestly island Molokai, called Mo-
lokai-a-Hina, whom Kulu-waiea (Wakea), husband of Haumea (Papa), takes during his wife's absence.[15] This is the
Hina called Hina-kawea, says Thrum, who is named as the
mother of the Maui brothers and wife of Akalana on the Ulu
genealogy.[16] The Kipahulu story of the malo, through wearing which Hina conceives the wonder child, is an obvious version of the Tuamotu story of Tiki hiding his phallus in a
heap of sand in order to beget a child by Hina.[17] The final
curious scene in the Maui Tuamotu story with its allusion to

14. *Ibid.* 148: 11–60.   15. For. Col. 4: 2, 6, 12, 18.
16. *More Tales,* 199.   17. Stimson MS.

the life of the crab as symbol of rebirth has also a parallel form in the Hawaiian. Kepelino writes: "According to the Hawaiian story, man lived like the crab, he came out of the first shell and lived in that soft condition until he grew hard again. Thus man lived, became old, creeping, yellow like the yellowed hala leaf, eyelashes few like a rat's, then he returned again to youth, became beautiful once more, the body grew as it had before, became old, and so on."[18]

Maui stories from other groups lack any reference to the "strifes" of Maui over the kava, and the killing of the Kia (post) brothers of Hina, with which the Kumulipo series opens. A close parallel occurs in the opening scenes of the legend of Iro (Hilo) from Rarotonga, not only of the assertion of rights in the kava feast but also to the mysterious birth of Maui.

Iro-ma-oata is son of Moe-tara-uri of Vavau and his cousin, the beautiful Akimano, wife of Pou-ariki of Kuporu. Moe-tara-uri seeks her out during the absence of her husband and leaves her before the child is born. In their games the child shows magical powers above those of his older brothers. When they go to learn the sacred chants, he follows and gets them so readily that his teachers marvel. Hearing his teachers sigh for the good food, kava, and pig which are denied them, he takes up the spear of his real father, of whose identity he is as yet unaware, and attacks with it and kills the keepers of these foods. When his supposed father Pou(post)-ariki is angry and uses words of insult, he obtains from his mother the secret of his birth and goes forth to make himself known to Moe-tara-uri.[19]

Although Maui is not here named and Iro's further adventures have little to do with the strifes of Maui, it is to be noted that Tongan Maui stories are much concerned, like this Iro story, with encounters with monsters, such as the dragging up of a great eel and the killing of a biting tree. The Maui fishing tale from Kauiki tells of fishing up Pimoe, a legend which is handed down today in the story of Kuula,

18. 48.
19. Savage, *JPS* 25: 138–149; 26: 1–18, 45–65.

god of fishing stations, and which is evidently closely connected with the tale of Tuna the eel, husband of Hina, and with the Tuamotu Turi story. The "biting tree" uprooted by Maui, or by some other hero of the South Seas, may be the kava strife noted in the Kumulipo series.[20]

20. A complete bibliography to date of Maui material is under preparation. The following are useful:

1. A classified list of references to Maui myths in the *Journal of the Polynesian Society* (*JPS* 38 [1928]: 15–16).

2. Article on "Maui" in Tregear, *Maori-Polynesian Dictionary*.

3. Dixon, *Oceanic Mythology*, 41–56 and notes.

For distinct centers see:

MAORI: White 2: 62–127; Taylor, 124–133; Grey, 10–35; Percy Smith, *MPS* 3: 145–146, 174–182.

TAHITI: Henry, 427–433, 615–621; Baessler, *ZE* 37: 920–924.

MARQUESAS: Handy, *Bul.* 69: 12–18, 103 (Tikitiki, 122–124); Von den Steinen, *Kunst*, 2: 110–112.

NIUE (Maui-Tikitikilaga): Loeb, *Bul.* 32: 209–213.

MANGAIA: Gill, 51–63 (77–80).

MANAHIKI: Gill, 63–76; Turner, 278–279.

RAKAHANGA: Buck, *Bul.* 99: 85–86.

TONGA: Collocott, *FL* 32: 45–58 (summary of text with French translation in *Anthropos* 12–13: 1026–1046 [1917–1918]; 14–15; 125–142 [1919–1920]); Gifford, *Bul.* 8: 21–24.

SAMOA: Fraser, *RSNSW* 25: 79–83; Stuebel, 64–65; Turner, 209–211; Stair, 238–239; Krämer 1: 393 (who equates Maui with Tagaloa-a-ui, child of the Sun).

This list does not take into account the equally important Maui equivalents such as Qat or Tangaloa in the South Seas, or the overlapping of the Maui cycle of adventures with those of other hero cycles, as suggested in the Iro cycle and that of Wakea and Tiki. The study of the Maui cycle now under way by Dr. Luomala will clear up many obscure points in existing Maui variants.

XVII

AIKANAKA-KAHAʻI CYCLE

THE Ulu genealogy used by the chiefs of Maui and Hawaii includes, as the twenty-eighth to the thirty-second in descent from Wakea, the names of five chiefs famous also in the genealogies and tradition of the South Seas. These five are Ai-kanaka (Kai-tangata), Hema, Kahaʻi (Tawhaki), Wahieloa, Laka. A comparison with southern groups shows a close likeness in the series, although the names of their wives differ widely.

HAWAII

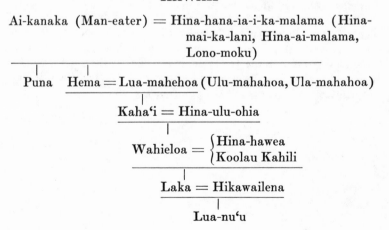

Ai-kanaka (Man-eater) = Hina-hana-ia-i-ka-malama (Hina-mai-ka-lani, Hina-ai-malama, Lono-moku)

Puna   Hema = Lua-mahehoa (Ulu-mahahoa, Ula-mahahoa)

Kahaʻi = Hina-ulu-ohia

Wahieloa = { Hina-hawea / Koolau Kahili

Laka = Hikawailena

Lua-nuʻu

MAORI

Kai-tangata (Man-eater) $= \begin{cases} \text{Awa-nui-a-rangi} \\ \text{Whaitiri} \end{cases}$

Punga   Hema = Kare-nuku (Kae-nuku)
                  Ara-huta (Hu-ara-hu, Ara-whita-
                  i-te-rangi)
                  Uru-tonga
                  Hina-pupu-mai-naua
                  Hine-piripiri

Tawhaki = Hine-nui-i-te-kawa (Hine-te-kawa)
          Maikuku-makaka (makaha)
          Tangotango
          Hapai-nui-a-maunga
          Hine-murutoka
          Hine-piripiri

Wahieroa = Hine-tua-hoanga (Hine-tu-a-haka)
           Matoka-rau-tawhiri (Matokarau)
           Kura

Rata = Tonga-rau-tawhiri

Tu-whaka-raro = Apakura

TAHITI

Ro'o-nui = Haumea (Nona or Rona)

No'a-huruhuru = Hina

Pu'a-ari'i-tahi = Te-'ura   Hema = Hina-tahutahu
                                          Hua-uri

Arihi-nui-a-Pu'a   Tafa'i-iri-ura = Hina
                     (Vai-ta-fa'i,   Tere (Te-ura-i-te-ra'i)
                     or -uri-i-te-   Ura-i-ti'a-hotu
                     tau-i-Havaii)   (Morning star)

Vahieroa = Maemae-a-rohi

Rata

TUAMOTU

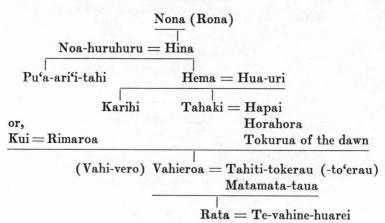

Nona (Rona)
|
Noa-huruhuru = Hina
|
Pu'a-ari'i-tahi   Hema = Hua-uri
| |
Karihi   Tahaki = Hapai
or,   Horahora
Kui = Rimaroa   Tokurua of the dawn
|
(Vahi-vero) Vahieroa = Tahiti-tokerau (-to'erau)
Matamata-taua
|
Rata = Te-vahine-huarei

RAROTONGA

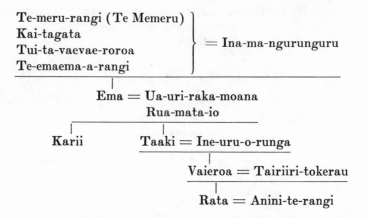

Te-meru-rangi (Te Memeru) ⎫
Kai-tagata   ⎪
Tui-ta-vaevae-roroa   ⎬ = Ina-ma-ngurunguru
Te-emaema-a-rangi   ⎭
|
Ema = Ua-uri-raka-moana
Rua-mata-io
|
Karii   Taaki = Ine-uru-o-runga
|
Vaieroa = Tairiiri-tokerau
|
Rata = Anini-te-rangi

The district of Hana in East Maui is the center of localization in Hawaii for the lives of the Aikanaka-Laka family, and traditional chants are preserved which tell precisely where each of the five was born, where the afterbirth, umbilical cord, and navel string of each were buried, the place where each was reared, the site of his house, the place of his death and burial, and sometimes other data, together with lists of place names of which it is doubtful whether they name places where the body rested on the way to burial or have some other significance, factual or spiritual. The circumstantial nature of these chants might argue for the actual existence of such chiefs on Hawaiian soil, but Kamakau, who records the chants in his *Moolelo Hawaii* (1869), tells how, in the time of Kua-li'i of Oahu and later in that of Kamehameha-nui of Maui, the genealogists got together and established the genealogical lines back to Puna and Hema, sons of Aikanaka, from whom Hawaiian chief families count their ancestry; Oahu and Kauai families from Puna, Maui and Hawaii from Hema, traditional settler in New Zealand with the Menehune. At that time the genealogical chant for each chief was probably harmonized with local tradition and crystallized into its present form. The legends have passed into nursery tales and lost the grim character preserved to them in less sophisticated groups, but as a whole they follow closely the pattern common to the whole area where these names appear.

The cycle tells of a woman from a cannibal group who weds a chief in another land and, becoming dissatisfied, returns home, leaving two children, Puna (Punga) and Hema. Hema wins a goddess as a wife, and when his child is to be born he goes away to seek a birth gift and is taken prisoner. His eyes are plucked out and he himself is thrust into the filth pit. His son Kaha'i (Tawhaki) goes to rescue him and to avenge his wrongs, accompanied by his brother Alihi (Ka-rihi, Kari'i), who does not share his godlike nature and is hence unable to endure the difficulties of the journey. He is guided by an old blind ancestress who is discovered roasting food and whose eyesight is restored in return for the information sought. Kaha'i's son Wahieloa is also taken captive, and his son Laka goes to seek his bones, carried across seas in a double canoe fashioned for him by the canoe-building gods and the little spirits of the forest who are his family deities.

AIKANAKA LEGEND

(a) *Thrum version.* Ai-kanaka (Man-eater) is a Maui chief, son of Heleipawa, son of Kapawa. He is born at Kowali-Muolea, at a place called Hoʻolono-kiʻu in Hana district and reared at Makaliʻi-hanau, and his home is on Kauiki hill. He is a good industrious man and a kind ruler. Hina-hana-ia-(i)-ka-malama (Hina who worked in the moon), or Hina-mai-ka-lani (Hina from the heavens), comes from Ulupaupau in Kahiki to be his wife and to them are born, first, imbecile children, then Puna-i-mua (Puna the firstborn), and last Hema. Hina's servants are Kaniamoko and Kahapouli. After the birth of Puna, Hina begins to enlarge her landholdings. The children's excrement has to be carried to the north side of the water hole at Ulaino and Hina wearies of their constant messing and the tapu involved in the disposition of the excrement. Hence on the night of Hoku (Full moon) she leaps to the moon from a place called Wanaikulani. Her husband leaps to catch her, the leg breaks off in his hand (hence she is called Lono-muku), and there she hangs in the moon to this day.[1]

(b) *Kamakau version.* Aikanaka, son of Kailoau, son of Heleipawa, is born in Kipahulu, Hana district, on East Maui. The place of his birth and the site of his house on the hill Kuekahi can still be seen. Strange stories are told of his wife Hina-hana-ia-ka-malama or Hina-ai-ka-malama (Hina fed on the moon). She is said to have found food from the moon in the shape of the sweet potato called hualani. Her husband cut off her foot and threw it to the moon where she lived.[2]

According to Malo,[3] Aikanaka died at Aneuli, Puʻuolai, in Honuaula, Maui, and was buried in Iao valley. An early school record makes Hana-ua-lani-haʻahaʻa the place of Hina's ascent and adds, "If her husband had not cut off her legs she would have reached the locality of the sun."[4] The *Moolelo Hawaii* (1838) reads: "Because the children made so much excrement she fled away and lived in the moon. As she flew up, her husband cut off her foot, hence she was called Lono-muku. What a grand lie!"[5] Nursery tales today center upon

1. Thrum, *More Tales,* 69–71.
2. *Ke Au Okoa,* October 21, 1869.
3. 323.   4. For. Col. 5: 658.
5. 41.

the weariness caused by the constant running to and fro from Kauiki to Ulaino, a distance of a mile or so, to deposit the children's messes, a situation made amusing by the dramatic way in which the story is told. The theme occurs in traditional Polynesian variants; in Maori it connects with the use of a latrine. A local version collected in Hana in 1932 makes the husband the one who wearies of cleaning the children or does not like being given the child to clean.

He takes large gourds [for which the neighboring district of Hamoa is famous], one under each arm, and leaping from the hill Ka-iwi-o-Pele [where the site of the house can be seen today] floats away to the moon.

A similar story is told in Mangaia of the god Tane.

Tane comes from Avaiki and marries a sister of Ina-of-the-moon. She becomes jealous and he weaves himself baskets out of coconut fronds and, using them for wings, flies away to his own land.[6]

In Rarotonga:

Ngata wins Ngaro-ariki-te-tara, the beautiful daughter of Kuiono, and after recovering her from Avaiki and again from the land Ka-opu-te-ra (of sunset) he abandons her forever because she has left their child with him to tend while she pays a visit to Variiri and the child is fretful.[7]

In New Zealand:

Hapai-nui-a-maunga (Great lifter of mountains) comes from heaven to wed Tawhaki. A child is born. He complains of its filth. She takes the child, steps off the roof gable and goes back to heaven.[8]

Maori. Whaitiri (or Awa-nui-a-rangi) of the heavens is a man-eater. She hears of Kai-tangata on earth and, taking literally a name perhaps signifying victory over enemies, comes

6. Gill, 107–114.   7. *JPS* 27: 185.
8. Taylor, 143; White 1: 115; Grey, 36.

to earth and makes him her husband. When she finds he is not really a man-eater she is disappointed. She bears him children, Punga and Hema (and others). He complains of their filth (or discusses her with others) and she returns to the heavens (having first made a filth pit for the children). Her husband tries to catch her by her garment in some versions.[9]

Tahiti. Nona (or Haumea), a cannibal woman of high rank, lives at Mahina (Moon) in North Tahiti. Her husband, a chief of high rank of the house Tahiti-to'erau abandons her. Her daughter Hina hides her lover in a cave which is opened by a spell. The mother listens to the spell, finds and devours him. The girl flees and is protected by a hairy chief named No'a (Noa-huruhuru) who kills the cannibal mother-in-law, Nona, and marries the girl. Pu'a-ari'i-tahi and Hema are their children.[10]

Tuamotu (Anaa). Nona is the daughter of Te-ra-hei-manu and the girl Hei-te-rara who is daughter of the ogress Ragi-titi. She desires Noa-makai-tagata and they sleep together. Noa insults Nona by complaining about her bad odor and she leaves him for another lover. Noa follows her, kills the new lover, and brings back Nona to his own land.[11]

Rarotonga. Te-meru-rangi is the father, Ina-ma-ngurunguru the mother of Ema, father of Taaki and Karii. Te-meru is also known as Kai-tangata and Tui-kai-vaevae-roroa.[12]

The Tuamotu version is related to the story told (at Ra'iatea) in the Tahitian group of Hiro and his beautiful wife Vai-tu-marie, parents of Marama (Moonlight). Hiro overhears his wife laughing with a neighbor about her husband's strong odor, and puts her to death. Her son Marama discovers and grieves over her death, but nothing comes of the incident.[13]

9. White 1: 87–89, 95–97, 119–121, 125, 126–128; *JPS* 19: 143; Taylor, 138–143; Wohlers, 15–16.

10. Henry, 552–555. 11. Stimson, *Bul.* 148: 60.

12. Savage, *JPS* 19: 142–144; Smith, *JPS* 30: 1.

13. Henry, 543–545.

HEMA LEGEND

Puna is brought up on Oahu, Hema on Maui at Kauiki, called Hawaii-kua-uli (Hawaii of the green back). Hema grows to be a handsome man and takes Lua(Ulu, Ula)-mahehoa from the upper Iao valley in Wailuku as his wife. In the fifth month of her pregnancy he sails after the birth gift called Apo-ula (Red feather band) to the land of the child's maternal grandparents. They are deep-sea divers and "it is a custom in that country to take men's eyes for fishbait." Hema's eyes are gouged out and he loses his wits ("caught by the aaia bird of Kane"). The last part of his chant reads, in Emerson's translation:

> "Hema sailed for Kahiki
> Seeking the birth gift (Apoula)
> Caught was Hema seized by the Aaia,
> He fell at Kahiki, at Kapakapaua,
> Remaining at Ulupaupau,
> There are the eyes of Hema."[14]

Maori. Hema is the son of Kai-tangata and Whaitiri. He weds Ara-whita-i-te-rangi (Arahuta) who becomes mother of Tawhaki and Karihi[15] or weds Kare-nuku, who becomes mother of Pupu-mai-nono, Karihi, Tawhaki,[16] or weds Uru-tonga and has Karihi and Tawhaki[17] or Hema, daughter of the same, weds Hu-aro-tu and has Karihi, Pupu-mai-nono, Tawhaki. Forbidden to follow her mother when Whaitiri leaves for her own country, she attempts the journey and is taken captive by Te-tini-o-Waiwai (The little spirits of the water).[18] Hema is slain by the Ponaturi, underwater people,[19] or killed and his wife taken captive at the settlement of the whale people Paikea, Kewa, and Ihu-puku,[20] or slain by the Patu-pae-a-rehe. In some versions[21] Karihi is called the "child" of Whaitiri.

14. Thrum, *More Tales,* 70–72; Kamakau, *Ke Au Okoa,* October 28, 1869; Malo, 323; For. Col. 6: 319; *Moolelo Hawaii* (1838), 41; Thrum, *JPS* 31: 105–106.

15. White 1: 88, 89, 128; *JPS* 37: 360.

16. White 1: 121; Wohlers, 17.   17. Grey, 36.

18. White 1: 54–55.   19. Grey, 37; *JPS* 7: 40.

20. Wohlers, 17; White 1: 121.   21. *Ibid.* 95–97, 125.

Tahiti. Hina weds No‘a-huruhuru (hairy), who has saved her from her cannibal mother Rona (or Haumea), and has two sons, Pu‘a-ari‘i-tahi and Hema. The mother favors Hema because he does not refuse to louse her hair and to swallow a red (and a white) louse which he finds in so doing. She accordingly promises him a goddess for a wife. He is to find Hua-uri (or Hina-tahu-tahu) at her bathing pool called Vai-te-marama (at the Vaipoo-poo river at Hanapepe) and catch her by the hair and carry her past four (or twenty) houses without letting her feet touch the ground; then she will lose her power and follow him. The first time he cannot resist her pleadings, lets her down, and she runs away from him; the second time he succeeds. Tafa‘i-iri-ura (-i-o-ura) is their child, Arihi-nui-a-Pu‘a is the child of Pu‘a. When her child is abused by the other children Hema's wife curses her husband and he tries to commit suicide by leaping head down from the A‘a-‘ura and is caught by spirits and carried to the Po (Tumu-i-Havai‘i) where his body becomes "a deposit for the spirits' dung" and his eyes are used "as morning lights at the mat-weaving place of Ta‘aroa's daughter." Hence in Tahiti a man with a skin disease is compared with Hema as "a place for the excrement of the spirits."[22]

Compare the Marquesan story of Kena who goes to the underworld after his wife and must carry her out in a basket and by no means let her out or she will escape. The first time he fails; the next time he succeeds.[23] See also the Hawaiian story of "Hiku and Kawelu."

Tuamotu. (*a*) *North islands.* Hema is son of Noa-huruhuru and Hina, daughter of the cannibal woman Rona. Hina sends her son to seize Hua-uri, "queen of Niue," and through the powerful incantations of Noa he brings her back "naked and wailing." When their son Tafa‘i is abused by the other boys Hema commits suicide and the "fairies of Matua-uru" catch him and confine him in a latrine.[24]

(*b*) *Fagatau.* Hema is the husband of Hua-uri, younger sis-

22. Leverd, *JPS* 21: 5–7; Henry, 555–561; Ahnne 49: 264–266.
23. Handy, *Bul.* 69: 120.   24. Leverd, *JPS* 20: 173–175.

ter of Arimata, and there is jealousy between the sisters over their sons Niu-kura and Tahaki. Hema and Hua-uri go to the sea after a special kind of sea urchin as food for their son. The goblin band of the Matua-uru seize and carry off Hema while Hua-uri escapes. They pluck out his eyes and fasten them to the belt band of the woman Roi-matagotago and use his body as a filth pit.[25]

(c) *Anaa.* Hema lives in the upper valleys and seizes Hua-uri who lives by the sea, daughter of Titimanu and Kuhi, while she is digging arum root in the uplands. Kuhi sends a magic bunch of feathers to find Hua-uri, and the wife, fearing lest her parents kill Hema, returns to her parents and wins their consent to the marriage, although they warn her that the man is not her equal. When her child is to be born she goes to her parents' home and is bidden by her mother pick and eat a louse from the mother's head. She picks first a black and then a red louse and the mother predicts that her second child will be famous. When this second child is to be born, Hema encroaches upon the beach where the goblins of Matua-uru catch crabs and is pursued and seized.[26]

Rarotonga. Ema is descended from Te Memeru, high chief of Kuporu. His wife is Ua-uri-raka-moana who dwells by the deep sea. Kariʻi, Taaki, and the girls Puapua-ma-inano and Inano-mata-kopikopi are her children. The older son Kariʻi refuses to bite the ulcer on her head; Taaki complies and power enters into him so that light shines from his whole body. Kariʻi is jealous because his father favors Taaki and offers his father Hema in sacrifice at the marae to "many gods." Hema's eyes are taken possession of by Tangaroa-a-ka-puta-ara, his body by the little gods. "Ema, heap of filth!" the gods call him.[27]

Samoa (Vaitapu). The brothers Punga (Puʻa) and Sema seek wives. Punga has many wives, Sema only a woman all sores named Matinitini-ungakoa. He is derided, but his wife dives three times and becomes beautiful, with a red skirt and light-

25. Stimson, *Bul.* 127: 50.   26. *Ibid.* 148: 60–68.
27. Smith, *JPS* 30: 1–2, 5; Savage, *JPS* 19: 143.

ning flashes. Her children are Tafaki (Tafa'i) and Kalisilisi ('Alise).

The Kaha'i (or Tawhaki) legend follows a more or less regular pattern, although with local variations. Hema is always the father (in one instance, mother); his wife is generally a goddess. A brother Alihi constantly fails in undertakings in which Kaha'i succeeds because of his godlike endowments or of the chants of which he has command. His cousins by his father's brother Puna (Punga, Pu'a) or his own older brothers often seek Kaha'i's life.

KAHA'I LEGEND

Hawaii. Kaha'i-nui (Kaha'i the strong) is son of Hema, a chief of East Maui living on the hill Kauiki in Hana district, and of Lua(Ula, Ulu)-mahahoa from Iao valley in Wailuku district. He is born in Iao valley at a place called Ka-halulu-kahi above Loiloa at Haunaka. His chant tells how he goes "by the path of the rainbow" and guided by cloud signs to seek his father, who has had his eyes gouged out on an expedition to foreign lands. His brother Alihi accompanies him but is unable to keep the pace. The chant, as translated by Emerson, runs:

> "Alihi's eyes were blinded,
> The horizon blinded his eyes,
>
> .   .   .   .   .
>
> The foundations of heaven were shaken,
> The kinsfolk of the gods inquired,
> Kane and Kanaloa asked him,
> 'O Kaha'i! where are you going?'
> 'I am seeking the eyes of Hema.'
> 'They are in Kahiki, at Ulupa'pa'u,
> There with the Aaia bird sought after by Kane
> You will find them on the borders of Kahiki.' "

On his return Kaha'i lands on the Ka-u coast of Hawaii and weds Hina-ulu-ohia at Kahuku and their child Wahieloa is born at Wailau (or Punalu'u). Kaha'i dies at Kailiki'i in Ka-u (hence

some say he never lived on Kauiki) and is buried in Iao valley,
or, as the chant says,

> ". . . on the plains of Kahului
> . . . at Keahuku. . . ."[28]

Maori. Tawhaki's relatives are jealous because all women love
him and they set upon him and leave him for dead. He restores
himself by his own power (or is restored by wife, mother, or sister) and leaves the country (calling down a flood upon those who
have attempted his life). He and Karihi his brother go to search
for their father's bones (and to release their mother from cap-
tivity in some versions). The bones are in the possession of an
underwater people called Pona-turi or Patu-pae-a-rehe (or, of
people like small birds) who cannot bear the sunlight but come
to land and sleep at night in a house called Manawa-tane. Approaching, he hears his father's bones rattle (and finds his
mother acting as watchman). He stops up the chinks until it is
broad day, and the spirit people are killed by the sunlight (or
killed as they attempt to escape from the house). Or Tawhaki
follows to the settlement where the father was killed, hears the
bones rattle, and avenges the father's death. He ascends to the
heavens guided by an old blind ancestress whom the brothers encounter roasting food and whose eyes he restores. She directs
him on his way, but Karihi is unable to make the ascent. She
also helps him secure a bird-woman as wife (Maikuku-makaha
by name) when she comes to her bathing pool; or a goddess
(Tangotango or Hapai) comes down from heaven to be his
wife; or he takes the wife of his enemy at the settlement he visits
(Hine-nui-i-te-kawa). Sometimes he loses her through a broken
tapu or because he hurts her feelings, and ascends to the heavens
in search of her.[29]

28. Kamakau, *Ke Au Okoa,* October 28, 1869; Malo, 323; For.
Pol. Race 2: 16–18; Thrum, *JPS* 31: 106.
    29. Grey, 36–48; Henare Potae, *JPS* 37: 360–366; Taylor, 138–
147; Wohlers, 17–20; White 1: 55–57, 57–58, 59, 61–67, 89–90, 97–
108, 110–111, 111–113, 113–114, 115–118, 121–125; Hare Hongi,
JPS 7: 40–41.

In the Maori, Tawhaki is represented as man or god at discretion.[30] He is god of thunder and lightning.[31] He causes a flood by stamping on the floor of the heavens.[32] At the top of the mountain he takes off his human form and clothes himself with lightning.[33] He learns from his sister Pupu-mainono incantations for walking on water without sinking.[34] From Tama-iwaho (Te-maiwaho) he learns incantations to cure diseases.[35] From Maru he learns war chants (such as the Maori still use when cutting off hair to prepare for war),[36] by means of which he climbs to the heavens of Rahua, keeper of the "elements of life."

The same incident may serve to embellish the legend of different members of the family cycle.

(a) Tawhaki disguises himself as an old man and is taken as a slave when he enters the settlement. Left to carry home the axes when the men quit work, he completes with a few strokes the canoe which the men are shaping, and brings in a huge load of wood besides. He goes to sit in a tapu place, unrecognized by his wife. The next day he appears in splendid person with lightning flashing from his armpits, claims his wife, and performs the proper ceremonies for his little daughter.[37]

(b) Tawhaki's descendant, Rata's son Tu-whaka-raro, has been killed by the Poporo-kewa people and his wife Apakura summons her son Whaketau to avenge her. He mingles with the wood gatherers, hears his father's bones rattle, and when recognized by those in the house, escapes through the smoke-hole and sets fire to the house Tihi-o-manono.[38] He asks a slave by which road Poporo-kewa comes, makes a slave summon him for the sweet-potato planting, lays a noose and catches him (as in the Rata story).[39]

The legend of Tafa'i in Tahiti belongs to the chief (ari'i) culture.[40]

30. White 1: 60.   31. *Ibid.*, 59.
32. *Ibid.*, 55.   33. *Ibid.*, 55.
34. *Ibid.*, 61–62.   35. *Ibid.*, 125–126.
36. *Ibid.*, 103–108, 111, 129–130.
37. Grey, 44–48.   38. White 2: 147–154.
39. See note 29, chapter xviii.   40. Handy, *Bul.* 79: 16.

Tahiti. Tafa'i's mother is a goddess from another world named Hina-tahutahu or Hua-uri (Ouri). His older cousin is Arihi (Arii)-nui-a-Pu'a. Anuenue (rainbow) is the canoe in which he sails. He is blond and handsome. He lives in the Tapahi hills of Mahina district, north Tahiti. His footsteps are to be seen in the hard rock.

The children of Pu'a kill (or beat) him because he excels them in sports, but he is brought back to life (by his mother) and later avenges himself upon the boys by turning them into porpoises of the sea. He descends to Po with Karihi (Arihi-nui-a-Pu'a) after his father and, helped by his old blind ancestress and guided by the dawn-star maiden, finds him kept in the spirits' filth pit (the Matua-uru) and his eyes being used "for morning lights at the net-plaiting place of Ta'aroa's daughters." He burns down the house with all inside, after netting the place to prevent escape, and secures the eyes from the girls.

Pu'a's children go on a courting expedition to Nu'u-ta-farata (some say to Hawaii) to woo a dangerous chiefess named Te-ura-i-te-ra'i (Redness in the heavens), or Tere, and refuse to let him go with them. He makes a canoe out of a coconut sheath, reaches land first, and after his brothers have been killed in the tests proposed, namely, to pull and prepare awa from the living awa plant (Tumu-tahi) and to slay for the feast the boar Mooiri (Moiri) who swallows men whole, he succeeds, eats the whole feast lest the creature come to life, restores his brothers to life, then deserts the chiefess. On the way home he turns his brothers into porpoises.

Tafa'i weds Hina of North Tahiti, famous for her long black hair. She dies and he pursues her spirit to Te-mehani, the last place on the island whence spirits take their departure to paradise or down to Po, and restores her spirit to her body. They live at Uporu in Mahina district of North Tahiti and Wahieroa is their son.[41]

For the episode of the awa root and boar-killing test see the Tahitian story of Hiro, who digs up the tree called Ava-tupu-tahi (Ava standing alone) and kills the boar Mo'iri

41. Henry, 552–565 and discussion 565–576; Leverd, *JPS* 21: 3–25; Gill, 250–255; Ahnne 52: 406–408.

and the keepers of the two, Taru-i-hau and Te-rima-'aere;[42] and compare the Mangaian version of Ono-kura, who fells the ironwood tree which has formerly restored itself and slain the feller, and kills the demon Vaotere at its taproot.[43] Other episodes of the Tafa'i story are drawn from familiar Polynesian themes. In one version Tafa'i's ancestral shark Teremahia-ma-Hiva (Nutaravaivaria) carries him over the ocean but swallows his brother. Tafa'i redeems his brother with a big load of coconuts, but later cracks a coconut on the shark's head and the shark deposits both brothers in the sea,[44] an episode also found in the Siouan Indian twin story and hence probably borrowed.

Tuamotu. Tahaki is son of Hema and Hua-uri; Niu-kura is son of Hua-uri's older sister Arimata. Both mothers vaunt the deeds of their sons. Niu-kura is jealous and sends Tahaki to dive, kills him with a spear, and cuts his body to pieces. His foster brother Karihi saves the phallus and testicles and the mother restores him to life. When Niu-kura and the other brothers go voyaging (or swimming) the mother (or Tahaki) invokes her gods and they are changed into porpoises (or whales) and live in the sea.

Tahaki and Karihi (Ariki) go to the land of Matua-uru(-au-huru), directed by old blind Kuhi (Uhi) who gives them a net to trap the spirits and offers to each of them one of her star maidens who come to her house at night. Karihi fails to catch one, but Tahaki catches the star called Tokurua-of-the-dawn; they struggle "way up to the floor of the upper heaven and down again to earth" but he holds on to her and she follows and lives with him. (He goes to a relative named Titi-manu and is sent to the house Maurua-of-the-region-of-the-gods "toward the flaming rays of the dawn" to woo Hora-hora and they have a daughter Mehau.) They find Hema in the filth pit, clean him up with coconut oil, restore his eyeballs (fastened to the belt of the woman Roi-matagotago), and kill the spirits (but save the woman).

42. Henry, 537–539.
43. Gill, 81–85; cited by Henry, 532–535.
44. Gill, 253–254.

Tahaki climbs the High-coconut-to-Hiti (Niu-roa-i-Hiti) ("goes to Niue," says Leverd) and is blown off naked into Hina's bathing pool. Since the "long girdle of Hiva" fits him exactly, he is recognized as the "grandchild" of Ituragi and Tuaraki-i-te-po and sent to woo the high chiefess Hapai. She at first rejects him, but finally recognizes his red body, perfumes herself, and gives herself to him (or recognizes him too late and he abandons her). Tane has not been consulted. He sets tests: to pass before his face, sit upon his three-legged stool, and pull up his sacred tree by the roots. From the hole thus made Tahaki can look down to Havaiki. For a long time the two are happy together, then he makes love to her sister Teharue. Hapai is jealous. He leaves her and she follows and laments his death at Fagatau.[45]

Rarotonga. Taaki is the son of Ema and Ua-uri-raka-moana. Ariki is his elder brother. Ariki is jealous of Taaki's superior accomplishments.

The mother predicts excellence for Taaki and Ariki has his father offered in sacrifice and tries to kill his brother. Taaki destroys three companies of fifty men sent to bring him to the bathing pool where Ariki plans to kill him, but follows his sister Ianao-mata-kopikopi and is cut to bits. His sister Pua-pua-ma-inano brings the pieces together and restores him to life.

Taaki sets out to seek his father by the road between heaven and earth called Nu-roa-ki-Iti. He passes two women beating tapa, climbs to the breast of his mother's sister Vaine-nui-tau-rangi (Altar of Tane), and goes to Tangaroa-aka-puta-ara after Ema's eyes and to the "house of many gods" after Ema's body, which is just about to be burned in sacrifice, and kills the "many gods."

At Rangi-tuna he finds Tu-tavake who gives him culture gifts, among them Maikuku.[46]

45. Stimson (Fagatau), *Bul.* 127: 50–77 (given by a chief of mixed Fagatau and Rekareka ancestry); (Anaa), *Bul.* 148: 73–89, 91–96; Leverd, *JPS* 20: 175–184.
46. Percy Smith, *JPS* 30: 1–13; 19: 143.

Moriori. Tawhaki is the son of Hema and father of Wahieroa by his wife Hapai. She is the daughter of Tu and Hapai-mao-mao. Since he will not allow her to give birth in the house Hapai leaves him and goes back to heaven. He goes thither on the path of the spider web to seek her. He gives sight to the old blind woman Ta Ruahine-mata-moai. He uses chants to insure calm winds.[47]

Samoa. Tafa'i belongs to a race of giants. He can hurl a coconut tree and once "plucked up by the roots a great Malili tree, eighty feet high" and "carried it off on his shoulder, branches and all." He can leave his footprint in the solid rock as if it were sand.[48]

Tafa'i's parents Pua and Singano (Sigano) have names of sweet-smelling trees. Sina-taeoilangi, a woman of the heavens, daughter of Tangaloa-lagi, is sought in marriage by Tafa'i. His messenger goes on the road to heaven and carries a present of musty food. This is rejected but Tafa'i's suit is accepted. The two brothers disguise themselves as if they were ugly lest they be slain by the people of the heavens, and she refuses to have anything to do with them. In the morning they make their bodies handsome and too late she sees the light flashing from them. They leave her and she follows. They abandon her trapped in a chasm, but Pua and Singano come and release her and take her to live with them in the uplands of earth. She goes to the sea after sea water for cooking in the hope of meeting Tafa'i. He sees and desires her, but she returns to the uplands and, mounting upon the housetop, takes her way toward heaven, bidding him follow. On the way she meets her father and his tribe bringing her marriage gifts and they persuade her to return to Tafa'i, where his sister turns herself into an ifiifi tree and shakes down abundance of food for the feast. From this union is born La (Sun), the heat of whose body is "like a whirlwind." La goes to live with his mother in the skies and the story of his adventures in far lands follows. Tafa'i takes Sina-piripiri and has Fafieloa (Wahieloa). Fafieloa takes Tula and has Lata (Laka).[49]

47. Shand, *JPS* 7: 73–80.   48. Turner, 136–137.
49. Pratt (from Wilson, 1835), 448–451, 455–458; Krämer 1: 456–457.

The Kaha'i cycle may be analyzed as follows:

(A) Ill-usage by relatives, (A1) avenged by their destruction.

(B) Expedition to a far land to rescue father (B1) from a filth pit into which he has been thrown, (B2) to restore his eyes (B3) and avenge his wrongs.

(C) Ascent to heaven (C1) guided by an old blind relative cooking food (C2) whose eyesight he restores (C3) and who gives him directions (C4) to find a wife.

(D) Winning of a wife (D1) whom he deserts (D2) or she deserts him (D3) and he goes to bring her back.

The two adventures therefore most commonly told of Kaha'i in Polynesian legend are the quest in search of his father Hema and a courting expedition, which may take the form of a search for a lost wife. The restoration to sight of an old blind ancestress roasting food, who directs his search and helps him to a wife from among her daughters, is a common episode in the story.

In Maori versions she is the blind ancestress Whaitiri, Mata-kere-po (Blind eyes), Te-ru-wahine-mata-moari, or Te-pu-o-toi, and she is found roasting ten taro, sweet potatoes, bananas, or other vegetables. He takes away one at a time until she is aware of his presence, then makes his relationship known, cures her blindness with a touch or a slap, with clay and spittle, incantations, or his brother's eyes and she shows him the spirit path to the heaven of his ancestors, in the shape of an arati'ati'a (notched ladder), hanging roots, a wall, spider's web, kite line, or rope fastened to her neck. In several variants the capture of Maikuku-makaha (her daughter) follows and the ascent to the heavens is made in pursuit of this wife.[50] Among the Moriori, the old blind woman to whom Tawhaki gives sight is Ta Ruahine-mata-moai and he ascends to the heavens by the path of the spider web.[51] In Tahiti, Ari'i and Tafa'i on their way to seek Ema find Kui (Uhi) the blind in Havai'i, steal her taro, avoid her

50. White 1: 56–57, 58, 62–63, 89–90, 100–101, 112, 116–117, 121–123, 128–129; Henare Potae, *JPS* 37: 361; Grey, 42–43; Wohlers, 17–18.

51. Shand, *JPS* 7: 73.

fishhook called Puru-i-te-maumau and her line "Shark of the firmament"[52] and kill her;[53] in Tumu-i-Havai'i they meet blind Ui, from whose four star daughters, named after the red feathers of the kula bird, Tafa'i selects a wife, the morning star Ura-i-ti'a-hotu, to direct him on the way.[54] In the Tuamotus, Tahaki and Karihi find Kuhi (or 'Ui) and Tahaki restores her sight by throwing coconuts at her eyes (from a tree named Te-niu-roa-i-Hiti) and wins the dawn star for wife.[55] In Rarotonga the place of the blind ancestress is taken by Vaine-nui-tau-rangi. Taaki climbs up to her breasts and gains recognition from her as descendant. In a Tane story, Tane, on the way to Iti-kau, goes first to Iti-marama, where he cures old blind Kui with a coconut plucked from a tree guarded by insects.[56] So in Mangaia, Tane swings over to Enua-kura (Land of red parrot feathers) on a stretching tree and restores the sight of old blind Kui and marries one of her daughters named Ina, whom he later deserts because she becomes jealous.[57] In Manihiki, Maui follows his parents to the underworld, restores the sight of Ina the blind, and obtains from her knowledge of coconuts and taro.[58] In a Samoan story told in Tokelau, Kalokalo-o-ke-La makes himself known to his old blind grandmother counting eight taro buds, restores her sight, and climbs a tree guarded by insects at whose summit he finds a spinning house and is given a shell to use as a lucky fish lure.[59] In Niue a divine child is cast out at birth, but survives and goes to seek his father. He finds an old woman cooking eight yams, whose sight he restores, and she tells him how to recognize his father.[60] In the Marquesas, the story of "Koomahu and his sister by the blind Tapa" tells how Koomahu climbs to heaven on Peva's beard after his sister, who has been caught on Tapa's hook. He finds old Tapa cooking bananas, restores her

52. Ahnne.   53. Gill, 251–253.
54. Leverd, *JPS* 21: 9–11.
55. Stimson, *Bul.* 127: 62–66; Leverd, *JPS* 20: 176–177.
56. Smith, *JPS* 30: 206–208.   57. Gill, 109–111.
58. *Ibid.*, 65–66.
59. W. Burrows, *JPS* 32: 168–170.
60. *JPS* 12: 92–95.

sight, and secures one of her star daughters as guide on the
way to find his sister. He finally climbs down from heaven
with his sister on the tree which he has planted below on the
earth.[61]

Although this adventure with the old blind ancestress is
not mentioned in the Hawaiian chant of Kaha'i, the episode
occurs in several other quest stories from this group. According to Westervelt, Maui, on his way to snare the sun, is directed by his mother Hina to his old blind grandmother who
is roasting bananas for the sun at a place up Kaupo valley
where there is a large wiliwili tree. The old woman gives him
another snaring rope and an axe, and hides him by the tree
until the sun appears.[62] In the Kana legend, Uli sends her
grandson Kana to bring back the sun. That she is conceived
as blind is shown by the statement that she has a rope
stretched from her door to the sea to guide her steps. Niheu
is killed in the ascent but restored by his brother on Kana's
return victorious.[63] In the legend of Kila, Moikeha's son on
his way to Kahiki visits the rat-woman Kane-pohihi (Ku-
ponihi), whom he finds blind and counting her cooked bananas.[64] Aukelenui-a-iku, on his way in search of the water of
life, finds at the bottom of the pit Old-woman-Kaikapu roasting bananas, steals them one by one, and restores her sight
with two sprouts of coconut, in return for which and her recognition of him as a grandchild, she directs him how to win
the water of life.[65]

The episode, in Kaha'i's quest after his father, of the destruction of the spirits who fear daylight by trapping them
inside a house is referred by Von den Steinen to stories of expeditions from the Marquesas islands undertaken after the
red (kula, kura, ula) parrot feathers, so highly prized for
ornament, upon one of which trips Hema is supposed to have
lost his life. The Marquesan journey to Aotona after bird
feathers is to the Cook group thirteen hundred miles to the
southwest from the Marquesas. The story is here connected

61. Von den Steinen, *ZE* 1933, 370–373.
62. *Maui*, 44–46.   63. Rice, 103.
64. Thrum, *More Tales*, 24–26; For. Col. 4: 162.
65. *Ibid.* 92, 94.

with Aka or Aka-ui (Laka), grandson of Tafaʻi, who goes
after the feathers to adorn his son and daughter when they
arrive at puberty.

KURA LEGEND

Aka's party get directions from Mahaitivi who lives at Poi-
to-pa in the neighborhood of Atuona on Hivaoa and has visited
Aotona and become a friend of the Kula bird, and his sons Utu-
nui and Pepu conduct the party. They set out from the north
coast of Hivaoa with a double canoe named Vaʻa-hiva carrying
140 rowers, eighty to a hundred of whom die of hunger before
they reach Aotona. Each of the islands at which they touch is
famous for certain scented plants, fruits, or bird feathers whose
names are mentioned, and the travelers are given free way when
their own names are spoken. At Aotona they build a house or
rebuild Mahaitivi's, sprinkle roasted coconut as a lure, and hide
until the "kula" have filled the house, thinking that their friend
has returned. When all are inside they close the doors and fill
140 bags with feathers, that the families of the dead may also
receive their portion.[66]

The theme appears in Maori story unconnected with the Kahaʻi cycle:

Tangaroa steals the child of Ruapupuke and sets him up
as a figure at the end of the ridgepole of a house at the bottom
of the sea where live the underwater people who fear daylight.
The father follows and, advised by an old woman, stops up the
chinks of the house until it is broad day and then lets the sunlight kill those within.[67]

66. Von den Steinen, *ZE* 1933, 9–21.
67. White 2: 162–163.

XVIII

WAHIELOA-LAKA CYCLE

THE story of Wahieloa (Wahieroa), son of Kahaʻi
(Tawhaki) duplicates that of Hema, and the story of
his famous son Laka (Rata) corresponds with the
journey made by Kahaʻi to restore his father or his father's
bones to his native land. In the Pele legend Wahieloa (Wahialoa, Wahioloa) is named as one of the husbands of Pele
while she is living with her parents at Hapakuela, "a place
unknown." Laka and Menehune are their children. The husband is "snatched away" by Pele-kumu-lani and Pele migrates to Hawaii in search of him.[1] Wahieloa's wife Hina-
hawea may be the Hina-kawea drawn out of the sea by Wakea. Her other name, Koolau (north Kahiki), corresponds
with South Sea versions, where she is a chiefess of North
Tahiti.

LEGEND OF WAHIELOA

Wahieloa is son of Kahaʻi and Hina-ulu-ohia, born at Wailau, Ninole, in Ka-u district on the island of Hawaii. He lives as
chief in Kipahulu at Kalaikoi and has by his wife Hina-hawea,
daughter of Hina-howana, a son Laka. Wahieloa sails to the
home of the child's grandmother on Hawaii after the birth gift
(Alakoi-ula-a-Kane), lands at Punaluʻu, Ka-u, and is seized and
sacrificed. His bones are guarded in the cave of Kaualehu (at
Koloa[2]) by Old-woman-Kaikapu. His son brings back his bones
to Maui and deposits them in Papa-ulu-ana at Alae, Kaumakani, Kipahulu.[3]

Maori. Wahie-roa (Long piece of firewood) is so named from
a great log of wood which his father Tawhaki has brought into

1. Westervelt, *Volcanoes,* 7; Thrum, *Tales,* 36; For. Col. 5: 524.
2. Malo, 323.
3. *HAA* 1932, 109. See also Kamakau, *Ke Au Okoa,* October 28,
1869; Malo, 323; Thrum, *Tales,* 111.

camp where his wife is living with her people. His mother is called Hine-nui-a-te-kawa[4] or Maikuku-makaha[5] or Hapai-nui-a-maunga.[6] His wife is Matoka-rau-tawhiri,[7] Kura,[8] Hawea,[9] or Hine-tu-a-haka.[10] He is killed by alien people across the sea led by Matuku. The story varies. Matoka-rau-tawhiri has a pregnancy craving for parson birds (tui) and Wahieroa traps them in the preserves of Matuku and is caught and killed. Or he goes to war with Pou-a-hao-kai and Matuku and is killed.[11] Or he is attacked and murdered by Matuku and Whiti, and his wife taken prisoner.[12] Or a party of travelers led by Whakarau arrive at Whiti-a-naunau, home of Wahieroa, wearing bird plumes which they say come from Pariroa on the seacoast belonging to Pou-haa-kai, Matuku-tangotango, and Hina-komahi, daughter of Tu-rongo-nui. These people go naked and are wild and roving in habit. The chief Manu-korihi leads an expedition of a thousand men to Pari-roa after feathers, a four months' journey from Whiti-kau in Whiti-roa. The expedition is successful, but Wahieroa is slain.[13]

Tahiti. Vahieroa is son of Tafa'i and his wife Hina and is born at his father's home in the Ta-pahi hills of Mahina in North Tahiti. He weds Maemae-a-rohi, sister of the ruling chief Tumu-nui. King Tu-i-hiti of Hiti-au-revareva [said to be Pitcairn island] takes to wife Hau-vana'a, daughter of Tumu-nui, the ruling chief of North Tahiti. She at first has rejected him, but when he prepares to leave her, love awakens and she insists upon accompanying him. They sail in the boat Are-mata-roroa. He invokes monsters who guard the way to let him pass but to attack Tumu-nui should he attempt to follow. When therefore that chief sails in the boat Matie-roa and the canoe Matie-poto in an attempt to recover his daughter, the entire party are swallowed up by the great clam. His younger brother Iore-roa (Big rat) and his brother-in-law Vahie-roa go to seek him and

4. White 1: 124.
5. *Ibid.* 90, 130.
6. *Ibid.* 67.
7. *Ibid.* 68; Wohlers, 19–20.
8. Grey, 67.
9. White 1: 77, but the name is doubtful.
10. *Ibid.* 75.
11. *Ibid.* 68–69, 90.
12. *Ibid.* 78; *JPS* 7: 39.
13. Best, *JPS* 31: 2–8.

are swallowed in their turn. The younger rat brothers are also lost. Vahieroa's wife Maemae-a-rohi, sister to Tumu-nui, who has been left as regent, rears her son Rata and herself sails with Tumu-nui's wife, leaving her son as regent in her place, and on her return is drawn in by the clam just as her son arrives to rescue her and restore the bones of the other voyagers.[14]

Tuamotus. (*a*) Vahieroa weds Matamata-taua or Tahiti To-'erau (North Tahiti) and on the night of their son Rata's birth the parents go fishing and are snatched away by the demon bird of Puna king of Hiti-marama, "an island north of Pitcairn and Elizabeth but long since swallowed in the sea." The bird Matata-ta'ota'o bites off the chief's head and swallows it whole. The wife is placed head downward as a food holder in the house of Puna's wife Te-vahine-hua-rei.[15]

(*b*) Vahi-vero is the son of Kui, a demigod of Hawaiki, and a goblin woman named Rima-roa. Kui plants food trees and vege-tables and is also a great fisherman. The goblin woman Rima-roa robs his garden; he lies in wait and seizes her and she bears him the son Vahi-vero. Vahi-vero visits a pool from which the beautiful Tahiti-tokerau daily emerges. Kui teaches him how to lie in wait and seize her and never let her go until she pro-nounces his name. Having mastered her, he finds that Puna, king of Vavau, is his rival. He goes by way of the pool to the place where Puna guards the girl in a house with round ends, and brings her back with him, leaving her sister Huarehu in her place. Tahiti-tokerau bears to him the boy Rata. Puna comes in shark form to avenge himself, kills Vahi-vero and takes his wife back and makes of her eyes lights for her sister to do sennit work by and of her feet supports for the sister's work basket.[16]

Compare the legend of Mamo and Rigorigo from the same locality, where eyes are plucked out and used as lamps and the body as a post to support the house.[17]

Rarotonga. Vaieroa is the son of Taaki and Ina-uru-o-runga and they live in Avaiki. Vaieroa's wife Tairiiri-tokerau has a

14. Henry, 468–476.
16. Anaa, *Bul.* 148: 96–111.
15. *Ibid.,* 495–496.
17. Stimson MS.

pregnancy longing for eels and the eels Pupu and Kavei are, in
spite of their sister's warning, caught, cooked, and eaten, hence
a rash comes on the child and as the parents seek a kind of seaweed to cure it they are swept out to sea and Vaieroa is swallowed by the sons of Puna (octopus, clam, etc.) and the mother's eyes are scooped out and given to Te-vaine-uarei on Motu-
ta'ota'o.[18]

Aitutaki. Vaiaroa and Tairi-tokerau, parents of Nganaoa,
are lost in the land of moonlight, Iti-te-marama, and Nganaoa
joins Rata's sailing expedition to that land under promise to
slay all the monsters that endanger them on the way. The parents
are found braiding sennit inside a monster whale that has swallowed them whole.[19]

Marquesas. Vehie-oa has by his first wife four sons and two
daughters. He lives with Tahi'i-tokoau (North Tahiti). His
plants are stolen and he is spirited away by Tui-vae-mona.
Tahi'i-tokoau goes down to Hawaiki to live with Teiki-o-te-po
whose wife is Vehie-oa's sister. At the advice of the two old
wives, each day of her journey to Hawaiki she gives a pig, until
on the tenth day she reaches the place. She has left tokens along
the way, a broken leaf, spittle, and tears, and her husband follows her with birds, a cock, and a drum with which to summon
the day to the realm of night. He sends the birds ahead, the
cock crows five times, the drum sounds, and it is day.[20]

Samoa. Fafieloa is the son of Tafa'i and his second wife Hine-
piripiri. Tula is his wife and Lata their son.[21]

The story of Laka, son of Wahieloa, is told today in Hana
district and the sites are pointed out of his canoe shed, Ku-o-
halau, his tree-cutting in the forest, with the rock table where
he "greased the mouths" of the forest deities who helped him
build the canoe, and the place where he launched his canoe,

18. Savage, *JPS* 19: 143, 145–146.
19. Gill, 145–146.
20. Von den Steinen, *ZE* 65: 38–41.
21. Krämer 1: 456.

together with the rocks into which his two sisters were transformed who swam after him.

LEGEND OF LAKA

(a) Laka is the son of Wahieloa and Hina-hawea (Koolau-kahili or -kahiki) and is brought up by his grandmother Hina-howana in Kipahulu district on the island of Maui. As the time of his birth approaches, his father sails after a birth gift for his son and, landing at Punalu'u in Ka-u district on Hawaii, is killed and his bones are thrown into the cave of Kaualehu guarded by old woman Kaikapu (or at the cave Makili and Makula at the cliff of Kupinai). When the boys jeer at Laka because he is fatherless he determines to seek his father's bones.

The tree cut down one day for the canoe, he finds restored to its place the next morning. Instructed by his grandmother, he first hides and seizes the leaders of the little gods of the forest who are doing the mischief, Moku-hali'i and Kupaaike'e who are his relatives, then "greases the mouths of the gods" with offerings, and the gods complete the two canoes for him in a single night. In the morning after the night of Kane he finds them standing outside his door ready to be lashed together and launched.

Four skilful men accompany him, father Prop (makua Pou-pou) to hold open the mouth of the cave, father Stretch (makua Kiko'o) to reach inside, father Torch (makua Kalama) to light the cave, and father Seeker (makua Imi) to hunt for the bones. Arrived at Punalu'u they bribe the old woman to open the door by offering her a dish of soup. She tastes it and slams shut the cave door, declaring it is not salt enough. Father Reach now puts out his hand and tries the salt of various seas until the old woman is suited with that of Puna. No sooner is the door opened to take in the bowl of soup than father Prop holds it open, father Torch lights it up, father Seeker finds where the bones are lying, and father Reach stretches in an arm and brings them outside. They kill old Kaikapu and return to Maui, landing at Kaumakani. The bones, together with the canoes and the bodies of his companions, Laka deposits in the cave at Papau-luana, whose entrance no man has found to this day.[22]

22. Thrum, *Tales,* 111–114; MS. by Jonah Kaiwaaea, Kipahulu, 1930.

(*b*) Laka was born in Hilo, at Haili, on Hawaii. His mother was Koolau-kahili(kahiki?). He rules over Koolaupoko on Oahu, dies at Kualoa, and his body is brought back to Maui by his son Luanuʻu, child of Hikawailena from Waimea (the shark aumakua Haiwahine) and laid in Iao valley.[23]

Kamakau quotes his chant, elaborating upon the searching party:

> Searched for by father Searcher,
> Lighted by father Torch,
> Dug for by father Digger,
> Uprooted by father Striker,
> Propped up by father Post,
> Reached after by father Reach,
> Danced for by father Dancer,
> Laka found them. . . .[24]

Old woman Kaikapu (Tapu sea) appears in several other Hawaiian stories. In the story of Kaumailiula her role is similar to that in this story. She lives in the land of Olopana and burns Kaumailiula and his brothers with fire because they arrive during a tapu period of whose rules they are ignorant. In the story of Aukelenuiaiku she is the old blind relative whose sight is restored by Aukele and who guides him to the water of life, and is represented as sister of his moʻo ancestress Ka-moʻoinanea and of his god Lono-i-koualiʻi(-iku-aliʻi?). Her local legend resembles the Tahitian story of the cannibal grandmother of Puʻa (Puna) and Hema.

Old Woman Kaikapu lives in a cave in Ninole, Kau district, on Hawaii. She is a cannibal and uses her pretty granddaughter Ninole to decoy travelers to her cave, whereupon she will take them out one by one and kill and devour them raw. She eats her own grandson, Ninole's brother, before she discovers who he is.[25]

The Laka legend is widespread in the south Pacific.

23. Malo, 323; For. Pol. Race 1: 191.
24. *Ke Au Okoa*, October 28, 1869.
25. Given by Mrs. Pukui.

Maori. (*a*) Rata is the son (or grandson) of Wahieroa by Kura (or Matoka-rau-tawhiri or some other). He teaches the art of cutting and polishing greenstone with the whetstone. His wife is Tonga-rau-tawhiri and their son is Tu-whaka-raro. Rata asks after his father and learns that he has been killed by Na-tuku-Takotako and his bones (or eyeballs) carried away "where the sun comes up." His mother sends him out to find a tree suitable for a canoe and gives him stone axes which he must "sharpen on the back of his ancestress" who is the daughter of Whetstone. The tree he fells returns to its place. He hides and catches the little people of Roro-tini, Pona-ua, and Haku-turi, who take the forms of the birds and insects of the forest. These spirits teach him to place an asplenium fern over the cut stump. The next day a canoe appears outside his door.

Ceremonies are performed for its successful launching. It is named Pu-niu (or nui), Aniu-wara, Ni- (or Ri-)waru, Tiu-rangi, Aniwaniwa, or Pakawai. Rata first slays some monster like the leader of the rat people, Kiore-roa,[26] or the swallowing monster Pouahaokai,[27] or he first slays Matuku, then Whiti.[28] Rata goes overseas to Matuku's (or Whiti's) land, persuades a friendly guard to give a false call, and when Matuku comes up out of his cave before the season to bless the crops he nooses or snares him (as Maui snares the sun).[29]

(*b*) *Best version.* Rata is son of Wahieroa and Hine-tua-hoanga. He learns from his mother that his father died at Pari-roa south of Tawhiti-roa, slain by Pou-haokai and Matuku-tangotango while accompanying a party after bird plumes. The tree he cuts down for his canoe is found erect in the morning and he is told to cover the stump with a special kind of fern and then convey the ferns so used to the priest Whakaiho-rangi, his ancestor, who utters building incantations. It is his "elders," the supernatural folk of whom the forest is full, who have done the mischief. The same priest teaches charms to insure the canoe Ani-waru against sharks, points out his route, and predicts suc-

26. White 1: 71; Wohlers, 21.   27. White 3: 3.

28. *Ibid.* 1: 79; Taylor.

29. White 1: 68–80, 90–94; Grey, 67–72; Taylor, 255–257; Wohlers, 20–22.

cess from the signs given him by the gods. He is accompanied by
Apakura as "controlling expert of the various supernatural
beings despatched by him as a protection." The party first slay
the people of Pouhaokai while they are scattered about looking
for food. Baskets full of the slain are brought to Matuku as
food, Apakura impersonating Pouhaokai. The house is then set
on fire and when Matuku tries to escape his neck is caught in
snares. His bones are made into spear points for spearing
birds.[30]

Tahiti. Rata is son of Vahieroa and Maemae-a-rohi, sister of
the ruling chief of North Tahiti, Tumu-nui. He is born after
Tumu-nui and his four rat brothers Iore-roa, Iore-poto, Iore-
mumu, Iore-vava, and his brother-in-law Vahieroa, father of
Rata, have all been swallowed by a giant clam while voyaging to
Tu-i-hiti, whose chief had made Tumu-nui's daughter his wife.
Rata grows into a giant and at a boar hunt loses self-control
and knocks men about fatally. His mother upbraids him and
when she sets forth to seek her lost husband, refuses to let Rata
accompany her.

Rata must have a canoe in order to follow her. He fells a
sacred tree in the grove of Ihu-ata. The little people of Tuoi
replace it until Rata hides and seizes Tuoi and the artisan Fe-
fera, releasing them only when they promise him the canoe. He
brings them a great offering of food and the next day it is completed and brought down to the beach, where a baptism ceremony has to be performed before the canoe is successfully
floated. It is named Va'a-i-ama (-i-a, or -i-ura).

Strong warriors, Matua-fa'auu, Matua-a-aro, Te-iri-poto,
Te-iri-roa, accompany him, and slay all the monsters enumerated in the voyages of Tumu-nui and the others lost in seeking
him. First they slay the great clam, recover the bones of the
dead, and also Rata's living mother, just fallen into the monster's mouth on her return voyage from Hiti-au-revareva, the
home of Tumu-nui's son-in-law. Afterward they slay the demon
bird Matutu-taotao and extract the skull of a relative from its
maw who speaks "in an audible voice" calling upon them to rescue his wife from king Puna in Hiti-marama. Rata escapes a fire

30. *JPS* 31: 8–13.

trap at king Puna's place and slays Puna (as in the Tuamotuan version) and recovers the woman.[31]

The four Tuamotuan versions of the Laka story are so similar that they must have come from a single source and probably by way of Tahiti, since the locale of Laka's home is laid in North Tahiti. The land of Hiti-marama, sometimes spoken of as a land swallowed up in the sea, is in one version called Aihi and identified with Makatea or Saunders island, seventy miles east of Tahiti. The story of the competition for Puna's wife is in the Tuamotus worked into the Matutu story with a consequent inconsistency in the causation. In Seurat's version the canoe builders are crabs and insects and a crab is the guardian on the way. From each of the monsters Rata recovers a part of his father's body and eventually restores him to life. His mother is in the power of an eel, as in the Tuna story.

Tuamotus. Rata is the son of Vahieroa (Vahivero in Seurat) and his wife Tahiti-to'erau (or Matamata-taua, or Tairiri-tokerau) in North Tahiti. He is brought up by his maternal grandmother Ui-ura (Kuhi, [K]ui, Ine-uru-o-runga, Tiau-tara-iti). When the boys taunt him because his clay boat is left behind in the race (or because he outdistances them with his toy boat), he learns from her that his parents have been seized by Matutu, demon bird of Puna, and his father's head bitten off and swallowed and his mother used as a food holder for Puna's wife (or daughter) Te-vahine-huarei (or father killed and mother taken to sacrifice on the altar). He sharpens an axe "on the back of his grandmother" and fells a tree for a canoe. The tree returns to its place. He hides and surprises To-a-hiti (Too-hiti-mataroa) and Ta-va'a, the leading artisans among the canoe-building spirits of the forest, makes them a handsome present of food, and the next morning a complete war canoe stands at his door. Puna has a number of sea gods whom he sends to keep back the voyagers. Guided by Ta-va'a, Rata spears them one by one (with his spear Taipu-ari'i): a giant bivalve, a shoal of monsters, a great billfish, a cavalla fish, and

31. Henry, 468–495.

a ghost-possessed rock (or branching coral which forms Faka-rava today). He slays the demon bird Matutu-ta'ota'o (Ma-tu'u). At Puna's home he is received with pretended friendship, escapes an attempt to kill him in his sleep, and plays tricks on Puna's men by betting his empty crab baskets for their full ones, then filling his own from theirs. He slays Puna by first slaying the warriors of Matutu who guard Puna, hooking the rooster who wakens him in the morning, and tying Puna in his sleep to the rock Papa-'ari'ari. He frees his mother (in Koro-ro-po) and secures the daughter of Puna (Tie-maofe or Te-vahine-huarei).[32]

Rarotonga. Rata lives in the island of Avaiki. Vaieroa is his father, son of Taaki, son of Ema; Tairiri-tokerau is his mother. He is brought up by his grandmother Ine-uru-o-runga (or Tiau-tara-iti) until the gods reveal to him that soon after his birth his parents were swept out to sea and destroyed by the sons of Puna (octopus, clam, etc.). He sharpens his axe by burying it overnight in the sand and when the little gods re-place the tree felled for a canoe, he makes an offering to the gods Atonga and Tonga-iti-matarau and they complete for him the canoe O-tutai and tell him of his parents' fate. A crew of ten men is selected for the voyage, each an expert in some art essen-tial to managing the canoe. When Nganaoa the kite flyer asks to join the party, he is refused. Twice taken in as a floating gourd and thrown out again he is finally accepted upon the promise to kill all the monsters on the way. This he achieves by entering their bodies in gourd form and stabbing their vitals; but for him all in the canoe would have been lost. At Great Fiji where Tukai-ta-manu is chief and Ina-ara-maunga his wife, he outriddles the riddling priest and hence the saying,

"It was said by the young priest Kairu-mauanoke
'Do not tempt voyagers lest you be outwitted.'"

He voyages to Motu-ta'ota'o and kills Te-vaine-uarei who has his mother's eyeballs.

32. Henry, 495–512; Leverd, *JPS* 19: 176–194; Seurat (from Hao and Amanu islands), 20: 481–485; Stimson, *Bul.* 148: 117–147.

Thence he voyages to many lands, remaining for a time at Vai-a-kura in the west of Tumu-te-varovaro. Returning to Avaiki, he attacks Kuporo and there his canoe is lifted and lodged in the treetops and he himself is slain by a great warrior named Vaea, but some say he escaped.[33]

Marquesas. Ata is the son of Vehie-oa and Tahi'i-tokoau. He is brought up by Tua-hoana and her sister, who find him sleeping in the cave where his parents left him when they went after crabs in Vae-tea and were carried away in the boat of Puna-iino which had come seeking victims for sacrifice. Ata plays with the Hana-ui children and although they give him green fire sticks to use and green breadfruit, his sticks alone strike fire and his breadfruit has the best meat; although he fishes in the sand with a thorn and the other children have fine hooks to cast into the sea, yet he catches all the fish and they catch none. The boys abuse him but the old women teach him how to wield a stick and throw stones. The boys taunt him about his parents and he learns the truth from his grandmothers. The temanu tree he fells for a canoe is erect the next morning. He thinks it may be a god and hides to see. Hope-ou-toi and Motuhaiki are discovered. He brings food offerings and they make the boat for him. He goes to the land of Puna-iino, takes seven men as a sacrifice, and bakes them in the oven in a feast of vengeance at Hanaui. Kau-tia, daughter of Puna, he takes for a wife. Koomahu carries her away. He returns weeping to Hana-ui and his companions go to the home of Koomahu and bring back the wife while Koomahu is away seeking his sister; when Koomahu returns he finds all gone.[34]

Aitutaki. Rata lives in a far land called Kupolu (Ukupolu). In search of adventure he finds a heron attacked by a serpent. The tree he is cutting for a canoe for a voyage to the "land of moonlight" returns to its place until he rescues the bird by killing the snake [a foreign interpolation], then grateful seabirds deposit the completed canoe at his door. Nganaoa, refused passage, follows in an empty gourd and is taken into the canoe on

33. Savage, *JPS* 19: 142–168.
34. Von den Steinen, *ZE* 1933, 39, 41–44.

condition that he kill all the monsters they meet on the way. These are a giant clam, an octopus, and a whale. Inside this last, Nganaoa finds his lost parents Tairi-tokerau and Vaiaroa sitting plaiting sennit. He builds a fire inside the whale [foreign interpolation] and leaves it to die.[35]

Mangaia. Una the moon is invoked in a canoe-making song to use the wonderful axe with which Lata felled forests:

> "Slash away, Una,
>   With the wonderful axe from another land,
>   That which enabled Lata to fell the forest."[36]

Vaitupu (*Ellice islands*). Rata is the child of Mafieloa and Tavini-tokelau, born when she eats an eel to satisfy a pregnancy craving. A tidal wave carries everyone away, but the child is saved. He finds a house, clothing, and adz, and adapts each to his use. A Sinota monster repeatedly erects the puka tree Rata has cut down for a canoe, until he has defeated it in wrestling. The monster Ulu-poko-fatu begs to come aboard, and accompanies and protects him from danger.[37]

Pukapuka. Lata of Samoa goes to pick out a log for a canoe and selects the favorite tree of a rival magician named Hinata. The two wrestle but find they are of equal strength. Hinata's chant restores his tree as before, but Lata has put another trunk into its body and has the log he wants. He selects for a crew "Head of stone," "Flat head," "Hole digger," etc., and voyages to see the world. As dangers approach, each man uses his special power and gets rid of the danger. Finally Lata dives into a giant clam, digs at the roots, the shell opens, and out he swims and divides the flesh among the islands, but forgets Puka-puka, which gets the unedible root. The voyagers come to the Witi people and win in competition with them, due to the special powers of Lata's companions. One of the tricks is that of a crab-digging competition, which Lata's man wins by putting the Witi man to sleep with stories and taking the crabs from the

35. Gill, 142–148.　　　　　36. *Ibid.,* 149.
37. Kennedy, 210–216.

other's full basket into his own, then making holes in the other's basket and pretending that the crabs have escaped.[38]

Samoa. Lata is a canoe builder who comes from Fiji, "visited Upolo and built two large canoes at Fangaloa," but dies before the deckhouse is completed. He builds a double canoe at Tafagafaga on the island of Tau off Manu'a and sails to Savai'i, where a southwestern district is called Lata after his name. Two hills on this island are called "the double canoe of Lata." From Savai'i he sails to Tonga and dies there and from him the Tongans learn to make the one-sided deckhouse after the Manu'a pattern, called fale fa'amanu'a. "Steersmen in the canoe of Lata" (Seu i le va'a o Lata) is a title still heard in Samoa in Turner's day.[39]

Tonga. Lasa (Laka) prepares to make a trip to Fiji. Haelefeke replaces the tree he has felled for a canoe, until on the fourth day Lasa hides and catches Haele, who then helps to build the canoe and advises his taking on board anyone whom he sees beckoning to him. Three helpful beings are taken on board in this way, a great eater, a thief, and finally Haelefeke himself. With their help the tests set by the demon of Fiji are successfully met, namely, an eating test, a catching test when fruit is shaken from a tree, a test as to which will first fill a basket of crabs. The thief waits until the contestant of Fiji has filled his basket, then puts him to sleep with a charm and empties it into his own.[40]

Santa Cruz. Santa Cruz people say that Lata made men and animals. They equate him with Qat.

The Laka story follows a fairly uniform type pattern, most consistently developed in the Tuamotu versions. Maori versions are without the trickster elements of the eastern islands.

(A) Discovery of his father's fate (A1) through taunts of

38. Beaglehole MS.
39. Turner, 264; Krämer 1: 455–457.
40. Collocott, *Bul.* 46: 15–16.

jealous companions, (A2) through discovery of superior
strength which has disastrous consequences upon his companions.

(B) Canoe building halted by spirits who replace the tree
he has felled.

(C) Dangers encountered on the voyage overcome through
(C1) a companion voyager, (C2) companions with special
skills.

(D) Swallowing monster slain, (D1) parent rescued from
the monster or (D2) from a cave.

(E) Competitive tasks won: (E1) filling baskets, (E2)
riddling, (E3) escaping a fire trap.

(F) Monster in a distant land tricked and slain: (F1) by
noosing, (F2) after a false call, (F3) after setting fire to
the house, (F4) by freezing.

(G) Woman sought: (G1) stolen mother rescued, (G2)
wife or daughter of enemy taken, (G3) both woman and
mother recovered, (G4) woman slain.

The motive of the tree that resists felling occurs regularly
in the Laka story. In the form of the reërected tree it appears
in the Kana story in Hawaii;[41] in New Zealand, in a folktale
of the Rata type in which two children who seek to build a
canoe to rescue their father from an ogress find the tree restored at the command of Tane;[42] in the Marquesas, in the
story of Taheta and his son Vaka-uhi, who, neglected by his
father because of the death of his mother in childbirth, attempts to build a canoe in which to leave the land, and finds
it each morning reset by the grandmothers, because they fear
the death of their grandchild on the expedition, but upon his
making offerings they build the canoe in a single night;[43] in
Samoa, in a fable of Toa in the form of a handsome tree replaced by his friend Pale, who has concealed himself from
woodcutters in the shape of a bent stick,[44] and in the story of
two chiefs of Upolo who cut down a tree in Raka's forest,
which Raka restores with an incantation;[45] in Dobu, of a

41. Rice, 96–98.   42. *JPS* 6: 99–100.
43. Von den Steinen, *ZE* 65: 343–344.
44. Turner, 219–220.
45. *JPS* 4: 100; Stuebel, 148.

mango tree which, when felled, returns to its place each night;[46] in Mota of the Banks islands, in a trickster tale of Qat, who fells a tree for a canoe, which Marawa the spider resets until Qat hides a chip;[47] among the Dyak in the story of Pulang-gana in which a clearing is restored as before until the proper offerings are made and incantations repeated.[48]

In other instances the tree resists felling except with a special instrument. In Hawaii, the legend of the Kalaipahoa tree which can be cut with a stone adz alone belongs to this type,[49] and the story of Maui told on Kauai, where a spear of lehua wood and a special ritual are required.[50] In the Ono-kura legend of Mangaia a demon living at the taproot of an ironwood tree destroys those who cut it down and restores the tree to position. Ono-kura kills the demon with his ironwood spade Rua-i-para, removes the roots, and forms weapons out of the hard wood.[51] In the Marquesas, the great tree Anianiteani cannot be felled by the avenger of Apekura's son until a special axe is secured.[52] In Tahiti, Tafa'i can cut the sinews of the great fish with a special axe alone.[53] In a Maori story, Te-Peri's brother is buried at the foot of a tree which resists felling until cut with the axe Tia.[54]

Among Hawaiians, the felling of a hardwood tree for a canoe is an occasion of great spiritual excitement as the feller feels himself drawn into close relationship with spirits of the forest whose anger he fears and whom he placates with propitiatory offerings and prayers. Special rituals attend the cutting and shaping of a canoe and its bringing down from the forest, or the cutting of the tree for the building of a new heiau. In Tahiti, "When canoes were hewed out in the mountain, Tifai (Mender) was invoked and there would come a wind, the men would lie inside the canoe with the ropes hang-

46. Fortune, 264.
47. Codrington, 158–159; and see Dixon, 325 note 14.
48. Gomes, 309–315.
49. Westervelt, *Gods and Ghosts*, 113.
50. Dickey, *HHS Reports* 25: 16–17.
51. Gill, 81–87; Henry, 533–534.
52. Handy, *Bul.* 69: 67–70.   53. Henry, 440–442.
54. *JPS* 1: 224.

ing outside, and the canoe would go down the mountainside of its own accord. When they came to low ground, the men got out of the canoes, picked up the ropes and sang, and the canoe was light to draw and was taken to the builders' marae to be completed."[55] Even today in Hawaii the canoe makers assure us that the difficult course of the canoe to the sea is achieved with such ease as could not be possible by human hands alone.

The Aikanaka-Laka legend emphasizes throughout this dependence of man upon the coöperation of spirit forces which control the material world whose resources he would utilize for his own needs. The cycle revolves about two major themes in Polynesian story, the winning or losing of a supernatural wife, and the voyage of adventure or revenge. These are developed by means of a multitude of details in which the supernatural forces of the mother's family are assembled in behalf of her child, either through direct endowment, instruction in magic incantations, or coöperation in the quest. The gods of a family, its aumakua, are thought of as restricted within a limited locality. A wife from a foreign land may control, through family descent, supernatural forces superior in power to her husband's but unable to exercise control within his territory. Competition against alien and inimical forces is necessarily set up by contestants who venture outside the area protected by their own gods. Death on an expedition to a foreign land or on a fishing trip into unknown waters is no natural occurrence but due to the malignity of evil powers. It must be avenged upon these powers in order to uphold the family honor. Even the preservation of an ancestor's bones from ignoble uses becomes a sacred obligation. Who is able to carry out such a revenge but one whom the ancestral gods have endowed beyond his fellows; specifically, one descended from divine parentage beyond the limits of the household into which he is born? The superiority of divine aid over brute force—the necessity therefore of propitiating the gods—is hence emphasized throughout the cycle. The characteristic Polynesian turn to this world-wide

55. Henry, 379–380.

theme is that of the necessity imposed upon the gods to ac-
knowledge the family claim and to succor and support their
offspring. It is through the idea of the kumu-pa'a, the "fixed
foundation," that such an obligation becomes inherent. In
the course of popular development and in groups where the
idea of family inheritance has been perhaps less firmly established than in Hawaii, the religious background gives way to
interest in trickery and native wit over dullard achievement
or to a realistic scene of human revenge, and the devices for
achieving a supernatural wife multiply down the line; but on
the whole the legend throughout the whole area unfolds a
family history of divine parentage through marriage with a
goddess, and the rise of an avenger equipped against the
mysterious forces of a supernatural world.

XIX

HAUMEA

THE mysterious figure of Haumea in Hawaiian myth is identified, now with Papa the wife of Wakea, who lived as a woman on earth and became mother of island chiefs and ancestress of the Hawaiian people; now with La-'ila'i, the woman born with the gods Kane and Kanaloa and the man Ki'i; again with the fire goddess Pele who sprang from the sacred thighs of Haumea. Myths connected with her name tell of her as a goddess from Nu'umealani who has power to change her form and to alter her appearance from youth to age or from age to youth through the possession of a marvelous fish-drawing branch called Makalei; and these, like the stories of Papa, are localized upon Oahu.

Of La'ila'i, Malo writes,[1] "In the genealogy called Kumu-lipo it is said that the first human being was a woman named La'ila'i and that her ancestors and parents were of the night (he po wale no), that she was the progenitor of the (Hawaiian) race.

"The husband of this La'ila'i was named Ke-alii-wahi-lani (the king who opens heaven); . . . he was from the heavens; . . . he looked down and beheld a beautiful woman La'-ila'i, dwelling in Lalowaia; . . . he came down and took her to wife, and from the union of these two was begotten one of the ancestors of this race."

The Kumulipo places the advent of La'ila'i, Kane, Ki'i, and Kanaloa in the eighth era and there follow the names of "Vast expanse of damp forest" and "The long-lived man of the two branches of chiefs," called "First chief of the dim past dwelling in the cold upland," whose genealogy extends to the eleventh era and ends with the death of Ke Aukaha Opiko-ka-honua (Navel of the earth) [who is perhaps Kaua-kahi]. The passage runs (as interpreted by Ho'olapa):

1. 23.

Many men were born,
It was the time when the gods were born,
Men stood up,
Men lay prostrate (the prostrating tapu prescribed for high
    chiefs)
They lay prostrate in that far-past time,
Very shadowy the men who march hither (marchers of the
    night),
Very red the faces of the gods,
Dark those of the men,
Very white their chins (because living to old age),
A tranquil time when men multiplied,
Living in peace in the time when men came from afar,
It was hence called calmness (La'ila'i),
La'ila'i was born, a woman,
Ki'i was born, a man,
Kane was born, a god,
Kanaloa was born a god, the rank-smelling squid,
It was day,
The womb gave birth,
The vast-expanse-of-the-damp-forest, was her next born,
The-first-chiefs-of-the-dim-past-dwelling-in-the-cold-uplands
    (Ku-polo-liilii-alii-mua-o-lo'i-po) her last born,
The long-lived man of the two branches of chiefs.

"The prolific one," La'ila'i is here called, and "woman from
a distant land." From her union with the gods and with the
man Ki'i arise strife and bickering.[2]

Haumea is also equated with her daughter Pele, from whose
familiar epithet honua-mea (of the sacred earth) some derive the name, but it may more naturally come from hanau-
mea (sacred birth). Haumea's children are born in the mythical land of Kauihelani (Kuaihelani), or Hapakuela, or Holani-ku. They are not born naturally but from different parts
of her body.[3] Children today who drool at the mouth are said
to be "born from the brain (lolo) of Haumea," that is, to

2. Kalakaua, 23–24, 50; Liliuokalani, 28–30, 65.
3. Westervelt, *Volcanoes,* 64–71.

have come out from her fontanel instead of by the regular passage, according to the lines of the Kumulipo describing the goddess's later births,

> Born from the brain were the generations of that woman,
> Drivelers were the generation from the brain. . . .

It is in her deified form as a spirit that Papa is identified with Haumea. The priests of Kane and Kanaloa of Maui told Ellis that "the first man" was "made" by Haumea.[4] The Kumulipo prayer chant, quoting the genealogy from Paliku, follows the names of the god Kanaloa and his wife Haumea with those of Ku-kaua-kahi (First strife) and his wife Ku-ai-mehana.[5] The *Moolelo Hawaii* of 1838 says of Kauakahi that he was "born from the head of Papa and became a god,"[6] and Haumea is called in Andrews' dictionary mother of the war god Kekaua-kahi and of Pele and "one of several names of Papa, wife of Wakea." In her human body as Papa, Haumea lives on Oahu as wife of Wakea; in her spirit body as Haumea she returns to the divine land of the gods in Nu-'umealani and changes her form from age to youth and returns to marry with her children and grandchildren. Some place these transformations on Oahu at the heiau of Ka-ieie (The pandanus vine) built for her worship in Kalihi valley.

Haumea is named by Kamakau among those who came with Kane and Kanaloa to the Hawaiian group, "at the time that the waters of Kane were brought forth from hills, cliffs, and rocks." During this same period came Kamaunuaniho, grandmother of Kamapua'a. The event is placed by Kamakau between the times of Paumakua and La'a (on the Ulu-Puna line).

Kamakau version. Haumea comes from overseas from Kahiki with her brothers Kane and Kanaloa. The party land at Keei, South Kona, Hawaii, and are first seen by two fishermen named Ku-hele-i-po and Ku-hele-i-moana, who hasten to worship them. By Ku-hele-i-po, Haumea has a daughter called Mapunaia-aala

4. *Tour,* 324.   5. Liliuokalani, 73.
6. 37.

(Springing forth with fragrance) or Kaula-wena (Rosy light in the sky). Haumea is said to have given birth to "strange noisy creatures."

Myths told of Haumea center about themes concerned with food supply for the life of man and marriage and birth for the increase of the family stock. By rebirths she changes herself from age to youth and returns to marry her children and grandchildren. She lives as a woman in Kalihi valley and transforms herself into a growing tree in which she conceals her husband from those who are leading him away to sacrifice. She secures for a chiefess a painless delivery in childbirth and receives in reward "the tree of changing leaves" out of which gods are made. She is possessor of the stick Makalei which attracts fish. With the stick (or tree) Makalei is associated a tree of never-failing food supply. Kamakau, summarizing the matter in his off-hand way, includes in the rebirths of Haumea the supernatural births by which the Pele sisters are said to have been born from different parts of Haumea's body. Back of the Haumea myth as we have it there is evidently a more primitive form, rejected, or perhaps forgotten, by Hawaiians of Kamakau's day.

Kamakau summary. Haumea has six renewals or rebirths, some say in other lands; for example, as Namakaokaha'i, as Pele, and so forth. She is said to have changed herself into a young woman at the heiau of Hale-papa-a (House of burning land) in Nu'umealani, a land in Pali-ku, and returned to marry her children and grandchildren. Her divine forms and her different bodies are worshiped by later generations as: Papa-hanau-moku (Papa giving birth to islands); Haumea-ka-hanau-wawa (Haumea giving birth noisily); Ka-haka-ua-koko (The place of blood); Hai-uli, because of her visits to the "blue sea" of Kahiki (on Oahu); Lau-mihi, from her gathering crabs (ku-mihi) and seaweed (lau) there; Kamehaikana, from her entering a growing tree—the last three names referring to the time when she lived as a woman in Kalihi valley.[7]

7. *Ke Au Okoa,* October 14, 1869.

MYTH OF HAUMEA AS PAPA

(*a*) *Makalei version.* Haumea as Papa takes Wakea for her husband and has by him a daughter, Ho'ohoku-ka-lani; Wakea takes the daughter to wife and she has the son Haloa. Papa is angry and returns to Kahiki. There she enters into the temple and by means of the mysterious stick Makalei she becomes a budding girl again. Haloa has grown "old enough to build an oven" and take a wife. She addresses herself to him under the name of Hina-mano-o-ulu-ae, becomes his wife, and bears to him the evil son Waia. Thereafter she continually reshapes her form by means of the stick and bears children to her sons and grandsons until the kahuna Uaia discovers her true nature and her power collapses. Kio therefore is the first of the line whom Haumea does not take as her husband, and from Kio spring the chiefs. The chant runs:

"Great Haumea, mysterious one,
　She returned and lived with her descendants,
　She came back again and slept with her children,
　Slept with grandchildren to the fifth generation, to the sixth,
　　　seventh, eighth, ninth, tenth,
　Ten tapus were brushed aside by the woman Hikawaoopua,
　By that woman Haumea.
　One body she had, many were her names,
　The petted royal one. . . ."[8]

(*b*) *Kumulipo version.*

"Many bodies had this woman Haumea,
　Great Haumea was wonderful,
　Wonderful was Haumea in the way she lived,
　She lived with her grandchildren,
　She slept with her children,
　Slept with her child Kauakahi, Kuaimehani was his wife,
　Slept with her grandchild Kauahulihonua, Hulihonua was his
　　　wife,
　Slept with her grandchild Haloa, Hinamano was his wife,
　Slept with her grandchild Waia, Huhune was his wife,

　8. *Kuokoa,* January 6, 1922.

Slept with her grandchild Hinanalo, Haunuu was his wife,
Slept with her grandchild Nauakahili, Haulani was his wife,
Slept with her grandchild Wailoa, Hikopuaneiea was the wife,
Kio was born, Haumea was recognized,
Haumea was recognized as withered up,
She was old, she was not desired, . . .
She was shown by Uaia to be worn out,
Dried up back and front,
She stamped on the ground, left Nu'umea,
The earth shook, the woman ceased living with many husbands,
From Kio came forth the chiefs. . . ."[9]

The myth of Haumea's transformation into a breadfruit tree, in which form she is worshiped as Kamehaikana (or -ua), is also laid in Kalihi valley on Oahu and its events are today minutely localized by old Hawaiians who know the legend and are familiar with the valley.

MYTH OF HAUMEA AS KAMEHAIKANA

(a) *Poepoe version.* Haumea takes human form and as Walinu'u becomes the wife of Makea and comes to live on the hill Kilohana in the uplands of Kalihi valley on Oahu. There they eat wild bananas, taro, and yam, with goby fish and shrimps from the stream. One day Haumea longs for seafood and goes across to Heeia after crabs and seaweed. As she fills her container she has a premonition that all is not well and hurries home to find that the men of the chief Kumuhonua, who owns the land, have caught Makea asleep and tied his hands, and are hurrying him away to have him burned for poaching. Just at the breadfruit tree which used to stand at Puehuehu on the stream Wai-ka-halulu where the bridge crosses Nu'uanu stream she overtakes the party and begs to give him a farewell embrace. At her touch his bonds fall away, the tree opens "like the door of a house," and the two disappear into the tree. It is decided to cut down the tree, but the attempt only results in death to the choppers.

(b) *Westervelt version* (1). Papa and Wakea sail from Ka-

9. Kalakaua, 62–63; Liliuokalani, 79–80.

hiki to Oahu and make their home up Kalihi valley near the cliff
Kilohana. Leleho'omao is the ruling chief of that section. He
finds trespassing going on and his men snatch and bind Wakea
while his wife is away at the sea, and carry him down to sacrifice
him at the heiau of Pakaka. Papa rescues him by entering the
tree with him, and as they flee up Kalihi she leaves behind fragments of her skirt, from which spring the wild blue morning-
glory vines of that region. All attempts to cut down the tree
fail until the men have rubbed their bodies with coconut oil.
They then carve from it the goddess Kamehaikana and it is worshiped on Oahu until taken to Maui, where it becomes a god of
Kamehameha. It is known as a god to win land and power and
to preserve the government.

(c) *Westervelt version* (2). Puna-ai-koae, after escaping
from his mo'o wife, goes to live above Kalihi-uka. He is found
asleep in the chief Kou's banana patch and is killed and his
body hung in the branches of a breadfruit tree. His wife Haumea comes to seek him. The two pass through the body of the
tree and escape. From the fragments of Haumea's skirt as she
flees up the valley grow the wild akala (Hawaiian raspberry)
vines.

(d) *Makalei version.* Haumea as the husband of Wakea is a
beautiful woman dressed in a skirt of yellow banana leaves with
a wreath of ti leaves about her head and neck. Kumuhonua is the
chief who catches Wakea. The tree stands at Nini, a short distance above Waikahalulu.

"Dark woman of Nu'umeha
 The lonely one, Kamehaikana,
 Kamehaikana, goddess of Kauakahi,
 Goddess of Kuihewa the shadowy,
 In the high dwelling place of the heavenly one of Haiuli,
 Goddess wife of Wakea,
 Haumea was a woman in the uplands of Kalihi,
 Lived in Kalihi and went to the sea,
 Entered the breadfruit called uu,
 Gained another body for herself, the breadfruit,

The body of the breadfruit, the trunk of the breadfruit was
   she,
The breadfruit branch was Kamehaikana,
Kamehaikana was she, many her names,
In them all was embodied Haumea."

   (e) *Kumulipo version* (*after Hoʻolapa*).

"Haumea, woman of Nuʻumea in Kukuihaʻa,
Mehani-nuʻu the impenetrable, Kuaihelani at Paliuli,
Beautiful, dark, darkening the heavens,
Kamehanolani, Kamehaikaua,
Kamehaikaua, god of Kauakahi,
At the parting between earth and heaven, in the high heaven,
Left the land, jealous of her husband's second mate,
Came to the island of Lua, of Ahu of Lua, lived at Wawau,
The goddess became the wife of Makea,
Haumea became a woman of Kalihi in Koolau,
Lived in Kalihi on the edge of the cliff of Laumiha,
Entered a growing tree, she became a breadfruit tree,
A breadfruit-tree body, a trunk and leaves, she had. . . ."[10]

   The myth of the gods formed out of "the tree of changing
leaves" which Haumea secures from Muleiula, daughter of
Olopana (perhaps Olomana) in return for acting as her mid-
wife and causing painless delivery, tells of the bringing of
these gods to Oahu.

MYTH OF HAUMEA AS PATRONESS OF CHILDBIRTH

   (a) *Hawaiian book of medicine*. Muleiula, daughter of Olopana, is about to give birth. Preparations are made for a cae-
sarian operation. Haumea appears and hears the lamentations.
She says, "In our land babies are born naturally without cutting
open the mother. The name of the remedy is Ka-lau-o-ke-kahuli
and its blossom is Kani-ka-wi. It is a tree to be fondled and its

10. Poepoe MS., BPBM col.; McAllister, *Bul.* 82: 83; Westervelt, *Honolulu*, 23–29; *Gods and Ghosts*, 160–162; "Story of Makaliʻi," *Kuokoa*, January 13, 1922; Kalakaua, *Kumulipo*, 62 (translation after Daniel Hoʻolapa); Thrum, *More Tales*, 185; Kamakau,
Ke Au Okoa, October 21, 1869.

blossom is beautiful." The girl ate of it according to instructions. When the child was coming Muleiula felt it being forced out by the plant. Haumea pressed herself against the thigh. After the baby was born, through Haumea's power the tree rose and flew and landed at Pu'ukumu, Waihee, on Maui, and there it grew.[11]

(b) *Westervelt version.* The divine ancestress Haumea comes to preside over the delayed childbirth of Olopana's daughter Mu-lei-ula in Kahiki. Mu-lei-ula owns a tree called "the tree of changing leaves" of which she is exceedingly fond. It has two blossoms called Kani-ka-wi, a blossom which sings with a sharp note, and Kani-ka-wa, whose notes come at intervals. Haumea agrees to deliver the child painlessly in return for the gift of the tree. She uses incantations and delivery follows. Haumea travels to Hawaii with the tree but finds no suitable place for its planting. She crosses to Maui and lays down the tree at Pu'u-kume beside the Waihee stream while she mixes kava to quench her thirst. When she looks for the tree it has taken root. She builds a wall about it and when the tree "blossomed" returns to the land of the gods in Nu'u-mea-lani. A man cuts down the tree with a stone axe and leaves it for the night. For twenty days and nights a storm rages and the tree is washed out to sea. A branch is washed up on the beach at Kailua and the fish leap about it. Of this branch is formed the god Makalei which draws fish. This was for generations a god of Hawaii. Another branch is made into the god Ku-ke-olo-ewa worshiped by Maui chiefs and used to hang bundles on. The trunk of the tree is found floating by the beach by an old couple who are in search of a god and they build for it the heiau Waihau. It is named Ku-ho'one'e-nu'u and becomes a noted god throughout the islands. The ruling chief brings it to Oahu and builds for it the heiau of Pakaka near the foot of the present Fort street in Honolulu and the chiefs of Oahu take it for their god.[12]

The myth is to be interpreted with reference to actual conditions as they existed in old Hawaii. The goddess Haumea

11. Buke Oihana Lapaau me na Apu-laau Hawaii, Honolulu, 1895, page 66.

12. Westervelt, *Honolulu,* 47–51.

was worshiped as patron of childbirth. She prescribed the technique for aiding delivery. The tree described as one "of changing leaves" which has blossoms that "sing" is probably the bamboo (ohe), used today for sorcery and out of whose joints the nose-flute was cut. Driftwood on the shore undoubtedly brought strange gods to Hawaii, even before the lumber industry of the Northwest Coast strewed Hawaiian beaches with logs from American forests.[13] The Japanese current is known to bring drift today to Hawaiian beaches from the Asiatic coast. The post on which to hang bundles is a common furnishing for a Hawaiian house. Even the idea of the stick to attract fish, which furnishes the theme for the myth following, may be referred to the old method of using a charred stick rubbed with odorous oils (laau melomelo) to attract fish.[14]

The romance of the stick Makalei "that attracted the fish of Moa-ula-nui-akea in the land where the sun goes down" (ka laau pi'i ona a ka i'a o Moa-ula-nui-akea-i-kaulana) is laid in the districts of Kailua and Waimanalo on the north side of the island of Oahu in the days of Olomana. It ran at length as a serial story in the Hawaiian newspaper *Kuokoa* from January 6, 1922, to January 10, 1924, when the writer, Samuel Kaiakea Kekoowai, died leaving the tale incomplete. The story is developed at great length with a wealth of descriptive detail, scraps of chant and story, domestic scenes—altogether a mine of folk material, through which runs the vein of the supernatural in strict accord with native traditional belief today in its compromise between the official religion accepted from foreign teachers and the family gods inherited through the irrevocable tie of blood and still to be held sacred and venerated by their descendants.

ROMANCE OF THE STICK MAKALEI

(a) *Makalei romance version.* An orphan boy whose brown head of hair shows him to be a child of the goddess Pele is brought up by his grandmother Niula (Ninula) at Makawao in the foothills below the cliff back of Waimanalo where the waters of a

13. *HAA* 1898, 122.   14. Malo, 277 and note 8.

little spring mingle with those of the Mauna-wili pond and flow
thence into the great fishpond of Ka-wai-nui. The people of the
district are summoned to clean the fishpond, but at night when
the fish taken from the pond are distributed to the helpers the
little orphan is off at play and gets no fish to carry home to his
grandmother. Twice this happens and the unfortunate omission
not only arouses the old lady's wrath but also "shakes the foundation pillars of Nu'umealani," and the goddess Haumea (Hau-
mea-nui-a-ke-aiwaiwa), the wonderful one of many forms from
Polapola, comes in the shape of a beautiful woman to direct the
revenge in such a way that her small descendant shall rise to
distinction in the land by attracting the attention of its chiefs.
By means of the stick Makalei which has been entrusted to the
keeping of his grandmother, the boy leads the fish out of the
great pond and conducts them into his own small spring. There
is great consternation among the chief's caretakers when this
loss is discovered. A kahuna consults a water gourd and is able
to discern the source of the trouble but not to discover what has
become of the fish or of the brown-haired boy the neglect of
whom has caused the damage. The rest of the story is occupied
in telling of the search for the child and the way in which he is
concealed by his supernatural ancestors until the time is ripe
for him to wed the chief's daughter and become great in the
land. The chief and his land agent win wives and the mysterious
Haumea withdraws to Nu'umealani with her mission fulfilled.

In Westervelt's story of Keaomelemele (Golden cloud),
the fish-attracting tree Makalei is brought from Nu'umealani and planted by the gods in the earthly paradise of Paliula (Paliuli) on Hawaii. Accompanying it is a tree of never-
failing vegetable food supply. In this garden of Paliula the
young virgin is reared until her marriage. Later the trees
are transferred to Oahu at the time of the marriage of a
younger couple.

KEAOMELEMELE TREE MYTH

The bird Iwa brings the tree Makalei from Nu'umealani and
gives it to Waka to plant in the garden of Paliula in the uplands of Ola'a on Hawaii. There Paliula lives under the care of

Waka. With the tree Makalei comes the tree Ka-lala-i-ka-wai (The branch in the water) or Makuʻu-kao (Supplying endless abundance). The first tree attracts fish (iʻa), the second provides vegetable food (ai); "Call this tree and food would appear." After Paliula has left the garden, the trees are brought thence for the marriage of a younger brother and sister on Oahu. The food tree is successfully conveyed up Nuʻuanu valley, but when the fish tree starts to ascend, the little people of the valley are frightened and raise a shout. The tree falls at Ka-wai-nui (near Waimanalo), thence fish are scattered through the waters all about the island.[15]

It is here evident that the fruitful trees are symbolic of the potential power of producing offspring in the maturing youth or maiden, thus furnishing a fresh branch of never-failing posterity upon the family stock. The southern parallel is contained in the story of Longa-poa, sometimes connected with that of Kae who visits the island of virgins, which is discussed under the romance of Keanaelike.

STORY OF LONGAPOA AND THE TREE OF PLENTY

Tongan version. Loau, king of Haamea in Tonga-tabu, sails "to the horizon," passing on the way the known islands of the Tongan group, then a "red sea," a "sea of pumice," a "white sea." At the horizon he steers for the whirlpool that leads to the underworld. Longapoa jumps out and eventually reaches an island where grows a tree (the puko tree) a branch of which, roasted, supplies an oven of food of every imaginable kind. The gods of the island give him a branch to take home with him, but warn him that it must be planted before a certain time. He forgets the warning, hence the puko tree does not produce food today.[16]

The idea is further developed in an enigmatical saying applied to spots originally planted or occupied by the gods, that if one has not visited this spot one does not know the place itself. Such spots are called the rootstock or beginning

15. Westervelt, *Gods and Ghosts,* 122, 149–150.
16. Gifford, *Bul.* 8: 140–141, 143–145; Fison, 79–81.

(kumu). The saying perhaps refers to the recitation of a genealogy that misses the final step needed to connect it with the ancestral stock.

Mrs. Pokini Robinson knew of a little water hole on Oahu up somewhere in Wahiawa of which the natives say, "If you bathe in that pool you have seen Oahu." On Molokai it is said that "no one knows Molokai" who has not visited the cave of Hina (Ke-ana-o-Hina) which divides Mapulehu and Kaluaaha. It is customary to place a gift of a lei at this sacred place and for women to wear a ti leaf protection in approaching it. In the district of Anahulu, according to an old Hawaiian of that district named Kahuila, there is to be seen the foundation of an old-style house where Pu'u-anahulu is said to have lived, from whom the district is named; and the saying is, "If you have not seen Pu'u-anahulu [the foundation spot] you have not seen Pu'uanahulu [the district]." Kilinahi Kaleo used the same phrase for the two rocks on the sea side of Kauiki called niu-o-Kane-a-me-Kanaloa (coconuts of Kane and Kanaloa). These are the kumu-o-Kauiki, the source from which the hill sprang, and if you have not seen these "you have not seen Kauiki."

On the island of Maui near the sea road to the wharf as it enters Keanae village from the western side one is shown the Kumu-o-Keanae, a small patch of ground planted with taro of which the saying is, "If you have not seen Keanae, you have not seen Keanae." This is the original source of all the taro cultivated in Keanae. The first earth was placed here when the taro patches were first formed. It is therefore sacred and belongs to the gods. Three or four taro tops planted here will supply enough taro for a whole family. If a load is pulled, the next day there will be as much left as ever.[17] A similar idea is reported from Pukapuka where a particular patch among the taro beds is called "the navel of the land" (te pito o te wenua).[18] In San Cristoval the legend is that the first yam planting came from a single yam brought by the serpent deity Argunua, which when sliced provided an unfailing supply of yam planting.[19]

17. Local information, July, 1930.
18. Beaglehole MS.   19. Fox, 83–84.

Haumea is regarded as goddess of fertility in the wild plants of the forest, and she is worshiped as presiding over childbirth. She is also feared as an ogress. The term haumia as applied to ceremonial defilement for women during the period of menstruation seems to be associated with these attributes. Haumia is known to the Maori as an ogress who devours her own children. As goddess of the fernroot she is invoked to ward off witchcraft.[20] The name may be preserved in a Marquesan deity cited by Garcia as Haumei, a god who devours, especially the eyes.[21] In Tahiti, Haumea is the ogress Nona, ancestress of the Tafa'i group.[22] In Vahitahi of the Tuamotus, Faumea is an eel-woman:

Tuamotus. Tagaroa sails to the land of Faumea. Faumea is a woman who has eels in her vagina which kill men, but she teaches Tagaroa how to entice them outside. He sleeps with her and she bears Tu-nui-ka-rere (or Ratu-nui) and Turi-a-faumea. Turi makes Hina-a-rauriki his wife. They go surfing. The demon octopus Rogo-tumu-here seizes Hina and carries her away to the bottom of the ocean. Turi weeps for her. Tagaroa, Tu-nui, and Turi build a boat and Tagaroa recites a canoe-launching chant. Faumea withdraws the wind into the sweat of her armpit and Tagaroa utters a chant for its release. He bids Faumea catch the girdle of Tu-nui-ka-rere, who slips away into the sky and is lost to her. Turi and Tagaroa sail out to Rogo-tumu-here's abode. Tagaroa baits his hook with sacred red feathers and Rogo is drawn up into the canoe. One tentacle after another Tagaroa cuts off until the head comes up. Tagaroa cuts that off and Hina is drawn out from it covered with slime.[23]

In Hawaii, Haumea is generally represented as living on Oahu, either up Kalihi valley, like Kapo, or, as in the Pupuhuluena story, on the north side of the island with her attendants, to whom, when she causes a famine to fall on the land, she leaves a supply of wild food plants to preserve them from famine.[24] In the story of Kaulu she lives at Nuihele in Kala-

20. *JPS* 9: 43; 28: 83, and see White 2: 167–172.
21. 42–43.   22. Leverd, *JPS* 21: 1–3.
23. Emory MS.   24. *HAA* 1926, 92.

pana, and Kaulu kills her by throwing nets about her as she sleeps, the last of which, Maoleha, which she is unable to break, is the same as that used in the divination ceremony of shaking out food over the land in the Makahiki festival,[25] the object of which is to insure food for the coming year. Kaulu, whose name means "growth in plants," is the famous voyager who robs the garden of the gods of cultivated plants, thus breaking the power of the goddess to vent her anger by withdrawing the wild plants of the forest, which must nevertheless be resorted to for vegetable food at certain seasons of the year when crops are maturing.

Thus it is in her character as destroyer or guardian of wild growth and patroness of childbirth that Haumea becomes, like La'ila'i, the producer or, like Pele, the destroyer of living things. Goddess of the "sacred earth," she is venerated as the spiritual essence of that ageless womb out of which life is produced in changing forms and which finally, in the body of a woman, bears to Papa, through union with Wakea, the human race, or, more specifically, the Hawaiian people in direct descent from the ancestral gods.

25. For. Col. 4: 530; 5: 368.

PART THREE
The Chiefs

XX

PAPA AND WAKEA

GENEALOGIES are of great importance in Hawaiian social life since no one can claim admittance to the Papa ali'i or ranking body of high chiefs with all its privileges and prerogatives who cannot trace his ancestry back to Ulu or Nanaulu, sons of Ki'i and Hinakoula. Chiefs of Maui and Hawaii generally trace from the Ulu genealogy; those of Kauai and Oahu from the Nanaulu. Both lines are respected alike. Both stem from Wakea and Papa and follow approximately the same succession down to the name of Ki'i as twelfth in line from Wakea. It is to be observed that on the Ulu line three Nana names follow those of Ulu and his wife Ulu-kou, and others occur down the line.

This association of names is also found in the Moriori genealogy, where the names Tiki, Uru, Ngangana follow those of the gods Tu, Rongo, Tane, Tangaroa, Rongo-mai, Kahukura as given in Tregear's *Maori Dictionary* (page 669) quoted by Stokes. In Maori, Uru-te-ngangana (Ulu-and-Nanana) heads the list of the family of gods from Rangi and Papa taught in the Whare-wananga or House-of-learning, and presides over the Whare-kura temple situated at the place where man was first taught the doctrines of Tane and where occurred the creation (naming) of land and sea plants and animals.[1] In Tahitian chants Uru is called the canoe bailer of Tu and Ta'aroa.[2] Nana is one of the artisans who shapes the man child Tane of Ta'aroa.[3] Uru-o-te-oa-ti'a is the son of Ti'i, the first man, and Hina-te-'u'ti-mahai-tuamea, the two-faced first woman. Three others are born of the same pair and from these descend chiefs and commoners (manahune) of Tahiti.[4]

From these comparisons it may be inferred that the names of Wakea and Papa as ancestors of the Hawaiian people de-

1. Smith, *MPS* 3: 82, 83, 118. 2. Henry, 356.
3. *Ibid.*, 365. 4. *Ibid.*, 402–403.

rive from old tribal tradition. In the South Seas, Wakea or
his equivalent is god of light and of the heavens who "opens
the door of the sun"; Papa is a goddess of earth and the underworld and mother of gods. The name of Wakea appears
in the Hawaiian word for midday, "awakea." "Papa" in Hawaii is "a word applied to any flat surface," especially to
those foundation layers underseas from which new lands are
said to rise—perhaps related in a figure to the successive
generations of mankind born out of the vast waters of the
spirit world and identified through their family leaders with
the lands which they inhabit. Papa-hanau-moku (Papa from
whom lands are born) is her epithet. Stories and genealogies
connect the Wakea-Papa line with the myth already noticed
of a marriage between a high chief from a distant land and a
native-born chiefess. A struggle is implied between an older
line and a new order which imposes the separation of chiefs
from commoners and of both from a degraded slave class, and
establishes religious tapus, especially as related to women, by
which so powerful a weapon is placed in the hands of the new
theocracy, chiefs working in harmony with the priesthood, as
to control conduct and effectually to subordinate the people
to their ruling chiefs.

Wakea, from whom all Hawaiian genealogies stem as the
ancestor of the Hawaiian people, "both chiefs and commoners," is regarded as a man in Hawaiian tradition, not as a
god as in southern groups. Stokes thinks him a duplicate of
Ki'i, twelfth in descent from Wakea, husband of Hina-Koula,
and father of Ulu and Nana-ulu. The southern equivalent of
Ki'i is Ti'i or Tiki, the first man, generally coupled with the
story of the birth of the first woman out of a pile of sand impregnated by Tiki, a tradition which Stokes sees reflected in
the Hawaiian euphemistic version of Wakea's infidelity to
his wife Papa and marriage with the young daughter Ho-
'ohoku-ka-lani (The heavenly one who made the stars). The
name indeed suggests that from this marriage descended the
chiefs, since stars are ascribed to chiefs in Hawaiian lore.

Wakea is called the son of Kahiko-lua-mea (Very ancient
and sacred) and his wife Kupulanakehau. To them are born
Lihau-ula (Liha-ula, Lehu-ula) from whom are descended

the priests (kahuna) and Wakea from whom come the chiefs (ali'i). From a third son, Maku'u, some say by another wife, come the commoners (maka-aina).[5] In the fourteenth era of the Kumulipo chant occur the names of Wakea, Lehu-ula (Lihau-ula) and Makulukulu-kaee-au-lani (Makuu) in connection with the name Paupani-a(wa)kea, a name applied either to Wakea alone or to the whole family group named above.

Paupani-akea is said to have been born to Kupulanakehau when she lived with Kahiko, the very ancient sacred one. The name may mean "End of the closing up of light," or "Opening up of light," possibly through the extending of the priestly line to include the chiefs. Malo, who does not name the third son, says that in the genealogy called Ololo, Kahiko (ancient) is the first kanaka (man).[6] Kepelino makes Kahiko an immigrant from Kahiki or "a descendant of La-'ila'i," who is the mother of the race on the Kumulipo genealogy.[7] In the chant of Kamahualele[8] about the birth of the islands, Kahiko is spoken of as

> O Kahiko ke kumu aina
> Nana i mahele ka'awale na moku.

> "Kahiko the root of the land
> Who divided and separated the islands."

The parceling out of the land among families of chiefs seems to be pointed to in this reference. Kamakau says that Kahiko-lua-mea was descended from Kane-huli-honua (Kane made out of earth) and Ke-aka-huli-lani (The shadow made of the sky) through their child Ka-papa-ia-laka; that he was a devout chief under whom the land was blessed. To his son Lihauula belonged the "priesthood of Milipomea" and to his son Wakea the temporal rule.[9] During the early years of settlement, reasons Kamakau, there were few people and each family governed itself. The kahuna class was first separated

5. For. Pol. Race 1: 112.   6. 23.
7. 190.   8. For. Col. 4: 20–21.
9. *Ke Au Okoa,* March 24, 1870.

from the rest of the family line and it was not until some hundred years later that chiefs came to be set up over the land. Human sacrifices he thinks were unknown.[10] According to Kepelino the chiefs eventually found their power restricted by that of the priests and they sought means of uniting the two offices under one line. Just how this was achieved is not made clear.[11] Two Wakea legends are given which may or may not have reference to a struggle to unite the priestly office with that of ruling chief and to establish a closed class of chiefs who might claim the right to the sacred office through descent from the gods. Wakea's fight for the controlling power is one of these legends; his infidelity to his wife Papa and marriage with their daughter Ho'ohoku-ka-lani is the other, out of which grow the stories of the birth of Haloa and of Waia who succeed Wakea on the genealogies.

LEGEND OF WAKEA'S FIGHT FOR POWER

Malo version. Kahiko at his death bequeaths the land to his elder son Lihau-ula "leaving Wakea destitute." Lihau-ula gives battle to Wakea the blond (ehu) against the advice of his counselor, who would not have him fight during the summer lest his men melt away. Lihau-ula is slain and Wakea takes over the rule. He fights with Kane-ia-kumu-honua and is defeated and obliged to take to sea; but as they are swimming about his kahuna bids him form a symbolic heiau and its sacrifice with his hand (described much like our own hand game of the church and the steeple), gather his people together, and offer prayer to his god, which done he renews the battle, is victorious, and wins the government (aupuni). Those who place the fight in Hawaii say that he was driven to the extreme western islet of Kaula and thence oversea; others say that he fought in Kahiki-ku.[12]

LEGEND OF WAKEA AND HO'OHOKU-KA-LANI

(*a*) Papa is the wife of Wakea. She (or some say the wife of his kahuna) bears a daughter Ho'ohoku-ka-lani who grows to be

10. *Ibid.*, March 17, 1870.   11. 60–67.
12. Malo, 312–314; For. Col. 6: 318–319.

a beautiful girl. Wakea desires her but finds no way to gratify his desire without arousing Papa's jealousy. His kahuna Komoawa suggests that he arrange tapu nights when husband and wife shall separate, and tell Papa that this is done at the command of the god. Papa is unsuspicious and consents to the tapus. On the second of the tapu nights when he takes Ho'ohoku, he unluckily oversleeps, although the kahuna chants the awakening song, and Papa discovers the trick. Wakea and Papa separate, one spitting in the other's face as sign of repudiation.[13]

(b) *Kumulipo version* (*twelfth era, translation after Daniel Ho'olapa*).

Great Papa bearer of islands,
Papa lived with Wakea,
Haalolo the woman was born,
Was born jealousy, anger,
Papa was deceived by Wakea,
He ordered the days in the month,
The night to Kane for the last,
The night to Hilo for the first,
The house platform was tapu (to women), the place where they
    sat,
The house where Wakea lived, . . .

and there follow a number of food tapus which further restrict women except of the highest rank.

LEGEND OF THE LAULOA TARO

(a) *Naua society version.* Ho'ohoku-o-ka-lani's first child by her father Wakea is born in the form not of a human being but of a root, and is thrown away (*kiola*) at the east corner of the house. Not long after a taro plant grows from the spot and afterwards, when a real child is born to them, Wakea names it from the stalk (ha) and the length (loa).[14]

13. *Moolelo Hawaii* (1838), 37–40; Pogue, 23–24; Malo, 314–315; Kepelino, 62–66; For. Col. 6: 319; Kamakau, *Ke Au Okoa,* October 14, 1869.
14. Kepelino, 192–193.

(b) *Lyman version.* The child of Papa is born deformed without arms or legs and is buried at night at the end of the long house. In the morning appear the stalk and leaves of a taro plant which Wakea names Ha-loa (Long rootstalk) and Papa's next child is named after this plant.[15]

According to Kepelino it is with this second Haloa that the union between chief and priest takes place, Haloa having assumed the three natures of god, kahuna, and chief.[16] His nature as god may perhaps be represented by the spirit of the unformed child which enters into him with the taking of the name of the plant which grows out of its body. It was an assertion of his power as a god that gave a chief the right to perform the sacred offices in the heiau which seems previously to have belonged to the kahuna alone.

Of Waia, child of Haloa according to the Nanaulu line and of Hoʻohokukalani according to the Ulu, tradition has nothing good to say. He is called a corrupt and evil ruler.

LEGEND OF WAIA

In his time appeared a portent in the heavens in the shape of a head which spoke, commending Kahiko as a just ruler and reproving Waia because he had failed to keep up religious observances, to be courageous, to care for his people's welfare, but took thought for his own pleasure alone and for the acquiring of possessions. "What king on the earth below lives an honest life?" asks the head, and the people answer "Kahiko!" "What good has Kahiko done?" "Kahiko is well skilled in all the departments of government; he is priest (kahuna) and diviner (kilokilo); he looks after the people in his government; Kahiko is patient and forbearing." "Then it is Kahiko who is the righteous, the benevolent man," says the head, and again it asks, "What king on earth lives corruptly?" and the people answer with a shout "Waia!" "What sin has he committed?" "He utters no prayers, he employs no priests, he has no diviner, he knows not how to govern," answer the people.

To the cruel chief Hakau, who is said to have been so eager

15. Thrum, *More Tales,* 238.   16. 62, 66.

over shark fishing that he would chop a hand or a foot from
one of his followers for bait, was given the sobriquet of Waia
and the chant runs:

> Harsh was Waia in cutting off hands
> Of his companions at Mokuhinia,
> He burnt the noses of the old men,
> Cut off the hands of lovers,
> Of women also who were weak,
> The heels of those who served,
> His sport was fishing,
> He consented to the lusts of his favorites,
> To the evil counsels of his friends.

A pestilence is said to have come in his day, called Ikipua-
hola, leaving only twenty-six persons alive. When the sickness called Okuʻu came in the time of Kamehameha, the medical kahuna Kama told his chief that this was the same disease
that visited the land in the days of Waia.[17]

The Wakea and Hoʻohoku legend is important on the one
hand because of its connection with the establishment of the
social order. It dates the regulation of the calendar with reference to tapu nights and the setting aside of certain foods
as tapu to women. Kamakau even goes so far as to assert that
until the time of Wakea plurality of wives was unknown. Certain it is that the keeping of tapu nights and food tapus
would necessitate the building of separate houses and the
cooking in separate ovens of food for men and women, as the
tapu upon intercourse during the period of menstruation led
to the women's occupying at such times a separate house called
the peʻa. The dedication of the tapu nights to the gods neces-
sitated a strict calendar system based upon the phases of the
moon, and as the priests alone kept these calculations, their
influence was greatly increased at this time.[18]

The relation of the story to the introduction of social
classes is left obscure. A legend ascribes to this period the in-

17. *Moolelo Hawaii* (1838), 40–41; Pogue, 32–33; Malo, 320–
322.

18. *Ibid.*, 50–61; Kepelino, 64–66, 98–113; Kamakau, *Ke Au
Okoa*, March 24, 1870.

troduction of the slave (kauwa) class through one of Papa's liaisons in revenge for Wakea's infidelity.

LEGEND OF THE ORIGIN OF THE SLAVE CLASS

After Wakea deserts Papa for Ho'ohokukalani, Papa lives with Wakea's kauwa Haakauilana and their son is Kekeu. From his wife Lumilani comes Noa. Noa lives with a second Papa and has Pueo-nui-weluwelu, who lives with Noni and has Maka-noni and another child. From this line spring the true kauwa and if any member of another class has a child by a kauwa, that child belongs to the kauwa class.[19]

Today, with the breaking down of class barriers, members of the slave class are indistinguishable from the ruling classes, but formerly the kauwa were carefully segregated on lands of their own, forbidden to mix with others, especially by intermarriage, and, when no criminal or captive was at hand for sacrifice to the gods, were drawn upon for such offerings. The term kauwa might, however, be used to show respect to a superior, as we say "your obedient servant," or to show affection, as of an older relative to a younger.[20]

It is likely that the Wakea-Papa marriage is meant to represent, either in these two themselves or in their parents, the highest marriage relationship of a marriage pair, that of brother and sister in a high-chief family, called moe pio (sleeping in an arch), whose offspring took rank above either parent, that of a god (akua).[21] So in archaic Japan, brother-and-sister marriage was the common practice until broken up by Chinese influence.[22] Ka-hanai-a-ke-akua, the boy brought up in Waolani on Oahu by the gods Kane and Kanaloa, is represented in Westervelt's romance of Ke-ao-melemele, perhaps patterned upon the Wakea-Papa episode, as married to his younger sister, whom he deserts for Pele's rival, Poliahu. As in that romance and in the legends of Papa's prototype

19. Malo, 96–101.

20. Kepelino, 142–147; Kamakau, *Ke Au Okoa*, November 3, 1870.

21. Kepelino, 195–198; Kamakau, *Ke Au Okoa*, October 27, 1870.

22. Chamberlain, xxxviii, 17 note 3.

Haumea, the scene of the Wakea-Papa adventures is laid on
Oahu. Wakea is born at Waolani on Oahu and he finds Papa
in Ewa district on Oahu, and there on Oahu the daughter
Ho'ohoku is born. Kamakau states that "the children of Wakea, up to the time of the disappearance of Haumea, lived
between Halawa and Waikiki and for the most part in the
uplands and valleys." The land called Lalo-waia (and hence
the name of Wakea's son Waia) was a fertile land. Wakea
(or perhaps his descendants) returned and lived there up to
the time of Kamehameha. Some of his descendants emigrated
to Kahiki and some peopled the other islands of the group.[23]
The story then resolves itself into that of a chief of god-like
rank, attached to the Kane and Kanaloa family of gods in
Waolani, who weds a daughter of a closely related Ewa
family living in the land, and unites the priestly office with
that of ruling chief. The chief later neglects his wife's family,
who eventually disappear from the land, and unites his interests with some other ruling line. The pattern occurs too
commonly in Hawaiian romance to give it special significance
in this connection.

Two chants in which the island births of Papa are made
the theme for an enumeration of the islands of the group are
so similar as to be certainly drawn from a common source.
Both date from the time of Kamehameha and are hence not
very early. Of the composers, Pakui is called the kahuna of
the heiau of Manawai on Molokai[24] and Kaleikuahulu is described as a native of Kainalu on Molokai, son of the ruling
chief Kumukoa and grandson of Keawe, whom Kamehameha
appointed to teach to some of the chiefs his knowledge of
genealogies.[25]

MYTH OF PAPA-HANAU-MOKU

(a) *Pakui version.*

Wakea son of Kahiko-lua-mea,
Papa, called Papa-giving-birth-to-islands, was his wife,

23. *Ke Au Okoa,* October 14, 1869.
24. For. Col. 4: 10 note.
25. For. Col. 6: 360 note 1.

Eastern Kahiki, western Kahiki were born,
The regions below were born,
The regions above were born,
Hawaii was born,
The firstborn child was the island Hawaii
Of Wakea together with Kane,
And Papa in the person of Walinu'u as wife.
Papa became pregnant with the island,
Sick with the foetus she bore,
Great Maui was born, an island, . . .
Papa was in heavy travail with the island Kanaloa (Kahoo-
    lawe) . . .
A child born to Papa.
Papa left and returned to Tahiti,
Went back to Tahiti at Kapakapakaua,
Wakea stayed, lived with Kaula as wife,
Lanai-kaula was born,
The firstborn of that wife.
Wakea sought a new wife and found Hina,
Hina lived as wife to Wakea,
Hina became pregnant with the island of Molokai,
The island of Molokai was a child of Hina.
The messenger of Kaula (Laukaula) told
Of Wakea's living with another woman;
Papa was raging with jealousy,
Papa returned from Tahiti
Bitter against her husband Wakea,
Lived with Lua, a new husband,
Oahu son of Lua was born,
Oahu of Lua, an island child,
A child of Lua's youth.
She lived again with Wakea,
Conceived by him,
Became pregnant with the island Kauai,
The island Kama-wae-lua-lani was born,
Ni'ihau was an afterbirth,
Lehua a boundary,
Kaula the last
Of the low reef islands of Lono. . . .[26]

26. For. Col. 4: 12–19; cf. 6: 360–363.

Another chanter called Ka-haku-i-ka-moana (The lord of the ocean) tells the story in a way to show that it is the ruling chiefs of each island upon whom his attention is directed.

(b) *Ka-haku-i-ka-moana version.*

Behold Great-broad-Hawaii,
Behold it emerge out of the underworld (po),
The island comes forth, the land,
The string of islands from Nu'u-mea-lani,
The group of islands at the borders of Kahiki,
Maui is born, an island, a land,
For the children of Kama-lala-walu (Child of eight branches)
    to dwell in.
For Kuluwaiea, the husband of Haumea,
For Hina-nui-a-lana as wife,
Was found Molokai, a god, a priest,
A yellow flower from Nu'umea.
The chief, the heavenly one, stands forth,
Anointed (?) with the living water of Kahiki,
Lanai was found, an adopted child
For Keaukanai when he slept
With Walinu'u of Holani (Oahu).
A sacred seed of Uluhina,
Kahoolawe was born, a foundling,
Uluhina was summoned,
Cut the navel cord of the little one,
The afterbirth of the child was thrown
Into the bosom of the wave;
In the froth of the billows
Was found a loincloth for the child,
The island Molokini
Was an afterbirth, an afterbirth was the island.
Ahukini son of La'a stands forth,
A chief from a foreign land,
From the gill of the fish,
From the whelming wave of Halehale-ka-lani,
Oahu was found, the wohi chief,
A wohi chiefship for Ahukini son of La'a.
From La'a-kapu as husband,

La'a-mea-la'a-kona as wife, . . .
At the tapu temple of Nonea,
In the lightning on the sacred night of Makali'i,
Kauai was born, a chief, an offspring of chiefs,
Of the families of chiefs of Hawaii,
Head of the islands,
Spread out by the heavenly one. . . .
Wanalia was the husband,
Hanala'a the wife,
Ni'ihau was born, a land, an island,
A land like the navel string at the navel of the land.
There were three children
Born on the same day,
Ni'ihau, Kaula, Nihoa, (then)
The mother became barren,
No more lands appeared.[27]

The conception of Papa-hanau-moku both as a human being—wife of Wakea and progenitress of the long line of descendants who form the common stock which peopled the group—and as a foundation land out of which islands were formed agrees with the Hawaiian belief that land forms arise as the material body of the spirit which informs them and which is in effect a god with power, in some cases, to take human form at will. It is this belief in the animate nature of land forms which gives poetic integrity to the conception and raises it above a mere poetic conceit. It is certainly with this double meaning that the chanters of Kamehameha's day composed their hymns of the birth of the islands upon the pattern set in the story which tells of Wakea and Papa and their loves and angers. The attempt to give it literal meaning is as foreign to the Hawaiian composer's thought as that to rationalize it as a mere metaphor. Kamakau would have us compare a current birth story, as follows:

Papa gives birth to a gourd, which forms a calabash and its cover. Wakea throws up the cover and it becomes the sky. He throws up the pulp and it becomes the sun; the seeds, and they

27. For. Col. 4: 2–13.

become the stars; the white lining of the gourd, and it becomes the moon; the ripe white meat, and it becomes the clouds; the juice he pours over the clouds and it becomes rain. Of the calabash itself Wakea makes the land and the ocean.

This charming conceit is exactly in the mood of Hawaiian riddling speech and it would be absurd, says Kamakau, to take it literally. He thinks that the myth is a poetic way of telling the story of beloved ancestors (who presumably belonged to different branches tracing back to a common stock) who lived as chiefs and whose names were after their death given to the islands where their descendants settled and ruled.[28]

The names in Kahaku's chant are not those by which the islands were known to the earliest colonizers of the group. Wakea and Papa were not the first settlers on the islands, says Kamakau. They belonged rather to the middle period of colonization and it was after their day that the islands were renamed. Hawaii, the firstborn, Maui, and Kauai were children of Wakea and Papa. Hawaii was called Lono-nui-akea in old days, Maui was Ihi-kapalau-maewa, Kauai was Kama-wae-lua-lani (The middle of the circle of the sky). Oahu was named after the good chief Ahu, son of Papa and Lua; of old it was called Lalolo-i-mehani (Lalo-i-mehani), Lalo-waia, Lalo-o-hoaniani.[29] The old name for Kahoolawe is said to be Kanaloa, although Emerson gives this name to Lanai.[30] A chant name for Kahoolawe was Kohe-malamalama (Glowing vagina).[31] Lanai was called Nanai or Lanai-kaula (Lanai the prophet), and a place on the island still bears this name. Both these islands were anciently inhabited by spirits alone and neither chiefs nor commoners ventured upon them.

Such is the story of Wakea and Papa, ancestors through Ki'i of the Ulu and Nanaulu lines from whom all high chiefs of the Hawaiian group stem. What the actual history was of the settlement of this ruling class upon the islands still awaits analysis. It was a period of colonization and of organization

28. For. Col. 6: 322; Kamakau, Ke Au Okoa, October 14, 1869.
29. Ke Au Okoa, October 14, 21, 1869.
30. Pele, 194.   31. For. Col. 5: 514.

under control of the priests and later under that of chiefs, a control united, according to the Wakea myth, in the person of Waia (compare Lalo-waia) or the still more mythical Haloa, son or grandson of Wakea, and follows a confusion of myths which tell of the creation of man out of black and red earth; of a flood which inundated the land; of a famous kahuna who at the command of his god led his son up to the hills for a religious sacrifice; of genealogies tracing back of Wakea and Papa "the first ancestors of the Hawaiian people, both chiefs and commoners" to mythical progenitors and to the gods; of stone and wood workers who live in the forest uplands and are called the Mu, the Wa, and the Menehune people; of the overwhelming of the first two by the last group and their final migration to a mythical land of the gods; of rival families of the gods (akua) and their struggle for supremacy; the demigods (kupua) who champion the cause of one or another overlord; the ancestral guardians (aumakua) venerated in the bodies of plants and animals or of physical nature, about whom and their worshipers the story cycles revolve. Out of all these elements the first period of Hawaiian history is compounded.

To the question of the meaning of the Papa and Wakea legend as it took shape in Hawaii no single answer can be given. Back of it is the Polynesian mythical conception of a dark formless spirit world presided over by the female element, and a world of form born out of the spirit world and to which it again returns, made visible and active in this human life through light as the impregnating male element. Back of it is also the actual picture of society in Hawaii, revealing a struggle for ascendancy among incoming settlers both in the Hawaiian group itself and in earlier lands—an ascendancy dominated by the idea of ancestry from a divine parent stock and hence of grades of rank as revealed in family genealogies.

XXI

GENEALOGIES

THE genealogists of each island are said to favor a particular account of the beginnings of mankind and the ancestry of the Hawaiian people. The Kumuhonua tradition, according to which Ho‘okumu-ka-honua (Founding of the race), as his name implies, is the original ancestor, is recited on Molokai. Hawaii and Maui genealogists favor the O-puka-honua (Opu‘u-ka-honua) or Budding-of-the-race. Oahu and Kauai follow the Kane-huli-honua (Overturner of the race) ancestral line.[1]

On the Kumuhonua genealogy a line of chiefs leads down from Kumuhonua, the first man descended from the gods, through Laka, or Kolo-i-ke-ao (Creeping toward the light), brother of Kolo-i-ka-po (Creeping toward the night), to Nu‘u (Ka-hina-li‘i) in whose time came the great flood known as the Sea-of-Kahinali‘i, and thence to Lua-nu‘u (Lu son of Nu‘u), called also Kane-hoa-lani, ancestor of the Mu and Menehune people; to Hawaii-loa, called Ke-kowa-i-Hawaii (The channel to Hawaii), and from him to Eleeleua-lani and from him to Ku-kalani-ehu and his wife Ka-haka-ua-koko, parents of Papa-hanau-moku the wife of Wakea.[2] Malo calls Kumuhonua the father, through his wife Ka-mai-eli (The digger), of the root of the land (mole o ka honua), which may be interpreted as the rootstock of the race.[3] An invocation for curing the sick begins:

O Kumuhonua of Mehani,
A spirit out of earth, a spirit out of heaven.

Te Mehani is the name in Tahiti of the famous mountain crater on the island of Ra‘iatea (called in old days Havai‘i)

1. For. Pol. Race 1: 188–209; Col. 4: 370–373, 404–407; *Moolelo Hawaii* (1838), 32–36; Pogue, 34–36; Kalakaua, *Kumulipo;* Liliuokalani, *Kumulipo;* Stokes, *JPS* 39: 1–41; Kepelino, 190–192.

2. For. Pol. Race 1: 181–185.   3. 21.

where souls of the dead congregate for their journey to the
other world.

The Kumuhonua legend includes the story of the creation,
by Kane and his associates, of Kumu-honua and his wife Lalo-
honua, of their placing in a fertile garden from which they
were driven because of disobedience to the laws of Kane (which
some say had to do with a "tree"), of the change made in his
name to Kane-la'a-uli as a fallen chief, and of his retreat to
Pu'u-ka-honua after his trouble with Kane. It is impossible
to say just what the legend originally implied. Kamakau
speaks of Kane-la'a-uli as "a noted chief who respected the
laws and proposed excellent reforms which he was unable to
carry through because of the greed of chiefs and so died."
Kepelino and Fornander papers make him responsible for
the coming of death into the world. Kepelino is writing for
the Catholic fathers and interested in interpreting genuine
old tradition in the light of Christian teaching. Kamakau is
a journalist, setting things down as he interprets them and
unrestrained by foreign criticism and, it would seem, without
access to either the Kepelino or Fornander papers.[4]

The Opuka-honua (Opu'u-ka-honua) genealogy opens
with the coming to Hawaii, after the islands are already peopled, of the chief Opukahonua and his younger brothers Lo-
lo-mu and Mihi and the woman Lana, and leads down to
Papa and thence to the Kamehameha line. According to the
Opukahonua legend the islands were fished up out of the
ocean by the great fisherman Kapuhe'euanui (The large
headed octopus).

Fornander version. Kapuhe'euanui lets down his fishline into
the sea from Kapaahu and fishes up a piece of coral, which the
kahuna Laulialamakua advises him to throw back into the sea
with prayer and the sacrifice of a pig, at the same time pronouncing a name over the coral, and for each piece he throws
there rises an island, first Hawaii, then Maui, then Oahu, and
so on.

4. For. Pol. Race 1: 77–82, 181–184; Col. 6: 267–269, 273–277;
Kepelino, 32–35, 42–49.

The incident is referred to in the lines of the famous chant of Makuakaumana when Paao's canoe appears off Moa-ula-nui-akea to invite a chief to come and live on Hawaii-of-the-green-back:

> A land found in the ocean,
> Thrown up out of the sea,
> From the very depths of Kanaloa,
> The white coral in the watery caves
> That caught on the hook of the fisherman,
> The great fisherman of Kapaahu,
> The great fisherman, Kapuhe'euanu'u. . . .[5]

The Kumu-uli genealogy, employed instead of the Kumu-honua on Kauai and Maui, is sacred to chiefs; to teach it to commoners is forbidden. The name is explained to mean "Fallen chief" (Ke-ali'i-kahuli) from kumu meaning "chief" in poetic diction and (kah)uli, "fallen."[6] It resembles the Kumu-honua up to a certain point, but differs in that it opens with the gods Kane, Kanaloa, Kauakahi, and their sister Maliu and wife Ukina-opiopio as ancestors of Huli-honua, and leads down through Laka instead of Pili to Wakea through Kahiko and his wife Kapulanakehau, instead of to Papa through her parents Ka-lani-ehu and Kahakauakoko. In the legend of Kuali'i it is quoted as the genealogical tree which leads down to Kamehameha.[7] It names Kane-huli-honua and his wife Ke-aka-huli-lani as the first parents after the group of gods named above. A variant on the twelfth branch of the Kumulipo says that at the close of the Ololo line were born Kumuhonua, Kane, Kanaloa, and Ahukai, the last three represented as triplets. Kahiko names follow among others, and the line closes with

Wela-ahi-lani-nui (Fiery-hot heavenly one) the husband, Owe the wife,
Kahiko-lua-mea the husband, Kupulanakehau the wife,

5. For. Pol. Race 2: 18–19; Col. 4: 20–27; N. Emerson, *HHS Papers* 5: 10–11.
6. For. Col. 6: 268.
7. For. Pol. Race 1: 86–87, 184–185; Col. 4: 404.

Wakea the husband of Haumea, Papa, and Hoʻohoku-ka-lani,
Haloa. . . .[8]

The Kualiʻi genealogy, as it follows the Kumu-uli down to
Wakea, is incorporated into a chant of 618 lines in praise of
the famous Oahu chief of the northern district who is said to
have ruled the whole island during the sixteenth and seven-
teenth centuries and descent from whom is claimed on the line
of Pinea-i-ka-lani, wife of Liloa of Hawaii. The story of its
composition illustrates the high position given to professional
poets among a people depending wholly upon oral memorizing.

Two brothers, Kapaahu-lani and Kamakaau-lani, desire to
better their position by securing a powerful patron. They are
kahunas and skilled composers. They compose a panegyric to
Kualiʻi, then stir up a conflict between him and a weaker rival,
join opposite sides, lead the two forces to a concerted spot, and
at the moment of joining battle, one brother chants the hymn of
praise from the opposing side and Kualiʻi, pacified, gives up the
battle; whereupon the deluded chief against whom the plan is
laid hastens to bestow upon his supposed savior lands and
honors, which the chanter loyally shares with his younger
brother.[9]

The Kumulipo genealogy (Kumu-[u]li-po, Beginning in
the darkness of night, that is, in the spirit world) is contained in a long chant of 2,077 lines divided into two periods,
the first that of the po or spirit world, the second that of the
ao or world of living men; that is, of ancestors who have lived
on earth as human beings. The first part tells of the birth of
the lower forms of life up through pairs of sea and land
plants, fish and birds, creeping reptiles and creeping plants,
to the mammals known to Hawaiians before the discovery by
Europeans: the pig, the bat, the rat, and the dog. The second period opens with the breaking of light, the appearance
of the woman Laʻilaʻi and the coming of Kane the god, Kiʻi

8. Liliuokalani, 71, 72; For. Pol. Race 1: 187.
9. For. Col. 4: 364–405; 6: 240.

the man, Kanaloa the octopus, together with two others, Moanaliha-i-ka-waokele (Vast expanse of wet forest), whose name occurs in romance as a chief dwelling in the heavens, and Ku-polo-liili-ali'i-mua-o-lo'i-po (Dwelling in cold uplands of the first chiefs of the dim past), described as a long-lived man of very high rank. There follow over a thousand lines of genealogical pairs, husband and wife, broken by passages containing myths familiar to us from other sources, those of Haumea, Papa and Wakea, Hina, and Maui.

The chant is said to have been composed about 1700 for the young chief Ka-I-i-mamao, son of Keawe-i-kekahi-ali'i-o-ka-moku, at the time he was dedicated in the heiau and given the burning (wela), honoring (hoano), and prostrating (moe) tapus which elevated him to the rank of a god. The child was born during the Makahiki festival and was hence given at birth the name of Lono-i-ka-makahiki. It is said that at the time of Captain Cook's arrival at Kealakekua bay in 1789 during the Lono festival, when sacred honors were paid him in the heiau of Hikiau as the returned god Lono, this chant was recitated by two officiating kahunas. It was given to Alapai-wahine, child by his own daughter, according to genealogists, of Ka-I-i-mamao and from her descended to the former king Kalakaua and his sister Liliuokalani who succeeded him. Kalakaua took an interest in genealogies and had the chant written down. When the German anthropologist, Adolf Bastian, visited the islands he studied the manuscript, recognized its importance, and made a partial translation into German which appears in his studies of sacred chants of Polynesia.[10] In 1889 Kalakaua had his manuscript version printed, and this has become, in spite of many textual errors and alleged tampering with the original, the standard text for the Kumulipo. In 1897 appeared Liliuokalani's translation.

There is no doubt that the first division of the chant is a reworking from old material. The conception of the birth from one form of matter to another, and from one form of life to another, corresponds with the text of the Wharewa-

10. *Heilige Sage,* 68–158.

nanga or school of learning belonging to the east coast of
New Zealand,[11] and to chants of the coming into being of living forms of nature collected in Tahiti, the Marquesas, and
the Tuamotus. In Easter island Métraux found a myth in
which three males and a female called Ra'ira'i (identical with
La'ila'i) people the island.[12]

The latter half of the chant from the dawn of light (ao),
although phrased in chant language difficult to render with
exactness into English, is nevertheless clearly designed to
give the genealogical history of the family of Keawe to which
the young chief belonged and from which the family of Kalakaua and his sister claimed descent. The first part must be
regarded as originally a simple and literal story of the development of natural forms on the earth. The antithesis between darkness and light which forms the structural basis of
the chant means, according to one Hawaiian informant (Kupihea), the division between the spirit world of the gods, which
includes all natural forms, and the world of men with which
the family history begins.

> Hanau ke po i ka po, po no,
> Hanau mai a puka i ke ao, malamalama.

> "Things born in the dark are of the night,
> Things born from and sprung up in the
> day, they are of the light,"

are the original opening lines, says Kupihea, which were replaced in transcription by the fine scene of tumult with which,
in our present copy of the chant, begins the birth of form in
the po.

It was the correspondence of the chant with the evolution-
ary theory of creation which interested early scholars. A Hawaiian friend (Mrs. Pokini Robinson) who was familiar with
old chief language and who read the chant for the first time
was convinced that the various stages of the po are so phrased
as to correspond with the development of a child from birth
to the time when the light of reason dawns and he begins to act

11. *MPS* 3: 136–137.   12. Easter island MS.

otherwise than from impulse, and she points out expressions belonging to infancy and the ceremonies connected with that period. If this is true the chant has certainly been a good deal mishandled by later retouchings with a quite different theme in mind. Dr. Handy finds a parallel in a Marquesan chant in which the development of the child within the womb of the mother is somewhat similarly handled. Much interesting speculation is also possible in matching the progress of births into plant and animal forms with the growth and expansion of the race and with particular incidents in its history. This historical point of view has much in its favor. It implies a comparatively late reworking, perhaps several such, of a genuine old original with its simple conception of the birth of prehuman forms in the spirit world (po) up to the coming of man, the image (ki'i, ti'i, tiki), who ushers in the world of human beings (ao), to correspond with the actual genealogical history of the Hawaiian line of chiefs from which the divine child to whom the chant is presented claims direct descent.

XXII

ERA OF OVERTURNING

TWELVE generations from the beginning of the race, on the genealogy of Kumuhonua, during the so-called Era-of-overturning (Po-au-hulihia), occurs the name of Nuʻu, called also Nana-nuʻu, Lana-nuʻu, Nuʻu-mea, Nuʻu-mehani. He is called "a great kahuna" and in his time came the flood known as Kai-a-ka-hina-liʻi, which may be translated as "Sea caused by Kahinaliʻi" or as "Sea that made the chiefs (aliʻi) fall down (hina)." Nuʻu himself is called Kahinaliʻi from this catastrophe, and after the flood he is known as Ku-kapuna, his wife as Ku-kekoa, and their three sons have names of winds that bring rain (nalu).

The story of Nuʻu as told to the missionaries shows a decided tendency to strain after biblical analogy.

(a) *Fornander version*. Nuʻu builds "a large vessel and a house on top of it" called Waʻa-halau-aliʻi-o-ka-moku. In this he is saved from the flood and after its subsidence Kane, Ku, and Lono enter the house and send him outside, where he finds himself on the summit of Maunakea on Hawaii at a place where there is a cave named after his wife Lili-noe. He worships the moon with offerings of awa, pig, and coconuts, thinking this is the god who has saved him. Kane descends (some say on a rainbow) and explains his mistake and accepts his offerings. In this version, as told on the island of Hawaii, he has three sons and his wife is named Lilinoe. Others say her name is Nuʻumealani. Some think he lands in Kahiki-honua-kele, "a large and extensive country."[1]

(b) *Kepelino version*. Nuʻu, called Nuʻu-pule (Praying Nuʻu) because he makes sacrifice to God, lives in the land Kahiki-honua-kele, in the mountains where Kumuhonua was made by God. This is after the flood, which came as a punishment for the sin

1. For. Col. 6: 269–270, 335; Pol. Race 1: 91–95.

of Kumuhonua. He built a Wa'a-halau-ali'i-o-ka-moku and survived the flood, in which his brother-in-law and those others who
jeered at him perished.[2]

Although Hawaiian tradition knows of the flood of Kahinali'i and the term Wa'a-halau-ali'i-o-ka-moku is familiar to
old Hawaiians and may be translated "Canoe like a chief's
house," the idea of a houseboat such as the legend describes
is not a native tradition. Old people on Hawaii told Ellis that
"they were informed by their fathers that all the land had
once been overflowed by the sea, except a small peak on Maunakea, where two human beings were preserved from the destruction that overtook the rest, but they said they had never
heard of a ship or of Noah, having always been accustomed
to call it the Kai-a-kahinarii."[3]

The story of a flood in which two are saved on the summit
of Mauna-kea has been told in connection with the myth of
the underseas woman drawn up to become wife of a chief of
Hawaii. Her father is Kahinali'i and her mother is named
after the waves of the ocean. The brothers in the form of
oopu fishes make the ocean waters rise to cover all mountaintops except that of Mauna-kea, where the chief, his wife, and
his family are saved. The name of Kahinali'i is to be recalled
as that of the father (or mother) of Pele in the flood version
of her migration myth, when the mother accompanies her in
the form of a wave and the brothers shout at the appearance
of a sea that covers the flat island of Kahoolawe. It is natural
to suppose that such a legend would arise about a volcanic
deity whose activities are likely to be accompanied by inunda-
tions. Among the Maori the mythical mother of the Pacific
Ocean is a deity known by the name of Para-whenua-mea, an
epithet said to refer to the devastation due to flood and closely
resembling Pele's familiar chant name of Pele-honua-mea.

A biblical version of a flood story recorded by White from
the Maori gives the name to a prophet who survives the flood
on a raft upon which a house has been built, and elaborate
flood stories outside the Polynesian area lay stress upon this
house building.

2. 34–43.   3. *Tour,* 333.

White (Maori) version. Para-whenua-mea and his son Tupu-nui-a-uta build a raft and put a house upon it with food of fern-root, sweet potato, and dogs, and they pray for rain and all are drowned except those in the raft. After pitching about on the sea for eight moons they land on dry earth at Hawaiki and pay homage to the god.[4]

Qat (Banks islands) version. Qat takes his departure from the world Gaua. Here he builds a great canoe on the plain. His brothers laugh at him and ask how he will ever get it down to the sea. He takes into the canoe his own family and living creatures of the island, "even those so small as ants," and shuts himself inside while he prays for rain. A deluge follows which tears a channel to the sea and he makes off, taking with him the best things of the island and leaving a lake where the plain had been. He is expected to return and foreigners arriving at the island have been taken for Qat and his brethren.[5]

Thomson (Fiji) version. The twin grandnephews of Nden-gei, the serpent god of the Kauvandra mountain on Viti-levu to whom men are indebted for fire, good crops, rain, and victory in war, have a pet pigeon which is their delight. During their absence Ndengei secures the pigeon to waken him in the morning with its cooing. The boys are angry and shoot the pigeon dead with the bow called "summer lightning." Ndengei proclaims war but Rokolo, head of the carpenters' clan, builds an impregnable fortress. Ndengei's seer dreams that if a vungayabi tree that stands near the wall is cut down the fortress can be taken. A flood follows the cutting of the tree, the fort capitulates, and the carpenters are exiled. They sail away and establish their craft on Rewa. For the boys Rokolo builds a wonderful boat called Na-wa'a-nawanawa (The lifeboats) and they sail westward and are never heard of again, although it is prophesied that they will return.[6]

Brewster gives a song-and-dance version of the myth called the Meke of Turukawa (Song of the pigeon). He adds that

4. 3: 172–181.   5. Codrington, 166–167.
6. Thomson, 134–140.

it is because of the scattering of the carpenters over the islands that Fiji outrigger canoes and Fiji woodwork excel throughout the Pacific. Tongans learned the art from the Fijians. The place is shown where the "ark" was built by Rokolo. The river Rewa gushed from the roots of the sacred myrtle when an arrow was shot into it. In the Lau islands it is said that the god of carpenters shot Ndengei's cock with an arrow and Ndengei sent a flood. In Tonga the story goes that Tangaloa Tufunga, god of carpenters, who fished up the Tonga group,[7] came down with his son from heaven and built on Fiji an impregnable fort. A Fijian god sent rain and floated the fort away with the carpenters inside, and thus the carpenters came to be scattered over the earth. In Dobu a magic mango tree closes up when an attempt is made to fell it, but when finally felled its fall is followed by a flood.[8] A myth of a tree rooted in the waters of the underworld is reported also for Hawaii by Mrs. Pukui, who had it from Ka-wahine-hula of Waipio valley:

FLOOD-TREE MYTH

Up Waipio valley is a kupua kawau tree which grows over the waters of Ka-wai-o-ulu (The water of growth [life]) and holds these waters together with its great roots. Were it not for this tree the water would fill the valleys of Waipio and Waimanu.

In the Marquesas a tree is planted over Tohe-tika's head to prevent his ever rising again. He causes it to rain and washes away the tree and drowns all the people.[9]

No natural catastrophe of this kind occurs in Polynesia without an explanation in the vengeance of an aggrieved god. Para-whenua-mea prayed for the flood because men would not listen to the teachings of Tane. The Maori say that in the days of Mataiho (Mataaho), Puta caused the land to be turned upside down so that all were destroyed because they would not listen to his teaching.[10] Another Maori story says

7. *Bul.* 61: 290.

8. T. Williams, 252–254; Brewster, 255–258; Fison, 27–31; Hocart, 180, 201–203; Gifford, *Bul.* 8: 201; Fortune, 263–266.

9. Handy, *Bul.* 69: 109.   10. White 3: 168, 181.

that a woman lifts a bit of tongue from a tapu oven and eats it and in consequence the whole two thousand of her tribe are overwhelmed in a flood to appease the wrath of the sea monster (taniwha) who is the guardian of the fishing ground.[11] In the Tuamotus, the spirit of the murdered Temahage, called Overturner-of-earth, is aided by his grandfather to submerge the island of Taiero, whose people were responsible for his death, and the neighboring islands.[12] Tana-oa overturns the island Fatu-uku and drowns everybody upon it because he overhears himself criticized by his wife's family; only he himself and his wife escape.[13]

The escape of a single couple or of a family group who have heeded the god's warning is a common ending to South Sea flood stories. A particular turn is given to some Tahitian versions where the husband proposes a more likely place of escape and the wife insists upon following the god's advice. The type is found on the island of Maui, where a low hill on the southwest side of the island which has escaped flooding by an old lava stream is explained as the place where a couple took refuge on the insistence of the wife during a volcanic eruption.[14]

Maori. Rua-tapu, child of Ue-nuku at Aotea, is angry because his father places the brother born of a royal mother ahead of himself, who is born of a slave mother. He takes a boatload of young chiefs far out to sea and drowns them all; only Paikea escapes. Rua-tapu promises to return "in the great nights of the eighth moon" and bids the people retire to the mountain in order to escape destruction. At the appointed time he comes upon the land in the form of a rushing tidal wave and all are drowned who have remained by the sea.[15]

Tahiti. Two friends go to fish and disturb the spot sacred to a sea deity called Rua-hatu-tini-rau in whose hair the hook is tangled. He is appeased by their prayers and bids them assemble all the royal family on a little reef as the land is to be submerged

11. *JPS* 10: 68–70.　　　　12. Montiton, 343.
13. *Bul.* 69: 96.　　　　14. Oral information.
15. White 3: 9–13, 23–31, 36–41, 48–58.

in revenge for the breaking of his tapu. Some scoff, but all the royal family are saved.[16]

Ruahatu, asleep in the sea bottom, is caught in the hair by a fisherman's hook and in anger sends a flood, but, pacified by the fisherman's offerings, tells him and his wife that they will be safe if they go to Toamarama islet. The man suggests climbing the mountain but the wife dissuades him and they alone are saved.[17]

Long ago Tahiti-nui and Tahiti-iki were submerged and, except for the birds and insects preserved by the gods, only a single couple and the things they saved survived. The man proposes fleeing to the lofty peak of Orohena, the woman foresees that it will be flooded and directs their way to Pito-hiti. This is the only land that emerges between Tahiti and Moorea. After ten nights the rain ceases. They remain in a cave in the mountain until the heavens are calm and clear. Nothing but bare earth remains on the land and they have nothing to eat but fish and red earth. Twins are born, and the third day a third child. Eventually Tahiti and Moorea are repeopled and plants and trees grow up and bear fruit and cover the ground.[18]

Andaman. Minni Cara once broke some firewood in the evening. A great storm came and killed many people and turned them into birds and fishes. The water rose up over the trees. Minni Cara and Minni Kota took the fire in a cooking pot and went up the hill to a cave where the fire was kept alight until the storm was over.[19]

The form of the name Kai-a-Kahinali'i is used by the Maori in speaking of Te-tai-o-Uenuku, or -o-Ruatapu, son of Uenuku.[20] Uenuku was "a very celebrated high priest and ancestor of many Maoris, living in Ra'iatea, Tahiti, and Rarotonga at the time of the great migration to New Zealand in the 14th century."[21] He stopped civil war, bloodshed, and cannibalism, says Skinner.[22] A tidal wave in the Marquesas

16. Henry, 445–448. 17. Ellis, *Researches* 1: 389–391.
18. Ahnne 44 (1932): 84–87; Henry, 448–452; Ellis, *Researches*, 1: 387–389.
19. Brown, 206–212. 20. Smith, *MPS* 3: 166–167.
21. *JPS* 29: 32. 22. *Mem.* 9: 42.

is called Tai-Toko, possibly from the ancestor Toko from
two of whose twelve sons the Marquesans claim descent.

In myth it is difficult to say in individual cases whether
terms like Kai-a-kahinali'i refer literally to an inundation or
tidal wave sweeping the land, a catastrophe which occurs all
too often in the South Seas, or are to be taken figuratively as
an invasion of some sort, the downfall of one leading family
and its gods and the rise of another. Although tidal waves on
the high islands are not so disastrous as the myth would represent, a small inhabited coral island is subject at irregular
intervals to a complete inundation from which a small rem-
nant may escape by clinging to the tops of the coconut trees.
Churchill records an earthquake which sunk the land where
two thousand lived,[23] and there are records throughout the
South Seas of occasions in which whole islands have disappeared utterly. In the Hawaiian group the sinking of populated coastal areas due to earthquakes or other volcanic phenomena must have left its traces upon old tradition. Such an
area on the Hilo coast still shows the tops of submerged coconut trees which once grew on firm land. Another important
area pointed out by tradition is the coast about the hill
Kauiki in Hana, East Maui, where Kane and Kanaloa are
supposed to have made their home. It is possible that the subsidence of this thickly populated area at a time of volcanic
eruption resulted in the rise of a rival power on Hawaii under
a reorganized priesthood which sought coöperation with the
goddess Pele.

23. Sissano, 13.

XXIII

MU AND MENEHUNE PEOPLE

LUA-NU'U (Second Nu'u, or cycle of time), called also Kane-hoa-lani, Lalo-kona, Pua-Nawao, Ku-ma-menehune, Ku-hooia, Ku-iiki, is placed as the twelfth name from Nu'u on the Kumuhonua genealogical line. Laka (Kupulupulu) and Pili are his sons. Maui, Kanaloa and Kaneapua, Waha-nui, and Makali'i are the mythical names belonging to his period. The names Pua-Nawao and Ku-mamenehune refer to him as ancestor of the Nawao and Menehune people. Ho-oia is an epithet applied to one who confirms the truth (oiai'o), i-ike to one who is keen-witted (ike). The name of Lalo-kona and the wife's of Honua-po-ilalo are said to be derived from his migration "to a remote country called Honua-ilalo to the south." The name Kane-hoa-lani, Malo equates with Kane-wahi-lani and calls him a god who rules the heavens.[1] It is the name given to the phallic stones called "stones of Kane" set up at the place of family worship, where prayer and sacrifice are offered to an ancestral deity for help in time of need. A legend is told of Lua-nu'u to explain why the highest peak rising cone-shaped from the ridge back of Kualoa on the north side of Oahu has the name of Kane-hoalani and the two lower peaks those of Ku-pulupulu and Pili-lua-nu'u.

The god Kane orders Lua-nu'u to perform a sacrifice, and as he finds no suitable place for this offering in the mountains of Kahiki-ku where he is then living, he is told to travel eastward until he finds "a sharp-pointed hill projecting precipitately into the ocean." He sails in his canoe with "his son Ku-pulupulu and his servant Pili" to the ridge back of Kualoa on Oahu and here performs the sacrifice.[2]

On the Kumuhonua genealogy Lua-nu'u becomes the father

1. 114. 2. For. Pol. Race 1: 97–99.

by a slave wife of the Nawao (The wild people), a Mu race
living on bananas in the forest (ka-lahui-mu-ai-maia-a-laau-
haeleele), and described by Fornander as "a people of large
size, wild, [who] did not associate with kanakas (men). . . .
Hunting people (lahui alualu holoholona) . . . numerous in
former times, but now . . . disappeared."[3] The Nawao are
ancestors of the Mu (silent) and Wa (shouting) people
listed as Namu and Nawa among the aumakua,[4] and all three
are invoked as Ku-a-mu, Ku-a-wa, Ku-a-wao by those who
go to the upland forest for tree felling and by the multitude
at the ohia-ku procession when bringing down a tree for the
god of a newly dedicated heiau. Any man who comes into the
path of such a procession may be seized for sacrifice.[5] A
sorcerer's invocation to such an aumakua runs:

> O Ku-a-mu, go thou to [name of victim],
> Enter him, head and tail,
> Let him become your bread and meat,
> Return not again until he is devoured of worms.[6]

By his chiefess wife Mee-haku-lani (Mee heavenly lord) or
Mee-hiwa (-black), Lua-nu'u becomes the father of the
Menehune people, "a numerous and powerful race from whom
the present race of Hawaiians is descended." The older
branch of the Menehune are descended from Aholoholo, a
wanderer, the younger branch from a son called Ka-imi-
puku-ku or Kinilau-a-Mano (Many descendants of Mano).
There are twelve "sons" in all of whom Luanu'u becomes ancestor (equated by Fornander with the twelve sons of Toho
[Toko] in Marquesan legends[7] from two of whom, Atea and
Tane, the Marquesans count descent). From one of these
twelve descends Hawaii-loa the navigator.

It is evident that we have here to do, in the legend of Lua-
nu'u and his forest-dwelling, banana-eating progeny, with
that period of early settlement noted in the chant of Kumulipo as directly following the dawn of day (ao) and the ap-

3. Col. 6: 271.   4. *Ibid.* 54.
5. Malo, 219, 238 note 20; *HAA* 1910, 61; For. Col. 6: 12–15.
6. Emerson, *HHS Papers* 2: 21.   7. Pol. Race 1: 53–56.

pearance of Kane, Ki'i, and Kanaloa, when the ancestors
dwelt in the uplands on the edge of the damp forests favorable to the planting of bananas, which were their principal
food—the period expressed in the names "Vast expanse of
forest" (Moanaliha-i-ka-waokele) and "Dwelling in cold uplands of the first chiefs of the dim past" (Ku-polo-liili-ali'i-
mua-o-lo'i-po). During this period and under Lua-nu'u, according to Fornander, the use of incision was introduced,[8]
and from such a reference to the rite as occurs in the Palila
legend it is at least possible to infer that incision began during this time to distinguish the Kane people from the "wild"
and was regarded as a necessary step to becoming a marriageable member of the ancestral stock. Ku-pulupulu, the
son of Lua-nu'u, is Kolo-i-ke-ao or Laka on the Kumuhonua
genealogy and the name itself refers to the wild fern growth of
those damp forests of which Laka is patron. The word pili
is a term applied to an indirect relation, a sort of hanger-on.
The Kumuhonua genealogy descends from Pili to Papa, the
Kumuuli from Laka to Wakea, husband of Papa.

On the side of mythology, Stokes thinks that Wakea's infidelity to Papa in the affair of Ho'ohoku is a misplaced episode belonging to Tiki in the south islands and should be related of Ki'i, who appears twelve generations down the line
on the Wakea genealogy as father of Ulu and Nana-ulu from
whom descend the high chiefs of the Hawaiian group. It is in
fact likely that the whole Kumuhonua line down to Wakea is
a mere threefold duplication of the Wakea line down to Ki'i.
Kolo-i-ka-po and Kolo-i-ke-ao, born to Kumuhonua's wife
after the two were driven out of their home by Kane's bird,
duplicate Haloa the taro plant and Haloa the son, born from
the unfortunate affair of Wakea with Ho'ohoku, from which,
however, sprung the line of ruling chiefs. If Kumu-honua as
the fallen chief who brought death into the world is the
equivalent of Wakea, then the "death" for which he was responsible is not natural death, which to a Hawaiian could occur only in extreme old age when a man "withered up and
flattened out like a lauhala mat," as they express it, but to

8. Col. 6: 270.

premature death as a punishment for transgression against
a law of the aumakua. Wakea's sin was not one of incest, but
of breaking the tapu upon intercourse with women during
the tapu of the god. This it was that caused Kane's anger
and drove the race down to death. This may be the explanation of the "excellent laws" made by Kumuhonua, alluded to
by Kamakau, which were the cause of his being driven out of
the land. They were laws of Kane and as such any infringement was punishable by death.

Stories of the Mu and Menehune forest livers, who are
placed by genealogists among the early generations of Kumuhonua's offspring, also include a legend of migration, but
generally not pictured as compulsory, away from their home
on this group to some mysterious other world of the gods. Besides this tradition of migration there have gathered a number of traditions about these Mu and Menehune people, most
of them from Kauai and Oahu, all of which represent the two
(or three) groups as former inhabitants of the islands, sometimes as aborigines but more often as introduced from abroad
and living in upland forests. The Menehune are called "human" as distinguished from the "wild" Nawao people, most
of whom they are said to have exterminated. To the Menehune, or sometimes to the Mu, is ascribed the building of
old heiaus, fishponds, and other stonework found about the
island. The legend of the Kauai chief Ola is connected with
these people, and that of the Oahu chief Ka-hanai-o-ke-akua,
the ward of Kane and Kanaloa at Waolani.

It is hazardous to attempt to untangle from these legends
the actual interweaving of fancy and fact which has gone to
their shaping. The "wao" is that part of the mountainside
inhabited by spirits alone and it is tempting to regard the
Mu and Wa of the Nawao family as nature spirits represented in the silent and noisy living creatures who dwell there,
like the rat and the gecko (mo'o) who play so important a
part in Hawaiian aumakua legends. But these aumakua creatures had their human offspring as well from whom Hawaiian
families count descent, and it is possible that certain short,
stocky family types of very primitive culture were referred
to such ancestry. Hawaiian families count the Menehune as

their ancestral spirits and helpers, and these little people play the part of benevolent godparents to their descendants. On the other hand, Hawaiians speak of eepa spirits who are tricky rather than helpful to mankind. A family story told in Kau district on Hawaii illustrates the benevolent activities of the Menehune spirits and many examples occur in old legends like those of Laka, Hainakolo, and Kawelo.

STORY OF KEAHIALOA

Ke-ahi-aloa (Eternal fire) is adopted by an older sister of her mother and taken to Kauai, where she is neglected, until finally she is taken in by an aged couple who find her nibbling raw potatoes in their garden patch and pity her starving condition. When she arrives at marriageable age her parents in Kau are made aware of her aunt's neglect and the father goes to seek his child, encouraged by a propitious dream in the form of his guardian shark who assures him of protection. Meanwhile the land agent of the district has chanced to see the beautiful girl and fallen in love with her. The night before the marriage mysterious sounds are heard. The Menehune people, her family gods, are preparing a sumptuous marriage feast. Her father arrives in time to give his blessing, and she decrees that never again shall an older sister be allowed to adopt a niece, but only a younger sister, and this rule is observed in the family to this day.[9]

LEGEND OF THE MU PEOPLE

(a) *Rice* (*Kauai*) *version.* After the deluge there were left three peoples who made their home on Kauai, the Mu (Ke-na-mu), the Wa (Ke-na-wa), and the Menehune. Kualu-nui-kini-akua (Kualu of the little gods) and his son Kualu-nui-pauku-mokumoku (Kualu of the broken rope) are chiefs of the Mu people in Kahiki. They travel from Ka-paia-ha'a (New Zealand) to Ka-ma-wae-lua-lani (Kauai) and there Ola is born. The Menehune are then summoned back from Ka-paia-ha'a to serve Ola. They live for some time at Lumahai, then at Wainiha, then at Lanihuli, then they migrate in order to preserve the

9. Green, 71–79.

purity of the race, because the people are found to be inter-marrying with the "Hawaiians."[10]

(b) *Kanehunamoku (Oahu) version.* The Mu are banana-eating people of Kuaihelani, one of the divisions of the floating land of Kane-huna-moku. They are sent for to Kauai to help Ola with his building. A few of them divide from the Menehune at Pele-i-holani on Kauai and travel over the ridges to a rocky gulch called Laau in the mountains of Wainiha where they live with their wives and find water in abundance and till the soil of the uplands. They are dwarf people, banana planters and hairy, with round stomachs as distinguished from the Menehune, who are smooth people with distended stomachs. After the work is completed for their chief Ola, all return to the floating land of Kueihelani and never return, but two Mu are left asleep under banana leaves.[11]

(c) *Green version.* When Paao comes to Hawaii he first visits Kahiki and brings thence the Manahune-nuku-mu-ai-maia (Bug-mouthed Menehune banana eaters), so called because of their small mouths, and they land in Puna.[12]

(d) *Lydgate version.* The Mu-ai-maia (Banana-eating people) are aborigines of Kauai, already there when "the first people" come to the island. They are a short stocky race with bushy hair, beards, and eyebrows, active runners, and with a guttural way of talking different from the Hawaiian. They know nothing of cooking food and live on wild plants. They live at Laau at the headwaters of the Wainiha where the wild bananas still grow which were their food. Campers must be on their guard lest these little people steal up and make off with food that is cooking by piercing it with sharp sticks. Hawaiians still fear to camp on the small plateau above the valley where the Mu made their home, believing it to be still haunted by their spirits.[13]

10. 34, 39–41.   11. *HAA* 1916, 144–147.
12. 121.
13. *HHS Reports* 29: 25–27; *HAA* 1913, 125–127.

LEGEND OF THE MENEHUNE PEOPLE

(a) *Rice (Kauai) version.* Menehune are a pygmy people "about two feet in height." Their food is a pudding of the starch plant (haupia), squash (pala-ai) made from a wild plant in the forest, sweet-potato pudding (koele-palau), and cooked taro leaves (luau). They live in caves. Their trails along the Kauai cliffs can still be seen and the hollows where they planted.

The sports in which they indulge are top spinning (olo-hu), quoits (maika), shooting arrows (ke'a-pua), hide-the-thimble (puhenehene), foot races, sled races, hand wrestling (uma or kulakulai), and diving off a cliff. Kahunas, soothsayers, astrologers belong to the company of the chief. "Story-tellers, fun-makers, minstrels, and musicians" furnish him amusement. The nose-flute and the ti-leaf trumpet, the ukeke stringed instrument, and the shark-skin drum are their accompaniments.

The Menehune migrate under their chief Maoli-ku-laiakea with Hema to New Zealand, hence the name Maori for the New Zealanders, and Raiatea for a place there. They are accompanied by the chief Aliikiola and his wife Lepoa. They return to Kauai to serve Ola as expert builders and craftsmen when he becomes ruling chief in Waimea, and increase in such numbers that the grown men can form two rows from Makaweli to Wailua. Papa-enaena is the guard who lays out the work required by the chiefs. A "bow-legged, deep-voiced" Menehune named Weli is sheriff for the chief and planted the breadfruit trees on the plain of Lumahai. A Menehune named Maliu once lingered in a Hawaiian house and was missed from work, but escaped punishment because he was able to report the discovery of a new spring of fresh water.

After living some time in the Lanihuli valley the Menehune are commanded to migrate because they are being troubled by thieving and the men are taking wives among the Hawaiians and destroying the purity of the race. Not a single expert craftsman is allowed to remain behind. Along the route they traveled, offerings of leaves are still made to certain rocks which mark the petrified body of one or another of their number who was so changed because of disobedience or folly, and who is still supposed to have control over the weather.[14]

14. 34–44.

(b) *Fornander (Oahu) version.* Mewa-lani (Lewa-lani, Heavenly space) has two sons, Lonohoonewa, father of Paumakua, and Kahano-a-Newa, Paumakua's uncle. Kahano introduces the Menehune people from Kahiki and establishes them on Oahu as laborers at Kailua in Koolau, and at Pauoa and Puowaina in Kona as servants for his mistress Kahihi-ku-o-ka-lani (identified by Fornander with Kahihi-o-ka-lani, wife of Nanakaoka and mother of Kapawa [or Hele-ipawa]). He "stretched out his hands to the farthest bounds of Kahiki and on them came the Menehune people to Oahu," and "when the sun vanished and the earth became dark Kahano brought the sun back again. . . ." Ku-leo-nui (Ku loud voice) is their leader "whose voice was heard all over the island" summoning them to work.[15]

(c) *Migration (Oahu) legend.* (1). Waha-nui, ruling chief of Honua-ilalo, oppresses the Menehune, and their god Kane sends Kanaloa and Kaneapua to lead them away from Kapakapaua-a-Kane, the place where Kumuhonua's sons Laka and Pili have taken refuge, to the Aina-momona-a-Kane (Fat land of Kane), or Ka-one-lauena-a-Kane, or Ka-aina-i-ka-houpo-a-Kane, the original continent which once connected all the island groups before it was overwhelmed and broken up by inundation. The four Ku days are to be kept as a memorial of this deliverance.[16]

(2). The Menehune have a heiau at Kukaoo. The "owl god" at Pu'u-pueo (Owl hill) summons the owls of Kauai and drives the Menehune out of the valley (or Kuali'i the great chief of Oahu is their persecutor).[17]

OLA LEGEND

(a) *Rice version.* Ola is the son of Kualu-nui-pauku-moku-moku (a chief of the Mu people) and the chiefess Kuhapu-ola from Pe'ape'a on the Waimea side above Hanapepe, whom the chief meets clandestinely. His name Ola is given when he is recognized by his father and thus "saved from death" (ola) for

15. Pol. Race 2: 23.
16. *Ibid.* 1: 99 note from Kamakau; Bastian, *Heilige Sage,* 126–127.
17. Westervelt, *Honolulu,* 131–132.

breaking the chief's tapu. He succeeds his father in the rule over the Waimea district. Desiring to bring water to the taro patches of the Waimea flats, he is advised by his kahuna Pi to proclaim a tapu and summon the Menehune people to his aid. Each brings a stone and the watercourse (Kiki-a-Ola) is laid in a single night. These people also build the heiau of Hauola named "after the famous city of refuge of his father at Kekaha." They camp on the flats above called Kanaloa-huluhulu, plant taro (which is still growing on the cliffs of Kalalau), and build a big oven (Kapuahi-a-Ola) between Kalalau and Waimea. They also make a road of sticks (Kiki papa a Ola) through the swamps of Alakai to the height above Wainiha.[18]

(b) *Knudsen version.* The chief priest of Ola's father's time is a powerful and designing man who causes any nominee from the chief's party to be assassinated. Ola is therefore brought up in retirement as if under the displeasure of his father and only at the age of twenty-four when he is able to defend himself by warlike skill is he publicly elected for the succession. The chief priest recognizes the youth as he appears before the people and hurls at him the sacred javelin, but Ola wards it off and the priest takes his own life. It is because of this event that the heiau at Waiawa on Kauai is called Hau-ola (Stricken with a spear).[19]

(c) *Thrum version.* Pi is the chief of Waimea who gets the Menehune to construct for him a dam across the Waimea river and a watercourse leading from it to a place above Kiki-a-ola. The Menehune are brought from the mountains of Pu'u-ka-pele and the sound ("hum") of their voices gives rise to the saying, "Wawa ka Menehune i Pu'ukapele ma Kauai, puoho ka manu o ka loko o Kawainui ma Koolauloa, Oahu" (The noise of the Menehune at Pu'ukapele on Kauai startles the birds on the fishpond of Kawainui at Koolauloa, Oahu).[20] It is Ola who builds the three-stepped heiau called Ahu-loulu at the foot of Pu'u-ka-pele crater cone on Kauai.[21]

18. 44–46.
19. Thrum, *More Tales,* 94–97.
20. *Tales,* 110–111.   21. *HAA* 1907, 40, 63–64.

(*d*) *Kanehunamoku version*. Kiki-a-ola is the chief of Waimea. Hulukuamauna the priest hears from Kane that only through Kanehunamoku and his people can the dam and watercourse of Waimea be constructed. The chief seems to be the sacrifice to be offered at its completion. The services of the little people are requested. Kanehunamoku receives from Kane a branch of red fruit as a token of the god's consent and grants the request. The Waimea chief also asks for the sacred chiefess Namaka-o-ka-hai for his wife, but this request is refused. After the completion of the work, Namaka and Kanehunamoku depart with the Menehune and the Mu from Laau to the floating land of Kueihelani and never return.[22]

A curious resemblance between some of the incidents in these Kauai stories and episodes in the legend of Umi on Hawaii may be merely fortuitous or may point to interchange of legends between the two islands. The story of the birth of Umi, although more fully elaborated, resembles that of Ola.

UMI STORY

On a journey into the country, Liloa finds a beautiful woman at her bathing pool and makes her his wife. He gives her his loincloth, whale-tooth necklace, and war club as tokens for the child. Umi becomes a nuisance to his supposed father because he gives away food lavishly, and his mother sends him to Liloa wearing the tokens. The chief makes him a favorite and eventually Umi usurps the place of the legitimate heir.[23]

OLA STORY

Ola's father has an affair with a chiefess from Pe'ape'a on the Waimea side above Hanapepe and leaves his malo and whale-tooth necklace for the child who is to be born. The child grows up mischievous and the mother sends him to the father living in Waimea. She follows with the tokens, tossing and catching nuts as she walks, according to the kahuna's instructions, and since none falls she is successful in freeing her child, whom she finds

22. *HAA* 1916, 144–147.   23. For. Col. 4: 178–185.

bound and about to be sacrificed for breaking the chief's tapu, and later she secures his succession to the ruling power.[24]

An incident in Rice's story of the "Bird-man of Wainiha" who handles invaders at a narrow pass resembles the account of how Nau held back Umi when he came to invade Hilo.

UMI STORY

Seeing the water muddied as it flows into the sea, Nau goes up into the hills to investigate. There he hides at the defile and thrusts each man with his spear until Pi'imaiwa'a leaps down from above and kills him.[25]

WAINIHA STORY

Lahi and his uncle Kane-alohi live in the Wainiha valley and go up to Kilohana to catch uwa'u birds for food, a kind of bird that seeks its nest in the cliffs by day, blinded by the light. Their first enemy is a "giant" whom they lure into a hole and kill. Their next is the chief with "four hundred" soldiers who objects to the depredations among the birds. They sit on a rock eating birds and watch the rippling of the water below for men approaching [hence a popular proverb]. The boy hides at the pass and throws all four hundred men over the cliff. The chief comes last and, recognizing Lahi as his own son, invites him to the village. He prepares a trap, but this the boy discovers and, burning down the house with his treacherous father and followers within, takes over the rule of the land.[26]

LEGEND OF THE TRAPPED WIFE

(a) *Lydgate version.* A band of banana eaters settle above the Wainiha Valley. A bird catcher from the village below becomes friendly with them and marries a pretty banana eater. Their beautiful daughter is sought as wife by the chief from her father's village, but is too wild to consent to leave her old home. The chief organizes a boar hunt. At Ipu-wai-nui he bids his fol-

24. Rice, 44–45.   25. For. Col. 4: 224–225.
26. Rice, 47–48.

lowers approach silently as he hears the sound of tapa beating. Her father, who desires the match, conceals the chief in the house, rolled up in a mat. When the girl enters she is caught by both father and lover, bound, and conveyed to the sea in a litter (manele). She becomes the chief's wife and mother of a beautiful daughter.[27]

(b) *Rice version.* In a cave below a waterfall at Holua-manu in the mountains above Makaweli lives a mo'o. A child of the family is fretful and is told to "Go to the mo'o and live with her." She obeys, the mo'o treats her kindly and the girl is happy. The family however wish to recover her and succeed in trapping her in a net. She is carried to Waimea where she becomes gradually reconciled, grows into a beautiful woman, and marries the ruling chief.[28]

OAHU CANOE LEGENDS

(a) Kahanai-o-ke-akua (Adopted by the gods) is brought from a foreign land and reared by the gods Kane and Kanaloa who live at Waolani heiau. Kahanai lives at the heiau of Kaheiki built by the Menehune and presided over by the kahuna who founded the priesthood called Mo'o-kahuna.

Kahanai wants canoes to visit his former home. Both Mu and Menehune set to work to furnish them. The Menehune get the work done first, hence the Na-mu-na-wa leave their canoes in the ditch, where they long remain. On his return, both classes of little people welcome him with shouts, the eepa in the uplands, the Menehune at the shore to lift the travelers from the canoe and later to prepare them houses. When the fish tree Makalei is brought to Oahu the little people shout so loud that the tree falls where it stands and cannot be brought up to Waolani. Hence the Menehune and eepa people (Na-mu-na-wa) are banished from Waolani.[29]

27. *HHS Reports* 29 (1920): 25–27; *HAA* 1913, 125–137.
28. 91.
29. Westervelt, *Honolulu,* 5–6; *Gods and Ghosts,* 90–91, 141–142, 144–145, 150; Thrum, *HAA* 1907, 56; Stokes, *HHS Reports* 33: 43–44.

(b) Kakae's wife wants a canoe to go in search of her brother and Kakae sends Ke-kupua to find a suitable koa tree for the purpose. Since Kakae is a descendant of the Menehune, the little people set to work to make the canoe, but day breaks before they can get it dragged down to the shore and it is left in the ditch at Kaalaa near Wai-ka-halulu where it goes by the name of Ka-wa'a-kekupua (The canoe of the kupua).[30]

The Kahanai story may be compared with a similar situation in a Samoan boat-building legend:

Mata-iteite comes seeking a husband and finally finds one to her liking. She begs to have a boat built and asks Tagaloa to send her boat builders. They work in the woods and are to be fed daily without being seen. One day the women, when they bring them food, slip in upon them secretly and they fly back to heaven. They are naked and have no axes but work with their teeth.[31]

Heiau said to be "built by the Menehune" are to be found among the oldest temple structures on each island. On Molokai they built a heiau on the cliff at Waikolu valley near Kalaupapa which no one has been able to reach either from above or below, and the Luakini heiau of Pakui between Ualapue and Manawai, said to be dedicated to Hina. On Maui the Pihana heiau at Wailuku was built by the Menehune "in a single night" from stones brought from Paukukalo beach. Hale-o-kane and Pu'u-kini are other Maui heiaus built by the Menehune.[32] It is said that in constructing a heiau it was the custom for a chief over a large district to line up all the men under him and pass the stones from hand to hand until all was in place, much like our own barn raisings in pioneer life. The time element is important in these Menehune structures, especially as the workers themselves become purely mythical beings and night is the time of their activity. Raffles reports a similar tradition from Java where, he says,

30. Thrum, *Tales*, 114–116.   31. Stuebel, 63–64.
32. Thrum, *HAA* 1909, 40, 46; 1892, 122; 1907, 56; 1929, 86; *Tales*, 116–117; Dickey, *HHS Reports* 25: 25; Westervelt, *Honolulu*, 131.

"The temples themselves were conceived to have been the work of a divinity, and to have been constructed in one night."[33] In Tonga a space between what was once two islands is filled in and trees are planted "in a single night."[34]

A Menehune class is known in other groups, especially in Tahiti, where the first migration from "Havai'i" (Ra'iatea) which settled Tahiti was composed of commoners alone and hence the island was known as Tahiti-manahune. Those manahune who remained agriculturists later formed the lowest social class of plebeians and were used for sacrifice. The warriors became chiefs and their families intermarried with the royal family of Opoa in Ra'iatea. Archaeological remains preserve the records of these changes in population. Two types of marae exist: the inland belonging to an earlier culture and represented on Necker island and occasionally on Hawaii by the platform structure; the later, the walled marae, common on coastal Tahiti and introduced there from Ra'iatea "by the 12th or 13th century" and from Tahiti into Hawaii between 1100 and 1400 when the great migrations took place which introduced the culture that prevailed in the Hawaiian group at the time of its discovery by Cook.[35] In the western Tuamotus the "Manahune" are known as ancient people of Tahiti, and former adversaries of the Tuamotuans, say the eastern Tuamotuans. They are sometimes spoken of as giants, as at Tatakoto and Vahitahi, but in Tatakoto as friendly giants.[36] In Rarotonga, among the clans of Tangiia's people over whom he makes Iro chief are the Mana-une, said to be found also in Mangaia and "known traditionally to the Maoris."[37]

Stories of spirit races who have relations with human beings are reported from Polynesian groups. In New Zealand the Patu-paierehe (or -paiarehe) are a wild race of spirits who inhabit the mountains. When Maui fished up the south island of New Zealand he left Kui in charge. The Tutu-mai-ao people from the other side of the ocean annihilated his

33. 2: 7.

34. Gifford, *Bul.* 8: 70; McKern, *Bul.* 60: 76.

35. Henry, 196, 229, 439; Emory, *Bul.* 53: 121.

36. Stimson MS. *Chant of Rua.*   37. Smith, *JPS* 28: 194.

people. The Turehu, a fairy-like people, came over the ocean
and annihilated the Tutu-mai-ao people. The descendants of
Maui now came to the island and lived among the Turehu
and after ten generations exterminated them and today they
are the Patu-pai-a-rehe (wild men) dwelling in the mountains.[38] They have reddish skin, hair with a golden tinge
called uru-kehu (Hawaiian ehu), eyes black or blue. Pipi,
wife of Ira the son of Uenuku, is famed as an urukehu.[39] Al-
binos are considered the offspring of Maori women with fairy
lovers. The Patu-paiarehe may be seen in the early morning.
They are full-sized, dress in white, are not tattooed, and
nurse children in their arms.[40] They are a very numerous
people, merry, cheerful, singing like crickets. They work at
night and cease working when the sun rises. Their skin is
light like that of a European. They do not bend down the
reeds when they walk. Their canoe is a stem of flax. From
them Kahukura learns to make netting for fish nets.[41] They
are a peaceful folk and have guardianship of the sacred
places (wahi tapu). They use wooden and bone flutes called
putorino and koauau. Their path is in the drifting clouds
and the low-lying banks of cloud.[42] Of the double rainbow,
male and female, the upper, which is male, is called Turehu.[43]

Moorea in the Tahitian group is the island of "fairy folk"
with golden hair.[44] The little lizard called mo'opuapua, which
lives on flowers, is the shadow form of these spirits among the
flowers.[45]

In Mangaia, "fairies" of the underworld associated with
Miru come through special apertures from Avaiki to take
part in a dance performed in honor of Miru's son Tautiti.
They bathe at sunset in the stream Aupara in the northern
part of the island or in the stream Vaipau or Vaikaute in the
southern, and dress their hair on the height above. When
they dance upon the fresh-cut banana leaves prepared for
them at one end of the dance floor the leaves are not dis-

38. White 3: 188–189.   39. *JPS* 27: 18.
40. Taylor, 153–154.   41. Grey, 178–183.
42. *JPS* 30: 96–102, 142–151.
43. *Ibid.* 28: 28, and compare Smith, *MPS* 3: 175–176, 182–193.
44. Christian, 45.   45. Henry, 383.

turbed. When the morning star arises they return to Avaiki.
They are associated with the worship of Tane. The Tapairu
or "peerless ones" are the four daughters of Miru, sisters of
Tautiti. Four male fairies also appear. In the sky are other
fairies of whom Ina is the most famous. Ngaru learned from
the fairies of the underworld the art of ball playing which he
taught in Mangaia.[46]

In Fiji, spirit people, invisible save to worshipers, pygmies
with "fuzzy mops of hair" like themselves of former days in
miniature, live in the woods and caves on wild bananas and
kava. Akin to them are the Luve-ni-wai, who are "water spirits." Young people of Fiji formed a sect who were supposed
to become votaries of these spirits and learn song and dance
from them. At their dance places a votary would sweep the
place with fans and hang garlands in hope of a vision. Mis-
carriages of women of rank were supposed to become such
spirits. They were friendly folk skilled in conjuring. Maui
was regarded as one of these little people.[47]

Two classes of spirits are described on San Cristoval, distinct but sometimes confused with each other. The Kakamora
are said to be from six inches to three or four feet in height,
from fair to dark, go naked with long straight hair to their
knees, are strong as three or four men, and fond of dancing
and singing. They do not use cooked food. They have a ruler,
male or female. They are described as harmless but tricky, or
as malicious and dangerous, and are differently named all
along the coast. The Masi are strong and stupid, easily
tricked, but otherwise like people. Their descendants are
skilled craftsmen and canoe makers and carvers in stone.
Their work may be left unfinished because the craftsmen are
called away by some trivial matter. The stories strongly resemble Hawaiian Menehune traditions.[48]

46. Gill, 256–264. 47. Brewster, 88, 222–224.
48. Fox, 138–154, 293, 345–346.

XXIV

RUNNERS, MAN-EATERS, DOG-MEN

KA-LANI-MENEHUNE, younger son of Lua-nu'u, had two sons, the older of whom, called Aholoholo (Runner), is said to have been "renowned for his swiftness." Legends tell of famous runners (kukini) employed by chiefs to act as messengers and especially to bring fresh fish from distant fishponds. Trained thieves too were employed to steal from an enemy, and for them swiftness of foot was an essential qualification. Chiefs looked doubtfully upon the first horses introduced upon the islands; their runners were swift of foot and could easily run down goats on the mountain. There is a well-attested incident told of a native Hawaiian in early days who staked his own speed on the race course against the competing horse and won the race. The names of famous runners and their deeds have passed into legend and sometimes into myth.

Ulua-nui, a famous runner of Oahu, could carry a fish from Kaele-pulu pond in Kailua around by way of Waialua and bring it in at Waikiki alive and wriggling.[1] Makoa (or Makoko), the swift runner of Kau, when Kamehameha had his awa preparing (at Kailua), was sent to Hilo to fetch mullet from the pond of Waiakea adjoining Puna, a journey which today would take a man four days, and returned with the fish still quivering.[2] A similar story is told of Kane-a-ka-ehu in the same period, who used to run back and forth between Kailua and Hilo by a steep and precipitous trail, starting when the preparations began for the feast and returning by the time the meal was cooked and ready. Other famous runners mentioned in the stories are Ka-leo-nui, sent by Ka-kuihewa to intercept Lono-i-ka-makahiki's kahuna on his way from Hawaii to help his master, who circled the island twice without finding the kahuna;[3] Ka-ehu-iki-a-wakea, the

1. Malo, 289 note 1. 2. For. Col. 5: 490; Malo, 289.
3. For. Col. 4: 310.

best runner of Aikanaka on Kauai;[4] Kalamea, the swift runner of Maui in Lono-a-pi'i's service who could go around Maui in a day;[5] Pakui, special attendant of Haumea at Kailua, who could circle Oahu six times in a day (see Pupuhuluana); Ku-hele-moana and Keakea-lani, the swift runners of Kakuhihewa, who could compass Oahu twelve times in a day;[6] Kama(or Kane)-a-ka-mikioi and Kama(or Kane)-a-ka-ulu-ohia, sons of Halulu of Ni'ihau, so fleet of foot that they could make ten circuits of Kauai in a day, and run on land or ocean, from earth to sky.[7]

Dwarfs (kupa-li'i) are mentioned in traditions of early migrations as "noted for their swiftness as runners."[8] It was said of the Menehune, to indicate their stature, that they were "below the knees of Naipualehu," a Kauai dwarf about three feet in height.[9] Kamakau says of the forefathers that "they often speak of the land of the dwarfs (ka aina o ke kupali'i), a land of people so small that it would take ten of them to equal one ordinary man." One of these little men was brought to Punalu'u in Kau district on Hawaii and lived above Kopu and Moaula and was called an ili (which is the name given to a small "parcel" of land) and a pilikua (back-clinger), and Wahanui brought some to Kauai.[10]

LEGENDS OF FAMOUS RUNNERS

Keli'i-malolo is born at Hana and noted as the fastest runner of Maui in the time of Kahekili. He joins a canoe trip to Kapakai in Kohala, Hawaii, and after a little run of about ninety miles to Kaawaloa and back finds the canoes not yet covered or the baggage removed. His friends challenge the truth of his story, contending that it would take two days to go and return from such a distance. His account of the places along the way however tallies with the facts, and at the end of the run he has been careful to leave two joints of sugar cane set up as proof of his story.[11]

4. For. Col. 5: 32.

6. Thrum, *Tales,* 104.

8. *Ibid.* 6: 277.

9. Thrum, *More Tales,* 214 note 2.

10. *Kuokoa,* December 22, 1866.

5. Thrum, *More Tales,* 81.

7. For. Col. 5: 164–166.

11. For. Col. 5: 490–495.

Kao-hele, noted runner of Molokai, is pursued in vain by Kahekili's men when they come to make war on Molokai. They station relays, but he outdistances them all, hence the saying, "Combine the speed to catch Kaohele" (E ku'i ka mama i loaa o Kaohele). At one time chiefs and people are crowded at a famous cliff for the sport of leaping into the bathing pool below, and Kaohele, finding himself headed for this cliff and closely pursued, leaps across to the opposite bank, a distance of thirty-six feet.[12] Kao-hele is runner and protector for four chiefs who live at the heiau of Kahokukano on Molokai and have a fishpond mountainward. He is killed by a slingstone in a battle with men from Hawaii but his chiefs escape.[13]

Manini-holo-kuaua (named by Rice as head fisherman of the Menehune at Haena on Kauai)[14] is known as a noted thief of Molokai, so strong he can carry away a whole canoe on his back and so swift he can escape all pursuit. His mo'o grandmother, Kalama-ula, lives in a cave in the uplands which opens and shuts at command, and it is his custom to run with his booty to this cave and hide it away there. When Ke-lii-malolo, the fleet runner of Oahu, comes to Molokai on a visit and in contempt of warnings leaves his canoe unguarded while he goes in for a bath, Manini lays claim to it and carries it away with all it contains to his cave in the uplands, into which he disappears before its owner can overtake him. Ke-li'i-malolo engages the help of the two supernatural sons of Halulu, Kama-aka-mikioi and Kama-aka-ulu-ohia, and sails with them to Molokai. Manini, in contempt of his grandmother's warning, seizes their canoe also, but is overtaken by one of the men, who overhears his command and orders the cave to shut just as he is entering so that he is caught and crushed within its jaws. Within the cave are found innumerable possessions.[15]

At the time of the discovery of the Polynesian islands, cannibalism was practised by Maori, Rarotongans, Paumotuans, and Marquesans. It was introduced late among the Tongans from Fiji and, although rare, was practised on Tongatapu

12. *Ibid.* 496; Malo, 289; Hyde, *HAA* 1883, 56.
13. *HAA* 1909, 53.   14. 42.
15. For. Col. 5: 164–167.

more than in other Tongan islands.[16] In Rarotonga cannibalism began as a means of revenge after a war; it was against
the law of the ali'i to practise it in time of peace.[17] Among the
Maori the story is told of Uenuku who practised cannibalism
in revenge for the death of his children.[18] Among one tribe it
was said to have been introduced by Kai.[19] Churchill finds
the practice noted by Friederici among the Sissano of eating
the bodies of dead relatives.[20] Brewster describes the Fiji
method of preparing a cannibal feast.[21]

Despite the fact that man-eating is ascribed to legendary
figures and that a class called olohe are sometimes spoken of
as cannibals, there is no proof that cannibalism was ever
practised in the Hawaiian group. Man-slaying however was
common and the lua or bone-breaking art was practised by
highwaymen. In North Tahiti, whence early Hawaiian migrations seem to have come, Mei-hiti is spoken of in chants as
a famous place for man-slayers.[22] The most celebrated of
Hawaiian man-eating legends, the story of Ai-kanaka of
Oahu, corresponds closely with one recorded from Tahiti, as
follows:

Ellis version. Cannibals lived on the island of Tepuaemanu
between Eimeo and Huahine. Men who went near the island
were found to be missing. At length the man-eater's wife discovered that her own brother Tebuoroo was to be killed and
eaten. She exposed her husband's habit and two men lay in wait
for him and stoned him to death.[23]

In Wahiawa on Oahu, near the place called Kukaniloko,
once sacred to the birth of chiefs, is a narrow ridge of land
forming a curving pathway between two steep gulches along
which men used to travel to reach the mountain timber. At
this defile, tradition says, the last cannibals of Oahu took
their stand and seized upon victims for their cannibal feasts.
Aikanaka (Man-eater) was the name of their chief, called in

16. Gifford, *Bul.* 61: 206, 227–229; Mariner 1: 265.
17. *JPS* 20: 201–207.   18. White 2: 127.
19. *Ibid.* 3: 21.   20. 18.
21. 28–29.   22. Handy, *Bul.* 79: 73.
23. *Researches* 1: 360.

legend Ka-lo-aikanaka, Ke-ali'i-ai-kanaka (The chief who eats men), Kokoa, or merely Kalo. The band lived beyond the defile at a place called Hale-manu (House of birds) or Hale-mano. There the foundation of a heiau used to be pointed out, and the large flat rock called the ipukai (platter) where their victims were laid, and the hollow where the oven was dug in which such victims were baked. The story is circumstantially related as follows:

(a) Ka-lo-aikanaka (Lo the man-eater) is chief of a band of strangers who land first on Kauai and are given lands near the foot of the mountain back of Waimea. Darker than the Hawaiians, with a different speech and no tapu laws, they have religious feasts at which human flesh is eaten. The chief himself is tattooed with figures of birds, sharks, and other fishes. Ka-lo's daughter is very beautiful with hair to her ankles, bright eyes, sparkling teeth, set off by pearl necklaces and anklets. Married to a Kauai chief, she is put to death for breaking the tapu. The band retaliate by a cannibal feast and are obliged to flee to Oahu. Landing first at Kawailoa and then going on to Waialua, they proceed upland and establish themselves eight miles east of Haleiwa in the mountains of Haupu. The chief's servant Kaa-nokaewa(or -keewe), also called Lotu, builds his house across the pass at a place called Kanewai, and pushes travelers over the cliff. Lotu's wife Kaholehua sees even her own brothers sacrificed to satisfy the chief's hunger when other victims fail, until the youngest, named Napopo, escapes to Kauai, learns the art of wrestling, and in a final struggle with Lotu falls with him over the cliff and both are killed together. The chief is then obliged to sail with his people to other lands.

(b) *Westervelt version (dated 1848)*. The man-eater lives at Hele-mano. Ke-ali'i-ai-kanaka is described as "either a foreigner or a Hawaiian." Little by little his band of warriors are killed in forays until he alone remains. Hoa-hanau, the brother of one of his victims, learns boxing and wrestling in Waialua, covers his body with oil, and in a struggle to the death, hurls the cannibal chief over the edge of the gulch.[24]

24. Dibble, 113–115; For. Pol. Race 2: 23 note 1; Kalakaua, 371–380; Westervelt, *Honolulu,* 194–203; McAllister, *Bul.* 104: 137–140.

Connected with a somewhat similar Aikanaka legend is the stone called Oahu-nui which is said to have the shape of the island of Oahu and which lies in the gulch between Ewa and Waialua. Those who would go "entirely around Oahu" used to visit this stone.

Lo-Aikanaka is the name given to a family of South Sea chiefs who are driven from the plains of Mokuleia into the hills to a place called Hele-mano, where they are received by the chief Oahu-nui east of that locality and the two chiefs exchange courtesies. Oahu-nui develops a passion for human flesh and finally the two chubby sons of his sister Kilikiliula, wife of Le-hua-nui, are sacrificed to his appetite during the absence of their father. Warned by a vision, the father returns, puts to death the chief and his sister, and abandons the place with his men. A curse hangs over the place. The headless body of Oahu-nui became petrified where it lay; his sister also turned to stone where she fell on the opposite hillside, and all who had partaken of the feast were turned to stone. None has ever dared to live there since.[25]

In romantic fiction Ai-kanaka is represented as the ruling chief on Oahu in the time of Halemano. He lives at Ulukou at Waikiki. Hearing of the beauty of Halemano's wife, he summons her to him and when she refuses to come he sends men to kill Halemano and the two are obliged to hide in the uplands of Wahiawa until they can escape to another island.[26] Dibble says that with Ka-hanu-nui-a-lewa-lani, who came from foreign lands to Oahu by way of Kauai, came also his younger brother Kawelo-ai-kanaka, both sons of Neva and both man-eaters, together with the followers who came with them.[27] It would be interesting to know whether this Kawelo bears any relation to the legendary Ai-kanaka who is dispossessed by his relative of a younger branch from Oahu in the Kauai legend of Kawelo, or whether he may be connected with Lono-ka-ehu and his man-eating dog Ku-ilio-loa, or whether the followers who came with the "two sons of Neva"

25. Thrum, *Tales*, 140–146.   26. For. Col. 5: 238.
27. 114–115.

have anything to do with the Menehune whom Ka-hano brought from Kahiki to serve the chiefess (or chief Kahanai) on Oahu.

Among the peoples said to have appeared during the fifth period of the Kumulipo, when the hog-man was building up his family line, are the dog people: "Hanau ka Huelo Maewe, he (p)aewe kona" (Born were the wagging tails; they had no fixed line of descent), says the chant. This seems to mean that they intermarried without regard to class distinction and hence built up no inherited chief class. The reference is to the Haʻa people, according to David Malo Kupihea, the hairless olohe people first discovered on Maui on the plains in Kula called Omaʻomaʻo. He says, "In the story of Alapai-nui on Hawaii it is said that messengers to Maui landed on the Hana side and found these Haʻa people and were afraid, so they went on to Oahu and Kauai. Both on Kauai and on Maui 'dogs' were taken out to fight Alapai-nui and they were still there in Kahekili's time. Some were in his army. They lived in the sand hills and they had mystical power of the demigods (kupua) in the form of big war dogs. These dog people still appear on Maui in the procession of spirits known as 'Marchers of the night.' They look like other human beings but have tails like a dog."

A Hawaiian will not touch a dog of the hairless variety; it represents an olohe. About Pearl harbor on Ewa beach, supposed to be the place at which "human beings" first landed on Oahu, many caves of the olohe (ka-lua-olohe) are to be seen. In Honolulu there used to be a pit called Hole-of-the-olohe near where Palm drive enters King street into which an olohe disappeared who was being pursued. These olohe were human beings; they were "born in the day."[28]

Olohe, or Haʻa people, were hence a well-recognized class in old days, skilled in wrestling and bone-breaking (lua) and with hairless bodies. It is said that they used to pull out their hair and smear their bodies with oil in order to give no hold to an antagonist. Legend represents them as professional robbers or even with man-eating habits, who used to station

28. Given July, 1935.

themselves at a narrow pass along the highway and kill and
rob travelers. Many such robber stations are pointed out today. Makua, one of the most western valleys in Waianae, is a
traditional haunt on Oahu. Here Makaioulu met two robber
women who were professional bone-breakers.[29] Similar olohe
legends occur on Maui and Hawaii.

LEGENDS OF OLOHE

Kapakohana, after killing the kupua Kalae-hina who has
terrorized the island of Maui, goes on to Oahu to challenge the
hairless cannibal (olohe) of Hanakapiai. Finding himself unable to overcome the olohe in wrestling, he pretends friendship
and gathers men to burn him while asleep in his grass house.
The olohe overhears the plot and, making a hole in the top of
the house, crawls into a tree, then begins eating the men until he
comes to Kapakohana, who grapples with him and eventually
kills him and sets up his bones to hang gourds upon.[30]

Kapuaeuhi, an olohe of Ola'a, uses his two strong daughters
to decoy travelers to his cave, where he has a stone, or, as most
say, a beam, which he causes to fall and kill the traveler as he
enters. Finally two cousins of a plundered man are successful in
setting upon and killing the daughters, then the old man himself, whom they leave in the cave. Some say that he lies there
yet, but since the death of the olohe no one has been able to
raise the stone (or beam).[31]

On the shore road toward Ka-u district just out of Kalapana
is a spot where the lava rock is contorted as if by a great struggle. A famous robber used to live in a cave above this road with
his two daughters. He hides himself along the road and the
daughters watch from the cave. If many people are coming together along the road they signal "High tide!" but when a
single traveler comes along they give the sign for "Low tide!"
and the olohe drops a great tree upon the man, thus disabling
him, and then kills and robs him.[32]

29. For. Col. 5: 490, 491.
30. *Ibid.* 210–213; Dickey, *HHS Reports* 25: 25.
31. Green and Pukui, 132–133.
32. Westervelt, *Gods and Ghosts,* 11; local information.

Uma, a dwarf skilled in the art of bone breaking, lives at Pue-huehu in Kohala in the days of Kamehameha the first. On a journey through the country, which is at that time infested by robbers, he repels every attack by his swiftness and skill.[33]

Similar conditions seem to have prevailed among the Maori.

Moko is a robber chief who establishes himself in a cave beside the highway traveled by those who trade up and down the coast. Finally he kills the brother of the chief Tu-te-wai-mate and the chief goes with a body of men to avenge the dead, but Moko takes advantage of his chivalrous warning to give an unexpected thrust which kills the avenger.[34]

Among dog-men represented as overthrowing the chief of a district and terrorizing the country, the most famous is the cannibal dog-man Kaupe who overthrew the government of Ka-hanai-a-ke-akua (Reared by the gods) and ruled the land from Nu'uanu to the sea.

Kaupe lives at Lihue on Oahu. He never attacks a high chief but eats some of the people both of Oahu and Maui. At last he crosses over to Hawaii and brings back a chief's son to sacrifice in the heiau at Lihue. The father follows to Oahu and consults Kahilona, the great kahuna at the heiau of Kaheiki just below the hill called today Pacific Heights, which was built by the Menehune and which becomes under Kahilona the center for the mo'o-kahuna class of priests; that is, for kilokilo who read the signs of earth and sky and sea. This kahuna teaches the chief from Hawaii the prayer to recover his son, which runs

"O Ku,! O Lono! O Kanaloa!
By the power of the gods, by the strength of this prayer,
Save us two, save us two!"

The prayer unfastens the boy's fetters and father and son flee and hide under a rock at Moanalua while Kaupe goes on to look for them on Hawaii. The father learns the prayer for killing an enemy, and overcomes Kaupe on Hawaii.[35]

33. For. Col. 5: 498–500.   34. White 3: 192–194, 291–292.
35. Westervelt, *Honolulu*, 90–96.

The story resembles one told locally of the heiau of Waha-ula in Puna district on Hawaii.

The smoke from the altar at Waha-ula is regarded as the shadow cast by the god of the heiau and hence to cross through the smoke is sacrilege. A young chief, forgetful of the tapu, allows himself to be touched by the smoke and is accordingly seized and sacrificed and his bones thrown into the bone pit. His spirit comes in dream to his father, who is the high chief of Ka-u, and the father sets out at once to recover his son's bones. After first encountering and killing the olohe who slays travelers along the sea road out of Kalapana, he arrives at the heiau. As the spirits dance at night, he recognizes and seizes the spirit of his son, who points out to him where the bones are to be found. Some say that the father restores his son to life, others that he merely gives the bones a proper burial.[36]

As a ghost god resting in the clouds stretched over the mountaintops of the Koolau range on Oahu, Kaupe's spirit body is today confused with legends of a dog-like creature called Poki, spotted or brindled in color and very long in body, who guards a certain section outside Honolulu, although he may appear at other places. Some say it is the spirit of the old chief Boki who in 1829 filled two ships for the sandalwood trade and sailed away and never came back, but the legend is doubtless much older. Travelers report having seen the creature and having made a long detour to avoid it. It sometimes appears as a form in the clouds, either resting or in motion. A foreigner reports seeing, as he was entering Moanalua valley from Honolulu just as the moon was rising, "a shapeless white form," a mist "convulsed with movement," which passed over the treetops from the Koolau range, preceded as it came by "the wailing of dogs" and followed as it passed by "a deathlike stillness."

Both the shape-shifting hog-man Kamapua'a and the dog-man Ku-ilio-loa, together with the spirit forms of Kaupe and Poki, are in some way connected with those signs in the sky called oila which the Hawaiians worshiped, believing that the

36. Westervelt, *Gods and Ghosts*, 1–13; local information, 1915.

animal shapes in such clouds could be used to foretell the movements of chiefs descended from their kupua ancestors because denoting the presence of their aumakua protectors in the heavens.[37]

Kamakau says of the dog-man Ku-ilio-loa (Ku long dog) that Lono-ka-ehu came to Oahu from Kahiki with his "great dog" Ku-ilio-loa to seek his brother. He pierced the hill Kane-hoa-lani at Kualoa, cleft Kahuku and Kahipa apart, and broke Ka-pali-ho'oku'i at Kailua. He found his brother in the heiau at Palaa near Kuone at Waialua and took him back to Kahiki.[38] The heiau named is the ancient heiau Ka-pukapu-akea said to have been built by Menehune out of kauila wood. The heiau of Lono-a-ke-ahu (Lono-ka-ehu?) at Keehu is said to have "worked with" that of Kapukapu-akea and at Kane-ilio at the lighthouse point stood the heiau of Ku-ilio-loa.[39]

Ku-long-dog is described as a dog with a human body and supernatural power, "a great soldier and famous warrior," who terrorizes Kahiki. His wives betray him to Kamapua'a and the hog-man conquers him by stuffing his own super-natural plant bodies between the gaping jaws of the dog and "eating his inwards"; that is, by performing the common folktale trick of allowing himself to be swallowed by a mon-ster and then cutting his way out. The contest follows di-rectly that with Lono-ka-eho, elsewhere described as the dog's master.[40] In the Ka-ulu legend the fight with Lono-ka-eho (The stone god) is similarly followed by an attack upon a "dangerous kupua" of Kualoa who waylays and kills travelers at the narrow pass about Kaoio point. Ka-ulu lifts the kupua and dashes him down, breaking his body into bits, one of which forms the rock islet Mokoli'i just off Kualoa.[41] The kupua is evidently not a "rat" as the story says, but the "great dog" of Lono, and the islet Mokoli'i (Little mo'o), by adding elided sounds and transposing, becomes Mok(u)-ilio (Dog island), the part played by the kupua as a waylayer of trav-

---

37. Westervelt, *Gods and Ghosts,* 128–132; *AA* 30 (1928): 13.
38. *Kuokoa,* January 12, 1867.   39. *HAA* 1907, 48, 54.
40. For. Col. 5: 332, 333.   41. *Ibid.* 370–371.

elers classing him unquestionably with the dog-men or olohe of other stories.

Ku-ilio-loa passes into legend as "the man-eating dog of Hina" whom travelers fear, in the Waha-nui legend,[42] and in that of Ka-ulu as the monster whom Ka-ulu tears into bits with his hands; hence dogs are small today.[43] Although these encounters take place on an ocean voyage it may be significant that Kane and Kanaloa, whom Waha-nui voyages to "tread upon," are represented in Hawaiian tradition as gods dwelling at Waolani on Oahu, the same island upon which is localized the Lono-ka-ehu legend.

Ku-ilio-loa, as "the great dog of Hina," is also connected with the Pele cycle of romances. The foster parents of Ke-ahi-wela (Hot fire) send Ku-ilio-loa in the shape of a dog to the Rolling island to save the girl from the wrath of her older sister, and he loses both ears and tail in the fight and goes to live on Kauai.[44] Na-maka-o-kaha'i, the analogous figure in the Aukelenuiaiku legend to the chiefess of the Rolling island, has a guardian dog Moela who is reduced to ashes when he touches Aukele.[45] In the Laieikawai romance, Aiwohikupua, a chief of Kauai, brings his kupua dog Kalahumoku to fight against the mo'o guardian of Paliuli named Kiha-nui-lulu-moku, and the dog runs home stripped, like Ahi-wela's pet, of both ears and tail.[46] Finally, Ku-ili(o)-loa, "a girl of fire," is the fifth child born to Kane-huna-moku and his wife in Kuaihelani.[47]

A somewhat similar story to that of Ku-ilio-loa is told in Tonga among the adventures of Muni-of-the-torn-eye. Muni comes to Fiji and finds the people harassed by a being "part man and part god," and wrestles with him in the cave where he lives until both fall dead. In another version a man-eating dog lives in a cave and terrorizes the people into giving up a man daily. The king's daughter is about to be sacrificed when Muni appears, takes her place, and slays the monster, this last evidently a foreign turn to the story.[48] See also Caillot's

42. For. Col. 4: 518.

43. Ibid. 524.

44. Rice, 31.

45. For. Col. 4: 54–61.

46. RBAE 33: 472–475.

47. HAA 1916, 143.

48. Gifford, Bul. 8: 121–122.

version where Maui kills the great cannibal dog of Fiji.[49] In Samoa one of Maui-ti'iti'i's feats is the slaying of a big red dog.[50]

The Maori are said to know two varieties of native dogs, one, generally regarded as sacred, with soft white hair and traced to the Pomeranian breed found on the shores of the Baltic, the other larger with coarse short hair and very strong, of Asiatic pariah breed.[51] The legendary dog Moho-rangi is left to guard the steep rock island of Whanga-o-kino when Tara-whata made it sacred for his reptiles. Po-nui-o-hine goes with her father to help kindle fire in order to remove the tapu on this island but forgets to veil her eyes and is hence turned to stone. Women today fear to go near this island and strangers veil their eyes lest they see the dog Moho-rangi.[52]

In a Dobu story a monster dog acts as the savior of the land by slaying an ogre and his wife who have devastated the country. A woman digs the dog out of a heap of rubbish and the inhabitants return and give him a wife to tame him down. He is believed still to roam the country.[53]

Another famous dog kupua of Hawaiian story is Puapua-lenalena (Pupualenalena), a great thief and runner of Waipio valley who can take the shape of a yellow dog and thus provide his master with all possible good things. He is finally engaged to steal for the chief the famous conch shell called Kiha-pu (or puana) which has been stolen from its place in a heiau on Oahu by the spirits of the valley. The place is still shown along the road leading down into Waipio where the spirit (eepa) beings lived who disturbed the chief's repose with their eerie sounding of the sacred conch, and a shell called Kiha-pu has been handed down by Kamehameha kings and is now preserved in the Bishop Museum, a small piece broken from it serving to motivate an incident which has since been incorporated into the legend.[54]

49. 279–305.   50. Stuebel, 66.
51. *JPS* 23: 173–175; 24: 69.   52. White 2: 192–193.
53. Fortune, 270–271.
54. For. Pol. Race 2: 72; N. Emerson, "Hula," 131.

(a) *Westervelt version.* Kapuni is brought up in the heiau of Pakaalana in Waipio. Two "gods," Kaakau and Kaohu-walu, look down into the valley and see him practising the art of leaping and they cut off a part of his body to make him lighter, teach him to fly, and take him with them overseas to Kauai. There they hear the sound of the Kiha-pu at Waolani: "The voice of Kiha-pu calls Kauai," is the saying. Flying across from Kauai to Oahu, Kapuni waits until the guards are asleep, then flies into the heiau and steals the Kiha-pu and hides it under the waves until he can reach the heiau on Hawaii where live the eepa beings to whom it is entrusted. The bones of Kapuni are worshiped as a god at Kaawaloa.

Kiha-lulu-moku has set a tapu, which is broken by the continual blowing of the conch by the gods on the plateau above. In the meantime the dog-man Puapualenalena has joined a new master who is a great awa drinker, and is sent to steal awa from the chief's tapu crop. The dog is traced and the chief agrees to pardon both man and master if the dog is cunning enough to steal the conch Kiha-pu from its new owners.[55]

(b) *Fornander version.* The dog Pupualenalena is a clever thief living at Puako on Hawaii. When his new master goes fishing he finds the dog eating the fish as fast as he pulls them up. The master promises him pardon if he will bring him awa from the chief Hakau's tapu crop. This the dog achieves, until he is followed and both master and dog brought before the chief. Hakau promises them their lives if the dog will bring him the Pu-ana (trumpet) which the spirits living above Waipio blow every night, disturbing the chief's sleep.[56]

(c) *Kalakaua version.* The Kiha-pu is owned by Kiha-lulu-moku in Waipio valley and if properly blown can control the hosts of the gods. Its sound is like weird music and if blown during battle it repeats the cries and groans of conflict. It was Lono (as god of sound) who gave it this power by blowing into it.

The Kiha-pu is stolen by a band of spirit beings under their

55. *Honolulu*, 105–111.   56. Col. 4: 558–561.

leader Ika (Iku) and carried away to Waimea on Kauai and thence to Oahu to a place in the neighborhood of Waolani. A rival places a magic mark upon the shell in the shape of a cross (pe'a) which takes away its power of sound. A kahuna tells Ika that the shell will not sound again except on Hawaii. On the way thither the shell is chipped by the waves and the sign lost. Above Waolani the spirit band blow the shell once more and Kiha engages the dog Puapualenalena to steal it back from Ika.[57]

(d) *Emerson version.* Kane and his companions revel all night above Waipio and blow blasts upon their conch shells which prevent the proper observance of religious ceremonies, until the chief Liloa sends the clever thief Puapualenalena to steal the Kiha-pu away from Kane, and this puts an end to the reveling.[58]

Emerson prints a hula on the subject, part of which reads:

> Meha na pali o Waipio
> A ke kani mau o Kiha-pu;
> A ono ole ka awa a ke alii
> I ke kani mau o Kiha-pu;
> Moe ole kona po o ka Hooilo;
> Uluhua, a uluhua,
> I ka mea nana e huli a loaa
> I kela kupua ino i ka pali,
> Olali la, a olali.

> "Wearisome the cliffs of Waipio
> With the constant sounding of the Kiha-pu;
> Ineffective is the chief's awa
> With the constant sounding of the Kiha-pu;
> The chief cannot sleep all winter,
> Vexed and worried
> With the search for someone who will find
> That cursed kupua on the cliff
> Where it gleams there."

57. 250–265.   58. "Hula," 129–131.

XXV

THE MOIKEHA-LAʻA MIGRATION

FROM Ulu and Nana-ulu, sons of Kiʻi, twelfth in succession from Wakea and Papa, all high chief families count descent. Hikapoloa, as well as the Waha-nui and Keikipaanea families of early legend, belong to the Nanaulu line. The important Maweke family is, according to Kamakau, the first of that line from whom men today trace ancestry. Their contemporaries are the Paumakua of Oahu, the Kuhiailani of Hawaii, Puna of Kauai, Hua of Maui, and the Kamauaua of Molokai. To the Ulu line belongs the late migration of chiefs introduced by Paao to the island of Hawaii, from whom most families of that island trace descent. Both legends, that of Paao and that of Maweke, are believed to have bearing upon early colonization of the Hawaiian group from North Tahiti.

The coming of Maweke and his sons to the Hawaiian group is dated sometime between the eleventh and twelfth centuries. Their descendants are supposed to have occupied the whole of Oahu and spread to the islands of Kauai, Maui, and Molokai, and hence, some say, the differences in speech and custom between these islands and Hawaii. Of the three sons of Maweke, Mulielealiʻi who inherited his father's lands on the south side of the island of Oahu, Keaunui who settled the western end of the island, and Kalehenui who took the north side, it is the children of the first about whom legends are told today. Of the three sons of Mulielealiʻi, Kumuhonua, Moikeha, and Olopana, it is the firstborn, Kumuhonua, who succeeds to his father's lands. Kamakau asserts that the two younger brothers, Moikeha and Olopana, make a sea attack upon him and are defeated and taken captive, together with Laʻa. However this may be, the Kumuhonua line of Oahu ruling chiefs ends with Haka. With Mailikukahi, who succeeds Haka, the Moikeha branch is established as the ruling line.[1]

1. For. Pol. Race 1: 166, 197–198; 2: 47–49; Col. 6: 239–257;

LEGEND OF MOIKEHA-OLOPANA

Olopana settles in Waipio on Hawaii and Lu'ukia, grand-daughter of Hikapoloa of Kohala, becomes his wife. They are driven out by a flood and retire to Kahiki where some say Moikeha is living, others that he was with Olopana in Waipio. Moikeha becomes infatuated with Lu'ukia and Olopana raises no objections; but a rival suitor, Mua, who cannot win her favor, pretends to her that Moikeha is defaming her publicly, and she will have nothing more to do with Moikeha. The chief therefore leaves his lands under the care of Olopana and paddles away in a canoe manned by companions whose names, as recorded, are perpetuated as place names on the Hawaiian group. His canoes beach on the island of Kauai, at Waimahanalua, in Kapa'a in Wailua. The pretty daughters of the chief Puna are out surfing. They take Moikeha for their husband and he succeeds at Puna's death to his father-in-law's lands. . . .

Moikeha's son Ho'okamali'i settles at Ewa on Oahu, Haula-nui-aikea remains on Kauai, Kila goes to Hilo, Hawaii. Other sons named are Umalehu, Kaialea, Ke-kai-hawewe, Lau-kapa-lala. His two wives are Ho'oipo-i-ka-malanai and Hina-uulua [but both names may belong to a single woman and "Sweetheart in the trade wind" may be a chant name for the Hina-uulua who appears on the Nana-ulu genealogy as wife of Moikeha and mother of Ho'okamali'i who succeeds his father].

On the journey from the south the party touches first at the easternmost point of Hawaii and the younger brothers of Moikeha (Kumukahi and Ha'eha'e) remain at Puna; the kahunas Mo'okini and Ka-lua-wilinau make their home at Kohala; Honua-ula lands in Hana on Maui; the sisters Makapu'u and Makaaoa land on Oahu [where Kila visits them when he sails after La'a, and Hi'iaka claims Makupu'u as relative in ghost form on her journey about Oahu]. The rest of the party go on to Kauai. These include the paddlers Ka-pahi and Moana-ikaiaiwe, the sailing master Kipu-nui-aiakamau, with his mate, especially skilled in maneuvering a canoe by backing water; the spy Kau-kaukamunolea, with his mate, who goes later as pilot with Kila

Stokes, *HHS Reports* 42: 41–48; Kalakaua, 118; Kamakau, *Kuo-koa*, January 5, 1867; Cartwright, 8–9, tables 2, 4.

to Kahiki; and the foster son of Moikeha, the chanter Kamahualele (Child of the flying spray). Between Lanai and Molokai, Moikeha has joined to his company a kupua called Kakaka-
uha-nui (Strong-chested Kakaka) who has such long legs he
can steady a canoe as he stands in the water and can stay under
water for a long time without breathing. It is he who, on the return voyage with Kila, wins a match in a diving contest with the
tide kupua Ke-au-miki and Ke-au-ka by staying under water
"ten nights and two" to their ten nights.

The fine chant calling upon Moikeha to make his home in Hawaii is supposed to have been composed by Kamahualele as the
canoe first sighted land, some say at South cape in Kau district,
others off the Hilo coast.

> Eia Hawaii, he moku, he kanaka,
> He kanaka Hawaii—e,
> He kanaka Hawaii,
> He kama na Kahiki,
> He pua alii mai Kapaahu,
> Mai Moa-ulu-nui-akea Kanaloa,
> He moopuna na Kahiko, laua o Kapulanakehau. . . .

> "Here is Hawaii, an island, a man,
>   Hawaii is a man indeed,
>   Hawaii is a man,
>   A child of Tahiti,
>   A royal offspring from Kapaahu,
>   From Moa-ula-nui-akea of Kanaloa,
>   A grandchild of Kahiko and Kapulanakehau.
>   It was Papa who bore him,
>   The daughter of Ku-kalani-ehu and Kahaka-ua-koko,
>   The island offspring from a single group,
>   Set evenly from east to west,
>   As if spread out in a row,
>   And joined onto Holani,
>   Kaialea the seer journeyed about the land,
>   Separated Nu'uhiwa, landed on Polapola,
>   Kahiko is the rootstock of the land,
>   He divided up and separated the islands,

The fishline of Kaha'i is broken,
Cut by Ku-kanaloa,
The lands are divided into sections, into districts,
Divided by the sacred bamboo knife of Kanaloa,
Haumea is the bird sailing to Kahiki,
Moikeha is the chief who dwells there,
My chief dwells in Hawaii,
He lives! he lives!
The chief lives and the kahuna,
The soothsayer lives and the slave,
He dwells on Hawaii and is at rest,
He grows to old age on Kauai,
Kauai is the island,
Moikeha is the chief!"[2]

LEGEND OF KILA AND LA'A-MAI-KAHIKI

(a) Moikeha wishes to summon from Kahiki a certain La'a (Sacred one) of peculiarly high rank, either a son or adopted son, left behind at the time of the migration to Hawaii. The object seems to be to insure the transportation of his bones back to Kahiki at his death. He tests his sons to see which will have endurance for the voyage to Kahiki. Kila's toy boat made out of a ti leaf passes directly between the father's legs; the other boys' boats miss the mark. The boys are jealous and try to trap Kila away to a dart-throwing contest in order to make away with him, but the father will not allow it. Before the expedition starts, Kila proposes to take a "god" along with him to protect him from his brothers, and the brothers are afraid to accompany him. On the journey to Kahiki, Kila first visits the members of Moikeha's company who have settled on other islands and at each stop there ensues a repetitive dialogue: "Who are you?" "Kila of the uplands, Kila of the lowlands, Kila born of the Woman-of-the-trade-winds, the child of Moikeha." "Is Moikeha then alive?" "He is alive." "What kind of life is he living?" "Dwelling at ease on Kauai where the sun rises and sets; where the surf of Makaiwa curves and bends; by the changing blossoms of the kukui of Puna; by the broad waters of Wailua. He

2. For. Col. 4: 18–21; Emerson, *HHS Papers* 5: 16–17.

will live on Kauai and die on Kauai." "What is the journey of the chief for?" "A journey to seek a chief." "What chief?" "La'amaikahiki." Kila goes on to Kahiki, stopping first at a place called Moa-ula-nui-akea-iki to get a food supply from his uncle Ku-pohihi the rat-man, then greeting his aunt Lu'u-kia, and finally ascending to Lani-keha at Moa-ula-nui-akea to find La'a. Kamahualele advises his consulting the aged priestess Ku-hele-po-lani. She tells him that when he hears the beating of Moikeha's drum Hawea from the mountains of Kapaahu where La'a is in hiding under tapu, he must sacrifice a man on the altar of Lanikeha, then go up with her to the heiau and hide himself inside while she, as a woman, remains outside, and when his brother comes to strike the drum and the priests line up and begin chanting, then he must address La'a and give Moikeha's message. Kila obeys these instructions and La'a obeys the message. By the sound of the drum beating off Kauai, Moikeha is made aware of La'a's coming.[3]

(b) Moikeha tests his three sons to see which one is ablest for a journey to Kahiki. Kila's toy boat strikes his father's navel and by this sign Moikeha knows that he will excel the others. Moikeha later fits out a canoe and sends Kila to avenge him upon his enemies in Kahiki. On the journey the long-breathed man Kakaka-uha-nui saves him from the tide kupua who would drag the canoe to the bottom. At a neighboring island to Kahiki lives Kane-pohihi, a rat-woman who is Moikeha's aunt. Kila finds her blind and roasting bananas, makes himself known, and is told that the chiefs are all dead, Kahuahuakai being the last of them; but Kila knows that La'a is still there, guarded by Hui-hui and Maeele. He is in need of food and his aunt in rat form nibbles the rope which releases the food that Makali'i has drawn up in a net out of reach.

At the tapu harbor of the main island, Mua, the lover of Lu'ukia who caused Moikeha's withdrawal, comes down to meet the canoe and, finding in Kila a man handsome enough to beguile Lu'ukia, whom he still hopes to win, determines to use him as a lure; for Lu'ukia, although her husband Olopana has dropsy and cannot enjoy her favors himself, has refused all

3. For. Col. 4: 132–139; Thrum, *More Tales*, 23–30.

lovers since Moikeha left her. Kila pretends to accept the plot, but has Mua killed. His warriors then defeat those of Makali'i, although half their size. He himself gives their leader such a blow that Makali'i lies stunned "long enough to cook an oven of food," then picks himself up and returns "up above," where he remains until his death and never shows himself on earth again.

Kila ascends, greeted by the wailings of the former people of the land, until he comes to Moikeha's ancient house, built with posts of kauila wood and battens of birds' bones, but now empty and overgrown with weeds. One by one the guards come to life as he enters. He goes to sleep on Moikeha's couch. Lu'ukia enters and, seeing his resemblance to Moikeha, embraces him, allows him to untie the cord with which she has been bound against the approach of men, and the two become lovers. (The mission to La'a is omitted in this romantic version.)[4]

(c) Kila is named in memory of Lu'ukia and is more beloved by Moikeha than any of his brothers. Moikeha hence instructs Kila in the art of navigation and the knowledge of the stars and makes him leader of an expedition to Kahiki after La'a. His place is on the high platform between the canoes while the two older brothers manage the canoes. The canoe calls at Waianae to acquaint Moikeha's former companion of the life the chief is living. At Kahiki, Olopana is high chief and Lu'ukia chiefess. La'a is the heir. The land is rich and people are living at ease. Olopana refuses to let La'a go until after he himself is dead; then he may go to Moikeha. On the return of the expedition, Kila settles at Hilo, Ho'okamali'i at Ewa on Oahu, Haulanuiaiakea on Kauai, and from all three descend chiefs and commoners of these islands.[5]

LEGEND OF KILA AND HIS JEALOUS BROTHERS

La'a-mai-kahiki returns to Kahiki after Moikeha's death and Kila becomes ruling chief of Kauai. The brothers are jealous and entice him away on an expedition to Waipio after their father's bones, which have been left hidden in the cliff of Haena.

4. For. Col. 4: 160–173.
5. Kamakau, *Kuokoa*, January 12, 1867.

They abandon him there and tell their mother at home that the canoe was upset, Kila seized by a shark, and the bones lost. He passes in Waipio as a slave, but often when he climbs Puaahuku after firewood a rainbow accompanies him and the priest of the temple of Pakaalana suspects his rank. When he is accused of eating tapu food, he flees to this temple. The ruling chief adopts him under the name of Lena and makes him land agent. It is he who devises the system of working a certain number of days for the chief. He is beloved for his industry. In the time of Hua there is a famine. His brother Kaialea comes from Kauai after food. Kila has him thrown into prison until he will confess the whole truth, but saves him from death. The mothers and brothers are summoned. When the mothers learn the truth they say the brothers must die. Kila intercedes and all are reconciled. The mothers are given the rule over Kauai and Kila remains in Waipio. Later he goes to Kahiki with La'a-mai-kahiki to deposit Moikeha's bones.[6]

LEGEND OF LA'A-MAI-KAHIKI'S TRIPLET SONS

La'a is received on Kauai by Moikeha and his kahuna Poloa-hi-lani. He settles at Kahiki-nui on Maui but, finding it too windy, removes to the west coast of Kahoolawe, whence he sails back to Kahiki. His principal place of residence is at Kualoa on Oahu. Here he has three wives, daughters of three chiefs of this region, all of whom give birth on the same night. Hoaka-nui-kapuaihelu, daughter of Lono-ka-ehu, chief of Kualoa, is the mother of Lauli-a-la'a; Waolena from Kaalaea, of Ahukini; Mano from Kaneohe, of Kukona. Mano's child came last, but when she heard that the other wives had given birth she used energetic means to hasten her child's arrival and hence her name of "Mano who slapped her abdomen" (Mano-opu-pa'ipa'i).[7] A chant [from Kamehameha's day] records the incident:

> "Ahukai (the father), La'a (the son),
> La'a, La'a, La'a-mai-kahiki the chief;
> Ahukini son of La'a,

6. For. Col. 4: 128–153; Thrum, *More Tales,* 30–45.
7. Kamakau, *Kuokoa,* January 12, 1867.

Kukona son of La'a,
Lauli son of La'a,
The triple canoe (triplets) of La'amaikahiki,
The sacred firstborn sons of La'a
Who were born on the same day."

TRADITION OF LA'A-MAI-KAHIKI AND THE HULA DRUM

(a) It is La'a-mai-kahiki who introduces image worship in the shape of the figure Lono-i-ka-ouali'i and the coconut fiber rope called Lanalana-wa'a. He is most famous as the bringer of the kaeke drum and the hula dance to Hawaii. When the people hear the noise of the drum and the nose-flute as his canoe passes the coast of Hawaii they say, "It is the canoe of the god Kupulupulu (Laka)" and bring offerings.[8]

(b) La'a sails with a company consisting of his kahuna Kukaikupolo, his astronomer Kukeao-ho'omihamiha, his diviner (Luhau-kapawa), his seer Maula, his drummer Kupa, and forty men to handle the canoes. They pass to the left of Hawaii and sail north past Maui and Molokai sounding the drum over the sea. A certain man named Haikamalama hears the strange sound from the Oahu coast at Hanauma bay and follows the canoe along the shore, beating out the notes on his breast to get the rhythm, and repeating the drummer's chant. When the canoe beaches at Ka-waha-o-ka-mano in Waihaukalua, he pretends, in order to get a good look at it, that the drum is well known on Oahu, and then makes an exact copy of his own.[9]

The names of Olopana and Lu'ukia in the Moikeha-Kila legend for relatives of Moikeha left behind in Kahiki make it probable that the Moikeha family migrated from the northwestern of the three land divisions into which old Tahiti was

8. For. Col. 4: 152–155.

9. *Kuokoa*, January 12, 1867. See also For. Pol. Race 2: 49–56; Col. 4: 112–173; Kamakau, *Kuokoa*, January 5, 1867; Thrum, *More Tales*, 20–45 (abridged from Fornander); Kalakaua, 115–135; Westervelt, *Hist. Leg.*, 79–92; Malo, 26; Emerson, *HHS Papers* 5: 14–24; Dickey, *HHS Reports* 25: 24–25; Stokes, *JPS* 29: 29–33; Cartwright, 8–9 and tables 2, 4.

divided; that is, from the Oropa'a (Olopana) division dominated by the powerful Oropa'a family. Puna-au-ia is the chief
district, through which runs the great valley of Punaru'u, a
name found also on Hawaii. Mou'a-ula-nui-akea as the former
name for the land division on the north now called Tahara'a
suggests the Moa-ula-nui-akea of the Kila story. Taputapuatea is a great marae (temple) at Opoa on Ra'iatea.[10]

The Oropa'a were a rugged family of warriors whose name
appears far up on the line of descent of the Pomare family.
Later they retreated into the mountains before invading peoples. Lizards (mo'o) were their family gods and lowering
clouds lying with fringed edges on the horizon are called after
the fork-tailed lizard.[11] Tipa, whose "shadow" on earth was a
species of lizard, was the healing god of sickness and disease
of the Oropa'a chiefs.[12] In myth there is an Oropa'a, god of
ocean, son of Tumu-nui and Papa-raharaha. The man-of-
war bird is his shadow, the whale his messenger.[13] In chant it
is said that "he lies with head upwards when the breezes come.
The white-foaming breakers are his jaws. He swallows whole
persons and fleets of people; he does not spare princes."[14]

Lu'ukia is not mentioned in Tahitian genealogies, but in
Maori tradition Tu-te-koropanga and Rukutia his wife (Olopana and Lu'ukia in Hawaiian) appear on the royal genealogy "relating to the period of occupation of the Society
islands." The names of Koropanga and Rukutia occur in
Tongareva as "two adjacent islands on the north side of the
lagoon." Rukutia introduces culture elements. "Be ye girded
with the mat of Rukutia," says a Maori chant, and again,
"Be ye tattooed after the manner of Rukutia."[15] Irapanga is
said by the Maori to have migrated with his children and sub-
tribes to Ahu (Oahu) and hence originated the people of Hawaiki, Maui, and other islands. To reach it they sail northeast from Tawhiti-nui. They name the big island Hawaiki-
rangi, and this is the old name for the Hawaiian group. From

10. Henry, 566–569; Handy, *Bul.* 79: 71–73; Buck, *Bul.* 92: 19.
11. Henry, 383.   12. *Ibid.*, 376, 383.
13. *Ibid.*, 387–388.   14. *Ibid.*, 358.
15. Henry, quoting Smith, 569.

here they migrate to Rangiatea (Ra'iatea) and Rarotonga. The Maori call Lanai, Ma'ui-pae; Molokai, Maui-taka.

In Hawaii the introduction of the bark-cloth skirt of five thicknesses commonly worn by women is ascribed to Lu'ukia, as well as the network cover used for water gourds and for the lashings of the outrigger of a canoe, supposed to be wrought after the pattern of the protection with which her thighs were bound against the approach of lovers after her quarrel with Moikeha. So sacred is such a form of canoe lashing that death is the penalty for intruding while the work is being done.[16] According to one story, the house of separation set up between Kawaihee and Waimea while she and Olopana were living at Waipio, to which she retired during her monthly periods, was a novelty in Hawaii. Waiauwia, a man of prominence in Waimea who followed her there, had never heard of the tapu for women at this time.[17] A cave is pointed out in Hana district on Maui where Lu'ukia is said to have taught tapa beating to the women of Hana. The cave goes by the name of Hana-o-Lu'ukia (Work of Lu'ukia), the long *a* representing a profession carried on, rather than incidental labor.

Hawaiian legend links Lu'ukia with the Hikapoloa family of Kohala on Hawaii, but some say she belongs to Tahiti and not to the Hawaiian group. In the Hainakolo romance she is a relative of Hainakolo belonging to Waipio or to Hamakua district, who adopts Hainakolo's child, brings him up as a waif, and later makes him her husband. In the Uweuwelekehau romance she is daughter of Olopana at Wailua on Kauai and takes as husband her cousin, who comes to her from Hawaii in the form of a fish but with the marks of a chief. An incomplete story from a school composition makes her the daughter of Hamau and Hooleia of Puako, South Kohala, and wife of Kama-o-ahu on Oahu. When her young brother Makahi comes to visit her and wins a betting contest in spear throwing with Kaaiai of Oahu, Lu'ukia's husband takes him for a former lover of his wife and insults him.[18] All these

16. Malo, 174; For. Col. 4: 112–115, 172.
17. *Ibid.* 156–159.   18. *Ibid.* 5: 564–569.

stories agree in making Lu'ukia the heroine of a love affair with a young husband, which makes trouble with her first husband or an older relative.

About the name of Olopana also certain traditions persist in Hawaii. He is said to have been afflicted with dropsy. After Moikeha's departure one version has it that as ruler of Moa-ula-nui-akea he makes himself so beloved that Moikeha's uncle sends him away and he emigrates to the Hawaiian group. He is said to have brought there the style of tattooing and to have enforced the tapu system. Some say there are three different Olopana chiefs mixed up in Hawaiian story, one belonging to Tahiti, another to the legend of Moikeha, a third to the Kamapua'a legend. In one romance, that of Uweuwele-kekau, Olopana is the older brother of Ku and Hina at Wai-lua, Kauai. Olopana and Ku quarrel and Ku, followed by his sister Hina, settles at Pi'i-honua, Hilo, Hawaii.[19] In the romance of Ke-ao-melemele, when Ku has an affair with Hi'ilei in "one of the large islands of the heavens," his wife Hina is taken by Olopana and their child is adopted by Ku and Hi-'ilei.[20] Here again the woman seems to be the wife of two brothers.

19. For. Col. 4: 192–199.
20. Westervelt, *Gods and Ghosts,* 132.

XXVI

HAWAIILOA AND PAAO MIGRATIONS

THE story of Hawaii-loa, called also Ke-kowa-i-Hawaii, belongs to the Kumuhonua legend and recounts
the peopling of the group from the south under four
brothers, sons of Aniani-ka-lani, named Ki, Kanaloa, La'a-
kapu, and Hawaii-loa. Ki peoples Tahiti, Borabora, Huahine,
Tahea, Ra'iatea, and Mo'orea. Kanaloa peoples Nukuhiwa,
Uapou, Tahuata, Hiwaoa, and the rest of the Marquesas. His
wife comes from the man-eating Taeohae and hence come the
man-eaters of Nu'uhiwa, Fiji, Farapara, Paumotu, and the
islands west. Hawaii-loa peoples the Hawaiian group, of
which there were at that time but the two islands, Hawaii and
Maui, but later the other islands "rose out of the sea."

(a) *Fornander version.* Hawaii-loa is born on the east coast
of Ka-aina-kai-melemele-a-Kane (Land of the yellow sea of
Kane). He makes long fishing excursions, sometimes of months
at a time, with his chief navigator Makali'i (Eyes of the chief)
who is an expert in star lore (kilo-hoku), and on one of these
they steer east and find a fertile land where coconuts and awa
grow. Some time after their return he migrates to this land with
his family and a great following, but as he alone takes his wife
and children, the whole Hawaiian race is descended from the one
stock. From time to time he voyages south to bring back mates
for his children out of his brother Ki's family. He brings Ki's
oldest son Tu-nui-ai-a-te-atua as husband for his favorite
daughter Oahu, and their son Tu-nui-atea is born at Keauhou
on Hawaii and the district of Puna named for the father's district, Puna-auia, in Tahiti. He brings Te-ari'i-tinorua (-double-
bodied) from Tahiti to become a wife for Tu-nui-atea; Ke-ali'i-
maewa-lani (Kauai) is their son, from whom the Kona people
are descended. The son and grandson of Tu-nui-atea, Ke-li'i-
alia and Ke-mili-a, are born in Tahiti, but the great-grandson
Eleeleua-lani or Ke-li'i-ku is born on Hawaii. Ka-oupe-ali'i is

his wife. From a child of Eleeleua-lani and a chief brought from Tahiti named Te-ari'i-apa (perhaps -oupe) are said to spring the Kohala people. Hawaii-loa's wife Hualalai bears her last child Hamakua and is buried on the mountain of Hawaii that bears her name.

Hawaii-loa discovers on one of his visits south that his brother Ki has abandoned the family gods Ku, Kane, and Lono and taken the man-eating god Ku-waha-ilo as his god. He therefore passes a law called Papa-enaena that communication shall be shut off with the islands to the south. He sails northwest with Iao as his guiding star and lands in the country of the "people with slanting eyes," travels west and north over the land, and brings back "some white men and marries them to native women." He voyages to Kapakapaua-a-Kane to teach his son Ku-nui-akea navigation and brings back two men whom he places under his young son Kauai as land stewards over the two rock islets of Lehua and Nihoa off Kauai, called after their names.

From Hawaii-loa's son Ku-nui-akea spring the high chiefs with the strict tapu (welo-ali'i); from Makali'i spring the commoners (welo kanaka). The kahunas belong to the chief class. In the time of Ku-nui-akea comes Tahiti-nui, a grandchild of Ki, from Tahiti, lands at the southwest point of Kahoolawe (Ka-lae-i-Kahiki), and settles East Maui, hence the name Kahiki-nui for a district of Maui. Thus the descendants of Ki and Hawaii-loa people the whole group.

(b) *Kepelino version.* Hawaii-nui is a fisherman from lands adjoining Kahiki-honua-kele. He knows the sea called "Sea where the fish run" (O-kai-holo-a-ka-i'a) which used to lie where these islands now lie. He sailed from Kahiki-honua-kele and discovered these islands, first Kauai, then Oahu, then the Maui group, then Hawaii, which he named after himself. The other islands he named after his children, and various land divisions after his eight navigators who sailed with him, of whom Makali'i was chief. To return to Kahiki they sailed west guided by the star Hoku-loa.

(c) *Thrum version.* After the chief's first visit to the Hawaiian group he returns to seek his brothers, whom he has left in the south, and finding his brother Ki in Kahiki he brings Ki's firstborn son Tu-nui-ai-a-te-atua to be a husband for his favorite daughter Oahu. Their child Ku-nui-akea is born at Keauhou in Puna on the island of Hawaii, a place named after Tu-nui's birthplace in Puna-auia in Tahiti. This child becomes a chief of the highest rank and from his line are descended the high chiefs (hoali'i) of these islands. Another grandchild of Ki called Tahiti-nui settles upon East Maui, from whom the district of Kahiki-nui is named.[1]

This Tu-nui-ai-a-te-atua is probably to be equated with Ka-hanai-a-ke-akua (The adopted of the gods) of Oahu story, who is brought up in Waolani by Kane and Kanaloa, marries on Hawaii, and becomes ruling chief over the island of Oahu with the Mu, Wa, and Menehune people as his servants.[2]

The names of certain families of chiefs survive out of this early period of intercourse with the South Seas, before migration legends to Hawaii begin to take on the color of actual history. The Waha-nui family of Oahu is one of these. The Kamauaua family of Molokai is another. The Pele migration and the coming of the "gods" Kane and Kanaloa perhaps belong rather to myth than legend, nevertheless they have their migration story and belong to the early period. Hika-poloa of Hawaii has a definite place in early tradition. The Keikipa'anea family of Kauai is represented by a riddling chief of early fame whose legend has been written out at length by a Hawaiian compiler under the name of Ka-lani-ali'i-loa (The great heavenly chief). Place names, chants, and ritual allusions, as well as family genealogies, unite to give these names traditional significance in spite of the fabulous nature of the legends to which they are attached.

Of Makali'i, the chief navigator of Hawai'iloa in the Ku-muhonua legend of the settling of the group, from whom are said to have descended the class of commoners (welo kanaka) as distinguished from the chiefs (welo ali'i) represented by the family of Hawaii-loa, no connected legend is told. In the

1. For. Pol. Race 1: 23–24, 132–159; Col. 6: 278–281; Kepelino, 74–77; Thrum, *More Tales,* 1–19.
2. Cartwright, *JPS* 38: 105–121; see also Ke-ao-melemele.

mythical story of Kaulu, Makali'i is represented as the seer of Kane and Kanaloa to whose place in the heavens messengers resort in order to make use of his powers of divination, and who is completely bullied into submission by the terrible Kaulu. In the Aukele legend he is connected with the Pele family as uncle of Na-maka-o-ka-ha'i and is again worsted by the young hero, who flies up to the heavens to make the acquaintance of his wife's relatives without waiting for her to give them warning of his coming. The story includes a glowing description of the wife of Makali'i:

"Her skin was as red as fire, on coming out of the house, her beauty would overshadow the rays of the sun, so that darkness would cover the land, the red rain would be seen approaching; the fog also, and after these things, then the fine rain, then the red water would flow and the lightning play in the heavens. After this, the form of Malanaikuaheahea would be seen coming along over the tips of the fingers of her servants, in all her beauty. The sun shone at her back and the rainbow was as though it were her footstool."[3]

As a settler on Hawaiian soil Makali'i is rather consistently connected with the island of Kauai. He is called a chief of Waimea on the Maweke-Moikeha line, and Nae-kapu-lani, wife of the chief Mano-ka-lani-po, after whom the name Kauai-o-Mano-ka-lani-po was given to the island, is called his child (-a-Makali'i).[4] Ku-ka-lani-ehu (Ku the heavenly blond), the parent of Wakea's wife Papa, is said to be sixth in descent from Makali'i.[5] In the Kahuoi legend Kinikuapu'u sails from Kauai with two fishermen whose names are constantly connected with Makali'i, as in the string figure chant which runs,

> There are Ieiea and Po'opalu,
> The fishermen of Makali'i;
> They are whipping the long fishcord.[6]

3. For. Col. 4: 74–79.
5. For. Col. 6: 279.
4. For. Pol. Race 2: 93.
6. *Ibid.* 214.

In the legend of Kamapua'a, Makali'i appears as ruling chief over the island of Kauai, who is driven into the uplands by his invading nephew just as, in the Moikeha-Kila legend, he is defeated and banished by his nephew Kila. His name is given to the month on the Hawaiian calendar "in which the food (plant) bears leaf," corresponding to our December or January when the sun turns north again, a season marked by the withering of the tender shoots of the ilima flower and the blossoming of the medicinal koolau.[7] At this season the legendary Makali'i prepared his land for planting, and because of his fame as an agriculturist the month was named in his honor. It was in the month of Makali'i, says the chant, on a night when lightning flashed, that the chief Kauai was born, the chief from whom the island ruled over by Makali'i is said to have taken its new name.[8]

According to the Hawaiiloa legend, the name of Makali'i refers to his post as navigator, "Eyes of the chief." In the Kila story the name is derived from the pattern called "Little eyes" of the net in which the plant foods of Kahiki were drawn up out of reach of Kila's expedition. It is during the seasonal festival of the Makahiki that the symbolic scattering of edible plants from the net of Makali'i takes place in order to decide the chances of the food supply for the coming year. Now the rat leaves the plains for the uplands and begins to nibble at the edible fernstalks while the owl, "thus deprived of its natural food," feeds upon berries, remarks Kepelino of the Makali'i season.[9] Something of this calendar meaning must enter into the legend of Makali'i as mythical navigator and seer of the early settlers of the northwestern island of Kauai who, through his knowledge of the stars, regulated for them the planting season and foretold success in agriculture.[10] Hawaiians call stars useful in such observations after the famous navigator. Not only is Aldebaran, traditional steering star for Hawaii-loa, named Makali'i,

7. For. Col. 4: 372, 386.   8. *Ibid.* 10.
9. 78–79, 84–87.
10. See Beaglehole, *Bul.* 150: 19 note.

but the Pleiades also are called "the cluster of Makali'i" (na huihui-a-Makali'i) or "nets of Makali'i" (na-koko-a-Makali'i). "Makali'i's rainbow-colored gourd-net hangs above" (Huihui koko a Makali'i kau iluna), is the saying.[11] Other stars are named "the bailers of Makali'i" (na ka o Makali'i), "the wives of Makali'i" (na wahine o Makali'i).[12]

The tradition of Makali'i as the regulator of food plants may come from Tahiti, where the Pleiades are also called Matari'i. When these first sparkle in the horizon toward Orion's belt (Mere) in the twilight of evening (November 20), the season of plenty begins, and it lasts until these stars descend below the horizon in the twilight of evening.[13] In Mangaia, the appearance of Matariki about the middle of December above the eastern horizon at sunset marks the new year. The story says:

The Pleiades were originally one star, and so brilliant that Tane was angry. He got Sirius and Aldebaran to help him, and pursued Matariki, who fled behind a stream. Sirius drained the waters dry and Tane flung Aldebaran and broke Matariki into six little pieces.[14]

In Samoa, (Maka)li'i is the descendant of Lu the wanderer (or circumciser, see Luanu'u), son of Lu-a-itu, who weds the daughter of the lord of Atafu north of Samoa. Li'i is swallowed by a fish and deified under the name of the Pleiades. Hence Atonga(-loa) is half spirit, half man.[15] In the legend of the settling of Manu'a, four children are offered to the sun: Li'i is swallowed by a fish and deified as the Pleiades, the other three reach and settle Manu'a, the sister as wife of its chief and mother of Lu-a-Tongaloa, who became the first chief of Upolo.[16] In Tonga, Mataliki "probably refers to the Pleiades," says Collocott.[17] Rakahanga people worship the Pleiades.[18] Mataliki is the principal god of Pukapuka.[19]

11. For. Col. 6: 272, 278.   12. Kepelino, 78.
13. Henry, 332.   14. Gill, 43–44.
15. *JPS* 4: 116.   16. *Ibid.*, 52.
17. BPBM Oc. Papers 8: 160.   18. *JPS* 24: 151.
19. Beaglehole, *Bul.* 150: 309.

PUKAPUKA MYTH OF MATALIKI

When Maui fished up Tonga, some gods who lived undersea wandered in the air. One traveled to a rock which had emerged from the water at the place where Pukapuka now is, and saw a godlike man come from it, so he swam away and did not return. This man was Mataliki. To him therefore the island belonged, and he was a god. He found a wife at an island called Tonga-leleva and they had two children, Te-muli-vaka and Te-mata-kiate. Tongaloa gods were invited to build up the island but, fearing union with Samoa, the Pukapuka people asked them to stop building reefs. The western division of the channel which the Sun made by stamping his foot, which marks the line of the taro beds, is called Te-muli-wenua (The back of the earth) ; the eastern division is Te-mata-wenua (The front of the earth).[20]

Hikapoloa has a place in legend as traditional ruler of Kohala district on Hawaii corresponding to that of Maka-li'i on Kauai. As an epithet attached to the names of Kane, Ku, and Lono it represents them as a joint godhead "before heaven and earth were created," an event which, so far as Hawaiian legendary history is concerned, seems to have taken place on Oahu and may be ascribed to the introduction of Kane worship and the setting up of a kahuna class. The phrase Ke-ali'i-Hikapoloa is said to be equivalent to "Almighty god."[21] "Taken by Hikapoloa" (Lawe aku la Hika-poloa) occurs in a chant of Kamehameha's day as a phrase for death.[22] The place in Kohala where the Makahiki god was kept, on the way up from the present heiau of Mo'okini, is called Hikapoloa.[23]

It is to this earlier period of colonization and the spread of new ruling families with their rival gods that, according to some interpreters, such an allusion as this from the fourth era of the Kumulipo refers with its indication of a new line of chiefs and the establishment of a family which becomes a determining factor in Hawaiian genealogical history:

20. Beaglehole MS.
22. *Ibid.* 453.

21. For. Col. 6: 272.
23. *Ibid.* 204.

Heap up the fire of La'a there,
The ape plant from over the ocean,
Those of the sea take to the land,
Creep this way and that,
The family of creepers multiply,
The ancient line and the new intermingle,
The new line becomes the genealogy of the chiefs,
Their offspring become the best of the land,
Fathomless, a deep darkness their rank,
Kane-of-the-night-of-deep-darkness is born.

Tradition ascribes to Paao the introduction of human sacrifice into the temple ritual, the walled heiau, and the red-feather girdle as a sign of rank; all typical, says Handy, of late Tahitian culture and not found in Samoa. Other institutions ascribed to him are the pulo'ulo'u tapu sign, the prostrating tapu (tapu moe or -o), and the feather god Kaili; some would call Paao rather than La'a-mai-kahiki the introducer of image worship. Most of these things characterize the Ra'iatea ritual. That Paao took his ideas from Tahiti is further indicated by reference to "Vavau" and "Upolo" as places where he owned land, probably old districts so named in northern Tahiti in the Aha-roa division of that island, and the name Aha-ula (later called Waha-ula) for the first heiau erected by his party on Hawaii suggests such a connection. Paao is said to have brought the puhala (pandanus) to Kohala. He brought soil from the hills and planted trees about the heiau, still standing, of Wahaula, some of which seem to have survived to Fornander's day. Stones near the heiau of Mo'okini are pointed out today as "Paao's canoe," his "paddles" and "fishhook," and the fields he cultivated are called "the weeds of Paao" (na maau o Paao) and left untouched for fear of storm. To him are ascribed those severities of religious observance which built up the power of chief and priest during this later period of migration from the south. The land was revolutionized and all the old kahunas were put to death during Paao's time, says Kepelino.[24]

24. 197.

PAAO MIGRATION LEGEND

(a) *Emerson version.* The priest Paao and his older brother
Lono-pele have a bitter quarrel. Lono-pele accuses Paao's son
of stealing tapu food and Paao insists on cutting open his son's
stomach to prove the accusation false. He broods over his son's
death and builds a double canoe to leave for other lands. Lono-
pele's son drums upon the canoes with his fingers while they are
under tapu and Paao has him slain for a sacrifice for the canoes
and buried beneath them, where the buzzing of flies reveals to the
father the child's dead body.

Paao acts as priest for the voyage, Makaalawa as navigator
and astronomer, Halau as sailing master, Pu-oleole as trum-
peter; and there are forty paddlers, besides stewards and awa
chewers. Na-mauu-o-Malawa (The grasses of Malawa), sister
of Paao, accompanies the party. Kanaloa-nui the canoe is called
(Or Ka-nalo-a-muia, The buzzing of flies). They pass under the
Kaakoheo bluff and the prophet Makuakaumana asks to be
taken aboard. Paao says all the places are full except the projection of the stern. Makuakaumana leaps and gains this position (but this incident probably belongs to the return trip to
Tahiti).

Lono-pele sends as storm winds Kona-ku, Kona-nui-a-niho,
Moae, Kona-heapuku, Kiki-ao, Lele-ula, Lele-kuilua, followed
by a north wind, Ho'olua, and a monster bird, the Iwa, called
Ke-kaha-ka-iwa-i-na-pali. Paao invokes Lono and first a school
of aku fish, then one of opelu come to quiet the waves. These fish
have ever since been sacred to the Paao family.

Paao lands first in Puna on Hawaii, where he builds the heiau
at Pulama [now called Waha-ula (Red mouth) but formerly
Aha-ula]. He goes on to Kohala and erects the famous heiau of
Mo'okini at Pu'uepa, the stones for which are passed from hand
to hand a distance of nine miles from the seacoast.

(b) *Kamakau version.* Upon Paao's prayer to the god of
ocean (Kanaka-o-kai, says Green), the aku and opelu fish
"leaped up and skipped in the waters and quieted the waves." At
the time of the prophet's leap, several other "gods" attempted

the feat and were dashed to death. His success is heralded in a chant:

> "You are like the flying fish
> Skimming easily through the sky,
> Traversing the dark waters of ocean,
> O Halulu at the foundation house of heaven,
> Kane, Makua-kau-mana,
> The prophet who made the circuit of the island,
> Who circled the pillars of Kahiki."

(Paao brings with him several mo'o kupua from Kahiki, all worshiped as sacred stones on Oahu today. These are Maka-pu'u, Ihiihi-lau-akea, and Malei.[25] Makua-kau-mana returns to Kahiki but Paao remains on Hawaii and his bones rest in the cave of Pu'uwepa in Kohala.[26] An early school composition makes Paao brother to Pele.[27])

PAAO AND PILI-KAAIEA LEGEND

Paao makes a return voyage to Tahiti (starting from Kapua in Kona district, says Thrum) in order to secure a relative of pure blood who can compete in rank as ruling chief with the blueblood families of other islands, Hawaiian chiefs having intermarried carelessly with families of petty chiefs. The invitation is preserved in an old chant (Emerson text):

> E Lono! e Lono- e! e Lonokaeho!
> Lonokulani, ali'i o Ka-ulu-o-nana,
> Eia na wa'a, kau mai a i,
> E hoi e noho ia Hawaii-kuauli.
> He aina loa'a i ka moana,
> I hoea mai loko o ka ale,
> I ka halehale poipu a Kanaloa,
> He koa-kea i halelo i ka wai,
> I lou i ka makau a ka lawaia,
> A ka lawaia nui o Kapuhe'euanu'u-la,
> A pae na wa'a, kau mai;

25. Green.   26. *HAA* 1932, 109.
27. For. Col. 5: 656.

E holo e ai ia Hawaii, he moku;
He moku Hawaii,
He moku Hawaii no Lonokaeho e noho.

"O Lono, Lono, Lono-ka-eho!
Lono descended from the gods, chief of the fertile land of Nana,
Here are canoes, come aboard,
Return and dwell on green-backed Hawaii,
A land discovered in the ocean,
Risen up out of the waves,
From the very depths of the sea,
A piece of white coral left dry in the ocean,
Caught by the hook of the fisherman,
The great fisherman of Kapaahu,
The great fisherman of Kapuhe'euanu'u;
When the canoes land, come aboard,
Sail away and possess Hawaii; a land,
A land is Hawaii,
A land is Hawaii for Lonokaeho to dwell in."

Lono-kaeho declines the invitation but sends in his place Pili-
kaaiea (or -auau), called a "grandchild" of Lana-ka-wai on the
Ulu line, but born and brought up in Kahiki. Pili wins the hearts
of the people and from him descend the chiefs of Hawaii on the
Ulu line down to the last quarter of the nineteenth century. The
priesthood established by Paao under the Ku ritual descended
through an unbroken line of kahunas to Hewahewa, under whom
the tapus were broken and the old heiau worship was abolished
after the death of Kamehameha in 1819.[28]

The Paao migration legend introduces stock episodes in
Polynesian stories of long voyages. Obstacles sent to oppose
a voyage are overcome through the interposition of a god, as
in the Waha-nui legend; not in this case referred to the god
who has made the supernatural leap to gain passage, but the

28. N. Emerson, *HHS Papers* 5 (1893): 5–13; Malo, 25–26;
Green, 120–124; Kamakau, *Kuokoa,* December 29, 1866; Thrum,
More Tales, 46–52; Remy-Brigham, 10–11; Westervelt, *Hist. Leg.,*
65–78; Kalakaua, 47–48; Stokes, *HHS Papers* 15 (1928): 40–45.

connection is here probably lost. The leap itself as a means of testing divinity is not an imaginary episode. Hocart says that in the Lau islands the choice of a ruling chief was determined by challenging the men of rank to jump off a point and catch at a banyan tree. Only the man brave enough to accept the challenge and strong enough to make the leap was worthy to be chief.[29] In Hawaii leaping down cliffs was practised as an asset in war.

The introductory episode occurs in almost identical form in the Maori, so much so as to lead Stokes to argue for an identity between Paao and Hiro (Hilo). It is, however, clearly a type episode attached to more than one figure in Maori story.

Maori. (*a*) Whiro-tu-tupua, after quarreling with his older brother Hua about the canoe they are building, strangles Hua's son Tao-ma-kati because he eats the choice bits given to the builders, and hides his body in the chips under the canoe (or kills him as an offering for the canoe launching). The body is revealed by a buzzing blowfly. The two fight and the child's father is defeated (and he and his family are killed and eaten).[30]

(*b*) Whiro kills Ngana-te-irihia because he snatches the choice bits of food, and hides the body under the canoe Whatu-te-ihi. A blowfly reveals the body. Whiro wins in battle with the child's father.[31]

(*c*) The body of the son of Manaia, who has been killed by Hoturoa (or Rata) while the canoes are building to sail to New Zealand, is revealed by the god assuming the body of a fly and buzzing about the body.[32]

(*d*) Uenuku kills Hoimatua's child for stumbling on the threshold, and Hoimatua's relative Turi kills Uenuku's in revenge and subsequently migrates in the Aotea canoe to escape Uenuku's vengeance.[33]

29. 209.
30. Best, *JPS* 31: 111–121; White 2: 14–17.
31. Hare Hongi, *JPS* 7: 37.
32. White 2: 187; Taylor, 263–264; Grey, 84.
33. *Ibid.*, 126–131.

Revelation of a murder by a buzzing fly is a common theme in Maori story. In the story of Hatupatu, parents send a spirit in blowfly form to find the body of their child who has been killed by his brothers for eating the birds they have preserved, and the spirit brings the child to life.[34] See also the Moriori story of Tu-moana's son who murders his sweetheart for laughing at him and her dead body is revealed by a buzzing fly,[35] and compare the Hawaiian story of Ka-hala-o-puna whose body is revealed by an owl or bird god.

The whole incident, like most Maori stories, corresponds closely with actual occurrences in human life. The supernatural element is introduced into the Paao legend only through the attempt to rationalize these occurrences in the light of belief in the part played by spirit forces in such happenings. The buzzing fly attracted by the odor of putrifying flesh is explained as a spirit emissary. Bad weather on a sea voyage is laid not to meteorological disturbances, but to the sorceries of an enemy; the schools of fish which come with clearing weather, to the cause and not the accompaniment of the change.

34. *Ibid.*, 115–116.   35. *JPS* 4: 211.

XXVII

RULING CHIEFS

TRADITIONS relating to the colonizing period in Hawaiian history emphasize the insignia of rank which became the tangible signs by which a man's position was assured in aristocratic society. These were: First, a family genealogy tracing back to the gods through one of the two sons of Ki'i, Ulu and Nana-ulu, and by as many branches (lala) as family relationship could be stretched to cover. Second, a name chant, composed at birth or given in afterlife, glorifying the family history not only of persons concerned but also of places made sacred by particular events or association. Third, signs in the heavens by which aumakua of the day recognized their offspring on earth. Fourth, a special place set aside as sacred to the birth of high-ranking chiefs. Fifth, the sacred cord (aha) stretched at the entrance of a chief's dwelling, under which all of lower rank must pass but which fell "of itself" before the approach of anyone of equal or higher position. Sixth, wealth, especially in lands, labor, and specialized objects such as foods, ornaments, colors belonging to ranking chiefs alone. Seventh, the power of the tapu, which gave the ranking chief immense personal privilege, although the ruling chief might have actually more power over lands and wealth; before certain captive chiefesses of Maui of incredible sanctity, according to Kamakau, Kamehameha himself had to remove his garment. Eighth, the right to officiate in the heiau as both chief and priest. Ninth, at death, the final deification of the bones and their laying away in a sacred (in later years a secret) place difficult of access, the most important such place in ancient times being the Iao valley on the island of Maui. Rank therefore depended primarily upon blood; but of equal importance was the conduct of life by which one could, by carelessness in preserving the tapus and in making proper marriages, lose caste and prerogatives under the severe discipline of the Aha-ali'i or so-called "college of chiefs," or could, through a royal marriage, raise the rank of one's descendants upon the family line.

The period during which political life became thus stabilized—through the building up of a ruling-chief class under a social system based upon strict religious observances—follows or overlaps the mythical migrations and colonization represented in legend by the arrival of the Kamau group and the activities of the kupua Kamapua'a, the coming of Pele and her family, the arrival of Kane and Kanaloa and their attention to the water supply, and the introduction of food plants.

Following the family of Akalana on the Ulu line appear three Nana names of chiefs who are said, like the Maui brothers, to have ruled the western end of Oahu in Waialua, Wahiawa, and Ewa districts. The last of the three, Nana-kaoko, has a wife, Ka-hihi-o-ka-lani, whose name resembles that of the chiefess as servants for whom Kahano son of Newa brought over the Menehune to Oahu. It is this Nana-kaoko and his wife who are the traditional founders on Oahu of the sacred place for the birth of chiefs at Ku-kani-loko in the uplands of Wahiawa, similar to that already set up at Holoholoku on Kauai. At Ho'olono-pahu (Sounding the pahu drum) the navel cord was tied and cut while the drum sounded. Afterbirth, cord, and later the navel string (piko) were carefully deposited, often in a heiau for safekeeping.[1] The site chosen is one frequently visited by thunderstorms, whose manifestations were regarded as the voice of ancestral gods of the heavens welcoming an offspring of divine rank. The drums perhaps simulated the voice of deity.

It was from the time of Heleipawa of Maui, whom some identify with Kapawa, that there began to be composed chants for a ruling chief in which were named his birth and burial places, the spots in which afterbirth, umbilical cord, and navel string were deposited, his house site, and other places sacred to his history. The site of the famous pleasure house (Hale-i-ka-lea) in Kipahulu built by Heleipawa was still to be seen in Kamakau's day, and the tapu spring of

1. For. Pol. Race 2: 272, 278; *HAA* 1912, 101–105.

fresh water, welling up in the sea at Kaui from a depth of twenty feet and walled up so firmly that the waves had not loosened the stones, where the chiefs of his day washed off the salt water when coming in from surfing.[2]

Another Maui chief, Haho, son of Paumakua and grandson of Hua-nui-ka-la'ila'i, was the traditional founder of the Aha-ali'i or ranking body of chiefs who might be distinguished by the use of the sacred cord called aha. They cultivated a metaphorical form of speech in order that their words might be concealed from the uninitiated. The awe attached to rank was accentuated by the dreaded tapu which attended the person of a chief. Those of highest rank never went abroad except at night lest their shadow falling upon the ground render it tapu. They were already gods, and at death their bones were separated from the flesh and placed in a receptacle (kaai) woven out of sennit or ie vine, in some cases shaped to imitate a torso, and worshiped as a family deity, while the soft parts of the body were laid away in some sacred place of burial like that back of the "Needle" in Iao valley. Kamakau records the names of chiefs down to Kalaniopu'u of Hawaii who were thus honored and enumerates also the names of their sacred cords.[3]

Many generations before Heleipawa and Haho, on the Ulu line, occur such mythical figures as Ku-hele-i-moana and his wife Mapuna-i-aala (Springing up in fragrance), daughter of Haumea; Akalana (Wakalana) and the Maui brothers; the Aikanaka to Laka group—all, except the first, famous names in southern tradition and all centering about the hill Kauiki in the fertile Hana district on the rain-washed eastern extremity of the island of Maui, where the sun rises out of the sea and the Kohala coast is to be seen beyond the channel of Ale-nui-haha (Great waves crashing).

From the time of La'a-mai-kahiki down to that of Umi, East Maui, comprising Koolau, Hana, Kipahulu, and Kaupo

2. Malo, 322–323; For. Col. 6: 319; Kamakau, *Ke Au Okoa,* October 14, 1869.

3. *Ke Au Okoa,* November 4, 1869; For. Pol. Race 2: 28–30; Kalakaua, 84–85; Malo, 323; Ellis, *Tour,* 270; Stokes, BPBM Oc. Papers 7: 4–5.

districts, was governed separately from the rest of the island and its chiefs were grouped about the fortified hill of Kauiki, famous in history, song, and story. Myths are told about its origin. Some say that it sprang from the navel of Hamoa. Others that it was born to the parents of Pele, or to the hill Kai-hua-kala by his wife Kahaule. Others relate how Ka-lala-walu (The eight-branched) brought the hill from Ka-hiki as an adopted child, but grew tired of its nibbling at her breasts and tried to leave it along the way, first at Kaloa, then at Kaena, then at the Ka-wai-papa stream. Others tell of the wanderings and death of Puʻuhele, little sister of Pele. The bay about Kauiki gives evidence of subsidence following some volcanic outbreak, and men say that formerly Kane and Ka-naloa planted a garden below the hill, and they point out two rocks below the hill on the inaccessible sea side which are called "the coconuts of Kane and Kanaloa" and the "root-stock" (kumu) of Kauiki. Mythical names are attached to the dwellers on Kauiki in ancient days. On the summit may be seen the rock placed by Aiai as an outlook for schools of fish entering the bay. Here Maui stood to push the sky higher because it lay so near the earth at Kauiki. Here lived Hina-hana-ia-ka-malama, she who worked at tapa making in the moon, and her husband, father of Puna and Hema on the Ulu line of chiefs.

All about the bay are crowded the memorials of those old days in the shape of a rock, a basin of water, a wave, a spring, a cave, or a mere name remembered from the time when chiefs and their followers thronged the bay, whose trifling deeds or misdeeds are still cherished in the memories of their living de-scendants. "If I told you all, it would fill a book," said old Kilinahi, watchman for schools of fish off the bay. Hawaiian verse loves to play with the memory of Kauiki. A hula begins,

> O Kauiki, mauna kiʻekiʻe,
> Huki aʻe la a pa i ka lani
> He poʻohiwi no kai halulu. . . .

> "Kauiki, mountain famous in story,
> Stretching upward to touch the heavens,
> A shoulder for the buffeting sea. . . ."

and a modern verse opens with,

> Healoha no Kauiki,
> Au i ke kai me he manu la!

> "Kauiki is beloved,
> Afloat on the sea like a bird!"

Hana is called "a land beloved of chiefs because of the fortress of Kauiki and the ease of living in that place." In time of war the hill was reached by a ladder of ohia poles bound together with withes. On the summit was spread a springy plant to serve as bed. Fishponds below furnished unlimited stores of fish. Heaps of awa root "delighted the nostrils of the dear firstborn chiefs."[4]

Maui chiefs who settled with their families in later days about Kauiki were Kanaloa and Kalahumoku, sons of Hualani the wife of Kanipahu, and half-brothers to Kalapana who ruled Hawaii; Eleio; Ka-la-ehaeha; Lei; Ka-mohohali'i; Kalae-hina; Ho'olae.[5] Much earlier, on the Ulu line, comes the name of Hua son of Pohukaina, said to be a contemporary of the prophet Naula-a-Maihea who came with La'a-mai-kahiki from the south. Two legends are connected with his name. One is the tragic story of his grandmother, the beautiful Popoalaea, put to death by her jealous husband. The other is the story of Hua's quarrel with his prophet Luaho'omoe (Ulu-ho'omoe) and the terrible drought that befell as a result of his impious conduct in condemning the prophet to death on a trumped-up charge. The story resembles the Kuula legend from the same locality and in fact Kuula the fish god is said to be descended from a son of the prophet whose death was attended by such evil results. Kepelino tells us that a struggle for power early arose between the secular and religious heads of the people, finally adjusted by uniting both powers in the person of the ruling chief, who became thus entitled to perform certain sacred offices in company with the priest. Both the Hua and the Kuula legend

4. Kamakau, *Kuokoa,* December 1, 1866.
5. For. Pol. Race 2: 78–79 note 2.

play up the priests' side of the contest. A story like that of
the chief Ka-lau-nui-a-hua (The long leaf of Hua, referring
to family descent) on the island of Hawaii shows the disaster
that follows when a prophet's warning is disregarded.

LEGEND OF POPOALAEA

Popo-alaea (Ball of red clay), a chiefess of rank in Hana
district on Maui during the rule of Kamohoali'i, is won as a reward of victory in strength-testing games by the chief Kaakea
(Makea) and he makes their home close to the crater above
Kaupo at a place called Koae-kea because there the koae birds
flock (or at the village of Hono-ka-lani). He is jealous, especially of her fondness for her younger brother. People bring malicious tales, and he sharpens his axe to kill her. She flees with an
attendant and the two women hide in the cavern at the pool of
Wai-anapanapa. At night they go to the village of Hono-ka-
lani for food. The people report seeing ghosts. He watches, and
detects her hiding place from the moving shadow of the fly
brush, waved by her attendant, cast upon the surface of the
water. Searching the cave, he dashes out the brains of the two
women upon the rocks.

Today, on the night of Ku, god of justice, the water in the
pool runs red. At some time each morning prismatic colors
(anapa) such as are sacred to divine chiefs play over the waters
of this pool as proof of her innocence. The water of the pool
makes even a dark skin look white when immersed in it.[6]

LEGEND OF HUA AND THE PROPHET

Hua's seer Lua-ho'omoe (Ulu-ho'omoe) arouses the chief's
anger and he seeks an excuse to discredit him and put him to
death. He therefore sends his men to the mountains after a certain species of bird found only on the coast. They appeal to the
seer, who points out the impossibility of the task to his chief.
When the men bring the birds from the sea, Hua pretends that
they have been trapped in the mountains and condemns the
seer for predicting falsely. The seer has the birds cut open to
show that it is seafood, not mountain berries, upon which they

6. Told by Sheriff Wahiako, Hana, July, 1930.

have fed. Hua nevertheless orders his death. A drought ensues
and fish disappear from the sea. Only for the two sons of the
seer, named Kaa-ka-kai and Kaa-na-hua, is a place provided
where rain falls, and thither they retire in secret. Naula-a-
Maihea scans the sky from the summit of Kaala on Oahu and
sees a cloud resting over Puʻu-o-inaina in Hanaula. He prepares
a great offering of swine for the sons of Hua and the drought is
broken.[7]

LEGEND OF KALAUNUIAHUA

Ka-lau-nui-a-hua consults the priestess Waahia as to the result of his war expedition and she consistently predicts disaster.
He attempts in vain to put her to death. Finally at her own
suggestion he has her body burned in the heiau of Keeku in
Kona. She puts a tapu against his coming out of the house
during the burning lest her god punish the land. As the smoke
rises, it takes the shape of two cocks fighting, then of two mud
hens. The chief can no longer resist tearing away the thatch
with his hand as he hears the shouts of the multitude at this last
portent, and the spirit of Waahia takes possession of his hand
through the god Kane-nui-akea. If he but points with his hand,
the land falls before him.

Hua conquers the chiefs of Maui, Molokai, Oahu, and proceeds with the captured chiefs to Kauai. Here the spirit leaves
his hand and enters that of a man of Kauai. His men are routed
and he and the three chiefs, Ka-malo-o-Hua of Maui, Ka-hoku-
o-Hua of Molokai, Hua-pouleilei of Ewa and Waianae are
taken prisoner by Kukona of Kauai, great-great-grandson of
Laʻa-mai-kahiki, according to the genealogy. Kukona treats his
prisoners with great magnanimity. On one occasion he feigns
sleep, overhears them grumbling against him and discussing a
plot to murder him, a proposal vehemently protested against
by Ka-malo-o-Hua, then pretends to awaken and repeats to
them the whole conversation as if it were a dream. As a tribute
to Ka-malo-o-Hua's good faith, he then dismisses the three
chiefs to their own lands with all the honors of war, but keeps

7. For. Col. 5: 514–519; Kalakaua, 155–173; Thrum, *HAA* 1924,
127–133.

Ka-lau-nui for some years a captive. There are in consequence no fresh invasions.[8]

The-long-leaf-of-Hua ruled on Hawaii as grandson of Ka-lapana descended on the Pili line. He was a restless and ambitious chief bent on the consolidation of the group under the rule of Hawaii, and his legend is not without interest for its bearing upon the resistance attempted by stubborn chiefs to the warnings of the priesthood. The incident of the magnanimous conduct of the chief of Kauai had a bearing upon later history, for even down to the time of Kamehameha, when chiefs consulted the memories of their archivists as to the conduct of the forefathers in like situations, the "peace of Ka-malo-o-Hua" was cited as precedent for securing a peaceful ending of hostilities.

It was during the time of Kakaalaneo of Maui that the division of lands is said to have taken place under a kahuna named Kalaihaohi'a (Hew the bark of the ohia tree) which portioned out the island into districts, subdistricts, and smaller divisions, each ruled over by an agent appointed by the landlord of the next larger division, and the whole under control of the ruling chief over the whole island or whatever part of it was his to govern. Land reforms and other means of strengthening the power of the ruling chief and stabilizing control over a growing population were carried out on Oahu also at about this time by Mailikukahi, successor on the Moikeha line of the last ruling chief of the elder Kumuhonua line, who was forced to retire because of his unpopularity. The names of Mailikukahi, his son Kalona-iki, and his granddaughter Kukaniloko are handed down in tradition as wise and just rulers. With Mailikukahi, Waikiki became the ruling seat of chiefs of Oahu. He carried out strict laws, marked out land boundaries, and took the firstborn son of each family to be educated in his own household. He honored the priests, built heiaus, and discountenanced human sacrifice. A raiding band from Hawaii and Maui he met at Waikakalaua gulch and pursued and slaughtered at Kipapa gulch. Punalu'u was

8. Malo, 328–332; For. Pol. Race 2: 67–69; Kalakaua, 175–205; Cartwright, table 4.

killed in the battle on the plain of that name. The head of
Hilo, son of Lakapu, was stuck up at a place called Poʻo-Hilo
in Hono-uliuli.[9]

Legends gather about the name of the ruling chief of
Maui, Kakaalaneo (Kukaalaneo, Kaalaneo), who lived in
the present Lahaina district on the hill Kekaʻa, owned fishponds in Hana district on the opposite end of the island,
planted a famous breadfruit grove, and took to wife the Molokai chiefess whom Eleio found for him and who brought
him the first feather cape seen on Maui, by whom he had the
mischievous son Kaululaau who killed off the spirits on Lanai. In his day the old name of Lele became attached to
Lahaina.[10] In the legend of the red-skinned kupua of Puna
Kepaka-ili-ula, Kakaalaneo is represented as a skilful
spearsman who "never misses a grassblade, an ant, or a flea,"
but in a contest for the favors of a lady (drawn direct from a
tale from *The Arabian Nights*) he is worsted by the kupua
and ignominiously slain.[11] This way of aggrandizing one
hero at the expense of another's traditional fame is no new
thing in Hawaiian story-telling, but the treatment of the episode marks it as a foreign imitation.

Tradition places in Kakaalaneo's time the arrival of a
party of strangers (haole) who played an active part in
court life and whose names were, according to Kamakau,
kept in memory as late as Captain Cook's day, for to the
question whether Cook's party were gods or men, the kahunas
expressed the opinion that they were "men from the land of
Kaekae (Kakae) and Kukanaloa." After regular voyages
between Hawaii and the southern islands had ceased, chance
seems to have brought some boats to shore which had drifted
from their course. One is said to have arrived off Mokapu
point on Oahu and another in the time of Ka-malu-o-Hua to
have been wrecked off the coast of Maui with five persons on
board, one of them a woman whom "Wakalana" took as his

9. For. Pol. Race 2: 89–91; Thrum, *More Tales,* 91–92; Kalakaua, 219–225.

10. For. Pol. Race 2: 82; Col. 4: 482–489; 5: 540–545.

11. *Ibid.* 4: 504–505; 5: 386–393.

wife and descendants of whom are said to be living on Maui and Oahu. A third party of strangers was brought back by Paumakua from one of his voyages. Kaekae and Maliu they are called, but a chant names them Auakahinu and Auakamea, or, in one version, Kukahauula and Kukalepa. They were priests, and it seems likely that the Kane and Kanaloa of the Haumea tradition have been here confused with Paumakua's people.[12] But all these arrivals are described so much alike and in terms so similar to such incidents recounted in southern groups, where the chance of a drifting boat making land with women on board is much more plausible, that they must be regarded as traditional rather than historical narratives.

Kukanaloa and Kaekae are the leaders of the party said to have arrived in Kakaalaneo's day, and the legend of their arrival and the chant that follows in which their names are played upon in listing names of chiefs will illustrate the type rather than fix the event. The last allusion in the legend is a pun upon the chief Lolale of Oahu who abducted the pretty chiefess of Maui, Kelea, while she was out surfing and carried her away to Oahu in the uplands of Lihue. She deserted him for his cousin Kalamakua in Ewa, by whom she became mother of the high chiefess Laie-lohelohe (The drooping pandanus vine), who became in turn the wife of her Maui cousin Pi'i-lani. All these names appear in the chant linked with the coming of Ku-kanaloa, together with the names of a wife and son of Kakaalaneo.[13]

LEGEND OF KUKANALOA

(a) The strangers land first at Keei in South Kona and then come on to Waihe'e, Maui, and land at a place called Ke-ala-i-Kahiki (The road to Kahiki). They are exhausted and the natives clothe and feed them. In looks they are light with sparkling eyes. When asked after their homeland and parents they

12. For. Pol. Race 2: 24–26, 81; Col. 6: 247; J. Emerson, *HHS Papers* 5: 13; Kalakaua, 182–184; Kamakau, *Kuokoa,* January 19, 1867.

13. For. Pol. Race 2: 82–87; Kalakaua, 227–246; *HAA* 1921, 58–62.

point to the uplands "far, far above where our parents dwell," and show themselves familiar with bananas, breadfruit, mountain-apple, and candlenut trees. The two leaders become Kaka-alaneo's property. There is no tapu place closed to them. They marry chiefesses and some of their descendants are living today. Kani-ka-wi and Kani-ka-wa (Whistle and Flute) they are called, "perhaps because their speech was as unintelligible as that of the lale birds that live in the hills."[14]

> Puka mai o Kanikawi, Kanikawa,
> O na haole iluna o Halakaipo,
> Puka mai nei Kukanaloa,
> Kupuna haole mai Kahiki
> Puka mai nei Kakaalaneo
> Me ke leo iki o Kakae,
> O Kaualua ia, o Kaihiwalua
> O Kelea, o Kalamakua,
> O Pi'ilani ia, o Laielohelohe.

> "Came Sharp-sound, Loud-sound,
> The strangers above Halakaipo,
> Came Ku-kanaloa,
> The stranger forefather from Kahiki,
> Came Kakaalaneo,
> With the soft-voiced Kakae,
> Kaualua (the wife), Kaihiwalua (the son),
> Kelea (the wife), Kalamakua (the husband),
> Pi'ilani (the husband), Laielohelohe (the wife)."

14. Kamakau, *Kuokoa,* January 19, 1867.

XXVIII

USURPING CHIEFS

PI'ILANI of Maui had by Laie-lohelohe two sons and a daughter named Lono-pi'ilani, Kiha-pi'ilani, and Pi'ikea. Lono-pi'ilani succeeded to the rule over his father's lands. Pi'ikea made a marriage, considered a misalliance by the blue-blooded chiefs of Maui and Oahu, with Umi, ruling chief on Hawaii. The story of the younger son Kiha-pi'ilani belongs with a series of popular legends recounted in great detail in which usurping chiefs on a younger branch wrest the ruling power from the legitimate heir through superior ability and power to govern men. Of these, the stories of Kihapi'ilani on Maui and of Umi on Hawaii contain no fantastic elements and the facts of their rule have substantial historic support. The corresponding legends of Kuali'i on Oahu and of Kawelo on Kauai bear the marks of handling as fiction to such an extent as to throw doubt upon their actual identity as historic figures.

The name of Kiha-pi'ilani is preserved locally about the island of Maui in connection with his feats of leaping from a height into a pool of water, called lelekawa, and for the famous paved road about the island with the building of which he oppressed the people. Men are said to have stood in line and passed the stones from seashore to upland. Parts of the road are still in place and may be followed where the trail cuts in a straight line up and down the deep gorges which break the windward slope of the island.

LEGEND OF KIHAPI'ILANI

Kihapi'ilani is brought up on Oahu, but when his uncle scolds him for wasting food he goes off to Lahaina to find his true father. He is dissatisfied to take the place of a younger son. When his father sets him on the left knee he jumps to the right, and he snatches from his father's right hand the food and drink intended for his older brother Lono. After their father's death Lono takes pains to humiliate him. The brothers come to blows. Kiha is defeated and saves himself only by leaping off a cliff down the hill Pakui. He hides himself in Kula district at Ka-lani-wai in the Makawao region with his wife Kumaka of a Hana family of chiefs, whom he passes off as his sister. The two live with a man named Kahuakole, whose son he is supposed to be. He proves a bad provider and is scolded for idleness. He steals a stick for beating tapa in order that his high-born wife may follow the custom of the commoners among whom they live, and himself goes off to the potato patch at Kaluaama in Haiku after potato slips. Offered "as many as he can carry away," he takes so large a load that an old man who sees him pass recognizes him as a chief and takes up his cause. He consults various kahunas as to the course he should pursue to win the rule from his brother. He goes back to Oahu, learns surfing and, returning to Hana district, surfs with the daughter of Ho'olae. The couple are repudiated by the father, but after a son is born, a reconciliation is effected and Kiha sends his wife to ask of Ho-'olae such lands as will give him control of the fortress Kauiki. Ho'olae recognizes at once that this is no common man to whom his daughter Kolea-moku has born a child, but the chief Ki-hapi'ilani. He nevertheless loyally refuses to desert his old chief Lono. Kiha therefore retires to Hawaii and succeeds in winning Umi's coöperation through the influence of his sister Pi'ikea. After the death of Lono, Umi sends an army to establish Kiha in the succession. Ho'olae defends Kauiki for Lono's son and sets up a wooden image so huge as to frighten off Umi's men, who believe it to be alive. Eventually Pi'imaiwa'a discovers the trick. Kiha has Lono's son put to death and asks that the lands may be made over to Pi'ikea's sons. The two lads come to Maui, but are despised and done to death and Kiha is established as ruler over his father's lands. It is his famous son Kama-lala-walu (Son of eight branches) who gives the name Maui-of-Kama to the island.[1]

1. For. Pol. Race 2: 97–99, 206–207; Col. 4: 236–255; 5: 176–181, 376–379; Thrum, *More Tales,* 73–86; Kamakau, *Ke Au Okoa,* December 1–15, 1870.

Between the periods of Hua and Pi'ilani, that is, between
Moikeha's time and that of Umi on Hawaii, were born at Kahinihini in Mokae, Hamoa, the twins, "Little and big sacred
ones of Hana," called Hana-la'a-nui and Hana-la'a-iki, from
whom respectively the chiefs of Hawaii and Maui count descent. From the great Kaupo families of Ko'o and Kaiuli,
descended from Kiha and his wife Koleamoku, came Kahekili's wife Kauwahine, mother of Kalanikupule, the last
ruling chief of Maui, and of a daughter, Kailikauoha, who
became the wife of the Maui chief Ulumehe'ihe'i Hoapili and
mother of Liliha, beloved wife of Boki of sandalwood fame.[2]

The island of Hawaii lying over against Kauiki, home of
the heaven-high chiefs of the Pi'ilani line, bred meanwhile
the offspring of the second of those usurping chiefs whose
final example is found in the well-known history of the first
Kamehameha. Umi of Liloa wrested the rule over Hamakua
from the unpopular Hakau, legitimate heir of Liloa, and
eventually brought most of the island under subjection, a
conquest completed six generations later by Keawe, called
"the first chief over the whole island." Liloa is said to have
died in 1575 at his home in Waipio valley, where stood the
most sacred heiau on the island, that of Paka'alana. To Liloa is ascribed by tradition the introduction of homosexual
practices.[3]

LEGEND OF UMI SON OF LILOA

Liloa has a son Hakau by his mother's younger sister, Pinea.
Later he begets Umi upon a pretty chiefess of low rank whom
he surprises at her bathing pool and with her consent makes his
wife. He leaves with her the usual recognition tokens and Umi
makes his way to his father's court and becomes a favorite.
Liloa at his death leaves the land to Hakau but the god to Umi,
and warns this favorite younger son to remain in hiding when
his father is no longer living to protect him. Umi withdraws
from Waipio with his three comrades Omaokamau, Pi'imaiwa'a,
and Koi, whom he has adopted from boyhood, and hides in the

2. For. Pol. Race 2: 126–127, 261.
3. *Ibid.* 73–78; For. Col. 6: 320; Malo, 334–335.

country between Hamakua and Hilo, where he takes two wives and engages in fishing and husbandry. The kahuna Kaoleioku observes a rainbow hovering over the boy's head as he repairs to the place where his god is hidden in order to lay before it the first offering of fish. To make certain of his rank, the kahuna lets loose a pig, and when the pig approaches the youth, the priest guesses his identity and takes up his cause against Hakau. The youths train themselves in all the arts of war. Four large houses are each filled with warriors from among the disaffected who hate Hakau for his cruelties and for his neglect of the common good. The two principal kahunas of Liloa, neglected and insulted by Hakau, secretly take up his cause. Hakau is apprised of Umi's preparations and induced to send his men to the forest to gather feathers with which to adorn his warriors in a raid against Umi. Thus left unprotected, he observes a long file of men approaching with bundles and is told that his people are bringing in tribute. Out of the bundles come hard tribute in the shape of stones with which Hakau is stoned to death. Umi brings the whole land under subjection and distributes its rule to his three comrades and the kahuna who has aided his conquest. At the advice of this kahuna he takes wives of high rank in order to overcome the odium of his inferior rank. Two of these are his half-sister Kapu-kini, daughter of Liloa, and his aunt Pi'ikea, daughter of Pi'ilani of Maui.

The subjection of Hilo comes about through a quarrel with the pretty daughter of its chief Kulukulua, whom Umi has won as an unknown lover. He makes fun of and destroys her necklace of wiliwili berries, boasting of his own whale-tooth ornament which alone is worthy of chiefs. The girl goes crying to her father and Umi is obliged to make good his boast and give up his own necklace to repair the loss inflicted upon the chiefess. A successful raid follows to regain the heirloom. Kau district is won from the blind chief Imaikalani, who, though blind, is famed for his stroke, which never misses. An attendant reveals to Umi that the chief has two "birds" (guards) who give warning when anyone approaches. The guards killed, the blind chief becomes helpless. But the most famous of Umi's battles is that fought with the invisible powers of the spirit world assembled to enforce a promise made by Umi's wife. Pi'ikea has promised her first daughter to her mother's family on Oahu to rear, according to custom in families of chiefs, but when her mother's supernatural relatives come to take the child, Umi resists and a war follows during which an invisible enemy strikes down Umi's men without their ever seeing who has dealt the blow. Meanwhile the child is born, and the relatives snatch the child and depart.

At Umi's death the body is entrusted to Koi to dispose in some concealed spot. Koi takes with him his sister's husband; the two arrange a substitute body to be publicly carried to burial while Umi's own body is borne away to the cliffs of Wai-manu. From this adventure the brother-in-law, the only other man besides Koi who knows the place of burial, never returns. Today, as the saying is, "Only the birds know where Umi son of Liloa lies buried."[4]

The legend of Umi is one of the most popular of all Ha-waiian prose sagas of heroes, embellished as it is with many stock episodes but still preserving the thread of historical ac-curacy. Umi is still famed as a farmer and fisherman. He laid out great taro patches in Waipio. Aku fishing was his de-light. He organized the people according to occupations. He kept up the worship of the gods and magnified the practice of human sacrifice. He built the heiau of Kuki'i overlooking the warm spring at Kapoho in Puna and that of Pohaku Hana-lei in Ka-u.[5] On the slope of the mountain just back of the hill Hale-pohaha were to be seen, before the lava flows of 1887 and 1907 covered them, the stone structures of "Umi's camp." Seventy-five huts were counted, all facing away from the wind and built of three slabs of pahoehoe lava rock, two set to-gether at an angle and a third forming the back, each hut large enough to hold two men. Larger huts, perhaps designed for chiefs, were supported by slabs within and built up out-

4. For. Pol. Race 1: 192; 2: 74–78, 96–108; Col. 4: 178–235, 244–255; 5: 176–181, 378–383; *Moolelo Hawaii*, 41; Ellis, *Tour*, 89, 274; Pogue, 81–86; Malo, 336–345; Kalakaua, 265–315; Thrum, *More Tales*, 98–103; Remy-Brigham, 18–29; Remy-Alexander, *HAA* 1888, 78–85; Kamakau, *Ke Au Okoa*, November 3—December 1, 1870.

5. For. Pol. Race 2: 101; Col. 5: 200; *HAA* 1908, 55.

side with stone walls shaped into a dome.[6] The place on Kauiki is still pointed out where the image stood which was later commemorated by Kamehameha as the god Kawalaki'i. Beside these tangible evidences of his fame, a number of popular legends surround the name of Umi. One tells of the revenge he took upon the man who crowded him unfairly in a surfboard contest when he was living in obscurity in the country. Another recalls one of his warriors named Mau-ku-leoleo who was so tall he could pick coconuts from trees and wade out into the sea several fathoms without wetting himself above the loins. It was said that a god, perhaps Kanaloa, gave him a fish to eat which caused his growth.[7]

No connected story is told of Keawe-nui-a-Umi. He is said to have subdued the warring chiefs over Hawaii and to have established a popular court in Hilo where story-telling flourished. Of his younger son Lono-i-ka-makahiki, who made a lucky marriage and rose to the position of ruling chief by his own ability, a long legend is recited, some of the incidents of which historians say belong to namesakes.

LEGEND OF LONOIKAMAKAHIKI

Lono-i-ka-makahiki is a younger son of Keawe-nui-a-Umi by his wife Haokalani. Reared at Napo'opo'o near Kealakekua in Kona district by his father's two prophets Hauna and Loli, he early becomes expert in the arts of war and of wrestling and learns to respect his father's gods. The old soothsayer Ka-wa'a-maukele at Kanokapa teaches him the art of competitive word play (ho'opa'apa'a) so that he is soon able to outwit all his comrades.

At the death of his father, Kaiki-lani-wahine-ali'i-o-Puna (The little heavenly chiefess of Puna), daughter of Keawe-nui's older brother, becomes the legitimate heir. Lono's older half-brother Kanaloa-kuaana is her husband. He tests Lono's skill by hurling forty spears at him at once, all of which Lono dodges. He therefore gives Kaikilani to Lono and the two rule the land.

---

6. A. S. Baker, *HAA* 1917, 62–70; and given by Judge Haselden of Waiohinu, Kau, December, 1914.

7. Ellis, *Tour,* 89; Kalakaua, 14, 279.

Lono and Kaikilani (or Kaikilani-mai-panio, another wife of Lono) quarrel. Lono accuses her of infidelity and strikes her down (or kills her). Her relatives on Hawaii rise against him. He retreats to the court of Kakuhihewa at Kamooa, Kailua, on Oahu. Here he is treated with some contempt as a nameless wanderer, but in a succession of contests in arts with which he is unfamiliar or at a disadvantage he wins every bet by his skill in word play and his quickness of memory. Thus he learns in a single night a new name chant from a visiting chiefess from Kauai whose favors he has won at a game of kilu, and is able to pass it off as his own; succeeds in a fishing contest by punning on the names of the fish he is supposed to have caught; visits other islands and excites envy by his great fly brush named Elee-leua-lani made of feathers not to be had save on Hawaii; displays a calabash containing the bones of the warring chiefs of Hawaii subdued and slain by his father and chants their names; wins a wife; and in general displays wit and talent to the credit of the somewhat despised chiefly house of Umi.

After the death of Kaikilani (according to one version), he wanders half-crazed through the uplands of Kauai, deserted by all his followers but a single man named Kapaihi-a-Hilina, who follows him through all the hardships of his forest life, cares for his needs, and constantly observes the etiquette demanded toward a tapu chief, never even crossing the chief's shadow. When Lono eats bananas the guardian contents himself with the skins. Upon Lono's restoration to reason this man therefore is raised to the position of favorite, which he enjoys until jealous enemies accuse him to Lono of familiarity with the chiefess, Lono's wife. Banished from the court, he raises a chant in which he describes their wanderings together in such touching terms that Lono's affection reawakens. No reconciliation is however possible until the slanderers are put to death.

The invasion from Maui under the ambitious chief Kama-lala-walu (Son of eight branches) occurs during Lono's rule. Lono visits Maui with his younger brother and war leader Pupukea and the two carry on a contest of wit with Kama-lala-walu and his brother Makakui-ka-lani, who is as tall and slim as Pupukea is short and stocky. Observing the Maui chief's ambition for conquest, Lono sends pretended deserters to represent

falsely the weakness of his own position, and thus lures Kamalalawalu into a raid upon the island in which the Maui chief is
completely defeated, his army annihilated, and he himself slain.
In spite of the disastrous result of this expedition, undertaken as
it was against the advice of his wisest seers, the glory of Kamalalawalu's name remains undimmed. Chants are sung in praise
of his glorious death and the island is called Maui-of-Kama because of his illustrious reign.[8]

The last great name of succeeding chiefs on the Ulu line
who ruled Hawaii before the historic period of Kalani-opu'u,
ruling chief at the time of Cook's arrival, and the rise of the
Kamehameha chiefs, is that of Keawe called chief over the
whole island (-i-kekahi-ali'i-o-ka-moku). He had many wives
and became, as the chroniclers say, "ancestor of chiefs and
commoners." When he died, his bones were encased in the
woven basket in which chiefs of high rank were worshiped.
"Keawe returned and rested in the kaai" says the chant.[9]

Contemporary with or somewhat later than Keawe of Hawaii was the rise to power of Ku-ali'i (Ku the chief) of Oahu,
said to have ultimately subjugated the whole group and been
succeeded in historic times by his "son" Peleiholani. The
Hawaiian chronologist records: "This chronology begins
with a famous chief and ruler named Kuali'i. He was called a
God, one of supernatural power, a soldier, a runner, swift of
foot. Five times he ran around Oahu in a single day. He loved
Oahu alone, he did not care for any other country. He is
said to have lived long, (until) he walked with a cane; four
times forty years and fifteen he lived, that is 175 years."[10]
The story of the famous genealogical chant of Kuali'i has already been related, in which through 610 lines he is glorified
as "a god . . . a messenger from heaven . . . a stranger
(haole) from Kahiki." Genealogists give him a place on the

8. For. Pol. Race 2: 114–125; Col. 4: 256–263; 5: 436–451; Kamakau, *Ke Au Okoa,* January 5—February 2, 1871.

9. Kamakau, *Ke Au Okoa,* February 2, 1871; Kalakaua, 333–349;
For. Pol. Race 2: 125–129; Col. 4: 26–29.

10. BPBM MS. col.

Kalona-iki line from Nana-ulu.[11] History and fiction combine in the account of his conquests.

LEGEND OF KUALI'I

Kuali'i is born at Kalapawai (Kapalawai) in Kailua on the island of Oahu. For the ceremony of the cutting of the navel string at the heiau at Alala, the drums Opuku and Hawea are used. He shows his strength when very young and is urged to save the people from the oppression of Lono-ikaika, whom he defies by usurping his place at the dedication of the heiau of Kawaluna in Waolani. A great army sent against him is repulsed and most of the chiefs slain, although he has but a single follower to wield the two-edged stone axe named Haula-nui-akea, called also Manai-a-ka-lani, which is his only weapon. Thus the southern part of the island between Moanalua and Maunaloa is brought under his rule. He lives at Kalanihale in Kailua and becomes proficient in the arts of war. At Kauai, to which island he goes after kauila wood for fashioning spears, he takes on Malana'ihaehae and Kaha'i as chief warriors and makes for himself the spear named Huli-moku-alana (Victorious overturner of islands). Returning, he meets a great army drawn up on the plains in Lihue and three men defeat twelve thousand. In three great battles, at Malama-nui, Pule'e, Paupauwela, he subdues the whole island. He goes to Hawaii and routs a chief named Haalilo, but returns to Oahu to repel a revolt of the Waianae chiefs at Kalena. He wins Molokai when called to help defend the fishing grounds of Kekaha against the chiefs from the northern half of the island, Lanai when called to aid Haloalena in a war with Maui. Kauai, hearing of his conquests, also hastens to make peace with him, and thus the whole group acknowledges Kuali'i as lord.

Four Lono chiefs rule Oahu before the time of Kakuhihewa: Lono-huli-lani rules the north side of the island and Waialua, Lono-ikaika the south side, Lono-kukaelekoa has Waianae and Ewa, Lono-huli-moku has Koolau-poko. It is hence against the Lono domination that Kuali'i rebels. His comrade in the first

11. For. Pol. Race 1: 195–196.

battle is Maheleana [a name given today to the place at the east point of Hawaii where winds divide (mahele) and blow east down the Hamakua coast and north down the Puna coast]. Later leading warriors are Kaha'i; Malana'i-haehae, called in chant

> "Offspring of mischief-making Niheu
> Who dammed the waters of Kekeuna";

and Paepae from the fishing grounds of Kekaha in Molokai.

Kauhi, son of Kauhi-a-Kama of Maui, becomes his battle leader as a result of the affair at Lanai. Haloalena, the amiable ruling chief of Lanai, has a hobby for collecting bird skeletons and will demote any district overseer who allows the bones of trapped birds to be broken. The mischievous son of Kauhi-a-Kama is banished to Lanai. There he breaks up the chief's skeletons. Haloalena sends to beg Kuali'i to join him in war against Maui. Kuali'i questions Kauhi and finds that the boy has twisted his father's innocent words of reproof for his conduct, when banishing him to Lanai, into an order to stir up war. Kuali'i is so pleased with the boy's daring that he takes him into his household and makes him leader of his soldiers.

Kuali'i takes as wife a very high chiefess of Maui born of a brother-and-sister marriage and hence of pio rank. Her name is Ka-lani-kahi-make-i-ali'i. During the rule of their son Peleiholani, Oahu is said to have prospered more than at any other time since Maili-kukahi.[12]

Certain elements in the Kuali'i tradition give the impression that we have here the legend not of a single chief but of a political movement led in the name of a god, perhaps belonging to the ancient Ku line and directed against the Lono worshipers. The names Ku-ali'i, Ku-nui-akea, Ku-i-ke-ala-i-kaua-o-ka-lani (Ku in the stone in battle of the heavenly one) and the repeated assertion of divinity suggest that some symbolic object is here impersonated as a god, like the feather god Kaili, who became in Kamehameha's day the war god Ku-kaili-moku, and was similarly handed down in a family

12. For. Col. 4: 364–434; Pol. Race 2: 278–288.

line as a god of victory in battle. The impression is strengthened by the chronological uncertainty of Kuali'i's period, the length and character of his chant, the story of his birth, ushered in by the sacred pahu drums, the boast of his speed, and by the fact that his antagonists on Oahu bear Lono names. His early act of rebellion in taking upon himself a ceremony which belonged to the ruling chief to perform was in itself an assumption of superior divinity.

Still more curious, if we are hearing the story of a mere rebel chief, is the personal inactivity that accompanies his conquests. In his first fight he is represented as too young to have learned the arts of war. He persuades his father to stay beside him for his own protection, gives his weapon into the hands of his comrade Maheleana, pulls the covers over his head, and sleeps until completely surrounded by the enemy. It is then Mahele, not Kuali'i, who gets up and mows down the hosts until most of Lono-ikaika's chiefs are slain. Again at Kalaupapa on Molokai he lies inactive in the bottom of the boat until it is lifted on the shoulders of the enemy to bring it ashore, when he and his companion mow down all the bearers with the famous battle-axe. Thus he wins all Molokai. Later, finding that his leading warriors are competent to fight alone, he does not go out with them to battle. Instead he goes secretly and each time brings back a feather cloak from a warrior he has slain. Since he is a swift runner and a fearless leaper, no one can keep up with him to discover his identity. The legend continues:

At the battle of Kalakoa a boy from Kaoio point sees him passing Kualoa. The boy's grandmother sends the boy out with shrimps to feed him and a fan to do him honor. The boy is careful not to use the fan himself and not to step on the chief's shadow. After the battle of Kukaniloko, when Ku bears away the cloak, the boy takes a finger and an ear of the dead warrior to whom it belonged. Ku is pleased with his daring and rewards him with his own loincloth, through which Ku is recognized as the slayer.[13]

13. For. Col. 4: 426–431.

The well-known motive of the disguised champion is here easily to be recognized as by no means an integral part of the Kuali'i legend. It occurs in several other kupua tales in Hawaii in which the hero plays the part of an inactive conqueror. It is as if the hero in such tales acts not in his nature as a human being but as a god to insure victory to those who are fighting his cause. This is a thoroughly native conception, one with which the romantic and no doubt borrowed motive of the disguised champion, in spite of the pains taken to work up the local color, is quite alien.

The episode of the disguised champion occurs in some South Sea groups.

Maori. Hatupatu's father sends his sons to slay his enemy Raumati. The brothers sail without Hatupatu, who follows by diving under water. The brothers still resist his company and refuse to give him any fighting men. He dresses clumps of grass in feather cloaks taken from the enemy and himself wears so many different costumes that he is believed to represent a host. All his brother's divisions are broken. Hatupatu rallies them and slays Raumati. Each of the brothers brings a head to his father as Raumati's but only Hatupatu can produce the true head.[14]

Tonga. A woman bears to Sinilau twelve sons who are made chiefs over the different island groups, but her first child is born in the form of a fat lizard called piliopo. A girl comes to marry him but is afraid of his form and runs home. Her sister shows no fear and he takes her home to his mother. When the young men go to match clubs, day by day a handsome stranger comes off victor. She finally sees the red paint of his cheeks under the lizard's skin and recognizes her husband.[15]

San Cristoval (Bauro). Taraematawa while in seclusion with the other boys of Bauro is drowned, but two girls find his body and persuade the old kahuna to restore him sound and well. All the men have gone out fishing save one lame boy. Tarae makes a tremendous haul of fish, then hides himself and the lame boy

14. Grey, 120–124.   15. Gifford, *Bul.* 8: 194–196.

claims the credit until the men watch and discover the true hero.[16]

With the semimythical legend of Kuali'i concludes the legendary history of Hawaiian chiefs up to the eighteenth century, and begins the narratives of heroes whose lives are so bound up with fictional elements as to class them with imaginative rather than with legendary story-telling. Although often believed in as true, the facts they record bear all the marks of conscious exaggeration and embellishment useful to the entertainer rather than to the historian. They belong to the field of story-telling as literature—equally true to the social background which they represent and much more revealing of the imaginative range of Hawaiian thought (conditioned as it is by tradition and circumstance and colored by fancy) and of the philosophy of life which shapes the moral action of the tale, but avoided by the scholar whose interest is in the purely external facts of Polynesian migration.

The scholar will in fact already have discovered such a play of fancy elaborating so-called legendary history as to discount the value of the distinction and to challenge its purpose. Fiction may be used to illustrate the general trend of a period or to emphasize the position of figures who play a part in it. But fiction is also useful as a subject in itself, with the idea of observing how the entertainer works up a traditional story to please his particular audience, what favorite characters occur, what types they present, and what embellishment either of background, incident, or interpretation, enters into the invention. This, in comparison with a similar type of tale told in other related groups and under a different setting, gives an insight into the way in which life looks to the mind of the composer. That words as signs of thought are used rather than tangible material, that the pattern followed is a story pictured to his mind out of his own knowledge of life, rather than an object to be bettered for its particular purpose, makes the completed form no less useful as an example of the culture which it represents. Story-telling is not to be neglected as an element in social life because it cannot

16. Fox, 119–121.

be exhibited on the shelves of a museum. Nor is it to be discredited by the historian because it plays havoc with calendar events. The comparison of stories over a related area gives, historically, evidence of a parent form, and an accumulation of such evidence may eventually help in the solution of worldwide problems of distribution.

PART FOUR

Heroes and Lovers in Fiction

XXIX

KUPUA STORIES

HAWAIIAN legends tell of the adventures of heroes who have two natures, part human, part god. The god nature is likely to be derived from some animal ancestor whose spirit enters into the child at birth. Hence the heroic struggles which take place between demi-gods, often in animal, plant, or stone form, competitors with more than human power whose character as shape shifters brings natural forces into play in the conflict and gives a mythical effect to the action. Such supernatural beings are called kupua. They may appear as human beings or in some other material form inherited from their divine ancestry, or their kupua nature may be shown in the power they are able to exercise with a weapon or with the mere grip of the hand. Competitions between rival kupua make up a large number of the episodes belonging to kupua stories. Such heroes belong to a period of conflict between warring chiefs. They perform prodigious feats of physical valor. They are the strong men of their district or island. Ruling chiefs give up their lands and hide from them, but on the whole kupua are more concerned to fight for some weaker chief whose cause they have made their own than to win lands on their own account. They are roving champions, passing from island to island, ridding the country of those who have held it in terror. They are experts in the use of the spear, slingstone, battle-axe, war club, as well as in boxing, wrestling, and word play. They are great rat shooters like Pikoi-a-ka-alala, great fishermen like Nihooleki, superhuman warriors like Kapunohu and Kepakailiula, performers of titanic labors like Kalae-puni and Kalae-hina of Hawaii, winners in cock fights like the chicken-girl Lepe-a-moa.

Geographical allusions abound. There is much riddling upon place names. Chiefs bear the names of districts they govern, chiefesses of hills or of bodies of water. Elaboration to

explain the origin of some physical feature or the derivation
of a name is by no means unusual. Kupua heroes leave their
mark upon the land they pass through. Thus the titanic
movement of supernatural forces is made realizable to the
listener.

There is humor in the exaggeration, as in our own tall-tale
telling. Kupua stories are admittedly fiction, although often
credited as fact. An old Hawaiian chuckles as he tells how Pikoi could shoot a rat asleep on the far point that lies faint on
the distant horizon. The traces of Kalaehina's activities are
pointed out today in various localities, sometimes with pride
as deeds of kindness, sometimes with accusation of malice as
a mischief maker, more often with a half-credulous grin as
for a wonder worker.

Kupua stories tend to follow a regular pattern. The kupua is born in some nonhuman form, but detected and saved
by his grandparents, generally on the mother's side, who discern his divine nature. He is precocious, becomes speedily a
great eater, predatory and mischievous. He is won over to
the side of some chief by a present of his daughter or daughters as wives, and sent to do battle with his rival or with some
dangerous adversary who is terrorizing the country.

The period covered in these legends is roughly that between the mythical figures of Olopana of Oahu, Kukuipahu
of Kohala, Kakaalaneo of Maui, down to such semihistorical
ruling chiefs as Keawe-nui-a-Umi and his son Lono-i-ka-makahiki on Hawaii, Kamalalawalu on Maui, and Kakuhihewa
and Kuali'i on Oahu. The island of Kauai, Kohala on Hawaii, and Ewa on Oahu serve as a sort of breeding ground
for these heroic figures. The Kauai legend of Kawelo with its
many exaggerated features stands perhaps midway between
the semihistorical figures of more or less authentic history
and these fictitious heroes, product of the free play of the
imagination upon whatever material, traditional or borrowed, comes best to hand.

One of the most popular of the kupua warrior legends, to
judge by the number of recorded versions and the fulness of
elaboration of the story, is that of Kawelo of Kauai, called
Kawelo-a-Maihuna-li'i (-son of Maihuna the chief) or Ka-

welo-lei-makua (Kawelo who cherished his parents) because
he defended his parents against their persecutors on Kauai.
The earliest recorded version is perhaps that by Jules Remy
published in 1862. The latest is that dictated to Pukui of
Honolulu by an eighty-five-year-old Hawaiian of Kauai
named Kaululaau shortly before his death, as it had been
handed down to him orally, and translated by Miss Laura
Green of Honolulu. The similarity in the chants and in the
episodes themselves proves the existence of a single traditional form, the changes and embellishments of which betray
the hand of an independent composer.

LEGEND OF KAWELO

(*a*) *Green-Pukui version.* Mano-ka-lani-po, ruling chief of
Kauai, has by his wife Ka-wai-kini a tiny son of extraordinary
rank and beauty called Maihuna-liʻi-iki-o-ka-poko (The little
chief Maihuna) who is brought up as a foster child of the high
chief Holoholoku. When the boy reaches the age to marry, a
wife is sought for him over all Kauai, but since none is found of
sufficient beauty, the foster father, directed by a dream, launches
his wife's magic canoe transformed out of a hibiscus blossom
and is carried by favorable breezes invoked from the wind gourd
of his ancestor Nahiukaka to Oahu, where he obtains the hand
of Malei-a-ka-lani, a high chiefess descended from Paao, daughter of Ihiihi-lau-akea and his wife Manana and brought up by
her grandmother Olomana in the Koolau mountains, and is
borne back with the bride that same day, to find that his wife
has already, with the help of the little Mu and Menehune people,
prepared a sumptuous feast for the marriage celebration.

Three sons are born to the two at Wailua, each birth preceded by a pregnancy craving satisfied only by the little Menehune people, who bring ice from the mountains of Hawaii, awa
planted by the birds at Panaewa, honey from the mingled blossoms of lehua and pandanus to be found only on Hawaii. Kawelo is the eldest born, Kamalama the second, Ka-lau-maki the
third. The boys are brought up under tapu and not allowed to
play with other boys. One day they run away and join the other
children in a spear-throwing contest. Kawelo wins, and eventually he becomes the champion spear thrower for Kauai. He

builds a shelter for himself of pili grass named Kahiki-haunaka. His god is Kane-i-ka-pualena (Kane in the yellow flower).

Kawelo longs to travel and persuades his brothers to accompany him to Oahu. Here he joins the expert fisherman Makuakeke in the sport of fishing for the giant uhu fish named Uhumakaikai. At night on his return his brothers meet him, each with a company of forty men, and hurl spears at him all of which he is able to dodge.

An expert in the arts of warfare named Kalonaikahailaau gives him his daughter Kane-wahine-iki-aohe (Little man-woman) as wife and teaches him all he knows, reserving only the art of stone throwing. When the call comes for him to return to Kauai and avenge his parents, driven from their land by Aikanaka, he sets sail with twenty-four young warriors, together with his warrior wife, his two brothers, and an adopted son named Kaelehaupuna. As the war party leaves the shore, his father-in-law appears and gives to the wife a snaring stick (pikoi) with which to defend her husband in battle. [This is in the shape of a block of wood like a rough dumbbell, to the center of which a long cord is attached, and is used to trip up or entangle an opponent in battle.]

The party sails for Kauai, lands at Wailua where Aikanaka and his men are, and, after declaring war, Kawelo mows down each antagonist with his famous war club, Kuika'a. Once they jeer at him, calling him "son of a cock (moa)" and "counter of cockroaches" because his grandfather has the name of Nahanai-moa, and Kawelo is about to retire in shame when his wife prompts him to retort to the taunt, "The cock roosts above the chief; the cock is chief." Kahakaloa fells him, but he recovers and in turn kills the other with a blow. When his old comrade, the giant Kaua-hoa advances, he tries to win the warrior over with a chant, fearing his mighty club, but the warrior wife catches the club with her snaring stick and it falls harmless. In the division of land that follows, the wife gets Hanalei for her courage.

Kamalama gets homesick and returns to Oahu, taking the family god with him, without which Kawelo is unable to foresee disaster. The adopted son who lives at Maulili takes a wife, to whom he betrays Kawelo's weak point in warfare. His enemies lure him to the plain. Three times they bury him in stones and three times he shakes himself free. The fourth time he seems to be dead and they leave him on a scaffold under guard until morning. He revives, does battle, and slays everybody. His brother, warned by their god, returns in time to insist that the traitor be also executed. Kawelo makes his permanent home at Wailua and dies of a good old age, but no one knows where he is buried.[1]

(b) *Fornander* (1) *and Rice version.* Maihuna and Malai-a-ka-lani have five children in Hanamaulu on Kauai: Kawelo-ma-hamahaia, Kawelo-lei-ko'o, Kawelo-lei-makua (the subject of the story), and Kawelo-kamalama, all sons, and Kaena-ku-a-ka-lani, a daughter. The maternal grandparents bring up Kawelo at Wailua with Ai-kanaka (Man-eater), son of the ruling chief, and Kaua-hoa (Battle comrade), all relatives born on the same day. Kawelo eats enormously and angers his fellows by outdoing Kauahoa in managing toy boats and kite flying. The place where he worsted Kauahoa in the latter sport is called to this day Ka-ho'oleina-a-pe'a (The kite caused to fall).

When the family move to Oahu, he angers his brothers by outdoing them in wrestling and they leave him and return to Kauai. Kawelo remains, becomes proficient in fishing, and fishes up the Uhumakaikai by means of a chant. When summoned to Kauai to avenge his family he sends his wife Kane-wahine-iki-aohe to obtain from her father the stroke called Wahieloa to prepare him for fighting. He bathes in the stream Apuakehau and gets a good meal of food. He sends Kamalama to spy upon the conversation of his wife's relatives and they believe him to be a god. At Waianae he builds a temple to his god Kane-i-ka-pualena and to the god Ka-lani-hehu which the messengers have brought him from Kauai. The chief of Oahu furnishes him with a canoe. An adopted son, Ka-ulu-iki, gets frightened at the start and returns to Oahu. The story of the subjugation of Ai-kanaka and his subsequent attack with stones does not vary essentially from Green's version. Aikanaka goes to live in the uplands of Hanapepe and it is this chief's daughter whom Ka-ele-ha makes his wife and to whom he reveals Kawelo's weak

1. Green and Pukui, 3–111.

point. Kawelo retires eventually to his parents' old home at Hanamaulu.

(c) *Fornander version* (2). Kawelo is born at Pupulima, Waimea. He-ulu is his father, Haimu his mother. He is a timid child and Kauahoa, his older brother, is adopted by Haulili of Hanalei lest he kill the younger child. Sea bathing is his favorite sport. He longs for the wives of his half-brother Aikanaka and his father says that a man to have wives must be an expert in fishing and farming. These accomplishments fail to attract, but when he becomes proficient in dancing they "fall upon him and kiss him." Aikanaka resents the loss of his wives and seeks Kawelo's life. Kawelo retires to Oahu with his brother Kamalama and becomes expert in spear practice. At the hill Pu'uloa he meets the beautiful Kou. With Makuakeke he goes fishing. With his wife Kane-wahine-iki-aohe, the girl skilled in surfing, he retires to Wahiawa after learning from her father all the arts of warfare except that of stoning. His parents on Kauai are meanwhile reduced to living on "fleas and popolo berries." He is out fishing when messengers arrive to summon him to Kauai and he first secures his catch, then with six strokes is at the landing. With ten warriors, his wife, and his brother he lands at Wailua. Haweo, Walaheeikio, Maumau-iki-o, and Kauahoa he meets and overcomes in single encounters. At the close of the war Aikanaka takes Kawelo's wife and it is she who betrays his weak point in warfare. The battle with stones follows other versions, but the story is left incomplete at the point where he takes position to meet his enemies after recovering from the last stoning.[2]

(d) *Westervelt version*. Kawelo has a kupua rat brother named Kawelo-mai-huna who helps him build a canoe in which he escapes to Oahu and who there thatches with bird feathers the house which the chief has set him as a task to build with his own hands.[3] Kawelo-aikanaka succeeds his grandfather Kawelo-mahamaha-ia, great uncle of Kawelo, as ruling chief over Kauai. When Kawelo, warned by the rat people, flees to Oahu,

2. For. Col. 5: 2–71, 694–721; Rice, 54–67.
3. Compare the story of Matandua, Fison, 75.

his own parents are already living there. He adopts a strong man named Ka-lau-meke who claims power through the rat family, and another named Ka-ele-ha. The rest of the story describes the catching of the uhu, the marriage with the warrior maid, the call to Kauai and defeat of Aikanaka's forces, and the battle with stones, without unusual features.[4]

(e) *Dickey version.* Kawelo-lei-makua is born in Wailua on the same day as Kawelo-aikanaka and Kauahoa Kame'eu'i. He goes away to Oahu with the help of his kupua brother Kawelo-mai-huna. Aikanaka becomes ruling chief of Kauai and oppresses Kamalama-iki-poki'i, younger brother of Kawelo. Kawelo comes to the rescue, lands at Wailua, and declares for war. At Wailua he slays all sent against him, including Kahakaloa. That night the brothers get some sleep by setting up images to resemble watchmen. The next day comes Kauahoa and gives Kawelo a stunning blow, but Kawelo revives and, with the aid of his wife's snaring stick, slays Kauahoa. Aikanaka wins the affections of Kawelo's wife. The stone battle is fought at Kalaheo and Kawelo left for dead, but his spirit warns his parents in Honolulu and they come and revive him and teach him the art of stone fighting (nounou) so that in the second battle (fought on the mountain called Nounou) he is victorious over Aikanaka. That chief he tears in two but saves his own treacherous wife. In his old age his people rebel and throw him over a cliff.[5]

(f) *Remy-Brigham version.* Kawelo is a giant of prodigious strength. To please the chiefess Kaakauhuhimalani he becomes a proficient agriculturist and fisherman, but she is untouched until he becomes expert in the hula dance. She then takes him for a husband and this gives him rank as a chief. Three older brothers named Kawelo-maka-inoino, Kawelo-maka-huhu, Kawelo-maka-oluolu (Kawelo with bad eyes, -angry eyes, -kind eyes) pour poi over his head and almost smother him, hence he chants a farewell to his wife and departs for Oahu.

4. *Honolulu,* 173–188; Thrum, *More Tales,* 149–163; *HAA* 1911, 119–128.

5. *HHS Reports* 25: 21–24.

He is welcomed by Kakuhihewa and secretly collects an expedition against Kauai. He sets out for that island and encounters evil monsters in the shape of the marine monster Apukohai, against whom he invokes the owl god, and the fish Uhu-makaikai, which he traps in a net [whose weaving pattern is described in detail] and which he kills after a fierce struggle. On Kauai his old friends and relations Kahakaloa and Aikanaka have joined the enemy. His friends Ka-lau-maki and Kaamalama follow him from Oahu. Ka-hele-ha deserts him for Aikanaka. Showers of stones are rained upon him. He prays to the gods and is saved. In the chant he accuses his enemies of putting to death his father Maihuna and his mother Malei by casting them over a cliff. He divides the land by giving Puna to Ka-hele-ha (who had deserted him), Kona to Ka-lau-maki, Koolau to Makua-keke, Kohala to Kaamalama, and Hanalei to his wife who has saved him with her snaring stick. He rules Kauai until he is old and feeble, when his people throw him over a cliff.[6]

(g) *Oahu temple story.* Kawelo is slain at the battle of Wahiawa and his body placed on the lele (altar) of the heiau of Kukui to decompose. It is struck by lightning and he comes to life again.[7]

(h) *Historical version.* Kawelo's grandfather was Kawelo-mahamahaia, an important ruling chief of Kauai whose heiau of the severest ritual class, Homaikawa, was dedicated to the shark god[8] and who was himself worshiped as a shark at death.[9] By his wife Kapohina-o-ka-lani he had five children, Kawelo-makua-lua, Kawelo-iki-a-koo, Koo-a-ka-poko, and two daughters, one of whom became the wife of her brother Kawelo-makua-lua, who succeeded his father as ruling chief of Kauai, and mother of Kawelo-aikanaka; the other, Malai-a-ka-lani, became the wife of Maihuna and mother of Kawelo-lei-makua, hero of this legend.[10]

Kawelo-makua-lua and his sister-wife are said to have first set up the practice of the prostrating tapu (kapu moe), called

6. 38–51.
8. *Ibid.,* 41.
10. For. Pol. Race 2: 292–295.

7. *HAA* 1907, 68.
9. Westervelt, *Honolulu,* 173.

burning-hot tapu of chiefs (kapu wela o na li‘i) because of the
death penalty imposed upon those who failed to observe the
tapu. It was carried to Oahu during the rule of Kauakahi-a-
Kaho‘owaha, father of Kuali‘i, whose wife has a Kawelo name,
and to Maui in the time of Kekaulike.[11]

The legend of Kawelo is recited at great length and is embellished with chants and episodes of a romantic character or
such as are typical of kupua stories. Accounts of his birth
contain references to the Menehune and Mu people and associate him with rat-men born of the gods, and it seems likely
that the kupua qualities ascribed in the Dickey and Westervelt versions to a rat "brother" were originally those which
belonged to Kawelo himself, or at least to his father. The
mysterious birth as a rat or other misformation in the midst
of a storm—hence the preservation of this embryonic form in
a gourd wrapped in a feather cloak until, when it is taken
down, feathers fly about, rain falls, and other wonders occur
and a being emerges who can take the forms of man, rat, fish,
or elepaio bird—certainly corresponds with the magical births
recorded of kupua heroes who belong in the same class as Kawelo.[12] Similar feats are told locally of Kawelo. He is said to
have wrested the "tongue of Hawaii" from that island and to
have brought it to Maulili pool on Waikomo stream in Koloa
district, where it projects from the cliff of Koloa on the eastern wall of the pool.[13] The account of the arrangements for
Maihuna's marriage closely resembles that given of Pi‘ilani's
to the Oahu high chiefess Laielohelohe. The legend must
therefore be taken rather as an example of fiction in the form
of a typical kupua hero tale than be judged for its historical
accuracy.

The story has some likeness to the San Cristoval legend of
Rapuanate the giant, who lived on Marau-raro.[14] All the
figures are conceived in the titanic mold characteristic of
kupua stories. The warrior of Hanalei, Kawelo's childhood
companion, is described as a giant 120 feet tall, as strong as

11. *Ibid.* 277–278.
12. Westervelt, *Honolulu,* 174–175; Dickey, 21.
13. *HAA* 1907, 92–93.   14. Fox, 162–169.

320 men, and carrying a club in the shape of an unrooted
koa tree from Kahihikolo "in whose branches birds perch
and sing." Before such an opponent even Kawelo's stout
heart quails and only the prompt action of his wife with the
snaring stick averts the club stroke and gives the hero a
chance to cleave the giant in two with a stroke of his own famous war club. We are here in a more sophisticated stage of
culture than is common in these kupua stories, where the hero's strength often lies in his hands and victims are rent apart
with an exhibition of physical violence. The motive is however curiously un-Hawaiian, since the war club does not seem
to have been developed in the group as it was in the islands to
the south. Kawelo's skill in dodging the spear is more nearly
in line with Hawaiian custom. Such a ritual spear-throwing
occurs at the Makahiki festival as the chief who represents
the god lands from the canoe sent out to break the tapu. This
has sometimes been interpreted as a mythical motive connected with sun worship, but nothing could possibly be more
unnecessary than such an interpretation of a natural gesture
by the ruling chief to proclaim his skill at arms during a festival especially given over to a display of athletic achievement.

Another characteristic motive common to such kupua hero
tales and which occurs episodically in this story is that of the
inactive hero. Kawelo sleeps until destruction becomes imminent. As the canoe approaches the land he warns,

> When Aikanaka's men approach, say no word,
> Only when they come very close awaken me,

and the enemy is allowed to lift the canoe and bear it up to
dry land before there comes the warning chant:

> We have passed the holes of the burrowing crab,
> We have passed the holes of the sand crab,
> Here we are at the rat's hole!

and he rouses himself to action and easily mows down twice
forty men with his terrible war club. During the first fight
Kawelo remains chanting beside his canoes while the rest of
the party engage the enemy on the plains. During the assault

with stones, he allows himself to be buried in stones before freeing himself of their weight. This motive of the inactivity of the hero, generally followed by some prodigious exhibition of strength, is sometimes rationalized by representing the kupua as smuggled on land wrapped up like a bundle. On the other hand it is replaced in the stories of Kapunohu, Palila, and Kalelealuaka by the probably borrowed tale type of the disguised warrior.

With due allowance for historical inaccuracies and for literary exaggeration, the story of Kawelo presents a true picture of Hawaiian culture. The foster father bears the same name as the land of Holoholoku which was made sacred to the birth of high chiefs of Kauai. Kawelo's wife, Little-man-woman, is true to the Hawaiian type of warrior maid who used to accompany her husband to war to hearten and assist him in actual warfare, as attested by old informants, in the days before the discovery by Cook. The practice of word play to destroy the morale of an opposing champion or to soften his wrath is also true to old custom. Battles may be ended by means of a laudatory chant, as in the Kuali'i legend. The incident in which Kawelo loses courage because of a taunt at his ancestry is characteristic of the actual fighting power believed to inspire such exchanges of insult.[15] Riddling allusions, often dependent upon punning with place names, win applause. There are homely folk incidents such as that of the paddlers who forget their message at the sight of a pretty woman and the consequent danger to the canoe [compare for the forgotten message the messenger sent from Tonga to determine whether men or women ought to be tattooed, who, in the perils of the passage, inverts the sexes, as in Brewster],[16] or of the champion who, believing he has done his enemy in "by a single blow," indulges in a hearty meal and struts about with the inverted food bowl over his head as a helmet. Though perhaps borrowed from one tale to another, such incidents add to the realistic effect of the action.

Two other kupua hero tales, those of Palila and of Kale-

15. Henry, 304–305; Brewster, 59.
16. 83.

lealuaka, follow the special type represented in the Rice version of Kamapua'a's adventures, the second part of which also appears as an episode in the Kuali'i legend, the first in that of Kapunohu. The type is that of a struggle between two chiefs for supremacy decided for the weaker chief by securing the aid of a son-in-law with kupua powers, followed by (or including) the episode of a disguised warrior who wins on successive days of battle and is finally identified as the seemingly inactive son-in-law.

LEGEND OF PALILA

Palila is a great warrior of Kauai, son of Ka-lua-o-Palena (The pit of Palena), chief over one half of Kauai, and of Mahi-nui, daughter of Hina. Ku is his god. He is born at Ka-mo'oloa in the northern part of Kauai in the shape of a cord and is rescued by his grandmother Hina from the rubbish heap and brought up among the spirits at the heiau of Alanapo in Humu-ula. He has two natures, one of a man and one of a spirit. His father is in conflict with the chief Na-maka-o-ka-lani (The eyes of the heavenly one) over the other half of Kauai, and just as he is at the point of defeat Palila comes to the rescue with the club Huli-a-mahi with which he fells whole forests of trees at a stroke. The hole called Wai-hohonu is formed where he sinks this club before his father. All are terrified and Hina has to roll over their prostrate bodies to make him laugh and end the tapu. She stands on the rise of land called Alea (Mauna-kilika) holding his robe called Haka-ula and his loincloth Ikuwa, and after circumcising him she returns with him to Alanapo.

The rule over Kauai being secured to Palila's father, the hero leaves home in search of adventure. Standing on the knoll called Komo-i-ke-anu he throws his club and, clinging to one end, arrives at the cliff Nualolo at Ka-maile, thence flies on to Kaena point on Oahu, and from there to Wai-kele where Ahu-a-Pau, chief of Oahu, is presiding over games. The shark-man Kamai-kaahui is terrorizing the country. By slaying this man he wins the chief's daughters Ke-alamikioi and Ka-lehua-wai but must first be "made human" at the heiau of Kane at Kahehuna before he can wed. Ahu yields his litter to the victor, and for the first time sets foot upon the ground.

Ahu fears his son-in-law and sends him on the circuit of the island without warning him of the formidable warrior Olomana, thirty-six feet in height, to whom the land from Makapu'u point to Kaoio point is sacred. Palila lights on his shoulder and cuts him through, casting off that portion called Mahi-nui toward the sea and leaving the peak called Olomana.

The whole of Oahu being now won for his father-in-law, Palila first goes fishing with Kahului at Mauna-lua, using his club with equal success as paddle and fishhook; but, finding his companion stingy, he goes across from Hanauma to Kaluakoi on Molokai, where he leaves "a part of his body" as the point Kalae-o-ka-laau; then, taking a dislike to Molokai on account of the name Ho'one'enu'u attached to a "tree" there, he flies across to Lanai, thence to Honua-ula on Maui, thence to Kaula between Hamakua and Hilo districts on Hawaii. There he finds Hina's sister Lupea living above Kaawali'i in the form of a hau tree. Since she is a kahu of Palila no hau tree will grow to this day where Palila's loincloth has been spread out to dry.

Kulukulua of Hilo district and Wanua of Hamakua are at war. Palila takes up the cause of the Hilo chief. No one knows who the invisible warrior is who cries each time a man falls, "Slain by me, Palila, by the offspring of Walewale, by the foster child of Lupea, by the o-o bird that sings in the forest, by the mighty god Ku!" until in the last fight he makes himself known. He slays the three great warriors of Hamakua each with a single stroke and hangs their jaws on a tree called Ka-haka-auwae (The shelf of jawbones) and becomes himself ruling chief of Hilo.[17]

LEGEND OF KALELEALUAKA

The father of Ka-lele-a-luaka is Opele-the-sleeper (Ka-opele-moemoe) whose nature is such that he passes into a trance every six months and lies for six months as if dead, after which there comes a storm with thunder and lightning and he awakens. During this trance his spirit "floats away into the upper air with Poliahu" and compasses the whole group in a day. Opele is born in Waipio valley on Hawaii in such a trance and his

17. For. Col. 5: 136–153, 372–375.

body is laid away in a cave. He awakens and calls to his parents
in a chant and when they come to the spot they find him sitting
in a tree braiding scarlet lehua flowers into a wreath. Cultivating the land is a passion with him and he plants crops at Kula
on Maui, at Kapapakolea in Moanalua on Oahu, in Lihue on
Oahu, but each time his trance seizes him just as he is about to
enjoy his crop, and others consume it. In one such sleep his body
is floated downstream and is found on the beach of Maeaea in
Waialua by some men from Kauai looking for a human sacrifice
for their temple of Lolomauna at Pokii (or of Kukui at Kaiki-
haunaka). For six months he lies on the altar without his flesh
decomposing, then there comes thunder and an earthquake and
he awakens. The old man at whose house he receives hospitality
thinks he will make a fine husband for his daughter Maka-lani
(or Kalikookalauae). He wastes no time in love making but goes
to work at once cultivating a huge tract of land and bringing in
a great catch of fish. When his wife is about to have a child he
warns her of his habit of trance, but her family (or the wife herself) cannot believe that he is not dead and they bind stones to
his feet and throw him into the sea, where within six months he
awakens during a thunderstorm and returns to his wife (or goes
back to his old plantation on Oahu).

The son Ka-lele-a-lua-ka grows up mischievous (in ignorance
of his true father, who has left him a spear as recognition token
and gone away to Oahu). Opele has given his own power to the
child and has no more trances. The boy can "jump up and down
precipices and run on water like a duck." He is challenged by
the ruling chief of Wailua who has heard his boasts, then by the
chief of Hanalei, and kills both as a sacrifice for the heiau he
and his father have built. With a lad named Kaluhe as companion he paddles across to Waianae on Oahu and, picking up
another lad nicknamed Keino-ho'omanawa-nui because he is too
lazy to clean his food before eating, he goes to cultivating at
Kahuoi in Ewa at his father's old plantation (or finds his father
at work and gives him the recognition token).

The boys live at a mountain house, Lele-pau, and amuse
themselves at night by making extravagant wishes, the sloven
for all kinds of fat food, Kalele for a house erected for him by

the ruling chief and the chief's daughters for wives. Kakuhihewa sees the boys' light burning night after night and, suspecting treason, comes (or sends a spy) to listen at the door. A spear is left at the door as a token that they are under the tapu of the chief, but since the kahuna Na-pua-i-kamau advises the chief that this is a man daring enough to win for him in the struggle then going on between Kakuhihewa and Kuali'i (or Pueo-nui), the chief fulfils the wishes of each and the two boys are housed splendidly at the court and have the chief's daughters as wives.

It was the lame marshal Maliu-ha'aino who was sent to execute the command. He proceeded so slowly with the other two boys that Kalele had time to be transported to Kuaikua to be bathed and circumcised in the midst of a thunderstorm and return to the party without being missed, when he picked them all up (but without their being aware of the miracle) and set them down at the chief's place. In like manner, when all the warriors go forth to fight the rival chief of Oahu's forces and the lame marshal starts out alone because of his slow progress, Kalele pretends to sleep, then sets for his wives some such fruitless task as filling a water bottle with the snout turned downward or cleaning and baking a fowl without cutting it open, and, disguising himself each day with plant wreaths of different localities, he overtakes the lame man and carries him to Punchbowl hill to overlook the battle, while he himself performs prodigies with his hands alone, driving back the enemy, killing the chief who is leading them, and carrying home and hiding the booty. On the last day of battle he forces Kuali'i (or Pueo-nui) to yield the rule over the land, but receives first a thrust from his spear by which he is later identified as the true victor. (In Fornander, it is a farmer at Halawa who sees him each time returning with the booty and on the last day gives him a spear thrust in order to identify him.) In the last battle he kills the sloven because he has each time claimed the conquest for himself, then brings out the feather cloaks and other booty taken from the bodies of the slain chiefs and he and his wives become chiefs over the land.[18]

18. For. Col. 4: 464–471; 5: 168–171; Thrum (from N. Emerson), *Tales*, 74–106; Dickey, *HHS Reports* 25: 19–20; and see BPBM MS. col.

In both these stories occur marvelous weapons and marvelous exhibitions of physical power. Palila fells whole forests with his club and is carried over land or sea clinging to its end. Ka-lele-a-luaka's strength lies in his hands. He is a swift runner and daring leaper. Opposing warriors, as in the Kawelo story, carry prodigious weapons. One spear can kill two hundred men at a stroke and is long enough to use as a windbreak or to dam a stream. Names of some of the warriors occur in other legends. Olomana is one of the mountain peaks back of Kailua said to have been named from a band of strangers (haole) who early reached these shores. Two of the warriors whom Palila meets in Hamakua on Hawaii are among the company of fish kupua who accompany Keanini from Kuaihelani when he comes to marry Hainakolo; one of them is said to have been slain by Lima-loa, the other to have become a sea deity and to have aided other sea gods in opposing Lohiau's passage from Kauai with Hiʻiaka to join Pele.[19]

Another tendency in Hawaiian legend, in which genealogical interest is strong, finds illustration in the Kalelealuaka story, where the action passes from the great deeds of the father to those of the kupua son. So in the Moikeha-Kila legend, the Pakaʻa-Kuapakaʻa, the Luahoʻomoe-Kuula, and the Aikanaka to Laka series. Attention is paid in the Palila legend to the circumcision ceremony by which the wild energies of the kupua seem to be made human and tractable, and to the tattooing of a warrior. The spot where Palila was tattooed for the fight on Oahu is pointed out on the edge of Kamahualele on Kauai at a place called Ka-eli-alina-a-ka-mahu (The digging and scarring by the hermaphrodite).[20]

Directly associated with the Kamapuaʻa legend are two kupua hero tales, one of which, that of Kapunohu, carries the same pattern as the two legends just discussed, although the theme of the disguised warrior is not developed; the other, that of Nihooleki, suggests the legend of Ka-lele-aluaka's father, Opele-the-sleeper, in that it is the tale of a great fish-

19. For. Col. 6: 345; Westervelt, *Gods and Ghosts,* 190–191; Thrum, *More Tales,* 224–225; N. Emerson, *Pele,* 160.

20. Dickey, *HHS Reports* 25: 29.

erman who becomes a reëmbodied spirit and friend of Kama-pua'a. Kapunohu enters the Kamapua'a story as a brother of two sisters, one of whom, named Koahua-nui, is repre-sented as the wife of Olopana, the other as the wife of Kukui-pahu, ruling chief over the larger section of Kohala district.

LEGEND OF KAPUNOHU

Kapunohu is born in Kukui-pahu's district. He gains the lead-ing ghost spirit of Hawaii, Kani-ka'a,[21] for his god. The spirit is one day glancing his spear Kani-ka-wi along the course when Kapunohu picks it up and runs with it until Kani-ka'a is obliged to call a truce. With the spear thrower as his god, he finds that he can hurl his spear through eight hundred wiliwili trees in line at one time. With Kani-ka-wi as weapon and the ghost god as his ally, Kapunohu avenges an insult from his brother-in-law by winning from him the whole district for his rival Niuli'i and marrying Niuli'i's daughters. At Kapaau in Ainakea, Kukui-pahu is killed and 3,200 men with him and their feather cloaks are taken. At the place ever afterwards famous as Lamakee he kills with his spear the warrior Paopele, who wields a club named Keolewa so great that it extends over a whole district in length, reaches up to the clouds of heaven, and takes four thou-sand men to carry. On Oahu he allies himself with his brother-in-law Olopana against Kakuihewa and slays that chief. Hun-gry after his exploit, he is bidden by his sister to help himself to what food he likes and he pulls up eight patches of taro. He goes on to Kauai, lands at Poki and at Waimea, and settles at Koloa. His greatest feat is winning a throwing contest, sling-stone against the spear Kani-ka-wi, in which he has staked his life against Kemamo, the strong man of Kauai. Kemamo makes a good cast, but Kapunohu's spear clears the coconuts at Niu-malu, enters the water at Wailua (hence the name Kawelowai) and, dashing up its spray (hence Waiehu), pierces the cliff at Kalalea and goes on to Hanalei.[22]

21. For. Col. 5: 428.

22. *Ibid.* 214–225; Dickey, *HHS Reports* 25: 34–35.

LEGEND OF NIHOOLEKI

The great fisherman Nihooleki is born at Keauhou in Kona, Hawaii, and comes to Oahu and lives at Kuukuua on Pu'u-o-kapolei in Waianae under the name of Keaha-iki-aholeha. He becomes ruling chief of Waianae and a mighty fisherman because of his famous pearl fishhook named Pahuhu, which attracts aku fish, and a double canoe ten fathoms in length manned by twenty paddlers in which he always goes out fishing. He travels to Waimea on Kauai, the birthplace of his wife who is high chiefess of that island, and becomes ruling chief. When he dies his body is brought back to Waianae and placed in a small house of poles in the shape of a pyramid, where his parents worship the spirit until it is strong enough to become a live person again. He goes back to his wife on Kauai under the name of Nihooleki and she does not guess that this is her husband's spirit. Reproached for doing nothing but sleep, he sends his wife to his brothers-in-law to secure first his pearl fishhook, which the spirit of his sister in the form of a black noio bird is guarding where it hangs from the ridgepole, and then his double canoe which has been pushed aside in the canoe shed, and, finally, paddlers to man it. The haul of fish he secures is enough for the whole island, and he gets as a third name at this time that of Puipui-a-ka-lawaia (Plumpness of the fisherman). He fishes first off Waianae, then comes to Keauhou, where he sends paddlers ashore each with a fish for his sisters. On his return to Kauai he carries two fish ashore to offer one to the male and the other to the female aumakua.

His friend Kamapua'a is afflicted with dropsy and in spite of her husband's instructions Nihooleki's wife, when Kamapua'a is brought in a litter to her door on a visit, turns him rudely away. Nihooleki therefore abandons his wife but gives her, as tokens for their child, a club and a feather cloak, and, as a name, that by which she had known him as her first husband. In this way the chiefess learns that her second husband is the reincarnated spirit of her first husband. Kamapua'a and Nihooleki go off together, diving under the sea to reach Waianae, where Nihooleki gives his friend recognition tokens by which his parents may know him and bids him marry his sister at Keauhou while he himself enters his tomb at Waianae and disappears.[23]

Other tall tales in which exaggerated feats of strength are the theme may be even more episodic in character and derive their subject matter from curious natural features of the district within which the kupua's power extends, or from contests with strong men of tradition. Among these are the stories of Kalae-puni and his younger brother Kalae-hina (Kalaikini, Kaleikini, Au-kini), sons of Ka-lani-po and Ka-mele-kapu, who are born and brought up in the Kona district of Hawaii, at Holua-loa.

LEGEND OF KALAEPUNI

Kalae-puni is mischievous and without fear. At the age of six he can outdo all his playmates; at twenty he is fully developed. He kills sharks with his hands at Kalahiki and pulls up a kou tree at Honaunau as if it were a blade of grass. The ruling chief Keawe-nui-a-Umi hides himself and Kalae-puni becomes ruling chief. At Keawe's request the kahuna Mokupane plots his death and has a pit dug at Ke-ana-pou on Kahoolawe and sets two old people to watch for a very old man with hair like bunches of olona fiber. When such a one floats ashore and asks for water the old people send him to the pit and then throw stones down upon him. The husband runs away but the wife finally hits him with a stone on the head and kills him.[24]

LEGEND OF KALAEHINA (KALAIKINI, KALEIKINI)

(a) Kalae-hina is so strong that he can throw a canoe into the sea as easily as if it were a spear, tear up trees by the roots, and split wood with his head. When the six canoes which his brother is building at Kupua in South Kona get stuck at the place called Na-wa'a-ho'okui in bringing them down to the sea, he hits on a plan to deliver five of them by sea from a different landing while he himself brings the sixth along on his back by the upper road. His brother therefore sends him to kill the chiefs of

23. For. Col. 4: 488–497.   24. *Ibid.* 5: 198–205.

Maui and seize the rule from Kamalalawalu. At Kauiki in Hana the chief is found holding competitive sports and Kalae-hina enters the games. When the chief sees how strong the new champion is he runs away and hides at Wai-anapanapa.

Kalae-hina becomes ruling chief over Maui and gets such a great name for strength that the men who work for him are silent from fear. Kapakohana, who has superseded Ola on Kauai because of his strength, comes to test himself with Kalae-hina. They wrestle and Kapakohana manages to push his antagonist over the cliff Kai-halulu and drown him in the sea, after which feat he cuts out his jawbone and exhibits it to the people.[25]

(b) The kupua Kalai-kini comes from Kauai of Mano-ka-lani-po in the form of a man to contend with the kupua of Hawaii. In Puna he strives to overthrow Pohaku-o-lekia in the form of a standing rock on the hill above Kapoho but is unable because Lekia is encouraged by his wife Pohaku-o-Hanalei, who stands in the form of a round-shaped rock beside the other. At Kapahua on the coast beyond Kalapana he stops up with kauila wood the spouting horn called "the blowhole of Kalaikini" in order to prevent the salt spray from spoiling the potato crop or, some say, for mischievous reasons.[26]

(c) In Waipio, Kaleikini tries to uproot a kupua stone called Nuhinuhi-a-Ua and attacks a kawau tree which is a great kupua called Ke-kumu-kewau which, if uprooted, would have caused a flood. He is called a native of Polulu in Kohala and can change himself into many forms. Once he wanted his sister to name a child after him but said nothing of his wish. Every child born to her he would throw into a certain pond, where it became a fish, until a kahuna advised the family of his wish. The fish are to be seen there to this day and are called uiui because of the squeaking noise they make.[27]

(d) In Hana, Kaleikini is described as a wanton mischief maker. He comes from Hawaii to Hana on Maui and tries to

25. For. Col. 5: 198–211.
26. Green (from Kalawe), 11–15; Remy-Brigham, 34–35.
27. Given by Mary Pukui from Kawahinehula of Waipio.

stop up the spouting horn near Kauiki called Puhi-o-Mokuhano, and he smashes the stone of Kane beside that of Kanaloa (Niu-o-Kane a me Kanaloa) because of its fame.[28]

Many Kupua stories center about the court of Kukui-pahu in Kohala district on Hawaii, and that chief is a favorite figure in kupua extravaganzas. In the story of Kaipalaoa the riddler, Kukui-pahu's wife is Kalena-i-hele-auau and it is she who instructs her nephew in riddling. In that of the riddler Kapunohu, the kupua's sister becomes Kukui-pahu's wife. In the story of Kepakailiula, Kukui-pahu marries his daughter to the red-skinned kupua. Actors in the story have traditional place names. Kukui-pahu names a land section in Kohala. Kaunalewa names the district on Kauai where Uweu-welekehau and Lu'ukia plant a coconut grove and where stands the heiau Lolomauna.[29] Keauhou and Kahalu'u are places on the Kona coast of Hawaii. Makolea is the name of a heiau at Kahalu'u presided over by Lono's god Ka-ili, where Lono-i-ka-makahiki is said to have celebrated some of his victories.[30] The story is patched up out of episodes drawn from both native and foreign sources and has, like others of these late compositions, no traditional value save as an example of how kupua elements were manipulated for stock entertainment.

LEGEND OF KEPAKAILIULA

Kepaka-ili-ula (Born with red skin) is born in Keaau, Puna, on Hawaii, child of Ku and Hina. He is born in the form of an egg and his mother's brothers Ki'i-noho and Ki'i-hele (Ki'i staying and Ki'i going) wrap him in a feather cape for ten days and ten nights and there emerges a beautiful child; at the end of forty days, during which he has lain wrapped in a red feather cloak, his skin and eyes have become red. His foster parents rear him in Paliuli, where the prodigious appetite he develops is easily pacified, since here all things grow in abundance without labor. As he approaches maturity his foster parents travel

28. Given by Kilinahi Kaleo of Hana; Thrum, *More Tales,* 68–69.
29. For. Col. 5: 198.　　　　30. *Ibid.* 4: 324, 330.

about the island seeking a wife for their ward and after reject-
ing the beauties of Hilo, Puna, and Ka-u they pronounce Makolea, daughter of the Kona chief Keauhou and his wife Kahalu'u, faultless. When Kepakailiula leaves Pali-uli to court his
wife, the place is shut up and no one has seen it since.

Since Makolea of Kona is promised to Kakaalaneo of Maui,
the lovers are obliged to meet secretly and are presently detected by the parents and the girl is sent away to Maui. Kepakailiula goes away to Kohala and takes to wife Ka-pua-o-ka-
onaona, the pretty daughter of Kukui-pahu, ruling chief of
Kohala. On two successive nights he paddles over to Maui, makes
Kakaalaneo drunk with awa and enjoys his bride, finally leaving him head down in a dung heap. Pretending a friendly visit
to Maui, he comes with a great following of canoes to meet Kakaalaneo and in a spear-throwing contest cuts the chief in two
with his war club named Olelo-kahi-e and keeps on slaughtering
the people until Kukui-pahu thrusts his young wife before him
to stay his wrath. The rule over both Kohala and Maui he gives
to Kukui-pahu and goes on to Oahu, where Kakuhihewa is so
afraid of him that he makes him his foster son and turns over
to him the rule of Oahu.

Makolea, while out surfing, is stolen away by Keaumiki and
Keauka, messengers of Kaiki-pa'a-nanea, famous ruling chief of
Kauai. Kepakailiula follows, makes friends with a leading chief
of the island living near at Waimea, and defeats the ruling
chief, first in a wrestling match and then in a riddling match
upon which the contestants have staked their bones, slays the
chief and burns him in an oven, and makes the friendly chief
Kaunalewa ruler over the island.[31]

Two animals besides the dog and hog found native here
before the arrival of Europeans were a species of bat (*Atala-
pha semota*), said to be found also in Chile,[32] and a species of
small rat inhabiting wild rocky places and living on roots
and seeds (*Rattus hawaiiensis*).[33] According to the Kumu-

31. For. Col. 4: 498–517; 5: 384–405.
32. Meinicke, 274.
33. See E. H. Bryan, *Hawaiian Nature Notes,* Honolulu, 1935.

lipo, in the sixth era of the po are born "the beings that leap in the night" and "keep the changes of the month."[34] Thus the rat kupua who is part human, part spirit, becomes a favorite theme for story-telling. When Kalanimanuia is brought back to life, he has the look of a rat until his human form is completely restored in all its beauty.[35] Na-maka-i-ka-ha'i has a rat-girl among her attendants.[36] In the Kila story it is a rat-man who gnaws the rope and lets down the food which Makali'i has hung up in a net. Kawelo's brother is said to have rat forms, and there is a folktale of Ohia-tree and his sister Rain who turns her forest family into rats with a slap each and herself into a spring of water.[37] Rat shooting, a favorite betting sport among chiefs on Hawaii and the unique example of the use of bow and arrow in this group, is also reported as a competitive sport of chiefs in Tonga,[38] and in Samoa the son of a woman with a rat's head has rat carpenters build a house for his marriage.[39]

The love of exaggeration characteristic of kupua stories is amply satisfied in the figure of the rat-man Pikoi-a-ka-alala (Pikoi son of Crow), which belongs to the period of Keawe-nui-a-Umi of Hawaii and Kakuhihewa of Oahu. He is born at Wailua on Kauai into a kupua rat family and is skilled in the art of shooting with bow and arrow. The two principal episodes of his legend are those of his contest in rat shooting with Mainele on Oahu and his successful shooting of the kupua birds who live in the forest of Hawaii and prevent Keawe-a-Umi from selecting a tree for the canoe he is building to go in search of his favorite Kapa'a. A famous riddler, he uses riddling puns as a legitimate way of winning a fantastic bet. But it is the fabulous skill of Pikoi in rat shooting which is the favorite theme for local tall-tale telling. He can stand on Kauiki on the island of Maui and shoot a rat lying asleep in Kohala across the channel.[40]

34. Liliuokalani, 27.   35. For. Col. 4: 550.
36. *Ibid.* 54.   37. Green and Pukui, 146–149.
38. Mariner 1: 224–228.   39. Buck, *Bul.* 75: 65.
40. Green, 69.

LEGEND OF PIKOIAKAALALA

(a) *Fornander version.* Pikoi-a-ka-alala is born at Wailua,
Kauai, into a kupua family who have the power of taking human or rat form. His father is Alala (Crow), and his mother
Koukou, his two sisters are Iole (Rat) and Opeapea (Bat).
When his koieie (koieiei) board wins over the others the boys
are jealous and push it into the rapids. He jumps in after it
and is borne down the Wailua river out to sea and cast up on
the beach at Kou on Oahu, where he is found by a man named
Kauakahi and carried to the home of his sisters, who have
married influential men on Oahu. He recites his family names,
is recognized, and the husbands sent for to prepare a feast of
welcome. While the food is preparing he joins a rat-shooting
contest and is taken as champion by the chiefess Kekakapuo-
maluihi against the famous rat shooter Mainele, the champion
of her husband Kaula-mawaho, ruling chief of the island. Mainele shoots ten rats with one arrow, but Pikoi puts up a prayer
to his rat family and strings ten rats and a bat by the whiskers
upon one arrow. After a betting contest in which Pikoi wins by
riddling upon the word iole (rat), the newcomer is acclaimed
victor and Mainele retires in disgrace. On his return to his sisters he eats up most of the food and the people say to each
other, "He eats like a god!"

Keawe-nui-a-Umi sends for the expert shooter Mainele to get
rid of some elepaio birds who prevent his canoe builders from
felling trees for their craft; every tree that the men attempt to
fell, the birds declare rotten. Pikoi gets his friend Kauakahi to
convey him with the party to Hawaii hidden in a basket, under
pretence of carrying with him his god, and when Mainele fails
to get the birds Pikoi takes successful aim by watching their reflection in a basin of water. Thus he becomes a wealthy man.

(b) *Westervelt version.* Pikoi has six rat sisters named after
the bow used for rat shooting (kikoo); he himself and his sister
Ka-ui-o-Manoa (The beauty of Manoa) who marries Pawa'a,
chief of Manoa valley on Oahu, have human form. The rat sisters teach him chants and he is furnished with a bow and arrows
by means of which he wins over all competitors on Kauai except

the dog-man Pupualenalena, whose skill is equal with his own. He accompanies his father to visit his sister, who lives with her husband at Kahaloa; they have also a place called Kahoiwai farther up Manoa valley. On the way he shoots and kills the great squid kupua Kahahe'e who pursues the canoe off Kaena. On the plain below Makiki valley the champion shooter of the chiefess Kaha-maluihi is losing to Mainele, the champion of her husband Kakuhihewa. Pikoi breaks up her bow and arrows, obtains his own from his father, and, employing his family prayer chant to invoke supernatural aid, he spies out rats invisible in the foliage save for their whiskers and strings them upon his single arrow by forties to the ecstatic cheers of the onlookers. For five years he hides until he is a grown man and his rat sisters have gnawed his hair short and colored his face, so that when he appears as a handsome man with a somewhat ragged haircut he is not recognized. The chiefess compromises him by riding in on the same wave with him and he is about to be killed by the chief's men when the former shooting champion is recognized and tested in a riddling match with Mainele in which he is acclaimed victor. His brother-in-law knocks dead forty of the men who have insulted him; his own "wise arrow" seeks out those who flee; and he becomes known as the "fire shooter" (Ka-pana-kahu-ahi), and dwells up Manoa valley in a great grass house given him by the chief.[41]

Cock-fighting was a favorite sport of Hawaiian chiefs as of Tahitian,[42] but without the use of artificial spurs such as are reported for the Dyaks of Borneo. High stakes were laid upon the game. A fine passage in the famous chant of Haui-ka-lani commemorating Kamehameha's first victory over Ki-walao on Hawaii compares the battle between the chiefs to a cock-fight:

Hawaii is a cock-pit, on the ground the well-fed cocks fight. . . .
He (the chief) is a well-fed cock . . .
Warmed in the fire-house until the stiffened feathers rattle,

41. For. Col. 4: 450–463; Westervelt, *Honolulu*, 157–172; Dickey, *HHS Reports* 25: 32; Kamakau, *Ke Au Okoa*, December 22, 1870.
42. Ellis, *Researches* 1: 221–223; Henry, 277–278.

Of varied colors like many-colored paddles, like piles of kauila
timbers;
The feathers rise and fall when the cock spurs.
The cock spurs north and then spurs south
Till one great blow of the spur
Hits the head, he flees severely wounded.
The chief bites like a dog,
Scratches the ground like a fowl,
The fowl scratches, the soft dust flies upward. . . .[43]

LEGEND OF LEPEAMOA

Lepe-a-moa (Comb of a cock), the chicken-girl of Palama, is
the kupua daughter of a high chief of Kauai named Keahua who
has incurred the displeasure of a sea-dwelling kupua named
Akua-peha-ale (God of the swelling billow) and been exiled to a
remote place in the mountains called Ka-wai-kini, where his wife
Kauhao, daughter of the chiefess Kapalama of Oahu, bears a
child in the form of an egg. Kapalama comes for the child and
keeps the egg wrapped in tapa and sweet-smelling plants until
it hatches into a many-colored bird and becomes, through the
power of a bird ancestress named Ke-ao-lewa who lives in the
heavens, a kupua with power to take either the form of a bird or
that of a beautiful girl. This child Lepe-a-moa is brought up by
her grandparents Kapalama and Hono-uliuli on Oahu.

Meanwhile on Kauai a boy is born named Kauilani. Storm
signs proclaim his rank as a chief and his father's parents, Lau-
ka-ieie and Kani-a-ula, bathe him in the spring called Wai-ui
and gird him with the malo Paihi-ku. Thus he gains supernatural strength. To destroy his father's enemy he first hems him in
by planting stakes, which grow into a thicket. The gods carve
images which come to life and fight for him. The malo Paihi-ku
gives his spear-thrust strength. Thus the demigod is defeated
and burned and his father restored to his lands.

Kauilani next goes to find his sister, tossing his spear ahead
of him and following its lead. Two women hide the spear; when
he calls "Koa-wi! koa-wa!" it answers. Over the sea he perceives
the kupua form of a bird ancestress, Ka-iwa-kalameha, then a

43. After Andrews; For. Col. 6: 382, 384.

rainbow, then sees by the shore his sister catching fish. He hides in her house and sees her change into her bird forms. As she falls asleep he seizes her and holds her fast. She tries to escape in her kupua bodies until the parents tell her in a chant who he is.

Kakuhihewa of Oahu is entertaining his sister and her husband Maui-nui and has bet his own lands against those of his brother-in-law upon a cock-fight. He now offers his daughter in marriage to the man who can produce a cock to win the bet for him. Kauilani, who is in high favor with the chiefess, promises to do this. The Maui cock is a kupua bird related to Lepe-a-moa's family and named Ke-au-hele-moa. A kupua in the form of an elepaio bird warns Kauilani not to let the cock see his sister before the fight. He wears her concealed in a garland about his neck until the fight begins. The Maui cock tries all its bodies in succession but the hen wins. At first the new wife is jealous of the beautiful sister, but after their girl child Kamamo is born and adopted by the kupua sister, Kauilani goes to live at Kakuhihewa's court.[44]

Tuamotu, Anaa. Taiva and Gaitua have a son born first as an egg. The wife conceals it, fearing her husband's anger. He however guards it as his own when the bird-child is discovered. This is Rogo-tau-hia or Rogo-rupe. See also Rua-toa, the boy covered with feathers, who rescues his father Hiri-toa from Puna's filth-pit.[45]

Tonga. The woman who eats her pigeon god bears a child with a pigeon head who later becomes a beautiful girl and marries the ruling chief of Tonga. Ulukihe-lupe is her name and her child Kauulu-fonua avenges his father and becomes ruling chief of Tonga.[46]

44. Westervelt, *Honolulu,* 204–245; also told in Thrum, *More Tales,* 164–184.

45. Stimson MS.   46. Gifford, *Bul.* 8: 62–65.

XXX

TRICKSTER STORIES

TRICKSTER stories are generally in the form of contests with the spirits who peopled the islands before the coming of man to Hawaii, and are only occasionally told of animal figures. In early days the southern islands of the group were all peopled by spirits, each with its chief spirit, Kani-ka'a of Hawaii, Keoloewa or Ke-ahu-ali'i of Maui, Pahulu of Lanai, Kaunolu of Molokai, Halali'i of Oahu. Lanai and Kahoolawe were long avoided by settlers through fear of the spirits who were their sole inhabitants. The Kaulu-laau of Lahaina who cleared Lanai of spirits has never been connected with the voyager Kaulu but may be a namesake. The tendency is to be seen on the one hand of centering such exploits about a single figure, on the other hand of a local detachment which gives rise to a distinct hero cycle on each island or even from district to district, hence a multiplication of trickster figures each with his own cycle of adventures, sometimes borrowed from district to district. Most of the stories on record are of wide distribution and must be referred to late foreign or south Polynesian sources. What original jests they supersede it is perhaps not too late to discover. The demigod Maui is archtrickster throughout Polynesia, but his deeds are rather typical of the kupua than of the trickster hero.

Pupuhuluena(-ana, Kupuahuluena, Puluana) is said to have been a kahuna who introduced food plants into the Hawaiian group, or, in localized versions, into Kohala district on Hawaii, by tricking the persons or "spirits" who owned the plants.

STORY OF PUPUHULUENA

(*a*) Pupu-huluena (Tuft of red feathers) lives along the steep cliffs east of Kohala where no food plants grow; the spirits have hidden them at Kalae in Ka-u district. He goes out fishing and follows the shoals of fish until off the Kona coast he sees Ieiea and Poopalu, fishermen of Makali'i, letting down a large-mouthed fishnet from their canoe. He makes friends with them by giving them oily kukui nuts in place of the sea beans (mohihi) they have been using to chew and spread on the water in order to see the fish entering the net. In return they help him get slips of food plants, which can be had only from the spirits ashore, since all their own food is cooked. The spirits must be made to believe that he has supernatural knowledge or they will never give up their food plants. He carves an image of wiliwili wood to set up as a god and weaves a basket of ieie vine in which he hides one of the fishermen. Brought ashore thus concealed, the native whispers to him the way in which to meet the tests by which those who have the food plants on shore attempt to put off the strangers. He is hence able to come ashore at the proper place and to name all the plants correctly as if revealed by his god. After he has stood some of them on their heads in a competitive game, they are glad to be rid of him. The tubers he planted are still to be seen growing at the foot of the cliffs east of Mohala.[1]

(b) Kula-uka lives above Kaumana on Oahu. At Lelepua lives the grandchild of Wailoa and Haumea named Kapahu. Kula-uka quarrels with his brother Kula-kai and, weaving a bird-form disguise out of ieie vine covered with feathers, he carries away Kapahu. When Haumea pursues, he throws out a stone which Haumea takes for her grandchild and which thunders when she tries to catch it. Haumea in revenge seizes the food from all the islands and retires to Nu'umealani.

Oahu, Kauai, Maui, Hawaii are afflicted by drought. Pupu-huluana and Kapala, strong men and swift runners of Kauai, come to Oahu seeking food and at Kailua in the land of Mauna-wili find Haumea's attendants, the men Olomana, Ahiki, Pakui, and the women Makawao and Hauli, living on popolo and ti plant left by the angry goddess for the subsistence of her own people. Olomana sends the swift runner Pakui with the Kauai men to Ololo-i-mehani, the land of Makali'i eastward of Oahu. They carve lifelike images of Ieiea and Poopalu, fishermen of

1. For. Col. 4: 570–573.

Makali'i, with humped backs like the uhu fishermen, real hair, eyes made of oyster shell. They bring back potatoes, taro, bananas, sugar cane, ape plant, ti, yams, hoi, arrowroot (pia), breadfruit, mountain apples (ohia), coconuts, and edible ferns. Thus these foods came to the islands.[2]

(c) There is a famine on the islands because Haumea has taken away the food. Pupuhuluana sails east to the land of Makali'i and on his return lands at Kalae in Ka-u district on Hawaii with food plants. His canoe, the "net of Maeha," and the fishermen of Makali'i, Poopalu and Ieiea, are to be seen there turned into stone.[3]

(d) It is Aukele-nui-aiku and his brother (Kane-)Apua who bring the first coconut to Hawaii. The first time Apua and his brother come from Kahiki they do not bring slips of food plants because they expect to find them growing here. Being almost famished, they return to Kahiki after plantings, and appear off Kaula-(u)ka's place in Kahiki with a load of pretended food in the shape of coral rock. Their not landing is laid to the rough surf. Of each plant they are shown they declare that it "germinates, sprouts, bears leaves and fruits in Hawaii," and hold up a piece of coral resembling the shape of the plant. The owners of the food plants cast all away as worthless and the voyagers gather them into the canoes and carry them back to plant in Hawaii. The first coconuts in Hawaii are planted at Kahaualea (where stands the heiau of Waha-ula) and at Kalapana in Puna district, Hawaii.[4]

(e) Kupua-huluena is a famous kupua who travels to foreign lands, names vegetables introduced at Keauhou, Hawaii, offers them upon the altars of the heiau of Kamauai erected to Kane, and distributes them for planting. Thus vegetable foods are introduced into these islands.[5]

2. *HAA* 1926, 92–95; *Kuokoa,* August 12, 1865.
3. Kamakau, *Kuokoa,* January 5, 1867.
4. For. Col. 5: 590–595.
5. *HAA* 1908, 72–73.

The device of a basket in which an accomplice is concealed as a pretended "god" occurs in the Pikoi-a-ka-alala legend, in which Pikoi is secretly conveyed to Hawaii concealed in such a basket as the god of his friend Kauakahi. In the Kaulu legend, the kupua's presence in the land of the gods is concealed by his hiding in a basket, where he acts as the pretended "god" of his brother and has to be properly fed to be effective. A bird disguise is woven by Maui when he goes in search of his wife who has been stolen by the eight-eyed bat.[6]

A few similar incidents are found in other groups, based on common customs or a common tradition. The use of oil to clear waters is noted in New Zealand.[7] Compare also the incident in Marquesan stories of emptying a gourdful of oil into the sea in order to look down to the sea bottom, or "into Havai'i."[8] The trick of pretending acquaintance with some coveted culture gift in order that its owners may not know how eagerly the stranger desires it occurs in other Polynesian travel stories. In Pukapuka, Wue travels. At Rakahanga he pretends that only children use swings in his country, and thus gets samples of this novelty to take home with him. So with other games which he learns at the different islands he visits.[9]

A similar famine story occurs in the legend of Makali'i.

(a) *Kepelino version.* Makali'i, the famous steersman of Hawaii-loa, is a great farmer who gathers up the food from Kahiki: bananas, yam, sugar cane, starch plant, hoi berry, and the gourd vines from which food calabashes and water bottles are made. But he is stingy and keeps all fast in a net (koko) until a rat nibbles the cord and lets them fall out. When the land is troubled by drought, rats (some of them two-legged) scatter his horde. Hence the saying, "But for the rat who spread these things broadcast over the group . . ." (E ole ka iole, laha ai no mea kanu ma keia mau pae-aina).

(b) *Fornander version* (1). In the Moikeha-Kila legend Makali'i, younger brother of Moikeha, remains in Kahiki as ruler

6. Thrum, *More Tales,* 252–259. 7. Taylor, 245, 280.
8. Handy, *Bul.* 69: 42, 68, 132. 9. Beaglehole MS.

over the land when his brother sails to Hawaii. He is good-looking, powerful, and brave, has the foreknowledge of a seer, and wields his war club Naulu-kohe-lewalewa with such force that its stroke forms a deep furrow in the earth. Foreseeing Kila's arrival, he has gathered up all the food of the land into a net called Makali'i and hung it up out of reach. "The net of Makali'i is drawn up above" (Huhui koko a Makali'i iluna) is the saying. Kila's grandaunt (or uncle), Kane-pohihi, climbs up in rat form and gnaws the strings of the net so that all the food is scattered over the land. Makali'i comes down from his home in the clouds to do battle with Kila, but Kila dodges the swing of his club and gives him a stunning blow, after recovery from which he crawls away thankfully to his home in the clouds and never returns to earth.

(c) *Fornander version* (2). Makali'i is a mythical ruler in Kapakapaua-a-Kane who in time of plenty stores up food which in time of famine he hangs out of reach in a net. The rats travel over the earth in search of food and find nothing. They look up to heaven and see the net. One climbs thither on clouds and rainbow and nibbles the ropes of the net at the center. The food falls and restocks the earth.

(d) *Emerson version*. Makali'i has hung up the vegetable food in a net attached to a cloud at Kaipaku, Hanalei, on Kauai. Puluena comes from Kohala seeking food and puts the rat into the net. A division of land in Kohala district is called Iole after this friendly rat. The chant runs,

> Hiu ai la Kaupaku Hanalei
> I na mapuna wai a ka naulu.

> "Hung up on the ridgepole of Hanalei,
> To the water springs of the rain cloud."[10]

References to the famine in the days of Makali'i are not uncommon. In Green's version of the Anaelike story the chief-

10. Kepelino, 78–79; For. Col. 6: 272; 4: 122–125, 160–165, 168–171; J. Emerson, *VCFL* 5: 3–4, 10–11.

ess of the Rolling island visits Hawaii at a time when Ma-kali'i has hung up the food in his net and there is little for man to eat; later in the story the rat nibbles at the net and there is food.[11] The famine myth is generally placed in a distant land. Only in Emerson's version is Makali'i said to belong to Kauai and the havoc of his horde to have taken place on the southern coast of Hawaii. At the southernmost point of that island, at Kalae in Ka-u district, rock formations are locally ascribed to objects in the legend: "the stars of Ma-kali'i [Pleiades], the house of Makali'i, his net, and the rat." The string figure to which the chant belongs shows the net with its eight compartments, each of which holds a single kind of vegetable food—taro, sweet potato, plantain, yam, arrowroot, fernroot, smilax, and another. The point at which the rat nibbled the cord is one which, if cut, will cause the whole figure to fall apart.

One of the ceremonies of the Makahiki festival consisted in shaking a netful of food out upon the ground to foretell what the crop would be like that season; if anything clung to the net it was a sign of scarcity. The ceremony, says a note, commemorated the time when "the kupua Waia let down from heaven a net whose four corners pointed to the North, South, East and West, and which was filled with all sorts of food, animal and vegetable (i'a and ai). This done he shook the net and the food was scattered over the land for the benefit of the starving people." In the prayer offered at this time for the net (ka pule koko), Uli is invoked as a god, and Kane and Kanaloa as the "life giver" and the "wonder worker." To this net Malo gives the name of Maoloha.[12] It is moreover from Makali'i that Kaulu (Kula-uka?) gets the net of Mao-leha in order to snare and kill Haumea. Now Haumea in one version of the Pupuhuluana legend is the one who has caused the famine which has started the quest after food plants. In Emerson's version of the net of Makali'i, Puluena is the man who comes seeking food. The names are evidently variants, and the food famine is thus closely connected with the stories of both Kaulu and Pupuhuluana. In the Kaulu legend Makali'i

11. 116, 118.   12. Malo, 197–198 and note 27.

is represented as the seer of the gods Kane and Kanaloa and lives in the heaven above Kuaihelani, where lies the vegetable garden of the gods. Kaulu wrecks this food plot by the trick familiar to folktale of appearing as a puny fellow and then gathering up the entire crop when told to take "all he can carry away." The same device of the chewed kukui nut to clarify the water with which Pupuhuluana bribes the "fishermen of Makali'i" to help him secure the food plants from the spirits is employed in the Kaulu story by Makali'i himself, under compulsion, in order to clear the ocean surface and find out where the fishes have hidden Kaulu's brother.[13]

Ka-ulu (The breadfruit) is known to Hawaiian legend as "son of Kalana" and a great voyager in the South Seas; to Hawaiian mythical fiction as a great trickster who wrecks the vegetable garden of Kane and Kanaloa, slays their pet shark whose spirit is accordingly placed in the Milky Way, terrorizes Makali'i into giving up the net Maoleha in order to snare Haumea, and kills Lono-ka-eho with the eight foreheads and his dog Ku-ilio-loa, who rule the north side of Oahu.

STORY OF KAULU

Ka-ulu is the youngest son of Ku-ka-ohia-laka and Hina-ulu-ohia born at Kailua, Koolau, on Oahu. Since an older brother Kamano has threatened his death as soon as he is born, he fears to take human form and appears in the shape of a rope, which is put up on a shelf and guarded by a kindly brother Kaeha (or Kaholeha) until he becomes a human being. Kaeha is carried away to lands in the sky called Lewa-nu'u and Lewa-lani (or Kuaihelani) where Kane and Kanaloa live and Kaulu voyages thither to find him. Kaulu's strength lies in his hands; each obstacle he encounters is overcome by means of their strength alone. These obstacles are strong waves, which he breaks up and hence the surf of today; long and short waves; the dog Ku-ilio-loa, which he breaks in pieces and hence the small dogs of today (and in another version the tides Keaumiki and Keauka, and gods and ghosts).

13. For. Col. 4: 526–529; 5: 364–369.

Kaeha hides him in a loulu palm leaf from which he speaks with the voice of a god and demands the awa cup given to his brother. The seer Makali'i warns the gods that Kaulu is among them and is all-powerful, but they fail to find him. He plays tricks on the spirits by putting stones into their sleeping places; they retaliate by refusing food to the brother and telling him to get it for himself. Kaulu "flies up" to the gods' provision ground; the guards turn it over and shake him off into space but he recovers footing and teases the guards into giving him "anything he wants." He takes everything they have, even to the rays of the sun, and they have to beg a piece of each to restock the land.

The gods endeavor to get rid of Kaeha by tempting him out surf riding, where he is swallowed by the chief of the sharks Ku-kama-ulu-nui-akea (or Kalake'e-nui-a-Kane). Kaulu first drains the sea to find his brother, then spits it out (and hence the sea is salt today) and seeks Makali'i. The thunderstone Ikuwa which Koeleele (or Kaaona) hurls at him he catches on his forefinger. Makali'i chews kukui nut to oil the surface of the sea and points out the chief shark to Kaulu. Kaulu teases the shark until it opens its jaws, then tears the jaws apart with his strong hands and out comes his brother with hair all worn away. The spirits again try to kill Kaeha in a swing, but Kaeha kills them instead by pretending to swing them. Those who survive catch Kaeha and hide him in a mussel (opihi) shell, but Kaulu urinates upon it and forces it to open its shell, hence that species of mussel is bitter today.

Kaulu returns with his brother to Papakolea in Moanalua and himself goes on to Kapalama, where he kills Haumea by trapping her in the Maoleha nets obtained from Makali'i; then to Kailua where he kills Lono-ka-eho with the eight foreheads and his dog Kuilioloa at Kualoa, and assumes the chiefship over Koolau.[14]

In this legend of Ka-ulu's birth and his fabulous adventures when he goes to find his brother in the land of Kane and Kanaloa, the trickster element is uppermost. As a kupua his own two hands are his "god" and, although the voyage and

14. For. Col. 4: 522–533; 5: 364–371.

the adventures in the land of the gods contain elements similar to other such travel tales, the emphasis of the story is upon the tricks he plays upon the spirits in contests of power.

(A) Birth in the form of a rope.

(B) Voyage in which obstacles are sent by the gods to obstruct the way.

(C) Tricking of the spirits in the land of the gods; (C1) disguise as a god; (C2) rough handling of the spirits until they are glad to be rid of the visitor.

(D) Carrying away food plants; (D1) all the food there is.

(E) Avoiding thunderbolts.

(F) Killing the gods' shark, which is thrown up into the Milky Way.

Similar stories of contests with spirits in order to win food plants from the gods come from Samoa.

Lele'asapai. The flying gods (aitu) in Alele have stolen all the chief of Samata's yam planting. He sends his grandson Lele'a-sapai to the spirits' land to the westward of Savai'i to bring them back. On the way Lele lands at Pulotu, where the ruling chief Savea Si'uleo pretends friendship and asks him where they sleep at night, intending to destroy them. His guardian god Saolevao sets a watch and guards them against the plot. Si'uleo sends him after kava, but misdirects him; again Saolevao sets him right. The spirits poison the kava they give him to drink, but Saolevao drinks the poison for him. Now allowed to go on to Alele, he hides at the spring and first kills the bearers who bring the chief of the flying spirits, then forces the chief to give him the yam plantings.[15]

Lefanoga. The young son follows his father Tagaloa-ui and his brother Tae-o-Tagaloa to the family gathering in the heavens. The family are shocked and give him the poisonous kava to kill him. He avoids the poison, uproots the whole plant, and brings it down to the Tagaloa people on earth.[16]

15. Krämer 1: 115–116.
16. *Ibid.* 416–418; Buck, *Bul.* 75: 147.

Losi. Losi sets out (usually with a boatload of god-like companions) after food plants and brings taro, coconuts, breadfruit, and the kava ritual from the Tagaloa in the heavens by outwitting the gods in all the tests they set him and defeating them in battle, teasing and bullying them until they will give him anything he asks in order to be rid of him. The tests consist in kava drinking, eating (sometimes poisonous food), surf riding, diving, catching fruit shaken from a tree, or in more magical feats like setting back the sun or stopping rain.[17] A similar story from Tonga tells of the voyage to Bulotu, the tests undertaken, and the food plants with which the voyagers escape from the spirits of Bulotu.[18]

The king shark of Kane and Kanaloa in Lewa-lani, called Ku-kama-ulu-nui-akea or Kalake'e-nui-a-Kane, whom Kaulu slays in this legend and whose spirit flies up to the Milky Way, has its prototype in the South Seas. In the Tuamotus the Milky Way is the sacred ocean of Kiho-tumu; the dark rift in the Milky Way is his sacred ship, called The-long-shark.[19] In New Zealand the Milky Way (Te Mangaroa) is called The-fish-of-Maui (Te-ika-Maui).[20] In Rarotonga Maui kills Te-Mokoroa-i-ata, the water monster who insulted Maui's father Tangaroa, and Mokoroa becomes the Milky Way.[21] In Tahiti Ire, "the handsome blue shark, beloved of Ta'aroa," frolics with the children until the gods of the sea warn the brothers Tahi-a-nu'u and Tahi-a-ra'i that there is danger of its becoming a man-eater. One breaks his spear between its jaws, the other aims at its heart. They are about to cut it up when Ta'aroa and Tu snatch away their pet to the Wai-ola-o-Tane and it bathes in the Milky Way.[22]

Kaulu and his wife Kekele, a quiet, handsome woman who loves all fragrant plants and who planted the hala groves of Koolau and used to wear wreaths of sweet-smelling panda-

17. Krämer 1: 392; Stuebel 4: 142, 143; Turner, 105–107; Fraser, *RSNSW* 26: 275–282; Buck, *Bul.* 75: 551.

18. Gifford, *Bul.* 8: 155–170; Collocott, *Bul.* 46: 14, 15–16.

19. Stimson, *Bul.* 111: 8. 20. *JPS* 7: 239–240; 8: 109.

21. *Ibid.* 7: 240; 8: 73. 22. Henry, 403–404.

nus about her, are not named upon the genealogical line to which Kaulu's forefathers belong but remain mythical figures. In the story of his adventures his parents are woodland deities. His own name refers to plant growth, especially the breadfruit, and is used in referring to a young person before puberty.

The theft of the awa plant from the garden of the gods connects Kaulu's exploits as a trickster with those of Maui as recounted in the Kumulipo. The arrangement of the strata of the heavens in which Kane and Kanaloa drink awa and surf with the spirits in the lower heaven (Lewa-nu'u) while their vegetable garden is tended in the heaven above (Lewa-lani) corresponds with a fishing chief's establishment who lives by the sea and has his vegetable food brought from the uplands. The looting of the patch corresponds with Maui's early exploit. Hina-the-tapa-beater, wife of the Nanamaoa who is represented on the Ulu line as son of the trickster Maui-a-kalana, is called the grandmother of Kaulu the voyager.[23]

Two traditions remain from the legend of Kaulu's voyages: one that he brought to Hawaii "the edible soil of Ka-wainui" called alaea, used medicinally by old Hawaiians and resorted to in Tahiti in time of famine;[24] the other that he visited the maelstrom called Moana-wai-kai-o-o, or Mimilo-o-Nolewai, an adventure, says Emory, often depicted in Tuamotuan tradition where actual whirlpools are common within the group, one within the lagoon of Takaroa "into which canoes are drawn, disappear from sight, and emerge again some distance beyond."[25] Lands visited by Kaulu in circling Kahiki are recited in a name chant:

> I am Kaulu,
> Offspring of Kalana,
>
> . . . . .
>
> He who visited Wawau (Borabora)
> Upolo (Taha'a), little Pukalia,
> Great Pukalia and Alala,

23. For. Pol. Race 1: 200–202.   24. Henry, 423.
25. Kamakau, *Kuokoa*, December 29, 1866.

Pelua, Palana, and Holani,
The isthmus (kuina) of Ulunui, Uliuli,
Melemele, Hi'ikua, Hi'ilalo, Hakalauai;
Spanned the heavens,
Spanned the night, spanned the day,
Made the circuit of Kahiki,
Kahiki is completely circled by Kaulu.[26]

STORY OF KAULULAAU

(*a*) *Fornander version.* Ka-ulu-laau (The grove of trees),
son of Kakaalaneo and Kanikani-ula, is brought up at Lahaina
(called Lele) on Maui, where his father lives and rules the whole
island of Maui. All the children born on the same day are
brought to the chief's place to be the boy's companions. Each
day he leads them into mischief, finally pulling up the breadfruit
plantings. The boys are sent home and Kaululaau exiled to Lanai, which is inhabited by spirits. In vain these man-eating
spirits try to discover the place which his god has given him to
sleep in. Each night they tire themselves out running to a new
place to which he has directed them, while he sleeps pleasantly
somewhere else, until all die of exhaustion except Pahulu and a
few others, who escape to Kahoolawe. The chief sees how his
son's fire burns each night on Lanai, is pleased with his courage,
and sends a canoe to fetch him home.[27]

(*b*) *Emerson version.* To trick the spirits, Ka-ulu-laau proposes a swimming test to a rock at which he takes his stand and
as they swim up to the rock one at a time, he holds the head of
each under water until he is drowned. The remaining spirits he
makes drunk in a feast house, gums their eyes while they sleep,
and then sets fire to the house. Only three or four escape. One he
ends with a mock club, another by tricking him to dive for his
own reflection in the water and then jumping in on top of him
and putting an end to him.[28]

26. Emerson, *HHS Papers* 5: 13–14, whose translation is here
for the most part followed; For. Col. 6: 321. The parenthetical identifications are Emory's.

27. Col. 4: 486–489; 5: 542–543.   28. *HHS Reports* 29: 16–19.

(c) *Kalakaua version.* Further adventures recounted of Ka-ulu-laau include the possession of a magic spear point with which he is able to sink into the ground a demon moʻo called Moʻoaleo, protect himself from Pele, and kill a giant bird which harries Oahu and is possessed by the spirit of Hilo-a-Lakapu, a chief of Hawaii who invaded Oahu during the rule of Maili-ku-kahi and was slain at Waimano and his head placed on a pole for the birds to feed upon near Honouliuli. Of akua blood, his spirit enters the monster and is driven forth only by pronouncing his name. This spurious version gives Kaululaau a half-sister Wao and a half-brother Kaihiwalua, father of Luaia. The kahuna Waolani is his friend. His land on Maui is called Kaua-ula. His wife from Oahu is named Laiea-a-Ewa.[29]

The motive of hiding from the spirits occurs in the Banks islands and in Samoa.

(a) Qat and his brothers go to the village of Qasavara and to escape death at the hands of the spirits hide each night through Qat's magic in a different crevice of the house, which the fool brother the next day points out.[30]

(b) In Samoa, Leleʻasapai is sent to recover yams stolen by the flying god of Alele. He comes to Bulotu and, helped by his guardian spirit Saolevao, avoids the plots laid against him, first by giving wrong information as to where he will sleep; second, by keeping awake all night; third, by climbing into the heavens and bringing down kava to drink; fourth, by avoiding drinking the poisoned kava. He then proceeds to Alele and kills the demon, but not the king for whom the demon stole them.[31]

Besides these two arch tricksters of Hawaiian tradition, similar tricks are told of other trickster figures who contend with the early spirit inhabitants of the islands.

STORY OF LEPE

A trickster (of Hilo, Hawaii) fools the spirits by feeding them salt dung, while himself only pretending to eat. When they play

29. 213–225.   30. Codrington, 163–164.

31. Krämer 1: 115–116.

hide and seek, Lepe conceals himself by standing on his head, and then plays them a vulgar trick. When they play sand digging he conceals dung in the sand so that they smear their hands. He goes to their feast painted black to escape recognition. He invites them to visit him in return, but as they approach he rattles gourds and sings, as if to companions, "Wake up! here come the spirits, our favorite food!" and all run away.[32]

STORY OF PUNIA

The artful son of Hina in Kohala, Hawaii, tricks the sharks who guard the cave of lobsters by throwing in a stone which the sharks all make for, supposing that he has himself leaped in, then diving in another place after the lobsters and escaping unharmed. Meanwhile the sharks quarrel as to which shark is his accomplice, and kill each other until the king of sharks alone remains.

To kill this king shark Punia prepares a long sharp stick, two fire sticks, kindling wood, food, salt, and a mussel shell and assures the shark that if it bites him and the blood flows it will rise to the surface and he will live again, but if it swallows him whole he will die. The shark accordingly swallows him whole and for ten days he lives inside the shark by making a fire and cooking the food he has brought and the meat which he scrapes out of the inside of the shark. When the shark becomes weak and makes for shore, he tricks it into carrying him to the sandy beach, where the fish is stranded and people come and dig out Punia.

On his way back to Kohala, Punia escapes the spirits by pretending that this fishing ground is familiar to him and thus enticing the spirits out to sea by ones and twos where they are at his mercy. Thus he kills all but one wary spirit.[33]

The first incident occurs in Samoa, where spirits called Alele rob the yams of the Tui Samata. He sends his grandchild La-le'a-sapai to recover them. The boy throws a club into their bathing pool and the spirits fight each other until

32. For. Col. 5: 422–425.   33. *Ibid.* 294–301.

all are killed.[34] The second motive, that of destroying a monster by being swallowed whole and cutting the way out, is of worldwide distribution. The third occurs in the Emerson version of Kaululaau.[35]

STORY OF HANAAUMOE

(a) *Fornander version.* Hanaaumoe, the great flatterer of the spirits of Oahu who devoured men, used to invite travelers from Kauai ashore with a chant warning of the dangers to be met from spirits of other islands and praising the safety of his own island. When the deceived voyagers came ashore, the spirits would give them a great feast and when they were sound asleep would kill and eat them. None escaped to warn other travelers. Finally the double canoe of Kahao-o-ka-moku, friend of the ruling. chief of Kauai, is tempted ashore and the whole party killed and eaten in this manner; "one smack and the people disappeared, all eaten up by the spirits." A lame man, however, has suspected danger and kept awake as long as he could in order to answer the guards who came to find if all were sleeping. Finally he goes to sleep in a hole under the doorstep and escapes detection. He returns to Kauai and reports the matter. The chief comes with a party to avenge his friend. Wooden images take their place in the Long House while the Kauai men conceal themselves. The spirits find the images tough eating. When all the spirits have fallen asleep, the house is burned over their heads and all consumed except the flatterer, who manages to escape.[36]

(b) *Rice version.* Kauai and Niʻihau fishermen are eaten by the gods who live at one end of Niʻihau. The fishermen make wooden images with eyes of mussel shell and place them in the Long House. While the gods are trying to eat the images, the

34. Fraser, *RSNSW* 24: 203–205.
35. Dixon, 69 and notes. Add MAORI: *JPS* 13: 95–98; Taylor, 157–161. SAMOA: Turner, 245–247. TONGA: *Bul.* 8: 79, 81–83. TOKELAU: Burrows, 172–173. NEW HEBRIDES: Turner, 337; Neuhauss, 550–551.
36. Col. 4: 476–483.

fishermen close the door and burn all to the ground with the gods inside.[37]

STORY OF WAKAINA

A cunning spirit of Waiapuka in North Kohala named Wa-kaina pleases the people by his singing, then deceives them into dressing him in a feather cloak, helmet, and native garment, and giving him a bamboo flute and other ornaments in which he promises to show them a new dance, and flies away with the whole costume.[38]

Wakaina accompanies Pumaia on one of his sightseeing tours on Maui. The people see them coming and to test whether they are spirits or not spread ape leaves for them to walk upon, since a human foot will tear the leaves but a spirit's will leave them untorn. Pumaia saves his friend by walking ahead and bidding him follow in the torn footprints. As they cross Lama'oma'o a prophet sees them coming and gives chase. The great owl of Kona (Pueo-nui-o-Kona) fights the prophet and his entrails become spread over the akolea ferns that used to grow in that place.[39] [Hence the name of "intestines of the prophet" for the endemic species of the dodder, called pololo and used for love charms, whose yellow stems form a tangle over bushes in some parts of the islands (*Cuscuta sandwichiana*).]

The trick of escaping with valuables while giving an exhibition of skill in dancing occurs in many South Sea groups. In Mangaia, Ngana the crafty persuades (H)ina to let him try on her ornaments, then flies up in the air with them through a chink in the wall.[40] In Maori, Whakaturia is taken captive and hung up in Uenuku's big house while the captors dance and sing. Tama-te-kupua suggests to him a way of escape by boasting of his own skill until he is released to dance and sing. He makes his escape through the doorway, which is then quickly closed and fire is set to the house.[41] A god caught stealing in the witch woman's sweet-potato storehouse is about to be cooked and eaten when he offers to dance

37. 68.   38. For. Col. 5: 418.
39. *Ibid.* 550–555.   40. Gill, 88–90.
41. Grey, 78–80; Taylor, 272–275.

and flies away with the witch's grandchild.[42] In Nukufetau of the Ellice islands a captive is released to dance. He leaps as high as the roof and is hence taken outside to show his skill, when he promptly flies away.[43] In the Lau islands, the tricky gods are tied and left in charge of the children. Freed to teach a new dance, they sing a magic song which sinks the ship and the children all perish while the gods disappear.[44] In Florida the incident is part of an animal story in which the turtle has saved the life of the heron and the heron reciprocates. The turtle is caught and tied in the house of his captors. By dancing for the children while their elders are away the heron distracts their attention from the escaping turtle. He then flies away with the ornaments he has borrowed from them for the dance.[45]

STORY OF IWA

The clever thief Iwa, son of Kukui, who "stole while he was yet in his mother's womb," lives at Kaalaea, Koolau, Oahu. Keaau seeks him to recover his lucky cowries used for squid fishing, which Umi has taken from him. Iwa dives under the hook, detaches the cowries, and fastens the hook to a bank of coral while he makes his escape. Afterwards he betrays the trick to Umi and steals back the shells from Keaau.

To test his skill as a thief Umi sets him two tests: to steal his tapu axe which hangs suspended to the middle of a cord passed about the necks of two old women in the temple of Pakaalana in Waipio while a crier makes the circuit five times each night of the tapued district, and to contend six to one with professional thieves in filling six houses with stolen treasure in a single night. Iwa personates the crier and asks the old women to let him touch the axe to make sure of its safety, then makes off with it so swiftly that no one can catch him. For the second test, he waits until the six professionals have filled their six houses and gone to sleep, then steals everything out of them and fills his own. He even steals the sheets from under Umi as he lies sleeping.

42. White 2: 59–61.
43. Turner, 286–287; *JPS* 29: 144–145.
44. Hocart, 208.   45. Codrington, 357–359.

Iwa owns a paddle named Ka-pahi (The scatterer), with four strokes of which he can cover the distance between Ni'ihau and Hawaii (the easternmost and the westernmost of the group).[46]

Stories of the clever thief Iwa do not strictly belong to this group. The tricks he plays are upon human combatants and resemble those told in Hawaii of such legendary heroes as Kua-paka'a in the court of Keawe-nui-a-Umi rather than of Laka and Kaha'i in southern cycles, who may be regarded as the great eastern Polynesian examples of tricksters in spirit land, as Lele'asapai is in western Polynesia. Iwa is the name of a bay below Kapoho in Puna district. Hiro (Hilo) is god of thieves in Tahiti, Iro in Mangaia and Rarotonga, Whiro among the Maori, not to be confused with the navigator of that name. In Tahiti the dragonfly is his agent. His "sky of the prophets" is below the "water of life of Tane" or Milky Way. Among the Maori he is one of the sons of Rangi, lord of darkness, as opposed to Tane, god of light. In Mangaia the will-of-the-wisp Uti is invoked to light the world against his thefts.[47]

46. For. Col. 5: 284–293; Westervelt, *Honolulu,* 148–156.
47. Henry, 391; Gill, 124–126.

XXXI

VOYAGE TO THE LAND OF THE GODS

THE Oahu Waha-nui (Big mouth) family is placed by Fornander in the early period of contact with the southern Pacific, contemporary with Hikapoloa on Hawaii, Kaikipa'anea on Kauai, Kamauaua on Molokai.[1] He is said to have been a great voyager, to have so oppressed the Menehune people as to induce their migration to the sunken land of Kane, led by Kanaloa and Kane-apua and directed by their god Kane, and to have been himself killed in a sea fight.[2] But the famous fictitious narrative (kaao) recording his voyage "to tread on the breasts of Kane and Kanaloa" connects Waha-nui with the island not of Oahu but of Hawaii.

STORY OF WAHA-NUI

(a) *Fornander version.* Waha-nui sets out from Hawaii with his seer (kaula) Kilohi to fulfil a vow he has made to sail to Ka-hiki and "trample" upon Ka-houpo-o-Kane-a-me-Kanaloa before returning again to Hawaii. Kane, Kanaloa, and Kane-apua, three gods with human forms, have been living on Lanai, but Kane-apua has angered his brothers by urinating in their water spring and they have taken bird form and flown away, leaving Kane-apua, who has no bird body, to shift for himself. As Waha-nui passes Kaunolu point on Lanai, Kane-apua hails him and asks to be taken aboard. Waha-nui points out that the canoe is already overcrowded. Kane-apua twice raises a storm which forces the canoe back and is at length given a place in the canoe behind the sailing masters Ho'okele-i-Hilo and Ho'okele-i-Kau. As they encounter various dangers of the sea he proves useful, first, in dispersing their fear of the island Kane-huna-moku when it looms up and is taken by the sailing masters for the great dog of Hina, Ku-ilio-loa; next, in quieting the two kupua hills Pali-

1. For. Pol. Race 2: 57.
2. *Ibid.* 1: 99; Col. 6: 272, 349–350; Kepelino, 68–74.

uli and Pali-kea (White and Black cliffs) which clash together
and destroy canoes; then in riding in safety a storm, sent from
the calabash that holds the bones of La'a-ma'oma'o, by diving
down and making the canoe fast with a rope made out of the intestines of his ancestress Hono-nui-kua-eaea where she lies with
her face turned upward to greet her grandchild; lastly, in quieting his own dog at the landing at Kahiki. He tells Waha-nui to
go until he comes to three men lying with their faces turned upward, who are Kane, Kanaloa, and Mauli. Waha-nui upon his
return worships Kane-apua and is given a pilikua, here described
as a double-bodied creature, "the bodies being joined together
by means of the ribs growing into each other," and told not to
show this wonder until he reaches Hawaii. Waha-nui cannot resist displaying it on Kauai and the ruling chief Kupakoili, advised by his diviner (kilokilo) Luluupali, kills the chief and all
his followers except one man, who dives into the sea and later
escapes to Hawaii and carries the news. The death of Waha-nui
is, however, avenged. His successor sends a plausible invitation
to the Kauai people to come to Hawaii, then massacres them
all; not one escapes.[3]

(b) *Kamakau version.* Kane-apua hails Waha-nui at the cape
Apua. Kilohi is the pilot, Moopuaiki the kahuna. The canoe
lands at Hale-o-Lono on Molokai, sails by the cliff of Kaholo,
passes the cape Kaunolu in broad daylight and comes to Apua,
where it is hailed by Kane-apua. After the storm the canoe lands
at Kaunolo-pau and sails by way of Ke-ala-i-kahiki on Kahoolawe. It is bound for Kahiki-kapakapaua-o-Kane to tread on
Ka-houpo-o-Kane, and Kane-apua warns him to tread upon it
all if he would live. On his return Waha-nui brings the pilikua
(dwarfs) and they become runners on Kauai. One is brought to
Punalu'u harbor on the Ka-u coast of Hawaii and lives above
Kopu and Moaula.[4]

Analysis of the Waha-nui legend shows that it follows a
traditional Polynesian type.

(A) A kupua is reluctantly admitted to an overcrowded

3. For. Col. 4: 516–523.
4. *Kuokoa,* December 22, 1866; January 5, 1867.

boat (A1) by means of a forced landing, (A2) or upon promise of help in overcoming obstacles, (A3) or through a disguise (the floating gourd), (A4) or through other proof of supernatural power.

(B) He wards off the dangers of the way.

(C) He sends the party home with a culture gift which they lose through disregard of a tapu imposed.

All of these elements seldom appear in the legend as preserved. In Samoa, Tangaloa joins two youths from Tutuila sailing home from Manu'a, who take him aboard only because the canoe will not move without him. He carries them to Fiji, saves them from the "pointing finger of Fiji," and sends them home with food plants and mullet, but the mullet (or all but the coconut) they lose because they forget the instruction not to bail out the canoe before coming to land.[5] In the Tonga version of the "Voyage to Bulotu" four gods sailing in a canoe are joined by a fifth, a woman Familie (Take care) or Haalefeke, who intercepts them at various places until her mysterious nature is recognized, and it is she who helps them come safely through the tests set in Bulotu. Through her, food plants are brought to Tonga.[6] In a Tuamotu story from Anaa, Tararo asks to be taken by Kio, king of Marama, on a courting expedition to Rarotonga and, when he is refused passage, calls up winds and forces the canoe to take him aboard, then himself wins the beauty of Rarotonga.[7] In an Aitutaki version of the Rata story, Rata, bound for Marama, refuses passage to Nganaoa, but when he comes floating overseas in a gourd he is allowed to join the party, after promising to destroy all the monsters of the way.[8] In the Tahitian Rata story it is "the priest" who encourages the expedition and names the opponents;[9] in the Tuamotuan, Tava'a, one of the family spirits of the forest, is found "sitting in the bows as a guide for the voyage."[10] In the Maori migration legend of the canoe Tainui, the female fairy Te Peri acts as directing god, seated at the bow of the canoe to guard

5. Krämer 1: 427–428; Buck, *Bul.* 75: 486; Churchill MS.

6. Gifford, *Bul.* 8: 155–170; Collocott, *Bul.* 46: 14, 15–16.

7. Stimson MS.   8. Gill, 145–148.

9. Henry, 494.   10. *Ibid.,* 502.

against dangers.[11] But for the warning spirit Saolevao, Le-le'asapai would never have succeeded in bringing down the yam planting from the flying gods in Alele.[12]

The floating-gourd trick in order to be taken into a canoe or to pursue one in which the supernatural being has been refused passage is to be found in Polynesian trickster cycles. In Hawaii it is told of the sorceress Hina-ke-ka (Hina the bailer). In the Marquesas, Tanaoa's brothers have gone off in a canoe and left him deserted. He follows in a coconut gourd and turns them all into porpoises, then himself wins the beautiful Meto with his flute playing.[13] White has a mixed story of Tautini who floats to land in a bowl-sized canoe after his uncle's fishhook.[14] In the Banks islands story of Qat, the trickster follows his brothers when they steal off with his wife and canoe, comes floating beside the canoe in a painted coconut gourd, and makes the landing before them.[15]

A common belief in spirit guidance dominates all these stories and may normally play a part in the make-up of any travel story. The incident of the guardian spirit or god through whose advice the hero wins success on a dangerous mission, whatever its objective, is therefore not necessarily borrowed from one story to another. But the particular treatment of the incident in the reluctance of those in the canoe to give passage and the repeated effort of the supernatural being to gain it, together with the fact that it is only through his help that the quest is attained, gives the tale a type form very characteristic of South Sea travel stories and which may derive from a common, perhaps borrowed, source. It is interesting to observe that an incident based upon reverence for a god is often diverted to farcical ends in the make-up of such a story. The helpful spirit is often, like Kane-apua in the Waha-nui legend, a trickster spirit whose troublesome acts distort the actual moral pattern of the tale.

The meaning of Waha-nui's vow is rendered obscure by the chant language employed. It must refer to some vengeance to be taken, such as Brewster describes from Fiji as

11. *JPS* 1: 224.
13. Handy, *Bul.* 69: 91–95.
15. Codrington, 161–162.

12. Krämer 1: 115–116.
14. 1: 171–172.

mbuturaki, which consists in knocking a man down and stamping upon him; "when a number of them got a victim down and jumped upon him, he generally bore their marks for the rest of his life."[16] In a Tahiti story Maui in a rage stamps upon the disk of the sun until it is cracked and weakened.[17] In Maori myth Tawhaki, angry with his parents because they did not avenge the attempt made against his life, "went to heaven and trod on the Toka-tami-whare," who were his ancestors.[18] Treading upon the prostrate bodies of relatives may be used as a mark of submission, as in the Hawaiian legend of Kamapua'a where his family submit to this treatment after their son has conquered the land. But the expression may well here refer to a voyage to ancestral lands circling the Pacific as in the Kaulu chant, Kane referring (in Hawaii) to the sun's path north of the Equator, Kanaloa to its path to the south.

Kane-apua's connection with Lanai is well established. Aiai, when he goes about marking out fishing grounds and setting up altars, finds him fishing off Kaunolu point on Lanai.[19] Fish gods named Kane-apua and Rae-apua were worshiped at Lanai in Ellis's day, and Kalakaua names them as worshiped by Molokai fishermen. Emerson calls Kane-(lau)-apua a healing and beneficent god from Lanai who is joined with his relative Kane-milo-hai as an emissary to save men from death. The akuhekuhe fish is said to be one of this god's forms. He is named as a brother of Pele, who is left as guard on an outlying island of the group.[20] He is named as the fourth son of Hina-ai-malama and Konikonia.[21] He is one of the bird brothers named in the legend of Aukele-nui-a-Iku and legend says that Aukele and his brother Apua bring the first coconut to Hawaii.[22] His connection with Kane and Kanaloa is that of a younger brother and lesser deity, who nevertheless by trickery gains his ends much like the younger Maui among the sons of Akalana.

16. 190.   17. Henry, 432.
18. White 1: 113.   19. Thrum, *Tales,* 238.
20. Ellis, *Tour,* 67; Kalakaua, 44; N. Emerson, *Pele,* ix, 194 note c; Emory, *Bul.* 12: 12–13.
21. For. Col. 5: 268.   22. *Ibid.* 590–593.

Waha-nui, the explorer of the Pacific and tyrant chief over the early Kane people on Oahu, is possibly represented in the mythical Ke-ali'i-wahi-lani who looked down from heaven and, beholding the beautiful woman La'ila'i dwelling on the island of Oahu, came down and made her his wife and thus became the father of "one of the ancestors of this race." An often quoted chant associates the name of Wahi-lani of Oahu with the adventure described in the legend of Waha-nui:

> O Wahi-lani, o ke ali'i o Oahu,
> I holo aku i kahiki,
> I na pae-moku o Moa-ula-nui-akea,
> E keekeehi i ka houpu o Kane a me Kanaloa.

> "Wahi-lani, chief of Oahu,
> Sailed away to Kahiki,
> To the islands of Moa-ula-nui-akea,
> To tread the sunken land of Kane and Kanaloa."[23]

The purpose of Wahi-lani's voyage in this chant is identical with that of Waha-nui's. The localization on Oahu is unmistakable and agrees with that of the Waha-nui family on Oahu, with the Wakea and Papa stories, and the traditional placing of Luanu'u, who is also called Wahi-lani, on the north coast of Oahu.

The name of Wahi-lani is, however, given to a chief of Kohala district on Hawaii in the time of Keawe-nui-a-Umi. This chief is named as one of those who accompany Keawe on his quest for Paka'a and he is jeered at by Paka'a's son as "not a chief by birth" but a petty chief, ruling over a land where sweet potato is the food and grasshoppers the fish of the land.[24] He (or his son) joins the rebellion against Keawe and is slain, and his bones are displayed by Lono-i-ka-makahiki together with those of the five other chiefs whom Keawe slew.[25] In both the Waha-nui legend and the Paka'a appear the Hawaii names of Ho'okele-i-Hilo and Ho'okele-i-Puna (or -Kau) for the sailing masters, and in both legends the

23. Malo, 311 and note 1.   24. Col. 5: 80.
25. *Ibid.* 72.

same device is used to force a landing by raising a storm. It looks as if the two stories took shape at the same time, when early legends were being relocalized and drawn into the cycle composed about the popular figure of Keawe-nui-a-Umi at the time when he held court as ruling chief on the island of Hawaii.

XXXII

RIDDLING CONTESTS

A STOCK episode of a kupua story is a riddling contest, called hoʻopaʻapaʻa, a term used to express the play of words back and forth in debate. The common situation is that of a famous riddler who has defeated all challengers but is finally outwitted and destroyed by an apparently mean antagonist. The most fully elaborated of these stories relates how a mere boy outmatches the most famous riddling chief of Kauai and avenges the death of his father in a similar contest. The event is commemorated in the name Kauai-of-Kaikipaʻananea, which means "The expert in riddling," from nane, "to riddle," although the word is also used for other games of skill such as flourished especially in the courts of chiefs of the island of Kauai and were thence carried to other islands.

In such a contest high stakes are set, even to life itself. In more homely usage the art consists in betting on a riddle to be guessed, in a brag upon which the opponent has been induced to put up a bet, or in merely playing with language in a way to entangle the opponent with contradictory and seemingly impossible meanings. Puns were delighted in as a way of matching an opponent or fulfilling a brag. Taunts after the manner of "stringing" a less sophisticated rival must be met with a jibe more bitter. One series of objects of a kind must be matched with another, or a forgotten item, no matter how trivial, added. One object proposed must be met with another analogous in every detail, or its antithesis. A spider web is thus matched with the dodder vine, a kukui nut with a sea urchin as it is cracked and eaten with the use of thumb and fingers and a pinch of salt added, the contestant being careful in every case to follow exactly the words of his opponent, which he must show to apply equally well to the parallel he has chosen. Real knowledge is necessary for such a contest.

The contestant must be prepared to match his antagonist
in material ways, and for this purpose he carried a calabash
of the type used for traveling, in which were stored objects
necessary for such uses. A famous riddler of the court of
Keawe-nui-a-Umi was Kua-paka'a who carried the bones of
the wind ancestor in his calabash and knew how to summon
each by name. Another was Pikoi-a-ka-alala who brags upon
his rat shooting and wins by punning on the word rat (iole).
He hits an old woman and claims to have "hit a rat" because
of the name haumaka-iole (eyes like a rat) applied to the
aged. He shoots at the topmost batten in the house, called
kua-iole (back of the rat), and again scores.[1] Folktales are
told of Kapunoho the great riddler. Two brothers whom he
encounters in the woods get him to put up losing bets against
their brags, first by pretending to be just covering, instead
of about to open, the oven of birds they are cooking; then by
serving up chicken in an eggshell in answer to the riddle
"chicken for the meat and chicken for the dish"; lastly, by
licking fingers dipped in gravy to fulfil a bet upon "eating
human flesh."[2] Sometimes court language is put to more serious uses. An uprising against a ruling chief is begun, according to tradition, while the chief and his rival are engaged
over a game of checkers (konane). Using the language of the
game, the rival's kahu declares that he knows a move by
which his master can "win the game." When the chief and his
master both give permission for him to "make the move," he
slays the chief who is his master's opponent not only in the
game of checkers but in that of politics as well.[3]

An example of the full riddling match from the Kalapana
legend shows the child challenger of the chief's riddlers playing upon the word hua, which refers to an offspring or fruit-
ing as the result of the swelling out of inner forces. The
rounding of the tuber or rootstock of the food plant is thus
matched with the rounded egg of the fish or bird, the fruit
of a tree with the rounded shapes of sun, moon, and stars in
the heavens. Competitive claims apply in one case to the

1. For. Col. 4: 454–463.   2. Ibid. 5: 418–421.
3. Ibid. 262–265.

depth down to the underworld, in the other to the height into the upperworld. The riddlers chant:

> The moon of Kaulua,
> The moon that bore the first breadfruit of Lanai, . . .
> The fruit of the taro swells down below,
> The fruit of the sweet potato swells down below,
> The fruit of the yam swells down below,
> The fruit of the pia swells down below,
> The fruit of the ape swells down below,
> Down, down, down to Milu and below that!

The boy answers:

> The moon of Kaulua,
> The moon that gave birth to the great turtle and placed it,
> The fruit of the seaweed swells below,
> The egg (hua) of the fish swells below,
> The egg of the turtle swells below,
> The egg of the chicken swells below,
> (At) the foundation of the house of Milu below,
> The foundation of the house of Milu, laid below, below, away
> below.

The men then name the fruits that ripen above ground, banana, breadfruit, mountain apple, and a half dozen others, and conclude,

> The coconut (niu) puts forth fruit above,
> Up to the flying clouds and above that.

The boy answers:

> Kaulua is the moon,
> The moon gives birth to a great turtle,
> At Po-niu-lua (punning on the word coconut) on Lanai is my
> fruit,
> The fruit is the sun that hangs above,
> The fruit is the moon that hangs above,
> The fruit is the stars that hang above,
> The fruit is the cloud that hangs above,

The fruit is the wind that hangs above,
The fruit is the lightning that hangs above,
Up, up above the flying clouds and above that!

The men jeer and say that their fruit still hangs above. The
boy continues:

There it is, there it is,
There hangs the great wind cloud,
The south wind is blowing,
The wind that goes roughly,
Beating the leaves of the trees,
Pushing against the trunks of the trees,
Making them fall below,
The trunk, the branches,
The leaves, the fruit,
Brushed off till they lie bruised and fallen below,
The breadfruit bears fruit above,
Struck by the south wind it falls below. . . .

and after enumerating all the other plants with fruit above
ground which falls below he cries, "Eh! the men are defeated
for lack of fruit that hangs above. Struck by the south wind
it falls below. I have defeated you!"

The illustration is from the most complete story of a riddling match which has been described in Hawaiian legend, of
which we have a number of variants. The competitors are a
powerful riddling chief backed by skilled practitioners, and
a mere youth who comes to avenge his father's death in a
similar match and who turns the old men's jeers back upon
themselves and matches their knowledge with a play of words
always to his own advantage.

LEGEND OF THE RIDDLING CHIEF OF KAUAI

(a) *Nakuina version.* A famous family of riddlers belong to
Kapalaoa on Kauai. The parents teach the art to their four
children. The brothers Hale-pa-iwi (House fenced with bones)
and Hale-pa-niho (House fenced with teeth) become riddlers for
the chief Ka-lani-ali'i-loa at Wailau and so great is their skill

that they are able to outwit all competitors. The sisters marry
on Hawaii, the younger sister to Kane-po-iki of Kona on Hawaii, to whom she teaches all she knows of riddling. He then insists upon challenging the Kauai champion, and his bones, staked
upon the outcome, are left bleaching upon the walls of Ka-lani-
ali'i. His young son Kalapana prepares to avenge his father's
death. Since his mother was not able to acquire the whole
knowledge of her parents' art before their death, she sends the
boy to her older sister Kalaoa who lives at Hilo-pali-ku; there
he becomes proficient in riddling in spite of his still childish appearance. At the Kauai court he is jeered by the nine men inside
the riddling house, just as at home he has been laughed at by
his playmates for his fat stomach and short legs. Only the
chief's younger brother, Keli'i-o-ka-pa'a, befriends him and sees
that he has fair play. In his riddler's calabash he carries grass
to spread out to sleep on, mats of choice weave, a block of wiliwili wood for a pillow, certain dried fish with punning names,
fire sticks, firestones, kindling wood, bundles of cooked meat,
awa root, a wooden dish and an awa dipper and strainer, a
water bottle, a feather holder, fish cords, a black beach stone,
a smooth pebble, a stone hatchet, and loincloths, all of which he
employs to prevent being shamed before the superior luxuries
enjoyed by his competitor. At first he is commanded to stay
outside the house, but when he counters by demanding that his
opponents then remain within they see that this will be incon-
venient and admit him to the house, which is divided into two
parts, one end finished neatly for the chief and his friends, the
other left rough for the contestant. However, by spreading
down his grass and mats and taking out fire, food, and drink,
he makes himself so comfortable that the chiefs are constrained
to begin the contest. At every turn they are outwitted and
finally each is hacked to pieces, according to the terms of the
bet, except the friendly younger brother, who is made chief in
place of the riddler. The boy returns to Hawaii without having
once lowered the sail of his canoe from the moment of setting
forth to that of his landing again.

(b) *Fornander version.* In the days of Pueo-nui-o-Kona, ruling chief of Kauai, the father of Kaipalaoa called Hale-pa-ki is

killed in a riddling contest with the Kauai chief Ka-lani-ali'i-loa.
Death is the wager and so expert in the art is the chief that a
fence of bones has been almost completed about his house. Kaipalaoa lives at Waiakea in Hilo with his mother Wailea who is
skilled in the art of riddling, but who sends him to her sister
Kalena-i-haleauau, wife of Kukui-pahu the ruling chief of Kohala, to complete his education. He then journeys to Wailua,
Kauai, and challenges the chief to a riddling contest, invoking
his own god Kane-pa-iki against the god Kane-ulu-po (god who
presides over the cock crow) invoked by the Kauai chief's instructors. He is met by ridicule because of his childish years,
but outriddles them all and has them all cooked in the oven prepared for himself and the flesh stripped from their bones in revenge for his father's death. (In the story of Pele and Hi'iaka,
Kaipalaoa is named as father of Wahine-omao and husband of
Puna-hoa.)

(c) *Kepakailiula episode.* Kaikipa'ananea is famous for his
skill in boxing, wrestling on all fours, "catch who catch can,"
and riddling. He abducts Kepakailiula's wife and that famous
chief comes to Kauai to recover her and takes the chief Kaunalewa of Waimea as his friend. After a successful boxing contest
he is challenged to answer the chief's riddles on pain of death if
he fails. The chief's public crier who "lives on nothing but the
king's excrement," and is hence avoided by all because of his
offensive smell, Kepakailiula bribes with kind words, fresh garments, and a good meal of pork and vegetables to reveal the
answers to the chief's riddles. These are

> "Step all around, step at the bottom,
>   Leaving, reserving a certain place"

and,

> "The men that stand
> The men that lie down
> The men that are folded."

Both refer to house building; for the first the thatch is trodden
down to the base all around, leaving an opening at the door, and
for the second, "the timbers stand, the battens are laid down,
the grass is folded." The two chiefs have staked their lives on

the result of the match and the oven has been heated by the Kauai chief in the expectation of securing the bones of his defeated antagonist. Upon his defeat, therefore, Kaikipaʻananea is thrown into the oven, there is a general slaughter of his men, and the chief Kaunalewa is made ruler over the island.

(d) *Pukui version.* A Puna chief (unnamed) fond of riddling sends out men to search for fresh riddles and, when they return, poses them with a riddle which must be answered by naming parts of the body containing the syllable ki (joint). As they do not understand what the chief is driving at, one after another suffers death. At last one young man, sent out in search of fresh riddles for the chief, encounters the old court jester who used to invent riddles for the chief's father and grandfather and who knows the chief's riddle. Pitying the young man, he teaches him the answer and how to turn the riddle against the chief himself. Thus the chief is slain and the young man escapes. This ends the practice of riddling in Puna.[4]

(e) *McAllister version.* Ka-mahalo-lani-aliʻi, chief at Moana-lua on Oahu, jealous of the admiration women show for the handsome Keliʻi-kanaka-ole (The chief without followers), challenges him to a riddling match, roasting in the oven to be the stake. Paeli, an upland man who has taught the chief the riddle with which he challenges his rival, takes pity on the handsome fellow and teaches him the answer. The riddle contains the description of a child's life from pregnancy to youth, and Keliʻi acts out realistically the interpretation, then escapes instantly and remains in hiding until the chief's death.[5]

Similar riddling matches are described in Scandinavian chants from the Elder Edda where gods in disguise challenge the old giants for their knowledge, and in such Indian legends as that of Rasalu at the court of the tyrant of the Punjab. In the South Seas riddling speech was a common accom-

4. *AA* 24: 328–329.

5. Judd, *Bul.* 77; Beckwith, "Hawaiian Riddling," *AA* 24: 311–331; Moses Nakuina, *Story of Kalapana,* 1902; For. Col. 4: 574–595, 510–517; 5: 396–405; McAllister, *Bul.* 104: 91–92.

plishment. In Tahiti, the study of enigmas and similes, called paraupiri, was a favorite pastime in the schools and women might take part as teachers. Artificial language, proverbs, and plays on words belonged to the ali'i period of Tahiti, represented by a dominating class similar to that of Samoa, Tonga, and Hawaii.[6] An example of such word contests is the dispute in song between the Raiateans and the Tahitians as to the comparative value of their countries,[7] or the piri sent by the chief of Tubuai to the priests of Tahiti, to answer which a priest of Ta'aroa from Tahiti came to Tubuai.[8] In the Marquesas, schools of learning were established in which pupils learned the legends, genealogies, and chants. The tuhuna o'ono was the reciter who taught the sacred lore, the oho au the building in which he worked. Contests of wit were held between the masters of learning and in ancient times the defeated tuhuna was killed.[9] Among the Maori, separate schools were held for experts in the secular art of agriculture, in the art of astronomy (which belonged to chiefs and priests alone), and in the ancient lore, including medicine and sorcery through incantations.[10] Riddlers must be well informed in the names of plants and stars. Geographical knowledge was important. See, for example, a song telling the place names from Wanga-nui to Wairarapa; the detecting of a plot of revenge through interpreting the riddling words of a chant; the word sparring with which a man who goes courting worsts his host; and Rata's visit to the house of Pou-a-haokai.[11] So in Niue an invading chief overcomes his elder in a bragging contest.[12] In Tonga a "court language" is used by the chiefs which consists in conveying a message in symbolic language. When a Tongan chief asks for "cuttings of yam to complete the planting of his little yam patch" he is asking for a girl as wife, and the chief of whom he asks her answers in courtly language that "the seed

6. Henry, 154.　　　　　　　　7. Ibid., 433–436.
8. JPS 19: 45.　　　　　　　　9. Handy, Bul. 9: 106–107.
10. White 1: 8–16.
11. Taylor, 307–309; Grey, 128; cf. Green, 83–85; JPS 22: 64–66; White 3: 3–4.
12. Loeb, Bul. 32: 26–28, 135.

yams are shriveled and old and it is too early to get plantings from the younger," meaning that one daughter is too old for him and the other not yet mature.[13] A third wife is jealous when she gets as her portion the tail of the fish and the rump of the pig, until her father explains to her that these parts are a symbol of lordship for her children.[14] "The double canoe is raised on the weather shore of Haakame," observes a man who sees a woman sitting on a hibiscus tree and dangling her feet in the sea. This same word play is employed in Samoa of which Mead says, "A village is proud of the reputation of being faigata [difficult] for the visiting orator," and "in this dextrous, graceful play with social forms the Samoans find their chief artistic expression."[15]

13. Gifford, *Bul.* 8: 43–44.   14. *Ibid.*, 36–37.
15. Krämer, 1: 110–112, 302–303, 344–347; *JPS* 34: 134–139.

XXXIII

THE KANA LEGEND

KANA, the stretching kupua, is the hero of a number of local legends explaining gashes in the contour of an island, or markings like a footprint in the rocks, or displacement of rock ledges as in some convulsion of nature. He travels about the islands destroying evil kupua, makes a journey to the entrance to the underworld to restore the stolen sun to his people, and, in association with his mischievous kupua brother Niheu (Sand crab), restores to her home and husband his mother Hina who has been abducted by a Molokai chief called Kapepe'e-kauila (The jagged lightning) and carried away to his home on the hill Haupu.

LEGEND OF KANA AND THE RESCUE OF HINA

(a) *Fornander versions.* The firstborn of Hakalanileo and Hina is born in the form of a rope and brought up by his grandmother Uli in the uplands of Pi'ihonua back of Hilo in a house called Halau-ololo. As the child grows, the house has to be lengthened from mountain to sea in order to contain him. The chief Kapepe'ekauila sails over on the hill Haupu to the island of Mokuola off Hilo bay. Hina climbs upon the hill to take a look about and is borne off to Molokai to become the wife of the Molokai chief. Her husband appeals to his son Niheu, who sends him to Kana, at the sight of whose eyes the father flees terrified. Kana joins the war party, but twice the weight of his hand sinks canoes prepared by all the canoe builders of Hawaii. Finally Uli digs up the canoe Kau-mai-elieli in the uplands of Paliuli. In vain the prophet Moi, brother of Nuakea, warns the Molokai chief of defeat. Kapepe'e trusts to his warriors to defend the hill. The messenger birds Kolea (Plover) and Ulili (Snipe) are sent to reconnoiter and the warrior snout-fish Ke-au-leina-kahi (or a monster turtle) is despatched to destroy the canoe. The warrior is slain with the club Wawa-i-ka-lani and a huge rock rolled from the cliff is caught by Kana and propped with a pebble to check its progress (or the canoe turned aside to avoid a deceptive reef). Niheu lands, breaks down a barricade of ulei and ti leaves, and would have escaped with his mother from the house Hale-uki had not the birds laid hold of his sacred hair and Hina run back when he put up his hands to ward them off. Kana now attempts to raise himself above the hill and the two contestants stretch themselves up into the blue sky. Kana's body becomes like a spider web and to prevent starving he lays himself across to Hawaii, and puts his head in at his grandmother's door. As his feet become plump again with her feeding, Niheu cuts at them with his stone axe to remind him of his task. Uli tells him that the hill Haupu is a giant turtle named Ka-honu-nui-mae-leka (or -maeaea) whose stretching power lies in its flippers. He breaks these off, crushes its back to pieces, and brings Hina back to her husband. From the pieces of the hill Haupu come the turtles today in Hawaiian waters.

(b) *Rice version.* Haka-lani-leo (Listener to the heavenly voice), child of Ku and Uli, weds Haka, ruling chief of Hilo district, and has ten giant sons, then a dwarfish son Niheu with strength and cunning beyond his brothers, and finally Kana, born in the shape of a rope and flung into the pigpen. Uli comes and carries it away to the uplands where she places it in a calabash of water and in a few days it develops into a child and in forty days has acquired forty feet in length and large bright eyes like the moon. Keoloewa abducts the beautiful Hakalanileo while she is out surfing and carries her away in his canoe to Haupu. The husband appeals to her sons, but Niheu is the only one able to tell where she is hidden and as his strength is good only for his own island he is unable to avenge his father on the Molokai chief. Kana appears among them in the form of a child and easily catches in his arms a great fish over which they are contesting in strength. His brothers bind him, but Uli appears and at her bidding he breaks the bonds. Niheu is now encouraged by this new supporter to attempt the Molokai expedition. He tries to fell a tree for canoes but each morning the tree is replaced, until Uli teaches him to make an offering to his ancestors and the forest god Kaikupake'e is caught and made to promise aid for the building. In two days all is complete. Kana in rope form joins Niheu for the launching and allows the canoes to run so swiftly over the shoulders of the giant brothers that all are knocked down and crushed to death. With a single helper called Stone the two brothers set out. The chief's bird scouts find the track of a giant on the sand but see no war party. In spite of Mo-i's warning the Molokai chief trusts to the stretching powers of Haupu and to his warrior swordfish. Stone kills the fish, Niheu fails when five hairs are pulled from his head, and Kana tries the stretching contest with the hill Haupu, using each of his five bodies in succession—human, rope, convolvulus vine, banana, and spider web. Fed and instructed by Uli, as in the other version, he crushes the backs of the turtles and so breaks their stretching power.

(c) *Forbes version.* The hairy chief Ka-pepe'e-kauila desires the beautiful Hina (or Hoohoakalani) and when she and her husband Hakalanileo come to live on the east side of Haupu he takes her for his wife and has all his hairs plucked out to please her. The deserted husband goes to seek a strong man to restore his wife to him but finds even such kupua heroes as Kamalala-walu, Niuloihiki, Kaulu, and Lonokaeho unequal to the task. His kupua son Niheu fails also in bush-pulling and canoe-building tests, but his son Kana merely scratches about in the sand and a double canoe called Kaumueli is ready to set sail. The two brothers embark and while Kana sleeps, Niheu with Kana's rod Waka-i-lani crushes down a ledge on which the canoe runs aground, wards off a wall of water, a monster fish, a sharp-toothed shark, and a turtle, all warriors sent against them by the Molokai chief. In the morning they free the canoe from entangling trees. Niheu, however, fails to capture his mother and the stretching contest follows. One of Kana's legs is named Keanea, the other Kaipanea. It is by pruning the kamani trees that Kapepe'e causes the hill to stretch upward. When these trees are destroyed the power of Haupu is ended.[1]

1. For. Col. 4: 436–449; 5: 518–521; 6: 158, 489–491; Pol. Race 2: 30–33; Rice, 93–102, 105; Thrum (from Forbes), *Tales,* 63–73; Malo, 298–301; Kalakaua, 67–94, 503; Dickey, *HHS Reports* 25: 21.

A comparison of the incidents in this story with similar fiction in the South Seas shows that the legend is not native to Hawaii, however exactly localized and firmly fixed in Hawaiian chronology, but reflects social customs or story themes found also in other parts of the Pacific.

The swimming hill Haupu as the means of the abduction has parallels in other groups. In a Tongan story the chief's rock at his bathing pool hears him wish for Hina from Samoa. It goes away to Samoa, its top covered with sweet-smelling herbs. Hina moves her sleeping mat to the rock and is carried back to the Tongan chief.[2] In Rarotonga it is said of Tinirau, "If he desired to visit any island, his island would take him there."[3] In Mangaia, Tinirau calls his island Motutapu to shore and embarks upon it.[4] In Dobu, Nuakekepoaki's "underwater swift-moving rock is still one of the terrors of the seas to all bold sailors who hug the reef between Dobu and the Trobriands." By means of it he carries off a beauty of Tarawa whom men have courted in vain.[5] The case of Anaelike and her swimming island in Hawaiian romance is similar to these instances. The fact that the word moku, meaning "cut off," is used for both an island and a ship may have given impulse to this myth of the navigable island. The Maori Nga-i-tahu tradition is that "some of the mountains which we now see were ships in days gone by."

The stabilization of the hill Haupu is represented as depending upon either cutting the flippers of the turtle upon which it rests or thinning out the kamani trees that grow at the water's edge. A note in Malo records an enigmatical folktale about the hill Haupu to the effect that the hill sinks and rises again due to the movements of a giant turtle, and only by killing the turtle can the disturbance be stopped. Mo-i, the kupua ruler of Molokai, refuses to do this and the plovers accordingly tear out his eyes and are banished to the barren hill of Maakuewa.[6] In San Cristoval a turtle holds up a rock at Haununu. When an earthquake occurs it clasps the rock, otherwise the island would go under.[7] The legend of the island

2. Collocott, *Bul.* 46: 27–28.   3. *JPS* 8: 118–119.
4. Buck, *Bul.* 122: 12.   5. Fortune, 267–270.
6. Malo, 126–127 note 29.   7. Fox, 133–134.

of Tahiti is that it was once part of Ra'iatea but a pretty
girl named Terehe went to bathe during a time of tapu at
Opoa and the gods were angry. There was a great convulsion
of the earth and the land came away in the shape of a great
fish which swallowed the girl and became possessed by her
spirit, and it swam away and formed the island of Tahiti. In
order to make the land stable its sinews must be cut. All the
warriors cut at the sinews in vain; finally the axe of King
Marere-nui-marua-to'a in the hands of the victorious warrior
Tafa'i cuts of itself and forms the winding gulfs of Tahiti,
after which the land becomes stable.[8]

The stretching contest of two kupua is told in Tahiti of
Hiro and his grandfather, who can reach up only to Hiro's
shoulderblades.[9] The Malay Nigritos of North Borneo say
that two magicians, father and son, contend and the father
wins because the son cannot attain the father's height.[10] The
story suggests the central Polynesian myth of Tane pursuing his father Vatea. In San Cristoval two serpents have a
stretching contest. In the Lau islands the kupua of Thakaun-
drove carries off a man's ornament while he is bathing. The
god Tui Vutu runs after him, wins in a stretching contest,
and brings back the ornament.[11]

The incident of the desecrated head of Niheu which causes
him to lose hold of Hina and permit her to escape to her new
lover is not found in other groups. Hawaiians call by the
name niheu (sand crab) a special method of head dressing,
skewered on top, and plastered with red clay (alaea) such as
is worn by the impersonator of deity who accompanies the
kahuna when he removes the tapu and purifies the land during the ceremonies accompanying the erection of a luakini
heiau.[12] The sacredness of the head of a chief, which must
never be touched if it can be avoided, even the cutting of the
hair being performed by a close relative, is reported also for
the Marquesas and the Lau islands, and is probably true for
other groups.[13]

8. Henry, 437–443, 558.   9. *Ibid.*, 539.
10. Evans, 195.   11. Hocart, 193.
12. Malo, 215 and note 13.
13. Hocart, 44; Handy, *Bul.* 9: 257–259.

But it is not detached incidents alone which correspond with southern fiction; the whole setup of the legend has parallels, perhaps even variants, in famous kupua legends from middle Polynesia. A kupua champion like Kana is represented with the powers of stretching to the heavens and terrifying by his gaze. Like Kana he is born in nonhuman form and preserved by a supernatural relative who recognizes him as a god. He develops human form and, in these South Sea stories, must be at once fed with human food and provided with a loincloth before he is able to live among men (as in similar Hawaiian stories the ceremony of incision is performed in the heiau). He obtains a weapon and a canoe famous in story. He serves as a champion against enemies who have terrorized the country. In many kupua legends he himself becomes a terror and his death is sought even by those he has protected.

The Hiro legend in the middle islands contains some of these traits. In Ra'iatea, Hiro is born a giant. He lives at Uporu on Tahiti with his maternal grandmother Cave.[14] In the Aitutaki version he is born in Enuakura and sails to avenge the death of his younger brother. The clan inimical to him he crushes to death by sending the canoe along their shoulders at the launching.[15] This Aitutaki version resembles the Kaha'i legend, and in fact episodes are readily borrowed from one hero tale to another.

A closer likeness to the kupua champion of the Kana legend is Hono'ura (Honokura, Ono) of Rarotonga, the Tuamotus, Ra'iatea, the Marquesas, Mangaia, and perhaps Rotuma. In Rarotonga, says Henry, Hono'ura is a contemporary of the Naea reputed to have fled to Hawaii. He is poet, warrior, navigator. His name occurs in the genealogies of chiefs. He lives in the mountains of Tahiti and his food consists in edible fernroot and fresh-water fish. His canoe is named Te-ivi-i-kaua. He weds Ata-nui and has a son named The-double-headed. He follows the chief Ta'ihia, wars with the Marquesans, and weds Ina. He dies at Tubai, but others say at Ra'iatea.[16]

14. Henry, 537.   15. *JPS* 12: 137–139.
16. 535–536.

HONO'URA LEGEND

(a) *Marquesan version.* Ono is born in the form of an egg
to Kua-iana-nei when her husband Tana-oa-kauhue is slain by
her second husband Aio. The egg enters a sacred temanu tree
beside the gods' house. His grandfathers Iipo and Iiao learn
this in a dream and rear Ono on air. Two of his brothers in succession are sent with offerings of fish to their grandparents.
They eat the fish on the way, and Ono kills them and tears out
their eyes, but subsequently restores them to life. In human
form Ono makes a great catch of fish. He is girded with a loincloth and engages in wrestling matches, in which he kills Na-
mahi-a-Tanaoa at Taaoa and Na-mahi-o-tu-Fiti, brother of his
Fijian wife Peautona, at Atuona. The Atuona people try to put
him to death. They set him tasks such as lifting a rock from a
pit and cutting down a giant tree, both of which he easily performs and escapes their designs for putting him to death while
so engaged. He bids them cast him into the sea, where he is
caught in a net and his head cut off. The body remains as a
coral formation off the coast. The head is cherished by his sisters and twelve births follow, each birth providing a portion of
Ono's now restored body. He goes again to live with his grandfathers. He sleeps and they plant a tree over him and flee in
fear. While he sleeps darkness reigns; when he stands up his
head towers above the clouds and it is light. In human proportions once more he contends with two magicians in magic and
gets possession of the island of Mohotani, where he dwells thereafter.[17]

(b) *Tuamotu version.* The grandson of a chiefess from Borabora and the chief of Ta'aroa, upland on the island of Tahiti,
weds a chiefess and a son is born "concealed in a great dormant
clod." He is hidden in the cave Po-fatu-ra'a on the side of the
mountain Tahu'a-reva where dwells the god Ra'a, and out of
the clod springs Hono'ura, "a giant with telescopic powers."
Three other shapely brothers are born to his parents. He is discovered in the cave living upon stones, which he alternately

17. Handy, *Bul.* 69: 104–107; Von den Steinen, *ZE* 1933, 364–
365.

swallows and rejects, and his mother hastens to bring him food
and a girdle. When he is brought out before the people his head
towers above the clouds. He is engaged to join an expedition of
vengeance against Tuamotuan warriors who have slain the young
chief Tuo-ha'a and carried away his body to the royal altar at
Takume. His weapon is the great spear Ruaipaoa. No one can
budge the ship Aere in which they are to sail until he gives a
shove. They pursue the enemy to Hiva (Nukuhiva), slay the
demon beast Tu-ma-tahi who guards Hiva, its chief Tu-tapu,
and the warrior billfish Te-a'u-roa who leads the attack on Tahiti and now guards Ta-kume. There they find the bones of the
slain chief, beguile and slay the hosts of the Toarere, and carry
back the chiefess 'Ata-ai (or Maruia) to Tahiti.[18]

(c) *Ra'iatea version* (*from text by Williams in 1846*). The
grandchild of Ta'ihia of Tahiti and child of the warrior chiefess
of Puna-auia is born "a nondescript," placed in a cave, and develops into a man of giant proportions. The well-formed brothers are sent to propitiate him with food and a loincloth in order
that he may join an expedition after masts for the chief's
canoes. When he shows himself his head towers to the skies.
They offer him a royal name, but he calls himself Maui-tua,
Maui-aro (Backwoodsman in front, -behind). In a wrestling
match he overcomes his warrior mother. The terrified father attempts to have him killed by throwing stones down upon him,
all of which he catches in his hands. On a voyage in the ship
Aere the sailors throw him into the sea in his sleep, but his
brothers pull him in and he kills with his spear Rua-i-paoa the
man-devouring beast (pua'a) which has been ravaging Ra'iatea.
On a second expedition after parrot feathers he attacks the Hi-
van warriors and finally leads his brothers against the giant
billfish of Hiva who has overcome Borabora, kills him and the
chief Tu-tapu, and takes back the chiefess Te-puna-ai-ari'i to
the chief Ta'ihia of Tahiti.[19]

(d) *Mangaia version.* Ono comes from the land whence came
an ironwood tree to the valley of Angaruaau which all have tried
in vain to cut down to make weapons out of the wood. It is

18. Henry, 516–534.   19. *JPS* 4: 256–294.

guarded by the demon boar Vaotere. With his spade Rua-i-paku
he kills the boar after uprooting the tree, and carves from the
wood the weapons of today. From the chips spring more ironwood trees. In a chant the destruction of Nukuhiva is lamented.[20]

(e) *Rotuma version.* Foouma is a tall boy who can walk across
the sea. He is brought up in a house built in the bush and grows
a fathom each year up to eight fathoms. He overthrows the people who have exacted tribute from his relatives and sets up and
defends a ruling chief.[21]

Still more closely related to the story of Kana at the hill
Haupu is the Apakura legend as told in the Marquesas. Apakura is descended from Kae and his wife from the island of
women. She has a kupua brother called Pakaha-ima-oa (The
long-armed one with fear-compelling eyes) or Haa-tau-niua.
Without his help, as in the Kana story, the other brother
who takes up her cause is unable to provide a canoe for the
journey of vengeance. Although the motive for revenge varies, the abduction of a wife as against the death of a young
relative, the action of these stories follows exactly the same
pattern, analyzed as follows:

(A) Search for a champion; (A1) one champion after
another discarded; (A2) a long-armed fierce-eyed champion
discovered.

(B) Building of war canoes; (B1) unsuccessful without
aid of the champion; (B2) or some supernatural helper.

(C) Prophetic warnings disregarded by the enemy.

(D) Outguards of the enemy met and destroyed one by
one.

(E) Defeat and death of the enemy; (E1) after a stretching contest.

APAKURA LEGEND

(a) *Marquesas (Handy version from Atuona).* Te-hina-tu-o-
kae, chief of Taaroa, has eight children only two of whom have
natural forms. The two human children are Apekua (called Pei-
kua) and the youngest son E-tia-i-te-toua. Apekua's son Pota-

20. Gill, 81–87.   21. Romilly, *Letters,* 129–138.

a-te-mau is affianced to the daughter of the chief Hatea-motua, but when he goes to get his bride he is not recognized and, in spite of the signs he shows and the warnings of Hatea-motua's priest, he is slain by Hatea-motua. Apekua seeks revenge, but each of her brothers turns a deaf ear to her plea until she comes to E-tia-i-te-toua, who arouses the allied tribes and sets out to build a great war canoe. The tree Aniani-te-ani resists felling and Etia is told in a dream to seek under a seven-branched coral in the sea for his brother Haa-tau-niua, who is called later Pa-kaha-ima-oa, "the long-armed one with fear-compelling eyes." This brother tells Etia where to find the adz with which to fell the tree. When the canoe is completed, Ima-oa stretches out his arm and snatches victims from Hatea-motua's household to serve as the dedicatory sacrifice. In vain Hatea trusts to his three defenders who have the bodies of a living vine which drags down canoes, weeds to entangle them, and a giant octopus to engulf them. All three are slain, the people flee, and Hatea-motua suffers a cruel death in revenge for his treatment of Ape-kua's sacred son.[22]

(b) *Samoa*. Sons of Tu-i-fiti go to make war against the chief Vaea of Vaimauga village (on Upolu). While they sleep Vaea comes down and sets their canoes up in the boughs of the trees. To appease Vaea they offer him their sister Apa-'ula. Her child is born on the return voyage. The brothers kill and eat the child. The mother goes back to Vaea to demand vengeance, but he is dead. His head speaks and tells her to apply to his brother Va'atausili. She meets an uncouth lad who tells her that he is Va'atausili. The lad enters a cave to sleep and his body grows long, straight, and beautiful. He tears up a coconut tree, goes with Apa'ula to Fiji, and kills her brothers. Tu-i-savalalo is the name of the child, from the place Savalalo where the father "stood" (tu) to watch the boat off.[23]

(c) *Moriori (Shand version)*. Apukura avenges herself upon Maurea for the death of her son Tu who goes with his nine brothers, concealed, to the house of Maurea and, being dis-

22. Handy, *Bul.* 69: 64–78; Von den Steinen, *ZE* 1933, 364–365.
23. *JPS* 18: 139–142.

covered, is killed and his eyes gouged out and eaten by the sacred woman Maurea. Apukura seeks her relative Whakatau to avenge her. As she passes along, each person she questions sends her on farther. Whakatau is finally found and proves to her his strength by leaping over a mountain. He refuses her request, she leaves him, he follows and is there before her. A canoe is manned and Whakatau is concealed among the rowers. Pairs of warriors approach and are slain. Whakatau hides in the house of the two leaders and, having put them to death, escapes and burns down the house and all within.[24]

(d) *Maori.* Apakura bears to Tuhuruhuru, son of Rupe's sister, a son named Tuwhakararo, next a daughter named Mairatea, who marries Poporokewa of the Ati-Hapai tribe. Her brother comes to visit her and is killed by a young man who is jealous of his sweetheart's attentions to the stranger. The younger brother at home, named Whakatau-potiki, determines to avenge his death. He gets up a great war party, comes to the home of Poporokewa, gets inside in disguise, kills the chief, and burns the house down with all those within.[25]

(e) *Rarotonga.* The oldest of Apakura's eight brothers becomes jealous of her son Turangataua because the nephew outdoes him in reed casting, and orders him killed and eaten. Apakura goes to seek vengeance, but no one throughout the land is found to avenge her. The sons of Tangaroa-maro-uka become her champions. Only two of her brothers escape and one of these makes the first settlement on Rarotonga. The last encounter is between Vakatau-ii and the oldest brother who has given the order for her son's death. Her champion would have been slain in the fight had not his brothers noosed the opponent.[26]

It may well be argued that such a succession of incidents is an exceedingly natural one for a revenge story which entails a journey overseas, and is to be recognized in the Kaha'i and Laka legends. Nevertheless, the similarity of incident in connection with the particular powers ascribed to the kupua in

24. *JPS* 4: 161–176.   25. Grey, 61–66.
26. *JPS* 30: 53–70.

each case makes it seem probable that the two legends are variants. The stretching contest in the Hawaiian story does not occur in the much grimmer and more realistic Marquesan. It is tempting to connect the curious difference between the habitats of the two heroes—one dwelling in Uli's "house" in the uplands which has to be made larger as the kupua grows longer, the other asleep under a seven-branched coral in the sea—with the Marquesan Ono story, where Ono's body grows into a coral reef while his head is born again to perform added feats. A cave in the uplands is the normal dwelling place of the wild champion in the Hono'ura story, before he is brought into public notice to perform some service for his chief. But the Rarotongan story of the noosing of the enemy in the last extremity makes it clear that the stretching power ascribed to the Hawaiian Kana is derived from his use of the fighting device of the lasso; possibly also his power to hold the canoe in mid-channel from the use of rope and anchor. An intention of this sort in the mind of the story teller is consistent with the concealment of the champion in a packet and with his inertia while Niheu engages in action, as in some versions of the story. It agrees also with the rope form in which he was born and in which Kana is worshiped by jugglers with the prayer,

> O Kana! O Kana!
> Rough line of hala root or bark of hau tree,
> Point and declare as to the sleeper,
> The foster child of Uli,
> Put on your rope body,
> Lay off your human form
> In this trick of yours and mine, O Kana![27]

A contemporary of Honokura in Tuamotuan legend may supply the abduction element of the Hawaiian Kana story. A Napuka legend tells how the beautiful Huarei, betrothed to the famous voyager Moeava, "had not her equal in all the surrounding isles"; how she was abducted by Patira, a giant from a distant place called Marama, so tall that he strode

27. Malo, 298.

from island to island; and how Moeva slew Patira in single
encounter with a stone from his sling as David killed Goli-
ath.[28] Here again the rope element may have significance in
connection with the wielding of the sling.

A journey to restore the sun to a darkened world is told of
Kana in much the same terms as that told of Kahaʻi's expedition in search of his father, with the kupua Niheu, whose
power is said to extend no farther than his own island, playing the part of Alihi.

LEGEND OF KANA RESTORING THE SUN

Niheu treats roughly the messenger of Kahoalei (-liʻi), ruling
chief of Kahiki, and the chief in anger takes away the sun,
moon, and stars from Hawaii. Uli sends Kana with Niheu to
bring them back. As Kana stretches to the sky to reach the
light, Niheu dies of cold and is left behind, but Kana bends over
to Kahiki and drops into the spring of two old relatives, who
give him fire to guide him ahead and wind to bear him behind
until he reaches the border of Kahoalei's land. He finds Uli's
brother Manu-a guarding the pit down which the food is kept
by the people below and handed up to those above. He puts
down a plump black hand which his relatives recognize and fill,
first with food, then with water, then with the birds called Kai-
wea (fishhawk) which signal the day, then birds and the cock
that crows for dawn, finally stars, moon, and sun, all of which
he places in the sky. The chief himself next emerges and returns
with Kana to tour the land, restoring Niheu to life on the way.
When Ka-hoa-lei reaches Hawaii he finds that Kana and Niheu
have both died and he rules there many years.[29]

The legend of the abduction of Hina is laid in the time of
Keoloewa, son of Kamauaua and ruling chief on Molokai,
whose name is in some versions given to the abductor; and
since Niheu is said to have as grandmother Hina-i-kapaʻi-
kua, wife of Nana-maoa of Oahu on the Ulu line, in common
with Kapawa who came from the south and was contempo-

28. *JPS* 28: 31–39.
29. Rice, 102–105; Ellis, *Tour,* 296.

rary with Pili whom Paao brought to rule Hawaii, the chronology harks back to an early period in Hawaiian annals. Nuakea, moreover, wife of Keoloewa, was a granddaughter of the Maweke family on Oahu, and her brother Mo-i is named as a famous kahuna in traditional history. Uli, the mother's mother who saves the unformed kupua from the rubbish heap and cares for him until he takes human form, is Uli-i-uka, sister to Uli-i-kai who taught the art of praying to death, and both are called sisters of Kuheilani, son of Hua-nui-ka-la'ila'i.[30]

Kana is thought of, like the gigantic Lima-loa, as a being who can step from one island to another (seventy miles distant) or wade through the sea from island to island, but some say this is another Kana from the brother of Niheu.[31] On Kauai is shown his footprint where he stepped over from the island of Ni'ihau to Ke'e near Kalalau. On the Puna coast of Hawaii is to be seen that of his brother Niheu, made when he was chasing the mischievous kupua who used to change into a goby fish and nibble Sandcrab's bait, and the hollow in a rock close by where Goby-fish hid from his pursuer. The hill Haupu, where lived the abductor, juts out as a steep headland from the precipitous north side of Molokai between Pelekunu and Halawa valleys. The mounds at the foot of Halawa valley, called "rocks of Kana," are said to have fallen from the heights of Haupu at the time of the fight with Kana; some say Molokini island was thus formed. A notch in the summit ridge of Haleakala on Maui is said to show where Kana leaned across the mountain in his rope form from Haupu to be fed at his grandmother's house in Hilo. The Kauai story is that he stood at Kipukai on Kauai and leaned across to Haupu and fed his starving brother through his own body.

30. Kamakau, *Ke Au Okoa*, July 21, 1870; For. Col. 4: 270.
31. Ellis, *Tour*, 296; Kalakaua, 502–503.

XXXIV

THE STRETCHING-TREE KUPUA

A POLYNESIAN type tale tells of a high chief who weds away from home and departs, leaving tokens with the mother for the child about to be born by which the child's paternity may be recognized. The story falls into an established pattern, but subject to infinite episodic elaborations and varying from romantic to realistic in treatment of details. In Hawaii a favorite carrier for the firstborn when he goes in search of his father is a stretching tree, sometimes spoken of as an "ancestor," who can take either tree or eel form, and this tree kupua in some cases goes by the name of Niu-ola-hiki or Niu-loa-hiki, variously translated Life-giving (ola) or Long or High (loa) coconut (niu) of Kahiki (hiki), the last word, hiki, being also sometimes explained as "traveling" and the whole name being interpreted as Long-traveling-coconut.

The tree as a pathway to another world occurs in Rice's version of the Kaanaelike romance;[1] in the Hi'iaka story, where one of Pele's brothers makes a canoe of his body in order to carry Lohiau back to Kauai after he has been for the second time brought back to life;[2] in the story of Maui's uncle Nu-lo-hiki, who turns himself into a canoe to bring Hina to her lover at Wailua on Kauai and then into a coconut tree up which Maui climbs to visit Makali'i in the heavens;[3] in the romance of Hainakolo, where Niu-loa-hiki is an ancestor god of Keaunini who, in the shape of a tall coconut tree, shakes down a leaf sheath to form a boat for the youth's journey in search of his father[4] and in the form of an eel accompanies him on his wedding journey.[5] In the story of Niauepo'o, who goes to seek his father overseas, an ancestor named Niu-ola-hiki in the form of a stretching tree serves as

1. Rice, 22.   2. *Ibid.*, 16.
3. Dickey, *HHS Reports* 25: 16–17.
4. Westervelt, *Gods and Ghosts*, 173.   5. *Ibid.*, 190.

carrier of the child. Closely related are the stories of Kala-nimanuia and of Namakaokapaoʻo.

STORY OF NIAUEPOʻO

Ku-alakai from Kahiki-nui-alealea meets Hina at Maniania in Ka-u district on Hawaii and leaves her with child. He gives her a feather cape and helmet, his loincloth and red canoe, and bids her send their child to seek him. The son Niauepoʻo asks after his father and desires to visit him, but refuses the sea road. Hina's grandparents give him a bow and an arrow whose flight he is to follow and invoke their ancestor Niu-ola-hiki to bear their child overseas in the form of a lengthening coconut tree. The boy clings to the tip, the mother utters a chant, and the god drops the boy down in Kahiki-nui-alealea. Here he finds the children playing games, competes, wins, and gains a boy companion named Uhu-ula (Red uhu fish). The arrow sent ahead to guide the way falls inside the house of the chief's grand-daughter and when the boys follow the arrow she takes Niaue-poʻo for her husband. The boys are discovered and killed and their bodies thrown into the sea, but the ancestor restores their spirits to life, Uhuula in the form of the red uhu fish and Niauepoʻo in his own form. Each night the boy comes out of the sea and uses the stone walk, bathing pool, loincloth, water gourd, drum, and sleeping mats prepared for the reception of the chief's son. The guards report to the chief, a watch is set, nets arranged to trap him, and as soon as he has eaten food he becomes a human being again and is joyfully received by his father. Hina, however, enraged by his former treatment, comes from overseas to avenge him and turns her husband into an alakai fish. The daughter she bears after her return is named Maniania (trembling), from the cold and fear experienced by her son while being carried overseas, and the name is today attached to the place on Ka-u where she lived.[6]

ROMANCE OF KALANIMANUIA

Ku, ruling chief of Lihue on Oahu, surprises the beautiful Kaunoa at her bathing pool and leaves her with his spear and

6. Green and Pukui, 179–185.

loincloth as tokens for their child, whom he directs to be named, if a boy, Kalanimanuia. The boy is brought up at Kukaniloko in ignorance of his birth until his supposed father scolds him for giving away food too lavishly, when the mother sends him to Ku with the tokens. Ku does not recognize the child and orders him to be thrown into the sea off Kualoa point. Night after night his spirit comes to the heiau, chants a song, and leaves at cockcrow. The heiau kahunas worship the spirit until it gains strength to take on human form. Ku recognizes his son and nets are placed about the heiau to snare the spirit, which is then worked over until it takes first the body of a rat and then becomes almost human in form.

The rat-like boy woos his sister Ihiawaawa, and jeers at her three suitors Hala, Kumunuiaiake, and Aholenuimakaukai as unworthy of her, but she will have nothing to do with him because he looks like a rat. The lovers determine upon a test of beauty, the falling of a suspended cord to determine the winner. The night before the contest Kalanimanuia hears repeated knockings at his door and there enter the soles of his feet (puakuakua), then the knees (moi), the thighs (lolelua), the hair (limuhuna), the eyes (hohoea). The next morning he appears at the contest as a splendid youth. Wind, rain, thunder and lightning hail his coming and the cord tumbles of itself in sign of a high ranking chief.[7]

STORY OF NAMAKAOKAPAO'O

Ku-ula-o-kaha'i (Standing breadfruit of Kaha'i) from Kahiki-papaialewa, a land in the clouds, comes to Oahu and meets Pokai at Hoaeae. On his return to Kahiki he leaves a garment, a girdle, and a feather cloak as tokens of their child's parenthood. Na-maka-o-ka-pao'o (The eyes of the pao'o fish) is born. While a mere baby he pulls up all the potato vines which his supposed father Puali'i has planted. When his father attempts to kill him with an axe, the instrument slips, as the child pronounces a chant, and cuts off Puali'i's own head and the child picks it up and hurls it a distance of five miles. Amau, ruling chief of Oahu, sends men to kill the child, but all are slain and

7. For. Col. 4: 548–553.

finally the chief himself, and the son sets up his mother as ruler over Oahu. He leaves the tokens from his father in a gourd at the foot of the Kaha'i breadfruit which is his father's imper-sonation on Oahu and travels to Hawaii, where he makes friends with some boys with whom he has wagered in a contest with arrows and is adopted as a friend by Namaka-o-ka-i'a, whose father Namaka-o-ka-lani is defending Kona district against Ku, ruling chief of Puna and Ka-u districts. Having established his friend's father, he sails to visit his own father (incomplete).[8]

Parallel forms of the same general pattern occur in south-ern Polynesian groups.

Maori. (*a*) Tu-huruhuru is son of Tini-rau and Hina. Hina flees with her brother Rupe when the child is born, but leaves the child in answer to her husband's supplication. The boys, jealous because he excels in hurling the throwing stick, taunt him as a bastard and the child goes disguised as a slave to his mother's settlement. Obeying his father's instructions, when ordered to bring Rupe water to drink he pours it on his uncle's nose and when his mother dances he sings a charm which loosens her girdle. Both beat him; he escapes and tries to drown himself but is recognized in time, and his mother and her brother return to Tini-rau for the baptism ceremony.[9]

(*b*) Tuahuriri is deserted by his mother's husband, son of the great chief Kahukura-te-paku, because she has had an affair with another man and he feels himself insulted. The mother of a boy whom the child has struck calls him a bastard and he in-quires for his father and goes to seek him at his home in Wai-mea. His party is about to be killed and eaten as strangers when he alludes to "the red battens of my grandfather Kahukura-te-paku's house" and repeats the name given to him by his father. Honorable recognition follows, but he still cherishes a grudge and on another visit is believed to have left a deadly plant which takes off many of his father's people.[10]

(*c*) Tautini-awhitia is born after his father has gone to live at another place. He excels in sport, and the boys taunt him as

8. For. Col. 5: 274–283.   9. White 1: 141–145.
10. *Ibid.* 3: 197–198, 200–202.

"fatherless!" He goes to seek his father in a canoe made of the rewarewa pod and his mother chants a charm for his safety on the sea. He arrives safely at his father's home and is adopted as a slave by a little son of his father and sent to live in the bush. Two pet birds of the same kind as those which his father had brought to relieve his mother's pregnancy craving before he was born are taught to speak and reveal his identity, and he is gladly received with honor.[11]

(d) Wharematangi is son of Ngarue by Uru-te-kakara. Ngarue leaves his wife because her relatives call him lazy, but gives her a name for the child, a dart, and a chant to guide him to his father's house. He excels in dart throwing but is jeered at by his playmates because his father's family has not avenged an insult from another tribe, and goes to seek his father. The dart leads the way, protected by the chant, and he is recognized by its shape and received gladly. An expedition of vengeance is speedily planned.[12]

Marquesas. Kae's son Te-hina-tu-o-Kae (Hina-tuu-o-Kae), child of Hina-i-Vaino'i (Vainoki), is mocked by the boys because he has no father. Hina sends him on her fish brother to the place where Kae lives. The boy bathes in the basin which Kae has prepared for his son; he tears up the bananas and sugar cane. The people, angry, take him to the old tuhuna and he is put in a hole to be strangled the next day. The lad chants his name. Kae comes, recognizes him, and puts him upon his head, thus consecrating the child,[13] or recognizes him only after having him first thrown into an oven.[14]

Tonga. Tongaloa Eitumatupua descends from the sky by a casuarina tree and takes to wife a woman of earth. A boy is born and called Ahoeitu. Tongaloa gives the woman a mountain of earth and a yam for the child's garden. The boy asks for his father. The mother sends him to the sky by way of the tree. She anoints him with coconut oil and gives him a loincloth. The father is catching pigeons. He takes the boy home and gives him

11. White 2: 173–175.   12. Best, *JPS* 34: 296–307.
13. Handy, *Bul.* 69: 56–63; Von den Steinen, *ZE* 1933, 347, 349.
14. *Ibid.*, 363.

kava and food and sends him to play at throwing-stick with his sky brothers. They kill him and eat him but throw away his bones and head. These are gathered up, the brothers are given an emetic, and with Malay apple leaves as covering he is brought to life. The brothers now love him and follow him back to earth, where he displaces the old Tuitonga and rules as far as Uea.[15]

Lau Islands: Legend of Vu. A woman is swallowed by a shark, escapes, and marries the lord of Notho in a strange land. Her son Vu never grows up but is stronger than other children. When they revile him because of his stranger mother he sails away alone to seek his mother's country.[16]

Each of the tales contains special incidents, emphasis upon which suggests the source from which the story is drawn. The tapu bathing basin and other preparations made to receive the expected visitor in the first two stories certainly belong to the Marquesas, where it is customary to prepare such a bathing basin, plant fruit and paper mulberry trees, and raise pigs in anticipation of a firstborn child,[17] and where the account of the arrival of Kae's child born to Vaino'i in the island of women almost exactly duplicates the episode in this Hawaiian story. The name Niauepo'o is a class title in Hawaii for chiefs of the highest rank, born from the marriage of close relatives among high chiefs. The singular episode of the restoration of the different parts of Kalanimanuia's body has a parallel also in a Marquesan story where Ono is killed and torn in pieces, but the twelve sisters save his "head" and each bears a child in the form of one of the missing members.[18] It is a variant of the theme of the ugly man grown handsome (by bathing, cutting up and making over by the gods, and so forth) and in this form is well known in Polynesian as in oriental and African story. For the slipping knife compare a Tonga version of Hina's flight from Sinilau, in which the parents do not recognize the children and attempt to kill

15. Gifford, *Bul.* 8: 25–29, 38–43.   16. Hocart, 212–213.

17. Handy, *Bul.* 9: 43, 75, 79.   18. *Ibid.* 69: 106.

them, but by pronouncing the family names they cause the knife to slip.[19]

The test of beauty in the Kalanimanuia story agrees with the Hawaiian custom of stretching a sacred cord (aha) which is supposed to fall of itself before a ranking chief, and the incident is therefore probably native to Hawaii. A story illustrating this custom is recited by people of Hilo to this day, as follows:

LEGEND OF LONOMAAIKANAKA

At the time when Lono-ma-ai-kanaka was living back of Hilo with some of his chiefs, one of the chiefesses wandered into the back country and lived with the commoners on popolo berries and wild ferns. After a time she longed for fish and proposed an expedition to the coast. At Ka-nuku-o-ka-manu (Beak of the bird) they approached Lono's encampment. Her friends were about to retire, but the chiefess ran forward, the cords fell before her, and she went and lay upon the chests of the chiefs and embraced their heads. Thus for the first time her friends of the back country knew that she was a chiefess of high rank, and they feared for their lives; but she dismissed them with honor.[20]

The stretching-tree kupua, called Niu-ola-hiki or Niu-loa-hiki in Hawaiian story, occurs in the Marquesas, Raro-tonga, and the Tuamotus, generally as an intermediary between earth and heaven, man and the gods, a child and his divine ancestors, youth and manhood; or, in one case, as a symbolic connection between this world and that of the dead. In romance a chief goes by this path to woo a divine chiefess; the canoe in which a hero sails upon adventure is called by this name.

In the Marquesas, Tanaoa outsails his brothers in a canoe made out of a coconut sheath and named Niu-oa-fiti, here translated "Distant coconut at Fiji."[21] Koomahu climbs up

19. Collocott, *Bul.* 46: 32.

20. Kamakau, *Ke Au Okoa,* November 4, 1869; told also to Mrs. Pukui by friends in Hilo.

21. Handy, *Bul.* 69: 91.

to heaven after his sister and, finding her waiting upon old
blind Tapa for whom she is roasting bananas, he restores the
blind woman's eyes with coconut water from the Niu-oa-i-
Fiti, translated "Long coconut palm in Fiji."[22] In the rite to
consecrate a new-born child, two mythical "coconuts" are referred to, called niu-oa-i-fiti and niu-oa-ani, one for furnishing food for the child, the other for the navel cord, but
whether invoked as gods is not made clear.[23] In Rarotonga,
to say that one "climbs the coconut tree Nu-roa-ki-iti" is
equivalent to saying that one commits suicide.[24] Ta'aki goes
to seek his father by the road between heaven and earth called
Nu-roa-ki-iti.[25] In the Tuamotus, in Fagatau, Tahaki climbs
Niu-roa-i-Hiti and finds himself precipitated into Hina's
bathing pool.[26] An Anaa chant quoted by Stimson says,
"The ship of Maui is the shell of the High-coconut-of-Ha-
vaiki." The tree Niu-roa-i-Havaiki grows from the head of
Tuna-te-vai-ora, the demigod whose wife Hina-tuatua-a-
kakai comes to Havaiki after a husband and becomes Maui-
tikitiki's wife.[27] In the Chant of Rua, a canoe called Niu-roa-
i-hiti is constructed in Nuku-tavake to sail to Vahitahi, which
was the original home of the Nuku-tavake people. The story
proceeds:

The chief as high priest performs ceremonies proper for the
occasion and despatches heralds to call the people together to
the court before the House-of-learning. During the ceremony
he becomes possessed by the god, who reveals that the demon
god Rua-tuputupua has taken possession of the ship. Chants
are uttered to free the ship from the power of the demon, invoking Tane, Tagaroa, Tu. Te-tahi the captain chants songs.
He sends one herald aloft to watch for land birds, then another,
who sees birds riding the waves. The land of Vahitahi, lying
twenty miles distant from Nuku-tavake, is now in sight. The
seer at Vahitahi foresees the ship's arrival and knows that it is
possessed by a demon. Every effort is now made to exorcise the

22. Von den Steinen, *ZE* 1933, 370–373.
23. Handy, *Bul.* 69: 91.   24. Smith, *JPS* 30: 202.
25. *Ibid.* 4.   26. Stimson, *Bul.* 127: 68.
27. Stimson, *ibid.* 33–35.

demon. The ship is hauled upon the reef with erotic songs intended to arouse the men to their highest pitch of energy. The songs describe the safe passage of the reef, the bringing of the ship to shore, its lodging there, and precautions to prevent the demon from escaping on land. All proceed in file to the temple. The demon is exorcised into a pool of fresh water and the ship cleansed with smoke from its influence.[28]

Besides these allusions to a stretching tree or a swift canoe with a name obviously a variant of that of the Hawaiian kupua, there are a number of legends told in the South Seas where a lengthening unnamed tree serves as roadway between earth and heaven. In Mangaia, Tane climbs a tree beset by insects whose top seems to reach the sky, from which he shakes down nuts upon his own homeland.[29] A ladder-like tree beset by insects is alluded to in the Samoan Ahoeitu story.[30] In one Samoan story a lad goes up to the moon on a tree;[31] in another a boy sent to climb a tree at an ogre's house finds that it stretches upward when he attempts to pick a nut.[32] In Tonga, a child born with strength in his hands goes up to visit his father in the sky on a casuarina tree that grows up from his own staff.[33] In the Banks islands a lengthening casuarina tree saves Qat and his brothers from Qasavara.[34] In Dobu a scabby-skinned man, deserted by his fellows, travels to the sky on a lengthening casuarina tree.[35] In San Cristoval, brothers cause a betel tree to stretch in order to rid themselves of a younger brother, and it lengthens to the skies and bends over to the boy's home.[36] A lengthening areca tree which a man climbs after nuts for his brother carries a man to the country of the skies.[37] In a tale from North Borneo, a man escapes to the sky by a lengthening tree which pigs, woodpeckers, and porcupines are attempting to fell.[38] In

28. Stimson MS.   29. Gill, 111–112.
30. Turner, 199–200.   31. *Ibid.,* 203.
32. Krämer 1: 144.
33. Fison, 49–57; Gifford, *Bul.* 8: 38–40.
34. Codrington, 164–166.   35. Fortune, 219.
36. Fox, 155, 159–160.   37. *Ibid.,* 121–123.
38. Evans, 251–255.

Whitsuntide island of the New Hebrides, Tagaro comes to earth and begets a son who follows him to the skies on an arrow which turns into an aerial tree root.[39] Again, a grandmother sends a child up a tree after fruit and when he gives her none she causes the tree to lengthen.[40] In the Lau islands the daughter of Turi climbed a tree and "flew like a bird right up to heaven and married the god Mbengga."[41]

In Hawaii, according to information given by a worshiper of Kane-huna-moku, the kupua Niu-ola-hiki in his tree form is the path that leads to the land of the gods, a land of "sacred coconuts," where Kane, Lono, and Kanaloa first made man. Here the "coconuts" are phallic symbols. The chant addressed to Ku and Hina by herb pickers is identical with that by which the mother of Niauepo'o summons the boy's ancestor to bear him safely to the far land of his father:

> O Life-giving coconut!
> Budded in Kahiki,
> Rooted in Kahiki,
> Forming a trunk in Kahiki,
> Bearing leaves in Kahiki,
> Bearing fruit in Kahiki,
> Ripened in Kahiki!

The myth of the "life-giving," or "far-traveling" coconut palm of Kahiki or Avaiki may be regarded as the symbolic expression throughout Polynesia of the blood tie which connects a migrating people to their original ancestral line. It is a claim upon paternal recognition. It is a living impersonation of the family line which carries the genealogy of the newborn child back over whatever distance of time or space to his ultimate ancestry and to all the honors and dignities which such ancestry implies. It is the claim made by a migrating people for recognition by others of their line of their divine patrimony. It probably has phallic meaning in connection with the sexual life of the child who becomes himself

39. Codrington, 169.   40. *Anthropos* 7: 42–44.
41. Hocart, 200.

an element in the preservation of the family line. The Tuamotu references strongly suggest ritual symbolism. So also
the eel form in Hawaii, employed, like the coconut palm and
the canoe, as a phallic symbol.

XXXV

ROMANCE OF THE SWIMMER

IN Hawaiian romantic fiction the treatment of kupua figures differs from that employed in the hero story, where exaggerated feats of prowess, often humorously treated, keep the level of the story above that of ordinary life. In romance the atmosphere changes. Love and marriage are always the theme, and chiefs of unexceptionable rank—hence of divine ancestry—the actors, with family gods as their protectors and animate nature to aid and applaud their moments of apotheosis. The world in which such persons live in actual society, built up as it is out of fictional illusion, is here represented in all the complexity of natural form with which their island world keeps them constantly surrounded. Lands beyond the horizon, dimly remembered as once within the range of voyagers, are here transmuted into dwellings in the air—a more direct reality to an island-isolated people because of the shapes and movements of clouds ever shifting into imitations of earth, of the flights of birds in the air and the swaying of wind in the treetops, and the indescribable sharpness of cliff lines and mountain slopes which at sunrise and sunset send their shadows across from island to neighboring island, or the roar of thunder, the patter of hail, and the sheet of lightning from the sky, and the constant sound of the sea broken into so many changing voices. The abundant life of the sea and the myriad forms of the forest are all worked into the living pattern of a society of endowed beings whose emotional reactions and solutions of problems of action are undoubtedly based upon those of the men and women who were their prototypes in actual life. Certain motives which recur, like the transformation forms with which a divinity attempts to frighten a wooer, may be fairy-tale embellishments, but they belong to the philosophy of life according to which natural forms are believed to be born into family lines, and hence to belong, as a living impersonation, to their descendants.

Some characteristics of kupua hero tales are here also, such as localization, place and family names. Themes are Polynesian in character and incident and whole tales are found duplicated in South Sea groups. But the Pele cycle certainly dominates these romances, if not that of Papa or Haumea. As in the Pele romances woman plays a leading role. She is the desired one, set apart from her fellows by supreme rank; the problem ever foremost is to find a suitable parent for her firstborn. Or she may be the helpful sister, virgin and gifted with special powers of sorcery or of foresight. Romantic as is the general tone of the story, the composer often passes into essentially novelistic treatment in passages so close to realism that the divinity is lost in the woman and the god in the human. Always, however, it is necessary to remember that, according to the fiction, if you will, of old Hawaiian life, rank is an actual acknowledgment of divinity and the human is the god.

The romantic tale of Aukelenuiaiku is said to have originated in Kahiki and to be one of the most noted of all Hawaiian stories. It tells of the wooing of Namakaokaha'i, older sister of Pele and related to the family of gods who rule the heavens, by a stranger chief who is aided by a mo'o ancestor to cross the seas, escape the jealousy of his brothers and every attack launched upon him by the goddess and her relatives, and finally to become her husband and rule over her desolated land. Later he becomes enamored of her younger sister and eventually leaves the land and arrives ultimately at Hawaii.

ROMANCE OF AUKELENUIAIKU

(a) *Fornander version.* Aukele-nui-a-iku (Far-swimming son of Iku) is the eleventh and favorite son of Iku and Kapapaiakea in Kuaihelani. His ten older brothers, Ke-kama-kahi-nui-aiku, Ku-aiku, Noho-aiku, Hele-aiku, Kapukapu-aiku, Hea-aiku, Lono-ea-aiku, Na-aiku, Noi-aiku, Iku-mai-lani, are all great boxers, able to overcome at a single blow Kealohi-kikau-pea, champion boxer of Kauai; the three champions of Oahu

named Kaikipaʻa-nanea, Kupukupu-kehai-ka-lani, Kupukupu-
kehai-iaku; and Kakaalaneo, champion of Maui; but they are
afraid to meet Kepakailiula of Hawaii and return home to boast
of their achievements.

They hate Aukele because their father has given to him the
inheritance of the kingdom instead of to his older brothers.
When he approaches the games they break up his arrow, which
they recognize as made differently from their own arrows, and
attempt to kill him, but he wrestles with and overcomes one
brother after another. They throw him into the pit of the
ancestress Ka-moʻo-inanea who eats men, but she spares her
young relative, describes to him the vacant land ruled over by
Na-maka-o-kahaʻi (The eyes of Kahaʻi) whose inhabitants, with
the exception of her immediate family, have been devoured by
spirits, and gives him a food-providing leaf, an axe, a knife, a
bit of her tail which contains her "real body" (kino maoli), her
feather skirt (pa-u) and kahili, which have the power to protect
him from flames and to reduce his enemies to ashes, and a box
containing the god Lonoikoualiʻi to warn him of approaching
danger. She then lifts him up out of the pit and he returns to his
brothers. A second attempt upon his life is made by leaving him
in a water hole with a stone rolled over the top, but a kind-
hearted brother releases him.

The brothers determine to leave the land of Kuaihelani. He
insists upon accompanying them and on the voyage the food-
providing leaf keeps them from starving. Arrived at Namakao-
kahaʻi's country the brothers are rash enough to declare war
and are all reduced to ashes when she turns her skirt against
them; only Aukele is saved by swimming ashore. Taught by his
god, he is able to win over the rat and moʻo servants Upoho and
Haapuainanea whom he first encounters and to persuade the
four bird brothers Kanemoe, Kaneapua, Leapua, and Kahau-
mana to promise him their sister in marriage. At the goddess's
house he reduces the dog Moela to ashes with his ancestor's
skirt, and avoids the poisoned food set before him, eating instead out of the bird brothers' food containers. Finally he prays
to them all by name and the goddess calls him to her, but he
avoids approaching her until she has first come to him. The goddess shows him all her forms and teaches him her magic powers

except the art of flying, and she makes him ruler over all her land.

He is however obliged to exert his power to overcome other dangerous relatives. The bird Halulu carries him to his nest on the cliff and keeps him there to be devoured, but he cuts off one wing after the other with his magic knife and finally the head, and the bird's mate lets him down on a rainbow to earth. Na-maka sends him to the heavens to make acquaintance with her relatives. The bird brothers have taught him to fly, and he out-distances his escort and has a successful tussle with Kuwahailo, who hurls lightning and thunder rocks against him.

The son of Aukele's oldest brother, Kau-mai-iluna-o-holani-ku (Rising above Holani-ku), was a playmate of his. He was a boy so sacred that nothing he asked could be denied and it was through his intercession that Aukele was allowed to join the sailing party. Aukele now mourns his death and his wife sends him after the water of life to restore his dead relatives to life. It is kept by Ka-moho-ali'i in a deep pit reached by flying east-ward to the place where the sun comes up and then descending noiselessly, directed by his granduncles Kane-naenae and Kane-naiau stationed at the brink of the pit, by Hawewe and Kue-manu farther down, and by an old blind grandaunt at the bot-tom, called old woman Kaikapu, sister of Kamo'o-inanea and Lono-ikouali'i, whose eyes he heals with two coconut shoots. She blackens his hands to look like Kamohoali'i's and the people below hand up the gourd Huawai-a-ka-ola (Water gourd of life) inside the net Palea-i-keahe-lanalana. He picks up the stick Ho'oleheleheki'i, and returns too swiftly to be overtaken by the angry owner. His own attempt to use the water to re-store his brothers and nephew is unsuccessful, but, with the few drops remaining, his wife brings them all to life and he shares the rule with them and even gives them his wife as well.

Finally Aukele's little son Ka-uila-nui-makaeha-i-ka-lani gets a box on the head from his sacred cousin, son of the oldest brother. The angry child curses him, his father, and uncles as "food of maggots rotting at the sea bottom." Enraged at the insult, the brothers set sail with their son and are drowned at sea.

As time passes Aukele is attracted by his wife's young cous-

ins Pele and Hiʻiaka and pretends to go fishing in order to meet
them. His wife discovers this and drives them from the country.
They migrate first to Kauai, whence they are driven again, and
flee from island to island until they finally reach Hawaii. Soon
after, Aukele decides to return to his old home. Kanemoe makes
a spirit body to remain with his sister and himself accompanies
Aukele. They pass to Kuaihelani and find the place empty. Ka-
moʻo-inanea informs them that the family have gone to Kauai
to live and they go on to the Hawaiian group. At Kauai, Iku
first defeated Ku-koae and became ruler over the island, but
later a battle was fought over Aukele's pretty sister, Kaomea-
aiku, and Ku-koae won the contest.[1]

(b) *Westervelt version.* Kukali is born at Kalapana on Hawaii, the son of a kahuna. Ku is his god. His father teaches him
magic until he becomes a powerful kahuna and gives him a
magic banana skin always full of fruit. He sets out on distant
travels. He is thrown into a pit with others and kills the bird
Halulu which sweeps the pit with its wing to devour men. He
descends the bottomless pit containing the water of life and is
warned by the wizard guardian against eating ripe fruit. He
finds Na-maka-eha (Four eyes), the sister of Halulu, successfully meets tests of strength, and returns to his old home on
Hawaii.[2]

(c) *Dibble version.* Waikele-nui-aiku is the favorite son of the
ten sons of Waiku. They have one sister. His brothers are jealous and cast him into a pit belonging to Holonae-ole, but the
kindly older brother charges her to take care of her relative and
he escapes. He flees to the country of Ka-moho-aliʻi, where he is
thrown into a pit with others but escapes by interpreting their
dreams (contamination with the Joseph story).[3]

Analysis of the Aukele romance shows it to belong to a
type of worldwide distribution known as the Jason type. The
familiar story is that of a hero who, having incurred the en-
mity of his family at home, travels to a far country and, after

1. Col. 4: 32–111.   2. *Gods and Ghosts,* 66–73.
3. 17.

meeting successfully a number of dangerous tests, secures a
sorceress as wife whom he later abandons for another woman.
Analysis:

(A) The hero leaves home (A1) after escaping death at
the hands of his brothers.

(B) He is protected by a family deity, (B1) by magic objects, (B2) by magic powers.

(C) In a far land he secures a sorceress as wife.

(D) He overcomes dangers, such as (D1) guards of the
chiefess, (D2) dangerous food, (D3) a giant bird, (D4)
gods of the heavens, (D5) transformation tests.

(E) He makes a journey to the underworld after (E1)
the water of life, (E2) sun, moon, and stars, (E3) the spirit
of a dead friend.

(F) He becomes enamored of a younger relative.

(G) He leaves the land, (G1) is driven out, (G2) is killed.

The names of the characters in this story have very old
genealogical associations. The title aiku in Tahiti is almost
equivalent to the Hawaiian akua, implying divinity or divine
rank. In Hawaii two classes of chiefs are named: one the
Iku-pau, descended from Kane or Kumuhonua and classed
as high chiefs; the other the Iku-nuʻu, or ordinary chiefs.[4]
Kapapaiakea, mother of Aukele, is Kapapaiakele, wife of
Laka on the genealogy of Hulihonua. Ke-alohi-kikaupea, one
of the contemporaries named as champion in a wrestling
match, appears on the genealogies as a chief of Kauai contemporary with the Kakuhihewa family of Oahu, from whom
Kauai is called in chant "island of Ke-alohi-kikaupea."

A number of incidents are common to other Hawaiian romances. The main pattern belongs to a group of similar
stories centering about the Pele family and the wooing of a
daughter of Kuwahailo, the man-eating god in the heavens.
The shaken skirt (pau), which reduces all to ashes, occurs
again in the Laieikawai romance and connects the actor directly with the Pele family. The moʻo ancestress of both
parties in a marriage is a feature common to many other Hawaiian romances. The son Lightning-flashing-in-the-heavens

4. For. Pol. Race 1: 41–42.

reappears in an explanatory folktale from Ka-u district on Hawaii which tells how the wiliwili trees on the beach of Paula came to have their shape and why there are mackerel in the sea.

STORY OF MOHO-LANI

Moho-lani (Divine mo'o) is the firstborn of four sisters and the only one to have a husband. The sisters are accordingly jealous. Two sirens of the sea lure away the husband and the sister goes from one to another begging to know what has become of him, but they turn her away with insulting words. Moho-lani appeals to the guardian gods of her son and he comes to her rescue in his lightning body. It glances over the sea bottom, cuts in pieces the sirens (from whose bodies spring mackerel), and restores the lost husband. The ungracious sisters are transformed into the crooked, spare-leafed trees that grow upon the beach.[5]

The mo'o woman in this story would seem to bear close relation to the goddess of the mo'o family wooed by Aukele, and the rescue of the husband from the toils of the sirens to be another form of the infidelity theme, in which, as in the Aukele story, vengeance is wrought upon the ladies of whose charms he has been made the victim.

Na-maka-o-kaha'i, the heroine of the story, appears in the Pele cycle as an older sister of the fire goddess. She is daughter of Ku-waha-ilo and Haumea in Holaniku, to whom also are born Pele-honua-mea, the Hi'iaka sisters, the Kama brothers, and the bird Halulu. Aukelenuiaiku becomes her husband in Kahiki, then later the husband of Pele, and it is because of this quarrel that Pele, the Hi'iaka sisters, Malulani, and Kaohelo migrate to Hawaii.[6] In Thrum's Kanehuna-moku myth she is called the chiefess of the Mu and Menehune people when they are summoned to build the watercourse for Kikiaola at Waimea on Kauai, and in that

5. Green, 96–99.
6. 'N. Emerson, *Pele*, ix, xiv–xv; Westervelt, *Volcanoes*, 7–13; Thrum, *More Tales*, 104–107; For. Col. 5: 576.

story she disappears on the land of Kane-huna-moku.[7] Her brothers in the Aukele legend have bodies of rock and her child by Aukele has two bodies, one of rock and one human. She herself has three supernatural bodies, a fire, a cliff (pali), a sea, besides the power of flying, of coming to life again if cut up into bits, and of reducing others to ashes by turning her skirt (pa-u) upon them. The land where she lives is called Ka-la-ke'e-nui-a-Kane (Great crooked sun of Kane) and is devoid of human life.

The name of the stranger is variously written as Aukele, Waikele, Kukali. Waukele (or Aukele) means "excellence in swimming" and, as his wife knows him by the name of "Man of the sea" (Kanaka-o-kai), as in the related Anaelike story, this seems to be its derivation. "Slayer of the great bird Halulu" seems, from its mention in Andrews's early dictionary, to be the feat for which Aukele is most famous. Halulu is the name of an ancient heiau situated on the coast of Kaunolu district on the island of Lanai and the man-devouring nature of the bird Halulu may refer to the human sacrifices demanded by the deity of the heiau. On the plateau above the heiau is a place called Namakaokaha'i. The rock islet on the east side of the Kaholo cliff off the west bank of Kaunolu has the name of Kaneapua, one of the bird brothers in the romance, and two carved stones worshiped by fishermen of Lanai have the names Rae(Lea?)- and Kane-apua. It is at Kaunolu that Kaneapua intercepts Wahanui on his voyage to the land of Kane and Kanaloa.[8] This identity of names between places on Lanai and the figures in the romance suggests that the composer has in mind the Lanai background in working up his romance. Lanai was thought of as a land of spirits ruled by the goddess Pahulu until they were finally driven out and obliged to flee to other islands. If the name of Aukele the swimmer is equivalent to that of Kelekele-iaku, grandchild of Kamaunuaniho, whose family dominated Molokai, and brother of Kamapua'a, the affair of the hog-man with Pele may have had its prototype in the highly elaborated and ancient tale of Aukele's winning of Namakaokaha'i. If

7. *HAA* 1929, 93–96.   8. Emory, *Bul.* 12: 12–13.

Lono is the god of the Kamaunu family, a connection with that family may be suggested by the name Lono-i-kou-aliʻi given to Aukele's god which he has from his moʻo ancestress. It is the same as the god Lono-i-ka-ou-aliʻi said to be brought by Laʻa from Raʻiatea and taken into the heiau at Wailua on Kauai when he landed,[9] and of the god Lono-i-ke-au-aliʻi (Lono in the period of chiefs) listed by Kalakaua among the gods worshiped in the heiau on Oahu.[10] The name of the goddess herself in connection with temple worship may be translated "The-eyes-of-the-sacrificed-one" (ka haʻi) and hence may have reference to the custom of offering the eyes of man or fish in a cup of kava in honor of Kahoaliʻi, who is probably identical with Ka-ou-aliʻi and Kou-aliʻi of the Aukele story.

9. For. Pol. Race 2: 60.   10. 50.

XXXVI

ROMANCE OF THE ISLAND OF VIRGINS

IT will be remembered that the story of Ola's building of the famous watercourse Kikiola concludes with the refusal by Namakaokaha'i, chiefess of the Mu and Menehune people, of an offer of marriage and her disappearance with her people on the floating land of Kane-huna-moku. Kaanaelike (Anelike) in the story of the "rolling" island of Ulu-ka'a is the same chiefess under another name. Ulu-ka'a and Kane-huna-moku are interchangeable names for that garden of delight in which the gods first placed Kumuhonua and his wife, ancestors of the Hawaiian people. Ku-waha-ilo is the parent of Anaelike as of Namaka-o-kaha'i in the heavens. The lover who comes swimming to her over the sea is the Man-of-the-sea of Namaka under another name. Even the poisoned food of the Aukele test is here suggested, although with a quite different turn. The son Eyebrows-burnt-off of Kaanaelike by her stranger husband is Lightning-flashing-in-the-heavens whom Namaka bore to Aukele. The concluding infidelity motive connects the story unmistakably with the Pele legend with its outgush of fire which desolates the whole land.

ROMANCE OF KAANAELIKE

(a) *Rice version.* Kaana-e-like (Striving to be alike), the granddaughter of Ku-waha-ilo, lives with her parents and eleven sisters on the floating island of the gods named Uluka'a. Keawe-aoho, ruling chief of Hawaii at Waipio, is greatly beloved for his good government. However, he shows such favoritism toward his fishermen that his head steward is jealous and withholds the food which the chief invariably portions out to them after a day's fishing. They are angry and on the next fishing expedition persuade him to swim out after a lost oar and abandon him in the sea, where he might have perished had not Ku-waha-ilo in the heavens coveted him as a husband for his granddaughter and sent the floating island to his side.

The chief finds food plants growing and recovers strength and beauty. He teaches Kaanaelike and her sisters, who have hitherto subsisted on berries and edible roots, how to make fire with fire sticks and to eat cooked food. "Man of the sea" he calls himself, and her parents send her to the heavens on a stretching coconut sprout to ask her grandfather's permission to marry the stranger. Kuwahailo is a man-eater. When he approaches, the earth quakes, trees bend, winds blow; first comes his tongue licking up his victims, then his body follows. Before entering his cave house he hangs up his tongue outside. He would have killed the girl whom he finds inside, but her sacred skirt protects her and he recognizes his grandchild. He instructs her to marry the chief and promises on his part to cease eating men. Then he lowers her to earth seated on the crook of his tongue, she weds the stranger, and a feast follows.

Meanwhile the bird sisters of the chief have been searching for him and they come to him in a dream and tell him how badly things are going at home since he left them. He grieves and the chiefess orders a canoe to be built for him with red sails, ropes, and clothing for the sailors. She warns him not to look back and follows him on the floating island as he is rowed to shore, but when he looks back the island has disappeared. He reëstablishes his rule on Hawaii and puts to death the guilty fishermen and steward.

His child is born on the floating island and named Na-kue-maka-pau-i-ke-ahi (Eyebrows burnt off) because of an accident to himself when he built the first fire for Kaanaelike. By the time the boy is six days old he can play games with the other boys and he goes to seek his father in a red canoe. He gives the waiting sailors outside a sign that if he is received the smoke will blow seaward, if killed it will blow landward. The attendants attempt to stop the boy and inflict injuries but he gets through to his father's house and sits on his lap and the smoke turns and blows seaward. The mother however prepares to avenge the boy's injuries. She comes with her eleven beautiful sisters who resemble herself, and sends each ashore in succession; but the

chief, warned by his son, sends each to a house prepared for her
and takes none but his wife.

There is a reconciliation and the chief and his son return to
Uluka'a, where they live happily until he is attracted by the
younger sister, Ke-ahi-wela. One day he pretends to go fishing,
another day bird hunting in order to be with her. He is detected
and the wife sends a fiery flood which consumes him and all on
the land save herself, the son, and the sister, who has turned herself into a heap of rock and finally escapes down the gullet of
the dog Ku-ilio-loa (Ku long dog) who has been sent to bring
her home to her foster parents; but not before Kaanaelike cuts
off its ears and tail with her sacred skirt, and hence bob-tailed
dogs today. The dog goes to live on Kauai, the son leaves his
mother, and she lives alone on the still burning island Uluka'a.[1]

(*b*) *Green version.* To Kane-ko-kai (Kane who owns the sea)
belongs the rolling island of Uala-ka'a (or koa) where he places
his twelve pretty daughters. The oldest, Analike (Almost alike),
swims to Hawaii and takes as her husband the handsome Kanaka-o-kai (Man of the sea) but tires of him and returns swimming to her island. He wanders inconsolable until instructed by
an old woman how to regain her by swimming past the Island-
of-silence covered with flowering red purslane, past the Island-
of-darkness, until he reaches a third island, shaped round like
a potato (uala), where he must land but avoid mistaking any of
her pretty sisters for his wife. All goes well and the wife receives him joyfully. Their uncooked food does not please him and
there is a great outcry among the girls when he cooks and eats
the plants to which he is accustomed at home. Kane-ko-kai
sends his youngest daughter mounted on the back of a huge dog
to reassure them and advise them to eat the food which the man
of Hawaii offers them.[2]

(*c*) *Lydgate version.* The chief Keawe-ahu of Kona, Hawaii,
rules harshly and is hence abandoned at sea by a ruse. A land
teeming with good things floats up beside him and he finds there
a wife in the person of a little Menehune girl who lives with her

1. 19–31.   2. 115–118.

father and mother and whom he teaches to make fire and eat cooked food. Her name is Ana-like, their child is Na-maka-o-ke-ahi (The light of the fireside). He becomes homesick and one day when the island floats near the Kona coast he seizes up the child and swims ashore.[3]

In this tale, as in many Hawaiian romances, the story tells of a highborn maiden kept apart in a tapu place, surrounded by maidens, and watched over by careful guardians until a suitable match can be found for their ward. The setting here is that of one of the floating islands of the gods. The journey of the child to seek his unknown father in a distant land, the mother's revenge for indignities to the child, here transferred to jealous wrath for the infidelity of the husband, are both incidents common to this group of romances. The broken tapu against looking back which results in the disappearance of the floating island, common also to the Maui cycle where the broken tapu prevents the successful joining of the fished-up island to the Hawaiian group, may perhaps be meant to symbolize the unsuccessful union between the two families. The recognition test, found also by Stimson in Anaa, where Te-horo-ruga comes from Vavau to woo Mo-ho-tu in the Po and the girl hides while her attendant maidens try vainly to tempt Te-horo by their charms, occurs in the Pele and Hiʻiaka story where Pahoa comes to Pele, who conceals herself in the guise of an old woman but is recognized by the heat of her hand.

The whole story represents a type thoroughly Polynesian in color but well known to European romance and folktale as the Fairy Mistress type. The taking of a wife who is more than human, the husband's homesickness (characteristically induced in this Hawaiian version by spirit sisters in the forms of bird messengers from home), the broken tapu, the search for the lost lover, the warning by the child of danger from his offended wife, the identification test for the recovery of the wife—all these are familiar incidents of worldwide distribution, perhaps most closely paralleled, although representing

3. Given by Mrs. S. Polani of Kauai, *HAA* 1924, 134–137.

a quite different background, in the American Indian tale of the Buffalo wife.

As a Polynesian story it may be reckoned as a Hawaiian variant of the story of Kae at the island of women.

ROMANCE OF KAE AND THE ISLAND OF WOMEN

Marquesas. Kae (Drooler) is abandoned at sea, swallowed by a fish, cuts his way out and reaches an island of women (Vainoki, Vaino'i) where the women seek pandanus roots as husbands. He weds Hina-i-Vaino'i to whom he teaches natural methods of childbirth without, as was the custom, cutting open the mother. When he finds that he as a mortal has wedded an immortal who can, when her hair grows gray, ride the surf and become young again while he remains as before, he becomes homesick and Hina sends him home on her whale brother Tunuanui. He prepares a house, bathing pool, and garden for his son Hina-tupu-o-Kae who is to follow him. When the boy comes on the whale Tunua-iki and treats the house, pool, and garden as his own, the guards are about to have him killed, but he is saved by a chant repeating his name and those of his family. Either he or Kae forgets to send the whale brother home properly but nothing comes of it.[4] Kena comes to a similar land of women in the second Havai'i when he goes to seek his lost wife.[5]

Maori. Tura joins Whiro's canoe party but when it enters a whirlpool he catches the overhanging boughs of a tree and lives among the Nuku-mai-tore, to whom he teaches the use of fire, the art of cooking, and the natural way of childbirth together with the ceremonies attending the birth of a child. When his wife Turakihau (Hina-kura) discovers gray hairs on his head he goes off and lives alone and becomes covered with sores. He lives upon the meat from a stranded whale until his son by his former wife comes to rescue him. From Tura proceed diseases and the incantations and ceremonies for their cure.[6]

4. Von den Steinen, *ZE* 1933: (Vaitahu) 347–349, (Atuona) 360–364; Handy, *Bul.* 69: 56–63.

5. *Ibid.* 119.

6. White 2: 8–15, 17–19; *JPS* 21: 110–116.

The Maori say that in Hawaiki-raro live the Nuku-mai-toro "in the midst of plenty," whose hair never turns gray, who eat raw food, and cut open women at childbirth.[7]

Rarotonga. Chief Ati of Rarotonga weds a fairy woman to whom he teaches natural delivery and she begs him to come to spirit land to teach the art there, but he is unable to follow her when she returns thither.[8]

The Marquesans say that in Rarotonga the people have no breadfruit, do not cook food, and cut open women to deliver children. The Marquesan legends of Pepe-ui represent the sister of Toni sailing to Rarotonga in a double canoe formed of two fishes, hiding in the chief's bathing basin where the chief finds her and takes her to wife, and teaching natural childbirth and the use of cooked food.[9]

Niue. A whale swallows a woman named Gini-fale and makes off with her to another island. She cuts it open with a shell she had in her hand when swallowed, marries the chief Lei-pua, and teaches natural childbirth.[10]

Tuamotus. Kuru comes from Nukutavake. He is swallowed by a shark, cuts his way out, and comes to the island of Nuku-mau-toru, where live warrior women who seek holothurians as husbands. He has children by one of the women, but when he takes his family home some of the children have wings and fly back. . . .[11]

Tangaroa is once swallowed by a whale but cuts his way out with hair gone and finds an island of women who use pandanus roots as husbands. His sister's child Hina comes to seek him, bears a child, and is about to be burned to death by the other women when she prays and rain falls and Rupe appears and bears her away. . . .[12]

Kae is a sacrilegious man, a gourmand, and a giant. He eats

7. *JPS* 14: 47 note 177; cf. *JPS* 3: 101–104; White 2: 30–34.
8. Gill, 265–267.
9. Handy, *Bul.* 69: 127–128 and note 22.
10. *JPS* 12: 100–102.   11. Audran 32: 319–321.
12. Seurat 20: 433–435.

a part of the feast reserved for the god and the spirit of the god enters a shark and swallows Kae on his way home, but Kae cuts his way out.[13]

Rotumah. Toak is taken to the land of spirits and teaches the king's daughter natural delivery.[14]

Rapa. Te Kopara visits the island of women.[15]

Isabel Island. A fish swallows Kamakajaku. He cuts it open with a piece of obsidian, leaps out, and follows the sun to the sky. There he teaches the use of fire to cook food. He opens up a stone where he has been forbidden to go, looks down to earth, and lets down a cane upon which to descend. The sky people give him a banana to plant and the seed of a dye plant. He comes down on the hill Gaji and lives long thereafter.[16]

The Kae story is not always connected with the teaching of natural childbirth and the use of cooked food. Interest is sometimes centered upon the whale-brother carrier whom Kae has cut up and eaten, whereupon avengers are sent who pack Kae into a canoe (or basket) in his sleep and bring him back to be killed (and eaten). The Maori say that with Kae cannibalism began.

KAE AND THE WHALE CARRIERS

Tonga. Kae escapes shipwreck and gets to Samoa by clinging to the leg of a great bird. Sinilau sends him back to Tonga with his two whales Tonga and Samoa. Kae orders the whales slaughtered, but Samoa escapes and Sinilau has two large baskets prepared and brings Kae back together with the dung of all those who ate of Tonga, through which Tonga is restored to life while Kae is killed and eaten. One of the teeth of the whale has been presented to the Tui-tonga, hence there is a vacant place when the whale opens its mouth too wide.[17]

13. Montiton, 343.   14. Romilly, *Letters,* 144–146.
15. Stokes MS. in BPBM MS. col.
16. Fox, 121–122.
17. Gifford, *Bul.* 8: 139–152. Compare also the story of Sangone, *ibid.* 49–54.

Samoa. Tinilau of Samoa sends Ae of Tonga home with his pet turtles. Ae kills them. He finds himself returned to Tinilau's house where he is killed.[18]

Moso the god carries a Savai'i man home on his back. He asks for coconuts to take home. The man is ungrateful and Moso seeks him out and kills him.[19]

Maori. Kae comes to the home of Tini-rau at Motu-tapu (to visit Hina or to perform the proper ceremonies for her child left with Tini-rau when she returned home, and recognized only by a chant when he came to seek his mother). Tini-rau sends him home on his pet whale. Kae has it killed and eaten upon reaching home and Tini-rau sends messengers, bidding them recognize Kae by the gap in his teeth where two have been knocked out. The messengers dance to make all laugh and show their teeth, then pack Kae into a basket in his sleep and bring him back to Motu-tapu, where he is speared to death.[20]

Tuamotus. Kae comes from Vavau to Motu-tapu and takes Rua-tamahine to wife. She has two whale brothers, Tutu-nui and Toga-mahutu. Kae is sent home on Tutu-nui. He lands at Vavau and cuts up the whale for food. Its spirit returns to Motu-tapu and Rua-tamahine comes to avenge her brother. As they play a game she blinds him, then packs him into a basket and takes him home, where he is killed and eaten.[21]

The revenge of the mother, motivated in the Hawaiian story of Niauepo'o by the father's nonrecognition of the son, in the Aukele romance by Namaka's jealousy of her younger sisters, may be a carry-over from this familiar ending of the South Sea Kae story.

18. Turner, 110–111; Krämer 1: 127–131.
19. Turner, 266.
20. White 2: 127–140, 145–146; Grey, 55–60; Taylor, 241–244.
21. Stimson MS.; Seurat 20: 435–436; Audran 33: 343–344.

XXXVII

ROMANCES OF MATCH-MAKING

THE romance of Hainakolo tells the story of a marriage arranged between two young people of closely related families, one living at Waipio on Hawaii, the other in a distant land called Kuaihelani. There is friction between the two and the husband leaves the wife for another or an earlier lady love. The wife with her little son goes home (or in pursuit) but her canoe is overturned and she just manages to swim home to shore with the child. There she loses her wits and runs wild in the forest. The child is drawn up in the fishnet of the guardian of the chiefess Lu'ukia, a relative of Hainakolo, who has the little waif reared carefully and takes him for her husband. When she finds him philandering with a younger woman, in a fit of rage she kills the son she has had by him. The father's chant of despair is heard by his mother, who comes upon the scene to help restore the child to life, and the identity of its father becomes known.

ROMANCE OF HAINAKOLO

(a) *Pukui version.*[1] The man-eating Ku-waha-ilo comes from Kuaihelani to Waipio valley. Maggots squirm from his mouth. Thus his face appears reflected in the pool where the beautiful Hina is bathing, but when he reveals himself in the form of a handsome man the terrible apparition is forgotten and she takes him for a husband. He abjures human flesh and provides for his family by fishing and cultivating. After three children have been born, Kama-ai-ulu-nui, a son, Hina-ai-ulu-nui and Hi'ilei, daughters, he returns with his son and younger daughter to Kuaihelani leaving the older daughter with her mother. When the children reach marriageable age, Kama returns according to promise to Waipio to wed Hina. To satisfy her pregnancy craving he ascends the mountain after snow, and because she

1. As related by her mother, unpublished.

follows him (ho'okolo) and grumbles (kolokolo) the girl who is born is named Hainakolo and an uncertain fate predicted for her. Five more girls are born, Lu'ukia, whose foster parents are Kaholoholo-uka and Kaholoholo-kai (Going upland and Going seaward), and the four Maile sisters, whose foster parents are Nakula-uka and Nakula-kai (Land plains and Sea plains).

Hina's younger sister Hi'ilei meanwhile bears to her husband Kaula-wena (Red dawn) in Kuaihelani a son named "Keaunini of-the-redness-of-heaven." Her husband's sister, the beauty of Kuaihelani, wishes this boy for a husband, but Hi'ilei has promised him to her own sister's daughter, and Keaukai and Keaumiki are sent to Waipio, where they find in Hainakolo a ravishing bride for their ward. A mo'o ancestress named Mo'o-inanea who lives at Waolani in Nuuanu valley on Oahu stretches her body into a bridge across which Hainakolo walks to join her husband in Kuaihelani. A son Leimakani is born, but after seven years Keaunini falls under the spell of his former sweetheart and Hainakolo sails for home with their child. Ku-waha-ilo is displeased and sends a storm which upsets the canoe and she is obliged to make the rest of the journey by swimming with her child.

At Waipio, Hainakolo leaves Leimakani on the beach and wanders away crazed to the heights of the valley. He is drawn up in the net of Lu'ukia's foster parent and brought up in concealment because of his beauty, under the name of Lopa-iki-helewale (Little worthless castaway). Lu'ukia sends each of her sisters in turn to report upon him but each, desiring him for herself, declares him to be a monster. Finally she learns the truth and takes him for her husband. When she finds that he has an affair with her youngest sister Maile-lau-li'i, in a fit of jealous rage she kills the child she has had by him, named Lono-kai-olohia. The father's chant of grief reveals his identity and brings his mother to the scene with reason restored, and the child is brought back to life by bathing and prayer. [Two pieces at the top and at the back of the head were not quite healed and that is why babies' heads today are soft in those places.] Keaunini's infatuation for the beauty of Kuaihelani is broken and he returns to live in happiness with Hainakolo in sight of the beautiful falls of Hi'ilei.

(b) *Westervelt version.* Kahuli is a chief who, when he turns, shakes the land of Nu'umealani. Two children are born to him by his wife Kahela, named Nakula-uka and Nakula-kai. They wed and bear a daughter Hi'ilei and the triplets Keaumiki, Keaukai, and the girl Hina. Hi'ilei goes to Honua-lewa (Cloud land) to wed Ku-(w)aha-ilo. Warned by her mother, she shows no fear when he appears to her in all his terrible forms. He makes her his wife and when he leaves her he gives her a rainbow as loincloth and the war club Kaaona for their son Keaunini-ula-o-ka-lani. The boy grows up in the tapu house at Kuaihelani under the care of his uncles and, discovering who his father is, sails away to Ka-lewa in a canoe made by his ancestor Niu-loa-hiki. His father, who fails to recognize him, he clubs to death in a contest, but not before he has made the acquaintance in Ka-lewa of his pretty half-sister. On his return to Kuaihelani, Keaunini dreams of a beautiful girl, falls ill with longing, and sends his uncles in search of her. They land at Waipio during a tapu period and are about to pay the forfeit with their lives when they are recognized by their sister Hina. She has come to Hawaii, married Ku, and lives at Napo'opo'o. Hainakolo, daughter of Ku and Hina, is the girl of Keaunini's dream. When the youth comes to Waipio for his bride, the little people Kana-mu and Kana-wa build him a tapu house and there is chanting and singing and ceremonies unknown to the simple livers in the valley.

Soon the young people neglect the tapu; they quarrel, and Keaunini returns to woo his pretty half-sister in Lewa-lani. When Leimakani is born, Hainakolo places him in a coconut gourd and swims out to sea to find her husband, but her rival drives her back with contrary winds and she lands at Waipio, leaves her child, and wanders crazed in the forest. Leimakani grows up as in the other story and is taken by Lu'ukia, a "relative" of Hainakolo, as a husband. After their son Lono-kai is grown, he goes to Kuaihelani to seek his grandfather's spirit, which has gone down to Milu, and restores it to the body, which lies in the tapu temple at Kuaihelani. The two return to Hawaii, Keaunini is restored to Hainakolo, and Lono-kai weds a beautiful chiefess of Molokai.[2]

2. *Gods and Ghosts,* 163–223.

(c) *Thrum version*. Keanini-ula-o-ka-lani is born at Kuaihelani of Haumea the wife and Ku-wa(ha)-ilo the husband, and
brought up by his adopted parent Makali'i until he comes to
marriageable age. His maternal grandparents Keaumiki and
Keauka sail in a coconut-tree canoe to the Hawaiian group,
visit each island in turn to view the recognized beauty of each,
and finally arrive at Waipio on Hawaii during a tapu season.
They are seized and bound, but Olopana recognizes them and
they find in his sister Hainakolo a suitable bride for their ward.
Keanini comes to Waipio after his bride. The couple return to
Kuaihelani, where a son, Lei-makani, is born. Keanini goes to
live with a former sweetheart, daughter of Makali'i, and Hainakolo and her son return to Hawaii. The canoe capsizes in mid-
ocean. Mother and son swim the ocean, reaching first Ni'ihau,
then Nawiliwili on Kauai, where they take canoe and eventually
arrive at Waipio. The story proceeds as in the two other versions. Lu'ukia is represented as a chiefess of Hamakua.[3]

(d) *Fornander story outline*. Olopana lives at Opaelolo in
Waipio valley and has two daughters, Lu'ukia-nui and Lu'ukia-
iki. His sister Hainakolo becomes the wife of Keanini. The child
of the two, Leimakani, under the name Lopa-iki-helewale, becomes the husband of Lu'ukia-iki but is taken away from her by
her sister Lu'ukia-nui, who bears him a child called Lono-kai-
lohia. Lu'ukia kills the child in a fit of jealous rage, but Hainakolo restores him to life. Keanini has another wife in Kuaihelani.[4]

(e) *Fornander historical version*. Hainakolo is the daughter
of Mulieleali'i and sister of Kumuhonua, Olopana, and Moikeha.
Olopana and Moikeha establish themselves in Waipio valley on
Hawaii where Olopana takes to wife Lu'ukia, granddaughter
of the ruling chief of Kohala district, Hikapoloa, and of his wife
Maile-lau-li'i, who comes from a chief family in Kona district.
Hainakolo becomes the wife of a southern chief in Kuaihelani
but is unhappy and returns to Waipio valley, where her spirit

3. *More Tales,* 220–227.
4. Col. 6: 345.

still haunts the mountain cliffs and valleys about Waipio. From their son Leimakani some Hawaiian families count descent.[5]

(f) *Kamakau version.* Keaumiki and Keauka, brothers of Keanini's mother from Hawaii, come from Kuaihelani by way of Keolewa and Ni'ihau seeking a bride for their ward and at Waipio find Hainakolo. They return by the west side of Ni'ihau. Leimakani is born at Kuaihelani and both (mother and son?) return to Hawaii and become ancestors of Hawaiian chiefs.[6]

The very popular Hainakolo romance is probably based on an old traditional source. Certain elements are common to all versions. Others have been worked in by different composers out of material suggested by similar situations. From Leimakani (Wind wreath), who appears in all versions, Hawaiian families today are said to claim descent, but it would be difficult to say whether the historical connection is derived or basic. The romance belongs to the period of Olopana's legendary sojourn in Waipio valley. The wooded heights about Waipio are the traditional scene of Hainakolo's madness. Her family in Waipio represent a simpler religion than that imported by the young chief from abroad. He brings the drum and tapu ceremonies unknown before on Hawaii. The priests of Olopana can cause thunder, lightning, and earthquake; Keaunini's priests blow toward the east and make land. The lightning, the blood-red sky, the dark cloud are his signs in the heavens. The little people, the Kana-mu and Kana-wa, are his servants. In a single night they fashion a tapu house thatched with feathers, with posts and rafters of polished bone, and all day within there is soft chanting and the sound of a drumming unknown before on Hawaii, while Keaunini and his party drink awa and eat sugar cane in honor of the gods. The bride's family offer pig and fowl before he emerges to take his bride.[7] His grandson invokes Lono in the underworld, in the sky; Kane in the darkness and hot wind, thunder, whirlwind, and storm; Laka,

5. Pol. Race 2: 49, 56–57.   6. *Kuokoa,* January 5, 1867.
7. Westervelt, *Gods and Ghosts,* 182–188.

Pele, and Hiʻiaka; Aukelenuiaiku in the underworld; and offers a pig to his ancestral gods (aumakua).[8] Keaunini travels in a coconut-tree canoe which is the body of his ancestor Niu-loa-hiki; in another version this relative accompanies him in eel form. From his man-eating father he inherits a rainbow for his loincloth and the war club Kaaona. The whole picture suggests the severe ritual introduced with the Kane worship by the Ku class of priests as against the simpler practices of an earlier period. It corresponds with the Hawaiiloa tradition of marriage relations sought between two branches from a common family stock who have been separated by migration. Situations, characters, and incidents reappear in a number of Hawaiian romances which turn upon marriage between children of chiefs, often of close relatives separated from childhood in foreign lands but brought together by a recognized claim to such an alliance. This claim is based upon the idea of rank for a child born of close interfamily marriage. Family aumakua aid in effecting the union. As in the two preceding romances, there is often an infidelity episode and a recall of the mother, in this case to cure an abused and unrecognized child.

In Thrum's version the incident occurs of a landing made in ignorance at a tapu part of the beach or during a tapu season, and the consequent sacrifice of the stranger to the violated gods. It was thus that Laka's father perished at the hands of Old Woman Tapu-sea (Kai-kapu). A folktale from Hana district on Maui uses the theme humorously.

A man from Hana lands with his family on a Kauai beach during a tapu season. He is shut up in a house for sacrifice the following day. He arranges with his child to get up on the roof of the house and complain of hunger because the food he is accustomed to get from the moon is not forthcoming in this strange country. Meanwhile he is careful to see that the guards hear the talk. They report to the chief and an expedition is arranged to see this wonder. When they reach Hana the whole party is put to death.

8. *Ibid.*, 206.

The terrible bodies with which Ku-waha-ilo in the Westervelt version attempts to frighten Hiʻilei in order that he
may have an excuse to devour her find a parallel in the Aukelenui legend when the chiefess Na-maka-o-kahaʻi tries to
frighten off her wooer, and in the Puna-ai-koae when the
moʻo is getting ready to eat up her young husband for spy-
ing upon her. Ku-waha-ilo's forms are whirlwind, thunder,
and lightning, a stream of blood, a moʻo, a caterpillar, a
flaming pit; Namaka's are a cliff, an ocean, a flame. All these
are aumakua of the Pele family. South Sea groups furnish a
similar belief in such transformation bodies. Among the
Maori, each god has its aria or forms in which it may appear.
For example, the offspring of the family of Tane-atua and
Pahau-nui can take the forms of a stream, "a dog that barks
at night" (wind), a little lake, a rock. The Kai of New
Guinea tell a story of Tabotaing, chief of the dead, who tries
to frighten a visitor who comes to fetch fire by appearing
first as a boar, then as a snake, and finally takes the form of a
man.[9]

The story of the marriage of Keanini's mother bears some
resemblance to the Tagaloa-Ui cycle from Samoa.

The sun god Tagaloa is angry because men complain that the
sun goes too fast, and he begins to eat men. Lua and Ui wish to
prevent this. As he rises in the morning Ui utters a propitiatory chant and offers herself to him. She receives the sun's rays
and becomes pregnant. The sun promises no longer to eat men.
She and her brother Lua swim away to Manuʻa where she makes
a house out of coconut for the son whom she now bears, and
names him Tagaloa-Ui.[10]

The episode of the child caught in a net and adopted by a
chiefess is also reported from Samoa in the story of Fiti-
au-mua.

A pregnant wife craves taro and eats that dedicated to the
chief. She is expelled and swims out to sea with the child. The

9. *JPS* 10: 17; Neuhauss, 202–205.
10. Krämer, 1: 403–409; Buck, *Bul.* 75: 155.

child is caught in the net of Saʻumani, a fisherman who is after
an offering for the chiefess who rules the land. The parents beg
his life and name him Fiti-au-mua. In wars in Samoa he is slain,
but a foster brother from his parents' adopted homeland
avenges his death.[11]

The theme occurs in an Oahu story of Aiai, son of the fish
god Kuula, and in the Kauai story of Uweuwelekehau which
follows, in which the waif caught in the fishnet is adopted by
Luʻukia and becomes her lover, but is not recognized as the
high ranking chief that he is and the chosen bridegroom for
the highborn chiefess.

The name of Keanini (Keaunini) has a number of local
associations not necessarily belonging to the character in this
story. A kupua stone called Keanini-pohaku which stood at
the Kaukuana gulch on Oahu is one of two stones said to represent "Keanini and his sister" from Kauai. Off Waikoloa
bay at Hana, Maui, a surfing wave that disperses before coming up to shore is called "the wave of Keanini" (ka nalo o
Keanini). The local story is that Keanini came surfing from
Hawaii and was about to land at Waikoloa when he saw two
nude ladies bathing and was too bashful to proceed. The
right and left points of the bay are named for these two
chiefesses, Popolana and Hoʻolae. In the vicinity of the heiau
of Kalahiki toward Mokuleia on Oahu it is unsafe to speak
of going fishing at night lest the shark god Keanini, represented by a huge rock "lying awash a few hundred feet from
the shore," should bring on phosphorescent lights and spoil
the catch.[12]

Important for Hawaiian connections are the Maile sisters,
favorite characters in Hawaiian romance, and the appearance again of the infidelity motive, here doubled from father
to son. Keanini's former sweetheart, who seems to have no
traditional name but is called variously Hapai-memeue, Ha-
pai-onemuu, Moho-nana, or Kaekae-nalu-kae, is to be compared with the similar situation in the Fornander romance of
Lau-kiamanu-i-kahiki which follows, in which the lover leaves

11. *JPS* 9: 125-134.   12. Thrum, *HAA* 1907, 53-54.

his sister-wife for a former alliance in Kahiki, and the girl, who has traveled to meet him clinging to the tip of a stretching tree, follows him across the sea on the back of a friendly turtle just as Hainakolo is conveyed on the back of her mo'o ancestress.

ROMANCE OF LAUKIAMANUIKAHIKI

Maki'ioeoe, a visiting chief from Kuaihelani to Kauai, leaves Hina with child by him and gives her a whaletooth necklace, a bracelet, and a feather cape as recognition tokens and bids her name the child Lau-kia-manu-i-kahiki (Leaf for bird trapping in Kahiki) and send the child to him in a red canoe attended by servants clothed in red. In Kuaihelani he makes a bathing pool and plants a garden for the child's arrival. A beautiful girl is born and brought up on Kauai without knowledge of her origin, until her supposed father scolds her for giving away food too lavishly. Learning the truth, she refuses to go by sea to Kuaihelani and two old grandmothers roasting bananas cause a bamboo to sprout, to the tip of which she clings until she is dropped at the chief's home in Kuaihelani. There she adopts a girl friend and the two string flowers in the garden planted for the chief's daughter and bathe in its sacred pool, where a turtle comes and rubs her back. She is not recognized and an oven is ordered built for the girl's death, but an aunt in owl form chants her name and lineage and displays the tokens, and the chief recognizes his daughter.

Light radiates from her as she sleeps at night. She becomes the wife of the chief's son Kahiki-ula when he comes to visit his father. On his return to his first wife at Kahiki-ku she is inconsolable and follows him riding upon a friendly turtle. At Kahiki-ku she takes the form of an old woman and enters the service of the household, recognized only by her former husband. His wife Ka-hala-okole-pu'upu'u treats her with ignominy. She does pretended service only and eventually burns down the house and consumes all in it except her half-brother, whom she then deserts and returns to Kuaihelani.[13]

13. For. Col. 4: 596–609.

ROMANCE OF UWEUWELEKEHAU

Uweuwe-lekehau is the son of Ku and Hina on Hawaii. Kane
and Kanaloa are his gods. He is kept under strict tapu as a high
chief. Olopana on Kauai has declared that his daughter Lu'u-
kia shall have no other husband than he. One day when Ku and
Hina have gone oopu fishing in the Wailuku river, the boy goes
to Kalopulepule river to sail his boat and floods wash him out to
sea. He is transformed into a fish and swims to Kauai. Fishermen catch him and bring him to Lu'ukia. He becomes her lover
in secret. When this is discovered, Olopana in anger banishes the
two to the barren country of Mana where none but spirits dwell.
He does not recognize the boy's rank because he has expected
him to come in a royal red canoe manned by a company of paddlers. The spirits supply the two with all things needful and
Mana becomes a fertile land where the hearts of the people are
stolen by kindness so that they follow to share their chiefess's
exile. The boy is finally recognized and becomes ruling chief of
Kauai. The two plant a famous coconut grove at Kaunalewa
and build the heiau of Lolomauna.[14]

ROMANCE OF HOAMAKEIKEKULA

Hoa-make-i-ke-kula (Companion in suffering on the plain) is
a chiefess of high rank and faultless beauty born in Oioiapaiho,
Kohala district. Her mother Pili bears first to the high chief
Ho'oleipalaoa the son Waikuaala, then this girl is born in the
shape of a taro plant and thrown out upon the rubbish heap.
Makapailu, Pili's mother, has a prophetic dream and, guided by
a rainbow, finds the child, wraps her in red bark cloth, and in
twenty days she has attained perfection of form. She is kept
under strict tapu, but one day when she and her companion are
stringing blossoms in the woods, the elepaio bird comes to them
with a song and, turning into a handsome man, hides the girl in
mist from her companion and lures her away to a young chief
named Ka-lama-ula (Red torch) living with his sister Ka-
nahele-i-ka-uka-waokele (Thicket on the forest upland), children of the chief of Kawaihae. His rank does not satisfy her

14. For. Col. 5: 192–199.

and she dreams of a handsome chief with whom she falls in love.
In a fog she runs away and wanders in the uplands of Pahulu-
moa, accompanied by a rainbow, until she is found by Puʻuhue
hiding in an olapa tree and taken to his chief Puʻuonale, ruling
chief of Kohala, who turns out to be the lover of her dreams.
The union of these two is accompanied by all the signs of high
rank and a child is born to them in the form of an image and
named Alelekinana; hence the saying, "Place the image on the
sea side of the platform" (Hoʻoku ke kiʻi i kai o kahua). Images
were first made for worship in Kohala and it was this image
which first gave the idea of carving the forms of gods out of
wood.[15]

ROMANCE OF KAPUAOKAOHELOAI

Ku and Hina, chiefs of high rank in Hilo, Hawaii, have two
children, the boy Hoʻokaʻakaʻa-i-ka-paka (Rolling in the rain-
drops) and the girl Kapua-o-ka-ohelo-ai (Blossom of the ohelo
berry). For twenty years they are brought up apart under
strict tapu without knowing of each other's existence. One day
at noon when the attendants are away the girl follows a bright
light and discovers her brother. They sleep together until time
for the guardians' return. This goes on for some days, until the
girl grows impatient of the slow-coming dawn and gets the
guards off early by waking the chickens and starting their
crowing. They are detected and the girl is banished to Kuaihelani, where her mother was reared. At Kauai, they find a messenger just come from Kuaihelani in search of a wife for its
young chief. No girl is to be found more beautiful than Kapua.
Forty days they sail before they smell the fragrant kiele flower
and know that land is near. Warned by her conductors not to
betray undue arrogance, she does not seat herself upon the
chief's tapa nor ascend his daughter's sacred platform until
taken by the hand. Even then she slips in the ascent because of
her loss of virginity and again at the sacred bathing place she
slips and the sacred eel bites at her. She would have been killed
at once had she not been recognized as daughter of Hina, the
chief's older sister, and of higher rank than his own daughter.
   The two girls become companions. She weeps for her hand-

15. For. Col. 4: 532–541.

some firstborn brother and her friend wishes to see him. For ten days she brings his spirit to her friend in sleep until the girl is so much in love that she sails to the east to see him, landing first at Kauai, then going on east to Hawaii and the harbor of Puna-hoa. The brother has been pining for his sister, but a couple of days of feeding and bathing restore his beauty. The chiefess follows a rainbow and finds him under the red tapa. Only after his spirit has first gone to his sister and lain with her does the sister permit him to lie with this new lover.[16]

ROMANCE OF KAUMAILIULA

Holua-loa and La'a-loa have ten children, five boys named Kalino, Lulu-kaina, Ahewahewa, Wawa, Mumu; and five girls, the four Maile sisters and Kaulana. Maile-lau-li'i, the eldest girl, becomes the wife of Hikapoloa, chief of Kohala district, and lives upward of Pu'uwepa. Ka-ili-a(a)la (Fragrant skin) is their child. He marries Waikua-aala and the two have four children, Lu'ukia, Kaumailiula, Ka-lehua-lihilihi-loloa, and Ku-kui-kupuohiohi-ho'owiliwili. Lu'ukia sails to Kahiki and weds Olopana, ruling chief of Kahiki. Olopana's daughter Kaupea hears so much from Lu'ukia of the beauty of Kaumailiula that she sails from Kuaihelani, finds him at Kailua, and takes him for her husband. She becomes pregnant and returns to Kahiki for the child's birth. Kaumailiula follows but lands in Kuaihe-lani on a tapu day when Kaupea is in labor and Lu'ukia and the chiefs are gathered in the tapu house prepared for the birth of the child. The whole party is seized and imprisoned. Old woman Kaikapu proceeds to have them burnt to death, but through the prayers of Kaulana they escape. The child is called Ka-maka-o-ke-ahi (Eye of fire), and from him is descended Kahihi-o-ka-lani (The branching of the heavenly one).[17]

ROMANCE OF KAULANAIKIPOKI'I

Kaulana-iki-poki'i (Dear little Kaulana) is the youngest of five sisters born to Kau-malumalu and Holua-loa, chiefs in Kona

16. For. Col. 4: 540–547.

17. Kamakau, *Kuokoa*, January 5, 1867; For. Pol. Race 2: 57–58; Col. 6: 246.

district. She is the only one endowed with a knowledge of sorcery. Maile-lau-li'i, Maile-pakaha, Maile-kaluhea, and Maile-lau-li'i are her sisters; her brothers are Mumu, Wawa, Ahewa-hewa, Lulukaina, and Kalino. The sisters go sightseeing and in Kohala the oldest, Maile-lau-li'i, takes first as husband the handsome salt maker Puako, then, dissatisfied with his rank, the ruling chief Hikapoloa at Koko-iki.

The chief sends his wife to ask from her family the lucky fishhook for catching aku fish. The hook she brings back proves worthless and Hikapoloa seeks to avenge himself. He invites the brothers to visit him and as they come up from the beach and stoop their heads in at the low entrance to his house he cuts off the head of each and consumes the flesh with fire. The sisters are meanwhile shut up in the women's house composing a chant for the child about to be born to Maile-lau-li'i. Kaulana knows all that is happening and succeeds by her magic in bringing about the birth at once, whereupon the father is summoned. Rain and high seas impede his way, his footsteps are entangled in ie and maile vines conjured up by the magic of Kaulana, and he is put to death. Kaulana has by her magic arranged that each brother should be reduced to ashes by a particular kind of wood and she now invokes the spirits of the wood (who are her family aumakua) to tell where the bones lie whose flesh they have consumed. Putting together the bones, she brings her brothers back to life and all depart for Kona and "abandon the proud land of Kohala and its favorable wind the Aeloa."[18]

18. For. Col. 4: 560–569.

XXXVIII

ROMANCES OF THE DANCE

THE group of romances just considered center about the marriage relations between a chief family resident in the Hawaiian group and a related family but of superior rank localized in Kahiki or on one of the other islands of the group or merely in a neighboring district. Specifically it refers to the Moikeha-Olopana marriage with Lu'ukia of the Hikapoloa family of chiefs who early settled Kohala district on Hawaii. In the long romance of Kalino from which Fornander summarized from Kamakau the story of Kaumailiula, Lu'ukia appears consistently as the granddaughter of Hikapoloa and his wife Maile-lau-li'i. The story provides Maile-lau-li'i, as in the Hainakolo romance, with a band of sisters whose kupua power lies in their fragrance and who are dominated by a younger sister represented as gifted with special powers of sorcery or merely of good sense, courage, and character. This figure is worked up more fully in the romance of Ke-ao-melemele (Golden cloud) which follows. Here she is represented as remaining unwed as a means to supernatural attainments, and as becoming skilled in medicine and in the hula dance. The Hainakolo theme of a propitious marriage made between two children of Ku and Hina who have been brought up separately, broken by the infidelity of the husband, centers, in this romance, about the girl Paliula and her brother, who is the firstborn of Ku and Hina, but brought up by the gods Kane and Kanaloa in Waolani. Ke-ao-melemele appears on the genealogical line of chiefs as wife of Ka-la-lili (Ka-lau-palili?), tenth or eleventh in descent from Kumuhonua.

ROMANCE OF KEAOMELEMELE

The guardian mo'o named Mo'oinanea who cares for the gods in Kuaihelani arranges a marriage with Ku for her grandchild Hina, and three children are born, a boy and two girls. The boy is at once conveyed to Oahu to be brought up at the heiau of Waolani in Nu'uanu valley under the care of the gods Kane and Kanaloa and is given the name Ka-hanai-a-ke-akua (Adopted by the gods). The little eepa beings called Nana-mu and Nana-wa act as his servants. The older girl named Paliula is carried to the uplands between Puna and Hilo districts on Hawaii and placed under the care of Waka. Two trees, Makalei which brings fish and Kalala-i-ka-wai (The branch in the water) or Maku'u-kao (Supplying endless abundance) which produces vegetable food, are planted in her garden to keep her provided with abundance of food. The third girl is brought up in a revolving house called Ke-alohi-lani in Nu'umealani where she is waited upon by clouds until she eventually follows her brother and sister to Hawaii. She is named Ke-ao-melemele (Golden cloud).

Ku and Hina travel about other islands of the heavens and take each a new spouse. By the chiefess Hi'ilei, Ku has a red-skinned son named Kaumailiula and Hina has by Olopana a daughter Kaulana-iki-poki'i (Beloved little one of the sunset) who is adopted by Ku and Hi'ilei while Hina and Olopana take the boy to rear. Kane and Kanaloa finally summon these two children also to Waolani.

Paliula has meanwhile become the wife of her brother Kahanai on Hawaii and been deserted by him for the beautiful kupua Poliahu who lives on the snow-covered summit of Maunakea. She travels to Oahu and wanders crazed in the heights of Manoa valley, then goes to Waianae, where she takes lessons in hula and, becoming an expert, travels on to Kauai and learns the dances of that island. Her sister Ke-ao-melemele in cloudland hears her chanting the hula and longs to join her sister. With Kapo, sister of the poison gods of Maunaloa as her teacher, Ke-ao-melemele becomes an expert. When her younger brother and sister arrive, she teaches Kaulana the dances until she is equally adept. Kaulana is also given instruction in herb medicine. The boy Kahanai has already freed himself from Poliahu, made a visit to his parents, and returned to Waolani, where he becomes an expert kahuna with knowledge of sorcery and sacrifice. Paliula becomes reconciled with him. Ke-ao-melemele takes Kaumailiula as her husband and the food-providing trees are brought from Hawaii for the marriage feast, but the fish tree is broken

and hence fish become dispersed about the islands. Ke-ao-melemele and her husband rule the islands. Kane sends for Ku and
Hi'ilei, Hina and Olopana, and the guardian mo'o to come and
live on Oahu, and Mo'oinanea shuts up forever the lands where
they lived and brings all her mo'o family with the chiefs to Hawaii. Kane-huna-moku that hidden land is called. Kaumailiula
and Ke-ao-melemele long rule over the islands and leave their
signs in the heavens to their descendants.[1]

Throughout the romance the signs of divinity established
for chiefs of divine rank in Hawaii form the machinery of
the story. At the birth of the firstborn chief appear clouds
and fog, thunder and lightning, red torrents down the cliff-
sides, strong winds and bending trees, high seas rolling landward. The rainbow (anuenue) sister of Kane and Kanaloa
acts as their messenger or hovers over the child of godlike
rank. The great bird Iwa bears the messengers of the gods
overseas. The marriage of the divine firstborn son to his sister by the same father and mother is the highest form of
union to which Hawaiian bluebloods can aspire; the issue of
such a union is a god (akua).

Other allusions to Kahanai in Hawaiian legend call him
chief of Waolani and make him the ward of Kahano and
Newa, that Kahano who is said to have brought over the
Kana-mu and Kana-wa on his own arm as on a bridge as
servants for his ward Kapawa. In traditional history he appears as a chief of high rank who comes from afar and whose
family colonize the island.

Ke-ao-melemele (Golden cloud) is born from the head of
Hina and not in the ordinary way. Ku-ke-ao-loa (Ku long
cloud) is her messenger; Ka-onohi-o-ka-la (Eyeball of the
sun) is her seer; Ke-ao-opua-loa (Living cloud) is her sorcerer. On nights of full moon one can see the Ali'i-wahine-o-
ka-malu (Chiefess of the shade) against the moon. Her messenger reveals to Ku and Hina all the lore of cloud forms, how
they meet, move, or separate; how the stars appear through
them and the course of the winds among the clouds; the
meaning of each change so intimately connected in Hawaiian

1. Westervelt, *Gods and Ghosts*, 116–151.

thought with the lives of chiefs.[2] It is because Ku sees in the
clouds the form of a beautiful woman that he is led to take
the journey northward during which he weds a new wife and
Hina a new husband.

Closely connected with the knowledge thus gained of the
shape and motions of clouds is that which governs the art of
the hula or dance. The movements of the dance are definitely
related in this nature romance to the motions of leaves and
blossoms swaying in various ways according to the particular
wind that blows. It is by watching the dancing trees, the
shifting clouds, and the shadows which they cast that the
girl learns their motions. Hiʻi-lani-wai teaches the hula to
girls at Waianae; Malu-aka teaches on Kauai. Kapo, sister
of the poison-tree gods of Maunaloa and proficient in the
arts of herb medicine and sorcery, teaches Ke-ao-melemele on
the dancing field near Waolani in Nuʻuanu valley until she
can dance in the skies and over the sea. Clearly these are the
Pele sisters, Hiʻiaka, Laka, and Kapo, all three goddesses of
the woodland and invoked in the hula dance. The Hiʻiaka sisters of Pele are called "shadow bearers" by Westervelt[3] and
her brothers are gods of sorcery. Hence the story seems to be
definitely connected with the Pele family and its guardian
moʻo and to represent the Kane worship established during
the time of the ascendancy of that god, which persisted down
to the time of the breakup caused during the wars of chiefs,
and retained its hold upon the people up to the coming of the
white men.

Equally interesting with this close relation of forms of nature with the movements of the dance is their employment in
the action of a love story, as illustrated in the account of the
birth and marriage of Lau-ka-ieie (Leaf of the trailing pandanus), goddess of the wildwood and sister to the wind god of
love, Makani-kau, and to the Hiʻilawe who was transformed
at death, his body into a stone and his spirit into the mist of
that waterfall in Waipio valley which is called after his name,
of which Hawaiian poets love to sing. The romance tells of
the kupua beings of the forest, associating plants, land shells,

2. Westervelt, *Gods and Ghosts*, 128–132.   3. *Volcanoes*, 69–70.

winds, streams, rainbows, and the red-feathered birds in a
single family line.

ROMANCE OF LAUKAIEIE

Hiʻilawe is born to Ka-kea (The white) and Ka-holo (The
runner), children of the cliffs, and is wrapped in moss and flung
away by the mother. Hina-ulu-ohia sees that the bundle contains a child and she recognizes the signs of a chief and takes the
child as her own. The father's sister Po-kahi (First night) has
for husband the bird catcher Kau-kini. Hina knows that she has
longed for the child, hence she brings her a beautiful girl perfect in form, who is named Lau-ka-ieie. The adopted parents
bring her up secretly with birds and flowers and singing shells
as playmates. When she reaches marriageable age she dreams of
the handsome chief Kawelona (Sunset) at Lihue, Kauai, and
her brother Makani-kau goes to seek him, choosing as his shell
carrier Pupu-kani-oi (Singing shell) because when all the sisters raise their hands her fingers are the longest. She takes a
husband on the way, but the wind chief goes on to the islet of
Lehua, where red iiwi birds have conveyed Kawelona, and finds
him willing to accompany the messenger because he too has
dreamed of the girl and is eager to wed her. Many kupua join
the marriage party as they proceed, Makani-kau in his shell
boat and Kawelona in his cloud boat. These kupua have leaf,
flower, bird, plant, shell, cloud, wind, fish, shark, sea-moss,
stone, or cliff bodies. The feast is celebrated in Waipio near the
heiau Kahuku-welowelo with music and dancing. Hina takes the
body of a lehua tree, and the girl after her death becomes the
ieie vine which wreaths the body of the forest goddess.[4]

Another romance in which the art of the hula is used to
win back a lover is that of Halemano and Kamalalawalu, the
beauty of Puna.

ROMANCE OF HALEMANO

Halemano is born at Halemano in Waianae on Oahu. Wahiawa and Kukaniloko are his parents. He has five brothers and

4. Westervelt, *Gods and Ghosts*, 36–48.

sisters, but only one, a sorceress sister Laenihi, enters in any way into the story. He is brought up by his grandmother and becomes faultless in beauty. Kamalalawalu is the beauty of Puna at this time. She has been brought up in seclusion with her favorite brother Kumukahi as her only companion and eight hundred dogs to guard and serve her. Huaa and Kulukulua, chiefs of Puna and Hilo respectively, court her in vain. She has seen the face of Halemano in dream and will have none but him. He too has dreamed of her and dies of love for her, but Laenihi restores him to life and teaches him how to lure the beauty of Puna to his canoe. Together they flee to Ukoa in Waialua, Oahu, and a great gift giving (ho'okupu) is held to celebrate the marriage.

Aikanaka who rules Oahu hears of her beauty and the two are obliged to flee. They live as castaways until the daughter of Kukuipahu, ruling chief of Kohala, becomes enamored of Halemano's beauty and entertains them royally. Several times the wife leaves Halemano for a new lover. He dies of grief, but again the sister comes to his rescue and proposes that he learn the hula in order to win back his wife's affection. The method succeeds. During a kilu game he chants eight compositions recalling to his wife their days of wandering together and the love they have enjoyed, and her heart is touched. She returns to him only to find that now he is weary of her love. Her former lovers finally come with a great fleet and carry her back to her home island.[5]

The story contains, besides the excellent picture of a kilu contest, a good example of the part played by the supernatural sister in Hawaiian stories in furthering the cause of a favorite brother, one brought up under the tapus of a god and whose wishes are never to be thwarted. Her sexual seclusion would seem to be imposed in order to cultivate her kupua power. Twice she brings Halemano back to life. She goes to Puna in the form of a fish. Her progress is accompanied by signs such as rain, lightning, thunder, earthquake, freshets that carry red earth into the sea. Coupled with these supernatural qualities are those also of practical wisdom. She rec-

5. For. Col. 5: 228–263.

ognizes the woman of his dream by a description of the wreaths about her neck. The plot for bringing the lovers together and that for winning back an estranged wife are shrewdly conceived and without magical machinery. The love story, told as it is with great detail, concludes on the familiar note of Hawaiian romance, that of a pair of estranged lovers. Stories which end with a happy married life must be suspected as a foreign innovation.

XXXIX

WOOING ROMANCES

THE romance of Laie-i-ka-wai (Laie in the water) is the story of a high tapu chiefess concealed at birth in a cave reached by diving through a pool of water and later reared under tapu in an earthly paradise prepared for her in Paliuli in the uplands of Puna by her moʻo guardian Waka, who hopes to gain wealth and position by arranging a marriage for her to some high chief. An impostor steps in on the eve of marriage and she is abandoned by Waka and her twin sister substituted in her place. Through a group of guardian girls, the abandoned sisters of a rejected suitor who has tried to use their kupua powers to win the chiefess and has then attempted to storm her tapu house by force, she wins a very high tapu chief from the heavens as a husband, her foes are punished, and she herself goes to dwell in the heavens with her husband. He proves unfaithful, his parents cast him out, and his wife joins her sister and is worshiped today as a goddess.

ROMANCE OF LAIEIKAWAI

Laie-i-ka-wai and her twin sister Laie-lohelohe are born at Laie on Oahu of Kahauokapaka the father, chief of the northern lands of the island, and Malaekahana the mother. Since the father has vowed to let no daughter born to his wife live until she bears him a son, the mother conceals the birth of the twins and gives them to her own relatives to rear, Laie-lohelohe to Ka-puka-i-haoa to bring up at the heiau at Ku-kani-loko, and Laie-i-ka-wai to Waka, who first hides her in a cave near Laie which can be reached only by diving into the pool which conceals the entrance, and then takes her to the uplands of Puna. Here she builds a tapu house for her ward thatched with bird feathers, and gives her birds to wait upon her and mists to hide her from the sight of men until such time as a suitable lover shall appear to make her his wife.

The first whose suit seems acceptable is Kauakahi-ali'i, ruling chief of Kauai and husband of Ka-ili-o-ka-lau-o-ke-koa (Skin like the leaf of the koa). The reappearance of his wife whom he had mourned for dead prevents the appointed meeting, but on his return to Kauai he relates the adventure and the young chiefs of that island are stirred by the story. Aiwohikupua meets her nightly in dream and goes to woo her, but even the presence of his four sweet-scented kupua sisters, named after the four varieties of maile vine whose scent they inherit, cannot shake her refusal. Enraged by the insult, he abandons the sisters in the forest. His fifth and favorite sister, Ka-hala-o-mapuana (The fragrant hala blossom) refuses to abandon them. Through her clever management she attracts the attention of Laie-i-ka-wai and the five are adopted as sisters and made the guardians of Paliuli. They drive off their brother upon his second attempt to win the chiefess, and a guardian mo'o named Kiha-nui-lulu-moku (Great mo'o shaking the island) completes his discomfiture. Another and more favored young chief from Kauai named Hauailike is also expelled by the watchful youngest sister.

Waka now arranges a match with Ke-kalukalu-o-ke-wa, younger brother of Ka-ili-o-ka-lau-o-ke-koa and successor with her to Kauakahi as ruling chief of Kauai. Just as the formal marriage (hoao) is about to be consummated, a young rascal from Puna named Hala-aniani, aided by his sorceress sister, carries her off on his surfboard in place of the legitimate lover. Waka finds them sleeping together and abandons the girl in a rage, stripping her of mist and bird guardians and of the house thatched with feathers whose protection her loose conduct has forfeited. The five sisters and the great mo'o, however, refuse to abandon their mistress. Since the Kauai chief has made her twin sister Laie-lohelohe his wife in place of their disgraced mistress, they determine to retrieve her fortunes by providing a more splendid match, and the clever youngest sister is despatched, with the great mo'o as carrier, to fetch their oldest brother who lives as a god in a tapu house in the very center of the sun in the highest heavens. While she is away on this errand the group leave Paliuli and travel about the island and, meeting an old family guardian and seer named Hulu-maniani, make their home with him as adopted daughters at Honopuwai-akua on Kauai.

Throughout the course of the story this old seer (kaula) has been following around the islands after the rainbow sign which hovers over the place where Laie-i-ka-wai is hidden, determined to make this new divinity his chief and thus provide for his own old age.

Ka-onohi-o-ka-la (Eyeball of the sun) looks favorably upon his sister's proposal and, putting off his nature as a god, he descends to earth, strips the enemies of Laie-i-ka-wai of their lands and power and, leaving Ke-kalukalu-o-ke-wa and the twin sister rulers over Kauai, gives to each of the sisters rule over one of the other islands of the group and takes Laie-i-ka-wai up on a rainbow to live with him in Ka-hakaekaea. All goes well until, on one of his visits to earth to see that all goes well there, he notices the budding beauty of his sister-in-law. He presses his attentions and succeeds in securing her. His wife in the heavens wonders what important affairs keep him so long on earth. In the temple at Kahakaekaea stands the gourd Lau-ka-palili which reveals to one who looks within what is going on below. Laie-i-ka-wai discovers her husband's infidelity and reports him to his parents, who live with her in the heavens. They banish him to become a wandering spirit, the first lapu (ghost) in Hawaii. Laie-i-ka-wai returns to earth and lives like a god with her sister. Today she is worshiped as Ka-wahine-o-ka-liula (Lady of the twilight, mist, or mirage).[1]

The story may be analyzed as follows:

(A) A girl child is rescued at birth and brought up (A1) by relatives, (A2) by divinities.

(B) She journeys from one place to another (B1) accompanied by signs.

(C) She is isolated under tapu to await marriage (C1) in a specially prepared house, (C2) with kupua guardians, (C3) in the midst of a group of maidens.

(D) She is visited by an unsuccessful suitor (D1) who attempts to win her in battle.

1. Haleole, Ka Moolelo o Laieikawai (The story of Laieikawai); translation, RBAE 33: 285–666; synopsis by William D. Alexander, contributed by John Rae, JAFL 13: 241–260; Kalakaua, 453–480; For. Col. 5: 406–417; HAA 1928, 79–87.

(E) She breaks her tapu for an unknown suitor, who turns out to be (E1) a high chief, (E2) of low birth.

(F) She secures a high chief for a husband.

(G) She is deserted for a younger relative.

The early publication of this romance has fixed its form as Haleole printed it; there are no variants. Westervelt's story of Paliula's marriage to her highborn brother in the romance of Ke-ao-melemele is obviously composed out of similar material. In both stories the mo'o guardian Waka (Waha) prepares for her ward a house thatched with feathers and a garden of plenty in the uplands of Puna in which she awaits a suitable husband. In both the girl is deserted for another woman. Poliahu plays a similar seductive role in both stories although of a minor character in the Laieikawai romance. Kahanai's journey to his bride in the form of lightning may be compared to Aiwohikupua's use of the lightning stroke at the boxing match in which he engages on the way to woo the beauty of Paliuli.

But the treatment of the two stories is entirely different. Haleole is novelistic in his handling of character. The supernatural character of the youngest sister of the Maile group becomes rationalized into a quick-witted and charming young person whose resources never fail under the most trying circumstances. Had her brother given her a chance, there is no doubt she would have won over the chiefess. When he proposes to take her home with him, she has spirit enough to refuse to abandon her sisters. She it is who keeps up their morale, devises ingenious methods for winning the attention of the chiefess, and brings it about that she and her sisters become her guardians. She it is who drives away unworthy suitors whom her softer-hearted sisters would have admitted, and when the chiefess whom she serves is won by an impostor and is stripped of her position of rank, it is she who makes the dangerous journey to a distant land to fetch back a bridegroom of sufficient rank to restore her mistress to honor. When the husband proves unfaithful, before daring to indulge his fresh passion it is her watchful eye of which he must rid himself. How human in fact is all this intrigue! How excellent a picture of the perfect chaperon!

From a rationalized wooing story the romance suddenly changes to a traditional pattern in recounting the messenger's journey to the heavens, an episode corresponding with that employed in the Kaanaelike romance where the girl on the island of virgins ascends to consult her parent Ku-waha-ilo about her marriage with the stranger. In Haleole's romance the members of the family dwell at different levels according to their rank as divinities. After voyaging for four months and ten days within the great mouth of the mo'o the girl messenger reaches Ke-alohi-lani (The shining heaven). Above is the garden of Nu'umealani, above this the heaven of Kahakaekaea to which she climbs by a spider web, although beaten back by hot sun and cold rain sent by her mother. There she finds her father lying face upward and, throwing herself upon his breast, makes herself known by chanting the family names. The coöperation of her mother, who lives above with her son but comes down during her monthly period to occupy her tapu house below, she forces by the artifice of securing the bloody garment which her mother has laid aside for the bath of purification at the end of her tapu period. The context makes it clear that the goddess wife fears lest the possession of this garment by her husband will in some way work her harm, a motive which suggests, in primitive form, the clothes-stealing incident in the swan-maiden story.

The actors in the story are not invented by the composer but drawn from familiar sources mythical or genealogical. The four sweet-scented Maile sisters, often accompanied by a fifth and favorite younger sister who has special powers of a god and by brothers who play a more or less active part in the story, are said to be even more popular figures in Hawaiian romance than the examples here brought together would argue. In the forests, wherever this fragrant myrtle vine (*Alyxia myrtillifolia*) abounds, is laid the scene of their wanderings. Their names are those given to the four varieties of maile which Hawaiians distinguish.[2] The kupua power of fragrance which they possess is entirely in accord with old

2. For. Col. 5: 614–619.

belief, and the association of women with flowers and of goddesses with fragrance in giving romance names to such kupua figures is no doubt ancient and is logically borne out in
this instance. Maile is associated with worship of the gods.
Old Hawaiians declare that the subtle pervasive scent of maile
still clings to those sites where ancient heiaus stood. Especially is the maile noted among the plants used for decorat-
ing the altar to the gods of the hula.

> O Laka ke akua pule ikaika,
> Ua ku ka maile a Laka a imua,
> Ua lu ka hua o ka maile. . . .

> "The prayer to the goddess Laka has power,
> The maile of Laka stands foremost,
> The goddess inspires her pupil as the maile
>   scatters its fragrance. . . ."

runs the chant.[3] Hence the Maile sisters in story may be a
modern replacement of an older family of sisters who group
about the figure of the volcano goddess and have as pet
younger sister the Hi'iaka-i-ka-poli-o-pele who plays so large
a part in the Pele legend and acts as patroness of the hula
dance.

Laie-i-ka-wai herself has some qualities of a volcano goddess. The course of her wanderings from Oahu, where she is
born, to Hawaii, where she makes her home, corresponds with
Pele's, who also establishes herself on the slopes of the same
mountain. Her garden paradise of Paliuli resembles the Fern-
house (Hale-ma'uma'u) which Pele makes cool and fresh
within the flames of the volcano, in which to receive her lover.
The scene in which Laie appears to defend her guardian's
boast of her power, when her skirt laid upon the altar brings
thunder and lightning, corresponds with the use, made by
other heroines connected with the Pele family, of the sacred
skirt (pa-u) to reduce their foes to ashes: with that of Namaka, who overwhelms the brothers of Aukele, and of Hi-
'iaka who destroys her mo'o enemies. This journey of the

3. N. Emerson, "Hula," 32.

young guardian to the heavens to secure a husband for her mistress corresponds with that of Hiʻiaka to seek Lohiau. The story ends in the infidelity of the husband and his affair with another sister, punished by his exile and disgrace while she herself becomes a goddess and is worshiped as "the lady of the twilight." So Aukele makes love to the Pele sisters. Kaohelo's lover turns to Hiʻiaka. Kaanaelike's husband dallies with her young sister and like Lohiau is overwhelmed in a stream of fire. Leimakani is unfaithful to Luʻukia. Keanini abandons Hainakolo. It looks as if a story so full of human interest as that of Pele's jealousy of Hiʻiaka had fixed the infidelity motive inexorably as an ending to Hawaiian romantic fiction. Possibly the situation should be referred back still farther to Wakea's infidelity with Papa.

The name Laie is probably to be analyzed as La(u)-ʻie, "Leaf of the ʻie vine," since the equivalent name of a Maui chiefess Laie-lohelohe refers to the "Drooping ʻie vine." This red-spiked climbing pandanus (*Freycinetia Arnotti*) which wreaths forest trees of the uplands is sacred to the gods of the wild wood, patrons of the hula dance, of whom Laka is chief. The epithet -i-ka-wai (in the water) belongs also to the food-producing tree Ka-lala-i-ka-wai planted in Paliula's garden. Love affairs of kupua beings often end in Hawaiian folktale in the transformation of lady into pool of water and wooer into a tree at its source, symbol of the act of reproduction, and the food-producing tree Ka-lala-i-ka-wai is another symbol for the reproductive energy of male and female which fills the land with offspring. This seems a more plausible explanation of the name of this important romantic figure than that generally given as derived from the watery home of the girl hidden in her infancy in a pool at a place on Oahu called Laie, which is still visited as the traditional scene of the incident.

Such an analysis would agree well also with the plant names of other women who figure in the story. The clever youngest sister of the Maile girls bears the name of a plant sacred to the hula dance and one of the most prized for its odor, the fragrant pandanus blossom. In other stories she is called Kaulana, equivalent to Ka-ula-wena (The redness in the sky),

which is a sacred name today in the Pele family. Kamakau
writes that Mapuna-ia-aala (Springing up of fragrance),
called also Ka-ula-wena (Red light in the sky), was the
daughter of Haumea when she came from over the sea with
Kane and Kanaloa and lived on Maui and was taken to wife
by Kahele-i-po, one of the two men of Maui who saw the
party land. Local tradition calls Kahala-o-mapuana "one of
a family of gods who lived on Kauiki in old days." An old
pandanus (hala) tree on Kauai which bore red fruit instead
of the customary yellow is pointed out today under the name
of Kahalamapuana. Kaha-ula (Kaha[la]-ula?) is one of the
gods invoked by Hi'iaka to bring Lohiau back to life.[4] According to Kalawe's chant, Kaha-ula is the god to whom the
maile vine is dedicated in the hula dance.[5] The clever little
sister of the Laieikawai romance called Kahalaomapuana is
the same as the youngest sister of the Ke-ao-melemele story,
Kaulana-iki-poki'i, she who remains virgin and becomes an
expert in medicine, that is, in sorcery—a sorcery which she
puts into practice in the Kaulana-poki'i and Kaumailiula romances by bringing the dead to life and entangling her
enemy in growing vines. She may thus be regarded as representing the deity of the Maile family of sisters as she would
appear in her human form for purposes of romance. Westervelt's translation of the chant to Kaulanapoki'i in the romance of Golden Cloud reads,

> A stranger perhaps is outside,
> A woman whose sign is the fog,
> A stranger and yet my young sister,
> The flower of the divine homeland,
> The wonderful land of the setting sun
> Going down into the deep blue sea.
> You belong to the white ocean of Kane,
> You are Kaulana-iki-poki'i,
> The daughter of the sunset,
> The woman coming in the mist,
> In the thunder and the flash of the lightning,
> Quivering in the sky above. . . .

4. For. Col. 6: 344.   5. Green, 3.

But this is not the whole story. In an invocation to Laka used in every hula ceremony, Laka is addressed as Kaulana-ula, translatable as "Sacred one above":

A aloha mai ia makou e Kaulana-ula
Eia no ka ula la,
He ula leo, he kanaenae aloha na makou ia oe, e Laka,
E Laka e ho'oulu ia.

"Grant us love, O Kaulana-ula,
 Here is the sacred gift,
 A gift given by the voice, a chant of affection from us to you,
  O Laka,
 O Laka, inspire us."

The charming figure of the wise woman in the Laieikawai romance and in that of Golden Cloud and of Kaumailiula represents at least a namesake of the goddess of the A-lala-lahe chant, "The woman of Hilihili-lau-ka-maile," who is Laka, the fecund goddess of the upland forests worshiped in the hula dance.

Many other details of the romance may be matched with Polynesian custom, symbolic value, or traditional theme. It is justly called the masterpiece of Hawaiian romantic fiction. The garden paradise, which appears also in the closely corresponding romance of Golden Cloud, represents the life of a favorite child of high ranking chiefs brought up under tapu, waited upon by relatives of lower station, and allowed to do nothing for himself. The early care for virginity was for the purpose of insuring for such a child a match of equivalent rank, preferably that of a brother and sister, in order that the offspring might be of the highest possible sacredness or even attain the rank of god (akua) and thus lift the family to wealth and fame. All the relatives of such a child were concerned in the matter. It was the guardians themselves who were the matchmakers. Although the custom of virginity for life has not been reported for Hawaii, the idea is stressed in the story. Kahala-o-mapuana is such a virgin figure. Malio, kupua sister of the Puna rascal, lives in solitude apart from men. The Maile girls remain virgin "at the command of our parents." Laieikawai loses her value for her royal suitor by her scandalous affair with the wrong husband and her kupua attendants fall away from her with the giving up of virginity.

In some Polynesian groups a virgin isolation is continued through life with the idea that virginity increases power with the gods and hence brings success in foresight or sorcery. Such an advocate with the supernatural world is prized in a family. Among the Maori a practice called puhi prohibited the firstborn daughter of a chief from marrying or doing any work except to sew, with the idea of making her an important person in the tribe.[6] In Samoa virginity is highly prized in a prospective bride. The leaves of the pandanus vine ('ie) were used to make the finely plaited skirt called 'ie-sina which became a special red garment worn only on the occasion of testing a girl's virginity.[7] Until this time the "village maid," called taupou, was isolated with a group of girl friends and kept apart from men until a suitable match could be arranged for her. In Tonga a "taupoou" goddess whom two lovers tried to approach at night is to be seen changed into a mound beside the road with her two lovers similarly transformed on the ridge at the back.[8] In the Lau islands girls were carefully kept in retirement before marriage and the custom of a virginity test is reported.[9]

The wooing value of fragrance, like the flower names of the women in the story, marks the love story, especially one which originally took shape, as it is said, in the mind of a composer from the Kauiki end of Maui where the girl Springing-up-in-fragrance was born to Haumea. The virgin period of the chiefess of Paliuli is thus surrounded by fragrance. In Tahiti an inauguration of the national marae is described at which "first born young virgins of the royal family of the kingdom represented their respective district" garlanded with fragrant single gardenia blossoms (tiere) as a sign of virginity. Brown says that in the Andaman islands a girl is,

6. Best, *TNZI* 36: 33; Mühlmann, 44.
7. Buck, *Bul.* 75: 275, 316–317.
8. Gifford, *Bul.* 61: 303.   9. Hocart, 155–159.

at coming of age, given the name of the odoriferous flower in blossom when she reaches puberty. This name she uses until after the birth of her first child.[10] In Tonga, flower names are given as nicknames to lovers. Love songs are called songs of sweet-smelling flowers, just as wooing is represented under the image of "hunting the pigeon" or "fishing."[11] In Hawaii, where the "fishing" symbol is common, a stick of sweet-smelling wood is used as a lure in actual fishing.[12] Association of fragrance with marriage occurs in the Kaulu story where the voyager takes a handsome wife named Kekele, a "quiet" woman whose favorite plants are the fragrant hala and maile vine, the 'ie'ie and other aromatic plants. Marquesans say that fragrant plants were first brought to Nukuhiva enclosed in a gourd to attract a husband for the sweet-scented girl Tahia-noho-uu of Hivaoa.[13] In a Tonga story a chief's rock crowned with sweet-scented plants is floated away to Hina's sleeping house by her wooer,[14] and there are innumerable references to scented plants in wooing stories throughout Polynesia.

The house thatched with bird feathers as an exaggerated symbol of the rank of its owner occurs also in Samoa in the house thatched with red feathers which the rats build for Alo, son of a rat-headed woman, and his wife Meto.[15]

The Halaaniani episode of the displaced suitor has a Tonga parallel in the story of Vaenuku who wins the love of the beauty of Tongatabu, daughter of the Tui Tonga:

He follows her to the bathing pool and she sees his golden hair and the dove tattooed on his back and arranges to flee with him. His rival overhears and in the darkness of night takes the place of Vaenuku and carries off the lady. At the marriage ceremony, although the trickster is given the lady, to Vaenuku is given the "virgin mat" because it is he who had won her consent.[16]

10. 93, 312.
11. Gifford, *Bul.* 6: 234; Collocott, *Bul.* 46: 63–65.
12. Malo, 279 note 8.   13. Handy, *Bul.* 69: 26 ff.
14. Collocott, *Bul.* 46: 27–28.   15. Buck, *Bul.* 75: 65.
16. Collocott, *Bul.* 46: 46–50.

The terms of Aiwohikupua's punishment are strictly in accordance with Polynesian custom. Mariner tells of such an occurrence in Tonga. When the case comes up of a chief who has revolted, the "king" is represented as saying that

it was not the custom at Tonga to kill those of whom one has no reason to be afraid, and that he did not think it worth his while to destroy a mere butterfly. . . . He then desired the culprit to consider himself for the future as divested of all power and rank—no longer to be the commander of men, but a single and unprotected individual; that his chiefship from that moment was null; and that consequently, he was never more to take his seat as a chief, at the cava ceremonies.

The result of the sentence was that, although his actual rank could not be taken from him, he was thereafter ignored by everyone.[17]

The idea that the sex of a child may be determined before birth depends upon the belief that the wish of the child is active within the mother while still unborn. In the Andaman islands the sex is determined by the side of the mother on which the child is felt, a male on the left because men hold the bow with the left hand, a female on the right because the woman uses her right for the net.[18]

The closest parallels to the incident of the rescued twins at the opening of the Laieikawai story come from outside the Polynesian area. The common custom of infanticide, as described by Ellis, often had in a chief's family, especially if the mother was of higher rank than her husband, some bearing upon rank and was not a merely arbitrary matter.[19]

Philippines. Long ago the Sun had to leave the Moon to go to another town. He knew that his wife, the Moon, was expecting the birth of a child and before going away he said to her, "When your baby is born, if it is a boy, keep it; if a girl, kill it." The Moon hid the baby girl but later the Sun found it and cut it into pieces and made the stars.[20]

17. 1: 174–175.   18. Brown, 90.
19. *Researches* (1829) 1: 333–340.
20. Laura Benedict, *JAFL* 26 (1913): 17–18.

Bantu. A father decrees the death of girl babies. A girl hidden away beside a pool changes into a bird.[21]

In the romance of Ka-ili-lau-o-ke-koa (With skin like the leaf of the koa tree), a betrothed chiefess at the seacoast escapes from her guards to seek a stranger hidden away in a tapu house in the uplands, who woos her with a musical instrument new to her and with a song. Her indignant family seize the lover and would have starved him to death but for a friendly younger brother of the chiefess who feeds him secretly until his high rank is made known. His rival, defended by the owl god and a mo'o kupua, attempts to kill him, but his wife saves his life with her throwing stick and Pele with her lightnings routs the foe.

ROMANCE OF KAILILAUOKEKOA

(a) *Dickey version.* Ka-ili-lau-o-ke-koa is the granddaughter of Moikeha and Ho'oipo-i-ka-malanai, high chiefs of Kauai, and daughter of La'a. At her home by the sea at Kapa'a she rides the curving surf of Makaiwa and develops skill in the game of konane. Twice she defeats a handsome stranger named Heakekoa from Molokai. She is betrothed by her father to Keli'ikoa from Kona district. Far up the Wailua river at Pihana-ka-lani in a house woven of flowering lehua branches and bird feathers, with birds as his companions, lives Kauakahi-ali'i, the adopted son of the sorceress Waha, with his sister Ka-hale-lehua (House of lehua). He invents the nose-flute (ohe), the sound of whose magic notes attracts the attention of the chiefess by the sea. Stealing out of the house at night with her attendant and a little white dog, she climbs the ridge called Kua-mo'o-loa-a-Kane (Long lizard-back of Kane), is beaten back by rain and mist sent by his sister, and presents herself at the home of her wooer. Here she finds a garden of plenty and a well-stocked fishpond, is hospitably received, and becomes his wife. Twice a band of fighting men attempt to storm her retreat but are driven back by rain and mist. Finally the parents accept the match and send gifts and an invitation to visit them at the seacoast,

21. Torrend, *Specimens of Bantu Folk-lore from Northern Rhodesia,* 93–94, 146–150.

whereupon the two appear splendidly dressed in feather mantles and attended by birds.

Keli'ikoa, however, plots to kill his rival. He lures him to a lonely place and would have made an end of him had not his wife followed, hit his enemy with a stone, and carried home her wounded husband. The angry rival engages as his ally Pi'ikalalau, the mo'o kupua who lives on the summit of an inaccessible cliff and can take the form of a mo'o or of a gigantic man with hog-like tusks. Again the wife rescues her husband by entangling the kupua with her throwing stick. Pele comes to the aid of Kauakahi with her lightnings, the owl to that of Pi'i. There is a great battle of aumakua which ends with the defeat of Pi'i, who escapes up the perpendicular cliff in mo'o form.

Kauakahi next goes to visit all the other islands in order to see whether there is another girl who can match his wife in beauty. None pleases him until he comes to Hawaii, where he makes an appointment with Laieikawai. The island of Kanehuna-moku appears off Wailua and he embarks upon it and does not return. Keli'ikoa makes another effort against La'a, but is again defeated by means of the throwing stick. At La'a's death Ka-ili-lau-o-ke-koa becomes ruler over Kauai and Ni'ihau.

In the Thrum, Rice, and Green versions the episode of the rival suitor does not appear and the story follows that of the Dickey version up to the reception at Kauakahi's house. From here on some variations occur.

(b) *Thrum version.* . . . At Kauakahi's house an identification test is presented in the form of a handsome stranger whom the girl successfully avoids for the true lover whose song she has followed. The girl's family carry the chiefess home and take her lover prisoner and shut him up without food or drink, where he would have starved had not a young brother of the chiefess named Kekalukalu-o-ke-wa cared for him secretly, until his rank is established and the kahunas give consent to the marriage. The couple rule over Puna district of Kauai. The brother becomes the young chief's favorite. At the point of death, he bequeaths to him the wooing flute and advises him to seek Laieikawai as his wife.

(c) *Green version.* . . . When the girl comes to seek her wooer, Kauakahi's sister, a sorceress who can take the form of a lehua tree or of a woman, conceals him for three months in the boughs of her tree form. At the marriage, signs in the heavens appear such as belong to the marriage of high chiefs. After a few months Ka-ili-lau-o-ke-koa falls into a magic sleep and is believed dead. Kauakahiali'i has two magic pipes called Kani-kawi and Kanikawa. The latter he leaves with the body of his wife and with the other travels about the islands to find a girl similar in beauty. A meeting is arranged with Laieikawai, but just as she enters the chief's house the restored chiefess appears and pipes the magic song with which he has once lured her to him.

(d) *Westervelt version.* Many years after Pele's exile from Kauai, two high chiefs of that island quarrel. Koa is filled with hatred for Kau and engages the mo'o kupua Pi'i-ka-lalau dwelling on the precipice Lalau to seize Kau. Pi'i in his human form is twelve feet in height with eyes as big as a man's fist and great tusks. Kau is lured far from home and attacked by this giant. His warriors flee but his wife throws her pikoi snare and Kau escapes, wounded. Pele now joins the fight in Kau's behalf and Pueo (Owl) in Pi'i's defence. Pi'i is defeated and, changing into mo'o form, he escapes up the precipice. Koa is later slain in battle.

(e) *Haleole version* (*in Laieikawai*). Kauakahi's wife Ka-ili-o-ka-lau-o-ke-koa falls into a magic sleep and he believes her dead. He travels about the islands to find another wife equally beautiful. Laieikawai of Paliuli, who dwells among the birds, at last measures up to the pattern and he has arranged a meeting with her, to be heralded by the notes of forest birds, when his wife awakes and appears in the house just as Laie stands on the threshold. [The story concludes as in Thrum's version.]

(f) *Malo and Dickey* (2) *versions.* Kauakahi lives at Pihana-ka-lani near the source of the north fork of the Wailua river in a beautiful house filled with birds arranged in four tiers, one above the other. One day he sees a water deity in the form of a woman combing her hair on a rock by the ocean and falls in love with her. He carves her likeness from memory and hides behind it, making gestures and speaking in so lifelike a way that the goddess comes out of the water and approaches the image, when he presents himself and persuades her to come to the mountains with him, and to be his wife. Her name is Uli-poai-o-ka-moku; the image he carves he names Ono'ilele. Arrived at his home at Pihana he transforms himself into an image like many others and obliges his bride to pick him out correctly, Kahihi-kolo, an old female relative, having shown her the room where he is to be found.

Warned by his friend, the god Kilioe at Haena, never to part from this image of himself lest his wife drag him after her into the water and he be drowned, he manages to substitute the image for himself when she plunges with him into the Wailua river, and his bird guardians carry him back to Pihana.[22]

The story is composed of three parts: first, the wooing of the girl by a high tapu chief; second, the fight with a rival suitor; third the infidelity of the husband, in some versions softened by the belief that the wife is dead. All three motives occur in the closely related story of Laieikawai. There is a male counterpart of the ladylove isolated in a tapu house and dwelling among birds. The anger of the parents until the wooer's rank is proved is worked out in the Laieikawai in the form of an actual affair with an unworthy suitor, atoned for by marriage with a high tapu chief from the heavens. The chief Koa takes the place of the militant Aiwohikupua in the Laie romance. The episode of the konane match occurs in both romances without motivating influence upon the central love story. Both composers evidently had in mind some common traditional source in representing the Kauai chief Kaua-kahi as one of the wooers of the beauty of Puna, an episode which occurs as a mere inthrust in the case of both romances. The popular songs connected with each romance—that which

22. Dickey, *HHS Reports* 25: 26–28, 35–36; Thrum, *More Tales,* 123–135; Rice, 106–108; Green, 50–54; Haleole in Beckwith, *Laiei-kawai,* 368–371; Westervelt, *Volcanoes,* 14–18; Malo, 117–119 note 17.

describes Laieikawai seated on the wings of birds in Paliuli, with its characteristic closing jibe for the scandal connected with her name, and the charming wooing song in the Kaili romance with its refrain: "O Kaili! Kaili! with skin like the leaf of the koa tree!" to words improvised by each reciter— were still to be heard some thirty years ago sung by old men who had belonged to the group about the king's court in the days when such song making was practised. Kauakahi's pipe song resembles the wooing song with which, in Marquesan story, Tana-oa, disguised as a little scab-covered fellow, woos the beauty of Fatu-uku who has resisted all other suitors:

O Meto, O Meto!
Like a crimson ray, O Meto!
Shining like a whale's tooth, O Meto![23]

A famous Maori story uses the unfamiliar music of the pipe to gain a sweetheart in a somewhat similar fashion to that employed by Kauakahi.

Tu-kane-kai lives on the island of Mokoia. He builds a platform on the slope of the hill and at night he and his friend Tiki go up there and play instruments, he the horn, Tiki the pipe. The sounds are borne to Rotorua and across the lake to the beautiful Hine-moa. She swims across the lake and hides in his bathing pool. A prominent rock on the southwest end of the Horohoro mountain at Rotorua is called by her name.[24]

Such a traditional wooing story seems to be the core of the romance of Kaililauokekoa. Different reciters wove into it incidents, out of a traditional stock of story material, which compare more closely with related romances. The departure of Kauakahi on the floating land of Kane-huna-moku and the identification test in the mermaid version resemble the Anaelike romance. The manner of the lure in this mermaid version corresponds with the device used by Konikonia to lure the underseas woman to his home. The skill of the wife with the throwing stick suggests another Kauai hero, Kawelo, and his warrior wife. In the Pikoi-a-ka-alala story

23. Handy, *Bul.* 69: 93–96.   24. *JPS* 1: 152.

Kauakahi is the friend who smuggled Pikoi over to Hawaii and Pikoi is, in the fullest version of the bird-shooting adventure, a native of Kauai. Heakekoa, whom the chiefess defeats in a konane match, is the name of the lover of Lono-i-ka-makahiki's wife Kaikilani, and it is his song from the hills while the husband and wife are playing konane that brings about the quarrel between the two and subsequent war between Lono and the chiefs of Ka-iki's family on Hawaii. It is the sound of the hula pipe also which lures Pele to her lover Lohiau on Kauai. A jealous sister in some versions impedes Hi'iaka's search. On the other hand, relatives place difficulties in the way of the goddess taking a mere mortal as husband. Here the Pele figure is seen once more drawn into relation with popular romance.

It is now possible to affirm that a dominating theme which runs through all Hawaiian romantic fiction and is used to motivate much of its action is the power of music to attract and of chanted song to awaken love. Equally dominant is sweet scent, so strongly associated with a former loved one or stirring the senses with its novelty. Both these elements attained formalized expression in the development of the hula dance, heightened emotionally by the religious setting which surrounded it. Nor are the movements of the dance in their old form to be interpreted as purely erotic imitations of the orgasms of love. Their appeal was often, as represented in these romances, to the imagination of the wanderer from home or of one estranged from friend or lover in recalling scenes of natural beauty which belonged to the old association and arousing in him love and longing. In the swaying movements of the dancers, their gestures of hand or fingertip, the onlooker saw, through the conventionalized symbol, the waving motion of leaves, the rise of a cliff side, the fall of water, the patter of rain, the movement of clouds across the sky. His senses were meanwhile filled with scent and sound, urging him to reawakened love for the scene itself or for the beloved friend or lover with whom it had been shared.

Romantic story-telling makes use of similar devices. Its great motivating force, like that of the related hula dance, is the background furnished by actual contact with the conflict between the fertility of the damp wild forest which furnished food to the early peoples and the fiery destruction wrought by volcanic outbursts. Both forces were apotheosized in the conception of a single goddess in her productive and in her wrathful manifestation as Laka or as Pele-i-ke-ahi. The loves and adventures of the Pele family, wrought as they were into religious rites and offerings, danced to with song and woven into wreaths of sweet-smelling plants, played an important part in shaping the treatment of love themes already traditional in memory or learned during the years of intercourse with southern groups. The more modern treatment of the story does not conceal the figures of those nature deities from whom the composer, through long convention, drew his pattern. The type remains, although the gods reveal themselves in the lives and loves of mortals.

REFERENCES

An asterisk (*) indicates Hawaiian material.
A dagger (†) indicates both Hawaiian and South Sea material.

AA : American Anthropologist.
AAAS: Australasian Society for the Advancement of Science.
AHNNE, E., "Légendes Tahitiennes," *Bulletin de la Société des études océaniennes,* 1931–1934, Nos. 40, 44, 46, 49, 51, 52.
AITKIN, ROBERT T., "Ethnology of Tubuai," Bernice Pauahi Bishop Museum, *Bulletin 70,* Honolulu, 1930.
*ANDREWS, LORRIN, *A Dictionary of the Hawaiian Language,* Honolulu, 1865; revision by HENRY H. PARKER, prepared under the direction of the Board of Commissioners of Public Archives of the Territory of Hawaii, Honolulu, 1922.
AUDRAN, PÈRE HERVÉ, "Legends from the Tuamotus," *Bulletin de la Société des études océaniennes,* Nos. 2, 5, 7, 14, 32, 33; translated by PERCY SMITH, *Journal of the Polynesian Society,* Vols. 27, 28, Wellington, 1918, 1919.
BAESSLER, ARTHUR, "Tahitische legenden," *Zeitschrift für Ethnologie,* Vol. 37, pp. 920–924, Berlin, 1905.
†BASTIAN, ADOLF, *Die heilige Sage der Polynesier,* Leipzig, 1881.
Die samoanische Schöpfungs-Sage und Anschliessendes aus der Südsee, Berlin, 1894.
BBAE : Bulletin of the Bureau of American Ethnology.
BEAGLEHOLE, ERNEST and PEARL, "Ethnology of Pukapuka," Bernice Pauahi Bishop Museum, *Bulletin 150,* Honolulu, 1938.
BEAGLEHOLE, PEARL, "Pukapuka Legends," collected 1934–1935 (Bishop Museum manuscript collection).
*BECKWITH, MARTHA, "The Hawaiian romance of Laieikawai by S. N. Haleole" (Text, Honolulu, 1863), Bureau of American Ethnology, *Report 33,* pp. 285–666, Washington, 1919.
"Kepelino's Traditions of Hawaii, Translated" (Text *ca.* 1860), Bernice Pauahi Bishop Museum, *Bulletin 95,* Honolulu, 1932.
BEST, ELSDON, "The Maori," *Memoirs of the Polynesian Society,* Vol. 5, 2 vols., Wellington, 1924.
Maori Religion and Mythology, Monographs of the Dominion Museum, No. 10, Wellington, 1924.
BPBM: Bernice Pauahi Bishop Museum.
BREWSTER, A. B., *The Hill Tribes of Fiji,* London, 1922.

*Brigham, William T. See Remy.

Brown, A. R. R-., *The Andaman Islanders,* Cambridge, England, 1922.

Buck, Peter (Te Rangi Hiroa), "Samoan Material Culture," Bernice Pauahi Bishop Museum, *Bulletin 75,* Honolulu, 1930.

"Ethnology of Tongareva," Bernice Pauahi Bishop Museum, *Bulletin 92,* Honolulu, 1932.

"Ethnology of Manihiki and Rakahanga," Bernice Pauahi Bishop Museum, *Bulletin 99,* Honolulu, 1932.

"Ethnology of Mangareva," Bernice Pauahi Bishop Museum, *Bulletin 157,* Honolulu, 1938.

Bul.: Bulletin of the Bernice Pauahi Bishop Museum.

Burrows, Edwin G., "Ethnology of Futuna," Bernice Pauahi Bishop Museum, *Bulletin 138,* Honolulu, 1936.

"Ethnology of Uvea (Wallis island)," Bernice Pauahi Bishop Museum, *Bulletin 145,* Honolulu, 1937.

Burrows, William, "Some Notes and Legends of a South Sea Island, Fakaofo of the Tokelau or Union Group," *Journal of the Polynesian Society,* Vol. 32, pp. 143–173, New Plymouth, 1923.

†Byron, (George Anson), *Voyage of H.M.S. Blonde to the Sandwich Islands, in the Years 1824–1825,* London, 1826.

Caillot, A.-C. Eugène, *Mythes, légendes, et traditions des Polynésiens,* Paris, 1914.

*Cartwright, Bruce, "Some Aliʻis of the Migratory Period," Bernice Pauahi Bishop, *Occasional Papers,* Vol. 10, No. 7, Honolulu, 1933.

Chamberlain, B. H., "Kojiki or Records of Ancient Matters (712 A.D.)," Asiatic Society of Japan, *Transactions,* Supplementary Volume 10, Yokohama, 1882.

Christian, F. W., *Eastern Pacific Lands; Tahiti and the Marquesas Islands,* London, 1910.

Churchill, William, *Sissano, Movements of Migration within and through Melanesia,* Carnegie Institution of Washington, Washington, 1916.

Manuscript from Samoa, "Helpful God Accompanying a Dangerous Expedition" (Bishop Museum manuscript collection).

Codrington, R. H., *The Melanesians; Studies in their Anthropology and Folk-lore,* Oxford, 1891.

Collocott, E. E. V., "Tales and Poems of Tonga," Bernice Pauahi Bishop Museum, *Bulletin 46,* Honolulu, 1928.

Notes on Tongan Religion, *Journal of the Polynesian Society,* Vol. 30, 1921, pp. 152–163, 227–240.

*DIBBLE, SHELDON, *A History of the Sandwich Islands* (1843); reprint, Honolulu, 1909.

*DICKEY, LYLE A., "String Figures from Hawaii," Bernice Pauahi Bishop Museum, *Bulletin 54,* Honolulu, 1928.

DIXON, ROLAND B., *The Mythology of All Races:* Vol. 9, *Oceanic,* Boston, 1916.

†ELLIS, WILLIAM, *A Narrative of a Tour through Hawaii . . . with Remarks on the History, Traditions, Manners, Customs, and Language of the Inhabitants . . .* (cited as *Tour*), London, 1827; reprint, Honolulu, 1917.

Polynesian Researches during a Residence of nearly Eight Years in the Society and Sandwich Islands (cited as *Researches*), 2d ed., 4 vols., London, 1831–1839.

*EMERSON, JOSEPH S., "Hawaiian String Games," *Folklore Publications of Vassar College* (cited as *VCFL*), No. 5, Poughkeepsie, 1924.

"Selections from a Kahuna's 'Book of Prayers,'" Hawaiian Historical Society, *Report 26,* pp. 17–37, Honolulu, 1917.

"Some Hawaiian Beliefs regarding Spirits," Hawaiian Historical Society, *Report 9,* pp. 10–17, Honolulu, 1902.

*EMERSON, NATHANIEL B., *Pele and Hiiaka; a Myth from Hawaii,* Honolulu, 1915.

"The Long Voyages of the Ancient Hawaiians," Hawaiian Historical Society, *Papers No. 5,* Honolulu, 1893.

"Unwritten Literature of Hawaii; Sacred Songs of the Hula" (cited as "Hula"), Bureau of American Ethnology, *Bulletin 38,* Washington, 1909.

*EMERSON, OLIVER P., "The Bad Boy of Lahaina," Hawaiian Historical Society, *Report 29,* pp. 16–19, Honolulu, 1921.

†EMORY, KENNETH, "The Archaeology of Nihoa and Necker Islands," Bernice Pauahi Bishop Museum, *Bulletin 53,* Honolulu, 1928.

"The Island of Lanai: A Survey of Native Culture," Bernice Pauahi Bishop Museum, *Bulletin 12,* Honolulu, 1924.

EVANS, I. H. N., *Studies in Religion, Folk-lore, and Custom in British North Borneo and the Malay Peninsula,* Cambridge, England, 1923.

FISON, LORIMER, *Tales from Old Fiji (Tongan),* London, 1907.

FL: Folk-lore (British).

*Fleming, Martha Ross, *Old Trails of Maui* (pamphlet), William and Mary Alexander Chapter of the Daughters of the American Revolution, Maui, 1933.

For. Col.: See Fornander, *Collection.*

For. Pol. Race: See Fornander, *An Account.*

*Fornander, Abraham, *An Account of the Polynesian Race, Its Origin and Migrations and the Ancient History of the Hawaiian People to the Time of Kamehameha I* (cited as For. Pol. Race), 3 vols., London, 1878–1885.

"Collection of Hawaiian Antiquities and Folk-lore" (cited as For. Col.), edited by Thomas G. Thrum, Bernice Pauahi Bishop Museum, *Memoir 4, 5, 6,* Honolulu, 1916–1919.

Fortune, Reo F., *Sorcerers of Dobu, the Social Anthropology of the Dobu Islanders of the Western Pacific,* London, 1932.

Fox, C. E., *The Threshold of the Pacific,* London, 1924.

Fraser, John, "Folksongs and Myths from Samoa," *Journal of the Polynesian Society,* Vol. 5, 1896, pp. 171–183; Vol. 6, 1897, pp. 19–36, 67–76, 107–122; Vol. 7, 1898, pp. 15–29; Vol. 9, 1900, pp. 125–134, Wellington, 1896–1900. See Powell.

Garcia, M., *Lettres sur les Iles Marquises, ou mémoires pour servir à l'étude religieuse, morale, politique et statistique des Iles Marquises et de l'Océanie Orientale,* Paris, 1843.

Gifford, Edward W., "Tongan Myths and Tales," Bernice Pauahi Bishop Museum, *Bulletin 8,* Honolulu, 1924.

"Tongan Society," Bernice Pauahi Bishop Museum, *Bulletin 61,* Honolulu, 1929.

Gill, William Wyatt, *Myths and Songs from the South Pacific,* London, 1876.

Gomes, Edwin H., *Seventeen Years among the Sea Dyaks of Borneo,* Philadelphia and London, 1911.

*Green, Laura, *Folktales from Hawaii* (cited as *Tales*) (text and translation), Honolulu, 1928.

*Green, Laura, and Pukui, Mary Kawena, *Legend of Kawelo and Other Hawaiian Folktales* (text and translation), Honolulu, 1936.

Grey, Sir George, *Polynesian Mythology and Ancient Traditional History of the New Zealand Race, as Furnished by Their Chiefs and (Priests),* 2d ed., Auckland, 1885.

HAA: Hawaiian Almanac and Annual.

*Haleole, S. N., *Ka moolelo i Laieikawai,* Honolulu, 1863; Kuokoa, 1865–1866; reprint by Solomon Meheula and James Bolster (pamphlet), Honolulu, 1888. See Beckwith.

HANDY, EDWARD S. C., "Polynesian Religion," Bernice Pauahi Bishop Museum, *Bulletin 34*, Honolulu, 1927.

"Marquesan Legends," Bernice Pauahi Bishop Museum, *Bulletin 69*, Honolulu, 1930.

"History and Culture in the Society Islands," Bernice Pauahi Bishop Museum, *Bulletin 79*, Honolulu, 1931.

"The Problem of Polynesian Origins," Bernice Pauahi Bishop Museum, *Occasional Papers*, Vol. 9, No. 8, Honolulu, 1930.

*Hawaiian Almanac and Annual. See THRUM.

*Hawaiian Historical Society, *Annual Reports*, 1893–; *Papers*, 1892–.

HENRY, TEUIRA, "Ancient Tahiti, Based on Material Recorded by J. M. Orsmond," Bernice Pauahi Bishop Museum, *Bulletin 48*, Honolulu, 1928.

*HENSHAW, H. W., *Birds of the Hawaiian Islands, Being a Complete List of the Birds of the Hawaiian Possessions with Notes on Their Habits* (pamphlet), Honolulu, 1902.

HHS: Hawaiian Historical Society.

HOCART, A. M., "The Lau Islands, Fiji," Bernice Pauahi Bishop Museum, *Bulletin 62*, Honolulu, 1929.

IZETT, JAMES, *Maori Lore, The Traditions of the Maori People with the More Important of Their Legends*, Wellington, 1904.

JAFL: Journal of American Folklore.

JENNES, D., and BALLANTYNE, A., "Language, Mythology, and Songs of Bwaidoga, Goodenough Island," S. E. Papua, *Memoirs of the Polynesian Society*, Vol. 8, Wellington, 1928.

The Northern D'Entrecastreaux, Oxford, 1920.

JPS: Journal of the Polynesian Society.

JRAI: Journal of the Royal Anthropological Institute.

*JUDD, HENRY P., "Hawaiian Proverbs and Riddles," Bernice Pauahi Bishop Museum, *Bulletin 77*, Honolulu, 1930.

*Ka Moolelo Hawaii (Hawaiian History) (written by scholars at the High School, and corrected by one of the instructors, adding dates and occasionally sentences and paragraphs), Lahainaluna, 1838.

*KALAKAUA, DAVID, *The Legends and Myths of Hawaii, the Fables and Folklore of a Strange People* (edited by R. N. Daggett) New York, 1888.

He Kumulipo no ka I-a-mamao a ia Alapai wahine, Honolulu, 1889. See LILIUOKALANI.

*KAMAKAU, SAMUEL M., "Moolelo o Kamehameha" (Life of Kamehameha), *Ka Nupepa Kuokoa* (cited as *Kuokoa*), Honolulu, October 20, 1866—January 9, 1869 (manuscript translation held at Bishop Museum).

"Moolelo Hawaii" (Hawaiian traditions), *Ke Au Okoa*, Honolulu, 1869–1871 (manuscript translation held at Bishop Museum).

KENNEDY, DONALD GILBERT, "Field Notes on the Culture of Vaitupu, Ellice Islands," *Memoirs of the Polynesian Society*, Vol. 9, New Plymouth, New Zealand, 1931.

*KEPELINO. See BECKWITH.

KRÄMER, DR. AUGUSTIN, *Die Samoa-Inseln*, Vol. 1, Stuttgart, 1902.

*LILIUOKALANI, *An Account of the Creation of the World According to Hawaiian Tradition, Composed by Keaulumoku in 1700* (translation of the *Kumulipo;* see KALAKAUA), Boston, 1897.

LOEB, EDWIN M., "History and Traditions of Niue," Bernice Pauahi Bishop Museum, *Bulletin 32*, Honolulu, 1926.

MACGREGOR, GORDON, "Ethnology of Tokelau Island," Bernice Pauahi Bishop Museum, *Bulletin 146*, Honolulu, 1936.

*MALO, DAVID, *Hawaiian Antiquities* (Moolelo Hawaii), translated from the Hawaiian by Dr. N. B. Emerson, edited by W. D. Alexander, Honolulu, 1903.

*MARCUSE, ADOLF, *Die Hawaiischen Inseln*, Berlin, 1894.

MARINER, WILLIAM, *An Account of the Natives of the Tonga Islands in the South Pacific . . . Compiled and Arranged . . . by John Martin*, 2 vols., 3d ed., Edinburgh, 1827.

*McALLISTER, J. GILBERT, "Archaeology of Oahu," Bernice Pauahi Bishop Museum, *Bulletin 104*, Honolulu, 1933.

McKERN, W. C., "Archaeology of Tonga," Bernice Pauahi Bishop Museum, *Bulletin 60*, Honolulu, 1929.

MEIER, P. J., "Mythen und Sagen der Admiralitats Insulaner," *Anthropos*, Vols. 2–4, Vienna, 1907–1909.

*MEINICKE, CARL E., *Der Archipel Hawaii* (Der Inseln des stillen oceans, eine geographische Monographie, Teil 2, Achter Abschitt; pp. 271–315, Leipzig, 1888).

Mem.: Memoirs of the Bernice Pauahi Bishop Museum.

MÉTRAUX, ALFRED (Easter island texts).

MOERENHOUT, J.-A., *Voyages aux îles du Grand Océan*, 2 vols., Paris, 1837.

MONTITON, Father ALBERT, "Les Paumotous," Les Mission catholiques, *Bulletin*, Vol. 6, Lyon, 1874.

MPS: Memoirs of the Polynesian Society.

MÜHLMANN, WILHELM E., "Die geheime Gesellschaft der Arioi, eine studie über polynesische Geheimbünde mit besondere Berücksichtigung der Siebungs- und Auslesevorgänge in Alt-Tahiti,"

Internationales Archiv für Ethnographie, Vol. 32, Supplement, Leyden, 1932.

MURRAY, J. H. P., *Papua or British New Guinea*, pp. 119–127, London, 1912.

NEUHAUSS, RICHARD, *Deutsch Neu-Guinea*, Band III: Beiträge der Missionare. . . . Berlin, 1911.

*PARKER, HENRY H. See ANDREWS.

*POGUE (Pokuea), J. F., *Ka Moolelo Hawaii* (after the version published at Lahainaluna in 1838), Honolulu, 1858.

POWELL, T., PRATT, GEORGE, and FRASER, JOHN, "Some Folk-songs and Myths from Samoa," Royal Society of New South Wales, *Journal*, Vols. 24–26; Vol. 29, pp. 366–393, Sydney, 1890–1892; 1895.

PRATT, Rev. GEORGE, "The Genealogy of the Sun, a Samoan Legend," Australasian Association for the Advancement of Science, Sydney, *Report of the First Meeting*, pp. 447–454, Sydney, 1887. See POWELL.

*PUKUI, MARY KAWENA. See GREEN.

RAFFLES, THOMAS S., *The History of Java*, 2 vols., London, 1817.

RASSB: *Journal of the Straits Branch of the Royal Asiatic Society*.

RBAE: *Report of the Bureau of American Ethnology*.

REITER, P., "Traditions tonguiennes," *Anthropos*, Vol. 2, pp. 230–241, 438–443, 743–750, Vienna, 1907.

*REMY, JULES M., Translated from the French by Brigham, William T., *Contributions of a Venerable Savage to the Ancient History of the Hawaiian Islands* (cited as *Contributions*), Boston, 1868.

Ka moolelo Hawaii (Histoire de l'Archipel Havaiien), Paris, 1862.

*RICE, WILLIAM HYDE, "Hawaiian Legends," Bernice Pauahi Bishop Museum, *Bulletin 3*, Honolulu, 1923.

*ROBERTS, HELEN, "Ancient Hawaiian Music," Bernice Pauahi Bishop Museum, *Bulletin 29*, Honolulu, 1926.

ROMILLY, HUGH H., *From My Verandah in New Guinea, Sketches and Traditions*, London, 1889.

Letters from the Western Pacific and Mashonaland (cited as *Letters*), 1878–1891, edited by Samuel H. Romilly, London, 1893.

RSNSW: Royal Society of New South Wales.

SCHIRREN, C., *Die Wandersagen der Neuseeländer und der Mauimythos*, Riga, 1856.

SEURAT, L.-G., "Légendes des Paumotu," *Revue des traditions populaires*, Vol. 20, Nos. 11, 12; Vol. 21, No. 2, 1905, 1906.

SHAND, ALEXANDER, "The Moriori People of the Chatham Islands,

Their History and Traditions," *Memoirs of the Polynesian Society*, Vol. 2, Wellington, 1911.

SKINNER, H. D., "The Moriois of Chatham Island," Bernice Pauahi Bishop Museum, *Memoir 9*, pp. 1–140, Honolulu, 1923.

SKINNER, H. D., and BAUCKE, WILLIAM, "The Morioris," *ibid.*, pp. 339–384, Honolulu, 1928.

SMITH, S. PERCY, "The Lore of the Whare-wananga: Teachings of the Maori College on Religion, Cosmogony, and History" (cited as *Lore*), *Memoirs of the Polynesian Society*, Vols. 3 and 4, New Plymouth, 1913, 1915.

STAIR, Rev. JOHN B., *Old Samoa*, London, 1897.

STIMSON, J. FRANK, "Tuamotuan Religion," Bernice Pauahi Bishop Museum, *Bulletin 103*, Honolulu, 1933.

"The Cult of Kiho-tumu," Bernice Pauahi Bishop Museum, *Bulletin 111*, Honolulu, 1933.

"The Legends of Maui and Tahaki," Bernice Pauahi Bishop Museum, *Bulletin 127*, Honolulu, 1934.

"Tuamotuan Legends" (Island of Anaa), Part 1, The Demigods, Bernice Pauahi Bishop Museum, *Bulletin 148*, Honolulu, 1937.

†STOKES, JOHN, "Notes on Hawaiian Petroglyphs," Bernice Pauahi Bishop Museum, *Occasional Papers*, Vol. 4, No. 4, Honolulu, 1910.

"An Evaluation of Early Genealogies Used for Polynesian History," *Journal of the Polynesian Society*, Vol. 39, pp. 1–42, Wellington, 1930.

"Honolulu and Some Speculative Phases of Hawaiian History," Hawaiian Historical Society, *Report 42*, pp. 40–102, Honolulu, 1934.

"Whence Paao?" Hawaiian Historical Society, *Papers 15*, pp. 40–45, Honolulu, 1928.

"Legends from Rapa" (Bishop Museum manuscript collection).

STUEBEL, O., "Samoanische Texte," Veröffentlichungen aus dem königlichen Museum für Völkerkunde, 4 Bd., 59–246 s., Berlin, 1896.

TAYLOR, Rev. RICHARD, *Te ika a Maui, or New Zealand and Its Inhabitants*, 2d ed., London, 1870.

THOMSON, BASIL, *The Fijians, A Study in the Decay of Custom*, London, 1908.

*THRUM, THOMAS G., editor, *Hawaiian Almanac and Annual: A Handbook of Information on Matters Relating to the Hawaiian Islands* (index compiled by Margaret Titcomb and Anita Ames, 1875–1932), Honolulu, 1875–.

Hawaiian Folk Tales, A Collection of Native Legends (cited as *Tales*), Chicago, 1907.

More Hawaiian Folk Tales (cited as *More Tales*), Chicago, 1923.

TNZI: Transactions of the New Zealand Institute.

TREGEAR, EDWARD, *The Maori-Polynesian Comparative Dictionary*, Wellington, New Zealand, 1891.

TURNER, Rev. GEORGE, *Samoa, A Hundred Years Ago and Long Before, Together with Notes on the Cults and Customs of Twenty-three Other Islands in the Pacific*, London, 1884.

†VANCOUVER, GEORGE, *A Voyage of Discovery to the North Pacific Ocean and Round the World . . . Performed in the Years 1790, 1791, 1792, 1793, 1794, and 1795*, 6 vols., London, 1801.

VCFL: Publications of the Folklore Foundation, Vassar College.

VON BÜLOW, WILHELM, "Samoanische Sagen," *Globus*, Vol. 69–75, 1896–1899; *Internationales Archiv für Ethnographie*, Vols. 11, 12, Braunschweig, 1898, 1899.

VON DEN STEINEN, KARL, *Die Marquesaner und ihre Kunst: Studien über die entwicklung primitiver Südseeornamentik* (cited as *Marquesaner*), 3 vols., Berlin, 1925–1928.

"Marquesanische Mythen," *Zeitschrift für Ethnologie*, Vol. 65, pp. 1–44, 326–373, Berlin, 1933.

*WESTERVELT, WILLIAM D., *Legends of Maui, a Demi-god of Polynesia, and his Mother Hina* (cited as *Maui*), Honolulu, 1910.

Legends of Gods and Ghosts . . . Collected and Translated from the Hawaiian (cited as *Gods and Ghosts*), Boston and London, 1915.

Legends of Old Honolulu (cited as *Honolulu*), Boston and London, 1915.

Hawaiian Legends of Volcanoes, Collected and Translated from the Hawaiian (cited as *Volcanoes*), Boston and London, 1916.

Hawaiian Historical Legends (cited as *Hist. Leg.*), illustrated, New York, 1923.

WHITE, JOHN, *The Ancient History of the Maori; His Mythology and Traditions*, Vols. 1–3, Wellington, 1887.

WILLIAMS, THOMAS, *Fiji and the Fijians*, edited by George Stringer Rowe, Vol. I, London, 1858.

WOHLERS, J. F. H., "The Mythology and Traditions of the Maori in New Zealand," *Transactions of the New Zealand Institute*, Vol. 7, pp. 3–53, Wellington, 1874.

YUPA: Yale University publications in anthropology.

ZE: Zeitschrift für Ethnologie.

INDEX